RED TIDE

BOOKS BY MARC TURNER

When the Heavens Fall
Dragon Hunters
Red Tide

RED TIDE

MARC TURNER

TOR

A Tom Doherty Associates Book
New York

RED TIDE

Copyright © 2016 by Marc Turner

All rights reserved.

Map by Rhys Davies

A Tor Book
Published by Tom Doherty Associates
175 Fifth Avenue
New York, NY 10010

www.tor-forge.com

Tor® is a registered trademark of Macmillan Publishing Group, LLC.

The Library of Congress Cataloging-in-Publication Data is available upon request.

ISBN 978-0-7653-3714-6 (hardcover)
ISBN 978-1-4668-3122-3 (e-book)

Our books may be purchased in bulk for promotional, educational, or business use. Please contact your local bookseller or the Macmillan Corporate and Premium Sales Department at 1-800-221-7945, extension 5442, or by e-mail at MacmillanSpecialMarkets@macmillan.com.

First Edition: September 2016

Printed in the United States of America

0 9 8 7 6 5 4 3 2 1

FOR JAMES

CONTENTS

DRAMATIS PERSONAE

The Olairian Court

Mazana Creed, *the emira of the Storm Isles*

The executioner

Kiapa, *the emira's bodyguard*

Jambar Simanis, *a Remnerol shaman*

Uriel, *Mazana Creed's half brother*

Mokinda Char, *a Storm Lord*

Imerle Polivar, *the old emira, now dead*

Cauroy Blent, *a former Storm Lord, now believed dead*

Dutia Elemy Meddes, *former commander of the Storm Guard, now missing*

Revenants

Jodren Labarde, *commander of the Revenants*

Twist, *his subcommander*

Tali and Mili, *the twins, former bodyguards to Imerle Polivar*

Erin Elalese

Senar Sol, *a Guardian*

Amerel Duquy, *a Guardian*

Noon, *a Breaker*

Emperor Avallon Delamar

Strike, *the emperor's bodyguard*

Tyrin Lindin Tar, *second in command of the Breakers*

Jelek Balaran, *a water-mage*

Kolloken Kanar, *a Breaker*

Gill Treller, *the First Guardian*

Li Benir, *a dead Guardian, Senar Sol's former mentor*

Jessca, *a dead Guardian, Senar Sol's former partner*

The Rubyholt Isles

Spear Clan

Dresk Galair, *warlord of the Isles*

Galantas Galair, *his son*

Magdella, *Dresk's wife*

Talet, *Dresk's chamberlain*

Qinta, *Galantas's Second*

Barnick, *Galantas's water-mage*

Drefel, *Galantas's quartermaster*

Faloman Gorst, *a krel*

Karsten Berg, *a krel*

Clamp, *a krel*

Worrin, *a krel*

Critter

Squint

Reska

Carlo

Vos

Scullen

Other Clans

CLAN LEADERS

Ravin Corre of the Falcons

Kalag Bluefinger of the Raptors

Malek Tenclaws of the Needles

Tolo the Unready of the Keels

Enigon Treach of the Squalls

Starboard Stonne of the Corals

Ysabel Tremeval of the Blades

OTHERS

Toben Stark, *a Raptor krel*

Tub, *a Needle krel*

Blist, *a Needle krel*

Cleo, *a Falcon krel*

Corm, *a Falcon krel*

Yali, *a Falcon krel*

Klipp, *a Squall krel*

Lassan, *a Needle*

Allott, *a Falcon*

Galitians

Ebon Calidar, *prince of Galitia*

Vale Gorven, *his timeshifter bodyguard*

Gunnar, a *water-mage*

Rendale Calidar, *Ebon's brother*

Lamella Dewhand, *Ebon's partner*

Silvar Jilani, *Galitia's ambassador to Mercerie*

Augerans

Commander Eremo al First, *leader of the Augeran expeditionary force*

Sunder al First, *his subcommander*

Hex, *a mage*

Ilabari Usco, *Eremo's Keeper*

Ostari Abrahim al Third, *an Honored*

Gilgamarians

Lydanto Hood, *Gilgamar's ambassador to Olaire*

Iqral, *a soldier*

Tia, *a racketeer*

Peg Foot, *Tia's minion*

Wirral Dray, *first speaker of the Gilgamarian Ruling Council*

Pettiman Teel, *Wirral's deputy*

Others

The Spider, *a goddess*

Romany Elivar, *a priestess of the Spider*

The Chameleon, *a god*

Karmel Flood, *a priestess of the Chameleon*

Caval Flood, *former high priest of the Chameleon, Karmel's brother*

Veran, *a former Chameleon priest, now dead*

Zalli, *Veran's widow*

Artagina, *high priest of the Lord of Hidden Faces in Olaire*

Fume, *an elder god, now dead*

Darbonna, *former high priestess of the dead god Fume*

Ocarn Dasuki, *prince of Mercerie*

THE LANDS OF THE EXILE

The Red Mountains

Camessil

Obenar

To Xavel

River Sametta

Mordella

Kolamin

Silver Hills

Linnar

Mander

Mercerie

KEN'DAH STEPPES

Forest

Kingswood

Korono

of

River Amber

Sighs

Majack

Culin

GALITIA

Koronos Hills

Estapharriol

White Road

Sun Road

Balshazar

Montenay

THE WAS

Bethin

Runesong Heights

White Mountains

Arandas

THE WASTE

Talen

Sun Road

GOLLOTHIR PLAINS

Cenan

Arap

Kal Kartin

Point Keep

Black Cliffs

Karalat

Helin

River Kal

Shield Road

High Fort

Sullen Sea

KAL

Kal Giseng

The Shield

River Renner

Javron

Kal Mecath

Renner

Mezan

Pallane

Wind Straits

Kerin

Amenor

Exile

Cortane

Bone Road

The Needle

Taradh Fold

Kerin Forest

Arkarbour

Taradh Dor

Sea of Bones

ERIN ELAL

Port Trinity

Melesse

Dram

Star

Maise

The Necklace

River Maise

Carros

Tresson Mountains

Brena

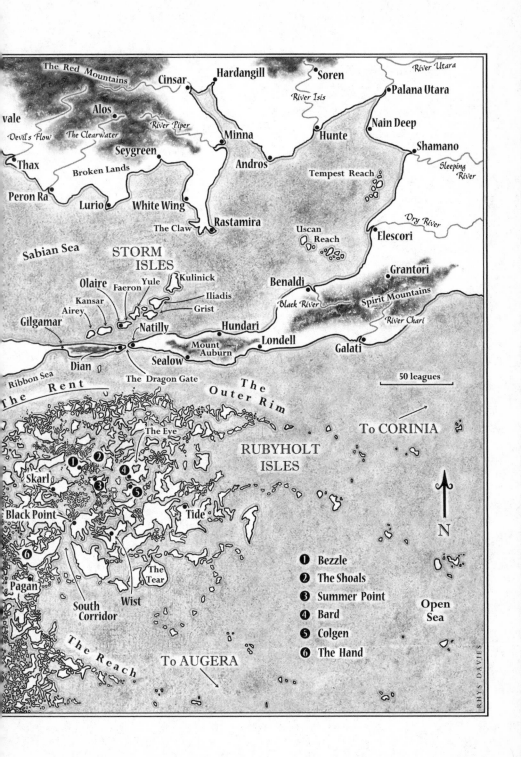

PART I

BLOOD FROM STONE

CHAPTER 1

STANDING ON the quarterdeck of the *Whitecap*, Guardian Amerel Duquy watched the headland fall away to reveal the city she had come to condemn. Bezzle, capital of the Rubyholt Isles. Judging by the smoke above the place, someone must have beaten her to the punch, damn them. But then the wind veered so it was in her face, and the sudden stink made it clear the haze was caused not by fires, but by the brine boileries and fish-glue factories clustered round the harbor.

If you *were* going to condemn a city, Bezzle was a good one to choose. Since Amerel had last been here, the place had bloated like a carcass in the sun. To the north was the Old Town with its crumbling buildings of pale blue-veined stone that shimmered in the midmorning sun. While to the south and west were districts of shanties that looked like they might slump into the bay with the next breath of wind. No more permanent than a castle of sand, but when you'd been invaded as often as the Rubyholters had, you didn't build things to last. At the ring of a bell the whole population would board their ships and melt away into the maze of waterways all about—as they had so many times before.

Even at this distance, Amerel could make out scores of ships bobbing at quayside. Among them was a Thaxian brigatina with its black-and-white-banded hull, an Androsian corrick with its high-rounded stern, along with a host of other vessels the Guardian had no name for. No two craft were of the same construction, but pirates couldn't be particular when it came to sourcing their fleet. Oh, the

Bezzlians would chafe at the name "pirates," but if there was a better word to describe them—to describe *all* Rubyholters—it wasn't the sort you would use in polite company. What else did you call a people with no culture, no trade links, no industry worth mentioning? A people whose very existence relied on the bounty they stole from the ships of Erin Elal, Corinia, Mellikia, and the Sabian League?

As the *Whitecap* entered a strip of water between two islets, its Rubyholt guide shouted, "Rift to starboard!" It was a cry Amerel had heard a dozen times during their passage through the Isles. As she now scanned the sea off the starboard bow, she saw a telltale shadow in the water that marked a gateway where this world overlapped with another. There were countless such gateways scattered across the Isles. Legend had it they were created in some apocalyptic clash between gods and titans in the Eternal War—a clash that had shattered a once hale continent into the tangle of islands and waterways that it now comprised, and burned holes through the fabric of the world to create portals to other lands. In the waters through which the *Whitecap* now sailed, there was evidence aplenty to support that tale. Amerel could make out flooded buildings of the same blue-veined stone as in Bezzle's Old Town, statues and obelisks draped in strands of fireweed, forests of columns reaching so close to the surface it seemed the *Whitecap*'s keel must scrape them as it passed.

The submerged ruins throughout the Isles had sunk more ships than even the rocks along Erin Elal's Bone Coast. But the underwater gateways posed a still greater threat to passing vessels, because beyond those gateways were otherworldly creatures waiting to ambush the unwary. Some were even large enough to take down a ship the size of the *Whitecap*. Earlier the vessel had passed the entrance to a channel called the Dragon's Boneyard, and Amerel hadn't needed their Rubyholt guide's gleeful commentary to guess how the waterway had earned its name. Now, as the *Whitecap* approached the rent, the wave of water-magic carrying it subsided. Doubtless the captain had slowed the vessel to avoid drawing the eye of any creature lurking below. Amerel, by contrast, would have raised the wave of water-magic as high as it would go, and fled for the safety of the harbor.

The combination of underwater gateways and submerged ruins made the Isles a perilous place for foreign ships—as Erin Elal's emperor, Avallon Delamar, had discovered to his cost a few years ago.

Incensed at the killing of one of his Circle in a hijacking on the Ribbon Sea, Avallon had sent twenty ships to the Isles to hunt down the pirates responsible. A week later, that force had limped back to Arkarbour, half its original size. Ten ships had been sunk or taken by the enemy, and what had the Erin Elalese accomplished to warrant such losses? Nothing, save to raze a dozen empty Rubyholt towns. Before, Avallon had promised to teach the pirates a lesson, and they'd learned it well enough. The number of raids on Erin Elalese ships had doubled thereafter. And while there had been fewer raids of late, the Rubyholt Isles remained an embarrassing blot off the empire's eastern seaboard.

Now, though, that stood to change. Now the Isles held—perhaps—the promise of Erin Elal's salvation, for in extending from the Rent in the north to the Hook in the south, they shielded the whole of Erin Elal's eastern seaboard from attack. And an attack was surely coming now that news had filtered through of the Augerans' appearance on Dragon Day eleven days ago. Even as the great and the good of the Sabian League were being feasted on by dragons, a stone-skin emissary was presenting himself to Warlord Dresk Galair of the Isles and his son Galantas, requesting an audience for a delegation to follow. That delegation was expected in Bezzle at noon tomorrow. Amerel could well guess the reason for its coming. *A pact between the Augerans and the Rubyholters.*

The significance of such a pact could not be overstated. True, the Rubyholters were too divided to pose a threat to Erin Elal themselves. But if they allied with the Augerans, the stone-skins would get guides to lead them through the Isles, maybe even staging posts from which to attack the empire. An invasion could be days away, and it was an invasion for which Erin Elal was not ready. How did you prepare for an enemy as strong as the Augerans when you were given only weeks to plan?

You didn't.

That point had been made to Amerel with mind-numbing frequency during a meeting with Tyrin Lindin Tar three days ago. With Erin Elal a virtual island, there was no way to prevent the stone-skins from landing. But *where* they made that landing was critical. The empire's eastern seaboard was the most vulnerable, because the major cities were located there, along with the Bone Road that connected them. The fate of those cities now lay in Amerel's hands. If she could turn the Rubyholters against the Augerans, the stone-skins would be faced with an unenviable choice: try to pass through the Isles without the Rubyholters' agreement, and face the same resistance the emperor's fleet had met all those years ago; or sail south round the Hook to attack Erin Elal from the west, and in doing so risk a clash with both the Kalanese and the pirate lords of Taradh Fold. Either option would cost them dear in ships and time. And it was time that Erin Elal most needed if it was to arrange a suitable welcome for their invaders.

Amerel swung her gaze back to Bezzle. Just one more day until the Augerans docked here, and the future of Erin Elal was decided. One day for her to set the Rubyholters against the stone-skins—a people they had no argument with, and whom they had never even encountered before.

No pressure, then.

The sun reflected bright off the waves, and Amerel squinted against the glare. Her eyes were scratchy from lack of sleep. Over the last few days, her dreams of blood had grown stronger as the threat of conflict loomed. In Arkarbour she'd taken cinderflower in an effort to shelter her niece Lyssa from the effects of those dreams. But while the drug delivered oblivion during the deepest part of the night, by dawn the visions would return. Now they pressed on her thoughts even through her waking hours . . .

A footfall sounded behind, and she looked back to see the Breaker Noon approaching. She'd done her best to avoid him during the two-day crossing from Erin Elal, but there were only so many places you could hide on a ship. The man was tall and lean, and had a curl to his mouth that suggested he found cause for amusement in everything he looked at.

"Ugly bastard, isn't he?" he said, pointing to his left.

Amerel glanced in the direction indicated, and saw carved into a nearby cliff a huge representation of Warlord Dresk Galair. She'd seen many such carvings during the *Whitecap*'s passage through the Isles. Most had been not of people, but of dragons or denkrakils or other monsters of the deep. It was a brave man who committed his likeness to stone when his dignity could so easily be stolen by an enterprising vandal. And such had apparently been Dresk's fate here, for one of his front teeth had been chipped away, and his eyes had been skillfully reworked to appear crossed.

Amerel said, "I think you'll find that image is quite flattering."

"You've met him, Princess?"

Princess? Did he know something she didn't? "No. But I saw him from a distance when I was last here—as I believe I mentioned in my briefing."

"There was a briefing?"

"Yes, there was. If you'd bothered to read it, you would know that a few years back our spy in Dresk's court managed to draw Galantas's suspicions. I was sent here by the Guardian Council to help."

Noon blew into his hands as if the sun had left him cold. "Help how?"

"By convincing Galantas that his misgivings were unfounded. Even at that time, Dresk and his son had their hands round each other's throats. I was able to . . . persuade Galantas—thanks to my Will—that his distrust was due solely to his dislike for his father's followers."

"As easy as that?"

"I never said it was easy. In truth, Galantas proved surprisingly strong-willed. But then he was only sixteen at the time."

"Age matters, does it?"

"Naturally. The young see things in such simple terms. They have none of the doubts that plague their elders. And doubts are what I feed on." Amerel leaned against the rail. "Using the Will to change someone's mind is like trying to change the path of an arrow in flight. Nudging it a fraction off course takes little effort. Turning it to face the other way is another matter entirely."

"But it can be done?"

"Given time, yes." The Will could be used as much to compel as it could to persuade. The problem was, people tended to notice when the mind of someone close to them was snuffed out like a candle flame.

Noon frowned. "It may yet come to that with Dresk. If he's meeting the stone-skins tomorrow, that doesn't give you much time to put him on a leash."

And that was assuming he granted Amerel an audience at all. The warlord had no idea she was on her way to Bezzle now. And she wouldn't be convincing him of anything from the wrong side of his fortress's walls.

The *Whitecap* had glided past the underwater gateway, and the wave of water-magic beneath the ship abruptly swelled again, lifting the ship into the air with a swiftness that made Amerel's stomach flip. Her gaze tracked the rent until it disappeared from view off the starboard quarter.

Noon studied her. "Aren't you worried the Rubyholters might recognize you, Princess? Your face isn't easily forgotten."

"I'll take that as a compliment."

It hadn't been meant that way, of course. Seven years ago she'd been in Arap, working to bring the city into the Confederacy, when an assassin in the pay of the sacristens had slipped nightspur into her wine. She'd been lucky to live. A month she had spent unconscious, another two in bed trying to coax her limbs to move. And even when she was back on her feet, the poison had left its mark, turning her hair as pale and fine as spider silk, and blackening the tiny blood vessels in her eyes so that the orbs appeared shattered. But that had all happened *after* her last visit to the Isles. There was little chance that anyone in Dresk's court would recognize her now.

Noon rubbed his hands together. "I must admit, I'm looking forward to seeing you lock horns with Dresk. As I heard it, the last Erin Elalese he met he left hanging upside down over a fire. This time tomorrow, that could be you."

Amerel didn't credit that with a response.

"Lot of bad blood between us and the Rubyholters," Noon went on. "Too much to be made right in twenty-four bells."

"I don't have to become Dresk's best friend. I just have to make sure he doesn't ally with the Augerans."

"If you say so. After what happened on Dragon Day, though, it wouldn't surprise me if he breaks out the bunting for the stone-skins. They sabotaged Dragon Day, right? Dresk has been trying to do that for years."

"A fact that Galantas will be quick to remind him of."

"Meaning?"

"Meaning even as I use my Will to steer Dresk to our cause, I will be using it to steer Galantas away from it. Persuade Galantas to speak in favor of the Augerans, and my task is halfway done. With luck, the chance for Dresk to spite his son will be reason enough for him to send the stone-skins packing."

Noon's expression was thoughtful. "What did you make of him? Galantas, I mean. The way our spy tells it, we're lucky Dresk is warlord and not his son."

"He tells it right." Even nine years ago there had been a steel to the youth that had left Amerel relishing their clash of wills. The latest reports from Bezzle suggested he'd lost none of his self-assurance in that time. Ambitious and charismatic, he was said to possess the ability to unite the Isles' fractured clans in a way his father never had. "Makes you wonder why the emperor has let him live this long," Amerel said with a pointed look at Noon.

"Is *that* why you think Avallon chose me to come with you? So I can put Galantas in the ground while you're charming his father?"

The thought had crossed her mind. "I've read your file," she said. "Lots of gaps in it." They'd been the most interesting parts by a distance. "Gaps that suggest you've been doing a few things your superiors don't want anyone knowing about."

The Breaker's expression gave nothing away. "I've read your file, too—"

"I didn't realize I had one."

"And I saw a few gaps in there as well. Like the time you disappeared in Kal for five months on a job that should've taken as many days. Five months on the run from the Kalanese, and you show up without even a scratch on you."

"I accounted for all my time in my report to the Guardian Council." A heartwarming tale of heroism and sacrifice, it had been—a tale Amerel had spent weeks dreaming up. She was thinking of reworking it for the stage.

"There were rumors that you'd gone over to the Kalanese. That you'd betrayed the empire."

And none as bad as the truth. "Yet here I am."

"Here you are," Noon agreed. "Betrayal's not something new to you, though, is it, Princess? I'm curious, why *did* you betray the Guardians and come over to the emperor's side?"

Amerel rolled her eyes. "Betrayal" was such an emotive word. And so ripe with hypocrisy. The First Guardian had flung it at her when she'd dropped by to tell him she was leaving the order. Like he thought it would make her feel guilty. Like he thought she owed him for all the murder and the blackmail she'd carried out in the Guardian Council's name. And perhaps he did think that, for along with the anger in his look, there had been a hint of hurt and indignation. It was for just such a look that she had gone to break the news to him in person, rather than slipping out the back door as Borkoth had done.

In response to Noon's question, she said, "Maybe the emperor made me an offer I couldn't refuse."

"Yeah, that sounds about right. That's the problem with you people born with a silver spoon in your mouth: all you can think of is that it should have been gold."

"What makes you believe it was money that swayed me? Maybe I just didn't fancy being the next Guardian sent through the Merigan portals."

"Maybe," Noon said. "Still, can't have been easy walking out on the Guardians like you did. Big fish like you. Leading light on the Guardian Council. Architect of the Confederacy."

"Please, you're making me blush."

"Makes you wonder, though. If you can walk out on your friends like that, how quickly might you walk out on the emperor when the squeeze is on?"

Amerel sighed. There was no pleasing some people. If she'd remained a Guardian, Noon would have called her a traitor for opposing Avallon's will. Yet now that she'd joined the emperor, he was condemning her for doing so?

He was right about one thing, though: Avallon couldn't count on her loyalty any more *now* than he could have done when she was on the Guardian Council. Maybe she wasn't a Guardian anymore—not really—but she wasn't a Breaker either.

Bezzle was drawing close, and Amerel shifted her gaze back to the city. Overhead, starbeaks circled on the turgid air. Protecting the entrance to the harbor was a line of islets, still smoldering from the fires lit in the run up to Dragon Day to ward off approaching dragons. One of those islets was scarred by claw marks where some beast must have tried to get at the men tending the fires. Along with the smell of charred wood, Amerel caught the acrid tang of dragon blood.

She scanned the harbor beyond. A forest of masts bobbed and twitched like the upthrust spears of some peasant army. On the greasy water, fishing skiffs rubbed shoulders with warships three times their size. Towering over them all was the steel-hulled monstrosity Amerel knew to be Galantas's flagship, the *Eternal*—a ship the warlord's son had claimed after it drifted unmanned through one of the gateways close to this island. Hard to believe such a thing could even float, yet Amerel had heard it was as swift as it was striking to the eye.

Movement caught her attention—a shape emerging from the

shadow of the metal-hulled warship. Amerel blinked as she saw a three-masted ship pulling up at one of the quays. Its sails were half-furled, but the Guardian could make out enough of the cloth to see the brightly colored patterns upon them, all intricate swirls and spirals like the weave of an Elescorian tapestry. She looked at Noon and saw he too understood the significance of what they were witnessing. Patterned sails. The ancient Erin Elalese texts were unequivocal on that detail.

That ship—it's Augeran.

Noon drew in air between his teeth. "Well, well," he said. "That certainly adds some spice to the pot."

The stone-skins had gotten there ahead of them.

Galantas Galair drew up as he entered the Great Hall. The air was heavy with blackweed smoke and the sour smell of unwashed bodies. His father's krels were already at the table to his right, while Dresk sat slouched in his throne at the end of the room, stroking his braided beard. Magdella was in the chair to his left, his chamberlain, Talet, behind. Of the stone-skins there was no sign. Still on their way up from the harbor, no doubt. But then it wasn't surprising that they should have taken longer to reach the fortress than a native like Galantas—particularly since he'd told Qinta and Barnick to intercept them, and delay them by whatever means necessary.

He leaned against the wall beside the door, his heart drumming from the briskness of his walk. Dresk was glowering at him through eyes made bloodshot from last night's drinking. For a heartbeat Galantas thought his father would order him to leave. Apparently Dresk knew better than to try, though, because he kept his silence. Hard to cling to the illusion of authority, after all, when even your own son defied you. Galantas met his glare with a smile, and it was Dresk who looked away first. He'd never been able to hold Galantas's gaze since that raid when Galantas had taken a sword strike meant for his father. And at the cost of his own left arm, too.

Galantas took in his father's tousled hair and swollen belly. His face twisted. This was the man who styled himself warlord of the clans? This was the man by whom the rest of the Isles would be judged? Nine years ago Dresk had put down a Raptor insurgency, and for the briefest of moments he'd had a chance to unite the clans under his rule. Instead he'd allowed the old rivalries to fester, while he wasted time chasing girls like the dew-eyed trophy sitting next to him now. And all so he could try to father on them another son to rob Galantas of his birthright—a birthright Dresk had already attempted to bestow on Galantas's younger brother, Kalim, before Kalim's untimely death on the Shark Run.

Galantas scanned the hall. The chamber was a mirror to its lord in its lost glory, with its stained rugs and its smoke-blackened tapestries. Mounted in one corner was the skull of a sea dragon, its mouth missing most of its teeth. The eyes of Dresk's krels gleamed in the gloom. Clamp was there, along with Worrin and Faloman and Karsten Berg. These were hard men, weathered by sun and sea and storm. Men who deserved a better leader than Dresk. Galantas had sailed with them all in his time; his blood had mixed with theirs on the decks of a dozen enemy ships taken. A few stared at him now with the reflected hatred of their lord, but most looked glad to have him here. And why not? The stone-skin messenger hadn't said why his masters wanted this audience. If their minds were on conquest, they weren't going to be dissuaded if they thought Dresk was the extent of the Isles' resistance.

It was more likely, of course, that their coming here was connected to Dragon Day. The Dianese governor, Piput Da Marka, had tried to hush up the events around the sabotage of the Dragon Gate. But a group of stone-skinned warriors running amok through your citadel wasn't the sort of thing you kept under wraps. Trouble was brewing between the Augerans and the Storm Lords. Perhaps the stone-skins had come here seeking allies for that fight, but if so they were going to leave disappointed. Galantas's people had more sense than to pick a scrap with an empire as powerful as the Sabian League. Besides, the Rubyholters weren't warriors, they were prospectors. And where was the profit in war? Where was the advantage in disturbing the flow of Sabian trade that was the lifeblood of the Rubyholt nation?

Footsteps sounded along the passage to Galantas's right. He looked across to see six stone-skins enter the hall. At the front was a huge warrior with swirling golden tattoos on his cheeks. Behind him came a man with spiked hair and a face crisscrossed with scars that made him look like he'd been sewn together from scraps of unwanted flesh. Both Augerans wore red cloaks, as did the four men who trailed after. The party halted a dozen paces in front of Dresk's throne. For a while no one spoke. Dresk frowned at the newcomers. The Augerans looked about them, taking in every detail of the hall. Finally one of their number—an older man with a receding hairline—stepped forward.

Galantas pushed himself away from the wall and circled to his left for a better view of the proceedings.

"Warlord," the balding stone-skin said to Dresk in heavily accented common tongue. "It is an honor to meet you. I am Commander Eremo al First of the Augeran empire."

Dresk rubbed his temples as if the man's words had given him a headache. "Never heard of it."

"Nor would I expect you to. My homeland lies beyond the Southern Wastes, hundreds of leagues from here."

"Then I'm guessing this ain't a social call."

Eremo inclined his head. "Allow me to introduce my companions. This"—he indicated the man with the scarred face—"is my mage, Hex, while beside him"—a man with eyes unnaturally far apart—"is my Keeper, Ilabari."

"Your Keeper?" Dresk said. "Tucks you in at night, does he?"

From the krels came a scattering of laughter and the pounding of fists on the table.

The Keeper stiffened, but Eremo merely smiled. "My people have strict rules when it comes to dealing with other cultures. My friend's job is to ensure I abide by them."

"Any of them rules say anything about turning up when you say you will?"

Galantas had heard enough. "Please forgive my father's ill manners," he said to Eremo. "Sender knows the rest of us have had to long enough." He advanced and offered his hand to the Augeran. "Galantas," he said.

Eremo gripped it. Galantas didn't squeeze—that would be immature. Plus the other man could probably squeeze harder. He'd expected the Augeran's skin to be as coarse as the granite it resembled, but it proved no more rough than Galantas's own.

Eremo took in Galantas's missing arm, his sharkskin cape, his necklace of shark teeth. Something in his look suggested he hadn't needed the introduction to know who Galantas was. "A pleasure," he said. His gaze shifted back to Dresk. "Apologies if my arrival has caught you unprepared. The crossing proved swifter than we expected. If you prefer, I can return—"

"What do you want?" Dresk growled.

The scarred man, Hex, was on the move, capering toward the krels' table. As he settled into an empty chair, those nearest to him edged back. He crossed his arms on the table, lowered his head onto them . . . and fell asleep. His snores reverberated around the hall.

Eremo didn't bat an eyelid. "You have heard, I take it, about the part we played in Dragon Day?" he said to Dresk.

"Nice bit of work," the warlord replied stiffly. Stiffly, because he'd tried to do something similar eight years ago, and failed.

"How did you pull it off?" Galantas asked.

"Anonymity helped," the commander said. "At first, the Dianese governor was wary of hosting our delegation on Dragon Day. But the opportunity to impress his guests with a few stone-skinned strangers proved impossible to pass up." He gave a half smile. "Somehow I doubt the trick will work a second time."

"Somehow I think you made your point the first. Assuming there *was* a point."

The commander regarded Galantas evenly. "You want to know why we targeted the Sabian League?"

The Keeper bristled. "We are not in the habit of explaining—"

Eremo raised a hand to cut him off. "Call it a preemptive strike, if you will. We had reason to believe our interests in the region would make conflict with the League inevitable."

Interests in the region? Galantas winced. "Sorry. I just felt a sudden pain in my pocket."

A lone krel banged his fist on the table in approval. Galantas would have to tip him later.

Eremo's tone remained affable, yet there was a tightness about his eyes that suggested his patience was already being tested. "Let's cut to the chase. We have unfinished business in these parts, and it is business that cannot easily be conducted across an ocean. We are looking to set up a base in the Isles from which to operate."

"A military base?"

Eremo nodded.

"You're going to war with the League?"

"Does it matter who our target is?" The commander looked about the hall. "Are you worried we might strike at one of your allies? Oh no, wait, you don't have any, do you?"

Galantas said, "There's a lot of water between not being allied with someone and being at war with them."

"We're not asking you to go to war. We're asking you to help us in ours."

"A fine distinction. I hope our neighbors appreciate it." From the bailey outside, the clang of a blacksmith's hammer struck up. Over it Galantas said, "You see the problem we face, Commander? What happens when you lose this war? What happens when you disappear back across the ocean, leaving us to pick up the tab?"

Some of the krels banged their fists on the table again. Eremo waited for the noise to die down, then said, "We will not lose."

Galantas pursed his lips, unimpressed. The words had been spoken with an unshakable assurance, but when did an invader ever embark on a campaign thinking it would fail?

Eremo swung his gaze to Dresk. "In addition to a base, we would need free passage through your waters, reliable charts—"

Dresk's snort interrupted him. "Charts?" He looked at his krels. "Hear that? The man wants charts!"

Laughter greeted his words.

Eremo's expression was wary. "I suspect your cartographers lack the skill of ours. We have collected more than a dozen different charts of the Isles, yet no two are alike in anything but the most cursory details."

More chuckling.

Galantas came to the stone-skin's rescue. "Those discrepancies are deliberate, Commander. Years ago, a neighbor used one of our charts to mount an invasion. Afterward the decision was taken to flood the market with false charts—so outsiders couldn't tell the real from the fake. Even if you *did* find an accurate chart, it would be covered in symbols you wouldn't understand, showing which waterways are passable and which are not."

Eremo's glance over his shoulder suggested whichever of his companions was responsible for intelligence would be enduring a testing half-bell when this was over. "Then you will have to explain them to us," he said to Galantas. "We will also need navigators to guide us through the waterways—until we know our way round."

"At which point we will cease to be of use to you."

Eremo ignored the comment. "Of course," he said to Dresk, "we don't expect you to give this help for free. Does the sum of fifteen thousand talents seem fair to you?"

Galantas's heart skipped a beat.

Dresk stared at the commander. The hall had gone still.

"Twenty thousand, then," Eremo said, a glint in his eye.

Galantas let his breath out slowly. Twenty thousand talents. More than a hundred million sovereigns. It was an outlandish sum. Absurd, even. With that money Dresk could buy all the ships in the Sabian League, and crews to man them besides. An awed muttering started up among the krels. Eremo was trying to dazzle Dresk with wealth, and Galantas was struggling to see past the glare himself.

Easy giving something away, though, when you intended to take it back straight after.

"This base you mentioned," he said to the commander. "Where would you put it?"

"That's something we'll need to reconsider, since you tell me the charts we've been working from are likely fakes."

"How long?"

"You mean how long would we need the base? Until we have established a presence on . . . the mainland."

That hesitation was telling. If he'd been about to say "the Sabian League," why not just say it? And why spend twenty thousand talents to sail *through* the Isles to the League when you could sail *around* them for free, with only a few bells lost? No, the more Galantas thought about it, the more he suspected the stone-skins' real target here was Erin Elal with its vulnerable eastern seaboard. "And then the base would be decommissioned?"

"Of course. It won't be much use to us afterward."

"Enough!" Dresk said to Galantas, but Galantas pressed on.

"How many of your ships would enter our waters?"

The commander cocked his head. "Surely you don't expect us to reveal the size of our fleet."

"Why not? You said you couldn't lose this war. Are we supposed to just take you at your word?"

"Enough!" Dresk said again to Galantas. "Your whining is making my head hurt." Then, to Eremo, "You said you ain't from round here. Where'd you get twenty thousand talents from?"

"We didn't get twenty thousand talents from anywhere. We got one, and produced copies."

"But still made from gold?"

"Yes."

"Show me."

Eremo took a huge coin from his pocket and tossed it to Dresk. The warlord missed with his snatch, but the talent landed in his lap. He inspected it by the dim light. "Where are the rest?"

"Somewhere safe. They will be available when you sign the treaty." The Keeper twittered in Eremo's ear, and the commander nodded and added, "My friend here has reminded me of something. In our agreement the twenty thousand talents will be expressed as a loan—"

Dresk scowled.

"But a loan repayable only after a thousand years."

The warlord stared at Eremo as if the stone-skin had started speaking in his native tongue.

"As I said," the commander explained, "my people have strange rules when it comes to dealing with other cultures."

"A thousand years?" Dresk said. "The treaty will have crumbled to dust by then. How will you prove the debt?"

"How indeed?"

"And the interest payable?"

"Nothing."

Galantas struggled to marshal his thoughts. What game were the Augerans playing? Why call the money a loan if you had no intention of asking for it back? That particular question would have to wait until later, though, for a more prickly concern had occurred to him. "What about the other Rubyholt clans?" he asked Eremo.

It was Dresk who responded. "What about them?"

"I assume the commander isn't going to want to pay our kinsmen on top of what he's paying us."

Eremo said, "You assume correctly."

"But you expect the other clans to abide by this treaty, correct?"

"I expect you to control your subjects." The commander swung to Dresk. "Is that a problem?"

"No problem," Dresk said, with a look at Galantas that warned him to be silent. As if Eremo wouldn't already know of the fractured relations between the warlord and the other tribes. As if he wouldn't know the risk of dealing with Dresk alone. The stone-skins would want to pass through the waters not just of Dresk's Spears, but of the other clans as well. And the leaders of those tribes would want a cut of the gold in return for not harassing Augeran ships. Somehow Galantas couldn't see his father sharing, though. How typical of him to see his position as warlord not as responsibility but as opportunity—to expect loyalty from the other clans, yet offer nothing in return.

Galantas's gaze slid from his father to Eremo. Could that be the stone-skins' true purpose here? Widen the rifts between Dresk and the tribes before attacking? After all, when a man like Dresk was floundering, heaping gold on him just served to hasten his journey to the bottom. Hells, the clans had fought over a lot less in their time. Twenty thousand talents, they would say, meant there was plenty to go around, and who could argue with them? Not Galantas, certainly.

And yet would a conflict between Dresk and the other tribes be a bad thing? If Galantas played his hand right, might there be an opportunity to speed his father's fall from power?

"What if another tribe breaches the treaty?" he asked Eremo.

"Then we hold you accountable, of course."

"Meaning?"

Eremo waved the question away. "Details. We can discuss them later. First I need to know if we have an agreement."

Dresk tossed the commander's coin from hand to hand, making a show of considering the offer. "Twenty thousand talents," he said.

Eremo nodded.

"For one base and free passage through the Isles."

"Yes."

Dresk grimaced like his arm was being twisted. "Agreed."

"Excellent. I will bring the treaty with me when I return. Shall we say, at the seventh bell this evening?"

Bring the treaty with him? So it had already been drafted, then? *So much for negotiating the details.* Galantas did not voice the thought, however. Sometimes knowing when to shut up was as important as knowing when to speak.

Eremo turned away. As he did so his scarred mage, Hex, abruptly stirred and sprang from his chair as if he hadn't been sleeping at all.

Galantas watched them make for the door. Strange, Dresk had been promised twenty thousand talents, yet Galantas couldn't shake the feeling that the stone-skins had gotten the better of the exchange. How could Dresk lose from the deal, though? War between the stone-skins and Erin Elal—if indeed that was their target—would disrupt the trade on which the Spears preyed, but twenty thousand talents would more than make up for lost profits. And if Erin Elal should come seeking revenge when the Augerans were gone, well, they'd tried invading before. Why should the result this time be any different from the last?

Eremo stopped by the door. "Oh, one final thing," he said over his shoulder. "We were attacked by two ships on our way here this morning. They ambushed us near some underwater ruins a league or so to the south."

Galantas knew the spot. It was a favorite place to pick off outsiders as they exited the South Corridor. "These ships . . . what flag were they flying?"

"A red feather."

Ravin, then. The clan leader of the Falcons wasn't the sort to let a profit sail past unchallenged. "Two ships, you say. But they let you pass when you told them you were meeting us?"

"Hardly."

Before Galantas could reply, Dresk said to his chamberlain, Talet, "Get the word out to the other clans. Make sure they don't bother our new friends again."

"Oh, I don't think that will be necessary," Eremo said, resuming his walk to the door. "We've sent out our own message loud and clear."

CHAPTER 2

STANDING ACROSS the courtyard from Romany, the priest of the Lord of Hidden Faces addressed his congregation in a wheedling voice. For half a bell he'd been dressing up his own wants and petty prejudices in the false trappings of his god's will, and criticizing faults in others that Romany had seen him display on numerous occasions. Now he was busy rewriting history. It seemed the Lord of Hidden Faces had not only predicted the events of Dragon Day, but actually orchestrated them too, with the intention of thinning the ranks of Olaire's elite. All in the name of the destitute and the downtrodden, apparently, so that they might throw off the shackles of their highborn oppressors and elevate their Lord to his rightful place of preeminence.

And in doing so promote the high priest, Artagina, and his brethren to the positions recently vacated by Imerle Polivar and her ilk. Though strangely the priest neglected to mention that detail.

His message seemed to be going down well with the locals, for the size of the temple's congregations had swelled since Romany arrived in Olaire eleven days ago. And what a day that had been. The dragons released into the Sabian Sea. The Storm Lord dynasty wiped out. With Imerle dead, Mazana Creed had seized the reins of power, but her mount was proving to be an unruly one, what with so many soldiers present in the city who had served the old emira. Then there was the problem of the simmering hostility between an ever-growing number of Storm Guard factions, and the rivalry between those soldiers and Mazana's mercenaries, the Revenants. Each night Olaire thrummed to the sound of conflict. And each night the Shallows and the Deeps emptied as their denizens took to the streets to profit from the chaos.

Sweat trickled down Romany's forehead, but her mask prevented her from wiping it clear. Gods, how she hated this slab of wood! Its size was such that aligning her eyes with the eye slits meant that her lips did not align with the mouth slit. That in turn meant that every breath she exhaled was trapped against her face. She wasn't the only one suffering in the heat. She could almost hear the flesh of the congregation crisping in the sun. And while a bald man at the front appeared to be swaying with rapture, it could equally have been from heatstroke. By contrast, the priest addressing them seemed in no discomfort. His sermon was evidently coming to a close, for he had moved on to the priesthood's favorite subject matter, and the topic with which they ended every speech: donations.

Yes, the Lord of Hidden Faces was the champion of the poor, but it seemed his worthiest servants were those who gave generously.

Romany had heard enough. She started following the colonnade round toward the archway that led to her quarters. She had acquired those quarters only yesterday when their former resident, one of Artagina's lieutenants, had been expelled following a quarrel with his master. As Romany stepped around a group of worshippers, she saw the high priest, Artagina, watching the sermon from the shade of a pillar. Eleven days ago he'd been the only one allowed to address the Lord's flock, but with the congregations growing, he'd been forced to share that honor with his deputies. As a self-made priestess of the god herself, Romany was looking forward to her turn to speak. She'd have a few choice truths to reveal when she did.

As she drew near Artagina, his head swung round. Through the eye slits of his golden mask, she saw his eyes narrow. "You, what's your name?" he demanded.

"The same as it was last week when you asked," Romany said, sweeping past.

At which time she'd given the same evasive answer, incidentally. For some reason it seemed to satisfy the high priest now as it had then, because he did not call her back.

She felt his gaze linger on her—a scrutiny she'd grown accustomed to since awakening in this new, much younger body. She wondered what had happened to her body's previous occupant that

it should have become . . . available to Romany. Who had the woman
been? What was her calling? The clues were not hard to find. The muscles in Romany's arms, and the calluses on her hands, pointed to a
history of manual labor. But the scars across her torso were less easy
to explain. She'd also inherited a bruise to her hip, together with a
badly stitched cut to her side. Most likely she'd been a dock worker or
a sailor. Or maybe even, Spider help her, a soldier. She shivered. No,
the possibility was too vulgar to countenance. How about a dancer,
then? That would explain the toned physique. But the scars . . .

A bad dancer, perhaps?

She entered a weed-infested passage open to the elements, and the
voice of the priest faded behind. Of course, none of this speculation
would have been necessary if the Spider had hung around long enough
after Romany's "rebirth" to answer her questions. Instead the goddess had told her simply to keep her head down, before vanishing to
who knew where. There had been no explanation as to where Romany
was or what she was supposed to do. The Spider hadn't even mentioned there was a war going on beyond the temple walls—though
Romany had discovered that soon enough when screams floated up
from the harbor as the Revenants attacked.

Romany had heard as many different opinions of what had happened on Dragon Day as there were people in Olaire. Curious to learn
the truth of it, she had constructed a sorcerous web across the city,
stretching from the Founder's Citadel in the west, to the Deeps in the
south, to the palace in the north. From conversations among Mazana
Creed and her entourage, Romany had learned about the attack on
the control room in the Dianese citadel, as well as the Chameleons'
failed play for power and the stone-skins' efforts to assassinate
the Storm Lords. She had also heard fragments of Mazana's plan to
strike back at the Augerans. Ambitious, certainly. It was hard to gen-
erate more than a superficial interest in the woman's machinations,
though, when Romany would, Spider willing, be returning soon to
the comfortable indolence of her home temple in Mercerie.

She reached her quarters and opened the door. From the smell that
greeted her, she might have pressed her face into someone's armpit.
She'd yet to find time to clear her rooms of the previous owner's
detritus—or rather track down an acolyte to do so. The floor, the
tables, even the chairs were covered in scrolls, clothes, and half-eaten
food. And seated in one of the chairs . . .

Romany had to still her features against the flood of relief that swept through her.

The Spider.

With her auburn hair and her enigmatic smile, the goddess looked exactly the same as she had the last time Romany saw her—as indeed she'd looked every time since the priestess first set eyes on her thirty years ago. It had been her second day as an initiate. A five-year-old Romany had barely been able to focus on the Spider through a mist of tears. Most of the girls in the goddess's service were orphans picked from the street, but a handful—Romany included—were sold to the priestesses by their parents. Sometimes that was done for profit; at other times, it was done because the temple promised a better life than the parents could offer their child themselves. There had been a time when it had mattered to Romany what her own parents' motives had been. Not now, though. Now, she was resigned to never knowing the truth, because all her efforts at tracking down her parents had come to naught.

A full ten years had passed before she'd seen the Spider again. A wild soul Romany had been at that time, opinionated and irreverent. Not at all like now, then. When she was called to meet the goddess, she had assumed the Spider meant to discipline her. Instead they had spent an instructive afternoon discussing the riots in Thax and the latest political machinations of the Mercerien padishah. The Spider, Romany had come to learn, wasn't interested in the devotion of her followers; she was interested in their shrewdness, their insight, their pragmatism. And Romany had caught her eye. At the time, her attention had been flattering. Now the priestess had a different take on it.

Seated in her chair, the goddess drummed her fingers against the pages of an open book on her lap. She chuckled as she read it.

"Ah, High Priestess, therrre you are," she said, with her familiar trill on the "r."

Romany shut the door, then tugged off her mask and tossed it onto the bed. "My Lady."

"I like what you've done with the place," the Spider said, glancing round. "And it seems congratulations are in order for your promotion. I could have sworn I left you with an acolyte's mask."

"Your memory must be failing you." In reality, Romany had taken it upon herself to swap the mask of plain wood for a priest's white as soon as the opportunity presented itself. Being an acolyte, with all the disdain and the . . . *work* it occasioned, was not for her, no matter that a white mask would earn her more attention from the likes of Artagina. She lifted an armful of scrolls from a chair and dropped them onto the floor before sitting. "What is that?" she asked, gesturing to the book in the Spider's lap.

"You mean you haven't read it? Shame on you! This is the Saradahn. The sacred text of the Lord of Hidden Faces."

"But . . . *you* are the Lord of Hidden Faces, aren't you?"

"Am I? Decades ago, when I first unleashed the Lord on the world, I compiled this book from the writings of a hundred dead religions from all across the globe. Writings that were carefully chosen to offer up as many inconsistencies and outright contradictions as possible. You can imagine the fun I had watching priests and scholars try to make sense of it all."

Fun? Clearly when you'd lived as long as the Spider had, you had to go a long way to find entertainment.

"And the amusement didn't stop there," the goddess went on. "Never once did I appear to my disciples to offer guidance on the text. Yet within a few years, a dozen sects had sprung up led by men or women claiming to have spoken directly to their Lord. Of course, the god had confirmed *their* understanding of the Saradahn to be correct above all others, and the quarrels and the inquisitions and the burnings duly started. If I had appeared at that moment to explain the lie behind the faith, do you think any of those people would have believed me? Would Artagina now?" She closed the book and set it down on a table. "So, to answer your question, yes, I *was* the Lord of the Hidden Faces once. Now I'm not so surrre."

A feathermoth as large as Romany's palm had materialized from somewhere, and was trying to settle on the priestess's arm. She waved a hand at it. "Why did you start the religion? What purpose did it serve?"

"It was necessary for a deception against Shroud, the exact nature of which escapes me now."

"And the deception failed? Is that why the Lord's faith died out?"

"The deception didn't fail. The faith died out because I destroyed it."

Romany opened her mouth and closed it. Then opened it again. "You killed them all?"

"The priests, the acolytes, yes."

The Spider's half smile hadn't slipped in the time she'd been talking, and Romany wondered if she was being made the butt of some joke. Yet the goddess's account would explain the overnight disappearance of the Lord's followers all those years ago. *A busy night that would have been.*

"Even the devout ones?" she said. "Even the true believers?"

"Believers in what? A Lord that didn't exist? If they believed in anything, it was in a god of their own devising. A god that justified exactly what they wanted to say or do. And you think I owed them loyalty?"

The feathermoth landed on Romany's head. She cursed and shook it off. "Do I take it then that a similar fate awaits Artagina and his crowd?" *Please?*

"Perhaps. For now, though, the high priest provides a useful screen for my other pursuits in Olaire."

Romany didn't like the sound of that, if those pursuits meant she'd be spending more time here. "I was hoping . . . My temple in Mercerie—"

"*Your* temple?"

"A figure of speech."

The Spider's fingers fluttered. "Why do you think I brought you back in this new body, High Priestess? For the pleasure of your company? Or as a thank-you for your efforts in the Forest of Sighs?"

When she said it like that, it did sound silly. The Spider, say thank you? *Absurd!*

"As I rrrecall," the goddess continued, "it wasn't even as if you died in the furtherance of your duties. To the contrary, your troubles started only *after* you stopped following my orders. A lesson in that, don't you think? And since we're on the subject of lessons, I trust there will be no recurrence of the . . . sensitivity you showed in your dealings with Mayot Mencada."

Sensitivity? Yes, how dare Romany? "What happened after that Mayot business? Has Parolla's mother been reborn?" After Romany had died at Danel's hand, she had witnessed from the threads of the Spider's web the Book of Lost Souls being destroyed, but not what came after.

"Not yet, but soon. Parolla and her friends are about to discover they were fools to trust the White Lady over the details of the child's birth. The goddess is not as purrre as her name would suggest." Another flutter of the Spider's fingers—at the feathermoth this time, now flapping between her and Romany. "But enough of that. You are anxious, I'm sure, to learn what I have planned for you in Olaire."

Anxious was the word. Romany gave a reluctant nod.

"How much have you been able to piece together of the events in the Founder's Citadel on Dragon Day?"

"I'm aware of *what* happened. I'm less clear on *why*."

"Why I helped Mazana Creed kill Fume, you mean?" The goddess leaned back in her chair. "From your history, you will know that Fume was taken prisoner by the titans toward the end of the Eternal War. But what you might not know is that *I* was the one who betrayed him. Once his high priestess and her followers located him, it was just a matter of time before they freed him. Imagine how cross he would have been with me after a few millennia of captivity."

"But he was mad, wasn't he? How do you know he would even have remembered your name?"

"You think I should have taken the risk? And even if he *had* lost his memory, you think it would have been a good thing to have a mad god obsessed with blood sacrifice on the loose? I couldn't let that happen, of course."

Romany sniffed. "How very public-spirited of you."

The Spider accepted the praise graciously. "When I learned of Mazana Creed's plans to overthrow Imerle, I saw a chance to dispose of Fume and gain a little something extra in the barrrgain."

"Mazana's debt to you."

"Precisely."

"And what *precisely* do you intend to ask from her in settlement of that debt?"

The Spider gave a secret smile.

The feathermoth had alighted on the table between the goddess and Romany—or rather on the blade of a throwing knife left by the room's former owner. Instinctively Romany reached out and picked up the weapon. The feathermoth took flight. Romany hefted the dagger, judging its weight. *Nice balance.*

She froze. Nice balance? Where had that thought come from? She'd never so much as held a throwing knife before, let alone used one.

That smile of the goddess's was making Romany's skin prickle.

"You never told me," the priestess said, "what you wanted my help for."

"I'm getting there. As you'll appreciate, when Mazana took some of Fume's power, she also took in part of his spirit. Which part exactly, and how much, remains to be seen."

Which part? Did Fume have a good side, then? Some inner child hiding behind the tyranny and blood sacrifice? "You're worried another of your creations might slip its leash?"

"If by 'another' you are referring to Mayot Mencada, I think you'll find he never escaped my control. Yourrrs maybe, but not mine. As the events after your death showed."

"Yet you think Mazana might be different?"

"I think I need to be alive to the possibility," the Spider said. "Oh, it's not like she's going to start hearing Fume's voice in her head. But she may begin to display an irrational dislike of both me and my followers." As opposed to a very rational dislike. "Whether it gets that far will depend on how well she is able to withstand the force of the god's persona."

"I've seen nothing yet to suggest she is under his thrall."

"Nor I." The Spider paused. "But the events of the next few days are likely to test her character to the full."

That prickle was back, as if every hair on Romany's body was standing on end. "You are referring to her plan to retaliate against the stone-skins?"

"In part."

The feathermoth flew past Romany's face, but she paid it no mind. "So you're sending me to keep an eye on Mazana."

The goddess nodded.

"And if she should fail your . . . test?"

"That would be inadvisable."

"You want her disposed of?"

"I thought I just said that."

Romany frowned. There was a note to the goddess's voice she could not place, a certain sharpness to her look that suggested there was a hidden message beneath her words. In some indeterminable way, it felt like Romany herself was being tested as much as Mazana. With no hint as to the reason or the stakes, naturally. "Is there no other way to rid the emira of Fume's presence?"

The Spider shook her head.

Behind the goddess, the feathermoth had alighted on the door frame.

Without thinking, Romany pulled back her right arm and sent the throwing knife spinning through the air. It flew true to its target and thudded into the wood, impaling the moth.

The Spider raised an eyebrow.

Horrified, Romany stared at her hand. Except it wasn't *her* hand, was it? Her skin had never been that tanned, and she couldn't remember picking up that crescent-shaped scar where her thumb met her palm. She experienced a sensation as if she were looking out through the eye slits of a mask again, only this one was made of flesh instead of wood.

"One other thing I should mention," the Spider said. "When you meet Mazana Creed, you might want to keep your mask on. And when you're around Senar Sol too." She considered. "Actually, it's probably best if you wear it at all times."

Romany's voice was a whisper. "What was . . . I . . . before?"

"An assassin, of course. Rrrather apt, in view of the task at hand."

An assassin. A part of Romany had suspected as much, but to hear it confirmed . . . *Oh, the indignity!*

The Spider said, "There are things about your body that will take more time than others to get used to. The spirit of your predecessor may have flown, but certain memories of the flesh will remain. Or at least I hope they will, since your predecessor had a most intriguing ability that I have come across only a handful of times in all my years. Tell me, High Priestess, have you sensed anything different about the street in front of the temple?"

Romany's mind was only just starting to function again. "Different?"

"You know, as in 'not the same,' 'unusual,' 'out of the ordinary.'"

Now the priestess thought about it, she *had* encountered something odd. Yesterday she'd left the temple to search for a bathhouse in the Jewelry Quarter. A stone's throw to the east, she'd encountered a spot that left her feeling nauseated when she passed through it, like when the Spider had transported her to Estapharriol along the strands of her web.

"What you're sensing," the goddess said, "is a point where the veil between two worlds has been eroded. Your predecessor was able to travel between those worlds, even when the connection between them was not strong enough to create a portal. With luck, you will have that ability too. Though I wouldn't recommend using it in this particular place."

Romany regarded her blankly.

"It leads to the Kerralai world," the Spider explained. "As your predecessor discovered to her cost."

"A demon followed her back to Olaire and killed her?"

"Not quite. It drove her to this temple, where the woman decided, with a little persuasion, to take shelter. Even from here she could sense the portal, and a nudge from me was enough to convince her she could make the jump to the world beyond, when in rrreality the distance was too great."

That explained how the assassin's body had become available for Romany to use. But it didn't explain why she needed to wear a mask in Mazana Creed's presence.

The Spider was only too happy to enlighten her. "You tried to kill her," she said. "Outside this very temple, in fact. You would have succeeded too, were it not for Senar Sol. And while I've taken the liberty of toning down the color of your eyes—they were a most conspicuous blue—I suspect both Mazana and Senar would recognize you if they saw your face again."

Romany could only nod in response. If someone tried to assassinate you, it wasn't the sort of thing you forgot. Yet now she was supposed to introduce herself to the emira? Spend enough time in her company to assess the extent of Fume's influence?

She sighed.

It seemed the Spider had brought her back from the dead just for the pleasure of watching her die again.

From the shade of a ketar tree, Karmel studied the town house across the street. Like the buildings to either side, its roof was missing as many tiles as remained in place, and its ground-floor windows had been boarded up. Unlike those neighboring buildings, though, the house—that of Veran's widow, Zalli—showed scars of the fighting that had raged through the city since Dragon Day. The planks over the windows were fire-blackened, and the front door was marked as if someone had taken an ax to it.

In the front yard was a white-robed figure attached to a cross. Not a person, Karmel realized, because it had straw protruding from the ends of its sleeves. But why was there blood round its neck and down its chest? She edged forward for a closer look. Then stopped. *Lord's mercy*. For while the body was made of straw, the skin of the face was all too real. Some woman's scalp and face had been peeled from her skull and pulled down over the head of the figure. Zalli's? No, the features looked too old. Blood-soaked straw bulged from her gaping eyeholes and from between her broken lips. Her skin at the forehead and cheeks had blackened in the sun.

"What is that thing?" Karmel said to Caval at her shoulder.

"My guess? A flesh-and-blood effigy of the White Lady."

"Meant as a warning?"

"Maybe. You said Zalli had the gray fever. Reason enough to stay away from this place, some would say."

Caval among them, judging by his tone. He'd been against coming here from the start, though. Not that he had argued with her, of course. He never did these days, even when she was wrong, and maybe she *had* been wrong to come. Veran's words on the journey to Dian returned to her. *Ain't no one ever caught the gray fever that's recovered from it. Ain't no one taken less than a year to die from it either.* Evidently Zalli's neighbors had feared the spread of the infection, and so put up the effigy to invoke the White Lady's blessing.

Because a tribute like this was sure to win the goddess's favor.

"Will the Chameleon heal Zalli?" Karmel asked Caval. "If we took her to the temple—"

"No."

"Why? Because Veran failed to kill me?" She couldn't keep the sting from her voice.

"Ah, even if he'd succeeded, the Chameleon wouldn't have lifted a finger."

"But he promised—"

"Veran walked out on the priesthood. Or had you forgotten? The Chameleon is not a forgiving god."

"Nor an honorable one, it seems."

Caval shrugged. "We are his servants, not he ours."

That last was something their father might have said, but Karmel did not voice the thought. Most of her thoughts these days were better left unsaid. She studied her brother. Caval looked more drawn than usual today, his cloak pulled close about him in spite of the heat, his right arm—the arm stabbed by Mili on Dragon Day—cradled in his left.

If Caval was aware of her scrutiny, he gave no indication. "Are we

going in?" he said. "Or shall we wait until someone out here recognizes us?"

He had a point. Eleven days it had been since the Chameleons'
failed coup. Eleven days hiding in rat-infested warehouses, or houses
abandoned after the fires on Dragon Day. On the few occasions Karmel
had ventured outside, it had always been at night for fear of encoun-
tering a familiar face. Yet now she stood in plain sight—

Caval put his hand on her arm. She looked left to see a squad of
Storm Guards approaching along Peer Street. One of the men sported
a black eye, while a second had a fresh cut across his cheek. Karmel
had heard rumors of tensions between the Storm Guards and Mazana's
mercenaries—tensions that had boiled over into outright conflict
after Dutia Elemy Meddes vanished six days ago. But it didn't have
to be the Revenants these soldiers had fought. Looters, the remnants
of Imerle's personal guard, another faction within the Storm Guards:
there was no shortage of trouble abroad in Olaire. It might even have
been Chameleons they'd clashed with, for the priesthood's play for
power on Dragon Day had been neither forgotten nor forgiven. On
Karmel's travels, she had seen several old friends swinging from
makeshift gallows, including both Imrie and Colley. She had cried
when she found them hanging together, knowing she was as much
to blame for their deaths as anyone.

A murmur of conversation from the Storm Guards reached her.
She was tempted to engage her power, but if the soldiers had already
spotted her, they would know she was a Chameleon when she disappeared. If, on the other hand, she remained in sight, there was
little chance of them recognizing her.

What about Caval, though?

"Let's go," she said to her brother, gesturing to Zalli's door.

Caval strode toward the house. "Best if I go first," he said. "I'm
not the sort of man you want at your back."

For a heartbeat Karmel could only stare after him. Then she set
off in pursuit.

She caught up to him at Zalli's door. Closer now, she saw someone
had carved "bitch" in the wood. Zalli's only crime had been to be
struck down by illness, but then blame was always attached to the victims. It made Karmel wonder whether the damage to Zalli's house
had indeed been caused by the fighting on Dragon Day, or whether
the woman's neighbors had tried to drive her out.

Caval pounded his fist against the door.

No answer.

Behind, Karmel heard the Storm Guards coming near. The tread of their feet was audible over the lapping of waves from the Shallows two streets away. She felt their gazes on her, but she did not look across. Nothing suspicious here, just two hooded strangers calling on a woman with a deadly and possibly contagious disease.

Caval knocked again.

Karmel clasped Veran's ring in her left fist. What in the Nine Hells was she doing here? With his final breath, Veran had requested that Karmel be with his wife at the end, but he'd had no right to ask that of her. She owed him nothing, and Zalli even less. What was she supposed to say when the woman opened the door? "Hi, I'm the person who killed your husband. I'm the one who left his body for the fish in a cave below Dian."

Or perhaps simply that Veran had died trying to save Zalli. That he'd been thinking of her at the last. Would that come as any comfort to the dying woman, though? Would that make her final days easier?

A part of Karmel wanted to push the ring under the door and walk away. But she knew she would not. What had happened in Dian hadn't been Veran's fault. He'd done it all for the sake of his family. Karmel might have done the same thing herself two weeks ago. *Forgive me, girl,* he'd said. *Just following orders.* Caval's orders, to be precise. The recollection made Karmel uncomfortably aware of her brother at her shoulder, and she struggled against an urge to edge away from him.

And yet were Caval's reasons for betraying her any less compelling than Veran's? If she could find it in herself to forgive Veran, could she not do the same for her brother?

Still Caval's knocking had drawn no response. He reached for the handle instead. Karmel shook her head. If Zalli had been forced to bar the door against an ax-wielding neighbor, she wouldn't have left it unlocked—

The handle turned, and the door opened.

Caval stepped inside. Karmel hesitated. She couldn't turn back now, though. The jingle of the Storm Guards' armor was just behind, and how would it look to them if she retreated having come this far?

The door opened directly onto Zalli's front room. The scent of dewflowers was so strong Karmel half expected to see the floor scattered with petals. Yet it could not mask the stink of sweat and smoke and corruption. The light streaming through the doorway cut a bright fissure through the darkness. Karmel saw the shadowy outline of bookcases against the walls, a chair pulled up to a fireplace. The windows to her left were boarded. Dotted about the room were vases filled with wilting flowers.

Karmel took a step inside, then stopped. She didn't want to go any farther. Veran's wife was nowhere to be seen. There was no point in calling out to her either, since she was obviously dead. Death left in its wake a silence like no other.

Then a shadow detached itself from the wall to her right and moved into the light.

Karmel felt the blood drain from her face. She turned for the open door.

At a gesture from the stranger it slammed shut, plunging the room into darkness.

Senar Sol blinked sweat from his eyes. The opening of the door had let in a welcome breath of air, but now that it was closed again he felt the heavy heat settle on him once more. His gaze lingered on Karmel. Their confrontation on Dragon Day had lasted for barely a handful of heartbeats, yet he'd clearly left his usual warm impression on her, for there was fear in her eyes along with something altogether darker. Caval put his hand on his sword hilt, his half smile suggesting he relished the prospect of a confrontation. When he stepped forward to shield Karmel, the priestess shuffled to her left as if spurning his protection.

Senar remained still, wary of doing anything that the Chameleons might misinterpret as a precursor to an attack. Earlier, the Remnerol shaman, Jambar, had assured him this meeting would not end in bloodshed, but the old man wouldn't have warned Senar if he was sending him to his death. True, the Chameleons didn't look like they'd put up much of a fight. Both were so haggard they might not have slept since Dragon Day, and Senar hadn't forgotten the wound Mili had inflicted on Caval's sword arm. He couldn't afford to take them lightly, though—especially here in the darkness, where he'd find it harder to follow their movements if they engaged their powers.

"Mazana Creed sends her regards," he said.

Caval showed his teeth. "Mazana Creed, is it? And here I was thinking you were Imerle's man."

"I am no one's man," Senar said, more sharply than he intended. Not even his own, he sometimes thought.

Karmel spoke. "Where is Zalli?"

"If you mean the woman who lived here, she is dead." Judging by the smell of the place, she could be buried under one of the floorboards. Neither Mazana nor Jambar had told Senar how the woman had died, or even her significance to her two would-be visitors. The Chameleons didn't seem overly distressed at her passing, though. If anything, Karmel's expression showed more relief than sorrow, while her brother's look was one of wry amusement.

"How did you find us?" Caval asked.

"Jambar told me you would be here."

"The shaman has taken to finding people, has he? Is that before or after he makes them disappear?"

"I'll ask him next time I see him," Senar said. If there ever *was* a next time. The Remnerol had proved impossible to track down these past few days, though only for the Guardian it seemed.

Karmel waved a hand at a fly buzzing round her. "What do you want?"

"Mazana Creed wants to speak to you."

"As she wanted to speak to Elemy Meddes?"

A fair point. Senar had heard rumors of Mazana inviting the dutia to a meeting at the palace before disposing of him. There were also stories of her tracking down and executing the Sabian dignitaries who had survived Dragon Day on the ship of that Gilgamarian Kalisch, Agenta Webb. Senar could believe them too, but as it happened, the emira had bigger plans for the Chameleons. And he wouldn't have agreed to fetch them if he thought he was leading them into a trap.

"It's been eleven days since Dragon Day," Karmel said. "Eleven. Why has it taken so long for her to track us down?"

To answer that question, Senar would have to tell the Chameleons what Mazana intended for them, and that was something he couldn't risk doing until she had prepared the ground. The Guardian himself had had three days to get used to the audacity of her scheme, and even now, when he considered it, he found himself shaking his head.

"We're wasting time," he said. "If Mazana wanted you dead, she would have sent a squad of Storm Guards in my place. Or the executioner."

"We're supposed to take your presence as a comfort, then?"

There was nothing he could say to that, so he kept his mouth shut. The silence dragged out.

Karmel stared at Caval. Of the two of them, Senar had assumed it would be Caval who called the shots. But a twitch of the man's shoulders in answer to Karmel's questioning look suggested he would leave the decision to his sister. Perhaps that was for the best too. There was a lightheartedness to Caval that left Senar feeling uneasy, for it indicated a carelessness of spirit that would make him impossible to predict.

Karmel looked back at the Guardian, her expression defiant. "You say Jambar foresaw this meeting. So tell us, do we come quietly?"

Senar scratched the stubs of his missing fingers. "Most of the time."

"And if we don't, do we leave here alive?"

"I won't try to stop you."

It hardly needed saying, of course, that Mazana wasn't the sort of woman to take no for an answer, no matter how politely the question was posed. Or that she could easily find the Chameleons again if she wanted to. It wasn't as if one could run far on an island surrounded by dragon-infested waters. If anyone knew that, it was Senar himself.

Karmel held his gaze, then took something out of her pocket. Senar tensed, but it was only a ring. A wedding band. The priestess tossed it aside, and it struck the floor before rolling into darkness beneath one of the bookcases.

"Lead on," she said.

As Romany strode through the palace corridors, her stomach pitched and heaved in time to the distant lap of waves against a seawall. The air was humid, as if it retained a memory of the water that had once filled these passages, and there were other signs too of the recent flooding: the waterlines on the walls, the silt that crunched beneath Romany's sandals, the stench of decay from some fish left to rot in a courtyard.

Behind the priestess walked a Storm Guard she'd met at the palace gates. He had insisted on escorting her to Mazana Creed, but he needn't have bothered. Thanks to Romany's sorcerous web, she knew better than he where the emira was to be found. At the last intersection, she had gone left when the soldier had continued straight on, and the man was now jogging to catch up to her. As he drew level, he started prattling about his respect for the Lord of Hidden Faces, no doubt working himself up to asking if Romany had taken a vow of celibacy. At the gates he'd relieved her of her knife. The priestess felt oddly incomplete without it.

As they turned a corner, the Storm Guard fell silent. Mazana Creed was coming toward them. She looked more like a courtier than a ruler, with her air-magic pendant and her dress cut so low it seemed its maker must have run out of material before he could finish it. She walked with a muscular stride ahead of six Storm Guards. Six body-guards to protect her in her own palace? Doubtless the emira feared trouble in the early days of her reign, though judging by where the soldiers' gazes were fixed, they must have been expecting an assassin to spring from her backside.

An assassin? Romany thought sourly. *I'm over here.*

Mazana slowed when she saw the priestess. Her expression darkened. Evidently she was no more pleased to see Romany than Romany was to be here. The emira was taller than the priestess, but not nearly as attractive as she probably thought she was. Her face had too many hard lines, and her eyes had a tinge of redness as if she'd been crying recently. Romany considered. How should she play this encounter? Of all the people to antagonize, a woman who had murdered a god was probably worst among them. If the priestess could nettle her, though, might Mazana send her away and thus force the Spider to choose another?

Romany could certainly have fun finding out.

She halted. Mazana drew up in front of her.

"You're not the priestess I've been dealing with," the emira said.

"The Lord has more than one, you may be surprised to hear."

"And, what, your sister couldn't face the walk down from the temple?"

"If it were that simple, I would have carried her here on my back."

Mazana gave a false smile. "We could share the burden, perhaps."

Romany sighed with feeling. "Alas, the Lord has chosen me to attend you."

"You are to join my councils, then? Is your god calling in his debt?"

"Yes, that sounds like a fair trade: the help my Lord has given you in exchange for the honor of me sharing your company for a time."

"And if I should choose to send you back to your god?"

Romany smiled behind her mask. Oh, this was too easy. "You would dare to refuse his order?"

Mazana was tempted, she knew. Romany could see it in the way she pursed her lips to keep herself from speaking. *Do it,* the priestess silently urged. It was the only way for Mazana to save face with the Storm Guards who had witnessed the exchange. The soldier who'd escorted Romany was shifting beside her, clearly unhappy at the association that came from standing at her shoulder. The men behind the emira seemed no less embarrassed. One was pretending an interest in a wall. It was missing a chunk of plaster where some weapon must have struck it during the fighting on Dragon Day.

When Romany looked back at Mazana, though, the sudden quirk to the other woman's mouth suggested she was enjoying their chat as much as the priestess herself. Romany scowled. Oh, amusing was it? Would the emira still be smiling if the priestess took off her mask? Would she be smiling when Romany buried a knife in her back?

She stiffened. Plunge a blade into someone else's flesh? Just the thought of it brought a bitter tickle to her throat.

Just then she sensed a ripple along her web. It came from the corridor behind Mazana. Someone powerful was approaching, though in a place such as this there would be no shortage of those, she supposed. She looked past the emira.

And blinked.

An old woman in a servant's livery was shuffling toward them like she was dragging the weight of the world behind. No one that Romany recognized. She had a squint and a stoop that made her long hair fall over her face. Looked harmless enough. But there were some who would have said the same about Romany, and as a priestess of the Spider, you learned to look past the *seeming*.

Sweat poured off the stranger. Perhaps it was just the heat. When you added in the darting eyes, though, and the hand tucked into her robe . . .

An assassin.

But an old woman? Didn't she know this was a young person's game? Was she trying to give the profession a bad name?

Romany's gaze brushed the stranger's. The woman's look was calm, but it was a forced calm with the merest hint of desperation mixed in. No prizes for guessing who her target would be: Mazana. Romany was less clear, though, on what she should do about the assassin. The Storm Guards hadn't noticed her yet, which meant she had a chance of reaching Mazana if Romany stayed quiet. Would it be a bad thing if the emira died now? Odds were, Romany would end up having to kill the woman eventually, and the sooner she went Shroud's way, the sooner Romany could return to Mercerie.

Yes, minding her own business seemed the most prudent course.

Alas, it appeared her gaze had already betrayed the stranger's presence. Mazana turned to look back just as the old woman reached the rearmost of her bodyguards.

The assassin sprang forward with unexpected agility. When she removed her hand from her robe, she was clutching a dagger that pulsed with dark sorcery. Plainly she knew nothing about wielding a knife, for instead of holding the weapon out in front and lunging for Mazana's chest, she lifted it high above her head.

Making it easy for the nearest Storm Guard to seize her wrist and stop the downswing before it even started.

The assassin had no second blade. She didn't think to butt the soldier in the face or drive her knee between his legs. Instead she engaged the man in a hopeless battle of strength. A second soldier made a grab for the knife. Teeth bared and sandals squeaking, the three antagonists lurched and grunted across the corridor like deadbeats fighting over a blackweed stick. The old woman was obviously stronger than she looked, because she kept her grip on the knife.

Then another Storm Guard stepped in and punched her in the face. *Sloppy,* Romany thought. The way he'd curled his fist like that, he could have broken his fingers when he hit her. Better to use the ball of the hand . . .

Gods, what was wrong with her?

The old woman was sent reeling by the punch. She collided with the wall and lost her grasp on the dagger, then slumped to the ground. The weapon fell to the floor with a ringing sound. There was blood on the blade, Romany saw. The assassin's? No, one of the Storm Guards had a cut to the back of his hand. He cradled it to his chest. He'd probably inflicted greater wounds on himself while shaving, but still he screwed up his face in pain like the hand had been lopped clean off.

Silence.

Romany waited.

The guard who had punched the assassin was shaking his hand

out. The others, even the ones who'd played no part in the scuffle, were huffing like they'd just wrestled a titan.

Mazana tapped a foot as she surveyed them. "Well done, sirs—oh, well done indeed! I thought I'd need a dozen guards to protect me from old women, but no, you've proved six is enough." Then she turned her gaze on the assassin. When she spoke, her tone was a mix of amusement and foreboding. "Well, well, Mistress Darbonna. What a pleasant surprise."

Romany tried to place the name among the others she'd heard since arriving in Olaire. *Of course, the librarian from the Founder's Citadel. The priestess of Fume.* The flesh round the old woman's left eye had started to bruise and swell. Her orbs were glazed, but she still stared at Mazana with a look of arresting malice.

"Leave it!" the emira snapped in a voice that could have flayed skin.

One of the Storm Guards had moved to collect Darbonna's knife. He froze at Mazana's command, and the emira bent to retrieve it herself.

Some instinct made Romany open her mouth to shout "no!" but it was too late.

Mazana's fingers closed around the weapon's hilt.

There was no flash of light, no roll of thunder. Romany didn't know why she'd nearly called out, yet her intuition told her something important had just happened. Something portentous. For an instant, Romany felt a sense of danger so strong she thought Mazana might turn toward her and plunge the blade into her chest.

Instead the emira lifted it with wary tenderness. It must have been an emotional moment, because the red tinge to her eyes became more intense.

A dozen heartbeats passed, then she glanced at Romany. Her smile was back, but there was a calculation in her expression too. Clearly she knew she might have died here, had it not been for Romany's awareness of Darbonna's approach.

The priestess sighed. She'd been sent to kill the woman, and the first thing she'd done was save her life.

She felt a tug in her guts, sensing what was coming next.

"Welcome aboard," Mazana said.

CHAPTER 3

AMEREL GAZED out of the window of her third-story room. For some reason, the Erin Elalese spy in Dresk's court had chosen to put her up in a brothel. From the windows below, painted ladies leaned out and shouted bawdy greetings to the people in the marketplace. The market was covered by a reeking haze from the fish boileries. Voices floated up from the murk, peddling coral birds and Elescorian brandy, fish-bone jewelry and Alosian patchwork dolls. Curled around the stanchions of one stall was a vast tentacle, thick as the trunk of a ketar tree. The shop's owner was doing a roaring trade, hacking off slices of the ever-shrinking limb for an unending flow of customers. At the next stall a man was selling plates with gold decorations that would have graced any king's banquet. Yet they were being hawked for the same price as the tentacle, and drawing less custom besides.

A market this size, you'd think it was the center of trade for the civilized world, but there were few signs of civilization on show. A woman lay facedown in a fountain to Amerel's left, and a man was urinating on her. At the center of the square, a crowd had gathered around a pit in which two naked men were wrestling in the dust and rubble. Beyond, a splash of color caught Amerel's eye, and a group of red-cloaked figures emerged from the throng with a gaggle of orphans and beggars in tow. Their stony complexions made them look like they'd just stepped from a rock face. So little attention did they draw from the Rubyholters, you might have thought walking statues were a common sight in these parts. No doubt someone somewhere in the market was selling them for a breeze.

She tracked the Augerans' progress as they disappeared and re-appeared among the stalls. One of their number was the largest man she had ever seen, yet she found her gaze drawn to the smallest member of the group—a man with spiked hair and a skip to his stride like he was dancing a step with each Rubyholter he passed. Amerel tried to read in the group's expressions how their meeting with Dresk had gone. She was too far away, though, to see their faces clearly, and in any event the longer she looked, the more she felt a sensation like she was being watched in turn. An irrational fear, perhaps, but still she withdrew into shadow before the stone-skins reached Harbor Road.

She shifted her gaze north. Behind the market was a stretch of rooftops that ended at the curtain wall of Dresk's fortress. Beyond the wall, the top part of the Great Hall was visible, along with a single tower flanking it—the other tower had collapsed in the time since Amerel was last here. A very different Amerel that had been, before she'd killed her first man as a Guardian and realized too late what all those years practicing with pieces of sharpened metal had been for. When she'd heard Dresk's spy needed help, she had volunteered to go. Foolishly she'd thought a diplomatic mission might spare her the need to blood her sword again. But she'd quickly learned that diplomacy was nothing more than the gilding on the scabbard of a hidden blade. In recounting to Noon how she'd steered Galantas's suspicions away from the Erin Elalese spy, she'd neglected to mention how she had fixed them instead on a servant in Dresk's court. She never found out what happened to that servant. Worse still, she knew she didn't care.

Noon was whistling behind her. She looked back to see the Breaker sitting on his cot, assembling the various parts of a crossbow. He wouldn't ask her, of course, but he'd be wondering what she planned to do next—as indeed she was wondering herself. Should she present herself to Dresk and press the emperor's case, as planned? Risky, now that the stone-skins were here. Or should she track down the Augeran commander and assassinate him? It might put a dent in the enemy high command, but could she be sure the stone-skins would hold the Rubyholters responsible? Might they not point the finger at Erin Elal instead?

It was a chance Amerel couldn't afford to take, for she had set her sights higher than thinning the enemy's numbers by one. Nothing less than a rift between the Augerans and the Islanders would do, and an unbridgeable rift besides.

Noon said, "While we're waiting for this spy to show, maybe now would be a good time to start my Will-training."

"Have you mastered the mental exercises they gave you in Arkarbour?"

"No."

"Then we have nothing more to talk about."

Noon fastened the shoulder slides to the sides of the crossbow's barrel before attaching the shoulder stock extension. "I thought you were supposed to be teaching me the Will, not the finer points of meditation."

The way he said it, you'd think meditation wasn't a priority for an assassin. "Before you can manipulate energies with the Will, you must first learn to perceive them," Amerel said. "But don't worry if you find it difficult at the start." She gave a half smile. "It took me years to master the art."

"Stone-skins aren't going to allow me that luxury, Princess."

"Yes, that is a problem. Makes me wonder why the emperor is so keen for the Breakers to learn the Will at all."

"Your friend Borkoth has been getting results. Heard a woman knocked him off his feet with her Will when he suggested how she could repay him for his training. And yet *you're* the one who's supposed to be the great teacher." He paused. "Anyone would think you're not as willing to share your knowledge as you'd like Avallon to believe."

He was right, of course. And not out of misplaced loyalty to the Guardians either. When the emperor had come knocking, it had been easy for Amerel to turn her back on the order, because she'd started the process herself many years previously. The hard part had been accepting Avallon's authority over her. At least in this small way, though, she could fight back. "A teacher is only as good as her pupil. You know how many Fenilar children make the grade? One in fifteen. The Will can't be learned like swordsmanship. Either you have the ability or you don't."

"But you said I can only use the Will if there's no doubt in my mind that I can do so. How can *anyone* know they can use it, if they've never done so before?"

"They can't."

Noon inserted the crossbow's trigger components into the stock. "And you don't see a contradiction there?"

"The Fenilar learn the Will as children. They are taught to believe they have the skill before they learn the cynicism that comes from failure."

"But only *Fenilar* children do the learning."

"Obviously. It's only by keeping the knowledge secret that the Guardians have been able to stop it falling into the wrong hands." Like the hands of someone who could challenge their privileged position within the empire, for example.

"There've been Guardians from outside the caste before, though, haven't there? Luker Essendar for one."

"And look how he turned out."

Noon grimaced. One subject, at least, on which they could agree.

Into the silence that followed came footsteps from the passage outside. They stopped at the door. Noon set down his crossbow and covered it with his blanket before moving to stand beside the doorway. Amerel closed the window and turned her back to it. Within moments, the heat in the room began to build.

Someone knocked.

"Enter," Amerel said.

The door opened to reveal a middle-aged man wearing a green shirt bearing the spear symbol of Dresk's clan. The years since Amerel had last met him had not been kind, for he was leaning on a walking stick. As he stepped into the room, Noon pushed the door closed. Talet half spun round, wincing as his weight came down on his bad leg.

"Come in," Noon said. "My compliments on your choice for our quarters. If nothing else they embarrassed our princess here"—he gestured to Amerel—"enough to bring some color to her cheeks."

Talet wiped sweat from his brow. "The brothel isn't for your benefit; it's for mine. Fewer questions this way if someone sees me arriving." He took in Amerel's black-lined eyes and white hair. "I preferred you as a brunette."

"So did I," Amerel said. Talet extended a hand, and she shook it. Best friends now. "You're late," she said.

Noon chuckled. "Yes, to business. Those pleasantries were starting to drag."

Talet's gaze remained on Amerel. "You're lucky I'm here at all. When I left Dresk, he was still talking to his krels. I took a risk leaving when I did."

"We'll sort you out a medal later. In the meantime you can tell us how the Augerans managed to turn up today when you said they'd be arriving tomorrow."

Talet shuffled to Amerel's bed and sat down. "I told you what *I* was told. The stone-skins' arrival took Dresk by surprise as much as it did you."

"They didn't send a message to say they'd be early?"

"No. And even if they had done, how was I supposed to get word to you on the *Whitecap*? With smoke signals?"

Amerel smiled faintly. "What did we miss at the fortress?"

Talet collected his thoughts before beginning his account of Dresk's meeting with the stone-skins.

"A moment," Amerel cut in after no more than a dozen words. "The Augeran commander spoke the common tongue?"

The spy grunted. "Better than Dresk, truth be told."

"And the other stone-skins too?"

"As far as I could tell."

Amerel exchanged a look with Noon. If the Augerans had learned the common tongue, that meant their coming here had been long in the planning indeed. She motioned for Talet to continue, and he took up his narrative again. Noon whistled when he heard how much the Augerans had offered to secure the Rubyholters' cooperation. After years of war with the Kalanese, Amerel doubted such a sum existed in the whole of Erin Elal.

"Did the stone-skins confirm that Erin Elal would be their target?" Noon asked Talet.

"No."

"But they did say where they'd be setting up this base they mentioned?"

"No."

"And Dresk didn't think to ask?"

Talet shrugged.

Amerel said, "What about the timing of the Augerans' campaign? Will they strike before winter?"

"Their commander didn't say. But he wants this agreement signed today. That suggests the stone-skins are looking to move quickly. Maybe there'll be some details in the treaty itself. If so, I'll be able to tell you when I see it later."

"You're sure Dresk will sign, then?"

"Of course. Before I left, the talk was not *if* he should sign, but whether he should share the money with the other tribes."

Amerel crossed her arms. "For the treaty to work, the stone-skins will need passage through all the Isles. Does Dresk have authority over the other clans' territories?"

"Depends who you ask. Dresk would say yes. The tribes may see things differently."

Noon was shaking his head. "Twenty thousand talents, and Dresk doesn't want to share? What's he going to do with all that money, pave the streets with gold?"

"It's not that simple," Talet said. "If Dresk keeps the money, the other tribes will call him greedy. But if he shares it, they'll think him weak. Better greedy than weak, Dresk will say. And he's probably right too."

Amerel turned to look out the window. To the east she saw Galantas's steel-hulled ship gliding between two of the islets that shielded the harbor. Leaving so soon? "What about Galantas?" she said. "Where does he stand on this?"

"His father was keen to accept the stone-skins' deal, so naturally Galantas had doubts. He spoke sense too, but it hardly matters now. The pigs are already lining up at the trough."

Pigs? "You would have turned down the twenty thousand talents yourself, then?"

Talet did not respond.

The Guardian gazed out the window again. Twenty thousand talents. Such a sum made Amerel's course here much clearer, for there was no point in her speaking to Dresk now. You didn't persuade a pirate to refuse that sort of money, no matter how strong your Will was. It would be like persuading him to stop breathing.

An idea formed in her mind, and she looked back at the fortress. On the battlements a lone guard was leaning against one of the merlons and vomiting over the side. Who knew, maybe he'd spotted an old flame passing by. How far to the wall? she wondered. Two hundred armspans? Close enough for that crossbow of Noon's?

Undoubtedly.

"When exactly are the stone-skins due back at the fortress?" she asked Talet.

"At the seventh bell. Why?"

Amerel considered not telling him, but she would need his help to make her scheme work. "Because I'm planning on killing their commander before he signs the treaty."

The spy's brows drew in. "Why?" he said again. "The stone-skins' agreement with Dresk will unravel long before the Islanders fulfill their part of their bargain."

"Will it?"

"Of course it will. I've already told you, the other tribes won't let Dresk dictate to them. When he refuses to share the money, they'll make a point of hunting down any stone-skin ship that strays into their waters. This could play out to the emperor's benefit."

"The Augerans will still have Dresk's scouts to guide them through the Isles. Not to mention the base he promised."

"Assuming he hasn't disappeared with the money by then."

"Assuming? You would risk the fate of the empire on an assumption?"

Talet shifted under her gaze. "If you're going to kill someone, kill Dresk. When Galantas takes his place, he'll send the Augerans packing."

"Assuming his opposition to the money doesn't die with his father."

"Assuming, yes."

Amerel let the silence drag out. Most likely Talet's claims about the durability of the treaty were true, but they weren't the real reason for his objection to her plan. He'd lived in Bezzle for years, so it wasn't surprising he'd built up ties among the Islanders. Stronger ties than those that bound him to Erin Elal? Amerel watched the thoughts race behind his eyes.

"If you assassinate the commander," he said, "what makes you so sure the Augerans will think Dresk is responsible?"

"Because I intend to kill him inside the warlord's fortress."

Talet barked a laugh. "And how are you going to do that? The stone-skins are bringing an empire's weight in gold, which means they'll be coming in numbers. And Dresk has already called in more men. I won't be able to smuggle you in."

"You won't need to. I can see as much of the fortress as I need to from here."

Noon came to stand beside her and looked across the marketplace. "You expect me to shoot the stone-skin from here?"

"The fortress is within crossbow range, isn't it?"

"Absolutely, Princess. You just have to convince the commander to climb to the wall and stand still long enough for me to line up a shot."

"Won't work," Amerel said. "If the Augerans are to believe that Dresk killed their leader, he has to die where only the warlord's forces can reach him. We'll take him out as he crosses the bailey."

Noon laughed. "I may be the best shot in Erin Elal, but even my chances of hitting a target I can't see are limited." His eyes twinkled. "No better than seven in ten."

Talet said, "Guardian, I urge you to reconsider. If you kill Eremo, the stone-skins aren't going to be content with recovering their money. They'll want revenge."

"We can hope."

"And Dresk isn't going to stand alone against them. He'll drag his people into the fight."

Now we get to it. "The Islanders are a piece on the playing board whether they like it or not. The only question is, who gets to play that piece first, us or the stone-skins?"

Talet scowled. "This isn't their war."

A bloodroach scuttled out from under Amerel's bed, and she crushed it beneath the heel of a sandal. "If the stone-skins attack the Isles, that's an attack that might otherwise have fallen on Erin Elal. Them or us, it's as simple as that."

" 'Them or us' means something different when you've lived here as long as I have. You're asking me to condemn friends—"

"I'm not asking you, I'm telling you." Amerel moved closer. "To listen to you, you'd think you cared more about the Isles than you do about your homeland. Perhaps you need to remind yourself where your loyalties lie." Not easy keeping a straight face with those last words. Next thing she knew, she'd be accusing him of betrayal.

Talet drew himself up. "You dare question my allegiance? Twelve years I've spent in this shithole! Twelve years wiping Dresk's ass and whispering poison in his ear to keep the tribes at each other's throats!"

"And why at each other's throats? To stop them uniting, of course. To protect the empire. Is that so different from what we're doing here?" Amerel stepped closer still. She'd given Talet a touch of the whip, now it was time to use her Will to salve his cuts. She lowered the pitch of her voice. It was the same voice she'd used to soothe Lyssa during the weeks after her mother's death. "You know the stone-skins. You know their history is written in blood. Once they've finished with Erin Elal, do you think a treaty with Dresk is going to stop them turning on the Isles? Better the Rubyholters face the threat head-on than get a knife in the back when they're least expecting it." Unless that knife was Avallon's, of course.

"They need time to prepare."

"So does Erin Elal." Amerel laced her voice with the Will. "And from what your reports say, the Islanders already have a warning system to protect them if they're attacked. When the stone-skins come, the bells will ring. And the Rubyholters will melt away, just as they've done a hundred times before."

Talet's face was getting a sheen of sweat to it. He tried to break Amerel's gaze, gave his head a shake as if he sensed her hold on him and was trying to free himself. But she had him caught as surely as a fish on a hook. He made to speak, then stopped himself. Finally he looked up in helpless appeal and said, "I have a son here. Surely the emperor . . ." His words trailed off.

A year ago Amerel might have laughed in his face. Not now, though. Not after Lyssa. Still, did he really think the emperor cared about his boy? That he could afford to? Avallon had the welfare of an empire to consider. And nothing—*nothing*—could be allowed to jeopardize the success of this mission.

Faced with the Guardian's silence, Talet tried again. "I need to make arrangements to move my son—"

"No," Amerel cut in. "Not until our business with the stone-skins is complete. If you move the boy, someone might ask questions. There will be time for that later."

"Could he come back with you when this is done? To Erin Elal?"

"If that's what you want."

The silence stretched out again. Talet stared at Amerel like he was weighing up what she'd told him, but she already knew what his answer would be. Doubts were what she fed on, and the spy was genuinely torn between his allegiances to Erin Elal and the Isles. A final nudge of her Will was enough to steer his course toward his homeland. The last part of his resistance buckled.

He hung his head. "What's the plan?"

From the quarterdeck of the *Eternal,* Galantas watched the waves being cut to foam by the submerged ruins. He knew this stretch of water well. Just beneath the surface off the port quarter was a domed roof whose high point you could stand on. Years ago, he'd won a bet here with a drunken Needle clansman over whether he could walk on water. Nice little earner that had been, and all part of the legend he'd created for himself. The sight of the dome now should have brought a smile to his face, but instead he found himself thinking about the ancient civilization that had built it. Dead that civilization might be, yet it had left a mark on these lands that had survived for centuries. What had the Rubyholters fashioned that would last that long? They didn't even build their own cities, merely grubbed about in the bones of the old, waiting for the next invader to sail through and raze them.

That had to change.

The headland to Galantas's left started to drop away to reveal Tinker's Strait—the narrowest part of the South Corridor. This was a favorite spot for Ravin's krels. Galantas had used it a few times himself. The cliffs to the west, along with the headland to the east, offered cover for ambushers, while the labyrinth of underwater ruins there meant a ship sailing through the strait without a water-mage would have nowhere to run once the trap was sprung. Galantas frowned. And yet the stone-skins *would* have had a water-mage for a journey across the Southern Wastes. So why hadn't they retreated when the Falcons broke cover? Or made a break for the open waters to the north?

Unless, of course, they'd wanted the confrontation.

Above the headland Galantas could see the topsails of two vessels. Their rigging had been torn loose in places, and there seemed to be something—no, some *things*—hanging from the lower yards . . .

"Sender's mercy," said Qinta, his Second, from beside him.

Bodies.

The yards had been transformed into makeshift gallows. Dozens of corpses swung back and forth in the breeze. Where the yards met the masts, more Rubyholters had been pinned to the wood—crucified, most likely. Still more bodies were piled on the main deck. Covering the dead, along with every inch of rigging, was a shifting white blanket of squabbling starbeaks. Galantas gave a low whistle. From Eremo's talk of sending messages, Galantas had known to expect a spectacle. When he'd walked through the harbor, though, he'd seen the stone-skin flagship without a scratch on it, and he'd wondered if he had misread the signs.

Something didn't add up, however. Ravin's Falcons were a steady bunch. There was no way two of their ships could have been routed by a solitary Augeran vessel, meaning Eremo must have had help from other stone-skins.

So where were these helpers now?

As the headland fell away, Galantas saw two boats plying the waters of the strait. The Augerans manning them were fishing from the waves the corpses of Rubyholters who must have died trying to flee the massacre. Tidying up after themselves, perhaps? Or checking to ensure there was no one who could report on what had happened here?

"Do you recognize the ships?" Galantas asked Qinta.

The Second crossed his tattooed arms. "Three-master's called the *Lively*. Yali is her captain."

Or *was* her captain.

The breeze picked up, and Galantas caught the smell of blayfire oil. One of the boats had drawn alongside the two-master and was unloading its grisly catch. The crew of the other boat, meanwhile, had stopped to stare at the *Eternal*. Galantas could make out four stone-skins on board. One wore a red cloak, the others black—

"Captain," Qinta said, pointing south.

Galantas looked in the direction indicated and saw an islet in the distance. Maybe a stone's throw across, it was little more than a tumble of rocks and yellow grasses.

Then he realized it wasn't the islet his Second had been pointing at, but a man swimming in the water near it. A survivor. *A witness.* Must have played dead all this time to avoid the stone-skins' notice. Now he started shouting to the *Eternal* and waving his hands in the air. Surprising reaction, really. Usually the best a drowning Islander could hope for from another clan was a boot on the head to speed his passage through Shroud's Gate. But clearly a swift death was better than what he'd get from the Augerans if they saw him.

And seen him they had. A wave of water-magic burgeoned beneath the nearest stone-skin boat, and it went shooting toward the man like a bolt fired from a ballista.

Oh no you don't.

Galantas gauged distances. The *Eternal* was closer to the swimmer, but the Augeran craft had the advantage of both weight and maneuverability. Galantas located his water-mage beside the ship's wheel. He was combing his long hair with a fish-bone comb.

"Barnick!" Galantas shouted.

The *Eternal* rose with a rush and fizz of water.

And the race was on.

Submerged ruins flashed past to either side of the ship. Ahead Galantas saw three towers beneath the waves like the prongs of a trident, and for an improbable moment he imagined them thrusting out of the sea to skewer the hull. The swimmer thrashed through the waves toward the *Eternal*. Just a few hundred armspans away now. Galantas gripped his shark-tooth necklace so tight, the teeth dug into his skin. The wind made his sharkskin cape billow behind him. He looked at the Augerans. The wave beneath their boat was of a size to match the *Eternal*'s. At the prow, the stone-skin in the red cloak leaned out as far as he could, as if he thought that would hasten their passage.

"Gonna be a close thing," Qinta said.

Too close for Galantas's liking. Maintain this course and speed, and they might beat the stone-skins to the swimmer only to roll over him and drown him beneath the hull.

"Barnick," he called. "A point to starboard."

The *Eternal* changed course.

The islet rushed closer. Was it just Galantas's imagination, or had the wave under the stone-skin boat grown larger? There was a corpse on the sea in front of it, and as the craft passed by, the body rose with the wave before falling behind amid a trail of white spume.

Qinta said, "Want me to get the lads to fire a few shots across their bows? Might spook them into slowing."

It might also end up with a stone-skin joining the corpses in the water. Galantas shook his head. He didn't want to start a war here. For while the prospect of losing his father twenty thousand talents was appealing, he might be inheriting that money soon. Besides, it looked like he was winning the race. The man in the red cloak gestured and shouted to the Rubyholters to give ground.

"Hold your course," Galantas shouted to Barnick.

"We're gonna bump 'em," Qinta said.

"It'll hurt them more than it hurts us."

The stone-skins must have reached the same conclusion, for the wave beneath their craft receded. Immediately Barnick slowed the *Eternal*'s rush so it did not overshoot its target. The deck tilted, and Galantas seized the rail. The quartermaster, Drefel, sprawled to the boards and swore. As the ship settled on the sea, the dregs of the wave that had been carrying it went hissing toward the islet. A crash, a spray of white, then a dozen nesting limewings took flight, squawking.

The swimmer was now abeam to port, bobbing on the swell. The wave created by the *Eternal*'s coming washed over him, and he went under before breaking the surface again.

"Get him up here," Galantas said to Qinta.

The Second nodded and moved off.

Some of the crew were whooping and jeering at the Augeran boat off the starboard bow. The stone-skins, by contrast, were silent. Bad losers, going by their scowls, but that just made the *Eternal*'s crew cheer louder. Galantas could see a handful of corpses at the bottom of the Augeran boat, all studded with crossbow bolts. The stone-skin in the red cloak was watching him. As his gaze locked to Galantas's, he lifted a sandaled foot and lowered it onto the face of a dead woman. Then he twisted it back and forth like he was putting out a blackweed stick.

A new wave raised the Augeran boat high and carried it toward the *Eternal*. The hulls of the two craft came together with a thud and a clank, and the red-cloaked stone-skin seized the rail and sprang over it. Tall bastard, he was. Taller even than Qinta, though not as broad. His skin was a lighter hue than that of the Augerans Galantas had met in Bezzle. The jeers of the *Eternal*'s crew died away. A hundred sets of hard eyes were fixed on him, yet he might have been a captain come to inspect his crew for all the apprehension he showed. He crossed to the stairs and climbed to the quarterdeck.

Qinta was waiting for him at the top. The stone-skin tried to move around to get to Galantas, but the Second blocked him.

"Qinta," Galantas said, and the Islander stepped back.

When the Augeran approached, he brought with him a whiff of blayfire oil. He stopped a pace away. Not a sailor, judging by the way he swayed with every shift of the deck. He stared at Galantas, and Galantas felt the gazes of his crew upon him. Anticipating the confrontation to come, no doubt. Some men might have been intimidated by that expectation, but Galantas was never more comfortable than when playing to an audience.

"Welcome aboard," he said to the stone-skin. "I am Galantas Galair of the Spears. And you are?"

"My name Ostari Abrahim al Third, Peer of Honored." The Augeran looked about him. "Curious is ship. Metal plates on hull made steel?"

Galantas nodded. Evidently not every stone-skin spoke the common tongue with the same fluency as Commander Eremo.

"Slow and heavy must make," Ostari added.

"It didn't seem to hold us back just now."

The Augeran pressed on. "Bulkheads on low decks, plates make tight against water?"

"Yes. There is also an inner skin of steel. Together with the plating on the hull, it makes the ship impenetrable to rams."

"Though is little use when defend enemy that tries to board."

"I wouldn't know about that." Galantas looked at his crew. "We're the ones who do the boarding, eh, lads?"

Chuckles greeted his words.

Ostari's smile was glacial.

There was movement at the corner of Galantas's eye. He looked across to see Squint and Critter heaving on a line over the port rail. A head of red hair appeared over the gunwale, and the two crewmen reached over and hauled the swimmer onto the deck. He lay gasping on the boards, curled up like a newborn. He was younger than Galantas had been expecting, maybe only fourteen or fifteen. The youth's gaze settled on the red-cloaked Augeran before shying away.

Ostari said to Galantas, "See you have something mine."

"Oh?"

"Boy on ship that attack us."

Galantas raised an eyebrow. "I saw your flagship in our harbor earlier. There was no damage to it."

"Did not say attack successful."

"But you took casualties?"

"Minor scrapes, that all."

"Explains why you felt the need to turn those ships"—Galantas gestured to the stricken Rubyholt vessels—"into floating gallows."

Ostari pointed to the survivor. "By law, his life mine."

"What law is that?"

"Augeran maritime law. Can quote sections, if want."

Galantas leaned forward. "I'll let you in on a secret," he said. "You're not *in* Augera anymore."

Ostari straightened. "And what your laws say done? I assume *have* laws here."

"Under our laws, a pirate must atone for his crime by serving the clan he attacked." If he was stupid enough to get caught, that is. And if he hadn't already suffered a more lasting punishment.

"Perfect," Ostari said, showing his teeth. "I promise care well of him."

Galantas let the silence drag out. He wanted the watching Falcon boy to feel his life being weighed. The more the youth convinced himself he was doomed, the more grateful he'd be when he was spared. "I think not," Galantas said at last.

"But is law, you say yourself."

Galantas snorted. The only true law in the Isles came at the end of a blade, as the Augerans had proved to the Falcons. Too late for them now to cry foul. They'd used the fight to send a message to the clans, and Galantas intended to send a message of his own. "If you feel aggrieved, you can take your complaint to the next gathering of clan leaders at the Hub. I'm sure they'll give you a fair hearing."

"I am sure. Must wonder, though, if your reaction be different if *we* victims, not Rubyholters."

Galantas did not respond.

Ostari studied him. "You said you Spear clan? Hear you agree today with us over sail through Isles. Bad start if let man go."

"The agreement isn't signed yet."

The Augeran nodded as if that was the answer he'd expected. Then he spun and headed back the way he'd come. His shoulder brushed Qinta's as he passed. When he reached the main deck, he cast a final look at the Falcon boy before vaulting over the rail and into his waiting boat.

The craft sped away.

Galantas watched it go, wondering how Eremo would react to this afternoon's events. Doubtless he'd complain to Dresk, but by that time the Falcon would be back among his own people. And Galantas suspected the treaty was too important to the stone-skins to cancel it over the fate of one boy. Of more interest was how the Falcon's clan leader, Ravin, would take the news of what had happened here—not just with regard to Galantas's intervention, but also to the stone-skins' treatment of Yali's men. He could have no complaint, of course, that the Augerans had defended themselves against raiders. But the butchery that had followed had surely crossed a line.

He looked at Critter and gestured to the survivor. "Bring him."

Critter hauled the Falcon to his feet and pushed him toward Galantas. The youth came slowly, his gaze fixed on the deck. For all he knew, Galantas might have spared him from Ostari just so he could kill him himself. Relations between the Spears and Falcons had been strained of late. Only a week ago, one of Dresk's krels had killed a Falcon in a dispute over some barren lump of rock no bigger than the islet off the *Eternal*'s bow.

Another shove from Critter sent the boy crashing into the steps to the quarterdeck. He climbed them in sullen silence and halted before Galantas, his red hair hanging across his eyes.

"Who are you?" Galantas asked.

Critter said, "What he means is, are you worth anything to us as ransom?"

Laughs from the crew, and Galantas made a calming gesture with his hand. "What's your name?" he said.

"Allott," the Falcon muttered.

"Allott, *Captain*."

The boy did not reply.

Qinta said, "I recognize him. You're Tusker's bastard, ain't you?"

Allott said nothing.

Tusker, as in Ravin's dead brother? That would make Allot the clan leader's nephew. *Better and better.* "What happened here?" Galantas asked.

Silence.

Qinta growled and stepped forward, but Galantas blocked him with his arm. *Okay, let's try something easier.* He indicated the two Falcon ships and said to Allott, "You were on board when Yali hit the stone-skins?"

A nod.

"On the *Lively*?"

Another nod.

"I've seen the stone-skin ship you attacked. It's a warship. Why would Yali take on a warship?"

Allott made to spit on the deck, then stopped himself. "He wanted its pretty colored sails, 's why . . . Cap'n. Didn't matter if there were no loot below, he said, so long as he got them sails. Said it would be easy pickings. Ship couldn't have a mage on board, the way it came tiptoeing through the ruins. And when we trained the glass on her, there were just a few men on deck. Yali had us ready to veer off late if more appeared, but they never did."

"So what went wrong? Another stone-skin ship?"

The boy shook his head.

Galantas waited. The Augerans in Ostari's boat were fishing the body they had passed earlier from the water. "What went wrong?" he repeated.

Allott's voice was barely a whisper. "Bastards used sorcery."

"Water-magic?"

"No."

A pause. "Is this the part where I keep guessing, and you tell me when I'm getting warm?"

Allott was a long time in answering. "It happened after we'd thrown the grapnels and made her snug. Stone-skins didn't do nothing to stop us boarding, just stood there like they knew they was done for. But before we could attack, our rigging . . . came alive."

Galantas stared at him.

"The lines tore loose like we was in a hurricane. Slipped their knots and started uncurling from the pinheads. Some of the lads got throttled. Others were lifted off their feet and left swinging from the spars. Yali himself got lines twisted round his arms and legs." There was a tremor in Allott's voice. "They pulled him apart. And all the while, there was this screaming coming from belowdecks, and this stomping, like the Sender himself were walking around down there."

A few of the *Eternal*'s crew sniggered, but Galantas could see from Allott's eyes that his fear was real. It was a fear that knew there were worse things in life than the cut of Shroud's blade. What manner of sorcerer, though, could do what the youth described? Not an elemental mage, for sure. "Did the same happen to your other ship—the two-master?"

"Shit if I knows. I weren't staying around to watch."

Qinta's voice had a note of scorn in it. "You jumped."

"What the hell else was I supposed to do? Draw that sword o' yours, show me how you'd have fought a Shroud-cursed rope!" The boy's shoulders hunched. "Some of the lads tried to escape onto the stone-skin ship, but the bastards cut 'em down. Only place to go was over the side. Don't tell me you wouldn't have done the same if you was me."

Ostari's boat had fished the last bodies from the water and now pulled up beside the *Lively*. Above the squawking of the starbeaks, Galantas heard Ostari shouting orders in his native tongue.

"How did you survive when the others died?" Galantas asked Allott.

The boy's look suggested he was wondering the same. "Just lucky, I guess. I were swimming, and these crossbow bolts were splashing all around me. So I grabbed one and flipped onto my back and held the bolt over my chest so it looked like I were shot. Then I let the current take me till you showed up." His face twitched. "Stone-skins cut their eyelids off, man—the ones that were crucified. Left 'em nailed there while the sun blinded 'em or the starbeaks took their eyes. I could hear 'em screaming. My ears were in the water, but I could still hear 'em."

Galantas regarded him impassively. What did the boy want? Sympathy? Would Yali have shown the stone-skins any more kindness if the raid had been successful? The Augerans had wanted to send out a message, and fear was a powerful statement in any language.

"Captain," Qinta said, "the stone-skins are pulling out."

The Augerans from one boat had joined their kinsmen in the other, and the workers on the *Lively* were climbing in too. After the last man jumped down, the boat rose on a wave of water-magic and set off north in the direction of Bezzle. Ostari was visible at the prow in his red cloak. Were they leaving the two ships behind? Together they'd be worth a lot of money. Galantas might even return them to the Falcons and add to the goodwill he'd earn from saving the boy.

Then he remembered the blayfire oil he'd smelled earlier.

The Augeran boat halted a short distance from the ships. A flame sparked to life, and a burning arrow arced toward the *Lively*. When it struck, the ship went up in a *whoof* of blayfire flames. Purple flames—as if they were so hot they needed another color. Fire crackled along the rigging. The starbeaks on the lines tried to take off, but the blaze caught them. They flapped about on incandescent wings before falling to the deck, their shrieks mixing with the screams of those still alive among the crew. Allott covered his ears.

Clouds of smoke boiled into the sky.

"Damned waste," Qinta said.

Galantas nodded.

Critter gestured at the boy. "What do you wanna do with him?"

"Take his fingers!" someone shouted.

"Burn him with the others!"

Galantas's gaze found Allott's. "No, he comes with us." He raised his voice to carry. "I know we've had our differences with the Falcons. They're bastards, I'll not deny it, but at least they're Rubyholt bastards." Laughs from the men, while Allott seemed close to tears. Galantas let his expression soften. "And right now I'm having difficulty remembering what it was we fell out over all those years ago."

CHAPTER 4

WHAT IS the meaning of this?" the woman said. "Who are you? How did you get in?"

Ebon drew up a handful of paces away, Vale beside him. The woman's accent marked her as a woman of breeding, yet there was a coldness to her eyes that hinted at something else. She'd drawn a dagger at Ebon's arrival, and her grip on it was unwavering. She tried to stare him down. There were few people, though, who could hold his gaze now. If you stared too long, Vale said, you started seeing the marks the Vamilian spirits had left behind. Sure enough, it was the woman who looked away first.

Alongside her, the elderly Galitian ambassador to Mercerie, Silvar Jilani, stood naked but for his sandals. Down his right leg, Ebon saw the scar he'd earned in service to Ebon's father during the Rook War. There was no glint of recognition in his eyes. They'd met only once before, though, and Ebon now looked more like a beggar than a prince in his travel-stained clothes and with his chin and jaw covered by three days' worth of stubble. Silvar glanced over Ebon's shoulder to the doorway through which the prince had entered, no doubt wondering what had become of his bodyguards—the bodyguards Vale had incapacitated moments earlier. Then Silvar shuffled behind his female companion like a child hiding behind its mother's skirts.

"Please, Ambassador," Ebon said, "there is no need for that. Your Honor is safe with us."

Perhaps it was his voice that Silvar recognized at last, for the old man's eyes widened. "Your Majesty?"

Ebon's gaze flickered to the woman. Her look of challenge had been replaced by one of appraisal. *Great.* All the work Ebon had put into keeping his coming here a secret, and Silvar had undone it in the space of two words. He should have known better.

Ebon bowed to the woman. "Madam," he said. "Forgive me, but I need to speak to the ambassador alone. I trust you will not hold it against me if I ask you to step outside."

Vale crossed to a door on Ebon's right. He opened it and looked through before gesturing to the woman. She sheathed her knife and stalked toward the timeshifter, her heels clicking on the mirror-bright floor.

Vale shut the door behind her.

Silvar's trousers lay discarded on the ground. He reached for them and started dressing. Ebon looked about him. The ambassador's house seemed too pristine to be a home. Most likely it was an oversized trophy cabinet to show off the man's collection of ebonystone statues and patterned vases. Even the furniture was trimmed with gold.

"Your Majesty?" Silvar said.

"Majesty no longer," Ebon replied. "My father has been reinstated to the kingship."

"But . . . I thought his ill health—"

"Was overstated by the Royal Physicians. They now expect him to make a full recovery." But only when Ebon returned to Majack to complete the task of healing him—a task he had started a week ago with the powers he'd inherited from the Vamilian goddess Galea.

"And your mother? She is well, I hope?"

Ebon ignored the question. He'd come here to get information, not give it. "I'm looking for my brother," he said. *And for Lamella,* he almost added, but there was no need to complicate matters by mentioning her. If he tracked down his brother, he would doubtless find Lamella too. "Is he here?"

Silvar hesitated.

Ebon stepped closer. "It's a simple enough question, Ambassador. Or do I have to describe your own prince to you?"

"Rendale was here."

The relief that broke over Ebon was like a breath of wind on a hot day. Up until now, he'd had no reason to believe his brother was alive, save for a single sighting of him fleeing Majack by boat on the day the city fell to Mayot's hordes. A week ago Ebon had left the capital seeking news of his brother in the villages along the River Amber. He'd drawn a blank, but then perhaps Rendale had feared to disembark close to Majack in case he encountered more of the undead.

That reasoning had sustained Ebon as far as the city of Mander on the edge of Galitian territory. Mander was sixty-five leagues from the capital. No Vamilians had traveled here, and thus there was no reason for Rendale *not* to stop in the city if he had come this way. But Ebon had been unable to find any word of him. It had been mere desperation that had made Ebon take his search to Mercerie on the shores of the Sabian Sea. In his darker moments, he'd acknowledged his brother's death as inevitable. Now it seemed his stubbornness would be rewarded.

There was something in Silvar's look, though, that told him to keep a check on his relief. *Was* here, the ambassador had said. "Where is he now?"

Silvar had finished lacing his trousers. He took a breath as if gathering his resolve. "There is no easy way to say this, Your Maj—Your Highness . . ." Another pause, and Ebon had to resist an urge to grab him by the throat and shake the words loose. "Your brother left Mercerie nearly two weeks ago—on a ship to take part in the Dragon Hunt."

Ebon stared at the ambassador, hardly able to comprehend what he was being told. In Mander he'd heard stories of what had happened on Dragon Day. Stories of treachery at the heart of the Storm Lord empire, and of dragons on the loose in the Sabian Sea. Each tale had been more outlandish than the last, but there had been one thing on which they had all agreed: the Hunt had been routed, the ships smashed or scattered. Ebon's thoughts were a whirr. But the Hunt took place at the Dragon Gate, many leagues to the south and east. Rendale shouldn't be there. He'd come to Mercerie as a refugee, and he would have known well enough to keep his head down in what was tantamount to enemy territory. He had no ship, no crew, and no reason to go looking for either. Silvar had to be mistaken.

When Ebon met the ambassador's gaze, though, there was no doubt in his eyes. Just disquiet . . . and something else the prince couldn't place.

Ebon suddenly felt his exhaustion. Moments ago he'd been offered a glimpse of hope, but now it was snatched away again. His legs wavered. How long had it been since he'd last slept? Two days? Three?

He sat down on a divan and looked across at Vale. There was no comfort to be drawn from the Endorian's expression, but when was there ever? He ran a hand over his shaved head.

"Tell me everything," he said to Silvar.

The ambassador collected his thoughts. "Your brother arrived here twelve, maybe thirteen days ago. Unlike you, he didn't think to approach me privately. He came to the embassy." From the censure in Silvar's voice, it was plain he considered that to be the cause of everything that came after. "He hadn't eaten for days. And he told me stories about undead armies that I confess I had trouble believing . . ." He left the statement hanging as if inviting Ebon to confirm or deny the truth of those stories. But the prince kept his silence, and so Silvar continued, "He said he managed to find a boat before Majack fell. Once he was clear of the city, he tried to disembark, but there were others on the boat with him, and they wouldn't stop. Eventually they reached Mander and tried to go ashore there. But they arrived in the dead of night, and no one answered their calls for help. One man tried to swim for shore, only for the current to take him. No one else risked it after that. And once past Mander, the country is practically a wasteland, so they let the river bring them to Mercerie."

"Was anyone with him when he came to the embassy?"

"Just some woman with a twisted leg. Miela, I think he called her."

Miela? Either Silvar had mistaken her name, or Rendale had deliberately given a false one. That surge of relief was back in Ebon, but it quickly faded. An image came to him of Lamella aboard a ship, a dragon bearing down on her. It felt as if a weight had lodged in his chest. "Where is she now? Did she go with him on the Hunt?"

"I believe so. I thought that strange at the time. . . ." Silvar paused again to give Ebon a chance to explain, then went on, "When Rendale arrived at the embassy, he was in poor shape. I told him to stay here until he recovered, but he wouldn't listen. He wanted to go home—at least as far as Mander. So I made arrangements to smuggle him out of the city."

Smuggle? "Did the Merceriens know he was here, then?"

"I didn't think so. But in view of your history with Prince Ocarn, I thought it best not to take chances."

Ebon nodded. He could see where this was heading. "What happened?"

"The Merceriens were waiting for Rendale when he left the embassy. Ocarn himself, in fact. Your brother hadn't taken even a dozen steps—"

"How did Ocarn know he was here?"

Silvar clasped his hands together. "I wish I knew. Someone must have seen him when he arrived at the embassy."

"Someone aside from yourself, you mean." Ebon made no effort to keep the edge from his voice. There would have been a constant flow of people entering and leaving Majack's embassy, why should Rendale have caught anyone's eye? There could be only a handful of people in Mercerie who would recognize his face. And what were the chances that one of them had been watching the embassy when he got here?

"I don't know what you're suggesting," Silvar said stiffly. "Only a few of my staff were aware who your brother was, and I can vouch for their integrity."

And who is going to vouch for yours? Ebon studied the ambassador. Silvar was a lifelong companion of his father's, so his loyalty should have been beyond question. Yet the man's unease in Ebon's presence went beyond the discomfort of someone forced into being the bearer of bad news. It would have been easy for Silvar to act the friend to Rendale while simultaneously passing a message to Ocarn. But what would have been his motive? Money? His lifestyle here would clearly take some maintaining.

Ebon pushed the questions aside. What was the point in speculating? The odds of him proving anything against Silvar were slim, and he had better things to do than hang around Mercerie to try.

The silence drew out, and the ambassador moved hurriedly to fill it. "When I found out that Ocarn had taken your brother, I went to the palace to protest. But my objections were ignored."

"You sent word to Majack of what happened?"

"Of course. By three separate messengers, in fact. Beyond that, I don't see what I could have done. Or what I *should* have done, indeed. Ocarn might count *you* his enemy, but he has no quarrel with your brother. Even if he did, his father would never allow a Galitian prince to come to harm." His voice turned beseeching. "There was no way of predicting that Ocarn would invite Rendale on his ship for the Hunt. Or what would happen on Dragon Day when he did."

The ambassador was right, of course, but that didn't make his words any easier to hear. The improbability of it all left Ebon with a feeling of . . . injustice. "What *did* happen on Dragon Day? All I've heard is rumors."

"Then you know as much as I do. Ocarn has not returned to shed light on it, nor has anyone docked here who took part in the Hunt." Silvar must have realized how little room for hope that left, for he added, "But if anyone is going to have survived the Hunt, it is Prince Ocarn Dasuki. He's taken part in every Dragon Day for the last dozen years, and never once has he come close to locking horns with a dragon. His ship would have been stationed far from the Dragon Gate. . . ."

The ambassador's voice trailed off, but it took a moment for Ebon to register why.

Footfalls behind him—from the hallway he'd passed along earlier. He rose and turned just as the door was thrown open. It slammed into the wall and rebounded, rattling.

"Well, well," said a voice from beyond. "What have we here?"

Karmel's steps faltered as she reached the end of the underwater passage leading to the throne room. All about, the walls of water were bright with trapped sunlight. The priestess had tried to suppress her memories of this place, but now they came crashing in upon her like the walls had done on Dragon Day. She saw again the bubble-shot waves, heard Imerle's bloodless voice lay bare the magnitude of Caval's betrayal. Karmel had been a fool to think she could keep the past buried. Trying to cover it up just meant it smelled worse when it was unearthed.

For all Senar's claims that Mazana merely wanted to talk, the priestess had expected to find the throne room filled with sword-wielding Storm Guards. Instead just three people were present. In Imerle's old chair sat Mazana. She was holding a knife which she turned idly in her hands. This was the first time Karmel had met the woman, and she struggled to recall what she knew about her. The fire to Imerle's ice, Caval used to say. Shrewd and capricious. Ruthless, too, for she had killed her father before taking his place as a Storm Lord.

And yet couldn't a similar charge be leveled at Caval?

Behind and to Mazana's right stood the executioner, his position and expression exactly as Karmel remembered them from Dragon Day. Had he even noticed what had happened since then? Or would he stir from his trance one day to discover, bemused, that the face of his mistress had changed? To his left stood an athletic woman wearing the mask of a priestess of the Lord of Hidden Faces. Unsurprising, perhaps, that Mazana had found a new patron after the Chameleon's fall from grace. But the Lord of Hidden Faces? Hadn't Caval said the god was a sham?

Senar Sol moved to one side of the chamber, as if he wished to distance himself from Mazana's entourage. In the sea behind him, a briar shark paused in chasing its tail to regard Karmel with black, unblinking eyes. She drew up. Since her confrontation with Imerle, the room had changed in a handful of telling respects. The leftmost throne was gone, while the one beside it was little more than a heap of bones sticking out of a hardened slurry of melted mosaic stones, like the leavings of a glassblower's furnace. Karmel doubted Mazana would hurry to replace those thrones; it wasn't as if they'd be getting any use.

It occurred to the priestess that she still didn't know the full story of what had happened on Dragon Day after Imerle dropped the sea on her. Some rumors said that Mazana and Imerle had fought each other for supremacy of the Storm Council. Others said they'd battled together against a host of stone-skin assassins, only for Imerle to fall at the last. It hardly mattered to Karmel which was true. The hunting down and hanging of so many of her friends proved that she and Caval could expect no kinder treatment from the new regime than they would have received from the old.

Which left her all the more curious to know why they had been called here.

"Caval," Mazana said. "So good of you to come."

Caval did not answer.

The emira's gaze shifted to Karmel. "This is your sister?"

Karmel nodded. A coldness had seeped into her—a coldness that had started as a tingling in her fingertips and was now moving down her arms to her chest. She wrapped her arms about herself. Strange, that chill. The ceiling of the throne room had been opened to the sky, and the rays of afternoon sunshine filled the chamber with a heat the watery walls trapped like a solarium. Mazana's cheeks were flushed, and there were beads of sweat on even the executioner's brow.

The emira turned back to Caval. "You'll be wanting to know why I asked you here."

Caval said nothing. He would, but he wasn't letting on.

"I was hoping," Mazana continued, "that you could do something for me. Something well suited to your skills as a Chameleon."

He blinked.

"No objections?" Mazana said. "Excellent!"

Caval found his voice at last. "You want me to *help* you?"

"You make it sound like such a sordid notion. If it makes it any easier, think of it as helping your fellow Olairians instead. I'd say you owe them for the chaos you unleashed on Dragon Day, wouldn't you?"

"You're offering me a chance to put right the wrongs?"

"Gracious of me, I'm sure you'll agree."

More silence. Karmel could hear the priestess of the Lord of Hidden Faces breathing behind her mask.

Mazana made a show of examining her knife, then said, "You know the part the stone-skins played in sabotaging the Hunt, of course, but did you also know the mischief they made closer to home? The killing of the Drifters. The attempted assassination of Imerle. Over the past few days, my agents have caught two of their spies stirring up trouble. Now it appears an invasion fleet is preparing to sail north from their homeland beyond the Southern Wastes."

"Heading here?" Karmel asked. The tightness in her chest put a hitch in her voice.

"Good question," Mazana said. "Alas, my shaman is ambiguous on that not insignificant detail, and the stone-skins we captured have proved similarly unforthcoming. All we know for sure is that an Augeran ship has docked in the Rubyholt Isles. The rest of the fleet will likely follow. For the time being, that fleet's destination remains unclear. There are some"—she glanced at Senar Sol—"who think it would be unwise to sit back and cede the initiative to the stone-skins. For once, they may even be right. In any case, it seems *some* response to the Augerans' action on Dragon Day is called for, if only to warn them against meddling further in my affairs."

Caval said, "So you want me to spy on their fleet when it arrives?"

"No. I want it destroyed."

Karmel waited for the punch line.

When it didn't come, Caval said, "Destroy it? An entire fleet?"

"Surely you're not worried about the blood you would get on your hands. After the stain they got on Dragon Day, I should think you wouldn't notice."

"I had a little help from the dragons in that regard."

Mazana looked from Caval to Karmel. "And yet the hand on the tiller was yours, was it not?"

The priestess could not deny it. Perhaps the controlling hand that day had been Imerle's, but there was no overlooking the part Karmel and her brother had played.

Mazana said, "You might be interested to know I dropped in on the Dianese governor, Piput, recently. Just to get his take on what happened when the Dragon Gate failed to come down. He told me he invited a party of stone-skins to the fortress on Dragon Day. When they tried to wander off, they were challenged. Only one man made it as far as the control room. Piput was at a loss to explain how that man opened a locked door, and then single-handedly overpowered the twenty soldiers inside. He thought the Augerans had help, yet the one name he didn't mention in his wild speculations was that of the Chameleons."

"Ah," Caval said. "And you think I should want it to stay that way."

"Don't you? You've seen the reprisals suffered by your fellow priests and priestesses in Olaire. Imagine those same scenes repeated across the League. If your deeds became common knowledge, how many would pay the price for your failed ambition?"

"Those people aren't my responsibility anymore," Caval said tonelessly. "I am no longer high priest. The Chameleon will pick another when he chooses."

Mazana sat forward in her throne. "But he hasn't released you from your vows, has he? You still have your powers. If you learned anything from Veran's example, surely it was that one doesn't leave the priesthood except on the Chameleon's terms."

The coldness that had gripped Karmel was becoming more intense. She had to grind her teeth together to stop them chattering. *She knows about Veran. She knows . . . everything.* But how? Caval hadn't told anyone else about the mission to Dian. And aside from Karmel and Caval, the only survivor from their meeting with Imerle was the executioner. Could he have informed Mazana?

Unless . . .

When Caval next spoke, Karmel could hear some of her own coldness in his voice. "You have been talking to the Chameleon," he said to Mazana.

"I would hardly seek to borrow his esteemed former high priest without asking him."

"And he gave you his blessing?"

"Of course."

Of course? Karmel was not so certain. And yet would Mazana tell a lie that could be so easily disproved?

A change had come over Caval. His expression was all hard edges. Senar Sol must have seen it too, for his hand strayed to his sword hilt. An unnecessary gesture, surely: if Caval tried to attack Mazana, the result would doubtless be the same as when he had tried to attack Imerle. But that didn't mean he wouldn't try. After Dragon Day he had hoped his days of service to the Chameleon were over. Now it was clear the god thought otherwise. What if Caval just wanted an end to it all? Would he force Mazana's hand, even if that meant taking Karmel with him?

Apparently not, for his shoulders slumped. The priestess wished she could feel more sympathy for him. But then she wished he had never betrayed her either.

To the emira Caval said, "What's in it for us if we agree to this mission?"

"Beyond the glory of doing your god's bidding?" Mazana shrugged. "As I said, one does not leave the Chameleon's service except on his terms."

Karmel rubbed her hands along her arms. Was the woman seri-ously suggesting the Chameleon would release them from their vows? Did she think them so naive? Because contrary to Mazana's earlier suggestion, if there was anything to be learned from Veran's example, it was that the Chameleon's word could not be trusted. What choice did Karmel and Caval have, though? If they refused to go along with the emira's wishes, they wouldn't leave here alive. And while they could agree to cooperate with the intention of running later, how far would they have to run in order to escape the Chameleon's reach?

They were trapped. They had been trapped from the moment they took their vows all those years ago.

Karmel said, "You're sending us to the Rubyholt Isles?"

"Us?" Mazana smiled. "No, I'm sending *Caval* to the Rubyholt Isles. You will remain here as my guest."

As a hostage against Caval's good behavior? Karmel looked at her brother. Since the events of Dragon Day, they hadn't spent more than a bell apart. And while on occasion their time together had seemed like one long, uncomfortable silence, whenever they'd been separated, Karmel had found herself hurrying back to him for fear he might have left while she was away. He met her gaze now, his look unreadable. Maybe he was waiting for her to signal her wishes. Or perhaps he didn't know what he wanted any better than Karmel herself.

Then he turned back to Mazana and said, "No. Either we both go, or neither of us does."

The emira pretended surprise. "Indeed? Are you so eager to put your sister in mortal danger again, then?"

Karmel's anger gave her a heat that thawed the cold in her chest. She suspected that whether she stayed or went didn't matter to Mazana; the woman was just doing this to toy with them. And to think there'd been a time when impressing the Storm Lords had seemed important to her. "Moralizing, Emira?" she said. "Shall we ask your father what he thinks of that?"

Mazana laughed. "Such commendable loyalty, my dear. Though I can't help thinking it is misplaced. Your brother did try to have you killed, after all. Are you sure you should be spending more time in his company?"

"If the alternative is staying here with you, absolutely."

"Enough games," Caval said to Mazana. "You have our answer. When do we leave?"

"This evening. I've chartered a merchantman to take you to Gilgamar. You will pick up a Rubyholt guide there before sailing south."

"What about the dragons? Last time I looked, the creatures were still making a nuisance of themselves."

Mazana sheathed her knife. "Yes, if only we had some way to keep them out of the Sabian Sea. You needn't worry, though. I'm sending someone to hold your hand as far as the Isles."

"This someone . . . a water-mage?"

"Yes."

"Ah, a good one, I trust."

Mazana nodded.

Caval waited for her to explain. When she did not, he added, "And the stone-skin fleet? Since you're so confident we can destroy it, I assume you have a plan."

The emira's slow smile brought a whisper of cold back to Karmel's chest.

Ebon watched the four newcomers enter the room—one man and three women wearing the uniforms of Mercerien soldiers. The man was the leader judging by the star adorning his collar. He'd rolled up his shirtsleeves to show off his heavily muscled forearms, and there were cords of muscle in his neck too. No way he'd followed Ebon here from the harbor; he must have been watching the ambassador's house and seen the prince enter.

Silvar looked at Ebon, waiting for his lead.

"Is there a problem?" Ebon said to the officer.

"I don't know, is there?" the soldier replied. "Maybe we should ask the ambassador's men out there." And he gestured over his shoulder to the hallway where Vale had left the two bodyguards unconscious.

Silvar said, "I commend your initiative in barging in like this, but your help isn't needed."

The soldier addressed the three women behind him. "See that?" he said. "The man here"—he pointed to Ebon—"was talking, and he didn't even have to move his lips."

"You think I am holding the ambassador under duress?" Ebon said. He drew his sword and passed it hilt first to Silvar, who accepted it with a grimace. "I'd say he is able to speak for himself now, wouldn't you?"

"Excellent. He can tell me who you are and what you're doing here."

"This is a Galitian matter. It does not concern you."

"I'll be the judge of that. Or rather my bosses will." The soldier beckoned Ebon forward with a finger. "You're coming with us."

"You're . . . arresting me? On what grounds?"

"On the grounds that, if you're important, my commander will want to speak to you. And if you're not, well, no one'll give a copper clipping what happens to you." His voice hardened. "You're coming with us," he said again.

"No, I am not."

The Mercerien showed his teeth. "Hear that, girls?" he said to his companions. "Got ourselves a tough one here." Then, to the prince, "This ain't the Galitian embassy. You can't hide behind that diplomatic shit."

Silvar said, "No, but this is my home. And I will thank you to leave before you do something we both regret." It was said without authority, though. Without intent. And the officer's smile only broadened in response.

Behind him his female companions shuffled apart to give themselves room to draw their swords.

Ebon studied the Merceriens. Four soldiers didn't constitute a threat, but could there be more outside? Then again, what did it matter? Four, eight, even twenty, they weren't going to stop him leaving. Rendale and Lamella weren't here, so Ebon didn't want to be either. And he reckoned he'd got as much as he was going to get from Silvar. No point wasting time trying to talk his way out of this. The sooner he made his move, the less likely he'd end up running into Mercerien reinforcements.

He glanced at Vale. No nods or other signals were needed. His look alone conveyed his intent, and the timeshifter's frown showed he had read it well enough.

On the ride back to Majack from Estapharriol, Ebon had tested the gifts unwittingly conferred upon him by the Vamilian goddess—not just to learn control, but also to explore the extent and the limits of his power. It had quickly become apparent that the abilities he was strongest in were those he'd used most often in the clashes at Estapharriol: shielding himself from destructive sorceries, cutting down foes with waves of glacial cold, hurling from his path anyone who sought to block him. That last skill would serve him well here. And while he was reluctant to reveal his magic to Silvar, what was the alternative? Leave the task of dealing with the Merceriens to Vale? That would mean the timeshifter having to use his own power, and in doing so, cut short his life. Why should the Endorian take the burden when the prince could now bear it himself?

Besides, after hearing what had happened to Rendale and Lamella, Ebon couldn't deny an urge to lash out.

The officer unsheathed his sword with a flourish. He would have expected Ebon's first move to be to retrieve his own blade from Silvar. Instead the prince gathered his power and *pushed* at the soldiers.

The officer took the brunt of the attack. He was lifted as easily as if he were made of straw and thrown back toward the open doorway. The back of his head struck the top of the frame even as the rest of his body passed through the opening. His head came forward and down, his legs going backward and up as he disappeared into the hallway beyond.

The women immediately to either side of him fared little better. They were punched back against the wall next to the doorway. Their heads cracked against stone, and Ebon's power pinned them there a moment before releasing them to crumple into unconsciousness. The final woman had been standing farthest from the officer. She was not so much lifted as spun about by Ebon's blow. She staggered into the wall, then bounced off and toppled into a statuette on a plinth. It fell to the ground and smashed. The woman landed on top of it, twitched once, and lay still.

Ebon stared at the devastation he had wrought. The floor trembled in the wake of his attack, and ripples of power set the room's curtains billowing. Truth was, he hadn't intended to hit the Merceriens so hard. But better too hard than not hard enough.

Assuming he hadn't killed anyone, of course.

The woman who had knocked over the statuette lay facedown in a pool of blood. When Ebon turned her over, he saw stone shards protruding from her skin. He tugged the largest splinters free, then touched a finger to a gash. When he released his power, the cut faded to a pale scar.

He wasn't healing her because he felt obligated to the woman; he was doing it because he wanted to hone his fledgling healing skills. Healing was a power Galea had never exercised through him, yet it was one he was intent on mastering. Outside Mayot's dome in Estapharriol, Ebon had repaired a gash to Vale's arm. He had the ability, but he needed practice, and so on the ride back to Majack, and with the prospect of healing his father to spur him on, he had taken to cutting his own arm so he could mend it again. Inevitably, his father's illness had proved a much more complicated beast than a mere flesh wound. It had taken Ebon several bells to get a sense of it, and many more before he'd suppressed it enough to sustain his father while Ebon went off to search for Rendale and Lamella.

Stone chippings crunched under Vale's feet as he entered the hallway. He tested the officer's pulse before meeting Ebon's gaze. "He'll live."

"Time to get out of here, then."

"You reckon?"

Rising, the prince looked across at Silvar. "I'll leave you to tidy up the mess," he said.

The ambassador could hardly object, but he nodded enthusiastically all the same. No doubt he was relieved to be rid of his guests. Ebon would be back, though. If the man had betrayed Rendale and Lamella to their deaths, there would be a reckoning.

Outside the house, the street was empty of Merceriens. Ebon made no attempt at stealth as he started retracing his steps to the harbor. He passed along an avenue lined by ketar trees shifting in the breeze off the Sabian Sea. To the east—down the hill toward the port—the buildings basked in the afternoon sunshine. A beautiful city, Ebon had heard Mercerie called, an enlightened city, with its fountains and its arched bridges. Though rumor had it its reputation would change if anyone thought to drain the canals that crisscrossed its Temple District.

"What now?" Vale asked as they passed a shrine to Hamoun.

As if he didn't know. "Mercerie is west of Dian, so odds are Ocarn's starting berth will have been west of the city too. If he was able to flee, he'll have sailed farther west, away from the Dragon Gate. What's the closest city that way?"

"Kansar. Or maybe Airey. But they're both in the Storm Isles, so getting there would mean a dash across open waters. If Ocarn kept to the coast, he'll have headed for Gilgamar."

"Then that's where we'll start our search."

"And if he ain't there?"

"Then we ask around, find someone who saw what happened to his ship. If no one knows, we continue on to Dian."

Vale looked across. "You want us to sail to Gilgamar? Across the Sabian Sea?"

"The overland route would take weeks. It would also lead us across the Waste. You think that road would be any safer?"

"Safer than a tangle with a dragon? Let me think about that."

"If we follow the coast and keep the land in sight, we can make a run for shore if we have to."

"And if we're trapped against a cliff?"

Ebon shot Vale a look to silence him. The Endorian should know better than to try to sway the prince once his mind was made up. Yes, they'd be taking a risk going by boat, but it was worth it for the time they would save. And yes, the chances of them finding Lamella and Rendale alive were slim, but it stood to reason that *some* ships must have survived the Hunt. Why shouldn't Ocarn's be among them?

Whatever the odds, Ebon had a duty to see this through. To follow the trail to its end, no matter where it led.

"The Sabian Sea is huge," he said. "That means there are lots of places a dragon could be, aside from the stretch of coastline we'll be following. At the speed we'll go, we should be able to cover the distance to Gilgamar in less than a day. Chances are we won't even see a dragon in that time."

Vale turned his head so his voice wouldn't carry, but Ebon caught his words nevertheless. "Only if our Shroud-cursed luck changes."

Floating in spirit-form, Amerel studied the bailey of Dresk's fortress. The yard ran southeast to northwest, with the gatehouse at one end and the Great Hall at the other. The hall was the same grisly sight she remembered from nine years ago. Its frontage was covered with mortar into which a collection of black and broken bones had been set. Above the main entranceway were the remains of a human rib cage, the ribs splayed. There were darker patches of mortar among the light, suggesting that someone had recently added new bones to the old. Some of those new bones were tinged red; others had shreds of flesh hanging from them—though a gaggle of limewings was working hard to put that right.

Amerel had seen similar . . . architecture before, of course: in Renner, and in Nain Deep, and among the ruins of the Gollothir Plains. There were few Guardians who had traveled as widely as she had in search of knowledge that would broaden her understanding of the Will. As a student, she'd found the theory behind the Will more interesting than the practice. So while her fellow novitiates were hacking chunks out of each other in the weapons yard, she'd been in the library learning what little she could from the ancient texts. So much had been lost during the Exile. Now the Guardians were ignorant of the most basic laws underpinning their powers. No one even knew how the Will could encompass such disparate elements as the spiritual art of Will-persuasion with the more physical applications used in swordplay.

Those unaware of how a Guardian's abilities worked thought that one simply had to wish for a thing to happen, and it would be so. If that were the case, though, why couldn't Amerel reverse the sun's path through the sky, or turn the sundial's shadow back to the time before she'd taken her Guardian's oath? There were rules governing the use of her power—the same rules, perhaps, as those that governed the forces of nature. Learn those rules, and she might expand the reach of her abilities, for as she'd told Noon on the *Whitecap,* a Guardian had to truly believe she could do something before she could do it in practice. For centuries that belief had come from knowing other Guardians had done the thing before. But that meant the order had gone stale on past successes. That it had not grown as it must do if it wanted to survive.

The problem was, where was Amerel supposed to find new learning to replace the lost? Scholarship required civilization to sustain it, and which of the empires around Erin Elal could lay claim to such a lofty ideal? None, she'd assumed. Then two years ago, she had stumbled across a book in a Talenese bazaar. A wondrous book written in High Celemin and containing theories on the movement of the continents, the properties of light, the cycles of the moon. Some of those theories Amerel had since disproved. Some she didn't understand. But some had expanded her learning in directions she'd never even considered before. And while thus far she had discovered few practical applications for that knowledge, the book in question—according to its cover—was only the first in a series of twelve. Imagine what mysteries she might unlock if she could locate the other eleven.

She'd asked the book's seller where he had found it, and he'd told her it had come from a barrow outside Arandas. Amerel had been skeptical. Those barrows dated back to the Fourth Age, so any book buried there would surely have crumbled to dust by now. Still, there seemed no harm in looking. It didn't count as theft, after all, when the tombs' occupants were dead.

Except that not all of those occupants *had* been dead.

Amerel's thoughts had taken her along paths better left untrod, but before she could change course, her gaze caught again on the splayed rib cage over the main entranceway. She felt a twist of agony in her chest. A blood-dream rose up to claim her, and she heard the grinding crack of her own bones as they were snapped back one by one to stand proud from her flesh. A scream bubbled in her throat. She tried to wrest herself free of her memories, but there were more visions waiting to rise in their place. Looking away from the wall, she scanned the bailey for somewhere safe to rest her gaze. It was difficult, though, to find *anything* that didn't spark in her a recollection of blood. A warped arrowhead, a splinter of stone, a sharpened stake: in the right hands, all could be used to create pain. And the Deliverer she'd met in that Arandian barrow had been so fabulously creative.

The Deliverers—those self-appointed moral guardians of the world—were said to purify their victims' souls in the cleansing fires of self-awareness. And perhaps Amerel's soul had been due a spring cleaning after what she'd done that time in Kal. Even now, though, she couldn't help thinking that the Deliverer's treatment of her had been . . . excessive. Hundreds upon hundreds of deaths he'd inflicted on her mind over the course of twenty-hour harrowing bells. Blade and fire, crucifixion and dismemberment; she'd experienced them all, only to be made whole again so the suffering could begin anew. Her face twisted. Here she was, the mighty Amerel Duquy, greatest exponent of the Will-persuasion to have lived since the Exile, yet she'd been helpless to withstand the images thrown at her that day. Through it all the Deliverer had stared at her with his blue eyes—eyes that burned with a feverish zeal. But it was hardly surprising that centuries of interment should have driven him mad. Immortality was seen by some as the ultimate prize, but try telling that to an immortal who'd been buried alive.

A burst of laughter brought her back to the present. She looked left to see four guards squatting over a pair of dice in the shadows of the gatehouse. One carried a fish-spine sword with a scrap of leather round the hilt. The others had scimitars pushed through their belts. Looking up at the battlements, Amerel glimpsed another guard with his feet propped up in a crenel, a battered straw hat tipped over his eyes. Two of his companions were exchanging obscenities with someone outside the fortress. The rest were slouched in what little shade was afforded by the merlons against the dizzying afternoon sun.

And to think Talet had said he wouldn't be able to smuggle Amerel into this place. She could have ridden through the gates on the back of a unicorn, and the guards wouldn't have spared her a second glance. Perhaps a change of plan was in order. Even if Dresk brought in extra men this evening to greet the stone-skins, a few more loafers on the wall wouldn't constitute a challenge to a determined party crasher.

Getting *out* of the fortress after she'd assassinated the Augeran commander, though, would be a good deal harder than getting in.

No, she would stick to plan A.

The fortress's bailey was fifty paces across, and the air above its flagstones shimmered. One of those flagstones near the center had an inscription carved into it, the words of which had faded to leave scratches like ribbon scars. Amerel pictured the stone-skins arriving at the guardhouse. Their route to the hall would take them close to the flagstone, but since Noon—waiting with his crossbow in the brothel's window—wouldn't be able to track their progress, he'd need a signal to tell him when to shoot. That signal would come from Talet, stationed in the highest window of the Great Hall's remaining tower.

Crossing to the engraved flagstone, Amerel rose into the air until she could see the brothel's window. She moved toward it, drifting past the battlements and over the marketplace, before turning to find some point of reference that would help Noon aim. There: a vertical crack snaking down from the parapet, filled with chokeweed. The height of the wall was such that Noon's bolt would have to skim the top if it was to drop in time to strike a target in the yard. But perhaps he could adjust the shot's trajectory to give the missile more dip.

Once it was past the wall, the rest would be up to Amerel.

There would be two chances for a killing strike—the first when the stone-skin party crossed the yard on arriving, the second when it returned from the Great Hall. Two chances, but Amerel wouldn't let that blind her to the odds of success. The Augeran commander would be vulnerable for only a moment as he reached the flagstone before passing out of range again. Then there was the risk that Noon's bolt might be blocked by a Rubyholter on the battlements, or by one of Eremo's kinsmen in the yard. Did it matter, though, if a stone-skin other than the commander was hit? If the Augerans thought they were under attack, they would doubtless lash out first and ask questions later. It just needed one of them to go for a weapon, and the mood in the yard would slide into the Abyss.

Amerel smiled as she flashed back to her body. With luck, this would be the shortest alliance ever to defile the annals of history.

CHAPTER 5

SWORD IN hand, Senar pounded through the palace corridors in the direction of the fighting. The sharp retort of steel reverberated off the walls. As he crossed an intersection he almost collided with a female servant coming from the left passage. There were more servants gathered in the corridor ahead, and they flattened themselves against the walls at his approach.

Ever since Mazana's betrayal of Elemy Meddes, Senar had been expecting an attack on the palace. In the aftermath of Dragon Day, a fragile truce had developed between Mazana's forces and those Storm Guards still loyal to the dutia. But that truce had ended with Elemy's disappearance. With Jambar's help, Mazana's mercenaries—the Revenants—had started hunting down the rebels, but they had yet to break the back of the insurgency. Just yesterday, a Storm Guard raid on the harbor had left seven mercenaries dead, and one of their ships ablaze. Now it seemed the rebels had struck at the heart of Mazana's power. It couldn't be a major offensive, though, because the clamor of metal had resolved into the ring of a handful of blades at most. An assassin, then. With Mazana the target?

Senar careered around the next corner, his shoulder brushing the wall.

Ahead a group of gray-cloaked Revenants was looking through an archway into a courtyard. No weapons in their hands, no tension in their bearings. A little of the tightness eased from Senar's chest. Matters had to be under control if the mercenaries were content simply to watch from the sidelines. At Senar's approach, a shaven-headed woman at the back of the group spun round. The sight of the Guardian bearing down on her with his sword drawn apparently wasn't deserving of a second glance, for she promptly turned away again, uninterested. Must have recognized him as Mazana's follower to have dismissed him so quickly as a threat.

Yes, that had to be it.

Sheathing his blade, he advanced to join the mercenaries.

The windows in the walls surrounding the courtyard were too high-set for him to look through, so he had to settle for the scant view afforded between the heads of the mercenaries in the archway. In the yard beyond stood a pale-skinned man holding in each hand a flail-type weapon made up of an iron staff with a weight and chain on the end. His face was covered in bruises, and he was stripped to the waist to reveal so many scars on his chest he might have been a joint of meat fresh off the butcher's block. Across from him was . . .

Senar blinked.

The executioner?

The giant circled the other man, his weight on the balls of his feet, the silver links of his armor shimmering. With a roar, he brought his sword round in a blow aimed at his opponent's midriff. The pale-skinned man swayed aside, then skipped forward and countered with a swing that sent the weight on the end of one of his weapons thudding into the threads over the executioner's stomach. The giant might not have felt it for all the reaction he showed.

Senar tugged his gaze away. If the executioner was here, then Mazana could not be far—

"You tricked us," said a woman's voice from behind him.

The Guardian turned to find the twins, Mili and Tali, a step behind him. They wore gray cloaks over their susha robes, and their long blond hair was held up with fish-spine combs. Alas, they hadn't lost any height since he'd last seen them.

"You tricked us," the twin on the right said again—Tali, he presumed, since she always spoke first.

"On Dragon Day, you said . . ."

". . . we were fighting the dragon . . ."

". . . in order to draw it away . . ."

". . . from the throne room."

"But you intended all along . . ."

". . . to go to Mazana's aid."

Senar couldn't decide if their indignation was genuine or feigned. "Ladies," he said. "You look well." On Dragon Day, Tali had shed more than her fair share of blood, yet now she looked the picture of health.

"The Revenants have a healer . . ."

". . . a good one."

"He healed me."

Senar glanced at their cloaks. "You have joined the mercenaries?"

Tali nodded. "Thanks to you . . ."

". . . we were lacking an employer . . ."

". . . and the attack on Olaire . . ."

". . . left a few gaps in the Revenants' ranks."

"Perhaps Mazana will leave us alone . . ."

". . . now she knows we are on the same side."

Senar was silent, thinking. Was there a message in those words for the emira? Unsurprising if so, considering the way Mazana had moved against the handful of Imerle's sympathizers who had survived Dragon Day.

He looked into the courtyard again. A stroke from one of the pale-skinned stranger's weapons was deflected by the executioner's sword. Half a dozen Revenants were watching the duel from one of the corners in the yard, and they scattered as the tide of battle brought the combatants close. The giant's next attack was intercepted by one of his opponent's flails, the blade tangling in the chain. The pale-skinned man smiled to reveal he was missing his front teeth at the bottom and top.

"Who is he?" Senar asked the twins.

"His name is Twist," Tali said.

"He is the Revenants' second in command," Mili added.

"So why is he fighting the executioner? I'm guessing it wasn't because of something the executioner said."

Tali shook her head. "Twist challenges everyone . . ."

". . . he considers worthy."

"He likes to . . ."

". . . test himself."

Senar adjusted his shirt cuffs. "And the executioner accepted his challenge?"

"Twist didn't give him a choice."

"He knew better than to ask."

The Guardian looked through the archway again and saw Mazana watching the fight from a terrace across from him. "Why hasn't the emira put a stop to this?"

"Why should she?"

"She knows Twist's reputation . . ."

". . . plus she is probably as intrigued as we are . . ."

". . . to know how this will end."

Senar said, "It will end with someone in a casket." Twist, most likely.

"Oh, we doubt that, Guardian."

"The duel is only to first blood."

Senar watched Twist duck beneath a swipe of the giant's blade that would have separated his head from his shoulders. "Did anyone think to tell the executioner?"

Tali seemed not to hear. "Twist challenged us, of course . . ."

". . . when we first joined the Revenants."

"And?" the Guardian said.

"He wanted to fight us singly . . ."

". . . but we only come as a pair."

"Just ask our mother."

Senar looked from one to the other. "So you never fought?"

Tali's smile left him none the wiser. "He will come for you, Guardian . . ."

". . . when he hears you fought . . ."

". . . the executioner on Dragon Day."

As one, the sisters gazed at the dragon scales emerging from the collar of his shirt. Senar resisted an impulse to cover them.

"Soon, too, before you grow . . ."

". . . a set of armor to eclipse the giant's."

Tali raised a hand to Senar's cheek, and he flinched. "Such a pity," she said.

"You seem sure the scales will spread," the Guardian said.

"Have they not . . ."

". . . done so already?"

"Perhaps." Senar had tried to deny it at the start, but it was becoming increasingly hard to do so as the days passed. In his mind's eye, he saw them spreading across his neck and face like a copper shadow. How long before they covered his whole body? How long before he was entombed in metal? He looked at the executioner. What a pair he and the giant would make then. And what a spectacle it would be if they ever fought again, each hammering uselessly at the other's armor until they slumped together finally in exhaustion. "Even if they have spread, the rate of progression is so slow it will take weeks for them to reach my face. Maybe months. Plenty of time in which to find a way to halt their advance, or even reverse it."

"As you say," Tali said.

For once Mili had nothing to add to her sister's pronouncement.

Senar beat a hasty retreat and made for a staircase leading up to the terraces.

Upstairs, Mazana was still standing where the Guardian had last seen her. She was wearing a sleeveless emerald-colored dress that accentuated the green of her eyes. Beside her was the Revenants' commander, Jodren Labarde, stroking his pointed beard. At Senar's approach, the man looked round. He'd been saying something to the emira, but he broke off now. The ever-present coral bird on his shoulder spread its wings and twittered. In the distance Senar could hear the low thunder of waves breaking against the seawall.

"Commander," he said. "Emira."

Jodren nodded. Mazana ignored him, unable to take her eyes off the duel.

In the courtyard Twist had blocked an overhand stroke from the executioner by bringing the staffs of his two flails together to form an X. Now he danced beyond the range of his assailant's follow-up. The threads sewn into the giant's skin were beginning to glow in the heat. Was that Twist's tactic to defeat his opponent? Keep the executioner at arm's length until he cooked in his armor?

As good a plan as any.

"You've been speaking to the twins, I see," Mazana said to Senar.

"They're two of mine now, Emira," Jodren said. "They signed up after Dragon Day."

The Guardian kept his gaze on Mazana. "And since the mercenaries work for you, that makes the twins yours as well."

"And that is why they wanted to talk to you?"

"That, and to offer their commiserations."

Mazana glanced at the scales on his neck, her expression studiously blank. Then she looked down into the yard again.

You had to admire the woman, the way she kept her emotions in check. To the casual observer, it might almost appear as if she didn't care.

"We missed you earlier," she said after a pause. "Our illustrious friend Jodren here wanted your opinion on his latest efforts to track down the Storm Guard rebels."

Senar shot the man a look. That seemed unlikely, considering how infrequently Jodren had sought his counsel previously. Indeed you could count on the fingers of one hand—of Senar's halfhand, even—the number of times they'd spoken before. The commander appeared equally confused by the emira's words.

"I have been at the Founder's Citadel," Senar said.

"Have you now?"

"To visit the library there," he explained. "I hoped to find something about the Augerans." Perhaps he should have been looking for information about his dragon scales instead, but the trouble with looking for answers was that sometimes you found them. And Senar wasn't sure they were answers he was ready to hear.

"The Augerans are a part of *your* people's history, not mine," Mazana said.

The Guardian shrugged. "It was a long shot, I admit."

"And?"

"And I found nothing. But that's hardly surprising considering the state the place was in." When he'd opened the door to the reading room, the floor had been scattered with papers that quivered in the draft he brought with him. Their crackle had been the first sound he'd heard since entering the fortress, save for the tread of his boots.

"Someone beat you to the prize?" Mazana said.

The Augerans, was she suggesting? An interesting thought, but there was a simpler explanation. "More likely it was the work of the citadel's new lodgers."

"Who?"

Senar shrugged a second time. "The same people who used to live there before Darbonna threw them out, I suspect. I didn't actually see them, because they took care to stay hidden. And after what happened in the fortress the last time we were there, I wasn't inclined to go looking."

"Could they be Storm Guards, Emira?" Jodren said. "The citadel was where a lot of the soldiers crawled to bleed out on Dragon Day."

Mazana did not reply, her gaze still on Senar. She rubbed her wrists like she'd just pulled free of someone's grasp. There was a certain expectation in her look as if she knew what was coming next.

"I thought I might speak to Darbonna," Senar said. "Since I understand you've now got her under lock and key." He'd tried to see the woman earlier, only to be turned away by Mazana's guards. "No one knows the library better than she."

There was sweat on the emira's top lip. Perhaps it was just the sun reflecting in her eyes, but the orbs seemed to take on a reddish tinge.

Senar looked back at her, undaunted. "There seems little point in me wading through hundreds of texts when I don't even know what I'm looking for. If Darbonna could confirm there's something worth finding . . ."

More silence.

It was broken by a cheer from the courtyard. Mazana looked down at the duelists. "Enough!" she called.

Senar followed her gaze.

And saw the executioner bleeding from a graze on his chin. The emira's command had been directed at him, for his sword arm was frozen in midswing as he was about to give answer to whatever blow Twist had landed on him. A heavy pause, then the giant returned his blade to the scabbard on his back before settling into his familiar relaxed stance. His gaze fixed on nothing. Twist, meanwhile, grinned like a youngling as he raised his arms to acknowledge the whooping of his fellow mercenaries. He tried to throw a comradely arm round the executioner's shoulders, but such was the difference in height between them that it ended up falling around the giant's waist instead.

The executioner looked at him.

Twist hurriedly withdrew the arm.

Jodren was evidently intent on basking in his second's reflected glory, for he said, "See, Emira! Didn't I tell you Twist would win? I think you may need a new bodyguard."

Senar eyed him dubiously. "Your man scratched his chin, Commander. If the duel had been for keeps, Twist would have needed a thousand such hits to win. Whereas the executioner needs to strike only once."

"If you say so, Guardian. I bow to your greater experience." A thought seemed to come to the mercenary. "As I recall, you crossed swords with the giant on Dragon Day. How did that go, remind us?"

From atop the bluff, Galantas looked down on the boy standing in shallow water at the midpoint of the channel. Nine sharks prowled the waves about Lassan, lured here by the blood dripping from a self-inflicted cut to his arm. Briar sharks and razor sharks mostly, but it was a blackfin that seemed to have taken most to his scent as it swum lazy circles about him. *Always the blackfins.* It was a blackfin that had given Galantas the scar on his leg that drew whistles when he showed it. The same blackfin, as it happened, whose teeth now adorned the band around his neck.

Who laughs last, and all that.

Years ago, Galantas had been first to make the Shark Run. After his mother's death, he had attempted the crossing for no reason that he could have articulated. He should have died that day. Caught in waist-deep water, he'd been helpless to evade a blackfin bearing down on him. Maybe it was shock that had caused him to freeze when others might have fled and, in doing so, drawn the creature to them. Or maybe he just hadn't cared whether he lived or died. Whatever the reason, the shark had paid him no mind, merely brushing his leg as it glided past.

It was only later that Galantas had recognized the opportunity for notoriety the Shark Run offered. He'd spent countless nights mapping out the seabed in the channel until he could walk it in his dreams. Only then did he risk a crossing in daylight, with both sharks and witnesses in attendance. He had repeated the Run many times since, earning grudging admiration from the fools who respected such acts of bravado. In time, more and more Rubyholters had sought to replicate his feat, until it became a rite of passage for the youths of every clan. More than that, though, it became the stone upon which Galantas's legend was founded. By his example were you judged an adult among your tribe. By his example did you prove your courage to your fellows. Every man who now risked the Run followed in his shadow. And succeed or fail, their imitation served only to add to that shadow's reach.

It was a hundred heartbeats since Lassan had last moved. Some of the spectators on the far shore jeered, perhaps thinking the boy's courage had failed. Galantas knew better. There was no such thing as a safe route across the channel, still less a guaranteed one, but there *were* paths less dangerous than others. In front and to Lassan's right was a stretch of shallow water that offered a straightforward means of progress, yet the route beyond that was treacherous. The simpler course lay directly ahead, but Lassan first had to traverse a section prowled by the blackfin. *Patience.* The key to success lay in reading the odds offered by each route, and in having the courage to run those odds when circumstances demanded it.

And luck, of course.

The blackfin finally moved away, and Lassan edged forward to ironic cheers from the spectators to Galantas's right. He scanned their ranks. Needles mostly, though there were a few Falcons and Squalls too. All sitting in their separate groups, naturally. Among the Needles was a girl in a red dress—a lover or a sister, perhaps—watching Lassan with hands over her mouth. There were no clan leaders or krels here, only sons and daughters: the next generation of Rubyholters. It was easy to tell those who had completed the Run from those who had yet to attempt it. For while the old hands followed Lassan's progress in silence, the virgins wearied Galantas's ears with their bluster and their feigned good humor.

Lassan appeared oblivious to them all. He'd taken a dozen steps along the deeper path, apparently unnoticed by the blackfin. But the cut to his arm was still dripping blood, and one of the briar sharks swam closer. Lassan didn't panic. Maintaining a steady pace, he waded toward shallower water. Soon the sea reached only to his calves. The briar shark was forced to halt. Its snout emerged from the waves, and Lassan played to the crowds by punching the creature on the nose. Galantas nodded his approval. The boy had spirit. He'd make a good leader if he ever commanded the Needles, and the odds of that happening were shortening by the moment. Galantas could see Lassan's elder brother, Flint, farther along the bluff. His expression showed the same conflicting emotions Galantas had felt when he'd watched his own brother make the Run seven years ago. Flint hadn't attempted the channel himself yet. If Lassan survived, he would have to do so.

A skittering of stones behind Galantas marked the arrival of Qinta and Barnick. Barnick lowered himself to the ground alongside Galantas, then took out a comb and started combing his hair. Qinta squatted on Galantas's other side. He looked down at the channel.

"That's Lassan, right?" he said. "Needle Clan."

"Yes."

"So what are we doing here?"

"Trying to watch."

The hint missed its mark. "You been giving the lad pointers?"

"Maybe."

Silence.

Galantas knew what his Second would be thinking: Galantas hadn't helped his younger brother, Kalim, when he had attempted the Run, so why was he helping this Needle boy? The answer was easy enough: because Lassan, unlike Kalim, had nothing to prove to Galantas. A memory came to him of his brother flailing in blood-stained water, but he scowled and pushed it aside. He was done blaming himself for Kalim's death. Hells, no one had helped Galantas when *he* made his first Run. So what if he'd pressed his brother into attempting the crossing? Kalim had been old enough to make his own decisions. And even with Galantas's help, there was no guarantee he would have survived.

No, the real fault here was Dresk's for making Kalim believe he was the warlord's rightful successor—and Kalim's for swallowing the lie. Once Kalim had made it clear he would challenge Galantas, he'd been left with no choice but to try the Run.

He brought it on himself.

Qinta dragged his gaze from the channel to track the course of a flock of limewings overhead. He frowned as they veered west.

"Are the birds speaking to you again?" Galantas said.

"They're heading dead away from us—you see how they changed direction as they passed over?"

"And that's a bad sign?"

"Means the omens are against our runner, aye. Means he needs to be careful."

Galantas clucked his tongue. "Careful on the Shark Run? I hope someone thought to warn him before he set out."

Qinta did not respond.

"If you're so confident about the outcome," Galantas added, "why don't you put money on it? There must be someone round here who's opened a book."

"I don't make money off the dead."

"Tell that to the crew of the last merchantman we took."

Another shark approached Lassan from the north. Galantas didn't recognize it from its fin—white, with a crimped edge—but there were lots of fish in these parts from beyond the underwater gateways. One of the spectators shouted a warning to Lassan. The boy had moved farther south than he should have done. But there was time yet for him to correct his course if he acted swiftly.

Galantas looked back at Qinta. "You delivered Allott to the Falcons?"

"Aye," the Second said. "Made sure plenty saw me doing it too. When they question Allott, wouldn't want him leaving out the part where we saved him."

"Was Ravin there?"

"No. But I got collared by one of his krels, Corm. He'd heard about Dresk's meeting with the stone-skins. Wanted to know if the rumors about the twenty thousand talents were true. News spreads fast, it seems."

Galantas had done a bit of the spreading himself—just a word or two in the right ears. Sometimes you had to shout to make yourself heard, but when the talk was of gold, a mere whisper sufficed. "You denied everything, I take it."

"Aye. That seemed the best way to convince Corm the rumors were true. He told me Ravin has called a meeting at the Hub to discuss the stone-skins."

"For when?"

"The day after tomorrow, at noon."

"Just the other clan leaders, or Dresk too?"

"Dresk too."

Galantas smiled.

"What, you don't think he'll go?"

"Of course he won't. He can't take twenty thousand talents with him, and who's he going to trust to look after it while he's gone?" Those talents had become a chain around Dresk's neck, shackling him to the fortress. A golden chain, perhaps, but no less restrictive for that.

Qinta said, "Maybe he'll send you in his place."

"I hope not. I'd hate to have to obey one of his orders."

The Second blinked. "You're going to the meeting?"

Galantas nodded.

"To support the claims of the other clans?"

Another nod.

Qinta chuckled. "Nothing quite like being generous with your old man's money, is there?"

"The money doesn't belong to Dresk. It belongs to all the Isles."

"And you're gonna offer to share it round if you take your father's place?"

"No." When it came to spending the gold, Galantas didn't trust the other clan leaders any more than he trusted Dresk.

Lassan was in trouble. He must have realized by now that he'd strayed off course, yet he seemed uncertain whether to continue on or retreat to safer ground. His attention was fixed on the white-finned shark. He'd forgotten the briar he'd punched, though, and the creature now drifted toward him from the north. Again the crowd shouted a warning. Lassan turned to face the new threat.

Galantas pursed his lips. The boy had just one option left: remain motionless and hope the shark passed him by. Instead he started thrashing through the water in the direction he'd come. He lost his footing and went under. Moments later he resurfaced, pleading for help. Kalim had cried for help too at the end. As if Galantas could have waved a wand and magicked him to safety. As if Kalim would have helped Galantas if the roles had been reversed.

The briar closed in on Lassan. A woman on the opposite shore screamed.

"Feeding time," Galantas said.

Qinta gave him an "I told you so" look.

Galantas pushed himself to his feet. "Let's get out of here."

Romany stretched out on her bed, her heart aflutter at the recollection of her time in the throne room. A bell had passed since the meeting with the Chameleons, yet still she was struggling to put the memory of that watery hellhole behind her. It didn't help, of course, that she could hear the distant rustle of waves. She'd chosen as her quarters a room far from the sea, but even here there was no escaping its sound, just as there was no escaping the damp air and the salty whiff that seemed to pervade every corner of this godforsaken palace. After the Forest of Sighs, she'd thought nothing would ever measure down to Mayot's hospitality and the discomforts of the ruined city of Estapharriol. Now she was beginning to wonder.

If there was a saving grace to Romany's day, it had come in the form of a bottle of Koronos white. And last year's vintage, no less! It was her new servant, Floss, who had found it. At Romany's command, the girl had spent most of the afternoon hunting it out in the palace's stores. Any goodwill Floss might have earned in so doing, though, had been promptly squandered when she revealed herself to be a devotee of the Lord of Hidden Faces and asked the priestess to say prayers with her at sunfall. Romany had declined, of course. It had been decades since she'd last sullied her lips with a prayer, and she saw no reason to start again now. It wasn't as if the Spider would have listened, after all.

She hadn't listened all those years ago when Romany had prayed for her parents to come back for her.

A mouthful of wine, then the priestess closed her eyes and surrendered her mind to her sorcerous web. Time to do a little exploring.

Something drew her to one of the courtyards. . . .

The clash of weapons greeted Romany, and she watched the Revenant subcommander, Twist, battling the Everlord, Kiapa, in the middle of a ring of cheering spectators. She rolled her spiritual eyes. Spider's mercy, didn't the fools have enough enemies outside the palace that they had to go fighting each other? A swing of one of Twist's flails tangled the sword of his opponent, leaving his second weapon unimpeded as it whistled for Kiapa's head, but the Everlord ducked beneath it and retreated. Twist surged forward, feinting with one flail before attacking with the other. Kiapa must have read his intent, for he stepped smoothly to the side before retaliating with a lunge that his adversary blocked.

Romany found her muscles twitching as she anticipated each move and countermove, mentally thrusting and parrying with the two men as they battled back and forth. And all the while a part of her wondered how she would fare with her newly acquired assassin's skills if she were ever pitted against one of them . . .

A knock sounded from the door to her quarters. A visitor. An uninvited one, needless to say. Floss, perhaps?

Sighing, she flashed back to her room along the threads of her web. *Well, well,* she thought as she hovered by her door. Not the servant after all, but someone far more interesting.

She would have to step carefully here.

Opening her eyes, she sat up in her bed. She'd taken off her mask earlier to give her face a chance to breathe, but she slipped it on again as she rose and made for the door. Outside waited the Remnerol shaman, Jambar. He wore a vacuous smile, but the stiffness of his posture betrayed his agitation. In one hand he held a bulging bag containing the knuckle bones he used for his readings. With the other hand he raised his monocle to his sole remaining eye and peered at the priestess through it.

"Greetings," he said. "May I have a few moments of your time?"

A welcome that courteous surely spelled trouble, but Romany nodded her agreement all the same. Her curiosity was piqued. While scouting the palace last week, she'd watched the shaman carry out numerous readings with his bones. Romany couldn't deny an interest in the workings of his craft, yet she'd been unable to make sense of his divinations, and alas he hadn't thought to provide his secret watcher with a running commentary.

Once inside, Jambar started pacing. "What is your Lord up to?" he said.

Romany stared at him. A strange opening gambit.

"More importantly, what are *you* up to?"

"You mean, at this precise moment?"

"Your Lord helped Mazana kill Fume in the Founder's Citadel, did he not? He must have known the god's bones would fall into my hands."

Even if Romany had been minded to speak, her guest didn't give her a chance.

"Why permit that to happen," the shaman pressed, "if he intended all along to rob me of the bones' usefulness?"

Rob him? "Has someone stolen the god's bones?" Romany asked, glancing at the bag in his hand.

Jambar clutched the bag to his chest as if she'd said that was *her* intent. For a while he studied her like he was trying to read her thoughts in her eyes. His smile began to irritate her.

"There are millions of possible futures," he said finally. "Every act of every person shapes what is to come. A shaman's art lies in distinguishing the momentous from the mundane—the actions that determine which path the arrow of time will follow. The deeds of a single person can change everything, you agree?"

Romany looked around the room. Perhaps there was something else she could be doing while she waited for him to get to his point.

"Then you must appreciate," Jambar went on, "that if just one person's part in the future's tapestry was missing, the whole picture would become at best distorted, at worst meaningless."

And finally he was starting to make sense. This one person . . . Romany herself? And her presence here was interfering with his readings? When she considered it, it wasn't surprising that he should have failed to predict the events that had seen her sent here by the Spider, or that the subtle spells she routinely weaved about herself should make it hard for him to see her future. Not surprising, but undeniably satisfying.

"I imagine that must be quite frustrating," she said. "To spend all your time piecing together a picture of the future only for someone to put their fist through the weave."

Jambar somehow managed to keep his smile in place even though the corners of his mouth turned down. "The question that interests me is *why*. *Why* am I unable to perceive you in the futures?"

"The answer seems obvious enough." Then, in response to the shaman's expectant look, "You're just not very good at what you do."

A muscle flickered in the Remnerol's cheek. "I know my worth. A man is no worse for being criticized than he is better for being praised. If you take note of what you are inwardly, you need not pay attention to what others say of you."

Romany retrieved her glass of wine and took a sip. It wasn't easy drinking while she wore a mask, but the important jobs were worth persevering in. "And yet you failed to predict the attempt on Mazana's life earlier. Unless, of course, you *did* predict it but chose not to warn her."

"You think my attention can be everywhere at all times? You think I just scatter my bones and read the future like a book?" He shook his head. "For a reading to be meaningful, I have to focus upon an individual or event—to assign value to each symbol on my board."

"And where has your attention been fixed of late that you've had no time to look to the safety of your patron?"

Jambar stepped forward. "Mazana Creed is not my patron. But perhaps my services can be of use to your Lord."

Romany raised a skeptical eyebrow.

"Do you think it is just my pride at stake here?" he said. "Do you consider me so small-minded? A man is born to help not himself but his fellows. I seek nothing more in my duties than the opportunity to serve the common good."

Romany had been taking another sip of wine as he spoke, and she had to swallow to stop herself snorting it out of her nose.

"If you know what happened on Dragon Day," Jambar continued, "you must be aware of the threat that is coming. The fate of the whole Sabian League is at stake, not to mention the lands about."

"You are referring to the risk posed by the stone-skins?"

The shaman nodded.

"And?"

"And what?"

"And what is the nature of that risk? You wish my god's patronage? Prove your worth to him now by telling me what you know."

Jambar said nothing.

"Why are the stone-skins here? When will they strike? Where?"

"All I see are possibilities."

"Possibilities are of no use to me," Romany said. "Possibilities I can get from the old wives sucking blackweed down at the harbor. Perhaps my Lord should recruit them as well."

The shaman did not respond. He was in an impossible position, Romany knew. Say nothing, and he would receive nothing back. But answer the priestess's questions, and he would give up his bargaining tool to get answers in return. Not that Romany would attach any weight to his predictions, of course. She could no more trust him to be honest than he could trust her to be the same. And if he *did* trust her, would that not prove him to be the fool she took him for?

The Remnerol tried to take another step forward, but he was already closer than Romany would have liked, and thus in the short time he'd been thinking she had weaved a few unobtrusive strands of sorcery about him. Now, as he sought to move, he found his path to the priestess obstructed. He tested the strength of the magic before settling back. The last vestiges of his sham good humor evaporated.

"Mazana Creed will hear of this," he said, his eyes narrowing in a manner Romany assumed she was supposed to find intimidating.

"From me, if not from you."

The shaman turned and stalked from the room.

Another day, another friend made.

Romany closed the door behind him and threw her mask onto a

chair. An interesting encounter that had been, as much for what Jambar hadn't said as for what he had. Judging by his unease, he clearly considered the stone-skins to be a threat, but a threat to *what* exactly? To Mazana Creed? No, the shaman had shown he cared nothing for the emira's fate. To the League? That, at least, stood to affect him directly insofar as he might be forced to move on before the enemy arrived. Was that the totality of his interest here, though? What did he really want beyond mere survival? Until Romany knew the answer to that question, there was little to be gained in trying to read the man or determine what he was working toward.

Lying back on her bed, she put him from her mind. Her web was calling to her, and she had to admit she was curious to know how the duel between Twist and Kiapa was progressing. When she returned to the courtyard, though, she found it deserted, no sign of the combatants save a tantalizing splash of blood at the center of the square. And to think she'd missed the entertainment just so she could cross empty words with Jambar.

Romany shook herself. Entertainment? How much lower could she stoop?

She was about to return to her quarters when she sensed a ripple along her web from nearby—a ripple she recognized from the assassination attempt on Mazana.

The knife.

She flashed across the intervening distance . . .

. . . To find herself in one of the palace's cells. Darbonna was chained to a wall, her arms shackled above her head, her feet to the floor. Her wrists and ankles were weeping from the touch of the manacles. The cell was lit by a solitary torch, but if the sweat on Darbonna's brow was anything to go by, it was giving off the heat of a forge. Her left eye was swollen shut where she'd been punched by Mazana's guard. Just now, though, she was probably wishing the other eye were closed too.

For in front of her stood the emira, that infernal knife in her hand. Mazana's eyes had their customary red edge, sharp enough to make them gleam in the darkness.

Romany toyed with the idea of withdrawing. Something told her Mazana hadn't dropped by to inquire after Darbonna's health. Things were about to head south for the old woman, and Romany had no wish to be present when they did. Except that she had been sent to the palace by the Spider to judge Fume's hold on Mazana. Was a conversation between the emira and the god's former high priestess something Romany could rightly miss?

Mazana was speaking to Darbonna as Romany arrived. ". . . He bled out, you know," she said. "The soldier you cut with the knife. The smallest scratch, yet the healers couldn't stop the flow of blood." She paused. "But you knew that would happen. Something to do with the sorcery invested in the blade."

Darbonna did not reply.

"What else can the knife do? It is sacred to your Lord, isn't it?"

No response. A bead of sweat collected at the end of the old woman's nose, then stretched and dropped to the floor.

Mazana raised the knife to Darbonna's wrist and stroked its point along her arm. The old woman shivered. "You don't scare me," she said.

"What's to be scared of? We're just talking here."

"There's nothing you can do to me that I haven't done a thousand times to others."

"And yet being on the receiving end is a telling change of perspective, I'd imagine."

Darbonna kept her silence.

"What else can the knife do?"

Nothing.

Mazana pressed the tip of the dagger into Darbonna's arm. A bead of blood formed and trickled down the weapon's blade. "And as simple as that, your life is ended. Of course, it will take a while for you to bleed out." The emira's voice was mild, but her look was heavy with threat. "Any preferences as to how you'd like to spend your remaining time?"

Still the old woman did not reply.

"What else can the knife do?"

Tell her! Romany silently urged. What did Darbonna hope to gain by holding out? She'd talk in the end—everyone did—so why not get it over with and spare herself the suffering? Spare Romany the discomfort of having to witness it too.

The fire from the torch seemed to catch in Mazana's eyes. She grabbed Darbonna's elbow with her free hand. Then she slid the blade into the flesh of the old woman's inner arm—above the elbow, just under the skin—until the weapon's point emerged from the other side.

Darbonna shrieked and thrashed, her chains clinking, but Mazana held her arm fast. Blood oozed from the cut and ran down her arm.

"What else can the knife do?"

Silence, but for ragged breathing.

Keeping the blade under Darbonna's skin, Mazana started drawing it up toward the old woman's shackled wrist. Darbonna gritted her teeth against the pain. She began muttering something over and over. A prayer to Fume, it might have been, but there was less reason to pray to a dead god than there was even to pray to the Spider. Then the agony became too much for her, and she screamed.

Romany's spiritual stomach clenched. The wine she'd drunk earlier was acid in her gut. The cell felt too small. She wanted to retreat to a less graphic distance, but she couldn't do so without passing through a wall, and so instead she half covered her eyes with her hands. Because watching the scene through her fingers was sure to rob it of its horror. The knife continued upward, passing as easily through Darbonna's flesh as a wire through cheese. So light was Mazana's grip on the hilt—her hand seemed just to rest upon it—that Romany wondered if the weapon would carry on cutting even if she let go.

The blade reached Darbonna's wrist and exited there. A long strip of skin peeled away from the arm to hang down like a ribbon, revealing wet red flesh beneath. Rivulets of blood streamed past the old woman's elbow and soaked into the short sleeve of her susha robe where it was gathered at the shoulder.

"What else can the knife do?"

No reply.

Romany closed her eyes. Her breath was coming as fast as Darbonna's. She tried to set her heart against the old woman's plight. Darbonna had tried to kill Mazana, she reminded herself. If the woman had approached from the other direction it might have been Romany, not the now-dead soldier, who ended up getting in her way. Plus she was a follower of Fume. His high priestess, no less. Hadn't she admitted to Mazana she'd done all this and worse herself?

It wasn't working.

Romany wanted to weave her threads about Mazana as she'd done about Jambar earlier. She couldn't save Darbonna—the woman had been dead from the moment she was cut. But at least she might spare her some pain before she bled out. If she did so, though, Mazana would discover she had an audience. How long before she worked out it was

Romany? How long before the executioner came knocking at her door to drag her off to this same cell? The Spider's words in the temple came back to her: *I trust there will be no recurrence of the . . . sensitivity you showed in your dealings with Mayot Mencada.* In the Forest of Sighs, Romany had tried to spare the Vamilians from Mayot's ill-usage, and she'd ended up with a knife in her back. Doing nothing now was the prudent thing to do. The only thing she *could* do.

That didn't make her stomach sit any easier, though. Through closed eyelids, she could still see that strip of skin hanging down. . . .

She opened her eyes again.

Mazana was holding the knife over Darbonna's chest as if wondering where to stab it. She was smiling at the old woman as if this were all some private joke between them, yet there was something in the set of her features that told Romany she wasn't enjoying this as much as she pretended. The point of the knife moved up and down, and from side to side, before stilling.

"Fascinating," the emira said. "I can feel the blade guiding my hand. It knows where a thrust would prove fatal and draws me away from that place. Does it want to prolong your suffering? Or does it wish to ensure as much blood as possible is drawn from your body before you die?"

Darbonna said nothing.

Mazana slid the knife into the old woman's chest, and the priestess screamed again. Her throat sounded as raw as the exposed flesh at her arm. A red stain bloomed on her robe over the wound, making the cloth stick to her skin.

Enough! Romany thought, preparing to withdraw. The Spider would no doubt mock her for her squeamishness, but if the goddess wasn't mocking her about that, she'd just be mocking her about something else.

The emira removed the knife from Darbonna's chest and made to push it in somewhere else—

And stopped.

Romany halted with her.

One of Mazana's fingers must have brushed Darbonna's bloody robe, for Romany could see the emira's skin glistening red. Then that skin started absorbing the blood like blotting paper. A stain spread through her flesh. Mazana's eyes smoldered. "Oh," she breathed, as if some truth had been revealed to her.

Darbonna was panting hard, wincing at each breath. And yet against all reason, her expression held a note of satisfaction. Her voice was a rasp. "Can I let you in on a secret?" she said to Mazana.

"I think the secret is already out, don't you? You might have spared yourself some trouble if you'd shared it sooner."

Romany's brows drew in. If the secret was out, it was doing a good job of hiding from her.

"Ah," Darbonna said, "but if I'd revealed it too soon, you might have been suspicious. You see, when I found you in the palace earlier I had no intention of killing you. One of your soldiers, yes, but not you. My aim was simply to deliver that blade into your hands, and to arouse your curiosity as to its powers."

Mazana's look was disbelieving, but a little of the glow had faded from her eyes.

"Aren't you going to ask why?" Darbonna said. "You were so full of questions a moment ago."

"Why?"

Romany found herself holding her breath. This was why she'd been right to stay.

Darbonna flicked her head to clear the sweat-slick hair from her eyes. "That day in the Founder's Citadel, only a handful of us escaped alive. After our attack on you failed, we retreated to one of the chambers above. That was where I felt my Lord die." Her voice cracked, and she swallowed before continuing. "Some of us wanted to follow our god through Shroud's Gate. Then, when we sensed you steal a part of his power, one fool even suggested we should start worshipping *you* in his place. I throttled that man with my own hands. But his blasphemy made me think. If you'd taken a part of our Lord's power, you had to have taken in part of his spirit too. Only a small part, perhaps"—her eyes glittered—"but a part that might grow if you had the Lord's own weapon in your hand. If you tasted of the blood delivered by its blade. Was I right? Can you feel his influence stirring inside you?"

"I feel nothing," Mazana said, but her words were given the lie by the tightness in her voice.

"I sense his mark upon you. I *feel* his taint—"

"Silence!" the emira said. She raised the knife again and held it to Darbonna's sternum.

The old woman's voice rose. "You think you defeated him in the citadel, but in the end it will be his victory over you—"

The last of her words dissolved into a scream as the emira plunged the dagger once more into her flesh. It seemed Mazana was no longer concerned about inflicting a mortal wound, for she twisted the weapon before pulling it out. She stabbed Darbonna again and again, her strokes becoming more frenzied. Blood spattered her dress.

Romany fled back to her body, wishing she'd had the sense to do so sooner.

CHAPTER 6

ENAR'S MOOD was dark as he strode along the corridor away from Jambar's quarters. The Remnerol hadn't been home, of course; he never was when the Guardian called. Three times in as many bells Senar had tried to surprise him with a visit, but how did you surprise a man who could read the future? A man who knew Senar would be looking for him following the unexplained disappearance of a young male servant yesterday.

The Guardian couldn't pretend, though, that it was the boy's fate alone that had brought him to Jambar's door.

Eleven days had passed since Dragon Day, and still Senar had heard no news of his homeland. About the Guardians. About whether his kinsmen had yet clashed with the Augerans. He'd tried showing his face this morning at Olaire's Erin Elalese embassy, but the ambassador had claimed to know nothing. He might even have been telling the truth too. Since Dragon Day, the only ship to have arrived in Olaire had come from Mazana's home island, and the cutting off of trade to the city had seen the flow of news end as well. And even if the stone-skins *had* attacked Erin Elal, how long would it take for word to reach Senar here? Weeks? Months? No, the best chance he had of finding out what was happening abroad was to track down Jambar and convince him to talk.

Of course, any information he wrested from the shaman would have to be digested with a healthy dose of skepticism. One moment the man knew the instant the Chameleons would set foot in Zalli's

house, the next he seemed barely able to foretell what day would follow this one. From time to time, Senar would see him in whispered
conference with Mazana, but the emira had been no more willing to
share the details of their conversations than Jambar himself. Among
the snippets Senar had overheard, though, one place had come up
more often than coincidence could warrant.

Gilgamar.

The Guardian's thoughts wandered as he turned into an unlit corridor. If Jambar was interested in Gilgamar, then likely the stone-
skins were too. Senar had assumed their actions on Dragon Day had
been geared solely toward ensuring the Storm Lords didn't interfere
in any clash with Erin Elal. But why were their agents still active in
Olaire? In the past few days, two Augerans had been hunted down
by that belligerent Watchman, Kempis Parr, and more were said to
be lying low in readiness for who knew what scheme. Neither of the
stone-skins caught had revealed their purpose, one dying of a self-
inflicted wound, the second holding out against Mazana's questioning
until his body expired. Perhaps Erin Elal wasn't their ultimate target,
after all. Perhaps their sabotage of the Dragon Hunt had merely been
the opening move in a wider campaign against the League. If so, their
first goal would be to obtain access to the Sabian Sea for their fleet.
That meant taking Dian and Natilly—or more likely Gilgamar, so they
could bring their ships through its canal.

Gilgamar. It all came back to Gilgamar.

So what was Senar still doing in Olaire? Olaire, where the heat and
the stink and the flow of unfamiliar faces wore on him more each day.
Olaire, where he woke each morning to a moment of disorientation
before remembering where he was. True, the dragons in the sea would
make sailing to the mainland a perilous undertaking, but was that
enough to keep him in Olaire? Should it be?

There had been times as a Guardian when he'd been away from
home for long periods, yet never before had he experienced the sense
of . . . separation he felt now. During the fifth Kalanese campaign, he
and Li Benir had spent months in the foothills of the White Mountains, raiding Kalanese spice caravans, or hunting the pashas as they
in turn hunted the sandclaws spreading west across the Gollothir
Plains. When food and water were scarce, Senar had had to drink
blood drained from the throats of alamandra. Yet still when he looked
back on that period, it was with fondness. Whereas he suspected he

might spend the rest of his life in Olaire and never develop that same sentiment.

Would things be any better if he returned to Erin Elal, though? What was there in Arkarbour he was so anxious to return to? He shook his head. When he thought of home now, it was of a time when it meant something to be a Guardian. But those days had long since passed. Servants of the people the Guardians might be, yet they'd lost their struggle for power with the emperor, and everyone hates a loser. It was easy to let his current discontent color his memory of what had gone before. To forget about Li Benir and Jessca dying, and about how dark the days had been before he passed through the Merigan portal. With the stone-skins' coming, he had felt a new sense of purpose. That purpose had leached away, though, as Senar came to realize the hopelessness of Erin Elal's plight. When the Augeran hammer fell, what chance did his people have of resisting? What difference could he make to the outcome?

The sound of fighting was coming from somewhere to his right, but he paid it no mind. Twist up to his tricks again, most likely. He realized his steps were leading him toward the cells. Mazana hadn't ordered Senar to stay away from Darbonna—she knew better than to try—but she'd made her wishes clear enough at the duel. Why, then, was he set on disregarding them? Because he wanted to speak to Darbonna about the library at the Founder's Citadel, yes, but also because he wanted to know more about the god she had once served. And not out of mere curiosity, either. In stealing Fume's power, Mazana had taken in part of his spirit. Senar had wondered at the changes that had come over her since Dragon Day. There was the redness to her eyes, but there was also the ruthlessness she had shown in sweeping aside the remnants of the old Storm Lord empire. Just putting down a marker for her enemies? Or something more—a consequence of the god's influence, perhaps?

If anyone knew, it would be Fume's high priestess. Most likely she would refuse to speak to Senar, yet where was the harm in trying? Of course, in ignoring Mazana's wishes he risked straining still further whatever ties existed between them. At least in doing so, though, he might better learn how strongly those ties were forged.

From ahead and to his left came a scream muffled by stone.

Senar's mouth went dry. He picked up his pace.

Three turnings brought him to the corridor with the door leading to the cells—the same cells Senar had been held in when he first came to Olaire. Standing outside was not the pair of Storm Guards he'd been expecting, but the executioner. Senar had become so used to the giant staring at nothing that he was surprised to find the man's gaze following him as he drew near. The Guardian stopped opposite him. There was a smell of singed hair about the other man, and Senar felt the warmth coming off his armor as it gave out the heat it had taken in through the day. The executioner's chest swelled with each breath, and there was a faint scratching sound as the metal links brushed against each other.

Another scream came from the cells, gurgling into silence.

Senar looked from the giant to the door behind. There was a grille at eye level, darkness beyond. Doubtless Mazana had told the executioner she was not to be disturbed, and there was as much point in asking him to move aside as there was in asking the door.

The Guardian, though, had no intention of asking.

He locked gazes with the executioner again. So steadfast did the man's presence seem, he might have set down roots in the stone floor. But Senar had learned from their duel on Dragon Day what force it took to stagger him. In combat the Guardian had only the time between sword strokes to gather his Will. Here, though, he could focus enough of his power that even the giant couldn't stand against it . . .

Footsteps sounded from beyond the door.

It opened.

Mazana stepped from the gloom. A scabbarded dagger was pushed through the belt at her waist. Her clothes were spattered with blood—no prizes for guessing whose—and the skin of her hands and lower arms was discolored by purple-red blotches like birthmarks. She did not seem surprised to see Senar. She even smiled as she came toward him.

Then she was on him, somehow managing to push him back against the wall and pull him toward her all at once. A jolt passed between them. She locked her arms round his neck and kissed him, her tongue darting between his teeth. Her breath tasted of mirispice. Senar stared into her red eyes, too taken aback to react.

Then she bit down on his lower lip. He gasped as he felt the blood flow. Mazana responded by biting harder, and the Guardian yanked his head to one side to free himself. A growl sounded at the back of Mazana's throat. She seized his chin and pulled his head round again, her fingernails digging into his skin. Gods, she was strong. Her breath was hot against his face. Senar raised an arm between them, not knowing if she meant to kiss him or tear out his throat with her teeth. She removed one arm from around his neck and reached between his legs.

He seized her wrist. Such was her strength, it was all he could do to hold her. A part of him didn't know why he was trying. Maybe there'd been times when he wondered how they would be together, but it had never been like this. As romantic encounters went, this was about as sensual as being mauled by a flintcat.

Behind, the executioner stood motionless, watching. All adding to the ambience.

Mazana strained forward, snapping her teeth at him. She was giving off so much heat, Senar might have been standing next to a bonfire. He could sense the abandon in her, and it made him all the more determined to resist. Before today she'd never offered herself to Senar because it would have meant something to him. Now he was refusing her because it would have meant nothing to her.

Her lips had darkened where she'd kissed him. Stained by his blood? Her flesh seemed to have absorbed it. Senar still had his arm between them, just below her throat, and he'd recovered enough of himself to add a touch of the Will to strengthen it. As Mazana continued to push against it, her smile stretched to a snarl.

Then abruptly the fight went out of her, and she pulled away.

Senar sagged back against the wall, breathless.

Mazana was panting too. Her face twisted in anger or disgust or both, and the Guardian wondered at the swings of emotion he provoked in her. He looked from her blotchy arms to the door behind her. "Where's Darbonna?" he said between breaths. "What have you done?"

As if he didn't already know.

Mazana did not respond.

"Why? Why did she have to die?"

The emira's lip curled. "A better question would be 'why should she live?' She tried to kill me on Dragon Day, then again this afternoon. Should I have let her keep trying until she succeeded? Do you think we could have become friends in time?" She stepped toward him. "But that's not what really bothers you, is it? The fact that she's dead. What bothers you is that I was the one holding the knife." Her voice was mocking. "What's wrong, Guardian? You don't think the one who passes the sentence should be the one to carry it out? Would my soul be less stained if I'd given the job to another? Maybe I should have got *you* to do it instead. Would you have killed her if I'd asked?"

Senar did not reply. She knew the answer to that already.

Mazana studied him, then snorted and looked at her hands. The blotches on her skin had paled. The flush in her face was fading, too. She was back in control, but that scorn was still in her voice as she looked at the door to the cells and said, "The Merigan portal you went through when you came here, it's along that corridor, isn't it? Why haven't you tried to use it since our illustrious friend Imerle passed away?"

"The gateway has a code. I don't know the symbol for Erin Elal."

"Then why haven't you asked me to take you to the mainland? A ship with a water-mage could reach Gilgamar in a handful of bells." She paused. "Perhaps it was because you thought I couldn't survive here without you. Or perhaps you were afraid I might say yes."

Senar crossed his arms. "You never offered before. Are you offering now?" The gods knew, he would have jumped at the chance just then.

The emira said nothing. She stood there rubbing her wrists. A smile formed at the corners of her mouth.

Then she spun and started along the corridor.

"Executioner, with me," she called over her shoulder. "Since the Guardian is unwilling or unable, I will have to find my entertainment elsewhere."

Scowling, Senar watched her go.

The gates of the Chameleon Temple were unguarded as Karmel strode through at Caval's side. The courtyard beyond was deserted too, and as the priestess and her brother followed the colonnade around, the echoes from the slap of their sandals faded into a pool of silence. They had three bells to kill before their ship left for Gilgamar, but from the pace her brother set, it was clear he intended their stay here to be a short one—just long enough for them to freshen up and gather a few possessions. Not that Karmel was complaining. She couldn't see the empty spaces in the shrine without thinking of the friends she had lost.

They reached the door to Caval's quarters. Inside, sunlight poured through the room's transparent west-facing wall, and Karmel shielded her eyes as she looked down on the city beyond. The fish market in Crofters Lane was thronged with people, seeking a share of the morning's meager catch. Also present was a sizeable force of Revenants, ready to prevent a repeat of last week's food riots. Prices had tripled now that grain shipments from Shamano and Elescori had dried up, and few of Olaire's fishermen were prepared to put out to sea if it meant risking a confrontation with a dragon. Mazana Creed had tried to ease their fears by ordering the remaining Drifters to accompany them to sea. But to no avail. The reluctance with which the Drifters had met the order told the fishermen all they needed to know about their chances of outrunning a dragon if they met one.

Dragging Drifters from their duties in the Shallows had created another problem. Even from this distance, Karmel could see the muck and trash that had accumulated in the flooded streets. There were fresh bodies there too each morning. With not enough space to bury them all, the grounds of the Founder's Citadel had been turned into a vast funeral pyre. The smoke from the fires formed a black smudge over the city, drifting south on the breeze.

Caval stood beside his desk, making no move to sit in the chair behind it. He was rubbing his left shoulder as if returning to the temple had made the pain of his old wound—the wound that had never properly healed after their father's beating—flare up again. He still had the bad dreams, still woke in agony each morning as if his collarbone had been broken anew.

"Can it work?" Karmel said. "Mazana's plan to destroy the stoneskin fleet, I mean."

Caval's smile was strained. "Reconsidering her offer to stay behind, are you?" Before she could reply, he moved to a bookcase and ran a finger along the spines of the books. He pulled one out and tossed it to Karmel. "Here, for the journey."

She snatched at it, missed, and it thumped to the floor.

"You should find that an interesting read, especially the parts about the Rubyholt. . . ."

His voice died away.

Karmel had heard it too—a sound from the corridor outside. A footfall? A muffled cough? Instinctively she employed her power, sensed Caval do the same.

The door handle swung down, the door inward.

A dark-skinned man in a stained white robe entered. His nose and cheeks were crisscrossed with the spidery red capillaries of a hardened drinker, and the sway in his step told Karmel he'd started early today. The sight of him tugged at a memory, but when the priestess grasped for it, it slipped away. Behind him came a man whose right eye was swollen to the point of closing and a woman whose face was so red she might have fallen asleep in the sun. Both wore green uniforms. And both were armed.

The drinker halted a few paces into the room. "Show yourselves," he said in an alien accent.

Or what? the priestess wanted to say. Her initial surprise at the strangers' appearance had given way to indignation. What right did they have to intrude on her home?

"Show yourselves, I am saying again."

Moving her eyes, not her head, Karmel glanced across at Caval. He tried to tell her something with his look—to stay out of sight, perhaps, while he dealt with these people. Then he surrendered his power and flashed Drinker a bright smile.

"How can I help?" he asked.

"The lady too, please," Drinker said, looking at the book on the floor beside Karmel.

"Lady?"

"I was seeing two people enter the temple, hearing two voices at the door just now."

Enough of this, Karmel thought as she let go her power. The man clearly knew she was here.

"See, just the two of us," Caval said to Drinker, perhaps hoping to convince him there might be more.

Drinker's lips quirked. Not taken in, then. "It is time I was introducing myself. I am Lydanto Hood, Gilgamarian ambassador to the Storm Isles."

Karmel covered her unease. Gilgamar was first stop on their forthcoming trip to the Rubyholt Isles. A coincidence that this man had called on them so soon after their meeting with Mazana?

Lydanto waited for a response from the Chameleons, but when they remained silent, he said to Caval, "And you, unless I am being mistaken, are Caval Flood, high priest of the Chameleon." He swung to Karmel. "You I am not knowing, though your face is—how do you say?—ringing the tower of bells."

It came to her then where she'd seen him before: on the deck of the ship, the *Crest,* that she'd hitched a ride back on from Dian. Another coincidence? She could only hope she'd kept enough of a low profile that day that he didn't place her.

The two guards took up station at the door. Karmel looked toward them, then said to Lydanto, "Do your greetings always come with armed men at your back?"

The ambassador's expression was unapologetic. "You would have had me make the journey to your temple without an escort? The streets are being dangerous of late, in case you were not noticing."

He did not ask his soldiers to withdraw, though.

Lydanto crossed to one of the chairs in front of the desk. It creaked as he settled into it. He withdrew a flask from a pocket in his robe, then unscrewed the cap and drank. His Adam's apple bobbed as he swallowed.

The silence dragged out.

"Well, this is cozy," Caval said. "We must do this again sometime."

The ambassador hesitated, his expression suddenly pensive as if he'd been building up to something, only to have second thoughts.

"How did you find us?" Karmel asked him, anxious to get this over with.

"Since Dragon Day I have been instructing my men to keep a discreet eye on the palace. You were seen entering and leaving earlier."

And the Gilgamarians had followed them here? Karmel hadn't spotted anyone when she checked her backtrail, but maybe Lydanto's watchers had guessed her destination and gone a different way.

"You've been looking for us?" Caval said.

"No."

"Ah, then why are we talking?"

Lydanto collected his thoughts. "For you to understand, I must first be going back a way. You have been hearing what happened on Imerle's flagship on Dragon Day?"

Caval's face gave nothing away. "Rumors only."

"Then you are doubtless aware that Imerle was inviting certain of her opponents on board to take part in the Dragon Day festivities. Among those opponents was Kalisch Rethell Webb, first speaker of the Gilgamarian Ruling Council, along with his daughter, Agenta. When the Dragon Gate went up, Imerle's mage, Orsan, was unleashing a wave of water-magic upon the *Icewing* in order to cripple it and thus render it—how do you say?—a sitting goose." He looked at Karmel. "Stop me if you are knowing this already."

There went Karmel's hope of him not placing her. But even if he recognized her from the *Crest*, he couldn't know the significance of her being on board that day.

"And then?" Caval said, continuing the pretense that this was new to him.

"And then fortunately the kalisch foresaw Imerle's treachery, and had his own ship standing by to rescue the *Icewing*. But not before the kalisch himself was being killed."

"Yet his daughter survived, I take it."

Lydanto nodded. "She was braving the dragons to sail back to Olaire in search of the vengeance against Imerle. Along with Iqral here"—he gestured to the male guard by the doorway—"she was in the palace when it was flooded. Alas, they were separated. That is the last time she was being seen alive."

"Ah, and you think we might know what happened to her?"

"You were in the palace too. Or at least the Chameleons were."

"Along with half of Olaire. Most of whom were trying to kill us, as I recall."

"Agenta would have been with a party of soldiers wearing the uniforms like Iqral here."

Caval's gaze flickered to the guard. "Very dashing."

Karmel frowned. What was wrong with her brother today? Was he looking for a fight? To Lydanto she said, "Even if we knew what this woman looked like, surely you don't expect us to remember one face among all the others we saw that day."

A ghost of a smile crossed the ambassador's face. "If you had been seeing the kalischa, you would not be forgetting her." His smile withered. "I am fortunate to be having some contacts at the palace. They are telling me the commander of Agenta's forces, a man named Warner Sturge, survived Dragon Day, only later to be dying of his injuries." Something in Lydanto's voice said he had doubts concerning the manner of the man's passing. "But there has been no word of Agenta. Perhaps she died on Dragon Day. Or perhaps, like Warner, she was suffering a wound and is now being treated at the palace."

"The palace," Caval repeated. "As in the place we just came from."

Lydanto regarded him coolly. "You may be assured I will be taking my questions to Mazana Creed in due course. But not before I have been exhausting all other options."

Karmel's skin prickled. Was that a threat? He'd put just enough emphasis on "all" to make it clear he would not leave without answers.

The ambassador went on, "I am not asking you to be telling me what you were doing in the palace on Dragon Day. I am not asking you to be telling me how Imerle met her end. I am just wanting to know if Agenta is alive. And if not, where her body can be found."

Caval made to speak, but Karmel got in first. "I'm sorry, there's nothing we can tell you. Before the palace was flooded, the only people we saw were Storm Guards."

"And after?"

"After," Caval said, "we were more concerned about steering clear of strangers than introducing ourselves."

Karmel had to offer Lydanto something, so she said, "When the corridors filled with water, we climbed to the terraces. If Agenta survived the flooding, perhaps she escaped that way too."

"And left Warner behind, injured? I am thinking not. And if she had been escaping, where is she now? Dragon Day was eleven days ago. It is not as if she could be getting lost for all that time."

Caval was in again. "It seems you've answered your own question, then. Better than we can, certainly."

Lydanto took a breath and blew it out. His gaze on Caval was steady, but his hands had a tremble to them. Karmel studied the man, trying to read his thoughts. There was suffering there, she realized. A suffering beyond that of an ambassador inquiring after the fate of his citizen. What had this Agenta been to him? How far was he prepared to go to hunt her down? Something in his expression told Karmel he wanted to believe the Chameleons' story, but how could he be sure of their honesty? Maybe a more . . . vigorous mode of questioning would get him better answers. Could he afford to pass up this opportunity?

Karmel looked toward the open door, wondering if Lydanto had reinforcements outside. Would he risk a confrontation with the Chameleons on home ground? Would he gamble his soldiers' lives when he had no guarantee Caval and Karmel were holding out on him? More to the point, could he question them more forcefully if he had to? Did he have the steel? The ruthlessness?

He stared down at his hands, perhaps deliberating the same.

Then he replaced the cap on his flask, rose, and crossed to the door. Without a backward look, he walked out.

Floating in spirit-form above the bailey of Dresk's fortress, Amerel looked up at the Great Hall's solitary tower. Where in the Matron's name was Talet? The spy was supposed to be at the second-floor window, ready to signal Noon when the stone-skins arrived. But with the seventh bell fast approaching, the opening remained dark and empty.

She'd been a fool not to make sure of Talet's allegiance at their meeting. Instead of using a nudge of her Will, she should have bludgeoned him with it until he was a mindless husk incapable of independent thought—until he'd forgotten the name of that son of his, along with the name of every friend he had in this godforsaken city. When had she ever settled for half measures before? Why should she start now with the stakes so high?

Never again. When you took half measures, you only got halfway to where you wanted to go.

Not a breath of wind stirred the rag that passed for a flag on the Great Hall's flagpole. From the distant harbor came laughter and shouting and whistling ashpipes. By contrast the Old Town round the fortress was silent. The sun had set below the western battlements, plunging the bailey into shadow. At the center of the yard, a group of Rubyholters waited to greet the stone-skins. Among them was Galantas, standing a pace ahead of his kinsmen and doing his best to look like his presence conferred an honor on the others in attendance. He wore a sharkskin cape and a necklace of shark's teeth.

Okay, he had a shark thing going on. Amerel got it.

A dozen guards were scattered around the bailey, and another thirty manned the battlements. They might as well have been made of straw for all the use they'd be in a scrap. A group of them sat with their legs dangling into the yard, passing a bottle between them. The next woman to receive it leaned back drunkenly and ended up tipping its contents over her face to a chorus of hoots and giggles. Farther along the wall, a man with a crossbow resting on his shoulder was standing in the exact place Noon's bolt would pass on its way to the engraved flagstone. But what did that matter now that Talet wasn't around to give the Breaker his signal?

She looked up at the tower window.

Nothing.

The seventh bell rang, and as the echoes faded Amerel heard footsteps outside the guardhouse. *The stone-skins.* Right on time, damn them. Looking left through the gates, Amerel saw a group of twenty Augerans approaching, eight of whom carried four huge chests between them. Only twenty warriors? It spoke of the stone-skins' arrogance that they considered twenty a sufficient guard to escort twenty thousand talents through the streets of a pirate city. But who was to say they hadn't started the journey with more men?

Behind them came a hungry-eyed crowd, drawn to the weight of gold as if it exerted its own gravity. A man shouted, "Just one coin, that's all I'm asking!" Another called, "Drinks are on Dresk tonight!" and his words drew a cheer. Somehow Amerel doubted the warlord's generosity extended even that far. He'd have to spend the money soon on *something,* though, that much was clear. When his subjects had spent their lives stealing whatever they wanted from whomever they wanted, they were unlikely to change their ways just because the "whomever" was Dresk himself. And while the warlord had a fortress and guards to keep the rabble at bay, who would protect him from the guards themselves?

The stone-skins entered the bailey, resplendent in their crimson cloaks. One of Dresk's men on the battlements gave a mocking wolf whistle, but the laughter that followed was forced. Even Amerel had to admit she was impressed by the size and build of the Augerans. Yet even more striking was their sense of self-assurance—a sense that, were the entire city to turn against them, they would still expect to win through unscathed. Judging by the quality of the forces arrayed against them, they might be right too.

Amerel recognized the commander, Eremo, from Talet's description. An upright man with a receding hairline, he wore an expression that just failed to disguise the disdain in which he held his hosts. Next to him was the man mountain Amerel had noticed from the brothel's window. His skin was a darker tone than that of his companions, and on his cheeks were golden tattoos in spiral patterns that marked him as one of the elite Augeran warriors referred to in the ancient texts as Syns. Behind him was a handsome man with a whiff of power about him—a power that felt so alien to Amerel he seemed like nothing less than a tear in the fabric of reality.

His was not the most unsettling presence among the group, though. For at the rear came the man with the spiked hair, skipping along like it was the first day of spring. His face was a patchwork of scars, and blood trickled from a cut beneath his left eye, making it seem as if he were weeping red tears. Just looking at him left Amerel feeling like there were bloodroaches crawling over her skin. That sense of being watched was back, too—the sense she'd first experienced when she'd observed the Augerans crossing the market. The urge to withdraw was strong, but what if Talet suddenly appeared in the tower window? Besides, having died a thousand deaths at the hands of the Deliverer, there was nothing in this world that held any fear for Amerel now.

No fear for herself, at least.

Galantas did not move to greet his guests, but instead held his ground so the stone-skins had to come to him. Eremo took in the defenders on the battlements, then went to join him. Walking a step in front of his kinsmen, the commander would have presented a clear target for Noon's crossbow bolt. But there was still no sign of Talet in the window.

Galantas and Eremo shook hands.

What now? Amerel wondered. All was not yet lost. Dresk and Eremo still had to negotiate the treaty, meaning there was time for Talet to take his position before the stone-skins made their exit. And if he never showed, Amerel could always return to her body when Eremo reemerged from the fortress, and tell Noon to shoot his crossbow blind into the yard. It wouldn't matter if he missed the commander, provided the stone-skins saw the missile and misinterpreted it as a Rubyholt attack.

In the meantime, Amerel would look round the fortress and see if she could find whichever rock Talet had crawled under.

As Galantas watched Eremo scrutinize the guards, a suspicion gripped him that Dresk had been played for a fool. That this talk of gold and treaties had been nothing more than a ruse to get the stone-skins into the fortress so they could mount an assault. Those chests didn't really contain twenty thousand talents. Hells, the black-cloaked warriors who'd carried them from the harbor weren't even out of breath. A couple of Red Cloaks had their swords out, and they seemed in no hurry to

sheathe them. But no, he told himself, if the Augerans intended treachery, they would have brought more than twenty warriors.

Then again, being outnumbered hadn't exactly hindered them
against Yali's ships.

Eremo looked less than pleased to find Galantas waiting for him.
Either he was anticipating a rough ride in the negotiations to come,
or he'd heard about the Falcon boy Galantas had rescued. In his party
was the warrior Ostari whom he had spoken to on the *Eternal*. The
man was trying to catch Galantas's eye now, but Galantas ignored
him. He watched the Black Cloaks set down the four chests. They hit
the ground with a reassuring clink. Meaning the money was real.
Twenty thousand talents! All that gold, and Dresk's plans for it probably extended no further than tipping it across the Great Hall and
squatting on it like some dragon of legend. When Galantas replaced
his father, he would use it to build a capital worthy of the Isles, to
unlock the wealth tied up in the karmight mines to the south, to recruit a force drawn from the best warriors and sailors and bring an
end to the years of infighting between the tribes.

Soon now. It would start with the clan leaders' meeting at the Hub
the day after tomorrow.

Dresk appeared in the fortress's archway. Judging by the glaze to
his eyes, he'd been drinking again. He beckoned Eremo to him, and
the commander set off across the yard, flanked by Hex and the warrior with the golden tattoos. The chest bearers lifted the chests and
followed, Galantas a pace behind. Dresk stepped aside to let the
stone-skins pass, but blocked Galantas with an arm.

"Run along and play, boy. This is men's work."

It was a moment before Galantas could speak. His father was spoiling for a fight, but Galantas knew this was a contest he couldn't win.
"Are you sure you won't need help with the big words?" he said at last.

Then, before Dresk could reply, he spun on his heel and walked
away.

Near the guardhouse, Qinta was speaking to two of Krel Faloman
Gorst's men. Galantas crossed to join them. He struggled to compose
himself. Not for the first time, Dresk had tried to shame him in front
of his kinsmen, but the fool probably thought he owed Galantas for
the indignity of Galantas saving his life in that Raptor raid nine years
ago. The irony wasn't lost on Galantas. As a child, he'd been warned
not to dishonor the warlord—had been pushed into excelling with

both sail and sword. Yet in the end it was Galantas's skill with a blade, rather than his lack of it, that had shamed Dresk.

Or shamed him in his own eyes, at least. To Galantas, his father had been immense that day, carving holes in the enemy ranks with each sweep of his broadsword. He'd saved Galantas's life a dozen times, so why should his son repaying the favor have caused such humiliation?

Pride. It was the only explanation.

And yet where is that pride now? Galantas wondered, remembering his father's drunken gaze.

The shadows in the yard were deepening, making the points of light in the Augerans' skin glitter. Galantas heard two guards speculating in overloud voices about whether those points would be valuable if they were cut out. The stone-skins' response was a scornful silence. Galantas understood their contempt. On the Ribbon Sea, the coming of a Rubyholt ship was feared like the coming of Shroud himself. Yet here the Islanders looked like nothing more than a gaggle of beggars, sniggering at the man handing out the alms.

So much would change on Galantas's watch.

At that moment, he noticed Talet moving through the guardhouse gates. Late for the meeting with the stone-skins? So who was advising Dresk in there? The chamberlain shuffled across the bailey like a condemned man on his way to the gallows, his cane tap-tapping on the flagstones. As he passed Galantas, he kept his gaze on the ground. Galantas's eyes narrowed. Talet was the closest thing Dresk had to common sense among his followers, yet Galantas had never trusted the man. He was about to call him back when he heard voices from the Great Hall.

Approaching voices.

He frowned. Was the meeting with the Augerans over already? Had Dresk changed his mind and sent Eremo packing? No, the stone-skins sounded relaxed—good-humored, even—and above them Galantas heard the rumble of his father's laughter.

Understanding came to him.

Dresk had signed the damned treaty without even reading it.

Amerel watched Talet cross the bailey. Had the spy experienced a late change of heart? Or was he only now returning from making arrangements to protect his son? Whatever the reason for his tardiness, his arrival had drawn all eyes to him like a pair of tits. Galantas in particular was looking at him, and if he was suspicious now, how would he feel when Noon's crossbow bolt found its mark? Once the dust settled on this evening's proceedings, Amerel would have a few loose ends to tie up.

Now wasn't the time to worry about that, though, for with Talet on his way to the tower, the game was back on.

The spy entered the fortress.

And not a moment too soon. From inside the hall came footsteps, a babble of voices. The Augerans back already? Amerel's first instinct was that it must be the chest bearers returning. But the first person to emerge from the building was the man mountain with the golden tattoos. *And where the bodyguard goes* . . . Sure enough, the next figure to appear was Eremo, rubbing his hands together. Good bit of business he'd done inside, apparently, and it wasn't often you could say that when you were the one handing over twenty thousand talents. Scarface followed him out of the door.

So much for the negotiations.

Amerel silently cursed. Talet had only just entered the fortress. The Guardian had to slow the stone-skins down, but how? What could she do that wouldn't alert them to her presence?

She gathered her power, still no idea what her next move would be.

Galantas came to her rescue. He stepped in front of the man mountain. It was like stepping into the path of an avalanche, and for a heartbeat Amerel thought the Syn would roll right over him. Instead the Augeran drew up. The two men stared at each other. Galantas had to crane his neck to look into the giant's eyes, but he wasn't backing down. It took a placatory word from Eremo to separate them.

Amerel looked back at the tower. Through the first-floor window, she saw a shadow—Talet's?—glide across a wall, but it moved slowly, slowly.

Galantas was talking to Eremo. Complaining about the speed with which the treaty had been signed, no doubt. The commander was all smiles and nods, but there was no mistaking the strain in the exchange. The Matron alone knew what Galantas hoped to accomplish here. Perhaps he wanted to show his kinsmen he could stand up to the stone-skins, but if you wanted to look big in front of your friends, you didn't do it standing next to a bodyguard the size of a cliff.

Did Amerel really care what Galantas was doing, though? All this tension meant that Noon's crossbow bolt would land like a spark on dry kindling.

A shout came from her left. The gates had been closed to keep the crowds outside, and a handful of people had pressed their faces against the bars, looking as resentful as sinners at the gates to paradise. Amerel shot another look at the tower window. Still no Talet, but maybe he was keeping out of sight until the instant came to give Noon the signal.

Time for her last preparations.

Floating up to the height of the battlements, Amerel checked to ensure she remained aligned with the engraved flagstone and the brothel's window. Then she sank back into the yard. Eremo must have grown tired of stroking Galantas's ego, for he broke away from the other man and started making his way toward the guardhouse again. This time Galantas let him pass.

Here we go.

Scarface skipped ahead of his commander. Amerel couldn't shake the feeling she would have been better off making this freak her target rather than Eremo, but it was too late to change the plan now. A clank sounded as the guards opened the gates. Amerel focused on the section of wall where Noon's bolt would appear. The sky above the rampart was darkening to bronze. Hard to stare into that relative brightness after peering so long into the gloom, but she dared not look away.

Any moment now.

Eremo was an armspan from the engraved flagstone. Assuming Talet had signaled to Noon, the Breaker's bolt would already be on its way. Amerel felt a blink coming on, opened her eyes wider against it. But the harder she tried to fight it—

A flash of black above the battlements. Noon's crossbow bolt seemed to hang in the air before dipping as it passed over the parapet.

A heartbeat for Amerel to judge its speed and trajectory.

It was the shot she needed—a fraction high and behind Eremo's position, but nothing she couldn't rectify with a nudge of her Will. A nudge was all she could afford to give it, too, for anything heavy-handed would rob it of its momentum. The bolt plunged into the shadows of the bailey, and Amerel squinted to follow its flight. On the battlements, a female Rubyholt guard must have heard the whisper of its passage, for she flinched as if she thought the missile was meant for her. Perhaps Eremo glimpsed her from the corner of his eye, for he paused and turned toward her.

Making himself a bigger target for Amerel to hit.

A last feather-touch to alter the bolt's flight.

Got you.

With Eremo facing away from her, she didn't see precisely where the missile struck, but it was somewhere high on the chest. He stumbled back under the force of the impact, his hands reaching up to the wound.

Then his legs buckled, and he collapsed.

There was a collective intake of breath from the Rubyholters. For a moment, the stone-skins stared at their commander as if their minds were trying to catch up to what their eyes were telling them. Amerel felt the scales of history waver on their pivot. Then one of the Augerans reached for his sword.

The yard exploded into motion.

Amerel didn't see what happened next because her blood-dream was already upon her. As she killed, so her victim's pain was reflected on her through the Deliverer's visions. It wasn't just one bolt striking home, though, it was six, seven, eight, each thudding into her body with the force of a horse's kick. Blood bubbled in her spiritual throat. Her vision was a blur, her chest a knot of agony, but she smiled nevertheless.

Here was justice.

What the hell?

It took Galantas an instant to register what had happened. Eremo down, and there was no mistaking the cause with that crossbow bolt sticking from his chest. The nearest stone-skins closed around their commander to shield him with their bodies.

"Hold your fire!" Galantas shouted, turning toward the section of battlements where the missile had come from. The faces of the guards there mirrored his disbelief. One man was frozen in the act of raising a bottle to his lips. Two had half drawn their swords, but none were aiming a weapon into the yard. A woman with a crossbow at her feet held her hands up as if to deny responsibility. Then her eyes widened at something behind Galantas, and she crouched to pick up the weapon.

From over Galantas's shoulder, a wave of black sorcery flashed toward the battlements, crackling like a hundred tindersparks and darkening the air in its wake. A man on the walkway flung himself aside, but the woman who'd gone for the crossbow was engulfed. The blackness clung to her as she fell screaming into the yard. Her flesh dissolved, and by the time she hit the ground she was naught but a sack of meat and bones that landed on the flagstones with a wet crack. She disintegrated into dust that was picked up and carried about the yard on a wind whipped up by the sorcery's passage.

The battlements themselves suffered a similar fate. The white stones crumbled to powder and were shredded by the breeze. Within the space of a dozen heartbeats, a section of ramparts twenty paces long disappeared, and the gap grew larger as the stonework at either end continued to melt. A guard sitting with his legs hanging over the bailey tried to scramble up and away, only for the walkway to dissolve beneath him. He toppled into the yard. Another Islander half scrambled, half crawled toward the guardhouse before a second volley of sorcery hit him.

"Hold your fire!" Galantas shouted again, this time at the Augeran mage.

Swords clashed behind him, and it dawned on him suddenly how much trouble he was in. The Islanders in the fortress might outnumber the Augerans, but the bulk of the defenders were on the battlements, and most of *them*—on this section of wall, at least—had already been removed from the fight. Galantas spun round. The stone-skin warrior with the golden tattoos was leading a charge against the guards at the gate. Ostari, meanwhile, had moved to engage Qinta, while another of the Augerans was attacking Faloman's men.

Leaving the route to the Great Hall open. Tempting, but Galantas would not retreat. The legend he had created didn't step back in the face of the enemy. Not a single pace.

Even as he drew his sword, he was thinking about the bolt that had hit Eremo. Had his father been behind it? Could that be why Dresk had refused to let Galantas enter the Great Hall? Because he'd wanted him outside when the commander was shot, and thus on hand when the stone-skins retaliated? It wouldn't be the first time Dresk had tried to engineer Galantas's death. There was that incident when Galantas had been set on by "thieves" in a Karalatian alley, then that "intelligence" about a Londellian trader that had turned out to be a warship. Would Dresk have risked war with the Augerans, though, just to rid himself of Galantas? And before he'd had a chance to spend the twenty thousand talents he'd acquired?

Ostari drove Qinta back with a series of lightning cuts and thrusts. Galantas moved to flank his kinsman. It seemed unlikely Qinta would need help dispatching a lone opponent, but suddenly Ostari was stepping past the Second and bringing his elbow round to hammer into Qinta's temple.

He toppled wordlessly.

Galantas sprang forward and aimed a cut to Ostari's midsection, only for the stone-skin to dance out of range. Galantas thought the man would retreat to join his kinsmen around Eremo, but instead he pressed forward again with a smile that said he was keen to avenge the insult done to him over the Falcon boy. Galantas glanced at Eremo. Through a gap in the Augeran shields, Galantas saw the commander's back arch as he coughed up bloody froth. His wound might be a mortal one, but for the time being he lived, which meant the stone-skins' first concern would be to get him to safety. That being so, Galantas didn't need to defeat Ostari to survive. He only had to hold him off until the Augerans withdrew.

A fact he was quickly grateful for as the stone-skin attacked. Ostari's sword seemed to come at him from everywhere at once, and it took all Galantas's skill to keep the questing blade at bay. His foe's style of fighting was strangely stilted, his sword arm jerking this way and that while his body remained largely still. There should have been little power behind his swings, yet each blow landed on Galantas's blade with the weight of a headsman's stroke. He hadn't faced an opponent like this since a raid on a Corinian merchantman when he'd fought a Belliskan knight wielding a sword as tall as the warrior himself. A feint from Ostari brought Galantas's blade low, and he only just recovered in time to block the real thrust to his chest. Still his opponent's sword deflected off Galantas's weapon to score a nick to his arm.

Behind, Eremo was being lifted onto a shield and carried toward the guardhouse. Not much longer to hold on, for Ostari wouldn't let himself be left behind.

Then a noise like the buzz of a needlefly sounded, and a crossbow bolt buried itself in the stone-skin's sword arm. He grunted as his blade was jarred from his hand, but he immediately rolled and scooped the weapon up in his left hand instead. Galantas had no idea whether Ostari was equally proficient with both hands, nor did he have any wish to find out. He kept his sword down to signal he wouldn't press the attack.

Ostari did not react to the gesture. He didn't look relieved. Hells, he didn't even look in pain.

But he didn't seem in any hurry to renew their duel either.

Over the Augeran's shoulder, Galantas saw the corpses of Faloman's men on the ground. The defenders at the guardhouse were also down, and the gates had been thrown open. Beyond, the Rubyholt crowd had vanished. Eremo was carried into the shadow of the guardhouse. Four of his kinsmen protected him with upraised shields. On the section of wall to Galantas's left, a handful of Rubyholters were aiming crossbows into the yard. A bolt struck an Augeran shield, and another one pinged off the ground beside Ostari.

The stone-skin's gaze didn't leave Galantas.

"Hold your fire!" Galantas shouted to the guards. It was too soon to think of healing the rift with the Augerans, but at least he could send a message that he'd had no part in the attack.

Ostari was now the backmarker. One of his kinsmen called out to him in their native tongue—telling him to withdraw, no doubt. With the stone-skins on the move, some of the Islanders on the walls had found the courage to start descending to the yard. Ostari had but moments before his line of retreat was blocked. He backpedaled. There were no taunts, no empty promises of revenge, but his look conveyed all that needed to be said.

The guards jeered at the Augerans as if they'd driven off the enemy by strength of arms. Galantas was the only Islander left standing in the bailey, and he stepped forward. The drama was done, might as well claim it as his own, so he raised his sword.

The jeers turned to cheers.

As the stricken Eremo was carried clear of the guardhouse, another bolt clanged off a shield.

"Hold your fire!" Galantas called again. How many times must he give the order before it was obeyed?

Even as he spoke, another missile flitted through the shadows. It took Ostari in the ankle. The Augeran gave a strangled curse. He tried to take a backward step, but his injured leg went from under him, and he crumpled to the flagstones.

His kinsmen couldn't have seen him fall, for no one turned to help. An instant later the other stone-skins were gone.

Part II

CITY OF SNAKES

CHAPTER 7

ROM THE prow of the boat, Ebon watched the last rays of light chase across the waves. As the sun sank beneath the horizon, shadows gathered in the water. Upon a bluff inland, a dozen hooded riders galloped south along the coastal road as if seeking to keep pace with Ebon's boat. On its wave of water-magic, though, the craft traveled at a speed no horse could match.

The elderly sorcerer responsible for that wave, Gunnar, sat on the rear thwart looking out to sea. His dark-rimmed eyes bore testimony to his weariness. On the journey along the River Amber to Mercerie, the prince had demanded a speed that had tested the man's reserves to the limit. Soon, though, Ebon would be able to take up the strain, for over the course of the last few days he had studied the signature of the other man's power until he was able to reproduce it. Ebon's mastery over the waves was a fraction of Gunnar's, but at least they could now take turns propelling the boat. One might have thought the mage would have welcomed the help, but it wasn't gratitude Ebon saw in his eyes when their gazes met. It was apprehension at the prince's abilities. The same apprehension Ebon had seen in his own father's face a week ago when Ebon had set about healing him.

Before the attack on Majack, Ebon's history of spirit-possession had made people regard him suspiciously. Now they had something else to fear about him. And all because of a power he had never asked for—a power he had acquired in the hope of helping the very kinsmen who now shrank from him. But he wouldn't have to endure their distrust much longer. Only until his father's health was fully restored. Then he would leave Galitia in case the Fangalar were looking for him. As to where he would go, though . . .

That wasn't a question he expected to have to answer anytime soon. After he found Lamella and Rendale—if indeed he *did* find them—his next task would be to look in on Parolla's mother, Aliana, when she was reborn. At the back of his mind, he could sense Parolla and Luker, as he had been able to sense the goddess Galea after they struck their bargain in the Forest of Sighs. Both were scores of leagues from his position, Parolla to the north, Luker to the west. Yet when the time came to contact them, he knew he'd be able to do so with a mere thought. Strange that he didn't share a similar connection with Lamella or Rendale, but perhaps that was because he hadn't seen them since he inherited his powers. Perhaps if he ever found them again, they would never be more than a thought away too.

If. Such a big word for only having two letters.

He shook his head. No, he wouldn't let himself think Lamella was dead. Now that he had given up the kingship, she was his whole purpose. He needed her. Years ago, when the spirits had invaded his mind, she'd been the only thing that had stopped him slipping away. The Vamilians were now gone, yet they'd left some mark on him, some malaise of the spirit that if left unchecked, might drag him down again.

But perhaps that malaise had nothing to do with the Vamilians. Perhaps it was just a result of the things he'd witnessed in Majack on his return from the Forest of Sighs. The palace gates had held where the city gates had not. When the Book of Lost Souls was destroyed, the undead's strings had been cut, leaving piles of bodies tangled about the palace walls. Worse still had been the hollowness in the eyes of the survivors as they looked for friends among the corpses. Silence had covered the city—a silence that, even after the trappings of life eventually returned, would no doubt linger long beneath the clamor and the bustle.

Where are you, Lamella?

If she was alive, he would find her. Gilgamar, Kansar, Airey: there were only so many ports that Ocarn's ship could have put in at. Ebon would try them all. Even if he tracked her down, though, how long would he be able to keep her? If the Fangalar were hunting him, she'd be in danger while she was with him. Was he searching for her just so he could give her up again? Did he believe things would get better if they were reunited? The last six years had been shades of gray, and when things were gray that long, you had to wonder if they would ever wash out to white.

Ebon's gaze shifted to Vale, sitting on the oar bench with his eyes closed. Without his chain mail the timeshifter looked older somehow. More frail. But his presence, as always, served to still some of Ebon's doubts. Duty, the prince had come to realize, was like a dozen leashes around your neck, all tugging in different directions. When you moved your head to ease the pull from one, you just increased the pull from another. Ebon had paid a heavy price for duty—but the Endorian had paid a heavier one still. A decade ago, when Vale first pledged himself to Ebon's father, he had looked ten years Ebon's senior. Now he appeared twice that, for by speeding the rate at which he moved through time, he condemned himself to age faster than those around him. And all of those years lost in the service of a people not his own.

"What are you doing here, Vale?" Ebon whispered.

The timeshifter must have heard him, for he opened his eyes. "Where else would I be?"

"Anywhere but here."

Vale considered the question, then shrugged. "I gave an oath."

"An oath I would have released you from long ago, if you had asked. Maybe I should do it now."

"And maybe you're not the one who gets to choose."

Ebon held the other man's gaze. He wasn't buying this talk of oaths. Ebon's father had given Vale to the prince as a bodyguard four years ago, after Ebon's first ill-fated excursion into the Forest of Sighs. But in the intervening time, the Endorian had become the closest thing Ebon had to a friend. That friendship cut both ways, though: it imposed responsibilities on Ebon just as it did the timeshifter, even if they were responsibilities of a different kind.

"Are you worried I'm losing my edge?" Vale asked. His voice was pitched low so it wouldn't carry to Gunnar behind.

The prince stared at him, uncomprehending.

"It's a problem with timeshifters. As they get old, their reflexes start to dull, so they use their power more to make up for it. So they get old even quicker, use their abilities more . . . It becomes a downward spiral. In Endoria, people are alert to the danger. A soldier reaches forty, he gets retired whether he likes it or not."

"And how old are you?"

Vale gave one of his rare smiles. "Wish I knew. Ain't easy keeping track of your age when you're shifting through time every other day."

"I've always wondered about your people. Why aren't they ruling the world with their abilities?"

"Who says we want to? Anyhow, it ain't as simple as you see it. One on one, there ain't many who can hold their own against a timeshifter. But wars ain't fought one on one. Put us in the field, and we die as easy as the next soldiers when the sorcery starts flying. Plus there ain't no more appetite for war in Endoria than there is anywhere else. Less, maybe. When a soldier goes on campaign, he can be away for months or years. That's hard, but it's harder still when you're shifting through time and you get home to find you're older than the ones you left behind."

"And is there someone waiting for *you* to go back?" Ebon had asked Vale the same question before, of course, but the timeshifter had always shrugged it aside.

"Not anymore," he said.

Was that why he had left his homeland all those years ago? To escape the memory of someone he'd lost? Ebon couldn't deny his curiosity, but he knew better than to push. Vale would tell him if he wanted him to know.

The Endorian turned away from the sun so his features were in shadow. After a while he said, "There was a war going on. Not much more than border skirmishes really, but the Alosi were proving headstrong enough that the Elders voted to give them a touch of the whip. The enemy was operating out of a forest on our western border, and a dozen squads were sent in to clear them out. Problem was, the wran in charge of my squad had lost a daughter to the raiders the week before. The Elders, in their wisdom, didn't think to stand him down." Vale's voice was barely audible over the rustle of water beneath the bow. "The other squads hit their targets and pulled back. We went on.

"We lost a couple of men, but the wran didn't retreat. One of those who died was his second, else he might have been forced to call a halt. You probably reckon timeshifting's a gift when the swords are drawn, but it can be a curse too. Because when the man across from you is that much slower, it stops being a fight and turns into slaughter. We all got our arms red. Most of the squad had been with the wran for years, so they weren't going to say anything. Even when we were through enemy lines, he didn't stop. Says he wants the Alosi to know how it feels to lose a daughter. Says it's only fair. Couple of us tried to put an end to it then, but the wran called our bluff. He knew anyone who ratted on him would be putting a noose around their own neck. So one night I left camp during my watch and didn't look back."

Perhaps Ebon should have been disturbed by the story, but instead he found himself wondering what he would have done in the wran's position—how he would react now if he found out Lamella and Rendale were dead. "And you've never been home since?"

"Home to what? If the squad kept together, best I could hope for was a charge of desertion. If I came clean on what happened, maybe the Elders would've gone easy on me." Vale's gaze was hard and level. "But then word of what happened would have got out to everyone else too."

Including the people he felt he could no longer go back to? "Is it better they think you dead?"

"I thought so at the time."

"But now?"

"Now it's too late to matter." Vale made a gesture with one hand to indicate the subject was closed. "What's the story between you and Ocarn? The ambassador said you two had history."

Ebon had been waiting for that question since Mercerie. "It happened a few months before you arrived in Majack—before I went into the Forest of Sighs the first time." Strange how he divided his life now into everything that came before that expedition and everything that came after. "My father was in Mercerie, trying to build bridges with the padishah, and he took me with him. I was only seventeen. I disliked Ocarn the moment I met him. Almost as much as he disliked me, in fact. He was a prince, I was a prince, that seemed reason enough for us to butt heads."

"And that's all there is to it?"

"Sadly, no. I am sure you won't be surprised to hear there was a woman involved. Ocarn's sister, in fact. She and I got on too well for Ocarn's liking, and it ended with her inviting me back to her room. Foolishly I agreed to go. Nothing happened between us, and I like to think nothing would have done. But Ocarn made sure of it by storming in. He accused me of dishonoring his sister, yet he tarnished her honor more than I had by shouting our indiscretion from the rooftops. And by demanding I face him in a duel. His father stepped in to stop it, but the damage had already been done—"

"Your Highness," Gunnar interrupted, his voice tight. "Up ahead."

The wave of water-magic beneath the boat receded.

Ebon looked south. Farther along the coast, a promontory jutted into the sea. Around it the water was chopped to foam by hidden rocks, while protruding from amid the white-flecked waves . . . *A ship.* Or the wreck of a ship, more accurately. The vessel was broken in half along its waist, the middle part sticking up from the sea to bare the craft's guts. One of the ships from the Hunt? What flag was she flying?

"Take us closer," Ebon said.

A wave of water-magic burgeoned beneath the hull again, and the boat drifted forward.

The sea was covered with a layer of detritus from the wreck: pieces of wood, lengths of rope, fragments of sailcloth, and so many scraps of paper someone might have ripped up a book and scattered its pages across the waves. Ebon's boat entered the wreck's shadow. The coming of dusk had drained the blue from the water to leave it the color of steel. The prince studied the ship's exposed beams where they had been snapped in two. The wood was twisted and splintered, yet there were no indentations he might have taken for a dragon's tooth marks. Nor was there anything on or around the vessel that showed which city it hailed from. Its masts were gone, snapped near their base, and there was no flag conveniently floating on the water.

"There's another one," Vale said, and Ebon looked up to see a second wreck appear from behind the flank of the first. Lying on its side in the shallows, just a section of its upturned hull was visible, blanketed in green fuzz. Each wave dragged at the ship, tugging it a handspan shoreward before releasing it to settle back again.

"Watcher's tears, there's more," Gunnar said, pointing.

Beyond the promontory, a stretch of shingle had come into view. Upon it were grounded the carcasses of three more vessels: a fishing boat with its nets tangled about it, a galley with shattered oars jutting from its oar holes, a Corinian corrick with its green-trimmed mainsail half covering it like a shroud. "It's like a ship's boneyard," Gunnar whispered, and the sun-bleached ribs of the corrick's frame did indeed look like the bones of some monster of the deep. Beyond the strip of fireweed marking the high-water line were rolls of cloth, splintered planks, rusting crayfish baskets.

But no bodies. Interesting, that.

Ebon scanned the waves again. The rocks around the promontory might account for one wreck, but five? *Some storm that would have been.* Yet what other explanation could there be? Might a dragon have set up home nearby and be preying on the vessels journeying through these waters?

Vessels like Ebon's own, for example.

"Let's go," he said to Gunnar, and the mage released more of his power to take the boat skipping south across the waves.

Inland, the setting sun had ignited the haze of dust, turning the sky russet and gold.

Karmel stood on the deck of the *Grace,* staring southwest toward Gilgamar. The wind of the ship's passage rushed in her ears. Two water-mages were on board, and the wave they had conjured up to carry the vessel thundered beneath its bows as if the ship were sailing on the cusp of a storm. It had taken a mere two and a half bells to make the crossing from Olaire. Faster than any dragon could follow, Karmel had been assured, but that hadn't stopped her scanning the seas with an intensity that had left her eyes aching.

The skyline behind Gilgamar was darkening. Occupying a narrow strip of land between the Sabian and Ribbon seas, the city seemed to comprise not one settlement but two, separated by a canal that cut straight as an arrow's flight through the middle. On the western side—the Lower City—were mismatched houses crammed together, or stacked one atop another, or slumped against their neighbor like each was the only thing holding the other up. By contrast, the properties to the east—the Upper City—were arranged in lazy avenues, and scattered with parks and gardens, all rising up a gentle slope to a huge stone structure at the top that sparkled in the last of the light. Above the building fluttered a flag for every city in the Sabian League. The Alcazar, seat of the Ruling Council.

The wave beneath the *Grace* began to subside. As the rustle of water faded, Karmel heard the hum of the city together with a multitude of clangs from the harbor on the opposite shore. At the point where the canal opened out onto the Sabian Sea was the wreck of a ship lying on its side. A victim of Dragon Day, most likely. The sight of it brought the day right back to Karmel. For a moment, she thought she could hear the screams of the dragons' victims, only to realize it was the calls of the starbeaks circling above Gilgamar on red-flecked wings.

Footsteps sounded behind her, and she looked back to see Caval approaching. There was that skip in his step that he always had after he'd taken oscura—as if he had to stop himself from breaking into a run. The once-whites of his eyes were now a dirty gray, and Karmel wondered how she'd missed the signs of his addiction before Dragon Day. Because she hadn't been looking for them, of course. Because she and her brother had grown too far apart for her to see. How differently might things have gone if she had been there to arrest his slide? Had the distance between them contributed to his fall? *A distance I allowed to develop as much as he did.*

Caval came to stand alongside her.

"I thought you said the drugs weren't working anymore," Karmel said.

"Does an addict need a reason for his next fix?" Caval uncorked a water bottle and took a swig. Slaking his oscura-thirst. Then his voice turned grave. "I'm sorry," he said.

The priestess waited.

"For leaving you alone on deck, I mean. I know sailors can be a rough crowd."

Karmel rolled her eyes. The day after Dragon Day, he'd said "I'm sorry," and she had thought he was apologizing for betraying her. Instead he'd merely been apologizing for something trivial—she couldn't even remember what. But he'd seen the expectation in her eyes, and from then on he had contrived to fashion false apologies out of ever more tenuous circumstances. It didn't matter that he hadn't apologized in truth, she told herself. He carried his regret with him everywhere. Better he feel remorse and not say it, than say it and not feel it. And better this forced humor than the sickness of spirit that seemed to consume him each time the oscura wore off.

"Ah, Gilgamar," Caval said wistfully. "The most soulless city in the Sabian League, it's said."

"Why?"

"No history—or at least none worthy of the name. Before the Dragon Gate went up, there was nothing here but swamps, and gal-

low crabs, and bandits extorting tolls out of anyone using the road
to Dian. Then the canal was built, and the place grew fat on the fees
it charged to ships passing through. The League stopped paying for
a while. But Gilgamar's Ruling Council was supported by the Storm
Lords, who themselves were in a disagreement with the League
over—"

"The payment of the Levy. Yes, I know."

Caval raised an eyebrow.

"Veran gave me a history lesson on the crossing to Dian. I never
had him down as a student of history . . . but then, the man was full
of surprises."

Her brother stared at her, then chuckled.

Karmel shifted her gaze to the far side of the city. In the harbor
beyond the canal, thirty ships bobbed at quayside in the shadow of
an immense seawall.

"The wall was built at the same time as the canal," Caval said, following her gaze. "With the Cappel Strait blocked by the Dragon
Gate, Gilgamar became the only link between the League and the
south. A link that couldn't be allowed to fall into enemy hands—hence
the wall. The chains came later, though."

"Chains?"

He pointed. "See those lines spanning the entrance to the harbor?"
Karmel could make them out now she was looking for them—like the
bowed rungs of a ladder. "Those are chains," Caval explained. "Thick
as pillars, and invested with earth-magic. Once Dragon Day started,
the Ruling Council needed some way to keep the creatures out of the
port. They've worked, too. In all the time they've been up, not a single
dragon has managed to get through."

One of the *Grace*'s water-mages was at the tiller with the captain—a
woman wearing a gray suit and a permanent frown. The two of them
were discussing the wreck obstructing the mouth of the canal. The
order was given to take in the sails, and a handful of sailors scrambled aloft. As the *Grace* drew near the wreck, it rose on a wave of
water-magic. The front of the wave broke against the ship in hissing
foam. Karmel could make out mangled beams where a dragon must
have seized it in its jaws. And swarming through the wreckage like
maggots over a corpse—

She shrank back. "What are those?"

"Blacktooth snakes," Caval said.

From a distance, the waters of the canal had seemed to run black with the grime of industry. Now Karmel was closer, she could see that the channel and the sea in front of it were actually seething with glistening forms. "So many."

"Ah, that's why you'll never see a galley pass through the canal under oars. Those without water-mages employ tugs instead. Not only do the snakes tend to mess up the stroke of the oarsmen, they also have a habit of slithering up the oars to greet the rowers."

"They're poisonous?"

"Deadly. But don't worry, you're safe up here on deck."

"You'll take care of me, will you?" Karmel said, echoing his words before she'd set off for Dian with Veran.

Caval's stare was appraising.

Karmel looked back at the wreck. "Where did the snakes come from?"

"From a tomb under the canal that collapsed a while back. Water rushed in, the snakes came out."

"No one's ever tried to get rid of them?"

"Tried, yes. Just after the collapse, in fact. A water-mage drained the canal so the tomb could be resealed to stop more snakes escaping. Then the snakes already in the channel were doused in blayfire oil and set alight. For two days afterward, the canal stayed clear. Then the snakes came back in greater numbers." Caval gave a humorless smile. "Gilgamar is not a place to visit in open sandals."

Or at all, if Karmel had had her way. There'd been a time as an initiate when she had found the monotony of temple life claustrophobic and had longed to discover what lay across the sea. Now she yearned again for those days when the entirety of her world had been bounded by the shrine's walls.

The *Grace* swept over the wreck, and the wave beneath it receded as it reached the canal. Guarding the entrance on the eastern side was a fortress, the lines of it soft in the gathering gloom. A crenellated wall ran the length of the canal, patrolled by soldiers. On the western side, the land immediately adjoining the canal was a wasteland of cracked mud and weeds and rubbish. From the line of houses beyond, a gaggle of townsfolk emerged, little more than silhouettes in the half-light. The *Grace* slowed to a crawl, yet its passage still sent water sloshing out of the channel. The handful of blacktooth snakes washed up on the land were snatched up by children and carried away. Some of the watchers shouted out to the ship for news. Others offered to sell blackweed or fish-bone jewelry or something called tollen, while painted ladies promised to pleasure the sailors in the time it took the vessel to sail the length of the canal.

It occurred to Karmel that there weren't any bridges spanning the channel. No, that wasn't quite true. Ahead she could see another fortress on the eastern side, and this one had a drawbridge that was currently raised. The bridge hadn't been lifted at the *Grace*'s approach, meaning it had to have been up already. When she quizzed Caval about this, he said, "The bridge is always raised at dusk. What better way to keep the rabble in their place than to prevent them ever leaving?"

"The poor aren't allowed into the Upper City?"

"Of course they are. They just need a good reason to be there. Written in blood, no doubt. And approved by one of their betters."

Along a street in the Lower City, Karmel saw a cart upended to form a barricade, yet there was no one manning it. From far away came the cry of a prayerseeker calling the faithful to worship. Covering the city was a nauseating sour-sweet scent like burned honeycomb.

Caval's voice interrupted her thoughts. "Well, well."

Karmel looked where he indicated. On the deck a short distance away, a male Untarian was mopping the boards. He was barefooted and wore a plain susha robe. From a cord around his neck hung a fish-bone charm. Karmel studied him, wondering what she was supposed to be seeing. Then it came to her. *Of course.* Mazana Creed had mentioned she was sending a water-mage to accompany them as far as the Rubyholt Isles. Karmel had assumed she'd been referring to one of the two sorcerers who had hastened the *Grace* here from Olaire. Now she realized she was wrong.

"Mokinda Char."

Caval drank from his water bottle. "Ah, he wears his disguise well, don't you think?"

Karmel wasn't sure how much of a disguise it was in truth. For while the other Storm Lords had always carried themselves with an ominous self-assurance, there had never been anything of that manner about the Untarian, even when he was emir. When she boarded the *Grace* in Olaire, she'd spotted him on deck and not given him a second glance. There had been no reason, though, to think he had survived the bloodletting on Dragon Day. As Karmel recalled, he had been sent by the Storm Council to investigate Gensu Sensama's death, meaning he would have been out of the firing line when Dragon Day came. Hadn't he always been in Imerle's pocket, though, not Mazana's? If so, why had Mazana let him live?

Mokinda must have heard Karmel say his name, because he looked in her direction. The priestess beckoned to him. He hesitated before setting down his mop and starting toward her.

"What are you doing?" Caval asked Karmel.

"Putting a little flesh on the bones of Mazana's story."

"I'd have thought you were used to being kept in the dark on missions."

Karmel forced a smile.

Mokinda halted in front of them. His gaze shifted from the priestess to her brother, then back again. "We should not be talking," he said. His diction sounded alien to Karmel's ears, even for an Untarian, for he stressed his "t"s with exaggerated care.

"Why not?" Karmel said. "You're not the first crewman I've spoken to since coming on board."

Mokinda did not reply.

Karmel considered her next words. If she was going to persuade the Untarian to lower his guard, she would have to do so by degrees. "Mazana said we were going to pick up a guide from the Rubyholt Isles. So where is he?"

"Waiting for us at the harbor."

"Does he know who you are?"

"Hardly."

"Does anyone on board?"

"Just the captain."

"And you're not worried one of the crew might recognize you?"

"Would you have done, if your brother hadn't prompted you?"

The *Grace* had reached the guardhouse with the upraised drawbridge. Ahead a second drawbridge came into view, this one without a fortress to protect it. Beyond, the canal opened out onto the harbor. The place had a stink to it that rivaled even the Shallows. Karmel could see the approach to the chains was bounded by stone walls that stretched back from the towers guarding the harbor entrance, forming a corridor of stone.

"Are you coming with us as far as the Rubyholt Isles?" Karmel asked Mokinda.

"Yes."

"Why?"

The Storm Lord blinked.

"I can understand why you escorted us to Gilgamar—in case we met a dragon in the Sabian Sea. But there's no reason to think there are any dragons between Gilgamar and the Rubyholt Isles. They'll have returned to the Southern Wastes by now."

Mokinda wouldn't be keeping his chips for long at the flush table, Karmel suspected, for his discomfort at her line of questioning was plain. That was good, because it meant she was on the right track.

"As Mazana explained it to us," she went on, "you've got no part to play in the destruction of the stone-skin fleet. No part. So what are you doing here?" Then, "Perhaps you've been sent to the Ruby-holt Isles for a different reason. Or perhaps Mazana is holding you in reserve in case Caval and I fail."

Mokinda's frown suggested that last was close to the truth . . . but not the whole truth. "Mazana has told you everything you need to know," he said.

"What we *need* to know maybe. I want the rest as well."

"What makes you think Mazana told me more than she told you?"

"She had to tell someone."

Mokinda did not respond.

Karmel bit back on her irritation, but what could she do? She had already accepted Mazana's mission; it wasn't as if she could threaten to back out if the Untarian didn't answer her questions. She tried a different tack.

"It was Jambar who warned Mazana the stone-skin fleet was coming, yes? So what else did he see in his bones?"

"As the shaman was so keen to impress on me, all he sees are possibilities."

"Yet some of those possibilities must be more possible than others. What trouble are we likely to run into? What are our chances of success?"

Mokinda finally met her gaze. "That depends on your definition of success."

"Completing the mission. Coming out the other side."

The Untarian winced.

"That good, eh?" Caval said.

Mokinda paused. He looked from Karmel to Caval, then made as if to speak before stopping himself. He wanted to tell them, the priestess realized. So why was he holding back? Maybe he was worried that Mazana would discover his indiscretion. Or maybe he thought telling the Chameleons would jeopardize the mission.

Most likely, though, he'd kept his silence because he knew his expression had already said enough about what awaited Karmel and Caval in the Rubyholt Isles.

He turned and walked away.

Ebon's boat drifted through the night. On the beach south of Gilgamar were dozens of fires, and about them were clustered figures wrapped in blankets, as if some ragtag army had arrived to besiege the city. A brooding silence hung over the camp that was broken by a distant scream from the town. Farther east, the echoing clang of metal against stone started up as if someone were trying to beat down a wall with a sword.

Ebon sat hunched on the oar bench, giddy with fatigue. Ahead and to his right, a line of torches marked the route of the canal through the city. As he approached the entrance to it, the hulking shadow of a wreck loomed out of the darkness. Each wave that lapped against its hull prompted a chorus of creaks. Gunnar—curled up now asleep in the stern—had warned Ebon about the blacktooth snakes infesting these waters, and the prince saw their moonlit forms twisting over the wreck. There were hundreds of them. Thousands, even. But they wouldn't be able to scale the outward-curving sides of his boat, he reminded himself. Strangely, that came as scant consolation as he steered the craft over the rustling black swell.

The wreck tilted acutely to one side, its rigging tangled between the shattered masts and spars. One of the spars extended across the entrance to the canal, just above the water level. Ebon released his power in a burst to lift the boat over it and into the channel beyond. To his right was an area of scrubland along with a collection of shanties. To his left was a two-story guardhouse with lights showing in its ground-floor windows. Beyond, a wall ran the length of the canal, built high enough to prevent someone in a boat such as Ebon's from scaling it. That wall gave the waterway the feel of a moat flooded to bar access to the eastern half of the city from the west.

At the end of the torchlit canal, Ebon could make out the dark curl of the harbor wall along with the masts of the ships at quayside. So few ships, but who was to say Ocarn's wasn't among them? One way or another, he'd be finding out soon. Worn thin as he was, he knew he should rest once his boat was tied up at harbor. But he also knew he wouldn't be able to stop himself—

A crossbow bolt flitted past his eyes and hit the water behind him with a *plish*. A second thudded into the oar bench beside him, throwing up splinters.

"Hold your fire!" Ebon shouted.

He didn't wait to see if the crossbowmen complied. Surrendering his power over the waves, he fashioned a shield between himself and the place where the bolts had come from—the guardhouse. One, two, three more missiles slammed into the barrier and cannoned away.

"Stay behind me," he said to Vale before looking at Gunnar. The mage had woken, but remained curled up in the stern. He watched Ebon through narrowed eyes.

The prince's outstretched hand signaled him to remain still.

Another crossbow bolt struck Ebon's sorcerous shield. If the shots were coming from the guardhouse, that meant the shooters must be Gilgamarian soldiers. He felt a rush of blood to his face. Were they so bored for something to do that they had to use him for target practice? He surveyed the battlements. Shadowy shapes had materialized atop the tower and the wall alongside it.

"Hold your fire!" he snapped again.

A voice floated down from the wall. "Canal's off limits between dusk and dawn. Toss your weapons overboard and throw us a line."

"We are strangers to Gilgamar. We seek news of a Mercerien ship that took part in the Dragon Hunt."

"Save it for the magister tomorrow. Toss your weapons overboard."

Surrender? Not likely. If Ebon gave himself up, he faced a night in a cell. And when he finally appeared before the magister, what was he supposed to say? That he was a Galitian prince? Galitia wasn't part of the Sabian League. It didn't have an embassy here, so there was no one in the city who could confirm his story. And who would believe that a prince had arrived in the dead of night with a mere two companions as escort? To make matters worse, Ebon had revealed he was seeking word of a Mercerien ship. If Ocarn *was* here, might not the magister summon him to verify Ebon's identity? Ebon couldn't expect help from that quarter. And if Ocarn was holding Rendale and Lamella against their will, the last thing Ebon wanted to do was give notice he was in town.

If he wasn't going to surrender, though, what options did that leave? Run the gauntlet of the canal in the hope of reaching the harbor? The waterway was only a few hundred armspans long, but there was no way of knowing how many soldiers lay in wait along its length, or indeed in the port itself. Ebon could probably extend his sorcerous shield to cover the whole boat, but this wasn't the time to experiment. For while *he* might be prepared to risk his life in his search for Rendale and Lamella, he couldn't expect his companions to take the same chance.

He ground his teeth together. If going forward wasn't possible, that just left going back.

Ebon looked up at the sky, trying to judge the hour. Somewhere around the fourth bell, he guessed, meaning it wouldn't be long until first light. He took a breath. *Patience.* If Rendale and Lamella were here, they weren't going to leave before sunrise. Perhaps it was best that he waited if it meant he could snatch some sleep.

"Gunnar," he said, his gaze still fixed on the tower's battlements, "get us out of here—back the way we came."

As the boat rose on a wave of water-magic, a guard shot a crossbow bolt to speed them on their way. It struck the boards a handspan from Ebon's foot and stuck there, quivering.

CHAPTER 8

SENAR HESITATED at the door to Mazana's bedchamber. He'd been tempted to ignore her summons from earlier, but his curiosity had won out in the end, what with the rumors sweeping the palace this morning. Were they why the emira had sent for him now? He knocked and heard her call to enter.

This was the first time he'd been in Mazana's quarters. To his left, a huge fish tank was set into the wall, screened behind a pane of sorcerously strengthened glass. The floor mosaic showed a beach of black pebbles, bright with spray. To Senar's right was an unmade bed, and on it sat Mazana wrapped in a towel. Her bare arms showed no sign of yesterday's blotches. Senar could see the shape of her body through the towel.

Next to her sat her half brother, Uriel, his fringe hanging over his eyes, his feet dangling over the bed. On his lap was a wooden bowl full of water.

Mazana looked up as Senar entered. Her gaze lingered on his swollen lip, and she gave a half smile. There was no shadow in her look from their encounter last night. Perhaps she'd forgotten it already.

"You wanted to see me, Emira," he said.

"So formal, Guardian? I can call you Guardian, can't I?"

"If you must," Senar replied.

Uriel spoke. "It's not working," he said to Mazana.

She turned to him. "Show me."

The boy tightened his grip on the bowl, his forehead creasing with that look of concentration only the young can muster. Nothing happened.

"Can you sense the flow in the water?" Mazana said.

"You mean, like currents?"

"Like currents, yes. Only these currents are there all the time."

"But the water isn't moving."

The emira smoothed his hair. "Remember when I put ink in the bowl that time? How the color spread through the water even though it was still?"

Uriel frowned some more.

"Shall I show you?" Mazana said.

He nodded.

"Follow what I'm doing. Close your eyes if it helps. The currents I'm talking about can't be seen."

The boy kept his eyes open.

Senar felt Mazana release her power. The water in the bowl began to glisten.

Uriel shifted on the bed. "It's getting cold."

"Yes. The slower the currents move, the colder the water becomes. Until . . ."

The surface of the water clouded to ice. The boy placed a tentative finger on it. It cracked, and he snatched his finger back. His look was disbelieving. "Can I have another go?"

"Of course. Why don't you stir the currents to life again, see if you can make the ice melt."

His brow furrowed once more.

Senar looked from Uriel to Mazana. He was struck by the resemblance between them: the copper hair, the full mouth, the high cheekbones. To look at them, you wouldn't know they were merely half siblings. Mazana must have sensed his regard, for she glanced up before looking away again. Senar felt like he was intruding on something, but the emira didn't appear to mind.

The ice in the bowl started to melt. Perhaps it was just the temperature in the room that caused it, for Senar had detected no more than a trickle of power from the boy. Uriel clearly did not think so, though, because his face split in a grin.

"I did it!"

"You did it," Mazana agreed.

He beamed pink, bounced on the bed and spilled some water. Then his smile faded. "Can I show Mother?" he blurted.

Mazana did not respond. Her gaze flickered to Senar in warning. Clearly the boy didn't know his mother was dead, or that Mazana had killed her—just as she had killed their shared father. That particular news would take some breaking when the time came.

"Is she coming here soon?" Uriel asked.

"I don't know," Mazana said.

"She's not coming soon, is she?"

"No."

"Because of the dragons?"

"Because of the dragons."

"But you'll hunt them down, won't you? Like you promised. When the bad men are gone."

The bad men?

Mazana nodded. "We'll talk about this later."

Uriel's face fell. He opened his mouth to protest.

"Later," the emira repeated. "I have to speak to Senar now."

The boy seemed to notice the Guardian for the first time. He flashed him an uncertain smile, then stood and carried the bowl of water to a doorway in the wall to Senar's right.

Mazana sat staring after Uriel as if she could see through the door that now closed behind him.

Senar flicked dust from his shirt collar. Beside the bed was a table, and on top of it was a breakfast tray. Mazana crossed to it and poured water from a jug into a cup. From the corridor behind Senar came the tread of feet as someone moved past the room. The footsteps died away again.

"Are the rumors true?" he said to break the silence. "Is Cauroy alive?"

Mazana searched his expression. He didn't know what she was looking for there, but he stilled his features so she wouldn't find it.

"Does it matter?" she said. "It's not as though he's going to come here and challenge me."

"He was ahead of you in the succession."

"So was the sadly departed Gensu. I count him more of a threat than I do Cauroy." She took a sip from her cup and looked back at Uriel's door. After a while she said, "You think I'm being too easy on him?" Then, before he could reply, "By his age, I was able to vaporize water and raise a wave as tall as you are. But then my father was such a good teacher. He always found ways to . . . motivate me to my best efforts."

Senar said nothing. He'd often wondered about Mazana's history, yet now that she'd opened a door on her childhood, he wasn't sure he wanted to look through. He had to say something, though, so he picked what he hoped was a less awkward avenue of inquiry. "What about your mother? Is she still alive?"

Mazana nodded. "She's on Kansar, sulking. My father treated her like a broodmare for five years, then set her aside when she couldn't give him a son. She still hasn't forgiven me for killing him, though. I don't know what's more stupid, that she thought he might one day invite her back, or that she would have accepted the offer if he did."

Senar looked at his feet. Less awkward. Right. He was beginning to see a pattern in his dealings with Mazana.

"What about you?" the emira asked. "Where are your parents?"

"Both dead. My mother died giving birth to me, my father in a mission when I was six."

"He was a Guardian too?"

"Yes."

"A good one?"

Senar inclined his head, wondering at the question.

Mazana's look was far away. "When I was growing up, I had a friend whose father was accused of trading in stolen cargoes. The charge was never proved, else he would have been fed to the dragons on Dragon Day. But thrown mud always leaves a mark, not just for the suspect, but also for their family. My friend never forgave him for that. The shame of it was something she always carried with her. She never stopped complaining about the unfairness of it all. But it is harder to be burdened with a parent's successes than it is to be burdened with their failures, wouldn't you agree?"

Again, Senar did not answer. When he thought of his parents, the word "burden" wasn't one that came to mind.

Mazana replaced her cup on the tray and stood. "But I did not call you here to talk about that."

Something in her voice gave Senar pause. "Oh?"

"I thought you might be interested to know a boat arrived last night bringing a messenger from Erin Elal. He's waiting for me in the throne room." Mazana's mouth twitched. "Whatever could be so urgent that he should have braved the Sabian Sea to speak to me now?"

Karmel blew into the mouthpiece of the blowpipe. A feathered dart shot across the cabin and caught the edge of the already-pockmarked bedpost. It tore out a splinter before deflecting off and under a table.

She lowered the blowpipe. Impressive. Ten darts fired, and all but the first had found its target. She'd been skeptical when Mazana Creed presented her with the weapon. Made from wood and wrapped in vine skins and resin, the blowpipe looked like it had been plucked from the hands of some jungle primitive. There was no denying the quality of its craftsmanship, though. The bore had been filed as smooth as a diplomat's tongue, and it was this smoothness that gave the blowpipe its consistency. Of course, Karmel still had to test it over distances greater than those permitted by her cabin. For while her targets in the Isles would be more difficult to miss than hit, the precise point where she struck those targets would determine the success or failure of her mission.

Blinking sweat from her eyes, she reached for another dart. The air in the cabin felt heavy, as if too much of the stuff had been crammed into too small a space. Over the rustle of water outside, she heard footsteps on the companionway ladder—Caval's, she knew instinctively. She'd barely said anything to him since their discussion with Mokinda. Another time, the Storm Lord's words might have had her seeking the reassurance of her brother's presence, but now she felt a greater sense of loneliness with him than she did when they were apart, for what loneliness was more lonely than that of distrust? Would that ever change? Karmel would have to try harder to make it so. The closer they got to the Rubyholt Isles, the less time they had to bridge the gap between them.

But wanting to do so didn't make it any easier.

Caval knocked at the door and entered. He was holding a roll of parchment—the crude map of Bezzle that Mazana had given them to memorize. He tossed it onto his bed, then looked at Karmel.

"You're going to want to see this," he said, nodding back the way he'd come.

Karmel set down the blowpipe on the sweating boards and followed him out.

Emerging onto deck, the priestess saw Mokinda standing alone by the starboard rail. He was frowning up at the cloudless sky like a farmer hoping for rain. Tracking the sun's course to gauge their progress? Were they running late for an appointment in the Isles? They'd only left Gilgamar at the fifth bell. At first the harbormaster had refused to lower the chains before dawn so they could leave. He'd changed his mind only after the intervention of some dew-eyed member of the Ruling Council, who had descended from the Upper City seeking news from the *Grace*'s captain. It would be a simple matter, of course, for Mokinda to make up time by throwing his will behind that of the ship's two water-mages. In doing so, though, he would signal his presence to the crew.

Along the port rail, a handful of sailors had lined up to cast a collection of objects into the sea: a bloodstained handkerchief, a lock of hair, a blackened bone, and so on down the row. Propitiations to the Sender, most likely. But that was not what Caval had called Karmel to see. A stone's throw ahead of the *Grace*, and stretching as far as the eye could discern, the waves were tinted black as if the ship were about to sail out over the Abyss. Bubbles rose from the depths, carrying on them the stink of rotten eggs. At the edge of the murk, dozens of dead honeyfish floated on the sea. As the fish drifted into darker water, they were sucked down beneath the waves.

"Gods below," Karmel breathed.

"You could be right," a voice said, and she turned to see their Rubyholt guide, Scullen, approaching. He smiled a slippery smile. "But round 'ere, we call it the Rent."

Karmel made no attempt to hide her scowl. The need to practice with her blowpipe hadn't been the only reason she'd chosen to stay belowdecks for the past couple of bells. After Scullen boarded the *Grace* last night, she'd felt his gaze lingering on her more often than she would have liked. His eyes explored her now.

She turned her back on him. "What is it?" she asked Caval.

It was Scullen who answered. "No one knows, petal. Ain't many souls volunteering to swim down for a better look, neither. The few that've tried ain't come back to tell what they seen. But the sharp ones round 'ere"—and from his tone, he considered himself among them— "reckon it's a gateway like them others scattered 'bout the Isles."

The stink of eggs became stronger as the *Grace* crossed the divide between blue waves and black. Karmel covered her nose with her sleeve. All that darkness below her, it made her feel as if the sea might drop away at any moment to leave her falling. Abeam to starboard, a kris shark flitted through the murky waters.

Caval pointed to it. "Ah, I thought nothing could swim here," he said to Scullen. "I thought everything was pulled down into the Rent."

"Not everything with fins," the Islander said. His lips curled back. "Barring water-mages, even the best swimmers will struggle t'keep their heads above water for more'n a heartbeat. My last captain once threw an Untarian over the rail to see how long she'd stay afloat. Woman went under before I could piss on her."

Karmel frowned. "Your last captain? I'd have thought a man of your distinction would command his own crew."

The Rubyholter's smirk wavered. "Eh?"

Caval raised his hands in a placatory gesture. "Ignore my sister's barbs, friend," he said to Scullen. "She likes to make her suitors work for her affections."

Karmel gave him her "not impressed" face, but her brother was all innocence.

"Your sister?" Scullen said with a wink, his good humor restored. As if seeing the competition trimmed by one had somehow guaranteed his conquest. "Travel with her a lot, do you?"

"Until someone takes her off my hands."

Karmel bit down on her tongue.

A gust of wind made the sails crack and set their shadows rippling across the deck. After the heat of Karmel's cabin, the breeze on her face was welcome. It struck her that the *Grace*'s pace had quickened. Evidently the ship's water-mages were keen for the vessel to clear the Rent as soon as possible.

Scullen leaned on the rail beside her. "One thing I'll say for the Rent—least there ain't no monsters lurking 'ere like those you find sniffing round the Isles. You heard of the Dragon's Boneyard, petal? Creature there's been known to take bites out o' dragons. . . ."

Karmel stopped listening. Bites out of dragons, indeed! The book about the Isles that Caval had given her had been full of such stories, and each one more preposterous than the last. It was all just a smoke-screen, she suspected, along with the tales about shifting currents and hidden cliff-top defenses. Nothing but propaganda to dissuade the Isles' neighbors from trespassing on their territory. And Scullen's presence on board was just another part of the myth. As if the *Grace* needed a guide to escort it through the Isles! True, there were only a handful of safe passages through the maze of islands that made up the Outer Rim, but after you'd sailed through them once, what was to prevent you coming back the same way after? Or making a chart of the route for others to follow?

"How long before we reach the Isles?" she said to Caval, talking over Scullen.

Again it was the Rubyholter who answered. "A turn of the glass to the Outer Rim. Another six before we get to Bezzle."

"Only six?" Caval said.

"Aye," Scullen said, still looking at Karmel. "Plenty of time for us to get to know each other."

Her brother nodded gravely. "You're a man of hidden depths, I'm sure."

Karmel paid them no mind. Her gaze had been snagged by a smudge on the horizon—a smudge that was resolving itself into the sails of another ship.

"That's a barquentine," Scullen said, following her gaze. "See how it's square rigged on the foremast, and fore-and-aft rigged on the main and mizzen?" He touched her shoulder, and she shrank away. "You've no need to worry 'bout pirates, though, petal. That there standard"—he pointed to the green flag he'd had the captain hoist below the *Grace*'s own—"tells anyone looking that I'm on board. Won't get no trouble from Rubyholt ships while I'm about, that I can promise you."

"Assuming the barquentine *is* another Rubyholt ship."

"What else could it be? Ain't no one fool enough to risk sailing these 'ere waters without our say-so."

Karmel thought back to what Mazana Creed had told her about the stone-skin fleet, but said nothing.

Senar strode along the corridor at Mazana's side. The sea was a whisper behind the wall to his right. Ahead he saw the executioner along with the priestess of the Lord of Hidden Faces, and Senar struggled against the instinct that he had seen the woman before somewhere. He shifted his gaze to the man standing behind and to one side of Romany. *The Erin Elalese messenger.* Senar knew all of the emperor's Circle by sight, but this man wasn't one of them. He was of a height with the Guardian but stockier, and his nose was so crooked it seemed to lie flat against his face. His clothes were all black, and he wore a heavy cloak ill-suited to the Olairian heat.

Perhaps Senar should have felt some sense of comradeship toward a fellow Erin Elalese, but the man was probably a Breaker, as well as a friend of the emperor's. And any friend of Avallon's was no friend of Senar's.

Two Storm Guards hauled on the doors leading to the underwater passage. They swung open to reveal a wall of water that receded at Mazana's gesture.

Senar followed her into the deep.

In the throne room, the Guardian took up a position to one side of the thrones. Mazana sat in the chair right of center, and the executioner and Romany stood behind her. At this early hour, the steely-blue walls of water gave off a palpable cold, so Mazana set the ceiling rising. The stretch of sea overhead grew thinner and brighter until the chamber opened out onto the sky in a wash of shimmering light. A fish slow to escape the vanishing waves flopped onto the floor at the feet of the Erin Elalese messenger, who had halted a short distance from Mazana's throne. He looked at it before flicking it with a foot into one of the walls of water. His expression showed nothing, but there was something in the set of his features that told Senar he was determined not to be overawed.

The battle lines were being drawn early, it seemed.

"Emira," the stranger said. "My name is Kolloken Kanar. Avallon Delamar sends his greetings."

"And in some style too," Mazana said, looking him up and down.

"When I left Erin Elal, I thought I'd be delivering this message to Imerle Polivar."

"You still can, if you like. We've got her head on a spike around here somewhere."

Not a hint of a smile touched the messenger's lips. "I hear you've done away with the Storm Council. That you alone now speak for the Storm Isles."

"For someone who's just arrived in Olaire, you are remarkably well-informed."

"When I got in last night, I stopped by the Erin Elalese embassy. The ambassador filled me in on what's been happening."

"Including the rumor about Cauroy Blent, I assume."

"He may have mentioned it."

Mazana's smile was warm, but there was an edge to her voice. "Remarkable coincidence, no? That the rumor should surface the same day you arrive."

Kolloken shrugged as if her implication had sailed over his head. "Shit happens."

Senar cleared his throat. "I am Senar Sol, a Guardian from the Sacrosanct."

The messenger turned his gaze on him. There was no surprise in his expression, but Senar's presence in Olaire was doubtless one of the things Kolloken had been briefed on by the ambassador.

"You came here by boat?" Senar asked.

"How else?"

"Where from?"

"Gilgamar.

"So you're a water-mage."

"No, but my traveling companion was. A man called Jelek Balaran. Maybe you've heard of him, eh?"

Senar had, of course. Jelek was the most powerful water-mage in Avallon's employ, perhaps the most powerful in all of Erin Elal.

"Where is he now?" Mazana said.

"Back in Gilgamar, I expect."

"He left you stranded here?"

"For a short while only." Then, "Emira, word has reached the emperor of what happened in Dian on Dragon Day, in particular the part played by the Augerans in sabotaging the Hunt. He asked me to pass on his commiserations for those who died." He paused. "But in your case, I'm guessing the commiserations aren't needed, eh?"

"I'm sure I don't know what you mean."

"Of course not."

Senar stared at Kolloken. The man's tone bordered on insolence. Plainly the emperor's hand wouldn't be strengthened if his emissary were seen to come before Mazana on bended knee, yet still the messenger must be close indeed to Avallon to risk antagonizing the emira like this.

Kolloken glanced at Senar before looking again at Mazana. "I assume the Guardian has told you about Erin Elal's history with the Augerans."

"If you mean the bit where they slaughtered you and drove you into the sea, yes."

The messenger didn't rise to the provocation. "As you might expect, Avallon is curious to know what brings the stone-skins to these parts. And after what happened on Dragon Day, he's assuming you feel the same."

"He wants to discuss an alliance?"

"He wants to discuss where our interests lie in common. And what we can do to move them forward together."

Senar saw an opening. "Has Erin Elal been attacked?"

"No."

The Guardian studied him. The man's tone left no room for misunderstanding, but could Senar trust his word? Avallon's best chance at securing an alliance with Mazana lay in convincing her that the stone-skins were targeting the Storm Isles, and that line wouldn't wash if Erin Elal had already been hit. "Did the emperor know the Augerans had returned before they showed their hand on Dragon Day?"

"You'd have to ask him that. I'm only a humble messenger."

Mazana said, "Does Avallon claim to know what the stone-skins' next move will be?"

"They've already made it." Kolloken left a pause for their interest to peak. "A group of Augerans is meeting with the warlord of the Rubyholt Isles. We don't know what they'll be talking about, but I reckon it's safe to say they won't be swapping honeyfish recipes, eh?"

If the man had expected a reaction from Mazana, he would be disappointed, for Jambar had long since warned her about the Augeran expedition. That was why she'd sent the Chameleons to Bezzle. "You think the stone-skins are going to use the Isles to launch a strike at the Sabian League?"

"Seems likely."

"Indeed? As I keep reminding Senar, the Augerans are *your* people's enemy, not mine."

"Right. Maybe one of their commanders held his map upside down on Dragon Day and thought Dian was a part of Erin Elal."

Senar said, "And maybe you rushed all this way for an audience with the emira out of concern solely for the Storm Isles' fate."

Kolloken did not respond.

When Mazana next spoke, there was a smile in her voice. "The emperor is suggesting a council, I take it. When? Where?"

"At Gilgamar. A delegation left Erin Elal the day after I did, heading for the city. It should arrive there today."

Gilgamar again, Senar thought. "Who's leading this delegation?"

"Tyrin Lindin Tar."

"Not Avallon himself?"

Kolloken looked at Mazana. "The emperor sends his apologies. He would have come if he could."

"Of course," the emira said. "He has a war to prepare for, after all. Now, unless there was something else . . ."

And just like that, the man was dismissed.

For a moment Kolloken held his ground. Mazana hadn't given him a yes or a no to his invitation, but he clearly knew better than to press her, because he gave a curt nod by way of farewell.

The executioner escorted him back the way he had come.

"Such a charming man," Mazana said after he was gone. "And such an eloquent speaker too."

"He's a Breaker, most likely," Senar said. "One of the emperor's new military elite."

"I thought that was the Guardians' role."

Senar made a face. Did she want some more salt to rub in with that? "Then you are three years late in your thinking. In another three, the Breakers will have replaced us entirely."

"That explains the hostility I sensed between you. You do know you two are on the same side, don't you?"

Were they? Senar wasn't so sure. Only a fool would believe there were just two sides in all this. Or that the various factions wouldn't be maneuvering against each other even as they plotted against the stone-skins.

Someone had to look past the petty rivalries, though. To focus on the common ground, rather than the divisions.

"Who were the others Kolloken mentioned?" Mazana asked. "Tyrin Lindin Tar?"

"She's the Breakers' second in command, and one of the emperor's most loyal supporters. A steady hand. One for the details."

"I like her already. And this water-mage, Jelek?"

"Jelek Balaran. A Mellikian. Or at least that's how he appears."

"Appears?"

"A few years back, one of the emperor's pet mages—an old man called Enko—contracted some mystery illness and vanished. Most thought he had died. Then three months later, Jelek arrives and slips seamlessly into Enko's role."

"You suspect soul-shifting?"

Senar shrugged.

The executioner returned along the underwater passage, and the floor seemed to tremble at his coming. Senar watched him take up position near the priestess of the Lord of Hidden Faces. *The priestess* . . . Senar had almost forgotten the woman was there. He couldn't see her eyes through the slots in her mask. For all he knew, she might be sleeping behind it.

Mazana must have been thinking the same, for she said, "Ah, priestess, you *are* still here. Perhaps you would honor us with your opinion on all this."

When Romany spoke, her voice sounded hollow behind her mask. "Do I have to have one?"

"As I recall, it was your Lord, not I, who wanted you here for your counsel."

The priestess sighed. "Very well. This man Kolloken knows more than he is telling, but that is hardly news to make the gods pause in their bickering. His job was not to answer your questions, but rather to lure you to Gilgamar for this council."

" 'Lure'? An interesting choice of word."

"Wasn't it you who implied Kolloken might have started the rumor about Cauroy Blent?"

Senar said, "You think there might be some truth to the tale?"

"Why not? If Cauroy *is* alive, he could have struck a deal with Avallon. As part of it, the emperor lures you"—Romany nodded at Mazana—"into a trap at Gilgamar, allowing Cauroy to claim the throne. And in return, Cauroy pledges to help Avallon in the war against the Augerans."

"But then why would the emperor start the rumor about Cauroy?" the Guardian asked. "What does he gain by doing so, save to warn us Cauroy is out there?"

Romany sniffed. "If Kolloken were here, he would doubtless say the same."

Senar frowned, sensing a double meaning in her words. *Does she think that I argue Avallon's case? That I am complicit in his schemes?*

Mazana swung a leg over an armrest of her throne. "What intrigues me most is how the emperor plans to make me fight his battles for him. Maybe it's true the stone-skins haven't attacked Erin Elal yet. But Avallon must think me a fool if he expects me to believe he is not their real target."

In Senar's experience, the emperor wouldn't care what she thought, so long as she did what he wanted. He would use every weapon in his armory to get his way, but if the result was an alliance against the stone-skins, didn't the end justify the means? If Erin Elal and the League were to meet the Augerans together . . . "The thing we're missing here is what the stone-skins are planning next. Why did they arrange this meeting with the Rubyholters? And how does it tie in with Jambar's warnings about Gilgamar?"

Mazana did not respond.

"What exactly was the threat he foresaw?" Senar pressed.

"There is nothing 'exact' about Jambar's predictions, as you should know. But he was clear that both the Augerans and your people have a part to play in what is coming."

Senar's tone was incredulous. "He thinks Avallon will move against Gilgamar? When his own borders are threatened?" He shook his head. "You can't trust the shaman, Emira, you must see that."

"Trust?" Mazana spoke the word as if it were new to her. "Ah yes, now I remember."

"Jambar wants Avallon dead more than he wants you alive. Erin Elal conquered his homeland. He is poisoned by his hatred of the emperor."

"We can't all have your objectivity," Romany muttered.

Mazana chuckled, then raised a hand to forestall Senar's retort. "This speculation is pointless. Jambar's visions may be accurate or they may not, but I cannot afford to ignore them. Gilgamar's canal is the gateway to the Sabian Sea. If either Erin Elal or the stone-skins should control it . . ."

Senar gave a grudging nod.

There was no need to finish that thought.

From the shadow of a building on Gilgamar's waterfront, Ebon studied the wall separating the harbor from the Upper City. It was taller even than the wall encircling Majack, and its guardhouse was manned by a dozen soldiers. Two of them were using their spear butts to prod at the amphorae in a handcart as if they thought the flasks might bite. Over the course of the last half-bell, Ebon had seen twenty people approach the Harbor Gate seeking entrance to the Upper City. All had been turned away, save three. It seemed the owner of the handcart was not going to be the fourth, for he began shaking his fist and screaming insults at the soldiers. Then one of the soldiers pointed up at a collection of withered hands and feet swinging by cords from the battlements above.

That quietened him down in a hurry.

Even as far away as Galitia, Gilgamar's Ruling Council had a reputation for brutality to its subjects. Judging by the number of body parts on display, it was a reputation well deserved. Ebon had once heard his now-deceased uncle, Janir, complain that beggars in Linnar were mutilating themselves in an effort to improve their takings. There would have been little point to that here, though, where every other man, woman, and child seemed to be missing a finger, an ear, or a nose. A girl in rags caught his eye, so thin she appeared to be made of bone entirely. Her left hand was missing, the stump a mass of puckered red flesh. If Ebon had possessed the skill to regenerate lost tissue, he might have given her back the hand. There was an emptiness in her eyes, though, that hinted at a deeper hurt no sorcery could heal.

He tore his gaze away and looked along the waterfront. Ocarn's ship was easily identifiable from the black-and-white-checkered Mercerien flag flying from its mainmast. Ebon had tracked the vessel down within moments of arriving at the harbor this morning. The heady rush of elation he'd felt on seeing it had faded when he noticed the damage it had sustained in the Hunt. The mizzen yard was down, the mast itself pitched at an angle, and the stern was hacked and scarred. From the crew guarding the galleon he had learned that Ocarn at least had survived Dragon Day and was now somewhere in the Upper City. Ebon hadn't risked asking about Lamella and Rendale for fear of arousing the sailors' suspicions. But if they were alive too, they would surely be with their captor.

Where, though? Odds were, Ocarn didn't own a house here, so the Mercerien embassy—if there was one—was the first place Ebon would check. But he wasn't getting much of a view of the place from behind this Shroud-cursed wall. He scowled. Three hundred leagues he'd traveled to get to Gilgamar, yet now with Lamella perhaps just a stone's throw away, he found his path to her blocked. When he finally got into the Upper City, what new obstacle would he discover barring his way? It was hard to shake off the feeling that she would always remain beyond his reach—that he would be cursed to chase her across the length and breadth of the Sabian League as punishment for abandoning her when the Vamilians attacked Majack.

When he tried to bring to mind a picture of her, the figure that formed was hazy, as if he were seeing her through a mist. Perversely, the easiest image to evoke was of their first encounter in the Kingswood, when his gelding had stamped on her. Her features were set in a rictus of agony, her right leg mangled and bloody. He sought to summon up instead a memory of the day four months later, when he'd brought her the piebald mare in an effort to give her back a measure of freedom. Yet the pained look on her face remained. Perhaps that was a truer measure of what she'd felt than the feigned smile she had conjured up. Joy, he supposed, meant something different to someone who lived with the constant hurt of a shattered leg. Maybe joy, as others knew it, was something forever lost to her.

Enough daydreaming; it was time to act. Ebon wasn't minded to introduce himself to the guards in case one of the soldiers recognized him from the canal last night. A part of him wanted simply to draw his power about himself and bludgeon his way through, but he wasn't Galea that he could hope to take on an entire city and survive. Most likely he'd find himself caught up in a series of running battles with the guardsmen. What chance did he have of finding a bolthole to hide in before the enemy took him down? And what chance was there then of him locating Lamella and Rendale with every soldier in the city looking for him?

There was always the option of going in at night. The gate, though, was closed between dusk and dawn, so how was he supposed to get inside then? Scale the wall and take the battlements? Curse his oversight, he hadn't thought to pack an army along with his water bottle and change of clothes.

If he got back in his boat, he could circle the city to the north or south, find somewhere to put in and approach Gilgamar from the east. But the guards on that gate would be no less vigilant than—

"Looking for a way into the city?"

Ebon startled.

The speaker was a man a head shorter than the prince. His right foot was missing, and in its place was a wooden peg. That peg had worn down to give him a lopsided look. He grinned to reveal an equally lopsided set of yellow teeth.

"For the last half-bell," the man said, "you been looking at that gate like you're hoping someone's gonna invite you inside. But it ain't gonna happen, mister. You wants in, you needs the right papers, and if you wants the right papers, you needs two folk in the Upper City who'll swear on your good behavior. If that's the way you wanna go, I can points you the way of the Petty Courts so you can start the stones rolling. Whole thing takes maybe a week, maybe a month. And even then you'll get a couple of them spearbutts"—he gestured to the guards at the Harbor Gate—"marching you wherever it is you're going. And marching you right back out again once your business is finished."

An armed escort wouldn't hinder Ebon if he could just get past the gate. But he didn't like his chances of finding someone in the Upper City to vouch for him, any more than he liked the sound of waiting a month for the process to run its course. "There must be another way inside."

"Oh, sure!" Peg Foot said, warming to his part. "Dozens, probably. Problem is, whatever plan you come up with has likely been thought of by someone else already. Or that's the way I sees it. And if your plan don't work, are you ready to pay the price?" He waved his peg foot about to show what that price would be. "I myself spent weeks sniffing out a way inside. Me and a few lads found this spot on the Ribbon Coast where the cliffs were climbable, then watched the walls for three days till we found a blind spot in the spearbutts' patrols. Bastards were still waiting for me when I hauled myself over the battlements. And I was the lucky one, 'cause I was first up the rope and not still climbing when the damned thing was cut."

Ebon's voice betrayed his irritation. "If it's as difficult to get inside as you say, why are we having this conversation?"

"That was then, this is now. Might be I can puts you in touch with someone who can help. The way I sees it, you got nothing to lose listening to what he got to say. Assuming you got a little coin in your pockets, of course."

"How little?"

The Gilgamarian grinned again. "I leave the details to the man."

"The man?"

"You wanna swap names, you can do it with him. But I doubt he gets up close and personal on a first date."

Ebon looked Peg Foot in the eye, trying to see past his smile. The Gilgamarian painted a grim picture of Ebon's chances of getting into the Upper City, but it was in the man's interests to smear the paint on with a trowel. And while Peg Foot's missing foot lent his story the whiff of authenticity, who was to say he hadn't been run over by a cart? *Or stamped on by a horse.* This might be a trap. Ebon might go down some dark alley to meet "the man," only to find a dozen of Peg Foot's friends waiting instead.

With Vale at his back, though, that was a risk he could afford to take. And if things didn't work out, well, as Peg Foot had said, what had Ebon lost? A bell or two wasted in the Gilgamarian's company was a price worth paying for the chance of an easy way into the Upper City.

"Okay," he said to Peg Foot, nodding. "Lead on."

CHAPTER 9

GALANTAS FOLLOWED the jailer along the corridor, Qinta a step behind. The only light came from the jailer's guttering torch. The cells to either side were empty and had been so since the conflict between the Spears and the Raptors nine years ago. On the day that Kalag came to discuss terms with Dresk, Dresk had unleashed his inquisitors on the Raptor prisoners so their clan leader had to listen to their screams while he negotiated in the Great Hall. Those screams had fouled the air, giving the place a baleful atmosphere as if the souls of the dead lingered beyond the reach of the torchlight.

The jailer halted and gestured to a wooden door. "In here."

Galantas looked through the grille. The cell beyond was so dark he could make out only gray shapes within the gloom. There was a cot against the right-hand wall, and on it lay Ostari.

"Open it," Galantas said to the jailer.

The key squealed as it turned in the lock. When the door swung inward, the complaint from the hinges was louder still.

Galantas took the torch from the jailer. "Leave us." The man bobbed his head. As he retreated into shadow, Galantas said to Qinta, "See that we're not disturbed."

Then he entered the cell.

His torch drove the shadows before him. In the flickering light, he saw white mold covering the walls, and in the corner was a drain crusted with blood and hair and—strangely—feathers. Needleflies buzzed around a stinking waste pail.

Ostari's wrists were shackled to the wall behind him by a length of chain—an unnecessary precaution to Galantas's mind, considering the wound to the Augeran's ankle. There were bloody bandages round his right shoulder and leg. Beads of sweat covered his brow. After the chill of the passage, the air in the cell seemed close, as if it had been warmed by its occupant's fever. The tightness to Ostari's jaw hinted at his agony, but his eyes showed only defiance.

"Have you been given something for the pain?" Galantas said.

Ostari did not respond.

Galantas sighed. You had to admire a man's refusal to accept that he was beaten. Unless he *was* beaten, of course, in which case that refusal just made him look witless. Ostari had been given up for dead by his kinsmen, so it was unlikely they'd be coming for him anytime soon. His only hope of limping out of here lay with Galantas, and the sooner Ostari understood that, the better.

"I hear your ankle was broken," Galantas said. "Has the bone been reset?"

Ostari gave a snort that turned into a cough.

"What, you think your healers could do a better job?"

Still nothing.

"You're right," Galantas said after a pause. "Why should you care if you never walk again?"

Silence.

Galantas pondered his next move. Was Ostari's apparent indifference to his fate genuine? Galantas was minded to call his bluff by leaving this place, but there was too much at stake here to walk away. Perhaps it was time he gave Ostari a taste of the welcome he would receive from Dresk's inquisitors.

No man, after all, was indifferent to pain.

Reaching out, he placed his hand on the blood-soaked bandages around Ostari's leg. The stone-skin flinched, his lips drawing back.

"What did you see in the yard?" Galantas said.

No reply.

"The shot that hit Eremo came from behind me," Galantas went on, "so I didn't see who fired it." He gave the stone-skin's leg a squeeze. "Did you?"

"Why matter?" Ostari grated.

"Your mage destroyed the battlements where the bolt came from. If the shooter was there—"

"If?"

"You must admit, it makes little sense for us to kill your commander after we'd taken his money. Of the two sides, I'd say we got the best of the bargain."

"Bargain be better if no need do anything in return."

Galantas removed his hand from Ostari's leg. His fingers were red, and he wiped them on the man's crimson cloak. It wasn't as if the stain would show there. "You think we planned to betray you all along? Then why weren't our guards ready to strike? Why weren't there ten bolts in the first attack instead of one?" He paused to let Ostari think on that. "And why didn't we attack your ship in the harbor at the same time? We could have killed every one of you, and your people back home would never have known."

Ostari showed his teeth. "If say so. But not *me* you must persuade."

"We've tried to contact your kinsmen," Galantas said. "Unfortunately they're not so keen on speaking to us. Every boat that approaches your ship is carried away by waves of water-magic."

"And want me messenger?" Ostari gave a dry chuckle. "Status in people less now captured. No Honored with indignity keep rank."

"Honored?"

The arrogance was back in the stone-skin's eyes. "Best in Augeran warriors. Survive longest trials of military."

There were questions that Galantas would have liked to ask on that score, but they would have to wait. "And this lost standing, there is no way it can be regained?"

Ostari did not respond.

From the Great Hall above came the clank of metal, the slam of a door. The fortress was stirring to life—meaning time was running out. Galantas had been careful to ensure as few people as possible saw him coming, but one of the guards would surely report his presence to Dresk. When his father roused himself from his drunken stupor, he'd be down here to find out what was happening. Even a fool such as Dresk couldn't be ignorant of the dangers of Galantas speaking to the stone-skins. Particularly since the warlord would no doubt be hoping to use Galantas as a scapegoat just as Galantas was hoping to use *him*.

Ostari surprised him by speaking. "If Eremo dead, you waste time. Subcommander Sunder replace. Spent life in shadow. Will want prove mettle by make someone pay."

"Someone like Dresk, maybe."

The stone-skin stared at him.

"I understand your people's wish for redress. But why should all of my kinsmen suffer? If it *was* Dresk's guards who attacked Eremo, they likely did so on my father's order."

"Or on yours, perhaps."

"And put myself at risk by doing so? In case you've forgotten, it was me trapped in that yard yesterday, not my father. If Eremo had died, I would probably be dead now myself." Galantas didn't believe that—he'd have found a way to come out on top, as he always did. But he suspected it was what Ostari wanted to hear.

"If Dresk falls, you take place," the stone-skin said. "You who spoke against treaty."

"For twenty thousand talents, I might be persuaded to change my mind."

"And why think Augera want you ally? A man who give up own father for ambition? A man who betray brother—"

Galantas's hand shot out and gripped Ostari's leg again. "What do you know about my brother?" The stone-skin's back arched, his chains clinking. He gritted his teeth, biting down on a scream. "You think you know me?" Galantas whispered. "You think I wanted my brother dead? It was never *my* loyalty to *him* that was in question."

He released Ostari's leg and took a breath to steady himself, annoyed that he'd let himself be provoked. "I think your people need reminding why they wanted this treaty in the first place. If you decline my offer, what are you going to do? Attack us? Everyone who's tried to do that before has failed. You know we have eyes in the outlying islands, watching for trouble. Approach in force, and you'll find Bezzle deserted by the time you get here. You've walked the city. You've seen the Great Hall. Is there anything you think we wouldn't hesitate to leave behind?" He gave his voice a more conciliatory note. "I'm offering you another way."

Ostari was still shaking with pain. Breath snorted in his nose. "As said, not me you persuade."

"But if I released you, you would speak for us?" Galantas wasn't stupid enough to think the man would support his cause, but surely Ostari would at least put the offer to his superiors as one that merited consideration.

The stone-skin was a long time in answering. He hid it well, but there was no mistaking his hope that he might soon be free of this place. "Dresk not know you here, yes? How free me without him agree?"

Galantas turned away, knowing he had his man. "Leave my father to me."

Amerel's hands were white where they gripped the windowsill. Her muscles were tight as rigor mortis, and her body trembled as if she'd overindulged in cinderflower. Again. The remnants of yesterday's blood-dream clung to her as a darkness at the edges of her vision. Or maybe that was just her exhaustion. Another night with no sleep. A night spent pushing back the images that awaited her behind closed eyelids. A night spent staring at the ceiling and listening to the whores ply their trade in the rooms around her—apparently they didn't sleep much either. In the end Amerel had used one of her mind exercises to empty her head. Nothing worse, after all, than having a few bells alone to think.

She swung her gaze to Dresk's fortress. It was the morning after the night before, and the stronghold looked decidedly the worse for yesterday's excitement. There was a gap in the battlements where the Augeran mage's power had struck. Echoes of that sorcery clung to the stonework. The sorcery was like death-magic, only more . . . final. As if such a thing were possible. What was Amerel supposed to feel, looking at the fortress now? Satisfaction? Guilt?

Something, surely.

She scanned the rest of the city. An unnatural hush had settled over Bezzle. In the market there were as many dogs as there were people—more, probably, if you counted the fare on sale at the butcher's stands. Over half the stalls were unmanned. Even the spectators at the fighting pit seemed subdued as they watched a wrestler pound his opponent's head against a block of rubble. In the harbor the Augeran ship had moved away from the wharf and now bobbed at anchor near the still-smoldering islets. Earlier a rowing boat—sent by Dresk, no doubt—had tried to approach it, only to be forced back by a wave of water-magic. Evidently the stone-skins did not want to talk to the warlord, and who could blame them?

But they weren't showing any signs of leaving, either.

The Bezzlians, by contrast, were leaving in droves. A steady flow of ships had departed the harbor during the course of the last bell.

On one of the quays now, Amerel saw a scuffle break out among a mob of Islanders waiting to board a Thaxian brigantine. Was Talet with them? Had he left on an earlier vessel? If not, he was doing a good job of keeping his head down. Twice Amerel had spirit-walked to the fortress to look for him, and twice she had returned frustrated. The more she thought about it, the more she was convinced his late arrival yesterday had been because he was arranging passage out of Bezzle for him and his son. Amerel couldn't decide whether she hoped he had managed it or not. If he'd fled, the chance of being exposed by him would have gone too. Yet a loose end didn't stop being loose just because you couldn't tie it off.

Footsteps outside the door signaled Noon's return from the harbor. He'd gone to warn the *Whitecap*'s captain they'd be sailing earlier than planned. As soon as he entered, Amerel sensed something different about him—a whisper of sorcery coming from his belt-pouch.

When she released the windowsill, her hands started shaking. She clasped them together. "What have you got there?" she asked.

Noon looked at his pouch. "A present from the emperor. Glass globes that go bang when they smash."

Amerel had heard rumors of their like. "Elemental sorcery?"

The Breaker nodded.

"It would have been nice to know you had them before I decided on my plan to deal with Eremo."

"What does it matter? We got the job done." He seemed anxious to change the subject. "It's all arranged with the *Whitecap*. A bell or two to load up—"

"We're not leaving," Amerel cut in. "Not yet."

"Oh? Some sights around the city you haven't seen yet?"

"We have another appointment with Talet—though he doesn't know it yet."

"You're going to kill him?"

Amerel looked at him askance. "Careful with that intuition of yours. You might cut someone with it."

Noon's expression hardened. "What's the matter, Princess? Is condemning an entire city not enough that you need Talet's blood on your hands as well?"

"Blood washes off, I've found." Sometimes it didn't even leave a stain.

The Breaker stared at some profanity carved into his bed's headboard. Maybe he was seeking to draw wisdom from it. "Talet doesn't have to die. If you're worried about him talking, bring him back to Erin Elal with us. It isn't as if he can do any more good here."

"And if Galantas is watching him? Or someone sees him leave with us? How far do you think we'll get before we're run down by that metal-hulled ship?" The darkness bordering her vision started to close in, and she blinked her eyes against it. "Talet has to die. You know it as well as I do."

"Maybe." The Breaker looked like he'd swallowed something that disagreed with him. The truth, perhaps. "Doesn't mean I have to like it, though."

"And you think I do?"

"No, of course not. I'm sure those bags under your eyes came from you wrestling with your conscience all night."

"Ah, my conscience, is that what's bothering you? Don't worry, I try not to let it bother me." It certainly hadn't in Arap, or in Helin, or in a dozen other cities on a dozen other missions. In any case, how did conscience figure into it when you were doing the will of the emperor? What task could be less than honorable when it advanced the empire's cause? "Talet has to die—you as good as admitted it. When he's cold in the ground, do you think it'll matter to him who put him there? Or whether we wrung our hands over his grave?"

"It should matter to you, Princess."

Should it? Amerel wasn't so sure. Maybe it had once, before she'd killed her first man on the road to Kerin, but after the second, or the third, or the tenth? "Next time there's an Eremo to eliminate, who do you want lining him up in the crossbow's sights? Someone who keeps their finger steady on the trigger? Or someone who hesitates and lets the moment pass?"

"Right," Noon said, "we can all sleep better knowing you're the one who's got our fate in your hands."

"And you're cut from a superior cloth, are you?" Amerel held his gaze. "You know how it goes. You draw your line in the sand, you step over it a couple of times, but you tell yourself you had good reason. Then one day you find the line has blurred, or is somewhere else entirely—if it exists at all."

"And you're okay with that?"

The Guardian shrugged. It didn't matter if she was or she wasn't; it was too late to do anything about it. Much easier to slide down a slippery slope than to climb back up after. And Amerel didn't think she had the strength to make the attempt.

"Why do you do it if you don't believe in the cause?" Noon asked. "Why haven't you walked away before now?"

Amerel spread her arms to take in the room with its peeling paint and its scuttling bloodroaches. "What, and give all this up?"

The Breaker muttered something under his breath.

A man's yelp sounded from the room below, somewhere between pleasure and pain. Hard to tell the two apart sometimes. Then something caught Amerel's eye, and she froze. Something under the door.

A piece of parchment.

Her skin prickled. A message? That hadn't been there when Noon returned, meaning someone must have come and gone while she was talking to the Breaker. And overheard their conversation, perhaps?

Noon picked up the note. The parchment had been sealed with wax. He broke the seal and unfolded the paper to read the message inside. His brows knitted. "It's from Talet," he said. "He wants to meet us at the third bell at his house in the Old Town. There's a map showing how to get there."

"The message is genuine?"

"Signature looks right. And there are no keywords to suggest anything amiss."

But the doubt in Noon's voice said he wasn't taking any comfort in that. A meeting in daylight, and at Talet's home besides? Why not here at the brothel, where the spy's presence could be easily explained? That was why he'd chosen this dump in the first place, wasn't it? And why in four bells' time instead of now?

A mystery, then, but not one Amerel was minded to dwell on. If Dresk or Galantas knew she was here, they'd be breaking down her door, not setting a trap in the Old Town. Maybe Talet had something to share about what Dresk was planning to do next. Maybe the third bell was the soonest he could meet.

If that was all there was to it, she should be grateful that he had spared her the trouble of tracking him down.

Standing beside the Spider, Romany watched Artagina pace along the far side of the temple courtyard. He was bellowing at a congregation of more than a hundred. The Olairians sat in silence amid a haze of heat, seemingly spellbound, and there must have been a certain sorcery to Artagina's words that he could have duped so many with them. Were there ever times, Romany wondered, when the priest was bewitched by his own lie? Did a part of him believe in his imaginary Lord? Or was he no more than the fraud she took him for, prostituting his passion to sustain the rotten edifice he had built around him? His sermon today was about faith, fittingly. He was telling his flock not to be concerned if their prayers were met by silence, for it was only in silence that true belief could be tempered.

True belief and true delusion both.

Romany looked around the courtyard. The temple of the Lord of Hidden Faces bore no resemblance to the Spider's temple in Mercerie. The shrine here was half derelict. Then there was the small matter of all the men cluttering up the place. The biggest difference, though, was in the absence of children. The Spider only ever took youngsters into her service. Adults could convert to the goddess's faith, of course, but none of them ever became priestesses. Why? Because the Spider liked to guide her disciples from an early age—to mold them into tools that she could use in her various concerns.

As Romany herself had been molded, perhaps?

Never! No hand, however subtle, could have steered the priestess's course without her knowledge.

During a pause in Artagina's speech, the Spider said, "The high priest has heard about your appointment as Mazana's adviser. You can imagine how surprrrised he was at the news. His own priestess elevated to the emira's right hand, and he the last to know about it. He has told one of his lieutenants to call on you at the palace later. But I don't suppose that's something you'll have to worry about, considering where you're going."

The goddess was smirking, fully aware of how much Romany detested sea travel. Mazana had arranged a crossing to Gilgamar, and her ship was due to leave in a bell's time. Though Romany hadn't completely abandoned the hope that she might find a way to miss it.

"Strangely," the Spider went on, "Artagina's opposition to the emira has waned since he discovered he has a seat at the top table, albeit vicariously. This morning he had the gall to issue an edict in Mazana's name, outlawing the practice of any religion other than his own."

"Thus usurping the same authority he was decrying only yesterday."

"The man's presumption is truly humbling."

Romany thought she heard admiration in the Spider's tone. "A presumption you have fueled by allowing him to remain in this temple."

The goddess appeared not to hear. "Did you know he has started making predictions? Apparently I need to clear my diary for next week, because anyone caught worshiping another deity then will be struck down by the Lord himself."

"And what happens when his god fails to show?"

The Spider looked at her as if she were simple. "Why, he makes a new prediction, obviously."

"And his followers simply forget about the first one?"

"Of course. Since the alternative would mean questioning the high priest's legitimacy, and thus the legitimacy of their own faith too."

That note of appreciation in the Spider's voice was back—more appreciation, come to think of it, than Romany had ever received from the goddess. She glared at Artagina through her mask's eye slits. Damned upstart! How would he react if he were ever to be confronted about his scam? What would he do if he heard his "Lord's" voice demanding that he confess his deceit? In fact, the more Romany considered it . . .

"Since we're talking about predictions," she said to the Spider, "what are your thoughts about Jambar's? Are the stone-skins truly the threat he claims?"

The goddess shrugged. "I am not a fortune-teller, nor would I wish to be. Can you imagine how borrring this game would be if I could foresee all the results?"

"Even if it means you are winning?"

"Especially then. What is winning, after all, without the occasional defeat to put it in context?"

Funny, the Spider had never tired of beating Romany in their clashes over a hafters board. "Who are these stone-skins? What is their interest here?"

The goddess shrugged a second time. "Truth be told, I've never bothered extending my web to their homeland. Many years back, they outlawed the worship of any member of the pantheon, which makes it rather difficult to enlist them to my cause."

"If that's the case, you must be keen to stop them spreading to this continent."

The Spider's fingers fluttered. "Empires rise, empires fall."

"This particular empire happens to be home to a great many of your temples. Temples the stone-skins would no doubt tear down if they got the chance."

"Temples like your own, you mean."

"*My* temple, is it now?"

The goddess chuckled.

That chuckle must have come at an inappropriate moment in Artagina's sermon, for a number of sets of disapproving eyes turned in the Spider's direction, including the high priest's own. The goddess waved a hand at him as if inviting him to continue, and after a heartbeat's silence he did as he was bid.

Romany had waited long enough to discuss the events of last night. She told the Spider about what had happened in the cell. "The blade Mazana took from Darbonna . . . did you know it existed?"

"No. I can't be expected to keep track of all of Fume's toys."

"And if you *had* known, you would have warned me, of course."

"There is that."

"Does blood extracted with the knife carry greater power than blood extracted with a normal blade?"

"Darbonna evidently thought so. And if anyone should know, it was she."

"Our course seems clear, then. You wanted to know if Mazana was feeling Fume's influence. From what happened last night, I'd say she is positively drunk on it."

The Spider looked at her. "I must say, you seem much more comfortable in condemning her now than you were when we last spoke."

"The woman's a monster!"

"Because she disposed of one of her enemies?"

"She didn't just dispose of her, she tortured her!"

"Whereas a knife thrust to the heart would have been entirrrely ethical."

Romany sniffed. The Spider's sermonizing was becoming as tiresome as Artagina's. "Do you disagree with my conclusion, then, about the danger she poses? Are you going to wait until she starts pulling legs off spiders to act?"

The goddess was a while in replying, and that pause left Romany feeling strangely uneasy. The Spider *never* had to think about a question. "No, I don't disagree," she said at last. "But as to the precise time that we move against her, I will leave that to you. The effect of

Fume's spirit should be slow to build, and it seems a shame to remove one of my own pieces from the board before I've had a chance to extract full value from it." She smiled. "But we can discuss that in more detail another time. Don't let me keep you any longer. Wouldn't want you to miss that ship to Gilgamar, now, would we?"

Ebon followed Peg Foot down a mud track scarred by wagon ruts. Moments ago, they'd left the tree-lined main avenue running east to west through Gilgamar with its orderly traffic and its armed patrols. The stone buildings had been replaced by ones made from wood and mud bricks. Everywhere Ebon looked, there were men and women sprawled in the shadows, drunk or drugged, while redbeaks watched from the rooftops, waiting to see which of the sleepers did not wake.

Peg Foot took a right turn into a road half blocked by the debris of a collapsed building. From the opposite direction came two women pulling a handcart piled with bodies as if the plague were in town. Beyond, an old man crooned to himself as he stirred up the dust with a broom of twigs. Ebon had to raise a sleeve to cover his nose and mouth. The smell of charcoal filled the air, along with the ever-present burned-sweet scent that Peg Foot had identified to him as tollen.

The Gilgamarian halted outside a wooden building with a door studded with metal bolts. Inside, a dog yapped.

"Here we are," Peg Foot said, gesturing to the door.

Ebon approached without hesitation. Perhaps he should have been more cautious, but overconfidence was the curse of the power he'd inherited—as dangerous, most likely, as whatever awaited him within. Besides, would nervousness serve him any better when he confronted "the man" Peg Foot had arranged this audience with?

The door had a scuffed sill a handspan tall, and Ebon stepped over it. He found himself in a room with a bar to his left manned by a barman wearing a bloodstained apron. Three men stood at the bar hunched over their cups, while another man sat against the wall opposite, stroking a one-eared mongrel dog. Half a dozen battered tables were scattered about the room. At one sat a young woman in a corset, plaiting her hair into pigtails. At another was a huge man with a bald, egg-shaped head, wearing a waistcoat with bulging buttons. He was eating a slice of bread and butter with a knife and fork.

Ebon drew up. Vale had entered behind him, but not Peg Foot, and no one inside the bar acknowledged his presence. So what next? He didn't have a name or even a description to work with. He hesitated before crossing to the bald man's table. The stranger's fork stopped halfway to his lips. He stared at Ebon, then gave a half smile and opened his mouth to reveal a set of pristine white teeth . . . and no tongue.

Great. This should be fun, trying to hold a conversation with a man who couldn't talk.

"Over here," a female voice said, and it took Ebon a moment to register that the speaker was the woman in the corset. So she was his contact? Not what he'd been expecting, but perhaps that was the point.

He sat across from her, putting his back to the bar. The woman had a heart-shaped face and wide brown eyes. Attractive in a way, though there was nothing of Lamella about her. She was young—maybe just a girl in truth—and the pigtails made her look younger still, yet there was a weariness to her expression that her makeup could not conceal.

"So you're 'the man,' are you?" Ebon said.

The woman giggled. "Silly. Don't you know what these are?" And she put her hands under her breasts and pushed them up.

Ebon shifted in his chair. "I believe so. My escort may need educating, though."

Under the table the woman's foot touched Ebon's leg. "My name is Tia. And yours is?"

There seemed no reason to withhold it. "Ebon."

"Ebon," she repeated. "You're a stranger to Gilgamar, yes? Your accent gives you away."

The prince kept his silence.

The woman's foot crept higher up his leg. "Our voices say so much about us," she said. "Not just our accents, but also the way we use words, the precision of our diction. Our hands, too." She took his right hand in hers and turned it to inspect the palm. "See? Your hand tells me you are accustomed to holding a sword, but that you've never pulled a plow or loosed a sail."

"Neither have you."

Tia's foot stroked his thigh. "Ah, but that is where the similarities between us end. For you are a man of breeding, aren't you? A man of refinement."

"So I keep trying to tell people." Time to move the conversation on. "I need to get into the Upper City. I was told you could help."

Tia paid him no mind, still gazing at his palm. She traced the path of a barely perceptible line that ran down from his middle finger. "This is the fate line," she said. "It tells me more about your life than all the other lines combined. A straight line is rare, for it shows someone who follows the course that fate has set for him. Boring. Where the line breaks up toward the top of the hand, as yours does, it shows a person who struggles against his destiny."

Ebon held her gaze, waiting. Her right hand had dropped beneath the table.

"Your left hand will tell me more, of course"—she reached for it—"for while the right shows how your reality differs from your desires, the left shows—"

Her right hand suddenly reappeared from under the table, driving something silver toward Ebon's exposed left palm. There had been no tensing of her body, no tell in her eyes to reveal her intent. But the prince had been expecting the move, all the same. His right hand snapped out to seize her wrist. The knife she was holding stopped a short distance from his palm. Tia struggled against him for an instant, her teeth bared, the muscles in her forearm standing proud.

Ebon's strength was greater than hers, though, and he held her fast.

From behind him came the whisper of steel as Tia's men drew their swords. The tongueless man pushed himself to his feet. Vale moved up to flank Ebon.

Ebon ignored them all. He tightened his grip on Tia's wrist, digging his fingers into her flesh until she surrendered her hold on the knife. It clattered to the table. Ebon released the woman and scooped it up.

He pushed his chair back from the table and made to rise. Then stopped himself. The sensible thing to do would be to get up and walk out, but some instinct made him hold. Had Peg Foot intended all along to lead him into trouble? Or had Tia simply mistaken Ebon for easy prey, and thought to empty his pockets now rather than work for the privilege? He needed to know which it was. Because if the woman *was* able to get him into the Upper City, he couldn't afford to give up on her so quickly. What guarantee did he have that there'd be someone else out there who could help? Or that he'd be able to track them down? And even if he *could* find them, who was to say they would be more trustworthy than Tia?

The woman watched him with a hint of a smile, her gaze shifting back and forth between Ebon and the knife. There was no unease in her expression, but doubtless she thought her henchmen standing by would give her the edge in a confrontation. Ebon would have to disabuse her of that notion if he was to get her to take him seriously.

Lowering the point of the knife, he cut a stinging line across his palm and watched the blood well up. A moment to let Tia take in what she was seeing, then he healed the wound and wiped the blood away to reveal a pale pink scar.

"And what does *this* line on my hand tell you about me?" he said.

Tia smiled in delight, and it made her look like the girl Ebon had first taken her for. "Nice trick," she said. "Does it work as well with a crossbow bolt through your eye?"

Ebon stabbed the knife into the table. "Are we done playing games?"

"If you insist." She motioned for the tongueless man to sit down.

"I need to get into the Upper City," he said again. "Can you help?"

"I don't like that word 'help.' You make it sound like you expect me to do it out of charity. But yes, I can get you into the Upper City. The question is, why do you want to go?"

"I don't see that that's any of your business."

"It is if you want me to help you."

Ebon leaned back in his chair. Most likely Tia wanted a sense of his need so she could judge how much to charge for her services. But she might equally be trying to find out whether she stood to gain by turning him in. Either way, he was not inclined to share more of his purpose than he had to. "I'm looking for someone."

"A survivor of the Hunt?"

Ebon raised an eyebrow, but it was a fair guess considering the timing of his arrival. "Yes."

"You've seen their ship in the harbor?"

He nodded.

"Then why not send them a message through one of the guards?"

"Perhaps I don't want them to know I'm coming."

Tia giggled. "An assassin, are you? I think not. Have you been to the Upper City before?"

"No."

"Then how are you going to track down whoever it is you're looking for?"

"With the map you're going to give me."

"A map, eh? That certainly narrows down your list of possible targets. No private houses on a map. There's the Alcazar, of course, but you don't need a map to find that. So . . . one of the courthouses? An embassy? Am I getting warm?"

Not a muscle in Ebon's face moved. "How soon can we go?"

"That depends. How many of you are there?"

"Two."

Tia's gaze flickered to Vale. "Tonight, then."

Ebon pursed his lips. He'd been hoping she would have false papers that could get him into the Upper City straightaway. "No chance of anything sooner?"

When the girl shook her head, it set her pigtails bouncing.

"When tonight?"

"I'll have to get back to you on that. Whenever it is, though, you should have enough of the night left to finish whatever it is you're planning to do."

"How will we get inside?"

"I don't see that that's any of your business."

"It is if you want my money," Ebon said. "If your help is just going to consist of a ladder to lean against the wall, I may need to look elsewhere."

Tia stroked her foot against his right leg again, and he lifted the leg and crossed it over his left. "I have a man on the inside," she said. "One of the guards. He'll look the other way when you climb his section of wall."

One man? "That leaves a lot of other sets of eyes to see me."

"Not if my man tells them to look the other way too."

Ebon frowned. It wasn't the people *in* on the scam he was worried about. "And you've got others into the Upper City this way before?"

"Yes. Well, a couple. The fact is, it only takes one person"—and she held up an illustrative finger as if she thought he might not be able to count that far—"to see something they shouldn't for my man to lose his head. That's not a risk you run every day . . . or without suitable compensation."

So they came to it at last. "How much?"

Tia regarded him appraisingly, no doubt trying to gauge how much money she could wring from him. He braced himself.

"Five thousand sovereigns."

Ebon gave a strangled choke. He might be able to raise that sum by selling the two rings he'd taken off before coming here, but he wasn't about to let Tia know that. "Five thousand sovereigns?" he repeated. A small price to pay if it reunited him with Lamella and Rendale, yet he had to go through the motions of haggling. "*Five* thousand?"

"Oh no, wait, you wanted a map as well. Five thousand and one."

"You are wasting my time. You said yourself, I am not from Gilgamar. No one travels with that kind of money. And it's not as if I've got friends here whom I can borrow it from."

Tia gave an innocent smile. "I'm sure you'll think of something. You could use that trick with the knife. There must be people who would pay good money to see that."

"One thousand," Ebon countered. "And I'll need directions to a moneylender fool enough to lend it to me."

"Four thousand."

"Two."

Tia's grin was growing broader by the moment. "Will you need help getting out of the Upper City as well as getting in?"

"No," Ebon said. With luck he'd be able just to walk through the Harbor Gate when morning came. And if not, well, breaking *out* should be a good deal easier than breaking *in*.

"Three thousand, then," Tia said. "And that's my best offer. Half payable in advance, half to be deposited with a countinghouse of your choice. Unless of course you've got something you can give me as surety for the second payment."

"Something like my good word, you mean?"

The girl snorted. "The countinghouse it is. First payment due by the ninth bell tonight, shall we say?" She reached for the knife wedged in the table and wiggled it free.

Ebon withdrew his hands. "You're not expecting me to bring the money here, I trust." Walking through the Lower City at night with his pockets full, how could that end badly?

"Of course not," Tia replied, with a look that said he was a fool if he thought he would ever find her *here* again. "Someone will track you down at the harbor to collect. You'll get more details then about tonight's arrangements."

"I'll be ready," he said.

For more treachery as much as for anything else.

CHAPTER 10

THE LAST chime of the noon bell faded, and still there was no sign of Galantas's prey. He looked at his companions crouched in the shanty behind. Qinta was examining one of his tattoos. Reska had his eyes closed. Carlo shifted his weight from foot to foot. But it was Vos about whom Galantas was most concerned. The man looked like he was going to be sick, and he wouldn't meet Galantas's gaze. It took a particular strength of character to stomach the bitter brew of kin slaughter. Maybe Galantas had misjudged Vos on that score. Catching the man's eye, he held out his hand for Vos's crossbow.

Vos set his jaw and shook his head. Galantas suppressed a smile. *As easy as that.* Some captains were quick to punish a crewman who showed reluctance to obey an order, but Galantas had always found it more effective to compel through example. Never ask a man to do something you wouldn't do yourself. He didn't want men serving under him who found this sort of task easy. He wanted men who could put aside their personal misgivings for the good of their clan. Men who trusted Galantas's judgment over their own.

Men with sense, in other words.

Through a broken window to his left, he saw a woman balancing a basket on her head pass the entrance to the alley. Beyond her, a jumble of rooftops sloped down to the port. Rising above the thatch and cracked tiles was the steeple of one of the water towers marking the course of Bezzle's underground aqueduct. Through the haze from the brine boileries, Galantas could make out the topmasts of the

Augeran ship. Its flag remained at full mast, which he took as a sign that Eremo still clung to life. Perhaps that explained why the stone-skins hadn't responded yet to the proposal Ostari would have put to them. Perhaps, while Eremo's fate hung in the balance, there was uncertainty in the chain of command.

And yet what option did the stone-skins have but to accept Galantas's offer? There was no way they'd be getting their twenty thousand talents back, so if they wanted a return on their investment, they had to do business with either Dresk or Galantas. And a choice between Galantas and his father was surely no choice at all.

He would have to play the next few bells carefully, though. For while he needed the Augerans' help to dethrone Dresk, he also needed to keep their involvement discreet, lest the other tribes think him their puppet. Then there was the problem of what to do with his father. Most likely the stone-skins would want to make a public display of Dresk, yet any repeat of the scenes on the *Lively* was certain to incite Dresk's followers to anger. The krels in particular would have to be managed, but Galantas had devised a strategy to keep them on side. A strategy that centered on Talet. The man was an administrator, and thus wholly expendable. With the right . . . persuasion, he might be convinced to back Galantas's story that it was Dresk who had ordered the attack on Eremo. Once Dresk's "treachery" was exposed, most of the krels would fall into line. A few, though, were too small-minded to ever be trusted in Galantas's service.

Hence his presence in this shanty now, waiting for Karsten Berg to appear. For years Galantas had been planning to move against Dresk's supporters. That was why he knew about Karsten's mistress, along with the route the man took when he called on her. Last month Galantas had intercepted a message from the mistress, inviting Karsten to stop by. He'd used that message this morning to lure his target into Bezzle's backstreets. The alley he'd chosen for the ambush was ideal. On one side was a windowless wall covered in nettle-claw and home to nesting spider jays, whose warble should conceal the sounds of any scuffle. On the other side were abandoned shanties, one of which now sheltered Galantas and his men. Someone had been here since he'd last checked the place over, for the table and chairs had been smashed so comprehensively the culprit might have planned to use them as firewood. There was no sign of that intruder now, though.

Meaning Karsten's final moments, when he got here, would be un-witnessed by all save Galantas and his men.

Galantas had always thought he would hesitate when the time came to act against Dresk, but instead he felt a thrill of anticipation. There was no going back now. His father would have learned of Ostari's release. He'd be looking for Galantas, maybe readying a strike against him, yet it would be Galantas who struck at his father first. At last he had a chance to repay Dresk for the insults and the petty betrayals—to start undoing the damage to clan unity his father had caused in his time as warlord. Ultimately he would be sacrificed for the good of his kin, and was that not the supreme duty of a leader? Dresk would serve his people in death as he had singularly failed to serve them in life.

Three figures entered the alley, and Galantas raised a hand to warn his companions. The warbling of the spider jays rose in pitch as the newcomers approached. Galantas shrank back against the wall. Karsten strode past the window in his familiar bloodred head-scarf. Behind him came two bodyguards, laughing at some jest. The house in which Galantas hid was located at a bend in the alley. As the voices followed that bend around to the right, Galantas made a fist to signal his men to move. Qinta took the lead, opening the door and slipping into the bodyguards' wake. Reska, Carlo, and Vos went after him, with Galantas bringing up the rear.

He trailed them around the bend.

It was over in moments. Blocking Karsten's way was a cart loaded with barrels. There was nowhere to run when Galantas's men at-tacked from behind, and more ambushers lay in wait behind the cart. Crossbows thrummed, a solitary scream sounded, and Karsten and his two bodyguards went down. Galantas nodded his approval. An unsavory task, but that was no excuse for sloppiness. His men had acquitted themselves well. Vos's expression was bleak, yet he hadn't held back from the attack. Today would either break him or put some steel in him; Galantas would find out which soon enough.

He laid a hand on the man's shoulder. He'd meant it as a reassur-ing gesture, but from the way Vos flinched, it might have been Shroud who'd crept up on him unawares.

Maybe later.

Galantas knelt at Karsten's side. The krel had taken a bolt in the chest and one in the gut, but he was still alive. He was looking up at the sky. His breaths came quickly as if he was determined to squeeze in as much life as possible from his final heartbeats. But that had always been his way. It was why Galantas admired him so much, maybe even liked him.

Galantas's crew had picked clean the corpses of the two bodyguards and were now bundling them into barrels on the cart. Galantas drew a dagger and rested its point on Karsten's neck. When the krel looked at him, there was hatred in his eyes.

"Your family is safe," Galantas said. "I'll see to it they're looked after."

"Go to hell," Karsten rasped.

Fair enough. Galantas would have said the same in the man's place.

He drew his dagger across the krel's throat, feeling the serrations bite.

From the quarterdeck of Mazana's flagship, the *Raven,* Senar scanned the sea all about. A stone's throw behind, a Revenant vessel glided on a wave of water-magic, while to the north and south sailed two brigatinas as escort, ready to draw off any dragon the convoy encountered. Beyond the southern ship lay the island of Airey, once home to the Storm Lord Gensu Sensama and now seemingly home to nothing but starbeaks. Every village the *Raven* passed was deserted, the inhabitants having fled inland. A wise move too, since the dragons had proved themselves willing to venture ashore to supplement their fishy diet. Yesterday Senar had seen one attack the Deeps, cracking open the partly flooded buildings like nuts to get at the tasty morsels inside.

From the number of claimed sightings around Olaire, a hundred dragons might have been prowling the Sabian waters. According to Mazana, though, the true number was only seventeen. Not sixteen. Not eighteen. Like she'd been in Dian on Dragon Day to count them as they passed under the gate. Rumor had it that some had laid waste to the Uscan Reach, then made their homes in the ruins of its settlements. But there were also rumors of a battle to the north between a dozen of the creatures and a denkrakil that had formerly had its tentacles wrapped around Olaire. In truth, Senar didn't care where the dragons were as long as it wasn't here.

Olaire's merchant guilds had petitioned Mazana to hunt down the beasts, but Senar knew she had no intention of doing so. For decades the Sabian League had bridled under the Storm Lord yoke, and in the farthest corners of the Sabian Sea, plans were no doubt afoot to ensure a new Storm Council didn't rise from the ashes of the old. A single Storm Lord, however powerful, couldn't hope to hold the empire in thrall. While the dragons were alive, though, the would-be conspirators would have something other than Mazana on which to focus their attention, thus giving her time to shore up her position. She hadn't confided her plans in Senar, but he'd heard tales that she'd started searching for new Storm Lords—albeit Storm Lords in name only. She hadn't spent all this time gathering power, after all, just to give it away again.

Jodren's coral bird flew across his line of sight, returning from one of the brigatinas. Senar watched the creature settle on the shoulder of its master, standing on the aft deck beside Mazana. Jambar was there too, staying close to his mistress so Senar couldn't corner him. Romany had yet to make an appearance on deck; the same for the Erin Elalese messenger, Kolloken.

That gave Senar an idea.

He looked around. None of the emira's entourage was watching him, so he headed for the companionway.

When he knocked at Kolloken's door, the man took an age to answer. The messenger's cabin was small, with a bunk against one wall and a desk bolted to the floor. Through an open window Senar heard the hiss of waves. A reflection of the sea shimmered on the white-painted ceiling. Kolloken sat at the desk, holding a piece of charcoal. In front of him was a roll of parchment held down at one end by a lantern. On the parchment Senar saw a charcoal drawing of a woman's features, the eyes two swirls of gray, the mouth caught in a self-conscious smile. Kolloken had captured her mood perfectly: mischievous, fey, unassuming.

"Impressive," Senar said.

"The days away from home are hard." Kolloken's gaze slid sideways. "But I'm sure you don't need me to tell you that, eh?"

Senar crossed to the window and closed it. In the sudden quiet he heard the creak of timbers, the sound of something rolling across the floor of the next cabin.

Kolloken's lips quirked. "Is this the part where I tell you everything I kept back from the red-haired bitch?"

A frown spread across Senar's face before he could catch it. "What news from home?"

"You mean, what news about the Guardians?"

"Yes, let's start there."

Kolloken went back to his drawing, sketching in the line of the woman's jaw. "Sacrosanct's still standing, if that's what you're worried about. Gill Treller's still haunting that tower of his. Though I reckon he might be getting a bit lonely, what with Borkoth and Amerel having come over to the emperor."

Senar covered his surprise. Borkoth's defection he'd known about, but now Amerel too? It shone a new light on the woman's presence in the Rubyholt Isles—though as to what that light revealed, Senar had no idea. "Were any more Guardians sent through the Merigan portal after I was?"

"No."

"Meaning Avallon first found out about the stone-skins shortly after I left."

Kolloken said nothing.

"Who else knows about them? Has the emperor told the Senate? The Black Tower?"

"Of course. It ain't the sort of thing you can keep secret for long."

Though doubtless Avallon had given it his best shot. "And have any Guardians returned since the news broke?" Before Senar went through the portal, the slide of the Guardian order had seen several of his once colleagues disappear into self-imposed exile. With the Augeran shadow now hanging over Erin Elal, perhaps some would return to the fold.

"One or two crawled out of the woodwork, yes."

"Who?"

"Myr Mellisan, Jeng Elesar."

Senar smiled. Names to remind him of how much he missed home. "Jeng was sent through the Merigan portal before me."

"Yeah. Seems it took him to one of the islands in the Southern Reach. Could have made it back to Arkarbour in a few weeks, but for some reason he only shows up last month—*after* he heard about the stone-skins."

"You think he should have hurried back for another go through the portal? Maybe next time he'd have got lucky and come out on the other side of the world."

Kolloken shrugged. "Would've been a risk worth taking. When the stone-skins come, we might need the portals to move men around."

"And how many Breakers have been sent through the gateways?"

Kolloken did not answer.

Through the window Senar saw Airey falling behind off the port quarter. The heat in the cabin was building, and he wiped a hand across his forehead. "How did Avallon first find out that the stone-skins were coming?"

"From one of your Guardian friends. Nova Quan. She was scouting a Tresson tribe when they got a surprise visitor."

"The Augerans are trying to stir up trouble among the clans?"

"Wouldn't you?"

He had a point. Since the Exile, Erin Elal had assimilated a dozen different peoples into their empire, and it wouldn't take much encouragement for those peoples to rise up against their conquerors. "What about the Kalanese? Any suggestion the Augerans have made contact with them yet?"

Kolloken had to think long and hard about the answer. Or perhaps he was thinking that he'd already revealed too much, for rather than answering the question, he said, "When I met our ambassador in Olaire, he mentioned you'd come round to see him earlier that day, asking for news. Said he was surprised you hadn't dropped by sooner to pay your respects."

"Imerle was watching me. She'd have thought I was a spy if I did."

"But I'm guessing she got less watchful after she died, eh?"

It was Senar's turn not to answer.

"The way the ambassador told it, you're Mazana's right-hand man now. That about right?"

If so, no one had bothered to tell the emira. "Having Mazana's ear has its advantages," the Guardian said. "After Dragon Day, her first thought was that the stone-skins had done her a favor. She saw their sabotage of the Hunt not as an attack against the League, but as a move aimed at stopping the Storm Lords from interfering in a future war between Erin Elal and Augera."

"And now?"

"Now she's at least prepared to withhold judgment—to listen to what Avallon has to say."

"So when the time comes, you'll be on hand to convince her to join forces with us. And to report to the emperor on her plans." Kolloken nodded. "I see it now. Quite a clever thing you've done, setting yourself up as her follower." He looked across. "A part you played so well in the throne room, I might say, that you had me completely convinced."

Senar was spared having to respond by approaching footsteps in the corridor. As they reached Kolloken's door, they paused as if their owner was considering whether to knock. Then they continued on.

The messenger's attention was back on his drawing. His charcoal hovered over the parchment as if he was struggling to recall some detail of his subject's face. "Be sure of your loyalties, Guardian," he said after a while. "A man can't ride two mounts at the same time. Emperor ain't gonna take chances with the safety of the empire. If he has to raze every city in the League to save Erin Elal, he won't hesitate, and I'll be happy to strike the first spark. Can you say the same?"

Romany stepped off the chattering gangplank and onto the Gilgamarian quay. The harbor was all but empty of ships, what with the dragons having cut off Sabian trade at the ankles. But the waterfront itself was thronged with people. Together with the usual froth of beggars, hawkers, and whores were gangs of unshaven men—laborers, most likely—gathered around upturned barrels, playing cards and smoking blackweed. As Mazana's party assembled for the walk to the Alcazar, the whole verminous mob descended on them like a flock of starving redbeaks, shouting their wares or their services in a dozen different tongues.

The Gray Cloaks closed ranks to meet the surge. For a while Romany knew what it must be like to be on a battlefield, jostled and screamed at, surrounded on all sides by a scrum of dirty faces, heaving and sweating, pushing and cursing. A man with half his teeth missing thrust a dead rat in her face like he thought she might have skipped lunch. Another shrieked something unintelligible until an elbow from a Revenant gave him cause to shriek in earnest. As he fell back, one of his fingers hooked around the edge of Romany's mask, nearly tearing it loose. She grabbed it and held it in place. *Spider's blessing.* That would not have been a good time to have her face exposed, with Mazana Creed and Senar Sol in close attendance. The chaos almost made the priestess want to turn and get back on the ship.

Or maybe not.

"Weapons out!" Twist bellowed, and with a hiss of steel the Revenants unsheathed their swords. The rabble came to its senses at last, retreating to a safe distance before starting up their caterwauling once more. Beyond the crowd, Romany glimpsed a man she thought she recognized—a man she had last seen fighting the Fangalar in the Forest of Sighs. But no, it could not be him.

He passed from sight behind the throng, and when Romany searched for him again, he was gone.

A hundred hard-fought paces along a road lined with wooden buildings brought the company to a fortified wall with a gate in it. Looking left and right, Romany saw that the wall extended the length of the waterfront. Had it been built to hold back an invader, perhaps? Or to keep undesirables from straying where they weren't wanted? That certainly seemed to be the message of the body parts hanging from the battlements. No mistaking the warning in those.

The gate was manned by soldiers who stepped with understandable reluctance into the path of the executioner—now walking at the head of the company alongside Mazana Creed. A few words, a flash of the emira's smile, and the guards parted again, though the majority of the Gray Cloaks were sent back to the ship to leave the company a mere twenty strong as it continued on.

Of all the cities in the Sabian League, Gilgamar—with its dearth of culture and its abundance of snakes—was among the last Romany had ever thought she'd like to visit. Within a quarter-bell of leaving the harbor, though, she found herself reappraising her view. The warehouses beyond the wall gave way to elegant buildings that put her in mind of her temple in Mercerie. But what struck her even more was the tranquility of the place. The port was a fading murmur behind, some marketplace a swelling buzz to her right, but the streets were free of the beggars and urchins that contested her every stride in Olaire. Instead there were powdered women in sedan chairs, or serious men in double-breasted jackets, or uniformed servants with the good grace to keep their gazes on the road. Aside from those servants, the only commoners Romany saw were accompanied by soldiers as they went about their business. This was how a city should be run, she decided: the great unwashed partitioned off from their betters, so they could do no damage to anyone but themselves.

On every street corner was a cage containing a mouse. It was only when Romany saw a blacktooth snake also trapped inside one that she deduced the cages' purpose. A sensible precaution to stop the serpents spreading too far from the canal, the priestess supposed. Indeed, the only surprising thing was that the authorities were using mice, and not condemned prisoners, to bait their traps. But perhaps that was just because they'd found a more grisly punishment for the reprobates. As the company passed a courthouse, Romany saw a line of stocks housing a miserable collection of ill-dressed, fly-ridden souls missing either a hand or a foot or an ear, and groaning like a chorus of the damned. Above the smell of corrupted flesh she caught a sticky-sweet odor. She wrinkled her nose.

"It's the tollen," a woman's voice said from beside her, and Romany looked across to see Mazana keeping pace, one arm around the shoulders of her half brother, Uriel. After last night, the priestess wasn't comfortable having the emira a mere knife's thrust away. But she couldn't let the woman know that.

"Tollen?" she said.

"A drug that numbs the mind to pain and grief." Mazana glanced toward the amputees. "Though having seen the lot of the underclass in this city, I can't imagine what they need to escape from."

Mazana Creed, champion of the poor and oppressed.

The company reached an intersection and turned onto a street leading up to the Alcazar—a huge building with a triangular frontage and turrets that became progressively smaller toward the margins. The road got steeper. After the walk up from the harbor, the old Romany would have been wheezing by now. The new Romany, though, was breathing no harder than when they had started out.

"Impressive, isn't it?" Mazana said.

"Most buildings are, compared to your palace."

"Ah, but my palace is on the coast. When you put a building on a hill, it has to make a statement. It was built by some tyrant who overthrew the Ruling Council at the turn of the last century. Alas, he didn't survive to see the last stones set in place. The Gilgamarians were never going to put up long with a despot, such is their love of democracy and equality."

Romany sniffed. "We are fortunate the winds of liberty never blew as far the Storm Isles."

"You think so? That is not the message preached by your high priest."

Not yesterday, perhaps. Romany thought back to the riots gripping the Shallows each night. "No, much better to allow the people the free rein they are enjoying in Olaire just now."

Mazana chuckled.

A hundred different flags hung limply over the Alcazar. The fact that Erin Elal's wasn't prominent among them suggested the emperor's delegation had yet to arrive, and indeed Romany hadn't seen a ship flying his colors in the harbor.

"See that flag at the center?" Mazana said, pointing. "The one with the swooping firedrifter? That's the crest of the city's former first speaker, Rethell Webb. And since it is flying at full mast, I'm guessing word has not yet reached Gilgamar of his sad demise on Dragon Day. That's hardly surprising, though. How is news supposed to cross dragon-infested waters when ships cannot?"

The Alcazar was now just a few hundred paces away, and from its central gate emerged an enormously fat man wearing a chain of office about his neck. A member of the Ruling Council, presumably. He strode down the slope toward the company at a pace that had a group of hangers-on trotting to keep up.

"My, my, someone's keen to meet me," Mazana said.

Overkeen, Romany would have said. A man that round, if he tripped and fell, might roll all the way down to the harbor.

The emira looked across at her. "If I didn't know better, I might think I had something he wanted."

Romany nodded. Like the power to clear the dragons from the Sabian Sea, for example. Gilgamar's infrastructure was sustained on the fees received from ships using its canal. With trade having ground to a halt, the Ruling Council would be feeling the loss of that income acutely.

"Before Dragon Day," Mazana said, "the Council was vociferous in its objection to Imerle's latest increase in the Levy. Is that still its position now, do you suppose?"

Galantas looked down from the first-story window of the temple of the Lord of Hidden Faces. It was over a bell since Faloman Gorst had entered the Speaker's hovel. Galantas knew the Speaker by reputation—a witch used by fishermen to dispel the ill fortune that would otherwise follow from finding in their nets such items as those that hung from the eaves of her house: a decayed fetus, a bloodstained susha robe, a mutilated doll of the White Lady. Of course Faloman was no fisherman, meaning he was here to avail himself of the Speaker's second talent: that of reading a man's future in a limewing's entrails. Waiting outside to ambush him, Galantas could only hope the Speaker's abilities were truly the sham he took them for.

He blinked sweat from his eyes. The roof of the temple had long since collapsed, and the sun beat down with a force that set the dusty air shimmering. Beside him Barnick was winding a finger through his hair. Galantas shared the mage's restlessness. Things were not going as planned. Talet had disappeared. The stone-skins still hadn't responded to Galantas's proposal. And after two and a half bells, Karsten's absence would surely have been noticed by now. His men would be searching for him, just as Dresk would be hunting for Galantas. And while the temple was as good a place as any for him to lie low, what happened when his father thought to seize the *Eternal* and force Galantas into the open?

He looked toward the harbor along the street known as the Gully. And froze.

The Augeran vessel was moving toward the quays!

Galantas allowed himself a smile. It seemed the stone-skins had finally come to their senses, though they hadn't yet raised a second flag in the agreed signal. No matter. Galantas needed to get down to the dock to meet them. A pity this chance to take down Faloman would have to go begging, but there'd be time later to deal with Dresk's krels.

Then Galantas noticed that the decks of the Augeran vessel were heaving with red- and black-cloaked figures.

A wave of water-magic swelled in the harbor, not under the ship but in front of it. It gained height as it rolled toward the wharf. Galantas lost sight of it behind the rooftops of the buildings along the waterfront, but he heard it strike home with a concussion that sent spray fountaining into the air. Screams sounded. The roof of one of the taverns collapsed. White-flecked water came fizzing along the Gully, carrying on it a boy wearing an eyepatch. The wave rolled past the doorway to the Speaker's hovel and lost speed as it climbed the slope toward the temple. It deposited the spluttering boy on the ramp beneath Galantas's vantage point.

It was a moment before Galantas's mind clicked into gear again. The stone-skins were attacking? Did the fools think they could take the whole city with one ship? He shook his head. Such a petulant move. Such a missed opportunity . . .

Then movement to the east caught his eye. Another ship was approaching Bezzle on a wave of water-magic—a second Augeran vessel, judging by its patterned sails.

The bells of the Meridian Watchtower started ringing.

Returning from her spirit-walk to the alley where Noon waited, Amerel lay for a time with her eyes closed. Her clothes were damp with sweat, and her fingertips were coated with dust from the cracked flagstones. From below came a murmur of water from Bezzle's underground aqueduct, while far off she could hear temlocks lowing. Otherwise all was silent. A breeze off the sea carried on it the smell of salt and rotting fireweed.

She had arrived in Talet's neighborhood well in advance of their meeting. She'd wanted to assess the lay of the land before calling on him, but she needn't have bothered. Talet's house was empty but for the spy himself. No crossbowmen on the roof. No swordsmen behind the curtains waiting to jump out and shout "boo!" The houses nearby were empty too, unless you counted the grayhairs and the odd woman cooing to a baby. And if *they* were the ones going to spring a trap, Amerel fancied her chances of fighting free. There was something about this idyllic picture that didn't fit, though. Something missing? Or something present that shouldn't be? She couldn't say, but there was no denying a certain feeling. . . .

A feeling. Yes, that would look good in her report to the emperor.

A stone was digging into her back, and she propped herself up on one elbow and opened her eyes. Noon was looking at her. "Well, Princess?"

"All seems quiet."

"You checked the other houses as well?"

"I thought you were doing that."

Noon squinted at her, then muttered something.

Amerel stood and dusted herself down. "Come on," she said, setting off down the alley in the direction of Talet's house.

The front door was unlocked. Nothing suspicious in that, though—he was expecting company, right? Over a hearth in the reception room were two crossed spears—the symbol of Dresk's clan—while through an archway was a graveled courtyard. The door to Talet's study was on the far wall. At the center of the yard was a pool in which floated a dead stoneback scorpion. To Amerel's left, through a partly open door, she saw a fish-scaling knife on the floor amid a scattering of child's drawings. She considered checking to see if anyone was hiding behind that door, but how many times did she have to search this place before she was satisfied it was deserted?

Sometimes nothing really did mean nothing.

She edged forward, stones crunching beneath her sandals.

Then in the distance she heard frantic shouts, the clanging of bells from the city's watchtower. She exchanged a look with Noon. Those bells, the signal to warn of an attack?

The stone-skins.

Amerel swung her gaze back to the door to Talet's study. A coincidence that the Augerans had come as she was due to meet the spy? It had to be. Otherwise Talet would have had to know what the stone-skins were planning, which in turn would mean he'd sold her out to the enemy. If this was a trap, though, why weren't any Augerans here? Had they only wanted to ensure Amerel was far from the harbor so she couldn't escape before the attack came? No, that couldn't be right. As Amerel understood the Rubyholt alarm system, those bells meant stone-skin ships had been sighted in the outer isles. It would take them longer to reach Bezzle than it would for Amerel to reach the harbor. But would the *Whitecap* still be there when she arrived? Would she be able to get to it with everyone in the city looking to flee?

Problems for later. First she had to deal with Talet.

She strode across the courtyard and flung open the door to his study.

The room beyond was exactly how she remembered it from her spirit-walk: roughly twenty armspans across and thirty deep; a concave wall opposite with floor-to-ceiling windows looking out on a garden. The place stank of moonblossom. At a desk near the windows sat Talet, his back to Amerel, writing on a sheet of parchment. Composing a farewell note to a friend, maybe? Or a tearful confession to Dresk?

When he did not acknowledge Amerel, she said, "Anyone else hear those bells?"

Scratch, scratch went his quill on the parchment.

Amerel took a step toward him. That feeling of *wrongness* was back, but she couldn't find the cause. She looked into the garden, expecting to see stone-skins storming toward her through the flowerbeds.

Nothing.

Scratch, scratch. That Shroud-cursed quill was like a claw across her eardrums.

"You wanted to see us?" Amerel said.

Still no answer.

She took another step closer. What game was Talet playing? Why invite her here if he meant to ignore her? His hair was thinning at the back, and through it Amerel could see his scalp was red from the sun. Her hand moved to the hilt of her sword. The spy's posture was strangely cramped, and there was something jerky about the movement of his writing hand. Over his shoulder Amerel caught a glimpse of the parchment he was writing on. . . .

She went still.

It was empty of words. No ink on the quill, no inkpot on the desk.

Scratch, scratch.

A clank of metal on stone sounded behind, and Amerel spun round to see that a portcullis had slammed down across the doorway through which she had entered. A portcullis in a house? How had she missed that on the way in? It wasn't an illusion either, for Amerel would have sensed someone trying to manipulate her thoughts.

Noon's voice was tense. "What's going on?" he said.

What indeed?

Amerel swung back to the spy.

To find him now slumped motionless over the desk. His shirt had disappeared to reveal that his back had been lashed to the bone. Judging by the bluish cast to his skin, he must have passed through Shroud's Gate several bells ago. *Of course, the moonblossom—to hide the smell of rot.* Amerel felt the gorge rise in her throat. Flayed to death—a particularly unpleasant way to go, and she should know. The blood-dream was already bubbling up in her mind.

She forced it down.

"Welcome," said a disembodied voice, and a figure materialized to her right.

Something told Amerel she shouldn't have been surprised.

It was the stone-skin Scarface.

Gesturing to Barnick, Galantas crossed to the stairwell leading down to the lower floor of the temple. He took the steps three at a time. When he reached the bottom, Qinta and Carlo were waiting for him, with Vos approaching at a splash along the Gully. Nothing needed to be said. That second stone-skin vessel changed everything. It meant the Augerans had found a way to bypass the Isles' network of watchtowers. It meant more of their ships would be coming. Bezzle was doomed, and it was a fate Galantas would share unless he could reach the *Eternal* and get out of here.

He set off toward the harbor at a run. The Gully was still flooded from the wave of water-magic, and his steps kicked up spray. He could hear the clash of blades from the waterfront, but he knew any resistance would quickly be swept aside. Men and women poured into the Gully from the wharfs, and Galantas had to fight against the flow. "Out of the way!" he roared, but he could barely hear his own voice over the tumult.

He drew his sword.

Faces melted past. To his left a bare-chested man tripped on the heels of a woman, and they went down together and were trampled by the press. Another man sought to escape a building overlooking the Gulley by throwing himself from a first-story window and using the crowd to break his fall. Galantas didn't see the jumper land, because a woman with blue-dyed hair had grabbed him by the shoulders and was screaming something into his face. He heaved her aside. This was hopeless. The *Eternal* was far to the south of here, so even if he could reach the waterfront, he'd have no chance of fighting through to it.

Brine Alley was on his right, and he dashed into it. Running parallel to the waterfront, it was three paces across and under a finger's width of water. Boarded windows and poster-filled walls flashed by. People streamed into the alley from the buildings to Galantas's left. Some carried possessions they had rescued from their homes—a model galleon, a bronze bust of the Sender, even a hafters board with a solitary piece on it. Galantas had to swerve to avoid the board-carrier and scraped his shoulder against the wall. "Out of the way!" he shouted again, but no one was listening.

From the waterfront came the sound of crumbling masonry as a building collapsed. There was a clash of swords, a thump of sorcery. Galantas tried to judge the progress of the stone-skin assault, but it was impossible to make sense of anything over the screams and sobs all about. A dozen paces ahead was a crossroads. People ran past from left to right, and behind them came the foaming dregs of another sorcerous wave. If Galantas could make it over the junction and into the alley beyond—

Two black-cloaked figures holding shields stepped into the passage. It was too late for Galantas to turn about, so he charged them.

They lowered their spears.

"Barnick!" Galantas shouted, and the water on the ground around the stone-skins vaporized in a hiss of scalding steam. The Augerans cried out, covered their eyes with their sleeves.

Galantas barreled into them.

He broke between their shields and sprawled into shallow water, the mist warm on his face. The wave of water-magic had retreated toward the harbor, leaving a scattering of runefish flopping on the flagstones. Voices from his left, the stamp of feet. More stone-skins? Galantas tried to rise, caught a stray boot in the ribs, and went down again.

Qinta's battle cry sounded. Grunts, curses, the clatter of swords. From Galantas's prone position, all he could see in the mist were the legs of the combatants. Perhaps it would have been safer for him to play dead, but his blood was up, and when a black-cloaked man came within range, he chopped at the Augeran's leg with his sword. Missed. A spear tip came for his chest. He rolled to evade it, heard it clatter off the flagstones. A female stone-skin reared above him, her spear drawn back to strike.

A mace cut through the murk, shattering her jaw in a shower of blood and teeth. She dropped with a mangled gargle.

Galantas scrambled to his feet. The mist was dispersing, and a look around revealed only one Augeran still upright, huddled behind his shield. Qinta and Carlo took turns putting dents in it. In the harbor beyond, a three-masted Rubyholt ship sped away from the quay—the *Wraith,* if Galantas remembered rightly. *Faloman's ship.* Didn't mean Faloman was on it, of course, and it occurred to Galantas he should be fleeing on the first ship he came to, rather than trying to reach the *Eternal.*

Then a wave of black sorcery struck the *Wraith's* port side, and its main deck and mast dissolved to dust.

That complicated things.

More Augerans pounded along the street toward Galantas. Barnick must have seen them too, because the water on the flagstones in front of them vaporized in white curls.

Time to go.

Galantas bolted into the alley beyond the junction. "Qinta, to me!" he called.

He scowled as he ran. The *Eternal* was lost. His ship was still more than a stone's throw away, and even if he could get to it, he would likely be annihilated by sorcery before he escaped the harbor. The realization left a bitter taste in his mouth. A captain without a ship was like a turtle without its shell. More important, the *Eternal* was part of Galantas's legend. Having the most celebrated ship in the Isles just meant his disgrace would be that much greater when he lost it. But it would be only a temporary loss. He would take it back, no matter the cost.

The bells of the Meridian Watchtower continued to ring. Ahead the alley was blocked by crates of gallow crabs. A woman knelt beside them, beseeching the skies as if she thought some immortal would reach down and lift her to safety. To Galantas's right the houses had given way to shops, and he careered into the backyard of one before scampering to the store itself. When he flung open the door he was greeted by the smell of galtane and caramir. An apothecary, then. He vaulted a counter and overturned a jar of silverspark flowers. It smashed on the floor, spilling petals. Glass crunched beneath his feet as he ran for the door.

He emerged breathless into the glare and clamor. In front and to his left, Tanner Road led deeper into the city. The press of people was thicker here than it had been along the Gully, but at least there were no red or black cloaks among them. And this time Galantas was moving *with* the flow, not against it. He risked a look behind and was relieved to see Barnick and Qinta with him. No sign of Carlo, Reska or Vos, alas, but Galantas had more important things to worry about just now. If he couldn't reach the *Eternal,* he'd need another way off the island.

And he'd need it fast.

CHAPTER 11

KARMEL PEERED southwest toward Bezzle. The city crawled with frantic motion like an anthill kicked to life. Mazana Creed hadn't said the place would be under attack when the Chameleons arrived, but the stone-skins' presence cast a new light on Mokinda's unease at the delays they'd experienced in Gilgamar.

The Storm Lord sat on the forecastle steps, conversing in a series of glances with the captain a dozen paces away. In close attendance were the ship's two water-mages, their furrowed brows suggesting they thought the captain should already have withdrawn. Scullen was there too. His cockiness had vanished a quarter of a bell ago with the first sorcerous concussion of the stone-skin offensive. Now he was leading the calls for the *Grace* to flee, his voice growing shriller with each heartbeat. Karmel might have enjoyed his discomfort if her own mouth hadn't been so dry.

The captain's silent discussion with Mokinda concluded, and she shouted at her mages to heave to. The *Grace* abruptly settled on the swell. A barge was on tow behind, and at an order from the captain it was hauled forward to the port side.

"That's us," Caval said to Karmel. He'd brought her gear up from the cabin, and now dropped her pack and blowpipe at her feet. The smell of oscura was heavy on his breath.

It took an instant for his words to sink in. "We're still going through with this?" she said. "We're going to land while the stone-skins are attacking?"

"Why not? The raid has only just started. There's no way the stone-skins will have taken the city."

"Not the whole city, perhaps, but their first target will be the warlord's fortress. And our route is going to take us across theirs. *Across* it."

Caval shrugged. "So the stone-skins see us, so what? We'll just be two more locals running for their lives."

But two locals who had never set foot in the city before. Two locals relying on a map that looked like it had been scribbled by a child. Karmel didn't voice the thought, however. What was she going to do? Cry off with a headache?

She picked up her pack and followed Caval.

Her brother crossed to the port rail where Mokinda waited. Steps were carved into the *Grace*'s hull, and Caval descended to the barge now floating below. Scullen demanded to know where the Chameleons were going, but Karmel paid him no mind. Never thought she'd be sad to leave *him* behind. She started down the ladder. The lower steps were slimy with growth, and when the time came to step into the barge, it seemed always that the boat would dip just as the *Grace* was rising. In the end Caval had to grab Karmel and haul her into the prow, where she sat down with a bump.

The priestess wouldn't need her blowpipe for this first part of the mission, so she stored it beneath a sailcloth cover. Across from her, Caval sat gazing up at the sky. There was no hint of nervousness in his expression. Sensing her gaze upon him, he looked over and said. "Your boyfriend not joining us?"

Karmel gave a weary sigh.

"You needn't worry," Caval added, "I gave him our details in Olaire. When he's next in town he promised to drop in."

"From a very great height, we can hope."

Her brother laughed.

Mokinda stepped down from the ladder onto the rear thwart. He settled himself on the oar bench, shipped the oars, and used one to push the boat away from the *Grace*. There was no more disquiet in his look than there was in Caval's, but then neither of them had fought that stone-skin in the Dianese citadel. *This is madness,* Karmel thought. On Dragon Day, just one Augeran had defeated her and Veran, yet now they were about to enter a city full of them?

Mokinda hauled on the oars. The *Grace* rose on a sorcerous wave, and a line of grim faces watched Karmel from the rail as the ship turned and started back the way it had come. Only when the vessel was far away did Mokinda summon up his own wave to carry the boat to shore—slowly at first, then faster and faster until the barge zipped across the water like a skimmed stone.

Ahead a deserted watchtower marked the northern end of a bay at the edge of the city. A handful of fishing boats were moving away from shore. All were brimful with people. Two boats yet remained in the shallows, and Rubyholters swarmed and fought around them like beggars around a corpse. Of the stone-skins, there was no sign. The city was alive with screams.

Karmel looked south toward the harbor. A thump of sorcery set the waterfront shaking, and left a black stain on the air that the breeze could not disperse. A forest of masts was visible over the rooftops. No telling how many of those masts belonged to Augeran ships, or what resistance the Bezzlians were putting up. With luck, the defenders would hold the enemy until the Chameleons reached their destination; though judging by the stampede at the beach, it was clear the locals didn't think much of their kinsmen's chances.

The priestess removed her baldric from her pack and strapped it across her chest. The last fishing boat pulled away from shore. There seemed to be as many people in it as had sailed south with Karmel on the *Grace*. Yet more Bezzlians swam alongside the craft, trying to heave themselves aboard, while those with a seat punched and scratched and shrieked at them to be gone. On the beach behind, two men wrestled back and forth with their hands around each other's throats, apparently unaware that the boat they fought over had left.

Mokinda's voice cut through her thoughts. "You'll have to wade the last part," he said.

It was only then that Karmel noticed how close to shore they were. Bezzlians were running along the beach toward them, and Mokinda halted the craft a short distance from the surf to ensure he didn't pick up any baggage for the outward passage.

"I'll see you at the meeting point."

Caval pushed himself upright and raised one foot to the gunwale. "Ready?" he said to Karmel. There was an unaccustomed concern in his look that suggested he would have called the whole thing off if she'd asked it.

She gathered herself, then nodded.

Amerel watched the Augeran caper into the center of the room and perform a clumsy pirouette. His face was a lattice of evenly spaced scars, as if someone had cut the lines in his skin so they could use him as a hafters board. Looking out from the devastation was the deadest pair of eyes Amerel had ever seen—deader even than the eyes that stared back at her from the mirror when she looked in it.

Noon stepped between her and the stone-skin. *My hero.* His expression was assured. Purposeful. After the mystery of that suddenly appearing portcullis, here was something he could understand: an enemy with a beating heart. The two men faced each other like duelists waiting for the referee's call. Scarface grinned, his head cocked to one side as if he didn't know why the Breaker was being so unfriendly. Noon reached over his shoulders for the twin shortswords scabbarded at his back.

Then his arms snapped forward. His hands were holding not his swords, but two throwing knives that must have been sheathed at his wrists. The daggers flashed toward the stone-skin.

A clever move, Amerel had to admit: lull the Augeran enemy into thinking Noon was reaching for one weapon, then surprise him with a strike from another. Scarface certainly seemed to have been wrong-footed, for he made no move to evade the Breaker's knives. The first thudded into his chest over the heart. The second took him in his left eye, and his head snapped back. That was one wound he wouldn't be stitching up after. Amerel waited for the stone-skin to fall.

But he didn't fall. Instead he took a step back and righted himself.

Then giggled.

He tugged the knives free and tossed them onto the floor. Where his eye had been was now a hole in raw pink flesh, leaking gray fluids. *But no blood.* He placed a finger in the hole and wiggled it around. Was this the point where Amerel was supposed to clap and ask how it was done? She watched the hole close, the skin drawing up around a new eye that formed where the old one had been. Scarface rolled the eye to test it, then sent his other orb turning the opposite way. His chest wound had healed too, leaving just a tear in his shirt where the knife had struck.

Noon hissed through his teeth. "What is he?" he asked Amerel.

She'd been pondering the same question. A necromancer of singular power might have survived his wounds, but death-magic didn't explain the portcullis, or the sense of incongruity Amerel got just from looking at the man. Then a memory came to her of her time in Kal three years ago, sipping ganja around a fire of bones and talking to the soulcaster Thorl. He'd told her of a peasant girl in a village in the White Mountains. A girl with a rare ability who had unwittingly killed her parents after an argument over something no less trivial than the way she wore her hair. Killed them in her sleep. Amerel had thought the tale fanciful at the time, but now . . .

"A dreamweaver," she said to Noon, watching Scarface's reaction for confirmation. "A man who can make his dreams manifest in the waking world."

The Augeran sketched a bow. "Hex is my name," he said in heavily accented common tongue. A hollow note to his tone signified his voice was being projected from somewhere else. *A sending.* "But please, no need for you to introduce yourselves. I already know all about you from our friend Talet here. Hee hee!"

Noon looked at Amerel. "You're telling me we're in his *dream*?" He glanced about the room. "So how come I can still see this house?"

"Because his dream doesn't replace our reality, it overlaps it. Here, we are subject to both."

Noon gestured to the portcullis blocking the doorway behind. "This is real?"

It was Hex who answered. "Quite real, I assure you. You wish to put it to the test? Please, be my guest."

Noon wasted no time striding to the gate. Crouching, he took a grip on the lowest horizontal bar and *lifted*. The portcullis did not budge. Veins stood out in the Breaker's neck as he tried again. Still no movement. Amerel was tempted to add her efforts to his, but Hex wouldn't have invited them to try if there had been any hope of succeeding.

The stone-skin hopped from one foot to the other. "Sooner lift the Dragon Gate than that barrier, poor fools. We're in my dream, yes, and here *I* make the rules."

Not *all* the rules, Amerel knew. Fragments of her conversation with Thorl were coming back to her. Dreamweavers, the soulcaster had said, could only *add* to the material world, not take from it, so while the stone-skin could conjure up any number of gates to cage her with, he could not make the floor disappear, or vanish the ceiling to expose her to the elements. How that might help, she did not know. But learning the rules governing Hex's power was a necessary first step to breaking them.

Even before that, though, she needed to determine how far the stone-skin's dreamworld extended. Escape that world, and she would escape his influence. She looked toward the floor-to-ceiling windows behind him. A pity she hadn't thought to make a break for them when Noon let fly with his knives, but an opportunity might yet present itself—

Three more portcullises dropped down across the windows, striking the floor with a *crack, crack, crack* that Amerel felt through her sandals.

Hex grinned.

My, aren't we pleased with ourselves.

She needed to buy herself time to think, so she pointed at Talet's corpse and said, "If he told you who we are, he must have told you it was us who shot your commander. So why can I hear bells ringing? Why are you attacking the city?"

The stone-skin lifted Talet's corpse from its chair as if it weighed no more than a scarecrow. Putting one arm behind the spy's back, he grabbed one hand and struck a pose like they were dancing partners. "Why not?"

"You must have thought Dresk could be of use to you, else you wouldn't have approached him in the first place."

Hex led Talet twirling about the room. The spy's lolling head bounced off his shoulder. "*Thought* he could, yes. Then we met him. What use is an ally who can't even protect us in his own fortress?"

"More use than an enemy, surely."

"But an enemy for how long? Listen!"

Through the doorway at Amerel's back, she could hear the tolling of bells together with the thrum and clamor of a population fleeing. Then above that, she caught a distant ring of steel on steel, a muted scream. The attack was already under way! But how could that be? The bells should have meant the stone-skins were in the outer isles. How could they have made it here so fast?

Hex nodded. "Right now Dresk is discovering his precious warning system is not all that he said. Within a few bells, this city will be ours, and the warlord and his clan either scattered or dead. Hee hee!"

"And when the other tribes unite against you?"

Hex gave her a hurt look. "Please. I may be a stranger here, but even *I* know the clans are as fractured as the lands under their sway. And when we recover our gold, we'll have twenty thousand reasons to keep it that way."

Amerel frowned. She'd probed Hex's thoughts with her Will—the gentlest touch so as not to draw his attention—and found his mind too strong for all but the most inconsequential manipulation. "So, with Dresk gone, you can pick the other clans off one at a time? Is that your plan? Or do you just want to make sure they don't interfere when you attack Erin Elal?"

Hex smiled a sly smile, then changed his jaunty step to a more sedate affair.

"Why come all this way to pick a fight with us?" Amerel pressed. "According to our texts, it was you who attacked us all those years ago. What reason did we give you to come back for more?"

"You really don't know?"

"You sent a delegation to Dresk, why not to Avallon? You've given us no threats, no demands. What do you *want*?"

The scarred man ignored the question. "It seems we both have much to relearn about the other." He halted his dance and released Talet's corpse. It crumpled to the floor. "In Dresk's fortress, I detected your power, yet didn't recognize it for a Guardian's. Were it not for your dreams—"

"My dreams?" Amerel cut in.

"Of course, your dreams—so much like my own." A wave of Hex's hand, and the light in the room started to fade. The windows clouded over with grime. Speckled shadows spread like mold across the floor. "I can share others' dreams without their knowledge, you see. Or sometimes *with* their knowledge, if that is my decree. Rarely, though, are someone's dreams so strong that they leak into their waking hours." He studied her. "And the cause of this . . . a Deliverer's powers?" Behind him, the desk and chair became blackened and warped, and the gates over the windows darkened to rust as if a century had passed in the space of a few heartbeats.

Amerel held his gaze. The freak thought he was in control here, but it wouldn't take much to rob him of that illusion. Somewhere nearby he was sleeping, and the surest way to bring this nightmare to an end was to wake him from that slumber.

How was she supposed to locate his body, though, if she hadn't found it earlier when she spirit-walked?

Gray-white slime leaked from the cracks in the walls, like brain matter from a cleft in a skull. The different trails joined before spreading outward to cover the walls in a gelatinous membrane that pulsed like a diseased womb. A hum reached Amerel's ears, rising in pitch as needleflies drifted out from pocks in the flesh.

Hex cocked his head. "Whatever did you do to earn a Deliverer's regard?"

Again Amerel kept her silence. She thought about Noon's sorcerous globes. A firestorm or an earthquake unleashed within the confines of this room might give Hex a rude awakening. But would one of her Will-shields protect her from the blast? Plus what guarantee did she have that the stone-skin was sleeping in this house and not in a neighboring one?

The dreamweaver considered her before shrugging. "Keep your secrets, then. For now. In truth, the cause for the deed concerns me not, but rather the problem the Deliverer's meddling begot. You see, he has left me with something of a challenge. Namely to think of a way to kill you that you have not already suffered. Hee hee!"

As the room continued to transform, Amerel felt an unfamiliar tickle at the back of her throat. Was this fear? It was so long since she'd experienced the sensation she barely recognized it.

Hex said, "But hark at me, chattering on when it should be you doing the talking."

"Talking?" Amerel said. "About what?"

"Oh, troop numbers and dispositions, the emperor's favorite color. I'm sure you'll think of something. The answers are of less interest to me than how long you are able to resist giving them."

Bulges formed behind the rubbery walls, and the membranes split in sprays of gray muck to reveal a wooden torture rack, a butcher's hook crusted with hair and dried blood, a winch and pulley linked by chains to—

Amerel tore her gaze away.

"Do you recognize this one?" Hex said, indicating a brass sarcophagus mounted on the wall. "The victim is locked inside and a fire lit below. In a matter of moments, the metal is aglow." He sniffed the air. "Is that the aroma of its last occupant I smell?"

Dark memories leapt unbidden into Amerel's mind. "If these things

are meant to spook me, you forget, I've already seen them in the Deliverer's dreams."

"And because you've known pain before, you do not fear it now? If
that were so, you would have welcomed your dreams, not hidden from
them." A man's screams started up, along with the clanking of chains.
The dreamweaver's expression turned thoughtful. "Too much, yes?
An overexuberant hand, and fear can quickly descend into farce."

A whisper of steel sounded as Noon drew his swords. Fear made
his voice sound brittle. "I've heard enough."

"Boring you, am I?" The dreamweaver's eyes glittered. "You should
have said. Pray, let me try you with this instead."

On the wall to Amerel's left, a swelling like a boil formed. It grew
from the size of a man's head until it filled half the wall. Then it burst,
and from it erupted . . .

Amerel's heart thundered in her chest.

Spiders.

Hundreds of them.

Galantas was being hunted. Each time he looked over his shoulder
he saw amid the crowds splashes of red from the cloaks of the chasing Honored. For the past quarter-bell he'd taken a winding course
through the Rat District in an attempt to throw off his pursuers,
yet they clung to his trail like dogs on a scent. If anything, they appeared to be closing the gap. They must have recognized him, and
that meant there'd be no shaking them off. After Dresk, Galantas
would be the scalp the Augerans prized the most. And to think he'd
always considered notoriety to be a good thing.

This would never have happened if he'd fled inland. Odds were, the
stone-skins didn't have the numbers to press the attack beyond
Bezzle's borders, but Galantas couldn't risk trapping himself on the
island. Word of the Augeran raid would spread across the Isles. Tonight, the clan leaders would meet at the Hub to consider their response, and Galantas intended to be there. All he had to do was find a
boat. That was why he was heading north through the city toward a
strip of beach known as the Drift. At this time of day a handful of
fishing boats were usually drawn up on the sand, just waiting to be
borrowed.

The problem was, half of Bezzle seemed to have had the same idea.

Most of the folk abroad were running in the same direction that he was, and there were only so many heels you could trip before people started noticing. He passed two men carrying a sideboard between them, and they stopped to point and swear at him like it was his fault the stone-skins were attacking. He lurched past, his breath sawing in his throat. Maybe he wasn't as fit as he could be, but he'd been trying to cut down on this running-for-his-life business.

Nearly there now. Galantas could see the sea ahead. The flagstones gave way to a dirt track, then to sand. At the top of a dune, he looked down onto the Drift—

And stuttered to a halt, cursing.

The boats were gone. He could make out grooves where their keels had been dragged to the water. On the glittering sweep of the bay, he counted eight boats. All were crammed to the gunwales with Bezzlians. In the shallows a handful of folk watched the craft retreat as if they'd come to see off loved ones, while around them bobbed half a dozen corpses of people who had fought and failed to claim a place on the boats. The water about them was tinged red. The sharks would be here soon, if they weren't already.

Galantas shaded his eyes and focused on the craft nearest to shore—a small fishing boat with a mast and oars. There were so many people on board it was a wonder it could float, and in the span of Galantas's gaze he saw a wave strike the bow and unseat a man perched on the rail. As he toppled backward into the water, he grabbed one of the oars in an effort to stop himself being left behind. Angry shouts sounded as the boat slewed around.

That gave Galantas an idea.

He staggered down the face of the dune. The beach was littered with nets and scraps of wood, like detritus washed up from a shipwreck. As Galantas approached the surf, waterlogged sand sucked at his feet. He waded out until the waves reached his waist. Only then did he pause to look back the way he had come. There was no sign of his Augeran pursuers, but Qinta and Barnick were just a few paces behind. They were both panting. As Barnick reached Galantas, he shot him a look. They both knew what had to be done. Maybe Galantas should have spent longer agonizing over the choice, but he'd worry about massaging his conscience when he was safe and dry.

"Do it," he said to Barnick. Then he gestured to the folk in the shallows. "Just give me a chance first to swim clear of this rabble."

Barnick nodded.

Galantas dived into the waves. His shirt was soaked through with sweat, and the sea felt blessedly cool after the heat of the chase. It wasn't easy swimming with one arm. Even with all the practice he'd had over the years, he kept rolling onto his side. The waves seemed to drag him back to shore faster than he could swim away from it. After a few dozen strokes he was done, and he started treading water. Over the crests of the breakers he saw snatches of the boat that was his target, its oars rising and falling in bright showers of spray. It was pulling away from him. His goal had never been to catch up to the craft, though. All he'd wanted was to put some distance between himself and the people on shore.

Qinta and Barnick drew up beside him. He looked once more at the boat.

"Now!" he said to Barnick.

Beneath the hull the sea swelled, and the craft was lifted into the air. It tipped to one side, pitching its passengers shrieking into the water—all except a bare-chested man who managed to grab the boat's mast with one hand. For a count of five he hung on, feet kicking. Then he lost his grip and fell onto the head of a woman just resurfacing. The now-empty boat settled on the sea and went shooting off on a wave of water-magic before its former passengers could climb back on board.

It reached Galantas in moments. As it approached, the wave beneath it receded, but its momentum still carried it into him. It bumped against him gently like a horse nuzzling its master. He wrapped his arm over the gunwale, too tired to clamber inside.

Qinta was first over the rail. He hauled Galantas dripping into the bow.

The boat rocked beneath them.

Shouts came from the bay and the shore. Swimmers thrashed toward them from both directions, yet none would get to them in time. A lone sandal lay in the bow. Qinta tossed it over the side just as Barnick scrambled aboard, his hair plastered across his face. The oars were still in their rowlocks, and Galantas pulled them free and stowed them in the bottom of the boat.

"Let's go," he said to Barnick.

The craft sped off on a curling course that took it wide of the swimmers in the bay.

Screams from the beach marked the arrival of the Augerans who had been hunting Galantas. Finding their quarry flown, they took out their frustrations on the unfortunates left behind, and a similar fate no doubt awaited the erstwhile passengers of this boat. If they had known of the danger Galantas was facing, though, they would have been more than willing to lay down their lives for him. And if they weren't, they damned well should have been. He *was* their lord now, after all.

Or soon would be.

He swung his gaze to the Old Town. The gates of Dresk's fortress had been shut, and a handful of guards manned the walls. Was Dresk still inside? Almost certainly, since the fool couldn't leave his gold behind any more than he could take it with him. Galantas pursed his lips. Strange. He'd been waiting for this day for as long as he could remember, yet instead of feeling triumph, he found himself wondering what his father was doing. Sitting in the Great Hall, perhaps, sensing the stone-skin noose tightening about him? Or looking out over the bay from the battlements, wishing he were in Galantas's boat?

For an absurd moment, Galantas wanted to turn the craft about and go back for him. But even if he could have rescued his father, that would only have brought more shame on the man. Galantas steeled himself. This was the father who had turned Galantas's brother against him. Who had dishonored the memory of Galantas's mother—his own wife—by spreading rumors of her infidelity so he could cast doubt on Galantas's birthright. Galantas should have let him die all those years ago in the Raptor raid. It would have been better for both of them.

He looked toward the harbor. Four Augeran ships bobbed at quayside amid the dozens of Rubyholt vessels. Among them was the *Eternal,* its metal hull gleaming in the sunlight. The waterfront was patrolled by red- and black-cloaked figures, and Galantas's expression darkened. Hundreds of Islanders would die today, but it was the loss of the ships that most troubled him—

"We got trouble," Qinta said, pointing.

A short distance to the south, a two-masted Augeran galleon rode on a wave of water-magic. As it neared the islets at the mouth of the harbor, it picked up speed.

It was coming straight for them.

Karmel slowed as she approached the corner around which the Augeran squad had disappeared. In all the time she and Caval had been following, the soldiers had yet to check their backtrail. That was no excuse for carelessness on the Chameleons' part, though, for one slip-up could cost them their lives. Caval swung wide to give himself a view along the street in case the stone-skins waited in ambush. But the enemy were already forty paces distant, and lengthening the gap with every heartbeat.

The Chameleons ran after them.

The Augerans had an enviable ability to sweep the roads clear of trouble. Two streets back they'd encountered a group of armed Rubyholters twice their size, but upon seeing the invaders, the Islanders had melted away like mist in the sun. Nor did the stone-skins seem interested in engaging the locals who crossed their path. They were heading for the fortress, Karmel suspected—now visible in glimpses over the rooftops to the north.

Ahead the street opened out, and stalls with striped awnings came into view. The Old Market. One of the landmarks on Mazana's map. The place looked like the Furies had swept through it. Fish-bone charms and pieces of broken pottery were scattered all about. Looters fought with stallholders for things they wouldn't want tomorrow and in some cases could barely carry now. A man staggered along with a rolled carpet on each shoulder, their ends sagging down to brush the ground. He passed two women wrestling over a ceramic pot while a bawling baby lay forgotten beside them. A man carrying an armful of sandfruits upended a spice stall. Baskets of spices fell to the ground, throwing up clouds of colorful dust.

The stone-skins ran through the wreckage, leaving footprints in the powder.

"This way," Caval said, heading toward an alley to the west.

The Chameleons entered a passage choked with rubbish. Karmel had to hurdle a section of road where the flagstones had crumbled to reveal the broken pipes of some decaying drainage system. The clamor of the city filled her ears—shrieks and groans, pleas for help or mercy. Beyond the next junction half a dozen men were fighting, no sides apparent. Karmel wondered if they even knew themselves who they battled, or why. A woman wielding a saber drove her weapon into a man's midriff. She looked around as the Chameleons approached and bellowed at them to stop, even stumbled a pace toward them, but Karmel and Caval skidded round a corner and away.

Buildings of blue-veined stone flashed past to either side. Caval kept looking back at Karmel as if he thought she might slip away, and a part of her wanted nothing more than to find a place where she could sit down and cover her ears. Mazana Creed had warned her, though, that there'd be no hiding from what was coming to Bezzle. And so Karmel let herself be tugged along by her brother's shadow, no idea where she was going anymore, just concentrating on sucking in each breath while the world slipped into the Abyss around her.

A left turn, and another, and another. Were they going in circles now? People ran in every direction, seemingly as lost as Karmel herself. Then abruptly Caval slowed, his arms coming out to shield Karmel from whatever lay ahead. Stone-skins? No, when the priestess looked past she saw only two Rubyholters, a woman pushed face-first against a wall, a man behind her with one arm round her throat, smiling a cutthroat smile. The woman had gone for a knife at her hip, but the man's free hand gripped her wrist to stop her from drawing it.

It was the same way Veran had held Karmel in that cave below Dian.

Something snapped in the priestess, and her anger came boiling up. She didn't know she'd been storing it inside, but it broke upon her now like a wave that had burst its dam. She pushed past Caval, her sword raised. Someone was shouting, could have been her. The man half turned. His eyes showed irritation at first, then widened in alarm. He released the woman, stepped back, and lifted his hands.

"Now, wait up there."

Karmel's sword slashed through his hands and cut into his face, tore his cheek open and smashed the bone beneath. Blood spattered the wall behind. The man went down with a shriek. The priestess stood over him, her sword poised to deliver a mortal stroke. He'd landed on his side, the flesh of his cheek flapping where she'd opened it from mouth to ear. Beneath, his teeth had been smashed to stumps. A severed finger with a wedding band lay in the pool of blood spreading about his head.

Karmel retched up bile. Her legs were weak, and she might have sat down in the alley if Caval hadn't seized her arm. The Rubyholt woman cowered against the wall, her face covered with blood, sobbing hysterically. She wouldn't meet Karmel's gaze. Probably thought the priestess meant to carve her up next, and Karmel's rage burned all the hotter. *You're welcome!* she wanted to shout, but she couldn't form the words.

Caval steered her away.

As the spiders poured from the wall, Noon gave a strangled curse and reached for one of the sorcerous globes in his belt-pouch.

Amerel seized his arm. "No," she said, "you'll kill us too."

Noon didn't answer. She wasn't even sure he'd heard her.

"No!" she said again, sharp enough to make him flinch. Then she gathered her Will and lashed out at the spiders. The air concussed amid the onrushing black tide, sending scores of broken creatures spinning into the air.

Still they came. Of course they did, this was Hex's dream—no matter how many Amerel killed, he could always make more.

Hex sighed. "Yes, I know, spiders are terribly unimaginative. I promise you my next creations will be more inventive. Hee hee!"

Noon tore free of Amerel's grasp and looked about with wild eyes. But there was nowhere to run. He sheathed his swords and drew a throwing knife before hurling it at one of the larger spiders. And some of the creatures were big enough to take a knife, too—huge black things with white on their backs like a dusting of snow.

"Fear not," Hex said, "their bite isn't poisonous."

Amerel did not doubt it. The dreamweaver had said he intended to question her and Noon, so he wasn't going to kill them so early in the game. What to do, though? Climb onto the desk? That would only delay the inevitable. Spin a Will-shield about herself to keep the spiders at bay? Hex would simply make the creatures rise from the floor instead, or conjure them up inside her barrier. No, better to meet his challenge head-on. Better to use what little time she had left to prepare herself. She set her jaw. This wouldn't be the first time she'd had to endure something like this. The Deliverer had liked spiders too, she recalled. Didn't everyone?

In her peripheral vision, she saw Noon drop to his knees and curl into a ball, thumbs pressed over his ears, hands covering his eyes and nose.

Amerel took a breath and let it out slowly. Her pulse was trying to run away from her, but she reined it in. There were a dozen different exercises the Guardians used to heighten their concentration. The one she had in mind, though, worked by blocking out the world around her. Focus was a hard thing to find with the wave of spiders rolling closer, yet force of habit saved her, and one by one the perceptions of her senses melted away: the dryness in her throat, the sweat on her brow, the knot in her stomach.

The spiders engulfed Noon, and he disappeared from view. The creatures had also reached Hex. The stone-skin could have disappeared himself if he'd wanted to, but instead he remained motionless as the spiders scuttled up his legs. He giggled like he was being tickled.

Amerel closed her eyes.

Even through her sensory detachment, she felt a whisper of movement on the tops of her feet as the first spiders reached her. She needed something else to think about, and what better way to distract herself than to consider how she was going to get out of here? Her first instinct was to use her Will to strike at Hex in the hope she might cause his dream to waver, but there seemed little chance of that if even a knife in his eye hadn't broken his concentration. The stone-skin was no more than a sending—a phantasm—and it was the conscious will *behind* that image she needed to target. Yet she still had no idea where Hex's body was sleeping. Somewhere close, no doubt, but did she have time to go looking?

No, better to target the dream than the man who'd fashioned it. She couldn't lift the portcullis behind her, couldn't shatter the metal from which it was forged, but perhaps she could interrupt the flow of power sustaining it. If she focused a Will-strike to the gate, she might be able to punch through. Reach the yard beyond, and she would escape his clutches. The dreamworld couldn't exist there too, else Hex would have sprung his trap the moment Amerel entered it on arriving.

Her hair stirred as a spider crawled across her head. *Ignore it.* She'd closed her mouth to keep the creatures out, but when she tried to breathe through her nose, she found one nostril half blocked by something inside. A wave of revulsion swept through her, a shudder that started at the tips of her toes—

Then suddenly the obstruction was gone, and she sensed a change come over her body: the release of a weight she'd barely noticed before; an abrupt silence where previously there had been a half-perceived rustle of tiny legs. Her skin tingled with the memory of the spiders, but the creatures themselves were . . . gone?

Unless that was just what Hex wanted her to think.

She opened her eyes. The room had grown darker, and she had to squint now to see the dreamweaver, still watching her, still smiling.

Yes, the spiders were gone.

A burst of relief made her shoulders sag, but she couldn't afford to lower her guard. If she didn't escape, those spiders would mark not the end of her ordeal but the beginning. And Amerel had no wish to see what horrors Hex summoned next from the throbbing walls. Now was the time to strike. She gathered her power, felt it swell within her like a long-drawn breath. To her left, Noon remained curled in a ball.

"Get up," she said to him. She couldn't tell him what she planned to do without alerting Hex, but if the Breaker was to escape with her, he needed to be ready to move.

He paid her no mind.

"Get up!" she said again. One chance she would give him to pull himself together. One chance, and even that seemed a mercy she could ill afford.

Hex spoke. "You control your fear well," he said to Amerel. "But not all fears are of the flesh. Take our friend Talet here." He pointed to the spy's corpse, and it rose in a series of jerky motions. "His greatest fear was for his son, but I made him betray the boy before the end. Can you imagine that? Giving up the person you care for most? Cursing yourself with your final breath? His mind broke long before his body did."

Fascinating stuff. What did Hex think Amerel was going to do, vow to avenge the spy? She should thank him rather for sparing her the task of killing the man.

Noon finally stirred. He rose on shaky legs, his expression as grim as their setting. It looked like Amerel wouldn't be the only one having bad dreams for a while.

"Now that those spiders are out of the way," Hex said, "we can move on to something with more . . . bite." He gestured to the torture implements lining one wall. "You may need some assistance taking your place in the more elaborate devices, but fear not, help is at hand. Hee hee!"

The walls bulged again, and figures started to squirm from the slime. First to emerge was a girl missing both feet, and she tottered toward Amerel with stilted steps. Behind her came a man with weeping red arms, the flesh peeled back to reveal the workings of the muscles. Talet, meanwhile, advanced on the Guardian with a knife in his hand. Her mouth twitched. Here was irony. She'd come to this place to kill the man, yet *he* could end up killing *her*.

"Who's first?" Hex asked. "No pushing, please."

Amerel edged back. A dozen freaks had now been . . . birthed from the walls, with more appearing each moment. The Guardian half turned toward the portcullis. Beyond, the yard remained empty of stone-skins, but there could have been a legion out there and she would still have chosen their company over Hex's.

No more putting this off. She needed to hit this with everything she had.

She struck at the portcullis with her Will. The gate and the wall around it rippled like they were naught but reflections in a pool. Then the center of the portcullis melted to leave a circle of brightness an armspan across, the bars immediately around it half translucent. Only an armspan? Amerel had hoped for something bigger, but Hex was already throwing his will in opposition to hers. The gap began to close.

She sprang forward.

The opening was too small to simply jump through, so she dived headfirst, felt a faint resistance like she was plunging through cobwebs. Then her feet clipped the bars at the bottom of the hole. Her dive became a sprawl. She stung her palms on the gravel in the yard, slipped as she sought to rise, then scrabbled forward on all fours to make way for Noon behind. The sounds of fighting in the city were suddenly loud and disconcertingly close. Regaining her feet, Amerel turned about so quickly she almost spun herself from her feet.

Noon had only just reached the portcullis. Still holding his swords, he flung himself through the hole. But the opening had nearly shut. His feet caught on the gate as Amerel's had done, his upper body pitching forward and down. Before he could pull his legs clear, the bars closed on them. Amerel thought the metal would sheer through his ankles. Instead it held him pinned. The sight of him was almost comical—face in the gravel, legs up in the air behind. But Noon wasn't laughing as he writhed and bucked and kicked. He released his swords, fingers scrabbling at the ground for something to grip.

"Help me!"

Amerel hesitated. Hex's dreamworld was expanding into the yard, the mold and the shadows spilling out from the study.

"Help me!" Noon screamed again.

He'd stopped calling her Princess, she noticed.

Amerel looked at him. One chance, she'd told herself, and hadn't she given him that? It wasn't her fault if he'd been slow to trail her through the opening. To her right a black flash seared the sky, and it was followed by the *whump* of a sorcerous explosion, the patter and groan of a building collapsing. Running feet sounded from along the street. Stone-skins on their way to Dresk's fortress, most likely, but it wouldn't require much of a detour to call on this place. Amerel stood a better chance of escaping if she left now. And if Hex had Noon to answer his questions, maybe he wouldn't feel the need to come looking for her afterward.

It was the right thing to do; even the Breaker couldn't deny it.

Her gaze locked to Noon's. She could see in his eyes that he'd read her intent. There was no pleading, no cursing—he just stared at her. She'd miss him, of course, but she could always find someone else to mock her and question her every action.

Behind, Hex's dreamworld edged closer, threads of sorcery creeping into the yard like tendrils of knotweed.

Scowling, Amerel struck at the portcullis with her Will. Hex must have anticipated the move, for the resistance she met was stronger than before. She didn't need to create a hole as large as the last one, though, just some wriggle room for Noon to pry himself loose. His left leg came free, the right twisted but held. The Breaker screamed his frustration. He flipped onto his back, braced his free foot against the door frame, and pushed.

Nothing.

Amerel tensed to hit the gate again.

No need. A final yank, and Noon's foot pulled out of his boot. He kicked like an upturned beetle, then rolled and staggered upright. He didn't thank her. He didn't even look at her, just gazed at the boot caught in the portcullis as if he was minded to try and retrieve it.

"Leave it!" Amerel said, not quite believing he had to be told.

The Breaker frowned.

Another magical detonation set the doors and windows rattling, but at least it had come from farther away than the previous one. Evidently the fight had passed the house by—

A sword scraped free of its scabbard.

Amerel swung round to see four stone-skins, all men, standing on the opposite side of the courtyard. One of them had no armor—a mage, probably. All wore red cloaks and the relaxed expressions of warriors who had never tasted defeat. As Amerel studied them, she shook her head in disgust. If she'd left when she had the chance, she might have avoided them. This was what she got for helping Noon. Offer your hand to someone hanging from a cliff, and more often than not they dragged you over the side with them.

She drew her sword. Beside her Noon was hopping about on one foot, pulling off his remaining boot. What, was he going to throw it at the stone-skins? The enemy held their ground. All they had to do was stop Amerel and Noon escaping until Hex's dreamworld expanded into the courtyard.

The Guardian wasn't going to let that happen.

She advanced.

Behind the Augerans, the shadows to either side of the doorway came to life. Two blurred figures—a man and a woman—materialized, steel glinting in their hands. The stone-skins didn't have time to turn. Four throwing knives and as many heartbeats later, the Augerans were on the ground leaking blood to the gravel.

Amerel stared.

Chameleons. A brother and sister too, judging by the shared square jaw. No one she recognized, but they clearly knew her to have come to her rescue. And that made her cautious. She looked between the strangers, waiting for one to speak. It was unlikely they'd killed the stone-skins just to turn on Amerel next—but no less unlikely than them coming to help her in the first place.

A pause, then the female Chameleon said, "Follow us."

A bolt of sorcery from the pursuing Augeran ship struck the sea to Galantas's right. The waves blackened before dissolving to dust.

Water crashed into the hollow left behind, with nothing to show where the magic had struck save a patch of hissing foam.

That had been too close for comfort.

The smaller size and greater maneuverability of Galantas's boat should have given him the advantage in the race against his hunters, but it seemed Barnick's counterpart on the stone-skin vessel held the edge in the ways of water-magic, for over the course of the past quarter-bell the Augeran ship had been steadily closing on them. Galantas was running out of options. Captown and Feng were too far away to reach. Abandoning the boat on some beach and fleeing inland would serve only to trap him as surely as if he'd stayed in Bezzle. And while it would be easy to shake off his pursuers in the maze of waterways that made up the Shoals, with the clan leaders due to meet there at the Hub this evening, Galantas didn't want to prompt a manhunt that might lead to the cancellation of the gathering.

Fortunately, there were lots of places around the Isles where a small boat could lure a larger vessel into peril. One was close enough that he might reach it before those bolts of sorcery reached him.

The Dragon's Boneyard.

Galantas smiled. If the stone-skins were intent on following him, it seemed only fair that he show them the best sights.

Barnick steered the boat north toward an opening between two cliffs, hugging the inside bend of a curve. The channel narrowed. Ahead the ivory-colored ribs of a dragon rose from the water. Three years ago, Galantas had seen that creature die—or rather heard it. He'd been standing on the cliff at Hangman's Drop after midnight. He remembered a weight of darkness below him, nothing but glints of moonlight off the dragon's armor. When it was ambushed by the monster that nested in the Dragon's Boneyard, its first trumpeting had suggested outrage at its attacker's audacity. But that trumpeting had quickly turned to squeals as it was overpowered and dragged beneath the waves. Next morning Galantas had seen one of the dragon's scales at the foot of the bluff. He'd always believed the creatures' armor to be impenetrable, yet the plate had been mangled like some hedge knight's shield.

Galantas had come this way only once before—in the Thousand Islands Race three years ago. The race followed a course that crossed the territories of all eight clans. It was hotly contested by the best sailors in the Isles, and the Dragon's Boneyard had offered Galantas a shortcut that promised victory. Barnick, as a water-mage, had been able to negotiate the channel in relative safety, so in the days before the race he had spent bells mapping out the contours of the strait together with the flooded ruins under the surface. That information had enabled Galantas to devise a plan to get them through the waterway and past the creature that dwelled there. In the race, he and Barnick had barely escaped with their lives. It had been worth it, though, to see the look on Dresk's face when he handed over the winner's purse.

Galantas had never imagined he'd have to come this way again. And three years ago he had been sailing in a boat specially adapted for the route he would take. If he wanted to follow the same path now, he'd need to make some modifications to the craft he was traveling in.

"Qinta!" he said. "Get the mast down! Use your sword."

Qinta had the sense not to question him. He clambered upright and drew his blade. Setting his feet, he delivered a crunching stroke to the mast at waist height. The weapon caught in the wood. He waggled it free.

"Faster!" Galantas said, and Qinta started chopping over and over at the mast, splinters flying, until he'd hacked out a sizeable groove. Then he resheathed his sword and put his shoulder to the wood, hit it once, twice, three times. It creaked and finally snapped and toppled. Galantas cut the lines attaching it to the sail and heaved the lot over the side.

The channel had now narrowed to the length of three ships. In the water ahead were threads of what appeared to be fireweed, but Galantas knew them to be the strands of a vast underwater web spun by the creature that dwelled there—the Weaver, it had come to be called, after the spiders of the same name that infested Bezzle's underground aqueduct. Its lair was at the foot of the southern heights, so Barnick steered the boat toward the cliff on the north side. As he did so, he let the wave beneath the craft recede. The slower pace would allow the stone-skins to get closer, but it would also reduce the Islanders' chances of catching the Weaver's eye.

The water seemed unnaturally still. Beneath the surface, Galantas could make out two towers that might once have guarded a road between the cliffs. To the west, the skeletons of four more dragons jutted from the water, while at the base of the southern bluff was a patch of shimmering blackness that marked the portal between this world and whatever hellhole the Weaver called home. As the boat drew level, Galantas held his breath. These were the critical moments, he knew. If the beast remained in its lair until the stone-skins arrived, its attention would surely be drawn to the larger ship.

Assuming it wasn't already lying in wait somewhere ahead.

Time crawled. The channel was in shadow, and the air had an unmistakable chill to it. Qinta frowned at a flock of starbeaks overhead, but when he opened his mouth to explain the birds' import, Galantas forestalled him with a raised finger. The boat crept forward. In keeping close to the northern cliffs, Barnick was forced to take the craft through the partly submerged rib cage of one of the dragons. Each bone was as thick as the trunk of a ketar tree. The boat was traveling toward the head of the creature, and as it cleared the chest cavity, Galantas glanced down to locate the beast's skull in the water.

Only to find it was missing, the bones of the neck bitten through.

Suppressing a shudder, he looked back the way they had come. The Augerans were still following, but the wave of water-magic under their vessel had subsided just as Barnick's had. They couldn't know what awaited them in the channel, yet the warning in the dragons' bones was clear. One set would have been a curiosity, two, a coincidence. Five, though . . .

The Augerans' caution was understandable, but it stood to play into Galantas's hands, because the lower their ship rode in the water, the greater the chance that their keel would tangle in the Weaver's threads.

Nearly there.

"Galantas!" Qinta said, pointing toward the rent.

His heart skipped a beat. Something moved in the darkness, spreading through the water like a bruise. Coming for Galantas's boat? The stone-skins couldn't be the Weaver's target because their ship hadn't yet entered the strait. Nor was that likely to change if they had seen the creature too.

Time to be going.

"Barnick!" Galantas yelled. "Go, go, go!"

CHAPTER 12

EBON WATCHED the boy pause in the shadow of the Mercerien ship's windowed stern. Dressed in three-quarter trousers and a shirt that looked like a sack with holes cut for arms, he took a stone from a bulging pocket and sent it looping over the rail. It landed with a clatter on deck. Another stone followed, then another. The third one drew a shout from a sailor on board, but no one appeared at the rail to investigate the source.

Just because Ebon had arranged access to the Upper City through Tia didn't mean he couldn't explore other options too. Gunnar had recently returned from scouting the entrance to Gilgamar from the direction of Dian. Alas, the guards stationed at the East Gate had refused to let him pass. Vale had received the same message at the Canal Gate. Not everyone was being turned back, though. A bell ago, Ebon had seen a party of gray-cloaked warriors and some metal-skinned giant enter the Upper City. He'd been tempted to tag along in the hope he would be mistaken for one of the group, but he'd hesitated at the crucial moment, and the chance had gone.

Tia it was, then.

Before he entered the Upper City, though, he needed to find out as much as he could about the circumstances in which Rendale and Lamella were being held. To do that, he needed to lure one of Ocarn's lieutenants down to the port. And so earlier Gunnar had posed as a sailor, and paid a guard at the Harbor Gate to take a message to the Mercerien embassy. That message had alleged a fatal dispute between two of Ocarn's crew. Ebon hoped that Ocarn would send someone to knock heads together, thereby allowing Ebon to snatch and interrogate the man. After three bells, though, there was still no sign of any visitor. With the afternoon drawing on, Ebon had decided to cut his losses and try instead to question a member of the Mercerien ship's crew.

Which was why he was standing here now, watching a boy in his pay throw stones at the vessel in an effort to lure a sailor onto the waterfront.

A bearded head finally appeared at the rail. The boy's next throw was inspired, skimming off the top of the man's skull. The sailor reeled back, clutching his head and screaming at the boy. Ebon couldn't understand the words because they were spoken in Mercerien, but he doubted the man was complimenting his tormentor on the accuracy of his throw.

Another stone sailed over the sailor's shoulder.

He stepped back from the rail.

Ebon wet his lips with his tongue. Ten heartbeats passed. Twenty. What would the sailor do next? Head belowdecks out of reach of the missiles? Throw the stones back at the boy?

Then a rattling clatter sounded as the gangplank crashed onto the quay.

As the bearded sailor crossed it, Ebon heard the force of his rage in the weight of his steps. The boy had seen his danger and fired off a final stone before turning to flee. *Wait,* Ebon silently urged him, for if the boy disappeared too soon among the crowds, the sailor would probably return to the ship.

The prince needn't have worried, for the boy moved away at a stuttering pace, feigning a limp to keep his pursuer interested.

The sailor had reached the end of the quay. His forehead was smeared red where the stone had hit him. He set off at a sprint after the boy, arms pumping, sandals slapping, bellowing at the people in his way to clear a path.

The boy vanished along the alley where Vale waited.

Ebon headed after them. "Stay here," he said to Gunnar over his shoulder. The mage's job would be to warn them if someone else got off the ship.

Gunnar nodded.

When Ebon rounded the corner, he saw the sailor already lying in a heap next to a mud-brick building that seemed to be melting in the heat. Vale stood over him, while the boy went through his pockets. Finding nothing, the boy rose and spat on the prone man. Damned imposition that, not carrying anything for a thief to steal. Ebon looked round to see if they had attracted attention. No one seemed to have noticed anything, though. No one ever did when blood was in the air.

Ebon tossed the boy a sovereign, and he scampered off.

"Help me get him up," the prince said to Vale.

Together they hauled the sailor to his feet, then Vale hoisted him onto his shoulder. Taking a route that kept them out of sight of the Mercerien ship, they made their way along the waterfront to where their boat was tied up between a Corinian galley and a salt-rimed fishing scow. Their craft bobbed an armspan below the level of the quay, so Ebon raised it on a wave of water-magic. He stepped on board, Vale following with his load. The Endorian dumped the unconscious sailor in the prow before tying his wrists and ankles.

Moments later, Gunnar joined them. Ebon released the wave supporting the boat, and it sank down onto the water between the shifting walls of wood to either side.

"Wake him up," Ebon told Vale. He had to speak over the spatter of bilge being pumped from a hole in the hull of the Corinian galley.

Vale scooped up a double handful of greasy water from the harbor and tossed it in the sailor's face.

The man spluttered and came to.

Ebon sat on the oar bench and gave the sailor a while to register his bound hands and feet, the three grim faces staring back at him. The Mercerien sat up slowly, in no hurry to get this started.

"I have some questions," Ebon said in the common tongue. "When we're finished, my mage here"—he pointed to Gunnar, sitting behind—"will take you east along the coast so you can walk back to Gilgamar. Or he can drop you a league out to sea and find out how well you swim with your hands and feet tied. Which would be your choice?"

The sailor squinted at him like he was trying to find the trick in the question. "I don't want no trouble."

"Good. You sailed with Prince Ocarn Dasuki from Mercerie?"

A nod.

"There were two Galitians on board." Not a question.

The Mercerien's eyes narrowed further. Now he saw where this was going. Another nod.

"Who were they?" Ebon said, taking his time.

"Some dandy from Galitia. Rendale were his name. A prince, I heard, but that could o' just been the lads talking."

"And the other one?"

"A woman. Never caught her name. No tits, twisted leg. The prince's woman, they said."

The prince's woman. The words left a sour taste in Ebon's mouth, like he'd swallowed some of the dirty water from that bilge pipe. "And was she?"

"Was she what?"

"Rendale's woman. Did you see them together?"

"Sure. They came up on deck to give us a show—"

Ebon rose and struck the man a backhand blow across the face. The Mercerien's head snapped round, and he fell against the side of the boat. He ran his tongue about the inside of his mouth as if checking for loose teeth. Then he looked at Ebon with a guarded expression.

Ebon sat back down on the oar bench. A crimson line ran down from one of the sailor's nostrils, and Ebon wished he hadn't already sold his rings, else he might have left a more permanent mark. And yet the sailor couldn't have intended to taunt him. He couldn't have known who Lamella was, or what she meant to Ebon.

Couldn't have known *before.* But couldn't fail to suspect now.

The prince's woman.

Ebon forced himself to calm. Rendale would never try to steal Lamella from him, just as Lamella would never let herself be stolen. There was another explanation for the sailor's words. Rendale knew of the enmity between Ebon and Ocarn, so he would know not to reveal Lamella's identity to the Mercerien. The only way for him to keep her close without arousing suspicion was to pretend the two of them were together.

Still the idea festered.

Vale righted the sailor, then took up the questioning. "Are they both alive?" he asked the Mercerien. "Rendale and the woman?"

Ebon's breath caught. In his rage he hadn't thought to confirm that detail, just assumed.

The sailor answered with a nod, but there was enough hesitation to give Ebon pause.

"But . . . ?" he prompted.

The Mercerien tensed as if expecting another blow. "Rendale got hurt on the Hunt. Half the mizzen yard fell on him. Left a lot of blood on the boards and had to be carried below, but when we got to Gilgamar, he were able to walk down the gangplank on his own."

"And the woman? Was she hurt too?"

"Not as I saw."

Vale said, "What happened out there? On Dragon Day?"

The sailor spat a gobbet of blood over the rail. "Gate never got lowered again after it went up, that's what. Shroud-cursed dragons everywhere. Ocarn were quick to turn tail once he smelled trouble, but this gold dragon rises out of the waves dead ahead of us, as big as the *Dawnspark* herself. No time to steer round, so we rams the thing. Hurt us more than it hurt the dragon. Then the creature's tail comes whipping down on the decks, over and over like it's beating on a drum. Friend of mine got impaled by one of its tail spikes. Dragon lifted him up and mashed him down again till we was all wearing bits of him." The sailor's gaze flickered to Ebon. "That's when Rendale took his hurting. Mizzen spar broke and came down on the quarterdeck."

"How did you get away?"

"Through luck, that's how. Damned water-mage of Ocarn's couldn't conjure up a wave big enough to wash your feet. He starts us off west, but the dragon's catching up to us like we're sailing through blood honey. So Ocarn gives the order to turn south."

"South," Ebon repeated. "Toward the Dragon Gate."

"Smart move, too. 'Cause while the *Dawnspark* might have been moving slow, there was plenty of other ships moving slower. We sees this galley limping along, its oars clacking together 'cause the oarsmen are all pulling at different times. Ocarn tells the mage to take us across its bows, hoping the dragon might stop for a look. Works a treat, too. And while the creature's munching on oars, Ocarn takes us west again. Sender himself must have been watching o'er us, 'cause we didn't see another dragon in all the time it took us to reach Gilgamar."

"Dragon Day was twelve days ago," Ebon said. "Have you been stuck on the ship all that time?"

"Yeah."

"What about Ocarn?"

"Disappeared into the Upper City when we got here. Ain't seen him since."

"Disappeared where, exactly?"

"The embassy."

"And he took Rendale and the woman with him?"

The sailor nodded.

"How do you get a message to Ocarn if you need to?"

"Dunno. Ain't needed to yet."

Ebon stood up abruptly. He suspected the sailor had told them everything he knew, and the Galitians' time would now be better spent watching the *Dawnspark* in case one of Ocarn's men turned up in response to Gunnar's false message. He untied the boat and tossed the rope to the mage. "Take him along the coast toward Dian," he said. "We don't want him walking back here before we've finished our business."

Gunnar inclined his head.

A last look at the sailor. The man spat bloody drool over the side. His expression suggested he didn't know whether to believe Gunnar would set him free, and perhaps killing him would have been the most sensible course. Even if Gunnar took him as far as Dian, he might steal a horse and be back here in a couple of days. There was no guarantee Ebon would have found Rendale and Lamella by then. Why take the risk? Why put their lives in danger when tossing the man overboard now would put the matter beyond doubt? It wasn't as if anyone on the waterfront would see anything, or care if they did.

A fishing boat emerged from the Neck with a flock of screaming limewings in tow. Ebon watched it disappear behind the hull of the Corinian galley.

Then he raised the boat on a swell of water-magic and stepped back onto the quay. Vale followed him.

The boat with Gunnar and the sailor in it moved away on a wave of Gunnar's water-magic.

Ebon looked back toward the Upper City. In the shadow of a ramshackle warehouse, a group of men was gathered around a fire in a can. A pushing match was under way, and one man stumbled into the can and tipped it over. His shirt went up in flames. The other men started whooping and dancing about him as he shrieked and writhed. Then finally he thought to run for the harbor to douse himself.

"Are we doing the right thing?" Ebon asked Vale. "Waiting until night?"

"You sought out Tia's help. May as well use it now."

"And if she betrays us?"

"If she betrays us, she'll probably just keep the money and not show. We can worry about that if it happens."

"If it happens, we won't find out until tonight—after the gates to the Upper City are closed. That means we lose a night when we could have been looking for Lamella and Rendale."

Vale shrugged. "Then we hit the gates as soon as they open tomorrow morning. If I go through fast, I might be able to lead the guards away, create enough of a stir to let you slip in unseen. Or we hand out a few sovereigns, find some scum to kick up the dirt."

"Then why aren't we doing that now? If we timed it just as the gates were closing, we'd have the fading light to help cover our tracks."

"Hitting the gates ain't less risky than hoping for Tia to come good. And Rendale and Lamella ain't going to thank us if we show up with half of Gilgamar's soldiers at our backs. Your choice, though. That's the privilege of command."

"My choice, yes," Ebon said. "And the only thing I know for certain is that whichever option I choose, it'll be wrong."

Vale shrugged again. "So pick the other one."

Galantas's boat cleared the dragon's skeleton and picked up speed. Behind, the darkness in the water drew nearer. Through the froth in the boat's wake, Galantas glimpsed flutters of black that might have been tentacles. The threads of the Weaver's web trembled at the creature's passage.

Sender's blessing, it was quick.

Galantas scanned the channel ahead. To either side, the cliffs dropped straight into the sea. Too steep for climbing. There were no caves they could shelter in, no beaches offering a safe exit from the water, meaning their only hope was to outrun the beast. Quarter of a league away, the strait opened out onto choppier water. This, Galantas knew, was where the Weaver's web—and thus its territory—ended. But there was no chance of the boat reaching that point before the creature overhauled it.

Not without a detour, at least.

To get where he needed to go, he'd have to run the precise course he'd followed in the Thousand Islands Race three years ago. First he had to take a bearing on the channel's underwater ruins. There were submerged buildings beneath the waves, flashing past in a gray blur. Galantas looked for a tower that reached almost to the surface. He might have missed it but for a telltale ruffle of water where the waves broke over it.

"A point to starboard!" he said to Barnick.

The boat changed direction.

Now that the craft's course was set, Galantas needed to consider distances. He scanned the northern cliff, looking for the mark he'd made three years ago. They were approaching Hangman's Drop, and the gallows was visible atop it. Below, a handful of stunted trees clung to the cliff, their roots half exposed . . .

"There!" he shouted to Barnick, pointing. A splash of white paint a hundred armspans away.

"I see it!"

Galantas looked at Qinta. The Second had not been involved in the Hundred Islands race, so he'd have no idea what was about to happen. "Get a grip on something," Galantas said. "And make sure you take a good breath."

Eighty armspans to their target. Galantas could see the shape of the building under the water ahead.

Sixty armspans.

Galantas looked round to see the Weaver closing. Its shadow rushed toward them like the coming of night. The sea bulged with its passage.

Forty armspans.

Twenty.

Galantas hunched down in the prow and braced his legs under the oar bench. The boat drew level with the mark on the cliff. "Now!" he shouted to Barnick. Then he took a deep breath, as much air as his lungs could take.

The boat began to sink.

Most people thought water-mages could guide a craft only over the waves, but there was no reason they couldn't steer *under* them too.

The timing of this maneuver was all-important. The boat traveled much slower underwater than it did on the surface. Dive too soon, and the Weaver might catch them before they reached their destination. Leave it too late, and they might overshoot their target. The mark

on the cliff was to show where to start the descent, but with the creature so near, Galantas wondered if he should have stayed above the
surface a while longer.

The sea closed over him.

Ringing silence in his ears. The waves tugged at him, and he tightened his grasp on the gunwale. From the Weaver behind came a
clicking noise, all stretched and distorted by the water. Like a black-
craw pecking at a snail's shell. It took all Galantas's will not to look
round. His pulse was beating double time. Not good. If he wanted his
breath to last, he would have to remain calm.

Calm. Right.

The sagging black threads that made up the creature's web shook.
They looked so delicate it seemed the currents must tear them apart,
yet stuck to one was the corpse of a briar shark, long dead and half
decomposed. Barnick guided the boat past. Ahead a shadow took
form in the water. Moments later an immense domed building became
visible. Across it Galantas could see carvings of ships made from
bones—carvings identical to those on the dome in the South Corridor
that he had walked across to win that bet with the Needle.

They were going to make it!

Then he saw the hole in the dome's side that the boat must pass
through. His elation faded. It was smaller than he remembered. More
a fissure than a hole, wide and shallow, with blackness beyond. When
he'd taken part in the Thousand Islands Race, it had been in a boat
with a mast that could be taken down entirely. Would the stub of mast
left by Qinta's sword fit through the opening?

The clicking sound became louder. To either side of Galantas, the
threads of the Weaver's web twitched. As the boat approached the
dome, Barnick aligned it with the place where the fissure was broad-
est. The front part of the craft passed through. Galantas looked from
the opening to the mast. Damn, this was going to be close. Barnick
steered the boat low, so its hull scraped the bottom of the hole. . . .

But the mast still snagged on the top of the fissure, bringing the
craft to a juddering halt.

Galantas fought down panic. His back prickled. He could *feel* the
pressure in the water caused by the Weaver's coming. Qinta looked
over Galantas's shoulder, horror in his expression.

Click click click.

Barnick reversed the boat a handspan before propelling it forward again. The mast struck the dome with a bang that Galantas felt through the boards. A puff of dust floated down, but the stonework held. The boat retreated once more for another try. *To hell with this.* Even if Barnick could batter a way through the fissure, how much of the dome would he bring down on their heads by doing so?

Time to move.

Click-click-click.

Grabbing the mast, Galantas hauled himself toward the bow. If he swam into the dome, he would likely drown there, but anything beat joining the Weaver for lunch.

Then the mast thudded into the dome a third time.

The stones at the top of the fissure crumbled, and the craft shot forward into darkness.

Cool water inside, and so much relief Galantas almost relinquished his hold on the mast. It was too early to count his blessings, though. The Weaver wasn't going to let them escape so easily. Would it try to smash through the dome and follow them?

Of course it would.

A muffled boom sounded behind. The whole building shook. When Galantas looked back, he saw the fissure had doubled in size, and another section of stonework broke away and toppled into darkness. Cracks radiated outward from the enlarged opening. Beyond, a huge eye stared at Galantas—or at least part of an eye, since it was bigger than the Shroud-cursed hole. Overhead, patches of light showed where the dome's roof was coming apart. But it only had to hold a few more moments. Galantas's boat was over halfway to the other side now. The exit from the dome was a pale arch on the opposite wall, growing larger with each thumping heartbeat.

A last look back. The Weaver's eye was gone from the hole. Maybe the creature had given up the hunt.

Or maybe it was smart enough to go around the dome and wait for them on the other side.

The boat glided through the opening and into sun-bright water beyond. No clicking noises to be heard. No sight of the beast either, though the strands of its web still quivered. Barnick steered the craft up at an acute angle through the swaying threads.

Galantas gritted his teeth. His breath was tight in his chest. It reminded him of that time he'd dived for sunpearls in the Outer Rim, but he'd managed to hold on then, and he was going to make it now too, because the boat suddenly broke the surface. He heaved in a lung-ful of air. A world of sound returned: the cawing of starbeaks, the fretting of the sea against the cliffs, Qinta coughing and gasping. The boat was full of water, and Galantas bailed with his hand until a ges-ture from Barnick set the liquid running up the sides of the craft and over the gunwales.

Galantas slumped back against the boards, his clothes sodden, his hair dripping.

The boat flew over the water. As it reached the point where the strait opened out, the sea became rougher. Qinta peered into the waves behind, his face as pale as Shroud's ass. "Do you . . . see it?" he croaked between breaths.

Galantas scanned the water. The strands of the creature's web were clustered thickly below the hull, but of the beast itself there was no sign. He grinned. They'd done it! A slice of luck along the way, maybe, but that was becoming a habit with him. How long could it last? When you diced enough times with Shroud, eventually the Lord of the Dead was going to throw a pair of sixes.

If that happened, though, Galantas would just match his score and beat him on the next cast.

Shouts from the east, and he looked back along the strait. He'd for-gotten about the stone-skins. At the entrance to the channel, the Augeran ship had halted. Was it ensnared in the creature's web, or had it simply abandoned the pursuit? A scraping noise reached Galantas, like claws on wood.

Then the vessel began to sink.

Cries sounded from the deck. A wave of water-magic burgeoned beneath the hull as the vessel sought to retreat, but it was going no-where.

In the sea below, shadows gathered.

Karmel followed Caval along the path through the long brown grasses in the boneyard. Ahead was a knot of trees, and sitting with his back to one of them was Mokinda. He didn't look up as they approached. Behind, Karmel heard screams as the stone-skins continued their attack on Bezzle. The boneyard, situated on a rise at the northern edge of the city, offered views of the fighting, but the priestess had no interest in watching. As Caval halted alongside Mokinda, she set her back to the action and waited for the Erin Elalese to catch up. Her hands trembled with the memory of what she'd done to the man in the alley. Had she killed him? She saw again his cheek gaping open. *He deserved it*, she told herself. As if saying it made it so.

Noon was the first of the Erin Elalese to reach the boneyard. His eyes had a haunted cast to them, and his face and forearms were covered by so many insect bites he might have fallen asleep on an anthill. It was Amerel, though, on whom Karmel focused her attention. She too had insect bites on her face. At the house, the first thing Karmel had noticed about her was her white hair, yet now it was the woman's eyes that stood out. Their whites were crisscrossed by tiny blackened blood vessels, making them look like orbs of shattered glass. There was no more life in them than there was in the graves all about.

In Olaire, Senar Sol had been reluctant to talk about his fellow Guardian. That reticence had told Karmel more than his eventual cursory description of the woman. His warning about her Will-persuasion had stayed with the priestess, though. *Be sure of your purpose,* he had said. *Else she will twist you round and round until you can't remember which way you started facing.*

It was Caval who broke the silence. "Senar Sol sends his regards," he said.

Karmel almost smiled in spite of herself. An astute opening, that, since it told Amerel the Chameleons knew not just who she was, but also what she was capable of. And that they'd be ready if she tried to use her power on them.

If the woman was caught off balance, she gave no sign. "I'd say some introductions are overdue."

As are some thanks, Karmel almost said, but she held her tongue.

"Ah, I am Caval, and this is Karmel. The one who doesn't speak is Mokinda."

"You are Chameleons," Amerel said, looking from Caval to Karmel. Caval nodded.

She swung her gaze to Mokinda. "But not you, I think."

The Storm Lord did not reply, but perhaps he didn't need to. There was something in Amerel's half smile that suggested she already knew who he was.

She looked back at Caval. "You mentioned Senar Sol."

Caval nodded a second time.

"I thought he was dead." There was nothing in her tone to indicate whether she was pleased or disappointed to discover otherwise.

"If so, he looked remarkably well for it. He works for Mazana Creed now."

"As do you, I take it."

"In this endeavor, yes."

"And what is 'this endeavor'?"

Caval looked at Mokinda. Evidently he was wondering whether the Storm Lord would take up the narrative, but the Untarian seemed happy to let Caval do the talking. Who better to lead the blind than the blind, after all?

Noon spoke. "How do you know us?" he said, scratching at a bite on his hand. "How did you know we were here?"

The questions were coming so fast this was beginning to feel to Karmel like an interrogation. "You have heard of the emira's shaman, Jambar Simanis?" she said.

Amerel inclined her head.

"Then you will know his reputation as a seer. He predicted you might need some help."

"And you just happened to be in the neighborhood."

The words were spoken casually, yet there was a weight to the Guardian's gaze that told Karmel she was on dangerous ground. But then the priestess suspected there was no such thing as safe ground within a stone's throw of this woman. "If you're wondering what else Jambar told us, no, we don't know why you're in Bezzle, or what you were doing back at the house. Nor do we care."

It was said with such feeling that it drew a raised eyebrow from Amerel. The Guardian drummed her fingers on the gravestone she sat on. A glance at Mokinda suggested she thought the Storm Lord might know more than the Chameleons did, and perhaps that was true. But it wasn't Karmel's concern, and so when Amerel looked back at her, she met the woman's gaze evenly.

The Guardian said, "Senar Sol told Mazana Creed about the history between Erin Elal and the stone-skins?"

"Yes."

"And because of this, the emira thinks we should work together? Or perhaps she seeks a favor in return for your help earlier?"

Caval said, "You are quick to discount her charitable nature."

Amerel's smile did not reach her eyes.

"Actually," Caval added, "Mazana believes you'd want to help us even if you weren't in our debt."

"Because you're planning a strike against the stone-skins? In revenge for Dragon Day?"

She was fishing for information, Karmel realized: about what Jambar had foreseen of the Augerans' next movements, and whether this was a revenge strike in truth, or a preemptive move against a further attack by the stone-skins on the Sabian League. Since Karmel did not know, she kept her silence.

"What is your target?"

"The stone-skin fleet," the priestess said.

"The stone-skin fleet," Amerel repeated. "What, all of it?"

"Yes."

The Guardian laughed. "And you need our help to destroy it? Why? There are three of you already."

"Our reaction was much the same when Mazana told us her plan."

Amerel tried to appear amused by this talk, but her fingers had ceased their tapping. "I'm listening."

A gust of wind set the grasses in the boneyard rustling. Far behind Karmel, a sorcerous explosion sounded, and she saw flames reflected in Amerel's eyes. She noticed a spot of blood on the back of her thumb—the man's blood. With a shudder, she uncapped her water bottle then used the water to wash her hands. "Are you familiar with the use of dragon blood to lure the dragons to Dian on Dragon Day?" she asked.

"It draws them like sharks."

Karmel nodded. "The blood of the creature killed in one Hunt is used to draw the dragons for the next. Except this year it wasn't one dragon killed, it was a dozen. A *dozen*. All that blood meant Mazana Creed was able to do some experimenting. When the gate was finally lowered on Dragon Day, many dragons were trapped in the Sabian Sea. The emira has been finding out how much blood it takes to attract them, and apparently the smallest drop is enough to draw them across the length and breadth of the Sabian Sea."

Another explosion sounded, closer this time, but Amerel didn't take her gaze from Karmel. "Go on."

"The rest I'm sure you've already guessed. Mazana has given us a flask of dragon blood, together with some blowpipes and darts. The plan is to reach the harbor undetected, then tip the darts with blood and use them to mark the Augeran ships."

Karmel wasn't sure how she'd been expecting the Erin Elalese to respond. With incredulity perhaps, maybe even excitement. Instead Noon grimaced as if he'd already had the idea himself and rejected it. Amerel's expression remained impassive. "The emira plans to release the dragons from the Sabian Sea?" she asked.

"No."

"Then she's relying on the dragons that have returned to the Southern Wastes. How can she be sure a mere drop of blood will lure them over such a distance?"

"She isn't. But if we do our job right, there'll be more than just one drop. Every ship we mark will make the lure stronger."

Noon snorted. "You'll be lucky to get close enough to mark even one. In case you hadn't noticed, there's a battle going on down there."

Caval said, "Ah, a battle needs two sides to fight it. This is a massacre. It'll be over before nightfall."

"Maybe, maybe not. But even if you're right, the city will still be crawling with stone-skins."

"Just as well, then, that Mazana Creed chose Chameleons for the job."

"You ever tried picking your way through a city at war? Stone-skins will be on the lookout for Rubyholt stragglers. Only takes one to spot you, and the game's up."

"You have a better idea, of course."

Noon looked at Amerel, then said, "Why not use crossbows to hit the stone-skin ships? We can fire them from a safer distance than blowpipes."

Karmel shook her head. "Mazana chose blowpipes for a reason. If the blood is to attract the dragons it has to come into contact with the sea. That means hitting the hulls just above the waterline so the waves wash over the darts. The only way you'll get that kind of accuracy is from close in."

Noon made to speak again, but Amerel gestured him quiet. "Why doesn't Mokinda swim round and mark the ships?"

Meaning she *had* recognized the Storm Lord? "Because the stone-skins are patrolling the entrance to the port. One of their water-mages would sense him coming."

"Then just pour the blood in the harbor. The Augeran ships are sure to get a dousing as the water circulates."

Not to mention the Rubyholt ships, too. "It may come to that," Karmel said. "But only if plan A fails. With so much blood in the harbor, the dragons would be drawn to Bezzle even if the stone-skins moved on."

"And you're expecting them to?"

There she went again, probing for information. Wouldn't Karmel have done the same in her position, though? What harm was there in telling what she knew? Except the priestess knew only what Mazana had told her, and that was nothing more than she'd already revealed.

Amerel's voice had a strangely soothing tone to it. "What is our role in all this?" she asked, indicating herself and Noon.

"Senar Sol said you can . . . spirit-walk?"

The Guardian nodded.

"Then your task is to pick a path for us to the harbor through the Augeran patrols. And watch our backs while we use the blowpipes on the stone-skin ships."

"Watch your backs," Amerel echoed. *Because you couldn't have found anyone in the Storm Isles to do that,* her look seemed to say. With the Chameleons able to make themselves invisible, she probably thought she was there to take the fall if trouble came calling. "How many Augeran ships are we dealing with?"

"More than ten, less than twenty."

"Then it's going to take more than one night to hit them."

"Agreed. We can decide after the first round whether it's safer to return here or bed down near the harbor."

"We start tonight?"

Caval said, "Unless you've got something else planned. The longer we stay in Bezzle, the greater the chance we'll be found."

Amerel's look was appraising. *And the greater the chance the stone-skins might leave,* she was no doubt thinking, and perhaps she was right too. But then wouldn't Mazana have warned the Chameleons of the urgency? Karmel shrugged the thought aside. What did she care? She just wanted to get on with things. To hell with the risks. At least while she was thinking about staying alive, she couldn't also be brooding on the events of Dragon Day, or on what had happened in the alley earlier.

Nightfall, she decided, could not come soon enough.

Romany watched Mazana run lazy circles around the two Gilgamarian councilors. And that was no mean feat, considering the size of them. The first, Wirral Dray, was the fat man who'd met them outside the Alcazar. He was also the new first speaker of the Ruling Council, now that Mazana had broken the news of Rethell Webb's demise. His deputy, Pettiman Teel, was only marginally less rotund.

"And so you see," the emira was saying, "it was actually Rethell's daughter, Agenta, who was responsible for Imerle's death."

Wirral wrung his hands. "I trust you do not think the Ruling Council had anything to do with this unsavory affair," he said. "Rethell was our first speaker, yes, but I have long had suspicions about the quality of his family's bloodline. As for his daughter, Agenta"—he smirked—"I have always regarded her as nothing less than—"

"A hero," Mazana cut in, her expression grave. "That's what you were going to say, isn't it? What else would you call someone who killed the traitor responsible for sabotaging the Dragon Hunt and murdering the other Storm Lords?"

Wirral's mouth hinged open, his chins wobbling. "Imerle . . . a traitor?"

"Unless you have a better word for it."

Mazana was toying with the Gilgamarians, Romany knew, using their ignorance of the events of Dragon Day against them. Already she had had them fawning over the Revenant commander, Jodren, before announcing that he'd spearheaded the attack on Olaire; then clucking their tongues over the near annihilation of the Chameleon population in the city before revealing that the high priest, Caval Flood, had made his own play for power that day. Mildly entertaining, to be sure, but Romany had more important business at hand. Already she had begun the task of spinning a sorcerous web about the Alcazar, and the last few moments had seen a discovery that required her immediate attention.

"If you'll excuse me," she said to no one in particular. Then she opened the door and stepped through before anyone could object.

Two Gray Cloaks flanked the doorway, and two more were stationed along the corridor. They gave Romany bored looks as she strode between them, but then no doubt mercenaries of their repute considered guard duty demeaning. The priestess passed the door to her own quarters and took a right turn before descending a staircase. The corridors were silent and empty of servants. There was a dustiness to the air that suggested this wing of the Alcazar had not been used for some time.

The passage that was Romany's destination looked the same as all the others. As the priestess entered it, she felt a sensation similar to that which she had experienced in the street outside the temple of the Lord of Hidden Faces in Olaire. *A crossover point between worlds—it has to be.*

She halted.

There was nothing in the corridor to suggest a portal was here— no ripple in the air, no subtle variation in the light. But the threads of her sorcerous web were quivering, and she felt a tug like she was edging forward even though her feet remained still. While she could detect nothing of whatever realm lay beyond the portal, her web at least gave her an indication of the size and shape of the gateway: roughly spherical in nature, and extending through the floor, ceiling, and walls to either side.

If she'd known the circumstances in which the portal had been formed, she might have speculated as to who had made it and thus what world lay beyond. Unfortunately, her knowledge of the Alcazar was limited to what she'd been told by Mazana Creed on the walk up from the harbor. Besides, gateways such as this were created by the release of powerful magics, which meant its formation must surely have predated the building. But by how long? Centuries? Millennia?

The only way to find out more would be to open the portal.

Romany considered. Where was the harm in trying? Since she could determine how far the gateway extended, there was no danger of her inadvertently trespassing on the realm beyond. There was still the risk, of course, that someone in the Alcazar might stumble across her while the portal was open. But for now the corridor remained empty, and there was no sound of approaching footsteps—no sound at all, aside from the slamming of a distant door. And if anyone *did* come near, wouldn't her fledgling web give her warning?

Her decision made, she shifted her focus back to the portal. How to go about opening it? She reached out with her senses, met a resistance like she was pushing through a heavy curtain. . . .

The gateway snapped open, spilling darkness into the passage. Romany stumbled back a pace, almost tripped over her own feet, and had to throw out a hand to the wall to stop herself falling.

Ah, as simple as that.

She smoothed her robe with her hands. With the benefit of hindsight, perhaps she could have been a *little* more circumspect in her questing. She could also have tried to exercise more control over the portal as it opened, for instead of confining it to the corridor she had allowed it to expand through the walls to either side—meaning that if anyone had been resting in the rooms beyond, they were unlikely to be resting any longer.

No inquiring shouts sounded, though, no screams of alarm. And with a touch here and a touch there, Romany was able to shrink the portal to a more manageable size, bounded by stone all about.

No harm done.

Overlying the corridor was the image of a dark, barren plain. There were no twin blue moons that would have indicated the world of the Kerralai demons. Sheets of dust swept across the ground, yet Romany could feel neither the grit nor the wind that stirred it. There was something strange about the movement of the dust. It seemed slow to lift in the breeze, then quick to fall to earth again. Aside from that dust, the priestess saw nothing apart from clumps of swaying grasses and a pile of rocks.

Rocks, great. As good as a map for pinpointing where she was.

She tried spinning her web through the portal, and the strands passed beyond easily enough. Good news, since it meant she would be able to explore the alien world without having to actually set foot in it. On the other hand, she had no way of knowing how far she'd have to extend her threads before she reached civilization. And then of course she'd have the challenge of trying to identify that civilization without being able to speak the native language. She scowled. And even if she *could* understand the locals, what guarantee did she have that they would know the name of the realm they inhabited? Did Romany know the name of her own world? "Home," was the best she could come up with, and she suspected that that name was shared by more realms than just hers.

She tutted her disgust. A fine ability this world-hopping was proving to be. Utterly useless, in fact, unless you enjoyed trying to—

A light went off in her head. Perhaps she had been too quick to
dismiss her new ability. Perhaps there *was* a use this portal could be
put to—a use that was made more valuable by the mystery and re-
moteness of the world that lay beyond. If, for example, Romany happened to be walking along this corridor with Mazana, what was to
stop the priestess opening the gateway and dragging the other
woman through? Ordinarily Mazana couldn't travel the portal—
only someone with Romany's ability could—but that would change
if the priestess seized her arm. And once on the other side, Mazana
would have no way of returning without Romany's help. True, the
emira wouldn't be dead, as the Spider had wanted, but she might as
well be. Plus the priestess wouldn't have to stain her hands with
the woman's blood.

She smiled. Were there no limits to the bounds of her genius? No
one would ever know where Mazana had gone, or be able to prove that
Romany was responsible for her disappearance. In fact, the hardest
part of the plan would be finding a way to separate the emira from
the executioner and that shadow of a Guardian—

A footfall sounded behind her, and she froze.

Then a man's voice said, "I thought it was you."

Senar watched Romany spin round. He couldn't have said what had
made him follow her when she left the meeting with the Gilgamarians, but he'd plainly been right to heed his instincts. The priestess's
hand moved to the hilt of her knife. He thought she would draw it,
yet sense prevailed. She'd fought him once before, after all, and come
off worst in the exchange.

"I knew I recognized you from somewhere," he said. "You're the
assassin I fought in Olaire. The change to your eyes threw me, but
when you opened that portal . . ." He studied her. "But you died—in
the temple of the Lord of Hidden Faces. The Watchman who found
you was clear on that point."

"If I died, then I can hardly be the person you think I am," the
priestess said in her usual scolding tone. Hers was a voice that made
you feel small just to hear it. Or smaller in Senar's case.

"Must I ask you to remove your mask?" he said.

"Alas, my faith forbids it."

"Lucky, then, that I am not a believer."

Romany sniffed. "You think me an assassin? If I'd wanted to kill the emira, I could have done so a hundred times before now."

The Guardian glanced at the portal. "But never with such a convenient means of escape at hand."

"And what makes you think there are no portals in the palace at Olaire?"

Senar moved closer. If he was going to read the woman, he needed to see her eyes, but the shadows cast by her mask's eye slits were too deep. "Two weeks ago an assassin tries to kill Mazana—an assassin uniquely able to open portals that others cannot even sense. Then shortly after that assassin dies, you appear. You, who are sworn to the god whose temple the woman died in. You, who just happen to have the same ability the assassin had." He waited for Romany's reaction, but she said nothing. "Any more coincidences like that, and I might actually start thinking your Lord exists."

"I am not the assassin you speak of."

That was it? That was the extent of her defense? "Then who are you?"

"Just a priestess of the Lord of Hidden Faces. A Lord to whom your mistress is indebted, I might add."

Senar took another step forward. Romany didn't retreat from him, but she didn't close her portal either. "Really? Because it strikes me your Lord wouldn't have let Mazana kill Fume unless he wanted her to. That she might have done him a favor even as he was doing her one."

"Fascinating conjecture."

This was getting Senar nowhere. He could have discovered Romany holding a bloody knife over Mazana's corpse, and she would still have sworn innocence. And probably found a way to blame him for the whole thing too. He pondered his next move. Striking at the woman seemed ill-advised when there was so much going on he didn't understand. Besides, if he drew his sword she could just escape by stepping back through the portal. Maybe it was time to try another line of attack while he had her on the back foot.

"What's happening to Mazana?" he said. "The Founder's Citadel changed her. Or rather Fume did when she took in his spirit."

"You think the god lives on inside her?"

"Does he?"

"The emira took in part of his aspect, that is all."

"An aspect that is becoming stronger."

"And yet an aspect no more or less dominant than her others. The desire for blood can be fought like any impulse."

"Can it be reversed?"

"No." Romany hesitated. "But there is something you could do to lessen the impact of the god's sway."

"What?"

"The dagger."

"The dagger she took from Darbonna?"

The priestess gestured, and the portal collapsed with a ripping sound, dispelling the darkness in the corridor. Daylight streamed through the windows to Senar's left, branding bright rectangles onto the wall opposite.

"It once belonged to Fume," Romany said. "Plunge it into someone's flesh, and it will drain every drop of blood in the victim's veins. To Mazana, blood is power. And of course power in the wrong hands is addictive."

"But if Mazana were to lose the dagger . . ."

His voice trailed off at the sound of footsteps behind. Had someone followed him, as he had followed Romany? He turned to see Kiapa approaching.

If the Everlord had heard anything of Senar's conversation with the priestess, it did not show in his expression. "Mazana wants you," he said, drawing up. "Both of you. The Erin Elalese are here."

As Romany followed Kiapa down the passage, she clenched and unclenched her hands. How could she have been so careless as to let Senar creep up on her? She'd been too fixed on the land beyond the portal and the opportunities it presented. For all her denials, it was clear the Guardian still believed her to be the assassin, and who could blame him? More important, her plan to drag Mazana through the portal was now in tatters, for Senar would never leave Romany alone with the emira. He might even tell Mazana what had happened here.

Would he want her to know they had discussed the knife, though, if he intended to steal it? Would he consider Romany a coconspirator in his efforts to stem Fume's influence?

She'd need to keep a close ear on their future conversations.

The Gray Cloaks standing guard outside the emira's quarters had been joined by two new soldiers. *Erin Elalese.* The men eyed each other with obvious suspicion, and the mood inside Mazana's chambers was no more welcoming when Romany entered. Four Erin Elalese had replaced the two Gilgamarian councilors. Introductions were under way. A rigid, heavyset woman in a soldier's uniform—Tyrin Lindin Tar, the priestess presumed—shook hands with Mazana. Judging by the sting in the women's gazes, they had each already recognized in the other all the qualities they looked for in a mortal enemy.

Such a positive omen for the negotiations to come.

Beyond the tyrin was a slab of muscle in a sleeveless white jerkin, while on this side was a young man with an armory's worth of metal pushed through his face. A Mellikian then, and a water-mage too, going by his blue robes. The final member of the Erin Elalese party was a balding middle-aged man with an assurance to his look that walked the line between confidence and arrogance. As his gaze met Romany's, he graced her with a smile that faltered as he caught sight of something behind her.

Or rather someone. Senar Sol, to be precise.

The Guardian's expression on seeing the man showed surprise and distaste in equal measure, but the distaste won out.

"Emperor," he said stiffly, inclining his head.

Part III

Deep Waters

CHAPTER 13

SENAR STOOD in the anteroom of the emperor's quarters, looking through a window at the courtyard below. A bench was barely visible amid the tangle of an overgrown garden, while weeds poked out from between the flagstones of the path running round it. Senar had insisted upon a meeting with Avallon. In the time he'd been waiting, he had watched the sun slide behind the Alcazar's roof to the west. Earlier there had been no meaningful discussions between the emperor and Mazana, Avallon claiming fatigue after his journey from Arkarbour. More likely, he had wanted a chance to speak to Kolloken about what the messenger had learned in Olaire. He might even be questioning the man now, for Senar could hear muffled voices coming from behind the door to his right.

Perhaps he should have been using this opportunity to get his story straight before he talked to Avallon, but instead he found himself thinking about his confrontation with Romany. He'd considered telling the emira who the priestess was, but something had made him hold back—a suspicion that, had he done so, Mazana would have asked him why he hadn't worked it out sooner. Plus if he told her about his conversation with Romany, he might end up having to tell her about the knife too—which would make the task of stealing it all the harder when the time came.

Not that he'd actually resolved to do so, of course. Odds were, Romany had been telling the truth about the dagger's influence on Mazana. But he didn't so enjoy being manipulated that he would leap to do the priestess's bidding without first questioning the color of her motives.

In the meantime, he would watch her like a crakehawk.

The door to the emperor's quarters opened, and Avallon's bodyguard, Strike, emerged. He wore a sleeveless white jerkin together with white trousers and sandals. The man was flintcat-aspected, and he motioned Senar inside with characteristic feline grace. Even flashed the Guardian a smile to see him on his way, showing off his gold front teeth.

The door closed behind Senar, Strike remaining outside.

The room beyond was five times the size of the Guardian's own, but the air was just as musty, as if this whole wing of the Alcazar had stood empty before the arrival of Mazana's and Avallon's parties. The floor was covered in white tiles the Guardian could see his reflection in. Across from him, doors opened onto a balcony, and in the distance he could make out the seawall as well as the masts of the ships in harbor. Inside, against the wall to his left, was a bed with mock-pillars for bedposts, while to his right was a desk so vast it could have fitted the Guardian Council around it. Behind it sat the emperor.

Senar blinked. And only the emperor. So this was to be a meeting between just the two of them? Most leaders saw enemies in every shadow, yet Avallon apparently saw no threat in a man he'd tried to kill ten months ago. Then again, Strike was doubtless waiting outside in the corridor. Senar glanced toward the open balcony doors. And the emperor had probably stationed someone out there, as well. Kolloken, perhaps, since Avallon would want him to hear Senar's story in order to verify it against what he'd learned in the Storm Isles.

Senar could do with some things being cleared up himself. In Olaire, Kolloken had told Mazana the emperor wouldn't be coming to Gilgamar. Had there been a change of plan? Or had Kolloken been lying all along? Because if he *had* been lying, maybe he'd lied too about the things he'd told Senar on the *Raven*. Like whether Erin Elal had been attacked. And whether the Guardian order still existed.

Senar studied the emperor. The man's skin was sallow, his eyes sunken. Thick black hair protruded from his creased shirt round the collar and cuffs. From the smell of him, he was still wearing the clothes he had traveled in, but there was no fatigue in his movements as he rose from his chair and came round the desk to greet the Guardian. He offered his hand. Senar looked at it. This was the man who had strong-armed him through the Merigan portal last year, yet now Senar was supposed to pretend it was design rather than chance that had seen him come out safely in Olaire? He shook the hand anyway; it seemed childish not to.

As if that had ever stopped him before.

"Emperor," he said.

"Guardian." Avallon's voice was the growl of a blackweed smoker. He leaned close, locking gazes with Senar for a moment longer than was comfortable before pointing to a chair. "Sit."

Senar did so.

The last time they'd talked, the setting had been very different: a room in the heart of Avallon's inner sanctum in Arkarbour filled with scowling portraits and high-backed leather chairs. It was a few days before the Betrayal. Senar hadn't been a member of the Guardian Council then, but the emperor had sought him out all the same, and tried to convince him of the need to act against the Black Tower. Senar recalled few of the words they'd exchanged. What had stayed with him, though, was the emperor's presence. Avallon's manner had been relaxed, but not familiar; earnest, but not insistent—so earnest in fact that at one point he'd overturned a lantern with an impassioned sweep of one arm. It had been a performance even Senar's master, Li Benir, would have been proud of.

But a performance all the same, as Senar had quickly come to realize. For with the Guardians weakened after their attack on the Black Tower, the emperor hadn't seen fit to make Senar's acquaintance again, even to explain why he had chosen to risk the Guardian's life by sending him through the Merigan portal. He'd done it for the good of the empire, Avallon would say. He might even believe it too. The problem was, what was good for the empire had a habit of being also what was good for the emperor personally.

Avallon poured himself a glass of wine from a decanter and took a sip. He looked at Senar over the rim.

"You still blame me for the Betrayal?" he said after a pause. "You still think I made up that stuff about the high mage contacting the Augerans?"

Senar shifted in his seat. It was a fair opening, albeit a predictable one. Two years ago, a whistleblower among the ranks of Erin Elal's mages had claimed the Black Tower was seeking to make contact with the Augerans. When the high mage refused to surrender himself for questioning, the emperor had ordered the Guardians to seize him. The seriousness of the accusations, together with the intransigence of the mages' Conclave, had left the Guardian Council feeling it had no option but to side with Avallon. The result had been an attack on the Black Tower that had seen the ranks of both mages and Guardians decimated—and the emperor's own hand strengthened as a consequence. At the time, Senar had believed the whistleblower was Avallon's puppet. But the mage had mysteriously, and conveniently, vanished before anyone could cross-examine him.

Could it really be a coincidence, though, that the Augerans should appear now, so soon after the whistleblower had made his claims?

"I think," Senar said to the emperor, "that the incident could have been settled without bloodshed, if that was what you wanted."

"And maybe if I hadn't acted when I did, the stone-skins would have turned up at our door sooner."

Senar did not reply. What was the point in arguing? They'd trodden this same ground so many times before, their prints were now well set. "Does the Black Tower know the Augerans are coming? The Senate?" He'd asked the same question of Kolloken, but it never hurt to get a second opinion.

Avallon's glass paused on its way to his lips. "The Senate!" he snorted. "Do you know what they did when I told them about the stone-skins? Called a Shroud-cursed vote to decide on how to respond. As if extending the hand of friendship were an option! For all I know, they're still talking about it now!" He made a gesture that set wine sloshing over the rim of his glass. "But enough of this. The Senate, the Conclave, it doesn't matter what they think. With war coming, even you can't deny the empire will face up better to the Augerans with a single man at the helm. Or that I'm the best person to steer our course."

Senar nodded. If only because the emperor had made sure there was no one else.

"Good," Avallon said. Then he smiled as if by yielding that point the Guardian had yielded all the others as well. "Good!"

Senar knew well enough not to relax his guard.

A breeze set the balcony doors rattling. From the direction of the harbor came the clang of a bell, the splash of water, the grinding of the chains as they were drawn tight across the Neck.

"Where did the Merigan portal take you when you went through?" Avallon said.

"To Olaire," Senar replied without hesitation. There was no escaping the need to share that truth. Better to seem open now in case he needed to keep something back later.

"Go on."

"I came out in a chamber next to the cells in the Olairian palace. They held me there until a couple of weeks ago."

Avallon stared at him. "They kept you locked up for ten months?"

"Yes. Perhaps Imerle couldn't decide what to do with me."

"I've heard a lot of words used to describe that woman. 'Indecisive' isn't one of them."

Senar shrugged. "If she'd released me straightaway, you'd have known the portal I traveled to was in the Storm Isles. By keeping me hidden, she hoped to muddy the waters."

"You agreed to keep it secret?"

"Yes."

"And Imerle believed you."

Senar's voice was flat. "Strangely, she didn't take much convincing. For some reason she thought my loyalty to the empire might have been tested by your sending me through the portal. For some reason she thought that gave me cause for grievance."

Not a trace of awkwardness showed in Avallon's expression. "And you allowed her to continue in that misapprehension."

"It seemed the safest course."

Outside, the clanking of the chains died away. The sky had dimmed to a sullen gray.

"Why were you released before Dragon Day?" Avallon asked.

The tone of the emperor's questioning was beginning to irritate Senar. Avallon had no authority over him, yet was interrogating him as if he were a subordinate. "Imerle never said," he replied. "But whatever the reason, she kept me on a leash short enough to make her distrust clear. I knew it was a matter of time before she turned on me."

The emperor's mouth was a thin line. He'd be wondering what Senar was holding back. He'd be wondering why Imerle had trusted the Guardian to keep quiet about the portal, but not about anything else. "So you threw in your lot with Mazana Creed."

The Guardian nodded.

"What do you make of her?"

"Mazana?" Senar wasn't sure how the question was meant, but he would use it to steer the conversation in a direction of his choosing. He intended to leave here with as many answers as he gave. "She is sharp enough to question your motives for calling this meeting, but also prudent enough not to sit idly by and wait for the Augerans to make their next move."

"Oh?"

Senar told him about Caval and Karmel's mission to the Rubyholt Isles. Avallon would hear about it anyway from Amerel.

The emperor's reaction was not what he expected. Avallon set his glass down on the desk with a crack, his look darkening. "When did the Chameleons leave?"

"Yesterday evening."

The emperor considered. "Meaning they'd have arrived in Bezzle this afternoon."

"Is that before or after Amerel did?"

Avallon's eyes narrowed dangerously—no doubt he thought Amerel's presence in the Isles was a secret. Senar, though, met his gaze without flinching. He'd survived the executioner's stare for the past two weeks; the emperor's look wasn't going to trouble him.

"Mazana's shaman, Jambar, knew Amerel was in the Isles," Senar explained. "He even anticipated she might run into trouble. The Chameleons were sent to lend a hand."

Avallon said nothing.

"What is she doing there?"

The emperor ignored the question. Snatching up his wineglass again, he started pacing the room. "This, *this,* is why the League should be working with us! This scheme of Mazana's . . . even if it works, the best the Chameleons can do is give the stone-skins a bloody nose." He rounded on Senar as if this were all the Guardian's fault. "The League, the Rubyholters, even the Corinians—they have to realize it's their war too, whether they like it or not. The Augerans may hit Erin Elal first, but they're not going to stop there."

"What's happening in the Isles?" Senar asked.

"What do you bloody well think's happening? The stone-skins are trying to negotiate safe passage. They want to attack our eastern seaboard."

A part of Senar had known that would be the case. But after Dragon Day, he'd let himself hope it might be the League, and not his homeland, that bore the brunt of the enemy's first assault. "And how do we stop them if they do?"

"We don't! That's why we've got to destroy their fleets before they reach us. That's why the Storm Lords are so important—or would have been if there were any of them left." He scowled. "Absurd, isn't it? If the Augerans hadn't sabotaged the Hunt, we'd have stood no chance of persuading the Storm Lords to back us. Yet now that they have done, there aren't enough Storm Lords left to make a difference."

So why are you so keen to ally with Mazana? Senar thought. He kept his silence, though.

Avallon gulped down his wine before wiping a hand across his mouth. "Tell me about Dragon Day. I want to know everything."

Senar told him, leaving out any mention of the events in the Founder's Citadel. When he reached the part about how he'd fought the dragon on the terrace, Avallon's gaze flickered to the scales at his neck.

"You didn't cross blades with a stone-skin, then?" the emperor said. "Did you see any of them fighting as a group?"

Senar shook his head.

"What's your assessment of their warriors?"

"From what I've heard, they are formidable. But the Augerans would have sent their best."

"Their best, yes." Avallon began pacing again. "These last few months I've had everyone I can spare poring over texts from before the Exile. Most of the writings can't even agree on whether the Augerans' skins are made from stone or not. And even when they *do* agree on some detail, how do we know that what was true then remains true now?" He refilled his glass from the decanter. "There's one thing we can be sure of, though, and that's the skill of their fighters. The Syns, the Honored, the Spawn—names to scare children with for eight hundred years." His gaze took on an intensity that pressed Senar back in his chair. "If they get a foothold in Erin Elal, we won't dislodge them again."

Ebon walked up and down the waterfront. The ninth bell had rung so long ago it seemed someone must have forgotten to ring the tenth and eleventh bells both. Tia's minions were late to collect the first half of Ebon's payment. There was no way, though, that they wouldn't show. If they vanished for good, it would be *after* they'd taken his money.

So where were they?

Ebon had watched the Harbor Gate close at the eighth bell, still undecided as to whether he should have been trying to break in. Now the decision was out of his hands, and he could only wait and hope that Tia came through. The more time that went by, though, the more stupid his choice seemed to be.

He pulled his cloak more tightly about his shoulders. Earlier he'd changed into his best clothes so he wouldn't look out of place when he reached the Upper City. Admittedly that meant he now looked out of place in his present surroundings, but there weren't many people around to show an interest in his attire. With the coming of night, the crowds at the harbor had melted away to leave only a handful of wretched souls, and the attention of those few was fixed on a woman atop an upturned barrel. She wore a white robe like a Beloved of the White Lady. Ebon had thought her a preacher at first, until he caught the smell of the tollen in the cups her assistants handed out. *A Seeker.* Oblivion in a glass she was serving, and there was no shortage of takers among her crippled and impoverished listeners. She had picked her audience well.

Ebon looked toward the Lower City. Above the creaks from the ships at quayside, a delirious hum was building as if someone had thrown wide the gates to the madhouse. In one of the streets a fire was burning, and shadows cavorted around it like they were engaged in some demonic ritual. As yet the bedlam showed no signs of spreading to the harbor—

"We got company," Vale said.

The prince stared along the waterfront. From the shadows of an alley appeared Peg Foot, and behind him strode four heavily armed men. Peg Foot's peg tapped a hollow note on the wooden quay.

"You're late," Ebon said as the man drew up.

"So we are. You got the money?"

Ebon nodded to Vale. The Endorian crossed to Gunnar in the boat and accepted from him two small chests. Vale carried them to Peg Foot and put them on the ground before retreating. One of the walking weapons racks collected them.

Ebon said, "The rest is deposited with a moneylender called Jilan Galamer."

"I know," Peg Foot replied with a smile.

Ebon didn't like what that smile signified. This afternoon Jilan had been only too happy to take the prince's gold. He'd even had a standard set of terms upon which it would be held pending the completion of Ebon's dealings with Tia. But then doubtless every moneylender in the Lower City was in Tia's pocket—together already with the money Ebon had deposited with Jilan, probably. "We're ready to go."

"Then *you're* early," Peg Foot said. "Ain't nothing gonna happen till the sixth bell."

Ebon stared at him. "The *sixth* bell? As in tomorrow morning?"

"That a problem? You asked Tia when you'd be going in, and she said 'tonight.' In these parts, morning don't start till the sun reaches its peak in the sky."

Ebon spoke through gritted teeth. "Tia also said I'd have time to conduct my business before first light."

Peg Foot shrugged. "Relax, man. Undo a button of that fancy shirt of yours. You're an intact, ain't you?"

"An 'intact'?"

"As in you still got all your bits on you. Once you're in the Upper City, you should be able to move around without no one asking questions. Or that's the way I sees it. Besides, it ain't as if we got a choice. Our man inside starts his posting at the sixth bell, so that's when we goes in. You could show up early if you wants, but the reception you gets will be a good deal less friendly."

Ebon kept his silence, not trusting himself to speak. He should have seen this coming. He should have pressed Tia more about timings at their meeting. But it was too late to remedy that now. What was he going to do? Ask Peg Foot for his money back? The man was more likely to give up his remaining foot. And while Ebon had little doubt that he could take back the gold by force, how was that going to make the sixth bell come sooner?

Peg Foot said, "We'll be back at the fifth bell to collect you and lead you to where we're gathering. Wouldn't want you to stumble down the wrong alley, now, would we?" Or not stumble down the wrong alley, perhaps. "Anyhows, look on the light side of things. A few extra bells means you gets a chance to sample the delights of the Lower City."

Ebon had seen enough of those delights already. Along the street leading to the Canal Gate he could make out a horseman dragging a motionless figure behind him by a rope. Then a swordsman emerged from an alley and cut the horse's legs out from under it. More attackers descended with flashing knives upon the squealing animal and its toppled rider. Dressed as Ebon was, he wouldn't last a quarter-bell down there, with or without Vale at his back. The best chance he had of avoiding trouble until morning was to get in his boat and sail to the center of the harbor.

"This city is sliding into the Abyss," he muttered.

"Every night, my friend," Peg Foot said. "Every night. And let me tells you, it's right cozy down there in the dark, damned if it ain't."

With that, he turned and hobbled away along the waterfront. His four companions fell into step behind.

Ebon watched them retreat until they disappeared down an alley, then looked over at Vale.

The Endorian said, "Told you you should have picked the other option."

Before Ebon could respond, a crackle sounded in his ears as if his hair had been set alight. He flinched and turned—

To see on the quay where the noise had come from . . . nothing, no one.

No, that wasn't quite right. There *was* something there, but it was hard to make out what in the gloom. A misty quality to the shadows. A hint of a form, insubstantial as smoke. Yes, Ebon was sure of it now: a figure, maybe a head shorter than the prince, wearing a tattered robe. It looked familiar.

Understanding dawned. *Mottle!*

But how? Ebon had heard nothing from the mage since they parted in the Forest of Sighs. When the old man hadn't returned to Majack, the prince had assumed he was dead.

Who cared, his friend was alive! He stepped forward to embrace the mage, only to stop in midstride as he remembered he was seeing just a spirit, a sending. Still he found himself grinning like a youngling.

Then his grin faded as he noticed more details of Mottle's ghostly image: the sunken eyes, the melted flesh, the scars on the old man's neck from what might have been tooth marks. He remembered Parolla telling him of her clash with a creature of fire—a tiktar—on that hilltop overlooking Mayot's dome. Of how the beast had engulfed Mottle before the two of them were snatched up by the vortex. Ebon had left the mage to face the creature when he set off to find Mayot. Left him because he couldn't let Parolla face the tiktar alone. Another friend abandoned in the name of his duty.

"Greetings, my boy," Mottle rasped. He sounded as dried out as a drunkard craving his next drink.

"You're hurt," Ebon said needlessly.

"The burns? Pah! The tiktar fared worse in our encounter. In any case, Mottle was able to use his arts to ease his discomfort until he found a Beloved to take away the pain. The scars remain, but Mottle believes they add a certain rugged allure to his otherwise scholarly gravitas."

"Perhaps I can help with those scars when we're next together."

"Perhaps you can," the old man said, regarding him with a beady eye. "Mottle has heard whispers of how you healed your father."

"Only whispers? Does that mean you are not in Majack?"

"Furies bless me, no, my boy. Mottle is in Olaire! The storm bore him east from the Forest of Sighs, yes? And your humble servant allowed . . . carried thence, believing . . . merited a rest . . ."

The old man's voice was becoming softer by the moment. "You're fading out, mage. I can barely hear you."

Mottle puffed out his chest like he'd been paid a compliment. "But of course Mottle is! Your humble . . . fifty leagues away! The Furies themselves could not . . . over such a distance, and even Mottle's . . . sorely tested by . . ." He waved a finger in the air. "In but a short time . . . fail, but before that he . . . usual brevity and insight. Now, as he was saying, the storm . . . east where by happy circumstance . . . momentous proceedings culminating . . . answer perhaps to the riddle . . . most cruelly in the Forest of Sighs . . ."

Ebon's impatience grew even as Mottle's voice dwindled. "Riddle? What riddle?"

"The riddle of . . . and the Vamilians, of course! The cause . . . ancient enmity. Mottle discovered . . . in a fortress not unlike—"

"Enough! Please tell me you did not track me down just to give me another of your history lessons."

The old man was taken aback. "Well," he said after a pause, "not *just* for . . . it is true."

"You know where Lamella and Rendale are?"

Mottle's face lit up. "Aha! So *that* is why . . . in Gilgamar!"

Ebon took a breath. And to think he'd been happy to see the old man again. But perhaps that had been as much to do with what he'd thought Mottle could bring to the search for Rendale and Lamella as it had to do with the mage's reappearance. It was an unworthy thought, but there would be time later to celebrate the old man's return. "How did you track me down?"

". . . Currents, of course. The Currents reveal all—"

"Good. Then they will have revealed to you where Lamella and Rendale are being held."

"No doubt . . . yet your humble . . . intent solely on your own—"

"Could you find them now?"

Mottle's expression changed, but Ebon couldn't read it because the old man's image was too faint. "Alas . . . storm is coming . . . clamor of impending conflict . . . drown all else. Like trying . . . one voice over . . . of battle."

Ebon cocked his head, tried to isolate the mage's whisper from the murmur of the Seeker's voice behind. "Conflict? Who? Where?"

"Why, Gilgamar . . . no less dread than the Vamilians . . . must flee . . . city fall . . ."

"Mottle, I can't hear you. Can you get to Gilgamar? Can you meet me here?"

Nothing.

"Mottle!"

The last shreds of the old man's image dissolved like smoke on the breeze.

Last light, and Galantas sat on the sandy ground of the Hub, listening to the cry of a blueback whale lost among the Shoals. Hundreds of Rubyholters sat round him, silent and still as they watched the shadowy figures of the clan leaders in the circle of standing stones. They were speaking in hushed tones, but Galantas could guess what they were discussing. Word had reached the Hub from the survivors of Bezzle: Dresk's fortress had been taken by the stone-skins, and the warlord himself was dead. Perhaps the reports should have sparked some reaction in Galantas, but he'd been expecting the news since the Augerans attacked, and in any event his father had been dead to him for years. Of more interest was the fact the clansmen thought Galantas was dead too—a misapprehension he had encouraged by keeping his hood up and his gaze down.

When he chose to make his appearance, he wanted it to be suitably dramatic.

Drama was never in short supply when the clan leaders met at the Hub. The last time they had been here was two months ago, when Kalag of the Raptors was accused of taking Erin Elalese gold to pick a fight with the Tridents. Some entertainment that had been. It was forbidden to draw weapons inside the stone circle, but there were no such rules for the rest of the island. More than twenty clansmen had finished the wrong side of Shroud's Gate that night. Galantas doubted even the coming of the stone-skins would stop the old rivalries flaring up now. He could see the tension in the postures of the clan leaders. Hardly fertile ground for Galantas's message of reconciliation, but that would just make his victory all the sweeter when it came.

Of the eight Rubyholt clans, only four were currently represented. There was no mistaking Kalag—Dresk's long-standing adversary—with his grating voice and his bushy beard, nor Malek of the Needles with his inch-long fingernails. Enigon was here from the Squalls with his blond good looks and his easy smile. Last of the four was Tolo of the Keels—a youth with watering eyes who had risen prematurely to his clan's headship following the deaths of his father and his elder sister to a fever last month. Rumor had it he had poisoned them both, but Galantas doubted he had the stones for that. Hells, the man hadn't even attempted the Shark Run yet.

Galantas had shaken hands with all of the other clan leaders in his time, but they'd known more of his reputation than they did of him. Enigon's Squalls were traditional allies of the Spears, yet Enigon had always been Dresk's friend, not Galantas's, meaning his support here was far from assured. Neither Tolo's Keels nor Malek's Needles had strong ties to the Spears, but Galantas hoped he'd find an ally in Malek at least. There had been half a dozen Needle ships in Bezzle's harbor when the stone-skins attacked. Malek would want them back, and he was the sort of man who would take any chance to get them.

Galantas shifted his gaze to Kalag. The Raptor leader had been the one who'd ordered the raid nine years ago in which Galantas lost his arm, and the man took delight in reminding Galantas of that fact whenever possible. In Kalag's own mind, he had probably already assumed the mantle of warlord. Of all the clan leaders, he had the strongest claim. Perhaps Galantas should have been content to cede it to him. Perhaps he should have concentrated on securing his own position as head of the Spears, but his gaze was set on the ultimate prize. Fortunately, no vote could be taken on the matter of Dresk's successor until all of the clan leaders were present, and it would be some time yet before the likes of Starboard Stonne and Ysabel Tremeval arrived, so far were their territories located from the Hub. That gave Galantas time to prove his worth. And he had a plan in mind to do just that.

Qinta nudged him, and he looked up. Striding toward the bloodline—the circle of shark's blood surrounding the stones that marked the point beyond which only clan leaders could pass—was a middle-aged man wearing his hair in a topknot. A blow from a mace had knocked out the teeth on his right side, giving his face a crooked look. Ravin, ruler of the Falcon Clan. Here was the man whose arrival Galantas had been waiting for. Here was the man above all others he had to win to his cause tonight. For if the Spears and the Raptors were the strongest clans in the Isles, the Falcons were an undisputed third. If it came to a clash between Galantas and Kalag, it was Ravin who would hold the balance of power. Fortunate, then, that he was also the uncle of the boy Galantas had saved from the stoneskins in the South Corridor yesterday.

Ravin kicked dust over the bloodline in the ritual gesture, then strode toward the standing stones. The conversation among the other clan leaders briefly broke off.

Galantas stood and brushed sand from his trousers. The stage was set, the other players assembled. He lowered his hood and paused to give the nearby clansmen a chance to recognize him. A murmur of anticipation went up, and he felt an answering buzz in his blood. This was his moment. This was his destiny, and his kinsmen's destiny too. He knew the path they must take to greatness, and if a thousand men, or ten thousand, or a hundred thousand must fall on the way, then so be it. The best leaders were those who could see farther than others. And that would be Galantas's task here tonight: keep his kinsmen's gazes directed to the horizon so they didn't notice him digging the ground out from under their feet.

He kicked sand over the bloodline. The chiefs had not seen him yet. Ravin was speaking to Tolo in his distinctive mangled voice.

". . . what I want to know is why the first warning of the attack came from Bezzle. What happened to the other watchtowers?"

"I'd like to hear the answer to that myself," Galantas said, stepping into the circle.

Ravin turned. He didn't look pleased to see Galantas. None of them did. Kalag in particular was scowling.

"Well, well," he said. "Seems some of the rats made it off the sinking ship after all. How's the arm, by the way?"

Galantas glanced at his empty short-cut sleeve. "What arm?"

The Needle chief, Malek, chuckled.

Galantas looked about the gathering. "Gentlemen," he said by way of greeting. Enigon gave him a nod. Tolo didn't spare him even that. The youth had acquired a tattoo since Galantas last saw him—a thin stripe along the line of his chin that was doubtless intended to look like a beard, but instead resembled a helmet's chinstrap.

Ravin was solemn as he offered Galantas his hand. "My commiserations about your father."

The man actually looked like he meant it, too. Evidently he expected Galantas to play the dutiful son, and it was a role Galantas could perform as well as any other. "Thank you," he said gravely, shaking the offered hand. Then he turned to Tolo. "You were telling us about your watchtowers," he said. The towers along the South Corridor—the direction from which the stone-skins had come—were mostly in Keel territory.

Tolo had the sullen eyes and uncertain speech of a boy half his age. "I don't answer to you."

"You answer to us," Galantas said, gesturing to take in the other clan leaders.

Tolo considered. At last he said, "The stone-skins attacked the towers just after the second bell. We've heard nothing from any of them since."

Ravin said, "Even Black Point?"

"Even Black Point."

The Falcon's brow furrowed. "Black Point is a Shroud-cursed fortress. No way the stone-skins could have taken it before someone rang its bell."

The accusation behind his words was clear: Tolo had accepted gold to ensure his men looked the other way when the Augeran ships came. And why not? If the stone-skins had twenty thousand talents to throw at Dresk, odds were they had money to buy the Keels' cooperation too.

Tolo looked at the ground. "Maybe they *did* ring the bell. Maybe the other towers didn't hear it 'cause they had already fallen."

"But *how* could they have fallen?" Galantas said. "Even I don't know where half your towers are, so how could the stone-skins?"

It was Kalag who answered. "You tell us. You got towers south of Bezzle too. Any o' them ring a note before the stone-skins came knocking?"

Galantas nodded as if that was the answer he'd wanted. "That shows the stone-skins were well prepared. That shows they've been planning to attack us for some time."

Kalag didn't let that slide. "Attack us? It was *your* damned city they hit."

"Tell that to the families of the Keels who died in the watchtowers. And what of the ships that were lost in Bezzle?" Galantas turned to Ravin. "The *Reef* was docked there, was she not?"

The Falcon nodded.

"Did her captain make it off the island?"

No response.

Galantas moved on to the Needle chief, Malek. "And the *Black Tide* came in this morning, didn't she?"

"Aye," Malek spat. "Shroud's own cursed luck. And she weren't alone there, either."

Galantas looked round the clan leaders. "The fact is, we all lost ships in the attack. Do you think the stone-skins didn't know that would happen? Do you think they'll give them back if you ask nicely?"

"You're forgetting your own part in this," Kalag said. "You owe us, boy. You stirred up the shit when you shot their commander. You can damn well clean it up now."

"What makes you so sure it was the Spears who shot him?"

Ravin spoke. "You know something we don't?"

"I know that by the time the stone-skin commander was shot, my father had already taken his gold. I know the Spears had nothing to gain from his death." Galantas made a dismissive gesture. "But that is a matter for another time. The reason we're here is to decide how to respond to the stone-skins' attack. And I say we strike back."

Kalag laughed. "The way I heard it, the stone-skins needed only five ships to take your city. They've got more than double that now."

Galantas raised his voice to carry to those beyond the bloodline. "What are you saying? That we should surrender before the war has even started?" Then, before Kalag could reply, "So what if the stone-skins have taken Bezzle? If the watchtowers had told us they were coming, we would have given them the city anyway. On land we may be no match for them, but on the sea we have no equal."

A murmur of approval from the clansmen met his words, but Kalag spoke over it. "If you had the ships, maybe. Pity, then, that you lost the best part of your fleet in Bezzle."

Enigon said, "Ah, but my dear Kalag, you're forgetting the stone-skins' twenty thousand talents." It was said with his usual grin, but there was an edge to his voice that suggested he was still smarting from Dresk's refusal to share the loot. "Easy to replace a few ships when you've got that sort of money in your pockets."

Galantas matched the clan leader's smile. "Alas, it seems my pockets have holes in them."

Kalag was loving it. "You lost the money? What, all of it?" He threw back his head and laughed. "Hear that, lads? The fool's lost twenty thousand talents!" The Raptor fished in his own pocket and pulled out a sovereign that he tossed to Galantas. "Here, boy, take this! Let no one say the Raptors didn't help the Spears in their time of need!"

Galantas caught the coin and looked down at it to see the face of Emperor Avallon Delamar looking back at him. Kalag was making this too easy. "Thanks," he said, tossing the sovereign back. "But *I* don't take Erin Elalese gold. Besides, while you might be prepared to surrender your ships without a fight, I don't give in so easily. Which is why I intend to take them back."

More murmurs, louder this time.

"How?" Malek said, his gaze intent. "Even if you had the numbers to retake Bezzle, the stone-skins would fire the ships before you could reach them."

"They won't have time."

"Oh? They've got ships outside the harbor and men inside the city. They'll see you coming long before you get there."

"Will they?" Galantas had them all hanging on his words now, and he took a moment to savor the sensation. Beyond the bloodline the assembled clansmen were silent. The only sound was the crackle of the torches and the murmur of the sea. "Imagine you're the stone-skins. Where would you expect a counterstrike to come from? From inland, of course, where most of my people fled. Or from the sea, as Malek says. But what if there was another way into Bezzle? A way the stone-skins didn't know about?" He kept them waiting an instant before explaining. "The Serpentine Aqueduct. It runs under the city from the north and comes out at the White Pool. It's wide enough for a man to walk along, and there's no way anyone in the city will hear you coming. I should know, I've used it enough times. And if none of you have thought about it, odds are the stone-skins haven't either."

Malek's eyes gleamed. "This pool, is it close to the harbor?"

"A stone's throw at most. The Augerans will have men on the waterfront, but they'll be spread thin. I'm guessing they'll be more worried about guarding their own ships than they are about watching empty Rubyholt ones. A small force should be able to reach those ships and launch them before the stone-skins respond."

"There's still the problem of the enemy ships outside the harbor. If they blockade the entrance, you'll be trapped inside."

"Those ships will have other things to worry about, because just as the land assault gets under way, a fleet of Rubyholt vessels will attack the port. The attack will be a feint, of course, aimed at drawing the stone-skins away."

Malek's expression was thoughtful. "And if the stone-skins pursue those Rubyholt vessels when they retreat?"

"Then we make them regret it. Earlier today I lured a stone-skin ship into the Dragon's Boneyard. It didn't end well for them. I suspect they might think twice now before following us into unfamiliar waters after dark."

Kalag sat down on a toppled stone. "And how are you gonna launch a sea strike when so many of your ships are in stone-skin hands?"

"That's where the rest of you come in."

Kalag stared at him. Then he laughed.

Galantas scanned the other clan leaders and saw the Raptor's amusement reflected there. Disappointing, but not wholly unexpected. He added a note of steel to his voice. "My father is dead, yet I see his influence lives on. Fifteen years as warlord, and all he could unite you in was contempt for his rule." He shook his head. "But the pattern was set before Dresk became warlord, was it not? I am old enough to remember the Third Clan War, but too young to have played a part in it. Remind me, what was it you fought over? Some worthless piece of rock no bigger than this circle."

"Spare us your history lesson, boy," Kalag said, but the Falcon leader, Ravin, held up a hand.

"This 'boy' "—he nodded at Galantas—"put his balls on the block yesterday to save one of my men on the *Lively*. If he's got something to say, I'm willing to hear him out."

Galantas suppressed a smile. He'd been counting on just such an intervention. That was why he'd waited for Ravin to arrive before making his own entrance. All he'd gained, though, was a chance to speak. Now he'd have to pick his words carefully, lest any inappropriate truths leak out.

"My lesson isn't over," he said. "Eight tribes we are now, but how many were there at the beginning of the Seventh Age? Fourteen." His voice turned bitter. "Six tribes we've lost in that time. And how many of those tribes fell to outsiders, do you suppose? Not one. You would think we'd have learned our lesson by now, but some of us"—he glanced at Kalag—"will still take foreign coin to pick a fight with their own kin. It's blood money, nothing less. And why do you think the likes of Avallon Delamar is prepared to pay it? Because he wants us divided. Because he remembers what happened the last time we fought against him."

Kalag wiped away a pretend tear, but Galantas ignored him. He'd always known the Raptor would not be for turning. It was Ravin's and Malek's support he needed.

"Enigon," Galantas said, "your tribe is descended from Xaver Jay, is it not?"

"It is."

"And Kalag, what of yours?"

Kalag did not reply, but he didn't need to. Every clan claimed descent from Jay—the notorious pirate and former Storm Lord who had founded the Rubyholt nation after he fled the Sabian League centuries ago. His likeness was carved into a hundred different cliffs around the Isles.

"Four years ago," Galantas said, "we fought against the Erin Elalese when they invaded. Malek, I remember at Summer Point when my father's water-mage took a stray arrow. You sailed rings round his attackers until Dresk could limp to the Shoals."

Malek nodded.

"And Tolo," Galantas went on, "as I recall, your father broke the blockade on Colgen as the enemy was preparing to attack the Falcons. Ravin repaid the favor when his catapults on the Dusk Strait took out an Erin Elalese ship chasing the *Mariana*."

More nods.

"A shame, isn't it," Galantas said, "that it takes an invasion to stop us fighting each other. And what has that fighting brought us to? Hells, the stone-skins just attacked one of our cities, and we can't even agree on whether to hit back." Kalag opened his mouth to speak, but Galantas forestalled him with a raised finger. "Shhh! Listen! Can you hear that?" Frowns and puzzled looks. Galantas cocked his head. "There, if you listen hard enough. Can you hear it now? That's the sound of the stone-skins laughing at us. The Erin Elalese and the Storm Lords too. Avallon sends his pitiful fleet into our waters. The Sabian League refuses to put an end to Dragon Day, or to pay us compensation for the damage caused by the dragons. And why should they? We're no threat to them. How soon do you think that will change if we keep fighting among ourselves?"

He paused to gauge the other clan leaders' reactions. Ravin's scowl could have signaled he shared Galantas's indignation, but it could equally have indicated disapproval at Galantas's words. Malek, meanwhile, was clicking his overlong fingernails together as if he wanted him to get to the point.

"Some of you may think the divisions between us go too deep to be mended," Galantas went on. "And if you look back, you'll find no shortage of feuds to pin a grievance on. Nothing sticks in the throat like a grudge, eh? But I prefer to look for the things we have in common. Our blood ties. The victories we've won." He looked round the clan leaders. "I'm offering you the chance at another. You all want to take back the ships you lost in Bezzle. So how are you going to do that? You don't want to help me, fine. I'll hit the harbor myself and take my chances with the stone-skin blockade. But what then? You could try your luck with your own raid afterward. How do you reckon that will go, though, once I've kicked up the nest? If we do this, we do it together."

And with that Galantas stepped back to signal he was done.

For a while no one spoke. The cries of the blueback whale sounded

from the east. A breath of wind tugged at the torches. All eyes were
on Ravin and Malek, yet it seemed neither man wanted to be first to
show his hand. Galantas resisted an urge to break the silence. He'd
said what he had to say. To speak again might be read as desperation. In any case, it wasn't as if he was asking for more than he was
offering. The others had probably expected him to plead for help in
retaking Bezzle, or to argue for some half-assed alliance against the
stone-skins. But this wasn't about war with the Augerans. This was
about proving the clans could work together.

And that Galantas was the best man to do the working for.

Malek's voice took him by surprise. "What's your assessment of the
stone-skins' capabilities?"

"They're good. Or at least their Honored are—that's what they call
their elite fighters. But they still bleed easily enough, for all that their
skin looks like stone. On land we would struggle to match them. At
sea . . ." He shrugged. "A single Augeran ship took out two Falcons,
but they had the advantage of surprise, and the damage was done by
their sorcerers. As for their seamanship, we will have to see."

"And this raid on the harbor you're planning . . . how many men
would there be?"

"Two hundred," Galantas said without hesitation. "We strike hard
and fast, target twenty ships at most."

"A water-mage on each?"

He nodded.

"When?"

"When do we hit them?" Galantas smiled. "Why, now, of course."

Kalag was incredulous. "Now?"

"What's the matter? Is it past your bedtime?" Then, to the other
clan leaders: "The longer we wait, the greater the risk of more stone-
skins arriving."

Kalag's look turned sly. "And who's going to lead this force?"

"Me. No one knows Bezzle better than I do."

"You?" The Raptor laughed. "A green boy? I was leading raids like
this when you were still a bulge in your father's trousers."

Galantas's expression darkened. Kalag knew he had lost the
argument, so he was trying to muscle in on the glory. "And age is
what counts, is it? Let us scour the Isles then, find the oldest grayhair
to lead the attack." Men like Kalag seemed to think they deserved

respect because they happened to have been born first. To Galantas's mind, that just meant they'd had more time to make fools of themselves.

"It ain't age I'm talking about," Kalag said, "it's experience—"

"Experience?" Galantas cut in. "And what experience is that? Of bending over and taking it from my father for fifteen years?"

Hoots from beyond the bloodline. Kalag turned red. He reached for his sword hilt, but Malek seized his wrist. "Enough," the Needle said, "Galantas is right. The city is his, the plan is his. He should have the command."

Galantas wanted to punch the air, but he kept his voice even. "And the sea strike? Who will lead that?"

"I will," Malek said. "But I have only three ships here to call on." He looked round the other clan leaders. "I'll need more than that if I'm to draw the stone-skins off."

Ravin grunted. He was frowning at Galantas as if Galantas had just asked for his daughter's hand in marriage. But he nodded his support all the same.

Enigon and Tolo followed close behind.

CHAPTER 14

ROMANY LEANED back in her chair and scanned the Erin Elalese delegation across the table. Avallon and Tyrin Lindin Tar were leafing through two leather-bound books, the emperor with genuine interest, the tyrin huffing in obvious irritation at Mazana Creed's tardiness. Two nameless soldiers were stationed behind her. The mage, Jelek Balaran, completed Avallon's party—unless you counted Senar Sol among their number, of course, and the priestess suspected not even the Guardian knew if you could. He stood to Romany's left at the midpoint of the desk, neither on one side or the other, as befitted his divided loyalties.

She studied the emperor. In all honesty, she'd expected a leader of his notoriety to cut a more imposing figure, but when did a man's substance ever measure up to his reputation? A charismatic ruler, the reports said, yet doubtless those reports had been written by Avallon himself. A merciless man, too, and that trait at least Romany had no trouble believing, considering the manner in which he'd crushed resistance to Erin Elalese influence in the Confederacy cities. That made her wonder what he'd do if Mazana refused to support him in his conflict with the stone-skins. Would he risk moving against her here, in Gilgamar, in the hope her successor proved more amenable? It seemed unlikely, but at least the *threat* of a confrontation might open up opportunities Romany could exploit. When the time came for her to act against Mazana, she would have no shortage of suspects onto whom she could shift the blame.

The door opened, and Mazana swept in, accompanied by Jodren and his twittering coral bird. The emira's gaze met Romany's, and the priestess saw nothing in her eyes to suggest Senar had told her of their encounter at the portal. Avallon rose and inclined his head, but Lindin remained seated. As Mazana took her place opposite the emperor, it struck Romany how unalike the two factions were. Avallon sat between two of his famed Circle, Lindin and Jelek— companions who would gladly lay down their lives for him, or some such nonsense. And who had Mazana chosen to be in her corner? A mercenary commander whose allegiance might be bought by someone else tomorrow; and Romany herself, who had been tasked by the Spider with killing the woman. It wasn't even as if Mazana had any more trusted allies outside the room, what with the other Storm Lords dead and the Storm Council disbanded.

The emira and Avallon inspected each other across the desk like opponents over a hafters board. Of the two of them it was clear Mazana held the advantage of the queen's pieces, for it was the emperor who had requested this meeting, the emperor who had most to fear from the stone-skins' coming. Avallon smiled. There was something about that smile that grated on Romany. Like it was given as a gift in the expectation Mazana and her party would bask in it. This meeting would doubtless be a novel experience for him, since he would be used to giving orders, not negotiating. Would he be able to keep his pride in check long enough to persuade the emira of his cause?

Mazana wouldn't make it easy for him, that much at least was clear.

"Is this it?" Avallon said, his gaze sweeping the emira's end of the table. "Will your shaman not be joining us?"

Mazana cocked her head. "I'd have thought you had enough shamans of your own, what with the Remnerol homeland falling inside your borders."

"I've got dozens. And all telling me different things. Whereas your man was apparently able to pinpoint the precise location of two of my people in the Rubyholt Isles. Senar Sol told me of the Chameleons' mission to Bezzle."

The emira glanced at the Guardian. "Did he now?"

Senar kept silent.

Avallon said, "Your shaman saw exactly where my agents would be—"

"Where they *might* be," Mazana corrected him.

"Nevertheless, you trusted his judgment enough to act on it."

"Enough to gamble the lives of two entirely expendable Chameleons, yes."

"Small stakes, big prize?"

"If you like."

A ghost of another smile crossed Avallon's face. "And this prize you sought . . . the destruction of the stone-skin fleet. A retaliation for Dragon Day?"

Romany saw where the emperor was heading with this. If he could get Mazana to acknowledge she saw the stone-skins as a threat, that would be a good first step toward establishing common cause between the Storm Isles and Erin Elal. Perhaps he had a point too. Mazana, though, was clearly not minded to concede it, for she said, "Just a little message to the Augerans that their involvement in Dragon Day did not go unnoticed. And a warning of what would happen if they interfered in my affairs again."

Avallon had to purse his lips to stop himself from arguing the matter further. He drank a mouthful of wine from his glass. "Your shaman was able to tell you that my agents were in Bezzle, but was he also able to explain *why*?"

"No."

"Then let me fill in the gaps. On Dragon Day, an Augeran emissary arrived in the Isles to request an audience with the warlord. The reason for the audience wasn't made clear, but I think we can assume the stone-skins wanted safe passage for their fleet. It was possible, of course, that Dresk would refuse. It was also possible the stone-skins' target would be the Sabian League, not Erin Elal. But there seemed no reason to take the risk. So I sent someone to turn the warlord against the stone-skins by whatever means necessary."

"Because you'll stop at nothing to drag your neighbors into your war."

Avallon waved the comment aside as if it were unworthy. "The meeting between Dresk and the Augerans was due to take place today—"

"Today?" Mazana cut in. "Oh, I think you'll find it happened before that."

The emperor stared at her, caught off guard. Romany could almost hear the cogs whirring in his head. He would be wondering precisely when the stone-skins arrived in Bezzle, and whether his agents had made it there before them. He would also be wondering how he was going to extract this information from Mazana without asking her directly.

Lindin Tar came to his rescue. "When?" she asked simply.

Romany rolled her eyes. With subtlety like that, the woman was wasted as a soldier. Faced with a barred door, she was trying to pick the lock with a battering ram.

Mazana surprised the priestess by answering. "Yesterday. The stone-skins arrived shortly before your agents did."

Avallon regained his poise. "Your shaman pointed the Chameleons to them because he foresaw they would need help. But help against whom?"

"The stone-skins, I presume. And before you ask, no, Jambar wasn't able to tell me whether your people succeeded in their mission."

"What of the Chameleons and the task you gave them? I don't suppose your shaman was any more forthcoming about the success of *their* mission either."

"I don't suppose so."

Lindin Tar scowled, but this once, Romany knew, Mazana was not dissembling. Several days ago, the priestess had overheard along her web a conversation between the emira and Jambar on this very subject. The shaman's lack of precision then had been met by Mazana with the same degree of skepticism now being shown by the Erin Elalese.

Avallon gulped down another mouthful of wine. Romany realized her gaze was following his hand each time he raised his glass. "Well," he said, after a pause, "we'll find out what happened soon enough when your people or mine report."

"Or when the stone-skin fleet arrives at your shore," Mazana said.

"Or yours. The Rubyholt Isles shield Erin Elal more than they do the Sabian League, yes. But free passage through the Isles would help the stone-skins strike at Dian or Natilly, too. Or Gilgamar, for that matter. Three important cities to the League, you must see that."

"Three cities that are accessible from the Ribbon Sea without having to pass through the Isles."

"So is the whole of Erin Elal's eastern seaboard, if you want to see it that way."

Mazana smiled as if to concede the point.

The patio doors had been thrown open against the heat of the night, and the needleflies drawn inside now buzzed around the lamps in the room. A feathermoth careered round and down toward a flame like it was being sucked into a whirlpool, and Romany had to stay her hand against an impulse to reach for the knife at her waist. The emperor's guards, she suspected, would not look kindly on a repeat of the display she'd given the Spider at the temple.

A fizz, a flicker of light, and the moth burned brightly before flopping onto the floor.

"Tell me," Avallon said to Mazana, "has Senar Sol told you anything of Erin Elal's history with Augera?"

"He has. More than I wanted to know, in fact."

"Truly? I admit my people's history with the stone-skins makes us the most likely target for their aggression. But I'd have thought you would want to learn as much as you could about a potential enemy."

"Are we talking about the Augerans or Erin Elal here?"

The emperor gave her the sort of look a long-suffering father might bestow on his wayward daughter. Then he slid across the desk to her the book he'd been reading when she arrived. "Take a look at this."

Mazana trapped it with one hand and glanced at it. "And to think they say history is written by the victors."

"Oh, come now, we only found out the stone-skins were here when they hit you on Dragon Day. That was two weeks ago. You think we could have written a whole new history in that time?"

"Of course not. Just as you couldn't have held back a book from your library if you thought it would harm your cause."

With a scrape of wood on stone, Avallon pushed back his chair as if he meant to rise, only to remain seated. "That text," he said, gesturing to the book, "dates back eight hundred years. It's the history of a war between the stone-skins and some of their neighbors."

"It's also written in Erin Elalese."

"There must be someone on your staff who speaks the language."

"Someone sufficiently educated, you mean?" Mazana looked at Romany. "Well, priestess?"

Romany hesitated, reluctant to be drawn into the conversation, yet equally loath to deny the full measure of her learning. "I have a passing knowledge."

"And?"

"And what?"

Mazana pushed the book over to her. "And what do you make of this?"

Romany did not look down. "It's a book. Almost certainly."

The emira raised an eyebrow.

With a sigh the priestess opened the cover, then stifled a cough at the puff of dust it released. The name of the book was written on the first page in the absurdly decorative style that seemed common to scribes the world over. *A Military History of Augera*. Catchy title, that. The author must have labored long and hard over it. Its pages crackled as she turned them. She'd read enough old books in her time to know the text was as ancient as the emperor claimed.

Avallon said, "I've taken the liberty of marking a few pages I think you'll find interesting."

"Don't count on it," Romany muttered.

"The first double page I've flagged"—he waited for her to turn to it—"shows the stone-skins' empire in the eastern part of a continent known as Crayland. Erin Elal, you'll see, is to the west, occupying an area greater than the one we currently control."

"And you're sure this map is accurate?" Romany said, peering at it. The coastlines seemed implausibly uniform, and whoever had drawn it hadn't bothered to include something as mundane as a scale. More amusingly, "There's a point inside Augera's borders marked 'The Abyss.'"

"I'm aware of it," Avallon snapped. "I think it's safe to assume the reference is merely figurative. Unless, of course, you believe the Void has taken root in the world, and the end of all things is upon us. Now, if I may be allowed to continue, the last double page I've marked shows the same continent just twelve years later. You'll notice Augera has now swallowed up the nations on its northern and southern borders, along with the patchwork of states that separated it from Erin Elal." He looked from Mazana to Romany to Jodren. "Twelve years it took them to annihilate an area the size of your Sabian Sea. And 'annihilate' is the word, since the stone-skins didn't enslave the native populations, they exterminated them down to the last soul. Men, women, children." He paused to let the import of his words sink in. "The writer of that book estimates the total dead at thirteen million."

Romany frowned. Sobering statistics, to be sure, but unlikely to induce even a flutter from Mazana's tar-black heart, or that of the blood-soaked mercenary commander sitting beside her. Particularly since there was no way of judging the mettle of the nations that had fallen beneath the Augeran sword.

Avallon rose and put his fists on the desk. "The Erin Elalese lasted a mere five years against the stone-skins before they were driven into the sea. Earlier, when the course of the war became clear, the then emperor ordered ships built in readiness for evacuation. Yet when the end came, it came so suddenly that only a fraction of the population escaped. You'll be familiar with the reputation of the Guardians as warriors without compare. During the Augeran conflict there were hundreds of them, yet even they were unable to turn back the enemy tide."

Mazana nodded gravely. "Yes, such a shame their numbers have fallen away in recent years."

The emperor's jaw clenched.

Jodren cleared his throat. "What's so formidable about these stone-skins?" he asked in a voice that said, whatever it was, he wasn't impressed. "What's the basis for their military success?"

"A pertinent question," Avallon said. "Every stone-skin—every damned one of them—joins a barracks at the age of six, and their place in society is dictated by how long they remain there. The first ones out spend the rest of their lives as servants. Only the very best last the course through to adulthood. Their elite division, the Honored, is probably bigger than Erin Elal's entire army."

"So it's a numbers thing."

"They had a few technological advantages over us when we first met—the quality of their steel, and so forth—though generally we had caught up to them by the end of the war." He hesitated. "There are also suggestions that stone-skin warriors are able to forge a mental link between them when they fight, though as to precisely how this works, and what benefits it brings, we can only speculate."

And why not? Romany thought. Speculation seemed to be far more prevalent among these Erin Elalese than actual facts.

Mazana gave a whistle. "A daunting foe, indeed. My commiserations to your people and anyone foolish enough to stand with them."

"If there is to be another war, the result will be different this time."

Romany snorted. The age-old cry of the habitual loser.

Avallon glared at her. "The circumstances of this conflict bear no resemblance to those of the last."

"Absolutely," Mazana said. "Your strength is down, while the Augerans' has likely grown."

"That's not what I meant. The enemy will have to conduct their campaign across an ocean, with all the challenges of transportation and provisioning that will bring."

"And yet I suspect their commander didn't wake up one morning and choose to invade because his coin flip landed heads. The stone-skins will have been planning this attack for a long time. Far longer, I'm sure, than *you* will have to plan a defense."

Avallon waved a dismissive hand. "There are risks in war no amount of planning can guard against. The Augeran fleet will be vulnerable when it crosses the Southern Wastes, particularly if we can persuade you to sell us your remaining stores of dragon blood. And if we have the stronger water-mages, of course." He threw back the remaining wine in his glass. "The stone-skins will know this too; hence their actions on Dragon Day. Clearly they were concerned enough by the Storm Lord threat that they chose to make a preemptive strike against you. Though why they should feel the need to do so when our two peoples are not allied—"

"Please," Mazana interrupted, holding up a hand. "I've heard this argument so many times from Senar Sol I can make it for you myself: Why would the stone-skins risk the enmity of the Storm Isles unless they knew their plans for us would make such enmity inevitable, yes?"

"If you've heard the argument before, you'll have had time to think up a response. So tell me, how *do* you explain the Augerans' actions on Dragon Day?"

"Their commander is obviously not a man who likes to gamble. He must have wanted the Storm Lords out of the picture to ensure we didn't interfere in his war with you."

Avallon appeared to consider this, his gaze not leaving Mazana's. Then he gave a smile that suggested he wasn't as irritated as he'd been making out. A smile that left Romany wondering whether, somehow, he had orchestrated the conversation so it arrived at just this point. "Ah, but there's the crux, isn't it? There *is* no war between Augera and Erin Elal. We've had nothing to do with them for eight hundred years. Yet suddenly their commander wakes up and—how did you put it?—throws a coin that lands heads?"

When Mazana next spoke, it was more warily. "You were enemies once; why not again? Clearly your previous war left scars slow to fade."

"Those scars would be on our side, surely. And even if you are right, why wait eight hundred years to come looking for redress? My people fled across an ocean, not the Abyss. The Augerans must've known we were here. The gods know, we've sailed enough ships along their coast over the years to keep an eye on them. It stands to reason they've done the same to us. So, I ask again, why have they come *now*?"

The room had gone still. All about, the Alcazar was so quiet they might have talked into the dead of night. *Why now?* A question so simple it was a wonder Romany hadn't considered it before, but its true import was only evident now that the emperor had spoken. Mazana's face remained expressionless, yet under the desk—out of sight of the Erin Elalese—one of her feet was tapping. She was plainly too proud to ask Avallon the next, inevitable, question, so Romany sighed and voiced it herself. "You have a theory?"

The emperor's gaze flickered to her before returning to the emira. "Maybe it has something to do with why the Augerans massacre the people they conquer. Maybe it's because they need the land."

"Maybe?" Mazana said. "You mean you don't know? You were at war with the stone-skins for five years, watched them wipe out your neighbors for the twelve before that. And no one stopped to ask why the Augerans were attacking?"

"Doubtless they did, but the knowledge did not survive the ages."

"Of course not."

The emperor set his fists on the desk again. "In case you've forgotten, a few things happened over the last eight hundred years that might have caused us to misplace the odd book. Things like—oh, I don't know—the relocation of our entire Shroud-cursed civilization! No doubt memories of the conflict were sharp for the hundred years after the Exile, but memories tend to fade when people die."

Mazana wasn't backing down. "And you think, what, the Augerans are here now because they've outgrown their homeland?"

"It fits, you must see that."

"If the stone-skins breed like ruskits, maybe. But their breeding habits are probably just another detail that has been lost to the mists of time."

Avallon leaned so far across the desk his chest almost touched it. "If I'm right, the Augerans won't stop when they conquer Erin Elal.

If I'm right, they'll come for you next. Your only chance of survival—yours, and all the other nations this side of the Southern Wastes—is to unite against them."

"Yes, you're always looking out for the best interests of your neighbors. The Remnerol, the Maisee, the cities of the Confederacy."

"And you have a better plan, do you? Maybe cling to the old hostilities, let the Augerans pick us off one by one?"

Mazana shrugged. "*If* you're right."

"If I'm right, yes." *And how could I be otherwise?* his tone seemed to say.

He was an emperor, after all.

As the last light faded in the west, Amerel sat in the boneyard looking down on Bezzle. She'd seen more than her fair share of conquered cities. After the siege of Cenan there had been riot and revelry, fire and smoke, snatches of laughter and shrieks of horror. Amerel could still picture the bodies piled up in the streets, taste the grease at the back of her throat from the burning corpses, see the people dashing every which way—some seeking escape from the madness, others seeking more of it. Even the Deliverer's dreams seemed bland by comparison. But weren't sights such as these the lot of a warrior? Victors or vanquished, she wondered sometimes who were the lucky ones. At least the dead only had to endure the night once.

Bezzle was different. There were still bodies, of course—lots of bodies. But instead of Cenan's nightmare cacophony, there was an oppressive silence broken only by an occasional scream or the crash of a splintering door. Groups of torchbearing stone-skins moved from house to house, dragging out survivors and butchering them. At Cenan, the besiegers had spent weeks camped outside the city, watching the walls turn red with the blood of their slain kinsmen. When they had finally overwhelmed the defenders, there had been a sense of release that had swept the Erin Elalese up and only set them down again several bells later. It didn't excuse what was done in the city, perhaps—who judged these things, anyhow? But at least it explained it. In Bezzle, by contrast, there was no abandon among the conquerors; just a cold, deliberate precision that brought the hairs up on Amerel's arms. An army capable of such a controlled display of ruthlessness was one to be feared indeed.

As the Guardian scratched a spider bite on her arm, she found herself wondering what had become of Talet's son. Had he left the city before the stone-skin attack? Unlikely, since Talet would have planned for them to flee together. Why had Hex pressed the spy into revealing the boy's location? Would he hunt him down now that he knew where he was? There seemed nothing to be gained by doing so, but would Hex need a reason? Thoughts of the boy made Amerel's mind turn to Lyssa. Was she safe? Was she missing Amerel, or glad to be rid of her? Perhaps a bit of both—a mirror to the Guardian's own feelings regarding her niece. After their first few tortured weeks together, it was hard to believe Amerel might ever come to miss the girl. But in time even the unspeakable can become routine.

Footsteps behind.

Noon drew up beside her and sat down on one of the gravestones. She could sense he was chafing to ask her questions about the Deliverer, but instead he said, "I didn't get a chance earlier. To thank you for saving me. If you hadn't—"

"I get it, you owe me," Amerel cut in. "Don't worry, I hadn't forgotten."

The Breaker looked across at her, and she thought he would get up and leave. Instead he gave a half smile and turned back to the city. Truth be told, she was impressed at how he'd kept himself together after the ordeal at Talet's house. Most men would have gotten surly or standoffish after having their pride pricked like that. But maybe Noon was just used to his enemies getting the better of him.

"Is that the White Lady's Temple burning?" he said, pointing to a blazing ruin at the edge of the Old Town.

Amerel nodded. "While you were resting, the stone-skins gave the shrine a good pounding with the same sorcery they used at Dresk's fortress. The priests held out for a while, but when their Beloved fell, the stone-skins barricaded the doors and fired the place." She plucked a blade of grass from the ground and rolled it in her fingers. "Fair to say the Augerans aren't believers."

"It's one thing not to follow a goddess, another to spit in her eye."

"Though if you *are* going to pick a fight with an immortal, the goddess of mercy and reconciliation is the one to choose."

The Breaker grimaced. "The people in that temple weren't a threat to the stone-skins. Just women and children, most likely."

"You think the Augerans were heavy-handed? Are there acceptable degrees of brutality in war, then?"

"Gotta draw the line somewhere."

"The people of Cenan will be relieved to hear it. You were there, weren't you, when the city fell?" Amerel had read his file; he could hardly deny it. "How many survived that night of bloodletting?"

Noon wasn't biting. He nodded toward the city. "This slaughter's gonna make it harder for us to get to the harbor. No chance of the stone-skins mistaking us for locals if there aren't any locals left breathing."

"Or maybe their diligence will work to our benefit. The more thorough they are in clearing the city, the less reason they'll have to patrol it after."

"Always a sunny side, eh?"

"I try my best to find it."

In the harbor a Rubyholt ship burned, perhaps as a beacon to guide in the rest of the stone-skin fleet. Even now, a three-masted galleon with patterned sails glided between the islets on a wave of water-mage. Light from the torches on the waterfront glinted off the armor of dozens of figures on deck.

Noon said, "Have you been keeping tally of the ships coming in?"

Amerel flicked the blade of grass away. "Yes. I make that fourteen."

"Any transports?"

"No, all warships."

The Breaker's brow furrowed. "A ship like that will have a complement of maybe four hundred. Say two hundred of them soldiers. Could be as many as two hundred and fifty. Multiply that by fourteen and you get . . ."

"A lot of men," Amerel finished. The Augerans would feel their loss keenly if she could make the Chameleons' plan work.

Perhaps sensing her thoughts, Noon looked toward where Caval and Karmel were practicing with their blowpipes. "You trust them to get this done?"

"Mazana Creed must have had some reason for picking them."

"That Caval's an oscura addict—you see how gray his eyes were? When the time comes for him to fire his blowpipe, it'd be nice if his hands weren't shaking."

"I'm sure his sister will keep him in line." From what Amerel had seen, it was Karmel who called the shots between them.

Noon picked at his boots—the boots he'd taken from one of the dead stone-skin warriors at the house. "There's bad blood there. The way they tiptoe around each other."

"What do you expect? They're family."

Karmel crossed to a tree to retrieve the darts she'd been peppering it with. She'd been steadily increasing the distance to her target, yet still hitting it with near-perfect accuracy.

"How much do you think they're not telling us about all this?" Noon asked.

"The Chameleons? Very little. Mokinda, on the other hand . . ."

"You reckon he's holding a crossbow to the Chameleons' heads?"

Amerel's smile was tight. "That's usually how it works."

If Noon noticed her tone, he gave no indication. "Stupid, isn't it. We've got every reason to work together, so why do I feel like I'm just waiting for a knife in my back?"

"No doubt the Chameleons think the same." Amerel had caught some of the looks Karmel had cast her way. It made her wonder what Senar Sol had said about her, and how he fit into all this. Was he some part of the emperor's master plan that Avallon hadn't seen fit to share with her? It was possible. Still, there was no denying the Chameleons had good reason to be suspicious of Amerel's intentions. "When they've finished marking the stone-skin ships," she said to Noon, "how much dragon blood do you think they'll have left in that flask of theirs?"

The Breaker stared at her blankly.

"Enough to mark another fleet, maybe? Or two. How valuable do you think that might be to the empire?"

Now he got it. Judging by his frown, he didn't like what she was implying, but he wasn't arguing against it either. "Maybe it won't come to that. Maybe they'll hand the blood over if we ask."

"Maybe," Amerel said. "I can be very persuasive when I have to be, after all."

Romany thumped shut the cover of Avallon's book. No more! She hadn't seen writing this dull since she'd peeked inside Abologog's

Fourth Treatise on Reverence. Information was conveyed without wit or insight, and in such a condescending tone she could almost hear the author's withered voice droning in her ear. And yet there was no clarity to the work. Some sections she had to read over and over to tease out the meaning, and she understood how Mayot Mencada must have felt trying to decipher the Book of Lost Souls.

She rubbed a hand across her eyes. Half a bell she'd been reading, and she was still only a handful of pages in. Mazana and Avallon hadn't set a time for the renewal of their hostilities tomorrow, but both would doubtless expect her to have finished the book by then. Thus far the stone-skins had barely set foot outside their borders in their first campaign against their northern neighbor. The only detail of interest was a hint that the Augerans had been a peaceful people before the war. As to what had precipitated their transformation into brutal empire-builders, though . . . the book was frustratingly silent.

Romany opened the cover again. The lamp on her desk flickered in the breeze coming through her room's solitary window. Then a distant clang sounded, and she tested the strands of her web for its cause.

This should prove entertaining.

She rose and exited through the door.

A hundred heartbeats later she found herself in a corridor next to an overgrown torchlit courtyard. A motley collection of Gray Cloaks and Erin Elalese soldiers were looking into the yard through the archways and windows surrounding it. In the yard itself was a circular paved area bounded by knee-high grasses and beds of wilting flowers. On the paving stones battled the Revenant subcommander, Twist, and the emperor's white-clad bodyguard, Strike.

Twist and Strike. It sounded like a move in some intricate fighting sequence.

Instead of the flails with which Twist had fought Kiapa, the mercenary wielded two shortswords with curved tips that Romany recognized as khindals. His opponent was armed with a longsword. Evidently the blade was imbued with earth-magic, for it cut through the air with preternatural speed. Its owner, too, showed freakish swiftness as he stepped back from a thrust to his chest before springing onto a bench to evade a low cut. There was something absurdly effortless about that leap—as if, had Strike wanted to, he could just as easily have jumped onto the roof instead. Romany realized with a start that he was animal-aspected. A flintcat, perhaps, judging by the tawny sheen to his eyes.

A disciple of the Beast God.

The watchers about the courtyard were hushed, perhaps because of the lateness of the hour, perhaps in recognition of the skill of the duelists. A Gray Cloak with a goatee beard moved along the corridor across from Romany, calling out odds in a low voice. It seemed that he had Twist down as the marginal favorite, though the priestess suspected that might be out of misplaced loyalty to his subcommander, for Strike had the edge in both speed and reach. The bodyguard's kinsmen must have shared that assessment, for the bearded bookmaker was finding no shortage of takers as he worked his way along a line of Erin Elalese soldiers. Romany wouldn't put it past the Gray Cloaks, though, to have arranged some sting on the foreigners. *Twist pretends himself hard-pressed to bring in the bets before breaking out his "A" game?* It wouldn't be the first time it had happened.

For a while the men fought back and forth across the courtyard, feet swishing through the grass, the initiative shifting between them with each sweep of a shadowy blade. Strike's sword made a whining sound with each stroke. As in the duel between Kiapa and Twist, Romany found herself contemplating how she would fare if she ever crossed blades with one of these swordsmen, and she was forced to concede she would be outclassed.

As an assassin, though, she would kill them before they even drew a weapon.

She watched Strike deliver a backhand blow that almost pierced Twist's defenses. His sword wailed as he drove his opponent past the archway on the opposite wall. In the shadows beyond the arch, a small red-haired figure observed the duel. . . .

Romany did a double take.

Uriel?

She tutted in disapproval. What in the Spider's name was the boy doing up at this hour? He wore his bedclothes, and his hair stood up at all angles as if he'd been roused from his sleep. Surely, though, there would have been someone stationed outside his room to stop him wandering off. There was no sign of Mazana Creed.

Whatever the explanation, this was no place for a boy of seven.

Romany stomped around the corridors, annoyed that she'd have to miss the duel to assume Mazana's mothering duties. At her temple in Mercerie, she had always left the care of the youngest acolytes to her juniors, but there was no one else here who could take the boy under their wing. Besides, how difficult could it be to handle a seven-year-old when she'd faced down tyrants and emperors in her time?

As she approached Uriel, she saw the Everlord, Kiapa, standing a short distance beyond him. Could he have been the one guarding the boy's room? If so, he would no doubt have welcomed the chance to bring his charge to watch the fight. That didn't absolve Romany of her duty, though. She drew up next to Uriel. He blinked over and over as if he was struggling to keep his eyes open, and the priestess noticed for the first time that he was missing one of his lower front teeth. Who knew, maybe Twist had challenged *him* to a duel earlier as well.

"Did your mother say you could be here?" Romany asked. Because that didn't make her sound old at all.

Uriel looked her way before returning his attention to the fight. "She's not my mother; she's my sister."

Of course she was, where was the priestess's head tonight? "Did your sister say you could be here?"

"No. But she wasn't in her room when I woke up. I came to look for her."

"She's probably looking for *you* right now. She's probably afraid you're—"

"No, she isn't," Uriel cut in fiercely. "Mazana's not afraid of anything!"

Except duty and decorum, perhaps. "Come with me," Romany said.

He made no move to comply.

In the courtyard, Twist had sought respite from his foe by retreating behind a bench, but Strike simply hurdled it and set about him again. The crash of the two men's blades came so rapidly the sounds merged to form one long metallic note.

"Why are they fighting?" Uriel said.

"They're warriors. What else would they do?"

"It's not fair. Why can that man"—he nodded at Twist—"have two swords when that man"—Strike—"only has one?"

To the contrary, it seemed to Romany that, of the combatants, it

was Strike who had the unfair advantage with his sorcerously imbued speed and his invested weapon. "That one"—Strike—"could use
two swords if he wanted."

"So why doesn't he?"

"You would have to ask him."

"But . . . he's from Erin Elal, isn't he?"

"Yes."

"Mazana told me not to speak to anyone from Erin Elal."

"Then we had best return to your room straightaway. Some
of these other people watching"—the priestess gestured to either
side—"are Erin Elalese too."

The boy considered this, then yawned and gave a reluctant nod.

Romany steered him down the corridor with a hand on his shoulder before letting the hand fall to her side—only to flinch as something touched it. It turned out to be just Uriel putting his hand in
hers. The priestess's reaction, though, had been entirely understandable considering the last child to hold her hand had been a Mercerien
urchin trying to part her from her rings. Uriel's hand felt warm and
uncommonly small in hers. They walked past a line of Gray Cloaks,
and Romany was grateful the warriors' attention was fixed on the
duel. Then she reached the end of the line and saw Mili and Tali
watching her. They gave her amused looks as she passed.

Oh, the indignity.

A grunt sounded from the courtyard, and there was a collective
intake of breath from the spectators. Alas, Romany had moved out of
sight of the duelists, and thus had no idea what the gasp signified. As
she and Uriel rounded a corner, she sensed the boy's gaze on her, but
when she glanced down he looked away. Then he looked back at her
again, his expression showing puzzlement and earnestness in equal
measure. The resemblance to his half sister was quite striking in that
instant. He opened his mouth to speak, but seemed to think better of
it. Probably working up the courage to ask her for a story. Romany
would have to go back to her room for that book on Augera, that was
sure to send him to sleep.

Uriel looked at her again.

Here it comes.

"Why do you wear that mask?" he said at last. "Is it because you're
very ugly?"

"Here he comes," Noon said.

Amerel looked up to see Caval making his way toward them along the alley leading to the harbor. Dressed in midnight blue, and with his power engaged, he was little more than a tremor in the darkness. He'd been gone for a quarter-bell, and Karmel's relief at his return was evident in her slowly released breath.

Caval's voice was a whisper over the gurgle of water entering the pool from the underwater aqueduct. "There's no doubt about it, the stone-skins are preparing to pull out. The waterfront is crawling with them."

Amerel swore. She'd feared as much on the journey through the city when they had only to evade a dozen patrols. She wiped sweat from her brow. "Any ships leaving *now*?"

"No, they're still making preparations. Though I did see one ship come in to dock before immediately casting off again."

Meaning this withdrawal was not in the stone-skins' original script. Meaning something, somewhere, had happened to make the Augerans change their plans. And Amerel was willing to bet that that "something" spelled trouble for Erin Elal. "Jambar never warned you of this?"

Caval looked at Karmel, then said, "No. He told us we'd have days, if not weeks, before the fleet moved."

Noon spoke. "Could it be the Rubyholters? Could the stone-skins have got wind of an attack?"

Amerel shook her head. Even if the Islanders had teamed up for a retaliatory strike, how big a force could they assemble at such short notice? Big enough to set the stone-skins running with their tails between their legs? The Guardian doubted it.

A cloud of needleflies swarmed about her, and she waved a hand at them. "What's the story with this blayfire oil we can smell?" she asked Caval. It had been burning her nostrils for the last half-bell. "Are the stone-skins getting ready to fire the Rubyholt ships?"

"If they are, they're not going to do it while their own ships are here."

Noon said, "So what's to stop us striking the flint now?"

"Nothing," Caval replied. "But if you did so, there's no guarantee you'd send the stone-skin ships up in flames with the Rubyholt ones.

The Augerans have got water-mages, remember? Difficult to make a fire spread when there are water-mages about."

Karmel said, "So what now?"

Amerel's voice was iron. "We go through with the original plan."

The priestess stared at her. "You're serious? Did you miss the part where Caval said the waterfront is crawling with stone-skins?"

"So we do this carefully. But we do it now. In a bell's time, the chance will have gone."

"If we do it carefully, we'll be lucky to mark a couple of ships before they leave."

"But a couple might still lure the dragons. And when they come, with luck they'll take down not just the marked ships but the rest of the fleet too."

Karmel looked unconvinced. "What about the plan B we discussed at the boneyard? Why don't we tip the blood in the harbor—"

"No," Amerel cut her off. "You said it yourself, if we do that the dragons will come here rather than to wherever the Augeran fleet is."

"Maybe to start with. But they'll get round to the stone-skins eventually." Then Karmel's eyes widened in understanding. "Except you're worried about where the fleet is heading *now,* aren't you? You think it's going for Erin Elal, not the League."

Before Amerel could respond, Caval said, "Even if we mark the ships, it'll be days before the blood draws the dragons. It's nearly two weeks since Dragon Day, so most of the creatures will be back in the Southern Wastes. There's no way they're going to get here before the stone-skins reach wherever it is they're heading."

"Maybe," Amerel said. "But maybe it'll take the Augerans longer than we expect to sail through the Isles. Or maybe there's a dragon nearby that hasn't made the trip south yet."

"That's a long 'maybe' to risk getting caught over."

Amerel couldn't disagree. And if the roles were reversed, there was no way she would have been persuaded to gamble her life. But then the Chameleons didn't have the Will to help with the persuading. She gathered it now and turned it on Karmel.

"We knew what we were getting into from the start," she said to the priestess. "We knew how many stone-skins would be here. So what if they're all at the harbor? That just means we had an easy ride getting through the city. Got to take the rough with the smooth." She lowered the pitch of her voice, gave it that rhythm she used when she lulled Lyssa to sleep. "The stone-skins are busy pulling out. They won't be expecting trouble. And as for hitting the ships without someone noticing, it's just a matter of picking the right targets. I saw close to twenty stone-skin ships dock. There must be some that aren't as well guarded as the others."

It wasn't working. Karmel looked about as convinced by Amerel's words as the Guardian was herself. Amerel needed to try something else—keep changing the point of her attack until she found what would work as a hook.

"We have to do this," she said. "We *have* to. Maybe the stone-skins are going to hit my people, maybe they're going to hit yours, it doesn't matter. Either way it'll be a bloodbath." Her voice was smooth as honey. "They've got Rubyholt guides now. They can strike anywhere they like on the Ribbon Sea coast, or along Erin Elal's eastern seaboard. Even at Arkarbour. The people there aren't ready. They don't have bells to warn them what's coming. If you think the slaughter's bad now, wait until the stone-skins sack Arkarbour. It's ten times the size of Bezzle. We'll be able to watch the bodies pile up from here."

Still no give in Karmel. The priestess seemed to be looking through Amerel rather than at her. Karmel opened her mouth to speak, but the Guardian plunged on. If appealing to the woman's reason wasn't getting her anywhere, she'd have to up the ante. "Please," she said, stepping closer. "I have a niece in Arkarbour. Her name's Lyssa. She's only six. Her mother—my sister—died a year ago. She's all I have left." Another step. "Please. She's the only reason I'm here. I can't lose her now. Maybe it's already too late for her, but I have to try. This is the only way. This could be her only chance."

Karmel said nothing. She held Amerel's gaze before looking at Caval. Her expression hadn't changed, but there was a vulnerability in her eyes. Caval stared back at her. The Guardian counted herself good at reading people, but she had no idea what their shared look meant. Maybe the Chameleons didn't know themselves. As the heartbeats dragged out, Amerel took a breath. Damn this heat! Sweat poured off her, making her spider bites itch. It seemed madness that they should be standing here arguing, when the stone-skins could stumble on them at any instant. Amerel forced herself to remain still, though, sensing the Chameleons' decision wavered on a knife-edge.

When Karmel at last turned toward the Guardian, Amerel still couldn't guess what her decision would be. If the answer was no,

Amerel would kill the Chameleons, take the blood, and carry on alone. She wanted to signal Noon to be ready, but she dared not take her gaze from Karmel. Her hand drifted toward her sword hilt.

Then the priestess nodded and turned away.

Amerel watched the Chameleons shoulder their packs and head silently toward the waterfront. Just two more shadows amid all the others. The Guardian could feel Noon's gaze on her, and she looked across. The Breaker was frowning at her like she'd set him a riddle he couldn't fathom.

She leaned in close and whispered, "That was easy."

CHAPTER 15

CAVAL PUSHED open the back door to the house and moved through, clearing the way for Karmel to follow behind. Once inside, she closed the door and waited for her eyes to adjust to the dark. She was in a room that made up the entire ground floor. There were flies everywhere, weaving through the murk. On the opposite wall was a window. Its shutters were closed, but through the gaps between the bars came strips of light that left bright scratches on the north-facing wall. The other side of the room was veiled in blackness. Karmel watched for any shift in the consistency of the gloom that might indicate movement.

Nothing.

She drew a throwing knife. Its hilt felt slick against her palm. The house smelled of wood smoke and mirispice. From outside came the rattle of bonechimes stirred to life by the breeze, the thud of a hull bumping into a quay—the hull of Karmel's target, most likely—then above that a *drip, drip* as of water from a leaky roof.

That was when she saw it: a pool of liquid—blood?—at the center of the floor. There was a stain on the ceiling above. Karmel's breath stuck in her throat. She looked at Caval, and he nodded to indicate he'd spotted it. If the blood was wet enough to drip, it must have been spilled recently. Karmel strained to hear any noise that might indicate someone was upstairs. A creak sounded. Probably just one of the beams settling down for the night, since it was unlikely that a stoneskin was up there taking a nap.

They'd be finding out soon enough. There was no way they could

unbolt the downstairs shutters without alerting the stone-skins on
the waterfront, so they'd have to try their luck upstairs. To Karmel's
right, a wooden staircase led up to a square of paler gloom in the ceiling. Caval moved toward it. Karmel waited until he reached the
bottom, then followed. Scattered across the floor were potsherds
and splinters of wood from a smashed chair, and the priestess lifted
her feet high before placing them down again so as not to kick something across the ground. For a moment she was back training in the
temple, stepping over pieces of glass in the courtyard as she closed on
the acolyte at its center.

Drip, drip.

She drew up alongside Caval, wishing she could see in his face
even a trace of her own apprehension. His expression, though, was
quiet, as if he'd done this before many times. All those occasions he'd
gone missing from the temple when she was younger, were they for
missions such as this? Each time he'd returned, he had changed a little
from the person who had left. The priestess was only now seeing the
effect of all those differences put together, and realizing she didn't
know what they added up to. He'd never spoken about his experiences, and she had never asked. Just one more thing they would have
to put right if they got out of this alive.

Caval climbed the steps and drew up when his head came level
with the ceiling. With his power employed, he would be invisible to
anyone lying in wait. He scanned the room above.

Outside, the bonechimes clattered again.

Drip, drip.

Earlier Karmel and Caval had discussed what they would do if
they were interrupted before they could shoot the dart. At the time
Karmel had felt reassured to think they were ready for all eventu-
alities. When you boiled it down, though, their plans amounted to no
more than hide or run if they could, fight if they couldn't—and *then*
hide or run. While hoping the Erin Elalese, waiting somewhere out
back, had something to contribute beyond showing them a clean pair
of heels.

Voices sounded on the waterfront, along with the measured tread
of an Augeran patrol. As the soldiers' footsteps died away Karmel
swung her gaze to Caval. He beckoned to her, then headed up the last
of the stairs and out of sight.

Karmel started climbing. The steps were smeared with blood, and she kept to the outer edges where the boards were unstained. The buzzing of the flies rose from a hum to a drone.

Upstairs consisted of a single room too, with windows looking out onto the harbor. Unlike downstairs, the shutters were open. A breath of air alerted Karmel to the broken pane of glass before she saw it. Light from a torch on the waterfront reflected in the panes, making it seem as if flames licked at the glass. Against the south-facing wall was a bed covered in blood-speckled rushes, and beside it was a pool of blood and viscera. Karmel could smell the stink of it even over the blayfire fumes. A woodcutter's ax was buried in the wall next to the bed. Not the weapon of a stone-skin soldier. Evidently the house's former occupant had taken a swing at one of his attackers before being cut down.

Karmel's fingers were cramping from their grip on her knife, so she sheathed the weapon before joining Caval at the window. Outside she saw the stone-skin ship that was their target, tied up along the waterfront to her left. In the darkness, the cordage hanging between its masts and spars looked like the threads of some vast spider's web. Figures moved on deck, and lights shone from the windows at the stern.

On the waterfront itself stood two black-cloaked Augerans. A stone's throw to Karmel's left, and moving farther away, was the patrol that had just walked past. To the north, more figures milled about on the quays, and Karmel heard the rattle of a gangplank, the rumble of rolling barrels. The stone-skins were preparing to withdraw, no question. But for now, the section of waterfront immediately outside the house was quiet.

She retreated from the window. Caval had already removed from his pack the flask of dragon blood Mokinda had given him. Thoughts of the Storm Lord reminded Karmel of their conversation on the *Grace*, and suddenly the breeze stealing through the window felt as chill as Shroud's breath on her neck. What the hell was she doing here, when the smallest mistake could bring an army of stone-skins down on her? She thought back to Amerel's words at the White Pool. Those words had had the ring of truth to them, but maybe that was just the Guardian's Will talking. In any case, what did Karmel care for the fate of the Erin Elalese? Or of anyone beyond herself and Caval? Was she here out of guilt for Dragon Day? Was she seeking redemption for the part she'd played in the deaths of all those killed by the dragons?

Because what better way to redeem yourself for a thousand deaths than by killing a thousand more?

She should give it up now, she knew. Leave her blowpipe on the floor and go back to the boneyard. How far would she get, though, before the Chameleon's chain around her neck pulled tight? The god had struck down Veran's wife with the gray fever; he could do the same to Karmel in an eyeblink. Or to Caval.

And if she did leave, how did she know her brother would come with her?

Caval must have seen something in her expression, for he raised a quizzical eyebrow.

"We're not going to make it through this, are we?" Karmel said.

He gave a half smile. "Anything you'd like to get off your chest while you can?" He'd spoken the words lightly, but Karmel sensed in them an invitation, maybe even a challenge.

She looked away. What did he expect her to say, that she forgave him for betraying her? She'd tried the words out in her mind a thousand times, but they didn't ring true now any more than they had before. She understood why he'd done what he'd done. Because he'd hoped to escape the memory of his childhood beatings. Because he and Karmel had drifted apart. But there were things Caval had done that she could not reconcile herself to, however hard she tried: the premeditation to his scheme, the way he'd maintained the lie until Imerle's revelations had rendered his deception untenable.

A part of her railed at her obstinacy. What did it gain her to hold on to her anger? To cling to it was to prolong the hurt, not just for herself but for Caval too, so why could she not give it up? Before tonight, she'd always told herself to be patient, but what if she no longer had time for that?

"Let's get on with this," she said, reaching for the blowpipe strapped to her back.

"Let's."

Karmel would be the one taking the shot, and she withdrew from her pack a cloth purse containing the darts of blackened tarnica. Each was stored in its own slot to ensure they did not clink together. Karmel selected one, then closed the purse and put it back in her pack so she was ready to make a quick exit if she had to.

Caval took the stopper off the flask of dragon blood. The vinegary fumes it gave off brought a mist to Karmel's eyes. She touched the tip of the dart to the inside neck of the flask, before holding the tip over the bottle's opening for a count of ten to allow any excess liquid to drop. Then she placed the dart in her blowpipe, taking care that the tip did not come into contact with the mouthpiece. The dart's feathers gave the missile a snug fit in the bore, ensuring it wouldn't slide along the pipe when it was tilted down.

Moving back to the window, Karmel checked no stone-skins were looking toward her. Then she lowered the tip of the blowpipe onto the bottom of the broken pane of glass. The weapon extended past the window, and Karmel extended her powers over it to make it invisible. She placed her left hand on the pipe where it rested against the glass. Her right gripped the shaft below the mouthpiece. The window was at an awkward height for her, too low for her to stand upright, too high for her to kneel.

Caval's hand settled on her shoulder. Her brother would be her eyes while she took the shot, and they had already agreed on the signals he would use to warn her of trouble: removing his hand meant "wait," a squeeze meant "abort." She focused on the stone-skin ship that was her target. It bobbed on the greasy waves, meaning she'd have to get her timing right if she wanted to strike the hull near the waterline.

Indistinct voices reached her from along the waterfront to the south. She ignored them. The angle of her shot would take the dart close to the heads of the two Augerans stationed below, but there was nothing to be done about that. Karmel tightened her grip on the weapon and raised its mouthpiece to her lips. A muscle in her leg trembled from the discomfort of her half crouch.

Caval's hand was steady on her shoulder. The coast remained clear.

Karmel adjusted the angle of the blowpipe, picturing the shot she wanted to make.

A sharp breath, then she blew hard into the mouthpiece. The expulsion of air was so loud it seemed the stone-skins must hear it. Karmel didn't look to find out. Instead she watched the dart flash across the waterfront. She couldn't see where it struck the ship because of the shadows, but the trajectory had been just as she'd planned.

First one done. Simple enough, though the prospect of having to repeat the feat a dozen times tonight didn't appeal.

Then Caval squeezed her shoulder in warning.

———

Floating in spirit-form above the waterfront, Amerel watched an Augeran guard take a step toward the Chameleons' house. He couldn't have seen the dart, else he would have raised the alarm by now, but clearly *something* had caught his attention. He growled a question at his female companion.

A shrug was her only response.

Amerel pursed her lips. If the man went looking for the Chameleons, he was unlikely to find them with their powers activated. But why take the risk when a touch of the Will might convince the stone-skin he was jumping at shadows? She gathered her power. . . .

Then she caught sight of someone looking down from a window in the house next door—just their eyes and a mop of blond hair above the sill. A boy, maybe twelve years old.

Amerel didn't hesitate.

Reaching out with her Will, she tapped on the glass of the boy's window. Not loud, but loud enough.

The boy froze at the sound, then flinched back and down.

But not before the stone-skins had looked up.

Karmel felt a stab of guilt as she listened to the *thud, thud* of the Augerans pounding on the door to the neighboring house. Perhaps the Rubyholters inside had done something to attract the stone-skins' notice just as Karmel fired the blowpipe. Most likely, though, it was her shot that had stirred the enemy to watchfulness. The Islanders might still have time to escape out the back before their front door gave way. But even as the thought came to Karmel, she heard a splintering of wood followed by a woman's screams, a boy's crying.

She looked at Caval. He shook his head as if to say, "Not this time."

Karmel scowled. Did he think she meant to rush out to save the Rubyholters as she had the woman in the alley? Maybe take on the stone-skin army single-handed? Did he really consider her so naive? So selfless?

Stepping back from the window, she returned the blowpipe to the straps on her back.

Galantas sloshed through water in the Serpentine Aqueduct. It was more than half a bell since he and the rest of the raiding party had started along the underground passage. They had brought only a handful of lanterns between them, and the darkness in the tunnel had a weight to it that served as a constant reminder of the tons of rock and soil overhead. The way led ever downward as if Galantas were descending into one of the Nine Hells, and that feeling was reinforced by the occasional muffled scream from the city overhead. Behind him someone muttered in the gloom—the same fool of a Keel, most likely, who had been complaining about the lack of room in the passage. At the Hub, Galantas had warned the other clan leaders how narrow the tunnel was, so of course Tolo had sent someone who was afraid of enclosed spaces.

Of the two hundred men in Galantas's raiding party, roughly half were his own Spears, meaning the other chiefs had entrusted him with a hundred of their own men. A hundred! Another time, the temptation to lead them astray might have proved irresistible, but in a tunnel with no paths leading off it, the opportunities on that score were limited. Along with the Needles and Falcons, Keels and Squalls, there were two Raptors whom Kalag had doubtless sent to watch Galantas in the hope he slipped up. Or to make sure he did, perhaps, by sticking a knife in his back? Galantas shrugged the thought aside. That was the one good thing about walking a tunnel as narrow as this: you had only to worry about the man immediately behind you. And Galantas had ensured it was Qinta stationed there.

A while later the air started to pale from black to gray. Ahead a low arch marked the place where the tunnel entered the White Pool. Galantas dropped to his hands and knees, then ducked his head under the water before crawling an armspan and resurfacing in the pool beyond.

After the chill of the tunnel, the air in the subterranean chamber felt like a warm blanket enveloping him. The room was gritty with flies. He waded to the side of the pool, then sat on the edge and swung his legs over. Qinta joined him. The floor was covered by a mosaic of a two-headed dog with more than half its stones missing. Men exited the water to gather in dripping huddles, while yet more warriors emerged spluttering from the aqueduct. It would take a while before the last of them cleared the tunnel, so Galantas looked for the crewman Squint, whom he had sent ahead to scout the waterfront.

Squint sidled up. His forehead was beaded with sweat, and there was something in his eyes that had Galantas bracing himself for bad news. Was there any other sort?

"The *Eternal*'s gone," Squint said.

"What do you mean, 'gone'?"

"She ain't where we left her, Cap'n."

"Then the stone-skins must have moved her."

"Not inside the harbor, they ain't—I'd have seen the gleam off her main trunk if that were so. She's gone I tell you."

Galantas's oath brought the heads of his nearby clansmen round, but he paid them no mind. The *Eternal* vanished. Could the stone-skins have scuttled her? No, that made no sense if the other vessels had been left untouched.

Qinta spoke. "We're gonna need another ship." Then, to Squint, "You see anything out there you like?"

Squint flashed the stubs of his teeth. "There's always the *Fury*. Handy girl to have in a scrap."

That she was. And while no vessel in the Isles could match the spectacle of the *Eternal*, the *Fury*—a devilship—had its own distinctive draw.

"The *Fury*'s a Raptor ship," Qinta said. "If we take her, Kalag's gonna want her back."

"Then he should be here now," Galantas snapped. "Where is she tied?"

"Outside Scurve's place," Squint said.

"Then that's our target. Qinta, tell Barnick and the others."

The Second moved away.

Galantas looked around. Some of the krels from the other clans watched him with guarded expressions, no doubt wondering what he had to discuss with Squint that he couldn't share with them. Among them was a barrel-chested Needle called Tub—Malek's right-hand man and a useful person to have in a knife fight. Next to him was Cleo, a Falcon, who was said to command the highest bounty of anyone in the Isles, after feeding half of Londell's monarchy to the Rent. With them were some of Dresk's krels—no, Galantas's own krels, he corrected himself. Clamp was there with his rainbow-dyed hair, and Faloman too, fresh from his appointment with the Speaker. There was no longer any need for Galantas to dispose of him. Once news had spread that the stone-skins had killed Dresk, Faloman—along with all of Dresk's erstwhile supporters—had quickly fallen into line.

As Galantas beckoned them toward him, he took a steadying breath. His most important task as commander was to project a sense of calm, so it wouldn't do for the krels to see his irritation about the *Eternal* and mistake it for fear. He studied their faces. Hard men, these. Confident. But then they were about to steal a few ships from an enemy, and what self-respecting Rubyholter hadn't trodden these same boards before?

"Gentlemen," he said, "shall we get down to business? Squint, tell them what we're dealing with."

"Easy pickings, to my eye," Squint said. "I counted just eight groups of stone-skins along our stretch of harbor, six men in each, maybe fifty strides apart." He looked around the krels. "If you're lucky, you should get a clear run at whatever ship it is you're going for."

"And if you're *really* lucky," Galantas said, "you'll get the chance to take out a few stone-skins on the way."

Chuckles from some of the krels.

"Any patrols?" Tub asked Squint.

"Just one that I saw, and only four men in it."

"There'll be others," someone muttered.

Nods all round.

Tub's gaze was still on Squint. "What about the streets behind the waterfront? Any movement there?"

Squint shrugged. "I didn't have time to walk every cobble, but from what I saw, it looked quiet. All the action is going down at the northern end—"

"Wait," Galantas cut in. "Action?"

"Aye, that's where most of the stone-skin ships are tied up. There's a steady stream o' traffic trampling the gangplanks, carrying barrels, crates, you name it. Bastards are reprovisioning, is my guess."

Tub looked at Galantas. "They're getting ready to pull out."

Galantas knew what the Needle was thinking: why risk going through with this raid when they could wait for the enemy to leave and take the ships without a fight? Galantas answered the unspoken question. "Because they'll fire the ships before they go, that's why."

"Ain't no 'might' about it," Squint said. "Whole damned harbor stinks o' blayfire oil. Stone-skins have doused some o' the ships."

Now he tells us. The krels muttered, and Galantas raised a hand for silence. "The stone-skins won't risk a fire while their fleet is in the harbor. If there's trouble, it'll come when we clear the islets, so make sure your decks are swabbed in case they use flaming arrows."

Cleo swatted at a fly. "What signal are you gonna give to start the attack?"

"I'm not," Galantas said. "No point in announcing ourselves to the stone-skins like that. You'll have quarter of a bell to get into position. When you hear the first shouts, go, and go fast."

A distant scream sounded from the city above. One of the krels stumbled back and trod on the foot of the man behind. Whispered curses. Their nerves were starting to bite now. Galantas felt another speech coming on, but if the stone-skins *were* reprovisioning, they might be dropping by the pool at any moment.

He looked around the krels one last time. Once this gathering broke up, the success or failure of the raid would be down to his companions. It didn't seem fair that Galantas would be judged on the mistakes or ineptitudes of the men working under him, but such was a commander's lot. And it wouldn't stop him claiming the glory if things went well.

"Any questions?" he said.

No response.

Galantas gave them a smile. "Doesn't feel right, I know, stealing our own ships when we should be stealing the stone-skins', but there's always tomorrow if they haven't moved on." He rose from his crouch. "Let's do this."

Amerel watched the Chameleons pick their way along the rubbish-choked alley that ran behind the houses on the waterfront. They stopped at a door hanging by a single hinge. Caval knew that Amerel would already have scouted inside, so he didn't hesitate to open the door and enter.

The Guardian drifted to the front of the house. Here the waterfront was lit by lanterns hanging from poles, and about them swirled hundreds of needleflies, salt-stingers, and feathermoths, thick as blizzard snow. Four stone-skins guarded the quay at which two Augeran ships were docked, the first a slim-hulled galleon with an eager look to it, the second a four-masted monster as large as anything in the Erin Elalese fleet. Its figurehead—a snake's flared head with a flickering tongue—was chipped on one side, and the hull along the port side showed damage in the form of three vertical gouges. Caused by a dragon's talons, perhaps? If tonight went as planned, the hull would be getting more such decoration soon.

On the waterfront were piled crates, casks, and nets of supplies along with wooden boxes and barrels of water. It didn't seem that anyone was in a hurry to stow them onboard the ships, but then most of the activity was taking place to the north of Amerel's position. . . .

Movement to her left caught her eye. She looked across to see four Augerans approaching—high-ranking ones, judging by the way the sentries snapped to attention as they passed. No Hex, thank the Matron. Amerel had thought the four-masted ship was deserted, but two sailors materialized from the shadows on deck and used ropes to maneuver a gangplank onto the quay. The newcomers walked across it and made their way toward the captain's cabin. Amerel was tempted to follow. Yes, their discussions would be in the stone-skin tongue, but she might still get the chance to overturn an oil lamp into a lap.

Then she saw a fifth figure approaching.

Her eyes narrowed.

A Syn.

This was not the same warrior who'd accompanied Eremo to Dresk's fortress—that man had been as broad around the chest as the barrels on the wharf, whereas this one was willow-thin and had shoulder-length blond hair. Just in case anyone should fail to notice the golden tattoos on his cheeks, he'd rolled up his shirt sleeves to show off more on his forearms. The sentries saluted him, a certain tension in their looks.

The Syn flowed up the gangplank and onto the deck.

Amerel blew out her cheeks. His being here changed nothing, she told herself. If she and her companions were discovered, it mattered not who sent them on their way through Shroud's Gate. Truth be told, a part of her would have liked the chance to see the Syn in action—provided it wasn't her he was fighting, of course. For while the ancient Erin Elalese texts agreed upon the Syns' martial prowess, none gave details as to precisely what powers they commanded.

Amerel decided she could wait a little longer to find out.

Light from the waterfront torches streamed through the first-floor window. Karmel edged forward with her back pressed to the north-facing wall, Caval a step behind. Just like in the first house, the downstairs windows had been barred, but the windows upstairs were open. Through them Karmel saw a squad of stone-skins immediately below her position. When one of the soldiers shifted his weight, a board creaked beneath his foot. The priestess froze. If *she* could hear *his* movements so clearly . . .

She had an unobstructed view of her two targets. The three-master was directly in front; the four-master, twenty paces to her left. Next to the smaller ship was a Rubyholt fishing boat still containing crayfish baskets filled with live crayfish. A stone-skin was unloading the catch, tottering under the weight of the baskets as he carried them two at a time to where more stone-skins waited to transfer them onto the three-master. Farther north, a group of soldiers laden with weapons and gear trudged along the quay to another Augeran ship. The thud of their boots set the waterfront rattling as if the whole rotting structure was about to collapse. Closer, a stone-skin patrol headed toward Karmel's position through a swirling cloud of flies. She waited for the soldiers to pass by before sliding her back down the wall until she was below the level of the window.

Caval crouched beside her. She brought her mouth to his ear. "There are too many of them. Someone will see the dart—"

A woman's distant scream cut her off. The same woman the stone-skins had found earlier? Caval signaled Karmel to wait, then raised his head to look out the window. He stared south, back the way they had come. Outside, a man's voice rang out, his tone disapproving. One of the Augerans below their position, objecting to the woman's treatment?

Caval ducked down again. "This is our chance," he whispered, removing the flask of dragon blood from his pack. "We're not going to get a better distraction."

"What distraction?"

"There's something in the harbor. Some . . . creature."

"A dragon?" Karmel said, thinking of the Augeran ship they had already marked.

"No. Something from beyond the rents, I'd guess."

And what do the woman's screams have to do with it? the priestess almost asked, but she could work that out herself. She hesitated. It seemed wrong somehow to take advantage of the woman's plight, but she couldn't have said why.

Karmel withdrew from her pack the purse with the darts and

passed it to Caval. He selected one and applied dragon blood to the tip. Then Karmel released her power, and stood, and set down the end of her blowpipe on the window frame.

The Augerans below had moved a short distance south in the direction of the woman's screams. The woman herself and her captors were mere shadows along the waterfront. A shouting match was under way between two stone-skins. The man unloading the crayfish baskets stopped to listen, and more Augerans gathered along the port rail of the three-master to look at something in the harbor that Karmel couldn't make out.

Caval's tap on her hip startled her, and she glanced down to see him offering her the dart. She took it and placed it in the blowpipe. The Augeran four-master was the more distant of her two targets, and thus the first ship she'd hit, since she would have more time to line up this shot than the next. Painted low down on the hull was a pair of eyes. Right between them was as good a place as any to put her dart.

Caval rose to stand behind her. His hand settled on her shoulder. To the south, something splashed into the harbor, and the screams of the Rubyholt woman were briefly cut off before starting up again. Karmel's gaze remained fixed on her target. She'd be shooting behind the backs of the stone-skins immediately below her, and even if someone else glimpsed the dart, maybe they'd mistake it for just another feathermoth flitting through the torchlight.

Okay, maybe not.

She brought the mouthpiece to her lips. Taking a breath, she blew down the pipe.

The dart flashed through the night.

Karmel was already reaching back, not looking for the next dart, simply trusting Caval to place it in her hand without stabbing her. Cold metal touched her palm, and she closed her fingers around it. She lifted the dart and inserted it in the blowpipe. All the while, she was waiting for someone on the waterfront to raise the alarm over the first dart, maybe send a missile winging back her way.

Nothing.

She swung the end of the blowpipe toward the three-master. The Rubyholt woman's screams rose in pitch, and the waters in the harbor swelled, sending a wave slapping against the hull of the three-master. Evidently the creature in the water was on the move.

Karmel focused on her next target.

Aim.

Deep breath.

Blow.

Amerel saw the dart flash across the waterfront, only to lose it against the backdrop of the harbor's black waters. She waited to see if anyone raised the alarm, but all eyes were on the Rubyholt woman thrashing in the harbor. The shadowy creature surged toward her. A chitinous arm broke the waves and wrapped itself about the Islander, then another arm followed, and another. The third one covered her mouth and cut off her shrieks. As she was tugged beneath the surface, her hands reached out for something to grab on to.

A wave hit the waterfront. Then the harbor was still.

Chuckles sounded from the Augerans who'd thrown the woman in the water, and who was Amerel to begrudge them their entertainment? She was the one who'd served it up, after all. The Rubyholt boy was next into the harbor. He must have been in shock, for he made no effort to stay afloat. Instead he sank soundlessly beneath the waves. Amerel should have looked away. Only one way this was going to end for the boy. The top of his head momentarily broke the surface before disappearing from sight again.

The blood-dream came on Amerel swiftly. She was in the sea, the cold tight about her. She sensed something huge beneath, and there was a crushing pain in her legs as she was caught and dragged down. She tried to gasp in a breath, only to draw in a lungful of water instead. The waves closed over her. Ringing silence in her ears. A pressure in her chest like her heart had ruptured. The pain didn't last long, though. It never did when you stopped fighting it.

He was only a boy. Amerel could have told herself she had acted on instinct, but she was done making excuses. There was always an excuse if you looked hard enough. Maybe the boy's death would save thousands of Erin Elalese lives, yet how did you balance the two sides of the scales? Amerel had no answer. Perhaps there *was* no right answer for someone with a shattered moral compass like hers. But that wasn't what troubled her just now. What bothered her was that these questions wouldn't even have occurred to her a few weeks ago. So why now? *No half measures,* she reminded herself.

Her thoughts were interrupted by a roar of voices from the south. She looked across to see dozens of figures pour onto the waterfront.

From the shadows of a doorway, Galantas studied the *Fury*. Its hull was painted crimson and sculpted to resemble flames, but it was the vessel's figurehead that most drew his eye. Scaled and horned, the carved demon had a forked tongue and black-lacquered eyes that seemed to swallow the light. Galantas had yet to sail aboard a devilship, but he remembered the last time he'd grappled with one off the Outer Rim. He'd expected the Corinian captain, outnumbered and outmatched, to surrender. Instead the merchantman's crew had come boiling over the *Eternal*'s rail, their eyes burning with a bloodlust inspired by the demented spirit bound to the ship's skeleton. Not a single enemy had let themselves be taken alive. And once the battle had turned against them, they had scuttled the ship rather than let her be captured.

He looked left and right. The stone-skins had lit only a handful of the harbor's lanterns to leave great pools of shadow on the waterfront. To the south, a group of six black-cloaked Augerans stood in a circle of light outside Scurve's inaptly named Palace of Delights, while to the north another party was stationed in front of a Needle barque Galantas recognized as the *Crakehawk*. That ship was the intended target of one of the groups in his raiding party, and when the time came to attack, Galantas meant to let them break cover first before making his own move for the *Fury*.

As the thought came to him, he heard a scream from along the waterfront. This wasn't one of the raiding parties attacking, though, just some woman and a boy. Galantas watched two stone-skins muscle the woman toward the harbor. There was a good chance she was someone he knew, but if she'd claimed as much, he would doubtless have denied it—especially if that boy of hers had his eyes. A splash sounded as she was thrown into the water. The boy followed soon after. Something about their plight seemed to amuse the stone-skins, though what that might be, Galantas couldn't imagine.

Then he saw a tentacle break the surface of the water.

Ah, that explained it.

He retreated into the shadows of the doorway. Perhaps the fate of the woman and the boy should have had him swearing bloody vengeance on the Augerans, but he couldn't save *all* his kinsmen. His energies were better directed at trying to help those among his people who yet lived. People like himself, for example. Still he found his grip on his crossbow was uncomfortably tight, and he had to force himself to relax his fingers.

The Needles chose that moment to attack. Ten figures sprinted out of the alley opposite the *Crakehawk,* screaming as they shot their crossbows. They clearly hadn't discussed their targets beforehand, because of the six Augerans facing them, only two were hit. One of the surviving stone-skins leapt to meet the Needles. Bringing his shield up, he blocked an ax-swing, then shoved his assailant back into his onrushing companions. A Needle woman, finding herself at the front of the group, drew up. A spear thrown by one of the Augerans caught her in the chest, and she went down.

Galantas frowned. The Needle attack had already lost momentum, and against the more heavily armed stone-skins, there could be no doubt as to how the skirmish would end. Why should that matter to him, though? All along the waterfront, other parties of Rubyholters were making a dash for the ships, and Galantas should have been doing the same. Indeed he *would* have been were it not for Kalag's two Raptors. The bastards would be out there somewhere, watching his every move so they could report back to their chief. And how would Kalag react if he found out Galantas had left the Needles to their fate? *He preaches unity,* the Raptor would say, *yet when the time comes to back his words with actions, he runs.* And wouldn't he have a point? Had Galantas's words at the Hub been nothing but empty rhetoric?

Perhaps. But there was no need for the other clans to know that. Besides, if he helped the Needles, their chief, Malek, would owe him one. And you could never have too many people in your debt.

He lifted his crossbow.

His men wouldn't like this, but they would follow him regardless, not least because they outnumbered the enemy ten to four.

"Pick your targets carefully," he said over his shoulder. "Let's show the Needles how this is done."

Karmel crept along the alley. The wall to her left was covered with peeling posters slapped one atop another, while to her right was a half-open doorway. Caval moved past it and stopped. Karmel halted this side, listening for movement in the building beyond, but hearing only distant screams and sorcerous concussions from the Rubyholt attack on the harbor. When the raid had started, she'd hoped the distraction might make her task tonight easier, but thus far it had served only to stir Bezzle to new life. Twice on the way here, she and Caval had been forced to engage their powers to hide from stone-skin squads heading for the fighting.

Caval looked through the door before entering the building. Karmel slipped into his shadow, her throwing knives a reassuring weight in her hands.

Three stairs led down to the common room of a tavern. The bar was to Karmel's left, while to her right was a wall illuminated by rectangles of light coming through the windows on the opposite wall. Beyond one was the silhouette of an Augeran stationed outside. To the left of his position was a door leading to the waterfront.

The tavern must have been flooded recently, for the floor was submerged beneath a finger's width of water, inky black with blood and shadow, and covered with rushes. A handful of bodies were scattered about the room. A barmaid was sprawled at the foot of the stairs where Karmel stood, apparently cut down trying to flee. Strange that the corpses had been left here when they'd been removed from the houses earlier. Strange, but not a cause for concern. It wasn't as if a stone-skin would be playing dead among them on the off chance someone stopped by for a drink.

Caval made for a staircase on the north side of the room. Each time he passed a body, a cloud of needleflies took to the air. Only when he reached the stairs and signaled the all clear did Karmel move herself.

The water on the ground was cold against her sandaled feet. She picked her way through the wreckage of a smashed table, her gaze twitching all the while to the silhouetted stone-skin. Still no movement from the figure. Karmel was beginning to wonder if it might be a statue rather than a soldier, but a statue outside a tavern? In Bezzle?

A flash of sorcery from outside smeared the south-facing wall orange and yellow, the glow reflecting in the water on the floor. Karmel stepped over the corpse of a bare-chested man. His head was held to his neck by a flap of skin, and bile rose in the priestess's throat. Death never looked pretty close up. Easier to observe it from a distance where you could pretend there were no victims at all. Like from the top of the Dragon Gate, for example. Her foot snagged on something—

A hand seized her ankle, and the bottom fell out of her stomach. Instinctively she tried to pull away. Nails dug into her flesh. She was about to strike out with her knives when her leg suddenly came free, and she staggered forward, tottered, made a despairing grab for the bar. With her blades in her hands, though, she couldn't get a proper grip on it. She fell to her knees, jarred them on the stone floor. Water splashed her face. An image came to her of the arm's owner rearing up behind, and she scrambled forward, half turning to look back.

A Rubyholt man was propped on one elbow, reaching out. He must have taken a stone-skin blade across the face, for his eyes were gone, and all that remained of his nose was a splinter of bone. But then how had he seen her leg to seize it? Unless he'd merely flailed out as she brushed against him, and had the fortune—or misfortune—to grab her.

"Help me," he croaked through blood-flecked lips.

Karmel silently swore, angry more at herself than at the stranger. What was she, a Shroud-cursed acolyte, that she'd panicked like that? A shock to be sure, but if she'd stopped to think, she would have realized the hand must have belonged to one of the Rubyholters. Outside the tavern, the "statue" came to life. Karmel heard the scrape of a sword being drawn from its scabbard.

Footsteps clomped toward the door.

Karmel froze in a half crouch, glanced across at Caval by the stairs. The merest flicker of his eyes toward the Islander told her to silence the man. It was too late for that, though. The door handle was already turning down.

"Help me," the Rubyholter said again.

Karmel looked back at the man, imploring him with her gaze to be quiet. Then she remembered he couldn't see her.

The tavern door opened.

Amerel reached out with her Will. It wouldn't be easy persuading the Augeran he'd imagined the commotion, for with the Rubyholt attack on the harbor, the stone-skin sentries had become wide-eyed watchful. She could only hope the Chameleons had the sense to shut the dying man up before—

The sound of shattering glass broke her concentration—a perception not from her spiritual body, but from her corporeal one. She muttered an oath. Before she'd started spirit-walking, she'd found a house not far from the White Pool to take cover in, thinking that it would be far enough from the harbor to guarantee no callers. But she hadn't reckoned on the Rubyholt raid. She could hear shouts now, the stamp of running feet, the hollow note of a sword striking stone. Some of the Islanders must have been driven back from the waterfront toward her hiding place. And while it was unlikely any of them would blunder into her building, was she prepared to risk her life on "unlikely"?

A moment's hesitation, then she returned her attention to the tavern. The southern half of the common room was bathed in light from the torches on the waterfront, but the remaining half was a tangle of shadows. The dying Rubyholt man lay pale-faced and shivering. He was whispering "help me!" over and over, though what good he thought anyone could do when half his face was missing, Amerel didn't know. There was no sign of the Chameleons. Evidently they'd engaged their powers, and if the Guardian couldn't see them, then the stone-skin wouldn't be able to either. With luck, he'd put the Rubyholter out of his misery and return to the waterfront, no wiser to the Chameleons' presence.

A scream sounded in Amerel's corporeal ears, so loud the culprit might have been standing next to her body. This was going to be a problem. Hard to concentrate on the inn, after all, when there could be an Augeran about to test his sword on her throat. She had to check, didn't she? Odds were, the Chameleons wouldn't need her help here, and of course they still had Noon to watch their backs.

Her mind made up, Amerel flashed back to her body.

Karmel squinted against the light streaming through the tavern door. Two Augerans entered, instead of the one she'd been expecting. Their skin glittered where the light caught their faces. Both were carrying swords, and both wore black cloaks.

The lead soldier, the shorter of the two, stepped inside and halted. His reflection wavered in the rush-covered water. He took in the corpses, the open back door, the blinded man. The Islander pleaded for help. Karmel waited for the Augeran to advance and finish him, but the stone-skin held his ground. Perhaps he understood the common tongue enough to wonder who the Islander wanted help from. It seemed he wasn't going to take a chance on the Rubyholt corpses remaining dead, for he stepped to his left and drove his sword into the back of a woman. The body made no sound.

Karmel's thoughts raced. There were corpses to either side of her position, and if the Augeran meant to stab them all, he'd probably end up treading on her toes at some point. So what to do? Stay still and hope he missed her? Or strike when he came close? If she picked the right moment, it should be simple to dispose of him. But what about the second Augeran? She'd need to silence him too before he raised the alarm—or Caval would have to do it. The problem was, Karmel was facing away from her brother just now, with no way to signal her intent.

And yet he'd be ready to support her if she moved, wouldn't he?

As the first stone-skin strode around putting holes in more corpses, his companion circled to the south-facing wall so he could check no one was hiding behind the bar. Karmel's breath was so taut in her chest, it ached when she breathed. A needlefly landed on her cheek. She was glad for the gloom about the room, else the motion of the insects might have alerted the Augerans to her presence. The injured Rubyholter crawled away, only to bang his head against the tavern's bar. He flinched as if he'd bumped into a stone-skin's legs, then started sobbing and begging for mercy. *Mercy.* One word in the common tongue Karmel suspected the Augerans hadn't bothered learning.

The first Augeran was now half a dozen paces away. He raised his sword in readiness to stab the closest motionless figure, then noticed it was the man whose head had been all but severed from his body. A neat trick that would have been, playing dead without a head. The Augeran must have made a comment to that effect to his companion, for the man chuckled, not a snatch of tension between them.

The first stone-skin approached the wounded Islander. At any other time, Karmel would have left the man to his fate. What was he to her that she should risk her life and Caval's to help him? She had no choice but to attack the Augeran, though, and the best time to do so would be when the soldier's attention was fixed on the Rubyholter.

She could make out the stone-skin's face. He was younger than she'd expected, maybe as young as the priestess herself. Hard to be sure of his expression in the gloom, but it was best to imagine a sneer or a snigger. That would make it easier to do what had to be done. Her grip on her knives was steady. When she struck, she would go for the Augeran's throat in the hope her blade would choke off any cry he made.

The stone-skin halted over the injured Islander and drew back his sword arm.

Karmel sprang forward, her right hand coming round.

The stone-skin half turned, his expression disbelieving. He tried to bring his sword up to parry Karmel's knife, but too late. The priestess's blade buried itself to the hilt in his neck. Her momentum carried her crashing into him, and he staggered backward, toppled over a corpse, and splashed down, shattering the reflections in the water.

Karmel righted herself, then pulled back her left hand with her second throwing knife, looking for the other Augeran.

The man was already on his knees. Caval's dagger protruded from his chest over the heart. He fell forward onto his face.

Caval swept past Karmel, making no effort to silence his footfalls. "Come on," he said. Then, when the priestess made to retrieve her knife from the first soldier's throat, "Leave it!"

There was an edge to his voice that could have been nervousness, but equally it could have been anger. Directed at her? She stumbled a pace after him before remembering the blinded Rubyholter. "Go back to being dead," she said to him, then set off after Caval.

Her brother had reached the steps leading up to the back door. He leapt to the top in a single bound.

The door burst inward and thudded into him.

CHAPTER 16

WITHDRAW!" GALANTAS shouted to his men. "Withdraw!"

Things weren't going as he'd planned. The stone-skins had spotted his group as soon as it broke cover, giving them time to bring their shields round against the volley of crossbow bolts that followed. Two of the warriors had survived, and now they retreated along the quay at which the *Crakehawk* was moored. Perhaps the remaining Needles, along with Galantas's Spears, would overrun them in time, but there was no longer any point in trying, for the Needle water-mage had just lost his head to an enemy sword stroke. Even if the Needles reached the ship, they wouldn't be going anywhere on it.

"To the *Fury*!" Galantas yelled. "Qinta, cover our retreat!" Then, to the Needles, "Pull back!"

The Needles needed no second invitation.

Galantas trotted along the waterfront. His mouth was dry as dust. Ahead a Needle two-master and a Spear warship he recognized as the *Saberfin* rose on waves of water-magic. They pulled away from the docks at the same instant, as if their captains had agreed on a race. Meanwhile, on the waterfront, Kalag's two Raptors loped toward Galantas, looking all about as if they were searching for someone. For Galantas, most likely. He drew his sword to make it look as if he'd been in the thick of the fighting.

Twenty paces behind the Raptors came yet more Islanders—Squalls, at a guess. They emerged at a gallop from a pool of shadow.

Anyone running that fast had to be fleeing something, and sure enough, a stone-skin in a red cloak appeared from the gloom behind them. Galantas blinked. *One man?* One man had put an entire party of Squalls to flight?

Reaching the quay where the *Fury* was tied, Galantas dashed toward the ship. With each step, the stink of blayfire grew fiercer until his eyes started to water. No question the devilship had been one of the vessels stained with oil, but there was no time to look for another. Some of his men had already climbed on board and lowered the gangplank. As Galantas clattered across it, he heard a high-pitched keening coming from the demon figurehead, no doubt roused to life by the prospect of bloodshed.

"Cast off!" Galantas called.

He stepped onto the main deck. There were a dozen little differences between the *Fury* and Galantas's beloved *Eternal*: the overloud creaking of the rigging; the exaggerated pitch of the deck; the fact it took him twelve steps instead of the usual fifteen to reach the ladder to the quarterdeck. Climbing it, he found Barnick waiting beside the ship's wheel. The mage shot him an inquisitive glance.

Against his better judgment, Galantas said, "No. Wait until everyone is on board."

The Raptors crossed the gangplank. On the waterfront behind, what had started as an orderly retreat by the Needles had turned into a stampede. The last of their number reached the quay just ahead of the first of the Squalls. Jogging at the rear of the Squall party, Galantas recognized the krel, Klipp. One of the best blades in the Isles, it was said, if only by Klipp himself. Intent on covering the retreat of his kinsmen, he drew his sword and turned to confront the red-cloaked stone-skin behind. It must have been a trick of the light, but when the krel swung his weapon, it seemed to pass through his opponent. The Augeran brought his own blade flashing across Klipp's throat, and the Squall fell in a spray of blood.

The stone-skin hadn't so much as broken stride.

"Crossbows!" Galantas shouted.

Three of his men rushed to the rail and leveled their weapons. The first bolt flashed past the Augeran's face, but he did not falter. As he entered the light from one of the lanterns, Galantas noticed golden tattoos on his cheeks like the ones Eremo's bodyguard had sported. Another bolt missed him, then another.

Hells, wasn't there anyone on this ship who could shoot straight?

On the quay the first Squalls had reached the gangplank. Behind, two women supported a male companion between them. He was limping. His two female friends looked back to see the Augeran closing—and promptly abandoned their kinsman to his fate. As they dashed for the *Fury*, the man gave a despairing cry and hobbled after them.

The stone-skin's sword punched through his back.

The women leapt to the deck.

"Go!" Galantas said to Barnick.

The ship sprang away from the docks. For the first time that night, Galantas found himself glad he was aboard the *Fury* and not the *Eternal*, for his own vessel, with its skin of steel plates, would not have proved as spritely at that moment. The Augeran warrior tensed. Galantas thought he meant to chase the ship along the quay and jump for one of its lines. *No, he wouldn't dare.* Galantas's crew, supplemented by the Needles and Squalls, now numbered around twenty, and the idea of the stone-skin attacking against those odds seemed . . . absurd. The Augeran must have thought likewise, for he spun and retreated the way he'd come. Jeers from the *Fury*'s main deck followed him along the quay.

The ship flitted out into the harbor. Galantas scanned the waterfront. There was fighting to the north and south, and every knot of combatants likely represented a ship that would not sail. The *Spirit* pulled away from its berth, but the *Breeze* was still tied up at the quay along with the *Swarm* and—

Someone stepped in front of Galantas, breaking his line of sight. One of the Raptors. The man's once-flamboyant mustache drooped in the heat. "I am taking command of this ship," he said. Then, louder, to carry to the crew, "The *Fury* is mine."

Galantas stared at him.

"She belongs to Kalag," Mustache added.

Galantas looked from the man to his Raptor companion. "He must want her very badly indeed if he sent *both* of you two heroes to claim her."

Laughs from the main deck, but Mustache held his ground. "The *Fury* is mine," he said again.

"If you want her, you'll have to take her from me. Draw your sword."

"My sword?"

"You know, the piece of metal in the scabbard at your waist."

More laughs.

"Why?" Mustache said.

"Because I want to see if you *can* draw it. The Sender knows, you made no effort to, back on the waterfront. Instead you just stood by and watched while your kinsmen here"—his gesture took in the Needles and the Squalls as well as his own Spears—"did all the work. And now you have the nerve to try to *steal* the ship from us." Because stealing was such a terrible thing.

The Raptor scowled but said nothing.

"What's your name?" Galantas said, beginning to enjoy himself.

"Toben Stark."

Galantas had heard of him—he was the krel who had won the Hundred Islands race the year before Galantas. "Never heard of you."

Toben looked round like there might be some way to extract himself from his predicament. Galantas, though, wasn't ready to put him out of his misery.

"Are you a water-mage?" he asked.

"No."

"What about your friend here?" He nodded to the other Raptor.

Toben shook his head.

"So tell me, if I had ceded you the command, how would you have gotten your new ship to safety? I trust you weren't intending to give an order to my water-mage. Or to one of the Squalls or Needles."

No response.

Galantas dismissed him with a snort. And to think that earlier he'd considered disposing of the Raptors when he had the chance. Much better to let them live for their entertainment value. He addressed his crew. "Someone find these fools a mop and get them swabbing the blayfire from the deck."

With that, he turned his back on Toben.

As the ship sailed into the black of the harbor, the screams and the clatter of blades fell away. Even the moaning of the *Fury*'s demon figurehead abated as the immediate threat of bloodshed receded. Gliding ahead of the *Fury* were a handful of Rubyholt ships. The white-hulled *Colossus* was there, along with the *Spirit*, and the black-sailed *Karmight*, and a few other vessels Galantas didn't recognize. He did a quick count. Nine in total, if you included the *Fury*. A poor return on tonight's efforts, but he would worry about that when he was clear of this place.

Thus far he'd been too busy to look for Malek and his ships, but now he peered into the darkness ahead. Rising from the distant waves were the islets that marked the edge of the harbor. Beyond, four stone-skin vessels with lanterns in their rigging were lined up like floating fortresses. Farther out was a row of seven Rubyholt ships, little more than shadows in the gloom. Between the two fleets, a heaving mass of water cut and foamed like a storm-tossed sea. A hissing sound reached Galantas, together with a growl and a thunder as if some titan were stirring in the depths.

"What's happening?" Galantas said to Barnick.

"They're battling for control of the seas—our mages and theirs."

"Who's winning?"

"No one."

Galantas wasn't so sure. For while Malek's ships swayed at the edge of the swell, the stone-skin ships sat perfectly still. In any case, a stalemate suited the Augerans just fine if it meant they could keep Malek's vessels at arm's length. But they hadn't counted on Barnick and the other water-mages in Galantas's fleet. Surely nine more Rubyholt sorcerers would tip the balance in the Islanders' favor.

"Get some lanterns lit," Galantas said to Qinta. "We need to signal our other ships."

The Second nodded and moved away.

Those ships began to reduce speed as they approached the stone-skin line. At the front of Galantas's fleet, an unfamiliar vessel—a Needle, most likely—had heaved to. The *Colossus*, trailing close behind, was slow to follow suit, and the two ships came together with a bump and a scrape that provoked a healthy exchange of views between their captains. Galantas looked at the line of stone-skin warships. Ordinarily it would have been easy to run the blockade, for the Augerans could guard only the gaps between the islets, and any water-mage worth his bones could conjure up a wave large enough to carry a ship over the rocks. What was the point in doing so, though, if the sea beyond was caught in the throes of a sorcerous quarrel? What mage could steer a steady course on that swell?

A speck of blackness arced out from one of Malek's ships. A catapult stone. It hung in the air, growing in size, before it landed with a splash between two Augeran vessels. The stone-skins' response was instantaneous. A blast of sorcery from the ship on the left cut a gash in the sky as it streaked toward Malek's fleet. Galantas didn't hear it strike home, but he saw the mainmast of the central vessel cut in two. It toppled onto the decks below.

Stones against sorcery. No prizes for guessing who would win that battle.

Barnick's voice was urgent. "Galantas, look!" he said, pointing.

The Needle ship at the front of his fleet had started moving again toward the stone-skin blockade. Its captain had evidently chosen to try his luck on the seething cauldron of water, and as the vessel approached one of the islets, the wave beneath it grew higher.

"What's the fool doing?" Barnick said.

Galantas did not reply. What was there to say?

The Needle ship advanced to within a hundred armspans of the Augerans. Then dozens of pinpricks of light blossomed on the decks of a stone-skin ship. They took flight. *Fire arrows.* Galantas heard their whistle even over the rumble of water beyond the islets. It was too late for the Needle captain to turn about, or do anything save wait for the deadly hail to land. Had the man's ship been doused with blayfire oil? The fact his crew had started throwing themselves overboard wasn't an encouraging sign.

Ten, twenty, thirty missiles descended on the vessel, and its sails became spotted with light.

Then its quarterdeck went up in purple flames.

Amerel opened her eyes. After the freedom of her spirit-walk, her body felt as stiff as the boards she lay on. Flies crawled over her, and she twitched and waved a hand at them, then rolled to her feet, cursing. Damned flies were everywhere tonight. Like the whole city had gone rotten.

From the street outside came shouts and the clatter of metal. Amerel crossed to the window and looked down. A contest was taking place between four red-cloaked stone-skins and twice as many Rubyholters—if you could call it a contest. The Rubyholters seemed to be doing more screaming than fighting, moving so slowly in comparison to their foes they might have been pushing through water. Half a dozen heartbeats later, it was over. The last Islander tried to make a break for it, but if you were going to flee, it was best to do so before you were surrounded. The man was stabbed simultaneously from behind and in front, as if the stone-skins wielding the swords both wanted him for their score. At least he hadn't attempted to join Amerel in the house.

She moved back out of sight.

Down a street leading to the harbor, the Guardian glimpsed a melee of combatants on the waterfront. A group of Rubyholters was trying to fight along a quay to where a three-masted ship was docked, but they made only stuttering progress in the face of resistance from five stone-skins. And all the while, more Augerans were arriving to support their kinsmen. On the water beyond, a barque was alight, sooty flames roaring into the night. Shrieking figures hurled themselves from the deck into waters made choppy by a dozen writhing tentacles. Amerel almost felt sorry for the stricken Islanders. How to plot your course to Shroud's realm, by flame or fiend?

Below her, the four Augerans set off at a trot in the direction of the fighting.

Amerel considered. This part of the city was getting a little crowded for her liking. True, her immediate danger had passed, but already she could hear more shouts to the south. Coming this way? It was difficult to tell. That left her with a quandary. Stay put, or make a dash through the streets in search of somewhere quieter? Maybe the chances of anyone stumbling across her hiding place were slim, but while the excitement at this end of the harbor continued, she would always have one eye on what was happening to her body rather than concentrating on the mission.

Time to move on, she decided.

She descended the stairs two at a time and opened the back door a crack. The street beyond was still and silent.

She slipped out into the shadows.

Ahead the road narrowed, the houses to either side leaning in. The cobbles were smeared with blood, and dark lines ran down to an open sewer at the center. Shutters lay scattered where they'd been torn from the windows of houses. In breaking into one building, the Augerans had destroyed not just the door, but also its frame and the stonework to either side.

At the next intersection Amerel caught sight of the harbor to her right, saw another ship burning—or maybe the same one. Then she was into darkness again. From a side street on her left came scuttling noises, and as she passed it she noticed a boy crouched over a man's body, rifling through the corpse's clothes. Scavenging? At a time like this? *They start them young in Bezzle.* The child must have sensed Amerel's regard, for he looked up and stared at her with empty eyes.

She hurried on. The sounds of fighting from the waterfront were fading, though whether that was because the buildings were blunting the noise, or because the Augerans had now stamped out the opposition, Amerel couldn't say. Indeed the loudest shouts seemed to be coming from—

Her step faltered.

From the direction she was heading in. That couldn't be right, could it? She was too far north now for it to be Rubyholt raiders.

The Chameleons?

For an instant, Amerel was tempted to turn and go back the way she had come. The problem was, three ships marked wasn't enough to guarantee the success of the mission. Moreover, if the stone-skins caught Caval and Karmel, they might learn from them what they'd been doing here. And even if the Chameleons died before they were questioned, the blowpipes, darts, and dragon blood were clue enough as to their purpose. If the Augerans found the marked ships, they could replace the affected boards, and Amerel's efforts tonight would come to nothing.

Then there was the chance that the stone-skins would use the dragon blood on Erin Elalese vessels as Amerel had intended to use it on theirs.

Drawing her sword, she took a right at the next intersection.

And turned straight into the path of a Rubyholter coming the other way. He was a brute of a man with eyes so large they seemed to fill his face. There was no time for him to swerve around the Guardian, so instead he lowered his shoulder and tried to go *through*.

Amerel threw up a Will-barrier.

The man ran headlong into it, crashed off, and bounced back with a grunt and a clack of teeth. He fell limp to the ground.

Two Augeran swordsmen materialized from the gloom behind him. Amerel wasn't going to outdistance them from a standing start, so she held her ground. The stone-skins slowed when they realized she wasn't running. They wore black cloaks and confident half smiles.

Confident? *Good.* An evening whipping hapless Rubyholters would have lowered their expectations nicely.

Amerel might not be the most skilled Guardian with a blade, but she had tricks aplenty to compensate. Transferring her sword to her left hand, she unsheathed a throwing knife in her right and hurled it at the Augerans. The throw went high of the man on the left, so high in fact that he didn't even have to duck to evade it. He grinned, then shouted something in his native tongue, his derision plain.

Using her Will, Amerel stopped the knife after it was past him, then reversed it and sent it flashing back at him, point first. It took the stone-skin between the shoulders, and he stumbled forward a step. He stared at her in indignation, as if he thought she wasn't playing fair. And why should she? A knife in the back cut as keenly as a knife in the chest, and with considerably less risk to the wielder. She felt an answering stab of pain in her own back as her blood-dream rose up.

The stone-skin crumpled to the ground.

His companion half turned to look behind him, evidently thinking an enemy was at his back.

Amerel charged him.

Realizing his error, the Augeran spun to face her again, swinging his sword off balance in a decapitating cut.

A nudge of Amerel's Will halted the weapon in its tracks even as her backhand stroke passed under his blade and severed his right leg above the knee. He screamed and toppled sideways, then dropped his sword and seized his stump with both hands. Black blood spurted between his fingers.

Amerel stepped past. No need to waste time finishing him off. She suspected he'd have trouble keeping up with her now.

A stone-skin surged through the back door to the tavern, sword raised to cut down Caval. Caval, though, had employed his power. To the Augeran he would appear naught but a shimmer, and the enemy hesitated.

Karmel's throwing knife was already on its way. Her target had been the soldier's chest, but her fear for Caval had made her snatch at the cast, and her blade thudded instead into his neck. Some luck for a change. The stone-skin grunted and tottered, would have fallen backward if Caval hadn't seized his cloak and heaved him down the tavern's steps. The Augeran splashed into the water at the bottom, his weapon clattering from his grasp.

Karmel drew her own sword in her right hand, another throwing knife in her left. Shadows gathered in the alley beyond the doorway, and a voice outside barked a question in a language she didn't recognize. An Augeran asking after his kinsman, probably. Odds were, the speaker was alone, for surely a group of soldiers wouldn't have lingered on the threshold. Either way, the Chameleons had to risk a sally outside before more of the enemy came through the front door. Karmel glanced that way now and saw a snarl of flies on the torchlit waterfront, the black hull that would have been her next target. But no stone-skins.

Yet.

She moved to the foot of the stairs. Caval winced as he drew his sword, and Karmel remembered the wound he'd taken to his arm on Dragon Day. Unlikely he'd be able to do much fighting with that. She gestured that she would take the lead, then crept to the top of the steps. Outside, the stone-skin shouted again, his voice directed out into the night.

Calling for backup.

His words dissolved into a strangled cry, then there was a scrape of metal on wood as something slid down the wall to the floor. The Augeran's head dropped into view, leaking blood from a hole in one temple. A crossbow bolt protruded from the wound.

"Friendly," someone said, and Karmel's wash of relief left her feeling light-headed.

Noon.

Karmel stepped over the stone-skin's body, and Caval followed her outside. Noon was waiting for them. He reloaded a small crossbow, his movements sure and precise as if this brush with the Augerans had all been part of the plan. Karmel shook her head. Was she the only one with a pulse around here?

"Trouble," Caval said.

The priestess looked left along the alley. Shadows approached, as if the darkness itself were drawing in on them. The slap of the stone-skins' steps sounded loud in the confines of the passage.

Noon was the first to react. He toppled a barrel toward the enemy before setting off at a run in the opposite direction.

"This way!"

Karmel dashed after the Erin Elalese.

Earlier the refuse piled in the alley had provided useful cover on the way to the tavern. Now Karmel had to jink through it, her eyes filled with the dark. She didn't see the overturned table until Noon hurdled it, jumped it late herself and clipped her knee, setting the joint buzzing. Thirty paces ahead, the passage was blocked by a hand-cart and its spilled contents. Noon veered through an open doorway in the wall to his left.

Karmel followed him into a yard. Flies seethed about. To either side rose brick walls, and set into the one on her right was a metal ring to which the bloated corpse of a dog was chained. At the far end of the yard was a house. Its ground-floor windows were boarded, and the wooden door between them had a disconcertingly solid look. Noon tried the handle, found it locked. He withdrew a step and shoulder charged it. The door barely flinched.

Karmel looked round. The walls were too high to climb without a boost up, and their pursuers would be on to them before they could scale them. No guarantee anyway that the next yard offered a better chance of escape. They had trapped themselves as surely as if they'd walked into a cell and shut the door behind.

The footsteps of the chasing stone-skins drew near. Caval took up position to one side of the doorway. Beside Karmel, Noon raised his crossbow, ready to shoot the first Augeran who appeared. The priest-ess signaled him to lower the weapon. Better to draw all the enemy in and ambush them, than to kill the first man and spook the others into waiting outside.

Noon nodded understanding.

Karmel transferred her throwing knife to her right hand and drew the arm back in readiness to throw. Then she engaged her power and went still.

Two black-cloaked stone-skins with shields trotted through the doorway and drew up. One of the soldiers was a woman—the first female Augeran Karmel could recall seeing. Her skin had a silvery cast to it against her companions' charcoal gray. Caval and Karmel would be invisible to her, and as she looked about the yard, her brow furrowed as she tried to work out how the three targets she'd been following had diminished to one. She glanced down at the dead dog as if the creature might be part of the mystery.

Karmel's raised arm was trembling. A third Augeran appeared in the doorway, also carrying a shield. Just three of them? There were no noises from the alley to suggest more were on the way. Perhaps Karmel's party would survive this after all. Noon lifted his crossbow.

The female Augeran's shield came up. "You will down put weapon," she ordered.

Noon ignored her.

Stone-skin number three moved up to flank his companions. Karmel's gaze shifted to Caval, undetected at the group's rear. Her eyes flickered to the rightmost stone-skin, indicating her choice of target. Caval blinked in acknowledgment.

"Down weapon," the female Augeran said to Noon again, enunciating the words with exaggerated care as if she thought he might have misunderstood her first command.

Caval attacked.

A step forward, an extension of his sword arm, and the leftmost Augeran stiffened as Caval's sword punched through his back. The other two stone-skins half turned, weapons ready.

Thunk went Noon's crossbow, and Karmel's arm snapped forward, her throwing knife flashing toward the second male stone-skin. It struck him in the chest. His female companion was already falling, Noon's crossbow bolt through her ear. Karmel's victim landed atop her, his arm curling around her neck in a macabre embrace.

Dead.

For a moment the priestess could only stare at the bodies, half expecting them to stir to life again. After Dian, she'd built the stone-skins up to be giants, but the soldiers she had met in Bezzle hadn't matched up to the man she'd fought on Dragon Day. Few could, she suspected.

Noon waved to get her attention, and Karmel remembered he couldn't see her with her power employed. She released it. The Erin Elalese leaned forward and put his mouth to her ear. "You two stay here," he said, looking from the priestess to her brother. "If there are more stone-skins outside, I'll lead them off."

Karmel was silent, thinking. She knew his suggestion made sense. Every one of the Augerans who had seen the Chameleons thus far was dead. If Karmel and Caval faded into the shadows, they'd likely escape detection, for the next stone-skins through the doorway would have no reason to go looking for someone they couldn't see—

"Down!" Caval hissed, hurling himself at Karmel.

His arms wrapped around her and his shoulder struck her chest, driving the air from her lungs. Her feet left the ground. A moment of weightlessness, then she thumped onto the floor, head cracking against stone. She slid an armspan across the yard before coming to a stop against the wall of the house.

She lay on her back, sucking in breaths, her brother on top of her. Before Caval's warning, she'd heard a rip of air, knew they'd been attacked by someone. With her head scrambled, though, she couldn't say how, or from where. No more stone-skins came through the doorway. Noon whispered something in an urgent voice, and Karmel lifted her head, only for the yard to do a flip. Vomit burned the back of her throat. Had she been wounded? It was difficult to know with so much of her body aching.

When her vision cleared, she saw on the ground a crossbow bolt together with a chunk of brick. She raised herself to a sitting position. Her elbows stung where she'd skinned them, and the back of her head felt wet. When she touched the spot, her fingers came back red. Noon crouched nearby, reloading his crossbow. He flicked his gaze upward. *Of course, the roofs.* That's where the stone-skin shooter must be stationed, south of Karmel's position. She looked that way, saw no one on the skyline.

"We need to move," Noon murmured, crossing to the doorway.

Karmel grunted her agreement. The Chameleons couldn't stay here now. She clambered upright, staggered. Caval's hand on her shoulder steadied her, and she looked across to nod her thanks.

Then froze.

Her brother was hunched up against a wound in his right side, his arm held tight to his body. Just winded? No, there was blood on his hand and sleeve. Karmel went cold all over. She didn't understand. She could still make out the chunk of brick and the Augeran crossbow bolt on the ground. How could the missile have hurt Caval if it had hit the wall?

Unless *two* bolts had been shot.

Seeing her expression, Caval gave a half smile to say he was all right. Putting a brave face on for Karmel's benefit? She wanted to ask to see his injury, but Noon was already beckoning to them from beside the doorway. Caval motioned the priestess forward.

She hesitated before joining the Erin Elalese.

Noon peered both ways along the alley before ducking back. He made a series of hand gestures. Karmel had no idea what half of them meant, but she garnered enough from the others to understand there were stone-skins nearby. "How many?" she mouthed, but Noon just shrugged. More gestures. He wanted the Chameleons to make a break south—back toward the tavern—while he covered their retreat. She explored his gaze, wondering if he meant to follow them or simply to hold off the enemy for as long as possible. If playing martyr was in his mind, Karmel wasn't about to argue. Caval's well-being was all that mattered to her now, and if abandoning Noon to his fate meant improving her brother's chances, so be it.

She looked across at Caval. He leaned against the wall, glassy-eyed, but he gave a nod to indicate he was ready.

Just then the shadows in the passage concussed. Screams came from the north, and there was a change in air pressure that made Karmel's ears pop. The handcart that had blocked her way earlier went flying past, along with the body of a stone-skin, limbs flopping. The clamor was fading when more cries sounded, to the south this time. A whoop and a clatter as of someone rolling down a roof, then a thump as they hit the ground.

Silence.

Footsteps approached, and a figure came into view. At first Karmel thought it was another stone-skin, but Noon lowered his crossbow.

Amerel halted in the doorway and made a sweeping gesture. "Shall we?"

Galantas watched the crew of the blazing Needle ship hurl themselves shrieking over the rail. The flames had spread across most of the vessel, yet the fire burned fiercest on the quarterdeck in a core of purple-white that seared Galantas's eyes. He covered his mouth and nose with his sleeve, wondering whether to order the retreat. The Needle ship might *look* a safe distance away, but the *Fury*'s blayfire-soaked deck didn't need a naked flame to set it alight—the fumes coming off it could be ignited by heat alone. Galantas had seen it happen two years ago in Colgen when a Londellian ship exploded as it entered the harbor. The Londellians had meant to use it in retaliation for Cleo's killing of—

A light went off in his head.

He turned to Barnick. "Mage, the Needle ship! Drive it toward the stone-skins!"

Barnick's eyes glittered with understanding. "A fireship," he breathed.

A fireship would leave the stone-skins with no good answer. Allowing it to ram their vessels clearly wasn't an option, yet if one of the Augeran mages threw his will against Barnick's, that would leave his companions short-handed in their struggle with Malek's sorcerers.

"Do it fast," Galantas said. "Don't give them a chance to react."

Barnick nodded.

A wave of water-magic roared into life beneath the Needle two-master. It rose into the air and rushed forward. The blaze on its quarterdeck left a glowing trail in the night.

Forty lengths away.

Thirty.

From one of the Augeran vessels a shaft of black sorcery shot out. It struck the fireship's bow, dissolving the figurehead along with a section of the hull. But the craft continued on its way. Galantas smiled. There was no time for the enemy to sink the vessel before it reached them.

A stone-skin mage must have countered Barnick's power at that moment, for the wave beneath the fireship started to dwindle. The craft sat down on the sea.

Barnick gritted his teeth. "Got a strong one here."

"So show him you're stronger."

The mage grunted.

The fireship halted twenty lengths from the stone-skins. The glare from its flames illuminated the closest enemy vessels, and the warriors at their rails retreated from the heat. The fireship shivered on the water, waves lapping about it as if in a quickening wind.

Then it began to float back toward Galantas's fleet.

Amerel led the party at a run along the alley. Her eyes watered from the blayfire fumes. A left turn, then a right, then left again, not knowing where she was going. Her only thought was to put some distance between herself and the harbor. She passed a deserted watchtower that was nothing more than a platform on stilts. On a corner of the next intersection was a gated compound, the yard of which contained the reconstructed skeleton of some monstrous alien creature. Its shadowy eye sockets seemed to follow Amerel as she dashed past and into the alley beyond the crossroads.

Darkness enveloped her, and she staggered to a halt, a stitch in her side. Her companions drew up round her. She cocked her head to listen for pursuit. Nothing could be heard over the rasp of her own breathing, the muted thrum of fighting at the harbor, the buzz of the flies about her—so thickly clustered she had to cover her mouth to keep from swallowing one.

Then a shout came from behind, a stone's throw away at most. It was answered by another cry to the south. Augerans calling to each other?

Amerel swore.

"Keep moving," Noon said.

The Guardian nodded. If they went to ground, maybe their hunters would pass them by, but why take the risk? Better to stay in front and wait for the stone-skins to tire of the pursuit. Before the Rubyholters had attacked, the Augerans had been on the point of pulling out of Bezzle. They weren't going to delay their withdrawal just to hunt Amerel down.

She pushed herself into motion.

The alley curled to the left. Amerel's footsteps splashed as if she was running through puddles, and it hadn't even been raining. *Blood,* she realized. Trampled into the ground were shirts and trousers, together with the washing lines they'd been hanging from. A cinderhound lapped at the ground, its muzzle stained red. It growled as Amerel approached before backing into a doorway.

A short distance ahead, the alley opened out onto a square.

The Guardian's steps faltered.

Swarms of flies, piles of corpses. The dead were heaped so high they had toppled over in places, spilling bodies into the blood-soaked pathways that lay between them. Some were bloated with gas. None had been relieved of jewelry or other valuables. And not one was wearing armor. The sight reminded Amerel of the carnage in Cenan ten years ago. There, though, the dead had been hacked or hewed or

carved open, whereas here most of the Rubyholters had been dispatched with a blade across the throat. Executed. *Murdered*. But
no, what was she thinking? This couldn't be murder; this was war.
Killing wasn't murder if you stole the victim's country while you
were at it.

A flock of feeding starbeaks took to the air in a whirlwind of feathers. If Amerel's hunters hadn't known before where she was, they
would now. She had to press on, but that meant passing between those
mountains of flesh. If one shifted at the wrong moment it might bury
her completely, and wouldn't that be a novel way to go? Smothered
by the dead. Even the Deliverer hadn't thought of that one. Along the
southern end of the square was a crude gallows. A woman was suspended from it. She hadn't been hanged by the neck. Instead her arms
had been bound behind her back, and she'd been lifted into the air
by a rope tied to those bonds until her shoulders cracked from the
weight of her own body. To either side were wooden crosses on which
seven Rubyholters had been crucified. Perhaps Dresk and Galantas
were among them, but Amerel wasn't minded to look too closely.

Then her breath caught.

One of the victims was a boy, maybe fifteen years old. There was
no reason to think it was Talet's son, and every reason to think it
wasn't: the boy looked nothing like the spy, and he had red hair instead of Talet's brown. But still the thought would not leave Amerel.

Even it if *was* the spy's son, though, what should that matter? She
wasn't the one who'd betrayed him to Hex.

"We should move," Noon said from behind her.

Ignoring him, Amerel walked toward the boy. Blood pounded
behind her eyes. The right side of his face was swollen with bruises,
and blood trickled from his mouth where he'd bitten his tongue. Flies
crawled over his eyes. Amerel wanted to reach out and lower his eyelids, but she resisted the urge. She felt sick. Her hands were clenched
into fists. Why was he here? What had he done to deserve this punishment? What *could* a child do to warrant it?

And yet hadn't she killed a boy herself tonight—the one who'd been
fed to the creature in the harbor? Oh, she couldn't have known precisely what his fate would be, but she'd known what the stone-skins
did to prisoners. *This is different,* she thought, and perhaps it was.
But not in any way that mattered.

Karmel moved alongside her, her expression pained. Her legs were speckled crimson from the blood they'd splashed through in the alley. "He's alive," she said. "His chest is moving."

Amerel did not respond. If he was alive, he wouldn't be for long.

Karmel drew a knife.

"What are you doing?" Amerel said.

"Cutting him down. We can't leave him here."

"Absolutely. Why take just the boy, though?" The Guardian gestured to the people on the other crosses. "Maybe some of these are alive, too. Maybe we should find a cart, take them *all* with us."

Karmel scowled. "We can't leave him here," she said again.

Amerel turned her anger on the priestess. "What are you going to do, carry him? Maybe you should save your strength for your brother. Odds are you'll need to carry *him* before long."

Caval's face was plague-pale, and his hands were bloody where they'd been clutching the wound at his side. The Chameleons exchanged a look. Caval pretended he was fine, and Karmel pretended to believe him. When the priestess turned back to the boy, some of the fire had gone from her expression, but she didn't back down. "We have to do something."

"What are you going to do?" Amerel said. "Kill him? Have you ever killed a child before?"

"What the hell kind of question is that?"

I'll take that as a no. The Guardian's voice was flat. "Best leave this kind of work to those whose hands are already stained."

Karmel looked across at her, her expression warring between relief and disgust. Disgust, really? The woman had the nerve to judge Amerel? You let someone unblock your latrine for you, you didn't turn your nose up at them afterward. You didn't disdain them for having the iron to do the jobs you couldn't.

Eventually it was Karmel who looked away.

Amerel stepped up to the boy. No one could have complained if she'd drawn her sword and put an end to him, but she had no intention of killing him in spite of what she'd said. Instead she laid a hand on his forehead. In Kal Giseng she'd experimented on countless Kalanese under the watchful eye of the soulcaster Thorl, testing the limits of her powers on her victims' minds. She had learned to use her Will to trap people in unending nightmares until they were driven to madness, to crush their will until they took to their beds and rotted away, to extinguish all conscious thought until they became mindless husks, dead to the world around them. It was this latter knowledge she now used on the boy, robbing him of his pain, his despair, his suffering. With a strong adult subject, the process would have taken bells to complete. The child, though, already had one foot in Shroud's realm.

Hard to believe she'd found a way to help someone with what she'd learned.

She stepped back, her work complete.

"What did you do?" Karmel asked.

The Guardian did not reply. She strode for the alley on the western side of the square.

Karmel stumbled along the road, Caval's arm draped about her shoulders. For the last tenth of a bell she'd been helping her brother walk, but the farther they went, the more she found herself supporting him. Now they weaved along the street like two revelers returning from a night on the bottle, and she staggered to a halt, heaving in breaths. Her clothes were soaked with sweat, her legs burning tired, her head pounding from the knock she'd taken in the yard. Amerel was a dozen paces ahead. Karmel called the Guardian's name, then hauled Caval to a gate across an arch in the wall to her left. When she pushed on the gate, it dragged across the ground with a squeal.

She found herself in a courtyard. There were closed doors ahead and to either side, a malirange tree in each corner. She guided Caval to the floor beside the gate, and he sat down with his back to a wall. His blood was all over Karmel's clothes where the two of them had been pressed together—so much blood she wondered if there was any left in him. His eyes were closed, his breathing a rattle. The hopelessness of his condition bore down on Karmel more heavily than his weight had a moment ago.

Amerel entered the courtyard and stood to one side, her gaze moving from the priestess to Caval, then back again. They couldn't stay here, Karmel knew. Thus far Amerel's spirit-sight had enabled them to evade the stone-skins that they might otherwise have bumped into. It wouldn't be long, though, before the enemy noticed Caval's blood trail. In the alley, Noon used water from his flask to wash some of that blood from the flagstones, but it was an empty gesture. After a heartbeat he abandoned the effort and retreated to the courtyard.

Caval coughed.

"Leave him," Amerel said to Karmel. "He's slowed us down enough already."

The priestess stared at her, disbelieving.

Caval gave a dry chuckle. "Don't mind me," he said to the Guardian. "Just talk as if I'm not here."

Amerel's gaze didn't leave Karmel's. "Either he dies here alone, or he dies with the rest of us a street or two away."

Beside her Noon made to speak, then changed his mind. He frowned and turned to look out through the gate, his shoulders set.

Karmel found her voice at last. "You can't leave him," she said, then realized she'd said the same about the crucified boy. Amerel had warned her then that Caval was fading, but the priestess had refused to believe. Even now she wouldn't give up. "If we keep going, we might find a healer somewhere."

"And maybe he'll come floating down in the arms of your guardian angel."

"The temple of the White Lady—"

"Was razed to the ground. Take a sniff. You can smell what's left of its priesthood on the air."

Karmel groped for a response, but none came. She wanted to shout at Amerel that the Guardian owed Caval for saving her when they first met, but that debt had already been repaid at the harbor. Besides, could the priestess really blame Amerel if she walked away? Karmel herself had been ready to abandon Noon not quarter of a bell ago.

She hated Amerel at that moment. But even more she hated that the Guardian was right. There was no way they would make it to the boneyard with Caval. More importantly, there was no way back for her brother from his wound. It was a realization Karmel had been hiding from since he was hit. *Hit by a crossbow bolt meant for me.*

"If you want to go, go," she said. "I'm staying." Then, when the Guardian didn't move, she added, "But you want the dragon blood, don't you? That's the only reason you haven't abandoned us already."

Amerel did not deny it. "We can't let the blood fall into the stoneskins' hands. You hit three ships tonight. Someone needs to finish the job."

"Take it, then," Karmel said. If she'd refused, the Guardian would just have taken it anyway.

Noon rooted through Caval's pack. He withdrew the flask and stepped back.

Caval stirred. "She's right," he said to Karmel. "You should go. I'll catch up to you at the boneyard."

Karmel shook her head, numbed.

"You have to go with them. . . . You have to go on."

She sensed a double meaning to his words, but she shook her head again. She couldn't have left him any more than she could have struggled on farther under his weight.

Amerel watched her for a time, her shattered eyes unblinking. Whatever she was feeling—if indeed she felt anything at all—was hidden from view. Karmel wished she had a fraction of the other woman's control.

Then for a heartbeat the Guardian's features shifted, and Karmel caught a glimpse of something new. Pity, she might have said if she didn't know better.

Amerel turned her face away.

A gesture to Noon, then she strode through the gate and into the night.

As the fireship drew closer, the vessels in Galantas's fleet retreated. All except the *Fury,* of course, because while Barnick was engaged in his struggle with the Augeran mage, he couldn't also summon a wave to carry the devilship away. Galantas scanned the other Rubyholt ships. Sender's mercy, did their captains really need a signal to know that their help was required?

"Where are those lanterns?" he shouted to Qinta.

At that moment, the sorcerous wave beneath the fireship reared up tall.

And bore the craft back toward the stone-skin line.

Galantas glanced at Barnick. "Seems our mages have finally woken up," he said.

Barnick nodded. "About time."

Beyond the islets, Malek's sorcerers were gaining control of the waters between the fleets. Waves buffeted the four Augeran vessels, driving them toward the rocks. And all the while, the fireship was getting nearer. Higher and higher it rose as each mage in Galantas's fleet added his will to Barnick's. The sight sent a tingle through

Galantas, for it was a reminder of the power the Islanders would wield if they acted together.

A second bolt of sorcery from a stone-skin vessel hit the fireship, but it did no more to slow the craft than the first had.

The fireship moved to within twenty lengths of the enemy.

Ten.

The Augeran line broke, two ships bolting north along the coast, two south. Cheers sounded from the *Fury*'s main deck. Some of the crew were even shouting Galantas's name—and not just his own Spears, either. A Needle dropped his trousers and presented his backside to the stone-skins for inspection. The fireship, its purpose now fulfilled, was abandoned by the Rubyholt mages. As the wave carrying it dissolved into foam, it crashed into one of the islets with a belch of smoldering embers.

A black fog of blayfire fumes hung over the water. Through it Galantas could see the seas beyond the islets, now settling to a ruffle. Malek's ships had turned about. Should Galantas try to link up with them? At the Hub it had been agreed he would head straight to the meeting point at Clinker's Bay, but that plan had assumed that Malek would be running from the stone-skins. There seemed little prospect of that now, since it was the Augerans who had been put to flight. . . .

Galantas's thoughts trailed off.

Because the two pairs of enemy vessels had curved away from shore on courses that would see them reunited. They came together in an inverted Y formation and went speeding off east on waves of water-magic.

Straight for Malek's fleet.

Galantas sighed. You had to hand it to the stone-skins. Whenever they were forced to take a step back, they always followed it with a larger step forward.

"Orders?" Barnick said.

Galantas hesitated. Malek's ships were slipping south into the night. Galantas's first instinct was to support them, but he doubted the stone-skins would chase them far into unfamiliar waters. Moreover, he had no idea what sort of reception Malek had arranged for his pursuers. If Galantas followed, he might blunder into a trap meant for the enemy.

Stick to the original plan; no one could criticize him for that.

"We sail for Clinker's Bay," he said.

Amerel peered around the corner of the alley. Thirty paces away, five red-cloaked Augerans fought a ragtag band of Rubyholters, fourteen strong. Thirteen strong, make that, for one of the stone-skins had just punched his sword through his opponent's parry and sheered his jaw away. The Islanders' superior numbers should have carried the day, but they were contriving to make of them a liability. One man nudged the sword arm of his female neighbor as she tried to block an Augeran's decapitating cut. The woman lost her head to an enemy stroke.

Twelve strong.

"What are we doing here?" Noon asked from behind.

"Making new friends," Amerel replied. If she was going to finish the work they'd started at the harbor, she would need the Rubyholters' help.

Noon scratched a spider bite. "Missing the Chameleons already, are we?"

Amerel regarded him coolly. She'd been trying to put them from her mind.

The stone-skins had formed a circle and fought with remarkable unity of will. The instant a female Augeran found herself confronted by three Rubyholters, one of her kinsmen came to her support, with no call for aid given. Their enemies, by contrast, continued to be more of a danger to each other than their foes. A Rubyholt spearman made a wild lunge at a stone-skin that was deflected into the path of another Islander. The spear took the hapless man in the gut, and he folded with a scream.

Eleven.

"So what are we waiting for?" Noon asked.

"For more of our friends to die, of course. Now be quiet. I'm concentrating."

This would take fine judgment. Amerel needed the Rubyholters grateful if she was going to secure their cooperation. Go to their help too soon, and they might think they could have defeated the stone-skins without her. Leave it too late, on the other hand, and they might break before she stepped in. She couldn't afford to wait much longer, though. The noise of the fight would draw every Augeran in the city—as it had drawn Amerel herself.

Another Rubyholter went down, then another. Nine left now.

The end was close.

Amerel unsheathed a throwing knife. "I'll take this side of the street," she said to Noon. "You go left."

The Breaker gave a mocking salute.

She slipped into the gloom, Noon a step behind. They made their way toward the fighting, the Guardian hugging the wall to her right, her companion veering away. The skin of Amerel's lower legs felt tight from the crust of dried blood. As yet no one had noticed her.

Another Rubyholter fell, leaving just eight alive.

Perfect. My lucky number.

To business.

Amerel chose an Augeran wielding two shortswords and sent her knife spinning end over end toward him. Not easy to pick out a target in the melee, but it helped when you could use the Will to correct the course of your blade in midflight. The weapon took the stone-skin in the neck, and he toppled sideways into the legs of a neighbor. That second Augeran staggered forward, half parrying a spear thrust from an opponent before taking a swing from an ax that shattered his ribs. Down he went. One of Noon's blades, meanwhile, had found its mark in the chest of a third stone-skin, and the woman was now on her hands and knees. That just left two Augerans on their feet.

Odds of eight to two in their favor represented an advantage even the Rubyholters couldn't squander. But they tried their best, bless them. Another Islander fell to a sword across the throat before the last stone-skins were cut down.

Silence.

Noon crossed to stand beside Amerel.

The Guardian stared at the huffing Rubyholters. The Rubyholters stared back. No shouts of thanks, no tearful adulation. Just suspicious looks, as if she hadn't made her cause clear with her intervention.

A Rubyholter on the ground groaned. Two Islanders knelt beside the man and peeled back his shirt to reveal a gaping chest wound. No way he'd be walking away from that, but his friends seemed intent on lugging dead meat around, for they hauled him up and carried him away. Another Rubyholter crouched beside a female comrade. Checking for life signs, Amerel assumed. Then she saw him pry a ring from the woman's finger. One of his kinsmen barked an order, and he rose and trotted after the others. They made their way toward a side street leading east.

Heartbeats later, the two Erin Elalese were alone.

Amerel looked at Noon, who shrugged.

They retrieved their throwing knives and set off after the Rubyholters.

The alley they followed was crisscrossed with red footprints and cluttered with gold-inlaid furniture, patterned tapestries, and ebony-stone statuettes, together with all manner of other dross. After a hundred paces the Rubyholters turned into one of the houses. Inside, the main room was decorated in an opulence out of keeping with the squalor of the house's setting. Elescorian rugs, Metiscan dream-paintings, and Mellikian clawbone furniture were all thrown to-gether in a riot of styles and colors only a thief could think appealing. The Rubyholter with the chest wound was lowered into a chair. He moaned. Should have been dead already, but there was nothing more stubborn than a man with one foot through Shroud's Gate.

Amerel addressed his kinsmen. "Are you going to shut him up, or do I have to?"

A shaven-headed spearwoman stepped toward her, only for one of her male companions to lower an arm in her path. The man's cheeks were pierced with a dozen metal studs, and his face was streaked with soot. There was no sigil on his clothes to suggest which tribe he belonged to.

"Who are you?" Pincushion said to Amerel in an accent so thick it took the Guardian a moment to decipher it.

"We're the people who saved your lives."

The spearwoman said, "We didn't need your help."

"Right. You were just letting the stone-skins even the numbers so they had a sporting chance."

The woman scowled. "If you'd missed with those pretty knives o' yours, we'd have been the ones wearing 'em."

Pincushion waved her to silence. "Set a guard," he said, his gaze still on Amerel. "Now."

The spearwoman glared at the Guardian, then shouldered past and went outside.

"Are you in charge?" Amerel said to Pincushion.

"Ain't no ranks here, missy. We ain't soldiers."

You don't say. "But you were part of the attack on the harbor?"

He nodded.

"Is Dresk alive? Galantas?"

"Could be."

"I need to see them."

No response.

Amerel tutted her frustration. "You don't trust me? Does my skin look stony in this light?"

Pincushion was a long time in answering. "Galantas was at the harbor. Maybe he made it onto one o' them ships that got clear, maybe he didn't."

Those were the options, yes. "And if he did?"

"Then he'll be with the others at the meeting point."

"Let's go."

Pincushion crossed his arms. "Ain't on this island they're meeting. Ain't even close. So unless you got a boat in your pocket, along with a water-mage strong enough to dodge them stone-skin ships, we ain't going nowhere."

Amerel paused, considering.

Then she smiled.

Karmel sat beside Caval, listening to his breaths become shallower. He shivered. About them the city was still, save for the occasional shout or the clash of swords from somewhere to the east. Survivors from the Rubyholt raid on the harbor, perhaps? Or had Amerel and Noon run into trouble?

The priestess couldn't find it in herself to care.

When Caval coughed, blood bubbled to his lips.

"Let me see where you're hurt," Karmel said.

He didn't move.

"We need to take the bolt out."

"Actually," he said, "I think we should leave it in. It might be the only thing holding me together just now."

Karmel didn't have the strength to argue. Or to pretend there was hope when there wasn't. A part of her had always known she and Caval wouldn't escape this cursed city; all the clues had been there in her conversation with Mokinda Char. The only surprise was that she wasn't dying now with Caval. So why had she allowed so many things to remain unsaid between them? Maybe they'd both been guilty of letting the wounds of Dragon Day fester. Of pushing Caval's betrayal to the back of their minds, as if by not talking about it they could somehow make it not have happened.

Caval ground his teeth against the pain of his wound. Karmel's own pain was a throb at the back of her skull. Blood ran through her hair where her cut had reopened.

"I forgive you," she said suddenly, the words tumbling out before she could stop them.

Caval gave a half smile. "Liar," he said. "But don't be hard on yourself. I wouldn't forgive me either." And he hadn't, she realized. Forgiven himself. Maybe he couldn't until she did. "If it makes you feel better," he went on, "I wouldn't have taken that crossbow bolt for you if I'd known how things would turn out."

"Liar."

He chuckled. "Still, it's not all bad. At least we have our faith to take comfort in, right?"

Karmel said nothing. Those last words had been laced with irony, yet she sensed a note of yearning in them.

"Do you think the Chameleon is watching?" Caval asked. "Do you think he's watching over us?"

With a smug smile, perhaps. Karmel took her brother's hand and grasped it tightly, as if by that contact alone she could stop him slipping away. A stone from the wall behind dug into her back, and she shifted her weight. From across the courtyard, the empty windows of the houses stared back at her. To the east a crackle of sorcery sounded, and the skyline flashed crimson. The clash of swords Karmel had heard earlier was escalating into a larger engagement. And judging by the frantic shouts in the common tongue, the Rubyholters were getting the worst of the exchange.

She looked at Caval. His face was beaded with sweat, his eyelids drooping. There were a thousand things she wanted to say to him at that moment, but she couldn't get the words out past the lump in her throat. Even on Dragon Day she'd thought that, given time, she and Caval would make their peace over his betrayal. Now, with the sands running out, she found herself questioning whether she'd done all she could to set aside her anger and hurt—if she'd even set it aside fully now.

She could sense Caval's fear in the force with which he gripped her hand. A memory sparked in her of the time they'd held hands like this on the day Karmel left home, but she pushed the thought aside. Too often since Dragon Day she'd sought refuge in memories of brighter times, as if by thinking of the closeness she and Caval had once shared, she could resurrect it in the present. A mistake. For as she'd come to realize, there was no greater grief than to remember times of happiness when times of sadness were at hand. Her expression hardened. *Times of happiness?* She'd never thought so when she was living through them. But sometimes you had to lose a thing to understand its worth.

Caval's head slumped against her shoulder, and she stiffened. His grip on her hand was failing. Was he still breathing? She couldn't tell. Her own breathing was leaden.

"Stay with me," she whispered, fighting back tears.

Then she froze.

Footsteps in the street outside, approaching quickly. Had the Erin Elalese returned? With help, perhaps?

A figure stepped into the courtyard. A male Augeran, tall and gaunt. *Just one?* the priestess thought dully. This stone-skin was not like the others, though. He had golden spiral tattoos on his arms and cheeks, and there was something . . . insubstantial about him, as if he had one foot in this realm and one in the spiritual. Karmel had seen him earlier, she realized, climbing the gangplank to board the four-masted ship she'd marked with dragon blood.

He looked in the Chameleons' direction. There was blood on the flagstones near Caval, but the stone-skin couldn't know the Chameleons were there. Not while they remained still . . .

Then it came to her. As Caval had faded, he'd released his grip on his power—meaning the Augeran would be able to see him. And that wasn't all he'd see. He would see Caval slumped to one side. He would see him seemingly supported by nothing more than shadows.

And thus he would know that Karmel was there too, for all that she remained invisible.

He drew his sword.

The priestess stared at him. She didn't think she had the energy to push herself upright.

The stone-skin came at her, and she rolled to one side. Caval's weight was a momentary drag on her shoulder, then she was up on her feet. Her brother slumped to the ground, his head cracking against stone. Karmel drew her sword just in time to meet the Augeran's first thrust. Her blade felt clumsy-heavy in her hand, and her fingers were slick with Caval's blood.

The bite of the weapons rang loud in her ears.

Through her tear-stung eyes, her foe seemed a blur to her. In Dian, the stone-skin she'd fought had been brute strong, but this one was smooth as quicksilver. He came surging toward her, light glinting off his tattoos, sword flickering every way. The priestess backpedaled, wielding her own blade with a speed she hadn't thought herself capable of. Yet she felt strangely detached from the fighting—as if she wasn't controlling her weapon, simply watching it flail about her as it cut the night to ribbons.

Her opponent pressed forward. Karmel needed all her concentration to keep him at bay, but she found her mind drifting to Caval. Was he still alive, and if so, was he conscious of her duel? If he'd had the breath, he would have scolded her about the sloppiness of her technique. She must have been doing something right, though, because her next attack—a backhand cut—appeared to take the stone-skin by surprise. He was late bringing up his weapon to block.

Karmel's sword whistled for his throat.

And passed straight through him.

She blinked.

As her blade exited the man's neck, he reached up and grabbed it with his left hand. At the same time he stabbed forward with his own sword.

Too late for Karmel to sway aside.

The weapon ripped into her. She felt a searing pain in her chest as if someone had lit a fire there.

And suddenly she was falling.

CHAPTER 17

AMEREL STOOD on the quarterdeck of Galantas's ship, the *Fury*, staring west across the moonlit bay. Above the shore of some nameless island, the skyline was stained orange. Bezzle's harbor was burning—she'd seen it earlier as she sped in Mokinda's boat with Pincushion and his friends toward the Rubyholters' meeting place. Perhaps the rest of Bezzle was too, considering the brightness of the glow. One city-sized funeral pyre. The stone-skins' ships, meanwhile, had pulled out and were now anchored beyond the islets. Awaiting the dawn, perhaps? Or further reinforcements?

To her right, Mokinda leaned on the rail. There was a silence about the Storm Lord that said he didn't want company. He hadn't been surprised when Amerel found him in the boneyard. It made her wonder if, thanks to Mazana Creed's shaman, he had known all along that the Chameleons would fail—and if they'd been ordered to save Amerel from Hex so there was someone to take on the baton when they fell. It made her wonder, also, if he knew what had become of Karmel, for the priestess hadn't been with him at the boneyard. Amerel wouldn't ask him, though. Deep down, she already knew the answer to that question.

She took a breath and let it out slowly.

In addition to the *Fury*, seven other Rubyholt vessels were anchored in the bay. None showed the faintest glimmer of light, but then the fiery stench of blayfire oil served as a constant reminder of the perils of naked flames. The ship's crew was hard at work scrubbing the oil-soaked boards. Amerel had learned some intriguing things while listening to their conversation: about Dresk's death and about the success—or failure, depending on who was talking—of the raid at the harbor. There were as many different views on that as there were tribes represented in Galantas's crew. Evidently the clans were intent on holding on to their grudges and petty rivalries. Amerel wasn't complaining, though. She might be able to exploit those fault lines in her imminent meeting with Galantas.

And thank the Matron it was Galantas, rather than his father, to whom she was about to speak. Dresk, after all, had been warlord, whereas his son was just one of many people wanting to take his throne. There was no right of succession in the Isles; a warlord had to earn his place. Judging by tonight's attack on the harbor, Galantas had already begun the task of trying to prove his worth. Odds were, he'd be open to any scheme that extended his notoriety. Odds were, he'd have no qualms about allying with an enemy if it served his purpose. Here was an ambitious man. A ruthless one too, if the rumors about him orchestrating his brother's death were true.

A man, in short, with whom Amerel could do business.

How best to approach their meeting, though? Admit she was from Erin Elal, or pretend to be from the Storm Isles? Relations between the Storm Lords and the Rubyholters had been strained for decades, their enmity fueled by Dragon Day and the devastation caused by dragons passing through the Isles. Had relations between Dresk and Avallon been more cordial, though? If Amerel admitted to being from Erin Elal, what reason could she give for being in Bezzle at the time of Eremo's assassination? A coincidence? Galantas was too smart to believe in such a thing. And how would she explain having the dragon blood in her possession? How would she explain being privy to Jambar Simanis's predictions?

No, she would have to be from the Storm Isles.

Noon moved alongside her and stared at the orange skyline. "This is just the beginning, isn't it?"

Amerel nodded.

"Doesn't matter what we do here. Doesn't matter if we sink every ship in this Augeran fleet. It's just putting off the inevitable."

"Let the stone-skins come. We'll drive them back into the sea."

Noon looked at her sharply. "You really believe that?" he said. Wanting to believe it himself.

"No."

The Breaker's attempt at a smile came out as a grimace. He looked over the bay again and massaged his temples with his thumbs. "Lady's mercy, what's that *noise*?"

"Noise?"

"You don't hear it? It's like a needlefly buzzing around in my head."

"Ah. That'll be the devilship."

He looked at her.

"Didn't you see the flames carved into the ship's hull when we arrived? Or the demon figurehead? We're on a devilship—a ship with a Krakal shade bound to it. That noise you hear is the spirit keening. When the ship goes into battle, the Krakal soaks up the crew's blood-lust and feeds it back to them fivefold. Makes them formidable in a fight."

The Breaker had a guarded expression like he thought she might be having him on.

"What, you don't believe me?"

"Oh, I believe you, all right. With that honeyed tongue of yours, though, I don't know if I believe you just because you want me to."

"You needn't worry on that score. If I'd used my Will on you, I'd have taken your doubts as well."

"Good to know. You ever sailed on one of these devilships before?"

"No. Heard about one, though. Some Corinian ship that lost its water-mage to bad lederel meat, then lost its bearings in a storm. Three months the crew was out at sea. Three months of dwindling food and fraying tempers, and with the Krakal whispering in the sailors' ears all the while. When they finally put into harbor, only twenty of them were still alive. They'd killed all the others. Eaten them too."

Noon's brows drew in. He squinted at Amerel, and she met his look evenly.

"What?"

The Breaker shook his head.

A boat glided between two ships in the bay. In the time that Amerel had been on board the *Fury,* the captains of three other vessels had come to confer with Galantas. The last had left quarter of a bell ago, making her wonder why he hadn't yet summoned her to his cabin.

"You were telling the truth to the Chameleons, weren't you?" Noon said. "About your niece, Lyssa."

"All the best lies have a grain of truth in them."

"I'm sorry about your sister."

"Why? Did you know her?"

Noon grunted. "This niece of yours, what's she like?"

"She's six."

A pause. "That's it?"

"Have you ever met a six-year-old before?"

"Maybe."

"It's not the sort of thing you forget."

"How come she ended up with you?"

"Because there was no one else."

"No other family?"

"Her father died of the same fever that took her mother. No grand-parents, no uncles, no aunts. Hence 'no one.' And believe me, I spent a long time looking."

Noon scratched a spider bite on his cheek. "Did you know her well before?"

"No." The day Cayda died was the first time Amerel had met Lyssa in years. The previous occasion had been after she got back from Kal. She and Cayda had been seeing each other less and less before then. Cayda wasn't a Guardian, and what was Amerel supposed to talk to her about when she returned from a mission? How she'd earned her latest scar? Things had come to a head after Kal. Lyssa had been four. She'd always been nervous in Amerel's company, but this time she'd cried when she saw her. Actually cried. No hiding things from a child. No clearer mirror to see yourself reflected in. Afterward Amerel hadn't spoken to Cayda about it, but they'd both known they would never see each other again. And so it had proved—until Amerel saw her sister's corpse on a slab in the mausoleum.

"Where's Lyssa now?" Noon said.

"With the emperor's lackeys somewhere. In Amenor, probably."

"A hostage?"

"Matron's blessing, no—how could you think such a thing? Aval-lon simply offered to look after her while I was away. Kind of him too, considering she has no one else."

Noon studied her. "Is she why you betrayed the Guardians?"

Amerel stared across the bay toward Bezzle. The orange glow had stolen the light from the stars. "I already told you, I didn't betray the Guardians."

Footsteps sounded behind, and Amerel turned to see a man with tattoos for arms approaching. "Galantas wants to speak to you," he said, as if Galantas had been the one who'd sought Amerel out.

"What a happy coincidence," she replied, gesturing for Noon and Mokinda to remain. The Storm Lord didn't even acknowledge her. "Lead on."

Awaiting her in the captain's cabin were Galantas and an unshaven man wearing the blue robes of a water-mage. The room was all lacquered wood and brass fittings, but the effect was spoiled by an old bloodstain in the middle of the floor. Galantas sat at a table on which was spread a chart showing the Rubyholt Isles. Behind him, a window looked out onto the bay. The moonlight trickling through it, and through the skylight overhead, was the cabin's only illumination.

Galantas sat straight in his chair, trying his best to look statesmanlike. He seemed to be coping well with the tragedy of his father's loss. He blinked when he saw her shattered eyes. Then his expression became calculating as if he was trying to place her face.

Not an encouraging start, but a nudge of Amerel's Will was enough to draw the sting from his suspicions. Lots of people in the world, not surprising if he'd seen a face like hers before.

"I need to speak with you alone," she said. He'd be more open to persuasion if he didn't have friends here to impress.

Beside her, Tattoo snorted.

Amerel kept her gaze on Galantas. "Your men already searched me for weapons when I came onboard. Quite thoroughly, I might add. I trust that won't be necessary again."

Galantas signaled his companions to wait outside. Tattoo flashed Amerel his best "behave yourself" look before making for the door. The water-mage followed and closed the door behind.

"My name is Cayda," Amerel said, surprising herself by choosing her sister's name. "Mazana Creed sent me."

"Interesting time for a social call."

"Hardly social. She has unfinished business with the stone-skins."

"Because of Dragon Day?"

Amerel nodded.

"I'd have thought she would want to thank them for what happened. She's done rather well from it personally."

"Indeed? Are *you* feeling grateful just now?"

Galantas turned to look out of the window, and the moonlight played across his face like silver fire. When he next spoke, his voice seemed to come from a great distance. "Curious," he said. "The stone-skins only arrived in Bezzle yesterday, yet here you are already. Word travels fast, it seems, and you faster still."

"Have you heard of Jambar Simanis?"

"Imerle's shaman."

"And now Mazana's. He foresaw the stone-skins' coming."

"He foresaw the stone-skins' coming," Galantas repeated. "Yet Mazana didn't think to warn us."

"Would you have done so, if the roles had been reversed?"

Galantas smiled without humor. "Relations between our peoples have been somewhat . . . erratic, it is true. As I heard it, the Storm Lords are still a bit prickly after my father tried to disrupt Dragon Day eight years ago. As I heard it, they're looking for ways to pay us back. And what better way to do that than by assassinating the stone-skin commander and putting the blame on the Isles."

Amerel waved a hand as if his insinuation was beneath her. "The commander was shot inside your father's fortress, right?"

He nodded.

"Big walls on all sides, only one way in and out. I assume you thought to search the compound after. Find any assassins, did you?" She paused. "If I were you, I'd look for the killer a little closer to home. I'd wonder if, by killing your father, the stone-skins haven't already avenged their commander's death."

Galantas did not reply, but Amerel could see from his look that his suspicions already lay with Dresk. No need for a touch of the Will to steer him further in that direction.

"You still haven't told me why you're here," he said.

"I came to destroy the stone-skin fleet."

There was a hunger in his eyes. "How?"

Amerel did not respond immediately. Better to leave him guessing for a while, let the anticipation build. She settled back and stretched out her legs. The ship rocked gently on the swell. "I believe congratulations are in order. For your raid on the harbor. It was your raid, wasn't it?"

Galantas inclined his head.

"As commander, you take the credit for its success. But by the same token, you take the blame for its failure."

"Meaning?"

"Lots of different clans represented in your crew. I overheard some of them complaining that you were quick to flee the harbor when you'd secured your own spoils."

Galantas's look suggested he knew who the culprits would be. "That *was* the plan, yes."

"A plan, your opponents will say, that succeeded in recapturing only eight of the ships in port."

"Doubtless those same opponents will argue that eight is less than zero."

"Doubtless. But don't worry, I'm sure you'll talk them round. Reasonable men, are they?" Let him chew on that. "How much stronger do you think your hand would be if you were to consign the stone-skin fleet to the sea?"

Galantas's frown suggested impatience. "I'm listening."

The shadows briefly gathered as someone crossed over the skylight. Amerel's gaze did not leave Galantas. "You will be familiar, I assume, with how the Storm Lords lure dragons to the gate on Dragon Day?" She proceeded to tell him what the Chameleons had told *her* about Mazana Creed's experiments with the dragon blood. "It seems the merest drop is enough to lure a dragon over dozens of leagues—lure it to something marked with blood, for example."

"Like a ship."

"Very good. My orders were to use darts tipped in blood to mark the stone-skins' ships. The hope was that they'd still be in Bezzle when the dragons came calling. Alas, Jambar Simanis didn't foresee that their fleet would pull out so soon."

"Were you able to mark any ships?"

"No," Amerel said. A lie, obviously, but Galantas might be less willing to take the risks she wanted him to if he thought the job was already half done.

"And you need my help getting close to the fleet? It's too late for that. The stone-skins started north quarter of a bell ago."

Amerel blinked. *North?* Had she heard that right? Erin Elal was to the west of here, but since she was claiming to hail from the Storm Isles, it wouldn't do for her to appear pleased at the news. She looked at the chart to give herself time to think. What was there to the north that might draw the stone-skins' eye? The Confederacy cities? No, they were on the wrong side of the Shield to be of strategic value.

Dian and Natilly? Or Gilgamar? What did they have to do with Erin Elal?

Assuming Erin Elal remained the Augerans' target.

She was missing something.

The Guardian looked back at Galantas. What now? Make her excuses, and withdraw to the quarterdeck to think things through? No, if she wanted to destroy the stone-skin fleet, she had to act now. Besides, did it really matter what the Augerans' first destination was? Who was to say they wouldn't change course for Erin Elal once they were clear of the Isles? Or sail there after they'd finished their business in the north?

"Can you get ahead of their fleet?" she asked.

"Why?"

"Because there are other ways to mark a ship than with a dart and a blowpipe. The Isles are full of narrow waterways, right? If the stone-skins were sailing along one, and we could reach the end of it before they did, we could pour the dragon blood in the sea. It would mark their ships' hulls as they passed through."

Galantas fingered the band of sharks' teeth around his neck. There was something about his gaze that reminded Amerel of that Arapian sacristen she'd clashed with seven years ago. The one with the rash and the weepy eyes. The one who had had her poisoned.

"It might work," he said. "But only some of the blood is going to mark the fleet. Most of it will stay in the sea. When the dragons come, they'll probably head first for the place where the blood is strongest—for the waterway where we pour the blood, rather than for the stone-skin ships."

Amerel had had this same discussion with Karmel over tipping the blood in Bezzle's harbor. This was different, though. "You're assuming the dragons are coming from the south. But what if they came from the north instead? What would the creatures be drawn to first? The far-off place where the blood was poured? Or the stone-skin ships sailing invitingly toward them?"

Galantas's eyes gleamed. "You mean to release the dragons from the Sabian Sea."

"Yes." She'd discussed the idea with Mokinda earlier. "The moment the blood is poured into the water here, the dragons in the Sabian Sea will sense it. By the time we raise the Dragon Gate, they should be queuing up to pass beneath."

"If the dragons are going to intercept the fleet, you'll have to get to the gate before the stone-skins arrive at wherever it is they're heading. How are you going to do that?"

"That's where my Untarian companion comes in. His name is Mokinda Char. Perhaps you've heard of him."

"Mokinda Char," Galantas said. "The Storm Lord."

Amerel nodded.

"Your companion is a Storm Lord . . . and yet you're the one down here doing the talking."

"It is because I'm not a Storm Lord that I am doing the talking. Mazana Creed trusts Mokinda as much as she would any rival. Now, you never answered my question. Can you get us in front of the stone-skin fleet?"

Galantas was silent, his face as empty as a blank page, and about as difficult to read. Did he believe her story? Had he spotted some flaw she had overlooked? She'd heard it said that when the mood took him, he could fire his kinsmen's blood with the power of his rhetoric. Yet she suspected the man sitting before her now was the real Galantas: cold, shrewd, calculating.

Not everyone could have her warm and generous nature, though.

Finally he looked at the chart. "It isn't as simple as a flat race. The stone-skins have Rubyholt guides now, so they're not going to lose their way. Our only chance of getting ahead of them would be at the Outer Rim." He rose and leaned over the table to point at the chart. "Assuming they don't change course, their best routes through the Rim will be here, here, and here. To find out which path they take, we'd have to be close behind. And then there'd be no way to get round and reach the end of the passage before they do."

Amerel peered at the chart, noticing for the first time the symbols scattered across it—symbols that doubtless denoted which of the waterways were navigable and which were not. "Are they more likely to take any of these three passages than the others?"

"At this time of year, no."

She pointed to a fourth waterway snaking between two of the three. "What about this—"

"Impassable," Galantas cut in.

"Even for a ship with a Storm Lord?"

"Even then." A look came over his face. "Except . . ."

"Yes?"

He hesitated, then stabbed his finger at an island with the symbol of a cross through a circle on it. "Liar's Crossing."

Amerel waited for him to explain.

"The island has a saddle of land running east to west, about a hundred paces wide. Liar's Crossing, we call it. No single water-mage can create a wave big enough to carry a ship over. But if your Storm Lord and my mage were to join forces—"

"We could use the crossing as a shortcut once we know which route the stone-skins are taking," Amerel finished.

Galantas nodded.

"Do I want to know why it's called Liar's Crossing?"

"Because everyone who's ever claimed to use it before is a liar."

Great. "Someone must have crossed it before, though?"

"Someone probably has."

"And that's the only option we've got?"

Another nod. Galantas was actually smiling at the prospect, but a man such as he would no doubt relish a chance to increase his fame.

Time to hit him with the last part of her plan. "Of course," Amerel said, looking through the window at the other Rubyholt vessels in the bay, "your other ships won't be able to follow us over the crossing after we take it."

Galantas sat back down. "Other ships? Is the dragon blood so heavy that it needs a whole fleet to carry it?"

"No. But you'll want those ships with you when you chase the stone-skins north."

Silence. No smiles this time.

"Think about it," Amerel said. "Let's say we mark the stone-skin ships with dragon blood. Let's say the dragons then destroy them. Who's going to believe you when you claim the credit? Who's going to believe it happened at all? You need witnesses—the more the better. And witnesses from other clans, ideally. Also, after we've crossed Liar's Crossing, Mokinda has to swim to the Dragon Gate to get it raised. He assures me he can swim faster than any ship can sail, but not by much. It'll take time for the gate to be raised, then for the dragons to pass beneath it and hunt down the fleet. Time *you* need to buy us."

"By harrying the stone-skins?"

Amerel nodded. "They can't ignore eight ships at their back."

"And when they turn on us?"

"You turn as well."

"Ah, thank the Sender. For a moment there I thought you wanted me to take on eighteen ships with eight. And with skeleton crews besides."

"I certainly hope it won't come to that. After all, I'll still be on-board with you at that time."

Galantas gave her a look. "Yes, you will." Then, "If we're not going to fight the stone-skins, how long can we hope to delay them?"

"Quarter of a bell? Half? Every heartbeat could be decisive."

Galantas leaned back in his chair. His expression was hidden in shadow. He tested one of the shark teeth round his neck against a thumb as if he thought it might need sharpening. "You realize," he said at last, "by destroying the stone-skin fleet, I'll probably save a Sabian city. Gilgamar, most likely."

"And in *not* destroying it, you'd pass up the chance for revenge on the enemy. How would that go down with your kinsmen?" Time to give him another touch of the Will. "Who's the greater threat to the Isles, the stone-skins or the emira? When did the Storm Lords last attack a Rubyholt city?"

"Thirty-one years ago," Galantas said without hesitation. "Or did you want months and days as well? My people have long memories."

"As do mine," Amerel said. "But I'm sure if you had to, you could find a way to spin our cooperation here to your advantage." Like the thought hadn't already occurred to him. She softened her voice. "You think these stone-skins will be the last you see of their kind? You think the next group will treat you better?"

"Certainly not. Especially if they find out I destroyed their fleet."

"You're right. They'd respect you more if you did nothing."

Galantas did not reply. His half smile was back though, and Amerel could well guess the reason. Throughout their most recent exchange, there'd been no animation to his words, no conviction. As if he'd asked the questions of Amerel solely to see how she answered. As if he'd merely been rehearsing arguments he expected to have again with his kinsmen. He knew whatever choice he made today would be denounced by his opponents. He was testing how strong the winds of reason blew in either direction, and he could bend either way, as expedience required.

Or as Amerel's Will dictated.

Not that she would need to use it in this instance. This wasn't about the future of the Isles, after all. It wasn't about relations with the Storm Lords, or avenging the deaths of fallen kinsmen. This was about doing what was right for Galantas, and when would he ever get a better chance to stake his claim to be warlord? Who could stand against him if he pulled off such a coup? True, there were a thousand and one ways this plan could go to the Abyss, but when had Galantas ever been one to play it safe?

Sure enough, he nodded and said, "I'll speak to the other captains."

Qinta and Barnick entered by the door Amerel had just left through. Qinta crossed to the window behind Galantas, while Barnick stood beside the chart table.

Galantas said, "I could swear I've seen her before somewhere."

"With hair and eyes like that," Barnick replied, "you're unlikely to ever forget her."

"Maybe. You heard our conversation?"

"Yes."

"And?"

"And if we're going to get ahead of the stone-skins, we need to move now."

Galantas's eyes were gritty from the blayfire fumes, but rubbing them only seemed to make them worse. His clothes and hair smelled of oil, as did the whole cabin. "There are gaps in the woman's story we could sail this ship through, yet still I found her logic persuasive. Eight ships we brought out of Bezzle. A success, I would argue, but still less than half of what I'd hoped."

"It was you who got the crews into the city unseen," Barnick said. "It was you who broke the blockade."

"But Bezzle still burns, along with who knows how many of our ships. Kalag won't let the other clans forget that." Galantas leaned back in his chair. "Cayda—if that's really her name—is giving us the chance to score a victory even the Raptors won't be able to dismiss."

"Assuming we survive long enough to tell of it."

There was that.

A board behind Galantas creaked, and he looked round to see Qinta staring out of the window. There was still no sign of Malek, alas—"alas" because if the stone-skins had killed him, it would make it easier for Kalag to claim the whole night had been a disaster.

"You hear that?" Qinta said.

Galantas cocked his head. Hear what? Shouts from another ship? A warning bell from a watchtower? All he could make out was the whisper of voices on the quarterdeck, and the swish of water in the bay.

Then he heard it. A flap of wings. *Birds.* Galantas glanced to the heavens. Qinta was looking for birds again.

"Startail," the Second said.

"You can tell that just from its wingbeat?"

Qinta shook his head. "Thought I glimpsed one earlier." His forehead creased. "As omens go, there's few worse things than seeing a startail pass."

"Then why the hell are you trying so hard to spot it now?"

The Second appeared not to have heard. "Coulda been a fish-crawler, of course—its markings are a lot like a startail's."

From the unhappiness in Qinta's voice, Galantas suspected seeing a fishcrawler was no better than seeing a startail. But then he was beginning to wonder if there was *any* type or configuration of birds that wasn't a mask for Shroud's baleful grin.

He turned to Barnick. The mage was combing his hair again. "Did you catch a look at Cayda's Untarian when you were on deck? Is he really Mokinda Char?"

"How would I know? It's been a while since I was last wined and dined in Olaire."

Galantas let that one go. "Keep an eye on him. If he uses his power, I want to know." Though by then it would probably be too late.

"You reckon he's going to turn on us?"

"If he's got any sense."

"Then why not take the blood from him now while he's not suspecting?"

"What makes you think he's not suspecting? In any case, we'll need his help when we try to make Liar's Crossing. Can the two of you get us over?"

"Maybe. If this Mokinda lives up to his reputation."

Not exactly the answer Galantas had been hoping for. Reputation wasn't always matched by reality, as he himself proved.

Barnick paused, then said, "You're really planning on shadowing the stone-skins north?"

"What choice do we have? If our only role in this business is to pour dragon blood into the sea, Kalag will call us the emira's puppets. We need some way to turn this into a victory, not just over the Augerans but over the Storm Islanders as well."

"How?"

Galantas had no idea. Then a thought came to him. "Who picked up Cayda in Bezzle?"

"One of our lads, Wex. He and his group traveled with her from the city. But it was *her* who found *him*."

"You're sure of that? Who's to say Wex didn't catch her nosing around the harbor and drag her here? Who's to say the idea to put the dragon blood in the water wasn't mine, not hers? Not Wex, that's for sure—he'll toe whatever line we give him."

"But the other clans on board won't." Barnick looked toward the door. "And if Cayda is supposed to be our prisoner, we're keeping her on one hell of a long leash. Maybe someone should be out there now paying her a bit more attention."

Good point. It seemed people other than Galantas were capable of having them from time to time. He looked across at Qinta. "Do it." The Second headed for the door. "And Mokinda's name doesn't leave this room, understood?"

Qinta nodded and left the cabin.

After he had gone, Barnick said, "What are you going to tell the other captains about this?"

"That the Augeran fleet is on the move. That the clan leaders want us to follow them and make sure they leave the Isles."

"And when they do? The other captains won't go beyond the Outer Rim without good reason."

"I'll worry about that if we make it over Liar's Crossing." Galantas rose. "Now, it's time we were going. Leave the wounded behind on the *Spirit* and get everyone from that ship over to the *Fury*." The addition of those men, along with Wex and his companions, would bring the devilship's complement up to forty. "If it comes to a scrap with the stone-skins, we'll need every man we've got."

Ebon followed the path up the sandbank and halted at the top. Ahead and to his right, the wreck guarding the canal's entrance rose from the sea. The hiss of the snakes swarming over it blended with the susurration of the waves. How long had it been since he'd last seen it?

Twenty-four bells. Twenty-four Shroud-cursed bells to end up back where he'd started. Except that now—if Mottle was to be believed— the sands were running out before Gilgamar was attacked. If only the mage had warned him earlier, Ebon might have risked it all on a dash through the Harbor Gate. As ever, the old man's timing left a lot to be desired.

Still at least Ebon now had Peg Foot with him. The Mercerien had arrived at the port at the fifth bell to escort the prince and Vale through the Lower City. They'd led a charmed life as they made their way north through the simmering streets. Trouble appeared always to be waiting beyond the next intersection, yet always by the time Ebon reached that junction, the way was clear. Throughout the journey, he had kept his power bunched tightly within him. There seemed little point in Tia betraying him now that she had his money, but equally there seemed little point in her going through with her part of the bargain. Except for professional pride, perhaps?

Yes, that sounded like Tia.

To his right, the beach stretched away to the canal. To his left, the sand curled to the northwest, glistening silver-white where the moon shone on puddles trapped by the retreating tide. Farther along was a multitude of fires surrounded by shadows. At the top of a dune, three figures stood guard.

"Ah, what a beautiful sight," Peg Foot said as he looked at the fires. "Enough to get the juices flowing, eh? All them sheep nicely rounded up like that."

"I thought these were refugees from the Hunt."

"Refugees, yeah, but not from the Hunt. From the city."

"You can't blame them for thinking they might be safer out here than in there."

"Blame them?" Peg Foot chuckled. "I don't blame them, I thanks them! Makes my job that much easier when the time comes to give them a shearing—as Tia likes to do from time to time."

And where was the shepherd to these sheep? Where were the soldiers who might have protected them from Peg Foot and his ilk? Sheltering behind the walls of the Upper City, of course. The same walls Ebon should have been scaling right now instead of listening to Peg Foot's poison.

"What happens next?" he asked.

"Next we waits for our ride. A boat will be along soon to take us to the fortress guarding the canal. There'll be a rope there for you to climb."

Ebon rubbed a hand across his eyes. The fortress. It had to be, didn't it? "I had some trouble with that fortress yesterday. At about this time of night, too. Knowing my luck, your man on the inside will be the same man who shot at me then."

"Ah," Peg Foot said with a wink, "but he ain't gonna sees you this time, remember? If we plays this right, no one will. They might sees the boat, of course, but Tia's arranged a little distraction at the Canal Gate."

"I am touched she should go to such lengths for me."

"Ain't for you she's doing it. Just protecting her investment. Next time someone needs to get into the Upper City, she'll want to send them this way too. And she can't do that if you're seen tonight. So make sure you gets up that rope and over the wall sharpish." Peg Foot grinned. "No stopping on the battlements to wave me off."

Ebon looked at him. "We'll see each other again, though, won't we? Get a drink maybe, catch up on old times."

The Gilgamarian laughed and clapped him on the back. "Here he comes," he said, pointing to Ebon's left.

A boat had materialized from the darkness to the west. Its passenger must have been using sorcery to propel it, for there was no splash of oars to accompany its progress. The boatman stood in the stern, robed and hooded like the ferryman in some Manixian fable of the underworld.

"Let's go," Peg Foot said, setting off down the beach.

Ebon's boots crunched over a ridge of shells and stones, then he skated down a sandbank and kicked aside a blacktooth snake in his path. Another fifty paces and the sands turned boggy. Peg Foot began to labor as the mire sucked at his peg. The wood left imprints that were quickly erased as water filled them.

Peg Foot brought them to a halt beyond the reach of the surf.

"That's far enough," he said. "Wet trousers might be hard to explain if you gets stopped in the Upper City."

Out to sea the boat had drawn level with their position. It looked like it might continue past, then the boatman brought its bow swinging round.

Peg Foot said, "You got your cover story straight in case you gets picked up?"

"We won't be," Ebon replied.

"Course not. Just remember, if you *does* get caught, keep Tia's name out of it. There's worse things that can happen to a man than losing a limb."

Like being possessed by Vamilian spirits and driven to the edge of madness, perhaps? Or seeing the hurt in your lover's eyes each day from a wound you inflicted on her?

Ebon grimaced. Yes, wasn't he quite the victim.

As the boat approached the shore, a wave built beneath it and carried it up the beach. It settled on the sand, just clear of the surf. Peg Foot was the first to climb in, his peg scraping the gunwale as he levered his leg over. Ebon and Vale followed before taking up seats on the rear thwart. The boatman gestured, and another wave of water-magic came foaming up the beach. Ebon gripped the rail. The boat tilted, stuck, then was drawn back onto the sea.

No one spoke as the boat glided east. It halted a dozen lengths from the wreck. Ebon could see thousands of moonlit characters scored into the ship's hull as if a storyteller, lacking paper and ink, had carved his tale into the wood instead. Snakes slunk along the masts and spars to drop off their ends into the water. Ebon pulled his cloak more tightly about him. The breeze off the sea was warm on his face, yet as he looked toward the guardhouse he felt a coldness form in his gut like he'd swallowed a lump of ice. What was the boatman waiting for? A signal from the soldiers?

Voices reached Ebon from along the canal, and small blazing shapes arced out from the Lower City toward the Canal Gate. Arrows, Ebon thought at first. Then they hit the fortress to the sound of smashing glass, and exploded in gouts of fire that ran down the walls like molten tears. Dark twisting shapes followed the incendiaries, thrown high to land on the battlements, or in the city beyond. It took Ebon an instant to recognize those shapes as blacktooth snakes.

Of course, the distraction Peg Foot mentioned.

The boat swept toward the entrance to the canal. Yesterday Ebon had lifted his own craft over the spar of the wreck that blocked the way, but tonight the boatman took their boat beneath it, forcing Ebon to flatten himself against the rear thwart. The fortress was only a stone's throw away now. Ebon's cold intensified, as if the building were giving off a chill. The tips of his fingers tingled. Something didn't feel right, but he couldn't have said what. Perhaps after enduring so many setbacks, he just found it hard to believe he might actually reach his destination without further trouble.

The boat glided to a bumping halt against the wall at the point where the fortress ended and the canal began. A knotted rope was lowered from the parapet. Vale was first to climb. Ebon didn't wait for the all clear before starting his own ascent. Grasping the rope, he pulled himself up from one knot to the next, his boots scuffing on stone. From the corner of his eye, he saw Peg Foot's boat moving off. He forced himself to take his time, make sure of his grip, since a slip now would mean a fall into the snake-infested canal below. And which of the powers he'd inherited from Galea would help him then?

The battlements edged closer. Vale had disappeared over the parapet. Disappeared and not reappeared. Ebon kept expecting to hear the clash of blades overhead, or see a guardsman reach out to cut the rope. Then Vale appeared above him. The Endorian grabbed Ebon's wrist and helped him climb the final armspan. Ebon rolled over the battlements and onto the walkway beyond.

He was on his knees straightaway. To his left was an archway leading to the gatehouse. To his right three Gilgamarian soldiers stood on the walkway, all facing away from him, shoulders pressed together so that they blocked him from the view of anyone farther along the wall. From the direction of the Canal Gate came the sound of more smashing glass, a louder crackle as if the flames had taken hold.

Immediately below Ebon, a deserted road ran parallel with the wall. Sitting on the edge of the walkway, he twisted and took his weight on his elbows before dropping the final way.

Vale followed him down.

Ebon slipped out of his cloak and tossed it onto the ground before setting off. He ducked into the first alley he came to. Some sixth sense warned him he was being watched, but that was probably just his nerves talking. He'd done it! He'd made it to the Upper City! The hard part was over; now he just had to locate the Mercerien embassy, find Lamella and Rendale, and spirit them away without Ocarn noticing.

His face twisted. Yes, it was all going to be smooth sailing from here.

From the quarterdeck of the *Fury*, Galantas stared west through his telescope across the slumbering sea. In the distance, the lights of the stone-skin vessels made their fleet look like a floating city. Still more lights indicated the position of sentry ships guarding the armada's flank. It had proved surprisingly easy for Galantas to overhaul the Augerans. On the journey north, the stone-skins had sent scout ships ahead through each channel they came to in order to confirm the safety of their route. One such ship was returning now from the passage through the Outer Rim known as Shroud's Gullet. A dangerous path to take when the seas were high. But with the waters currently as mild as a lullaby . . .

Galantas snapped his telescope shut. The enemy's course was set. He couldn't afford to linger here longer if he was going to brave Liar's Crossing and arrive at the end of the Gullet before the Augerans did.

He signaled Barnick to turn the ship about.

It took a few hundred heartbeats to reach the bay where the other Rubyholt ships were anchored. Galantas saw their masts before he spotted the Crossing itself: a saddle of rock between two ridges that formed the backbone of an island near the western end of the Rim. From his vantage point, the notion of a ship cresting that saddle seemed absurd. According to legend, Xaver Jay had once made the Crossing to escape a pursuing dragon. A Falcon vessel had tried to repeat the feat three years ago, but it had fallen short, and was now marooned up on the rock. Galantas could make out the shadow of it near the top of the slope. He hoped his own ambitions would not similarly be left high and dry when this was over.

Barnick brought the *Fury* round to face the saddle, then glanced at Galantas for the signal to go. It was clear from his look that he hoped Galantas would call off this madness. Earlier, the mage and Mokinda Char had paced out the Crossing. The thoroughness of Mokinda's preparations, together with his confidence on his return to the *Fury,* had given Galantas cause for optimism. Barnick's expression . . . less so.

"Ready when you are," Galantas said.

The sorcerer gave a weighty sigh.

The ship rose on a wave of water-magic and moved forward. Mokinda had said he would add his power to Barnick's only when it was needed. Now he spoke from beside his Rubyholt counterpart.

"You might want to narrow your focus," he said. "Don't waste your strength making the wave any wider than it has to be."

Barnick scowled, but nodded.

Galantas looked at Mokinda. The "suggestion" he'd just put to Barnick was typical of the way he conducted himself. So unassuming. Timid, even. Not at all what Galantas had expected of a Storm Lord, and Mokinda Char in particular. Eight years ago, the Untarian had been emir during Dresk's failed attempt to sabotage Dragon Day. The Storm Lords had responded by battering every settlement in the Outer Rim with waves as tall as the Bleakpoint Cliffs. The year after, Mokinda had passed a decree that said any Rubyholter caught in Sabian waters would be thrown to the dragons on Dragon Day. Galantas had lost many friends to that law before it was repealed by Imerle Polivar in a rare gesture of conciliation. But then maybe the rumors were true—that Mokinda had been merely a stooge for more uncompromising forces on the Storm Council. Gensu Sensama, Thane Tanner, Imerle herself.

What a loss they would be.

"A point to starboard, I think," Mokinda said to Barnick. "The gradient is less steep that way."

The *Fury* changed course.

As the island rushed closer, Galantas saw the gentler slope Mokinda had been referring to. Across it were speckles of gray from limewing nests. Galantas looked back at the other Rubyholt ships. In due course they would follow the stone-skin fleet through the Gullet, but for now they'd been ordered to stay put while Galantas attempted the Crossing. Succeed or die, he didn't want his efforts to go unwitnessed.

"Now!" Mokinda said to Barnick. "Give it everything you've got!"

The murmur of water beneath the *Fury* built to a roar, and the ship surged into the air. Galantas's stomach jumped with it. The ship climbed to a seemingly impossible height—as high as the saddle itself—yet still it continued to rise until Galantas could see a strip of moonlit sea beyond the Crossing, another island in the distance. The rumble of water grew louder. Someone in the crew shouted for people to hold on to something. Like having a grip on a line would save them if the hull cracked open on the saddle. Strangely, none of Galantas's crew from among the other clans had asked to be returned to their own tribes. It was as if they expected him to make the Crossing. As if they trusted him, even.

When the *Fury* reached the island, Galantas felt a drag on the ship's momentum. He looked over the rail. Far below, the wave devoured the shore in a flood of foam. But it was already receding. The *Fury* started to sink. Ahead, limewings took to the air in a raucous cloud. Qinta's head twitched from side to side as he tried to make sense of their passage.

He frowned.

The deck trembled. Galantas could make out the jutting ribs of the Falcon vessel that had failed to clear the Crossing. Amid the debris were white patches that might have been bones. Lots of bones. Moments later, the *Fury* rolled over the wreck to the sound of cracking wood. The saddle hastened closer, yet for every length the ship moved forward, it seemed to sink an armspan too. Some of the crew shouted prayers to the Sender. The demon figurehead, sensing their mood deteriorate, started wailing.

"We're not going to make it!" Barnick said.

Galantas had reached the same conclusion. The *Fury*'s quarterdeck was only just level with the top of the saddle, so there was no chance the lower parts of the ship were going to clear it. *Time for Mokinda to enter the game.* He glanced at the Untarian, but the Storm Lord's expression was so distant he might have been looking past the plane of this world into Shroud's realm beyond.

"Help me, damn you!" Barnick said.

Mokinda pursed his lips as if considering the request. Then he nodded. There was no flourish as he released his power, but all at once the deck ceased quivering, and the *Fury* began to climb once more. Yet slowly, oh so slowly. Galantas clutched his shark-tooth necklace so tight the teeth dug into his flesh. Was this all Mokinda had? It had to be, since the Storm Lord had no reason to hold back. Perhaps he'd left his intervention too late. Perhaps with most of Barnick's wave now spent, there was too little water for Mokinda to work with. At the rate the ship was rising, it might *just* make it over the saddle. But what of the land that lay beyond? Was there enough energy left in the wave to carry them all the way back down to the sea?

Not a chance.

The voice of the *Fury*'s figurehead went up an octave. There was a note of glee in it, as if the ship reveled in the threat of its own annihilation. If there had been time, Galantas would have ordered one of his men to shove a rag in its mouth, but the saddle was already upon them. As the *Fury* reached it, he expected to hear a grinding sound as the keel scraped rock. It never came. Still, there could be no more than a few armspans of water now supporting the weight of the ship.

For an improbable heartbeat, the devilship seemed to pause at the crest of the rise as if taking in the view. The downslope was blanketed with trees, while beyond . . .

Galantas started laughing, for he understood now why Mokinda had saved his strength. Rising up to meet the *Fury* from the sea below was a wave of equal size to that which had carried the ship to this point. With perfect timing, it caught the vessel as if it were a baton passed between the two bodies of water, and bore it down toward the distant swell.

Standing on the *Fury*'s quarterdeck, Amerel peered through the darkness at the huge stone carving overlooking the entrance to the strait. Lines in the cliff hinted at the features of a bloated, demonic face so lifelike it seemed the beast had been trapped in the rock. The warning behind the image was plain: *Do not enter!* And yet wasn't this one of the waterways that offered safe passage through the Outer Rim? Was the carving meant as a caution against the perils of the Isles as a whole? Or was it an attempt to trick strangers into taking other, more dangerous routes?

In the strait, currents stirred the waters into patches of silver foam, and their rustle mixed with the fizz of the sorcerous waves carrying the stone-skin ships. For now, those ships remained hidden behind a bend in the waterway. Amerel hefted the flask of dragon blood and looked inquiringly at Galantas beside her. He'd know better than she would how far away the Augerans were.

Galantas shook his head.

Wait.

When it came to tipping the blood in the sea, Amerel needed to get her timing just right. Do it too soon, and the blood might disperse before the stone-skins arrived. Leave it too late, though, and the Augerans might see the *Fury* waiting at the exit to the passage. It was unlikely they would deduce the significance of liquid being poured into the water, but why take the risk? And why take the risk of a chase through the Outer Rim when Mokinda had already departed on his swim north for the Dragon Gate?

She drew the stopper from the flask of dragon blood. When the signal came, she wouldn't be able simply to pour the blood in the sea, in case some splashed back onto the *Fury*'s hull. Instead she would have to throw—

Galantas touched her arm, and she startled, almost dropped the flask.

She glared at him, but he wasn't looking at her. He was staring along the strait. When Amerel followed his gaze, she saw shimmers of reflected light on the waves. *The Augeran fleet.* There were sounds now too: the creak of wood, the flap of a flag, the groan of ropes.

"Do it," Galantas said.

Amerel nodded.

With an underarm throw, she tossed the flask of dragon blood up and out over the waves, then used a nudge of her Will to set it spinning so its contents were sprinkled as widely as possible. She lost sight of it in the darkness, but there was a plume of spray where it landed. A whisper of water-magic told her Barnick had used his power to stop the flask from immediately sinking and taking its contents to the bottom of the sea.

Eight, nine, ten heartbeats, then Galantas tapped his mage on the shoulder, and the sorcery faded.

Amerel looked along the strait again, saw ripples of brightness moving along the cliffs at the bend.

A wave formed beneath the *Fury* and carried the ship away.

PART IV

RED TIDE

CHAPTER 18

GALANTAS WATCHED the three Needle and Falcon krels enter his cabin. Cleo and Tub he remembered from the White Pool. The second Needle was a tall man called Blist with an unkempt beard and body odor that masked even the lingering smell of blayfire. Galantas's own krels came after them: Seagle and Worrin and the rainbow-haired Clamp. He'd briefed them earlier on his plan to trail the stone-skins north, but he wanted them here—along with Qinta and Barnick—to bolster the numbers and thus make it harder for the Needles and Falcon to turn down his request for help. He needed their ships, not just to witness his triumph, but also to strengthen his fleet.

A decanter of Elescorian brandy and seven glasses had been placed on the chart table. Galantas gestured to the decanter as the krels sat down.

"Help yourselves to brandy," he said. "This was a Raptor ship before I claimed it, so the drinks are on Kalag."

Worrin chuckled dutifully, but the Needles and Falcon gave no reaction. Nor did they make any move toward the decanter. Evidently they wanted to keep their heads clear; they would know something was afoot from the fact they weren't sailing back to the Hub.

Galantas poured some brandy into a glass and leaned back in his chair. He'd already decided how he would play this. Ordering Tub and the others to follow him north was out of the question, so the next best thing was to present his plan to them as a done deal, and hope they didn't have the stones to challenge him. How much of the background should he reveal to them, though? Whatever story he used now he'd have to repeat to the other clan leaders in due course, so it made sense to keep things vague in case he needed some wriggle room later. Most important, he'd have to make sure the krels never got the chance to interrupt him with questions. If he let them start picking holes in his tale, he suspected they'd never stop.

"We don't have much time," Galantas said, "so I'll keep this short." Unless it proved hard to sway them, of course, in which case he'd speak for as long as was necessary. "Yesterday, before the stone-skins came, I captured three Storm Isle agents in Bezzle. They were carrying a flask of dragon blood, which they'd been ordered to use to mark some ships in the harbor. When I asked who their target was, they said the Augerans. That might be true, though it does leave open the question of how they knew the stone-skins would be arriving when they did."

Blist opened his mouth to speak, but Galantas raised his hand to forestall him. "Later," he said. Then, "After the attack on Bezzle, I had the idea of using the blood against the stone-skins in the same way the Storm Islanders had intended to. But the priority was to get our ships back, and then the Augerans pulled out after they fired the city. Opportunity missed, you might think. No way now to mark the enemy's ships." He paused. "Except there is another way. That is why I ran the Liar's Crossing earlier—so I could reach the end of the Gullet before the stone-skins did. So I could pour dragon blood into the waters their ships were about to sail through."

He waited a heartbeat to let the implications of his words sink in, then nodded and said, "Right now the Augerans are sailing north in ships marked with dragon blood. And in a few bells' time, the Storm Islanders will raise the Dragon Gate to release the dragons that were trapped behind it on Dragon Day." He smiled. "Anyone else curious to see what happens when the stone-skins meet the dragons?"

A hint of a smile showed on Cleo's face, but the two Needle krels remained impassive, waiting for him to show the rest of his hand.

"Unfortunately there's a problem," he said. "Judging by the course the Augerans have set, you can guess their destination as well as I."

"Gilgamar," Tub said.

"Gilgamar," Galantas agreed. "Which means there's a chance they might reach the city and be tucked up safe behind the harbor's chains before the dragons catch up to them." He sipped his brandy. "But not if we can slow them down on their passage north."

Cleo's smile beat a hasty retreat to leave his expression as pained as the other two krels'. Galantas spoke quickly to head off the inevitable outburst. "Let's be clear," he said. "I'm not talking about fighting them. We are seven ships to their twenty, with barely enough men to keep them on the water. But the Augerans won't know that. They'll see us on the horizon and think we're a threat. They'll try to engage us, but we won't oblige them. If they turn, so do we. If they head north again, so do we." He put his fist on the table and leaned forward. "We'll sail rings round those whoresons until they count it a blessing when the dragons show up."

Approving murmurs from his own Spears. Tub nodded along like he'd written the speech himself. The mood in the cabin had thawed a fraction, but Galantas still had work to do.

"Now, I won't lie to you," he lied. "This isn't how I thought it would go. If the stone-skins hadn't left Bezzle so soon, I'd be at the Hub now discussing this with the other clan leaders." He looked at the two Needles. "And if Malek had been at Clinker's Bay, we'd have had his ships with us on the journey north." Because the Needle chief was sure to have gone along with Galantas's scheme. "But the fact is, Malek isn't here, and the stone-skins aren't going to wait for him to show. We have to play the hand we're dealt. The job of finishing this falls on us.

"I can live with that, though. I know you weren't picked for the raid on Bezzle by accident. You were chosen because you're the best. Tub, I heard about you capturing one of the stone-skins and throwing her to that creature in the harbor. And Cleo, I saw the parting gift you gave to the enemy when you set alight the sails of one of their ships with some of your own flaming arrows." The two men shifted in their chairs, apparently uncomfortable with his flattery. But liking it at the same time, he saw. "Seven ships we may be, but I say that's more than enough to put the stone-skins in their place. And do you know why? Because there's no one else out there who can match our seamanship. Ask the Erin Elalese. Ask the Storm Islanders. Now it's the Augerans' turn to learn that the hard way."

All empty words, obviously. Once the Rubyholters left the Outer Rim, they would give up home advantage. On the open seas, seamanship counted for little compared with the strength of a ship's water-mage, and at Bezzle the stone-skins had proved they held the upper hand on that score. In Barnick, though, Galantas had one of the few Rubyholt sorcerers who could go toe-to-toe with the enemy. And Galantas was willing to sacrifice his other ships if it meant taking down the Augeran armada.

"Now, I know what you're thinking," he said. "You're thinking we've done our bit. You're thinking the stone-skins are probably already doomed, thanks to the dragon blood on their hulls. And you may be right. But this isn't the time for half measures." His voice was grave. "We all lost friends in Bezzle. I can only hope Malek's failure to show at Clinker's Bay doesn't mean we've got another clan leader to avenge." Tub's and Blist's expressions made it clear they'd already considered that possibility. "If I had my way, the raid on Bezzle would mark not the end of the tribes working together but the beginning. And I sure as hell don't want to be the one who has to return home and explain how I let the Augerans escape because I wasn't prepared to see this through."

No mistaking the bitter note of threat in that one. Now it was time to sweeten the brew.

"But let's not pretend it's all bad news, eh? I'm sure you haven't forgotten the twenty thousand talents the stone-skins gave to my father and then took back." They probably *had,* actually, but the reminder now had their eyes shining like the coin Eremo had tossed to Dresk in the Great Hall. "I'm guessing that money went north with the Augerans. I'm guessing it's onboard their flagship. Who knows, if we see where that ship goes down, we might be able to send our mages back to recover the loot. Twenty thousand talents. Split seven ways, that makes each of us"—he looked up at the ceiling and muttered some numbers as if he were doing the sums—"a shitload of money."

Grins all round. Even Blist mustered a half smile, but then gold had a way of lightening even the blackest mood.

Galantas took a final sip of brandy, then set down his glass. He had the krels now, no point saying anything further if it risked breaking his spell. "Any questions?" he asked, rising.

The other krels rose with him. Tub's jaw had a determined set to it. "Then let's get to work."

Standing in the gloom outside the Mercerien embassy, Ebon peered both ways along the street. The paving stones here were clean and free of cracks, the railings so bright they might have been buffed with the family silver. At this early hour—just before the seventh bell—the only person abroad was a man walking a Shamanon toy dog. Now was the time for Ebon to make his move, before the streets filled with witnesses and the embassy came to life. A lone figure moved in the darkness beyond the building's ground-floor windows.

The dog walker moved away.

Ebon nodded to Vale along the road, then approached the embassy's door and knocked. After a dozen heartbeats, he heard the grind of a key in the lock, the snap of a bolt being thrown back. The door opened to reveal a woman. Her rosy cheeks gave her a matronly look, though she could only have been a few years Ebon's senior. He looked past her, trying to take in what he could of the atrium beyond. Glistening white floor tiles, a double staircase, a crystal chandelier. And no people.

"Can I help you?" the woman said, her tone at once courteous and dismissive.

Ebon summoned up a smile. "My name's Tanner," he said, doing his best to hide his Galitian accent. He pretended to wait on her recognition. "I'm a physician. I understand you are expecting me."

The woman looked him up and down, no doubt wondering where he'd hidden his bag of medicines and instruments.

Ebon cleared his throat. This had seemed like a good idea when he'd dreamed it up earlier, but he was swiftly reconsidering. "I received a message from my associate," Ebon continued. "Something about a man hurt on Dragon Day."

The woman's look turned wary. "He's not here anymore. He left yesterday. I don't know where he was taken."

Taken? As in under guard? Or in a casket? "Is he dead?" Ebon asked, trying to sound offhand.

She shook her head no, but her look said more "I don't think so."

"But his condition had deteriorated since he arrived here?" Ebon pressed, conscious that every question took him further out of character.

A shrug. The woman looked over her shoulder as if seeking support from someone behind. The atrium, though, remained empty.

This was Ebon's chance to pounce, while her back was turned. Instinctively his hand started forward to seize her arm. If he dragged her out under threat of violence, no one would see what happened. But could he be certain she knew more than she was saying? Once he grabbed her, there would be no going back. And if he did abduct her, was he prepared to do what he had to to make her talk? Where could he take her to question her? What would he do with her afterward? Because if he released her then—and how could he not?—she would reveal to Ocarn that he was in the Upper City.

He pulled his hand back an instant before the woman turned to face him again. "My summons came from Prince Ocarn Dasuki himself," he said. "Is he here now?"

The woman shook her head.

"But he's due back soon?"

A nod this time. She appeared to have lost the power of speech.

"I'd rather not have to speak to him directly to clear this up. If you can tell me anything, anything at all, that would help me track down my patient, I would be much obliged."

The woman didn't even consider it. "I can't help you," she said. "Come back later, maybe there'll be someone here who can."

And with that, she closed the door in his face.

Ebon stared at the grain of the wood. He felt dizzy. A bell ago he'd thought he was in sight of his destination; now it seemed he was no closer than he had been this time yesterday. A flush rose to his cheeks, and that made him think of the woman who'd shut the door on him. Who he'd *let* shut the door. He wanted to knock again, but suddenly Vale was alongside him, taking him by the arm and leading him away down the street.

Ebon shook him off as they passed a fountain.

"What did she say?" the Endorian asked.

Ebon told him. Hearing it all again, it seemed so obvious the woman knew more than she had let on. Her reaction when he first mentioned Rendale had been telling, as if she'd been warned not to answer any questions. He swore.

They took a right turn. In the distance the masts of the ships in the port were visible over the harbor wall.

"So what the hell are we supposed to do now?" Ebon said. "We know Rendale was here, but not where he was moved, or why." He didn't give Vale a chance to respond. "I'm done with treading softly. If Rendale's condition has deteriorated, every bell could count. Then there's Mottle's warning about that coming 'storm.'"

"I see no clouds," Vale said.

He had a point. In the time since they'd arrived in Gilgamar, there had been no sniff of conflict brewing. Who was this enemy more dread than the Vamilians? Gilgamar wasn't at war. And while Ebon had heard whispers of alien forces sabotaging the Hunt, was there *anyone* who hadn't had the finger pointed at them for what happened on Dragon Day? If he looked hard enough, he'd probably find someone blaming him for the attack on the Dianese citadel.

They turned right again.

Ebon said, "The only way to be sure of getting answers is to speak to Ocarn himself."

"Then we snatch him first chance we get. The woman said he was due back soon, so we wait for him to come and leave again, then grab him when he goes."

"I'm not waiting that long."

"You want to send him a false message when he gets here? Try to lure him out?"

"I want to pick him up before he reaches the embassy. Can it be done?"

"We don't know which way he'll be coming—"

"Can it be done?"

Vale considered. "Maybe. If we do it right."

"Then let's do it right!" Ebon snapped. The Watcher knew, they'd be getting no second chance at this. If Ocarn learned they were in the Upper City, he would set men to hunting them, maybe move Rendale and Lamella beyond Ebon's reach.

Their path had brought them in a circle back to the embassy. Ebon could see it up ahead on the right. Farther along the street, walking away from them, was a man in a red cloak flanked by two Gilgamarian soldiers. At this distance, the stranger's skin resembled granite. He was gone before Ebon could get a better look.

He halted.

Vale stopped alongside. "You stay here," he said, "keep an eye on who comes and goes. I'll have a look around and see if I can find somewhere we can take Ocarn when we grab him. With luck, I'll be back before he shows his face."

"Make it somewhere quiet, Vale. I suspect he'll need a lot of persuading to tell us what he knows."

"He'll talk."

Ebon nodded. He didn't need his friend's reassurance in that regard. Ocarn would tell them what he knew, even if Ebon had to put his hand down the man's throat and drag the words out.

He watched the timeshifter move away along the street and duck into an alley.

Then he felt cold metal touch his neck.

"Easy now," said a voice in his ear. "Nice and easy."

Senar frowned as the door to Mazana's quarters swung inward and a female Gilgamarian servant stepped inside. A short time ago, the same woman had come to advise them that an Augeran emissary sought an audience. Senar had urged the emira not to receive him without the emperor here, but she'd laughed and said there was no need for Avallon to be present when he had Senar to report on what took place. The Guardian wouldn't limit his role to one of observer, though. He had no choice but to be the emperor's voice at this meeting and to try his best to disrupt proceedings.

The servant drew up just inside the room, puffing like she'd been chased here by the man she escorted—an impression reinforced by a certain wildness about her eyes that reminded Senar of the luckless horses he'd tried to ride in his time. The reason for her unease became apparent when her stone-skin charge capered into the room. It might have been quarter of a bell before dawn, but there was a skip to the man's step like he'd sprinkled sugarcrack on his oats this morning. His hair stuck up at all angles, and his face was a lattice of scars as if his flesh had been sliced up and sewn back together. One of the scars beneath his left eye wept blood. Senar wondered what all those scars denoted in their bearer. Besides lunacy, of course.

As the stone-skin reached the center of the room, he spun like a dancer, then bowed to Mazana.

"Emira," he said, "allow me to introduce myself. I am Hex of the Augeran Empire."

A heavy silence followed his words. Romany was inscrutable behind her mask. Mazana stared at the newcomer like he was some apparition stepped from a bad dream.

The Gilgamarian servant hastily withdrew.

"A privilege to make your acquaintance," the emira said at last. "I assume you are here to apologize for your kinsmen's conduct on Dragon Day."

"Apologize for what, pray tell?" Hex replied. "You seemed to have emerged from the affair rather well. Hee hee!"

Mazana clutched her hands to her chest. "And you did it all for me, yes? I'm curious, how would your leaders have responded if they were the ones attacked in my place?"

"I'm not here to justify what happened on Dragon Day—if indeed it needs justification. I bring a message from Subcommander Sunder, leader of the Augeran expeditionary force."

Senar sat up straighter. *Sub*commander Sunder? Meaning Amerel's attack on his superior had succeeded?

"You are referring to the force currently docked in the Rubyholt Isles?" Mazana said.

Hex did not reply. If he was surprised at the extent of her intelligence, he gave no indication.

"Tell me, how did your discussions with the warlord go?"

"Excellently, if you'll forgive the boast. Dresk Galair made for a most genial host."

Senar's eyes narrowed. *Boast, host?* Was the man rhyming his sentences?

Mazana said, "You must have made quite an impression on Galantas too, if he agreed to ferry you here from Bezzle. His ship, the *Eternal*, was recognized as it came into port—as I'm sure was your intent." She paused then went on, "No doubt there's a good reason why one of your own ships could not have made the journey."

"No doubt."

Senar's thoughts were a whirr. Because Caval and Karmel had already destroyed the stone-skin fleet, was that what Mazana was suggesting? No, even if the Chameleons had marked the Augeran ships, it was too soon for the dragons to have swum north from the Southern Wastes.

The stone-skin gave a smile that creased the scars on his face. "If your questions are finished, perhaps I can deliver my message. Subcommander Sunder extends his regards and requests that you deliver to him at once the head of the Erin Elalese emperor, Avallon Delamar."

The emira blinked.

From beside her, Romany gave a snort that degenerated into a fit of coughing.

If there had been any wisps of sleep still clouding Senar's head, they were blown away now.

"The head of the emperor," Mazana repeated sardonically. "Of course. Was there anything else while you're here?"

Hex performed a clumsy turn that set his red cloak swirling. "Would you have me believe it is not in your power? Your forces in Gilgamar outnumber Avallon's, that much I know. The servant who brought me here swore it was so. Hee hee!"

Know, so. The man was indeed rhyming his words. To Senar, this whole meeting was beginning to get an unreal feel about it. Did the budding poet intend to give them a recital when they were done?

Mazana fiddled with that knife of hers again. "My *forces* are guests of the Ruling Council," she said. "Perhaps you should speak to them."

Hex looked disappointed. "Oh, come now. My grasp of your politics is rudimentary, for sure, but the Council's support you can doubtless procure. Does it not pay you tribute? Is it not relying on you to clear the dragons from the sea?"

The emira did not respond.

From the corridor outside came footsteps, then raised voices. Avallon, perhaps, come to object to the meeting? Whoever it was, they wouldn't get past the executioner stationed outside.

Hex's foot started tapping along to whatever music was playing in his head. "I sense your mind is not yet resolved," he said to Mazana. "So think on this. The emperor comes before you offering his hand, but it is not the hand of friendship, as he claims. Rather consider it the hand of a shipmate in a storm, offered in desperation as he slips overboard. Clasp it, and you risk being swept to your doom, even as he."

Mazana considered this before looking at Senar. "He has a point."

The Guardian scowled. "And you think you would fare better with the stone-skins as allies? What does it say for their credibility that they should send such as this"—he gestured to Hex—"to speak with you?"

The Augeran's nose was in the air, scenting like a bloodhound. He held up a hand. "Wait, what's this I smell? Cynicism. Desperation. With just the merest hint of *Guardian* as well."

Senar studied him. "You've encountered one of my kind before, have you?" Amerel, most likely.

"Encountered, yes. And taken her measure in the doing."

Meaning Amerel was dead? Senar wasn't sure how he felt about that. He'd grown up with the woman at the Sacrosanct. An earnest type she had been, more at home among her books than on the road. For a while she and Jessca had been fast friends. But Amerel had drifted apart from Jessca in the same way that she had drifted apart from everyone else—and by her choice too, it had seemed. Cracks had appeared after her very first mission with her master, Colat. But not everyone was made to be a Guardian. The privilege brought with it a heavy . . . responsibility. Some bent under that load, and some broke.

Outside, the Erin Elalese voices took on a demanding tone. Demanding of the executioner? Good luck with that.

Hex swung his gaze to Mazana. "No doubt the Guardian has told you what happened when our two peoples last met. No doubt he has told you that, this time, the result is not set. Unlike him, though, you don't have to let your judgment be colored by mindless optimism."

"Then what should I base that judgment on? Your words here?" Her voice had a smile in it. "Or perhaps on the information I gained from your kinsmen. You know, the ones I recently caught stirring up mischief in Olaire. Caught, and interrogated."

Mazana was bluffing, Senar knew. The only stone-skin she'd taken alive had died before he could give up anything useful. Hex wouldn't know that, though, and it was heartening to see the first hint of sourness creep into his features.

"Careful, Emira, who you choose to provoke," he said. "Perhaps you think the Storm Isles safe behind the Dragon Gate. But the lessons of Dragon Day you would be fool to disdain. We reached you there once, we can reach you again. Hee hee!"

Mazana said, "So that would be the stick. Time for the carrot, I think. If I agree to deliver the emperor's head, what do you offer in exchange?"

Senar opened his mouth to protest, but she waved a hand to forestall him.

"Besides our eternal gratitude?" Hex shrugged. "Nothing."

"Nothing," Mazana repeated.

Senar threw up his hands. "This is a joke! The fool can't even be bothered to pretend his offer is genuine. But then his purpose was accomplished the moment he set foot in this room. Did he try to arrange this audience in secret? Of course not. Because the only reason he is here is so he can sow distrust between you and the emperor. The longer this meeting goes on, the more damage he stands to inflict."

In the corridor, the voices faded away. And with them any chance of an alliance between the Storm Isles and Erin Elal, perhaps?

Hex hopped from foot to foot. "I offer nothing, Emira, because 'nothing' is the limit of my authority. Subcommander Sunder leads the expeditionary force, not the Augeran empire. I am certain, though, that when the Triad hears of your cooperation, you will be paid in keeping with your service." He spread his hands. "Like the emperor, I could have offered something beyond my power to provide. The fact that I was open with you, that should make your doubts subside."

The emira rubbed at her wrists. "You can't offer me an alliance against Avallon. You can't even guarantee you won't attack the Storm Isles again." She pretended to consider. "Perhaps if I knew *why* you were planning to attack Erin Elal, I would be better able to judge your intent." It was said lightly, but clearly the matters she'd discussed with the emperor yesterday still preyed on her mind.

Hex did not respond.

"If revenge is your motive," she went on, "I might wonder at its cause. If conquest is your goal, I might wonder whether your ambitions stop at Erin Elal's borders."

The stone-skin sighed. "Alas, I am but a humble messenger in this. I am not privy to my superiors' innermost counsels."

Mazana turned to Senar. "Where have we heard that before?"

Romany closed the book. Fifty pages in now, and every one of them had been an exercise in tooth-clenching tedium. And what had she learned from the accounts of Augera's conflicts with its neighbors? Nothing, save that those neighbors had possessed a modicum of sophistication, thus giving context to the ease with which the stone-skins had overrun them.

If there was any entertainment to be found in the book, it was in the author's description of Erin Elal's hapless attempts to forge alliances with the kingdoms separating it from Augera. It seemed Erin Elal had not been afraid previously to engage in its own spot of empire-building, and having played the wolf for so long, its new sheep's clothing had drawn suspicion from its would-be allies. That suspicion had hastened Augera's victory, and no doubt Avallon would argue history was in danger of repeating itself now. Indeed the more Romany read of the book, the more she wondered whether that had been his whole point in giving it to her. If that was so, it was a grievous insult to the priestess's intelligence. Imagine thinking she wouldn't see through such a feeble attempt at manipulation!

Time to do some more exploring along her web, she decided. Conversations didn't overhear themselves, after all.

Closing her eyes, she allowed her mind to drift free of her body.

Hex's quarters first. As Romany glided toward her destination, she was surprised to find that her web in this part of the Alcazar was corroding. It was almost as if she were back in the Forest of Sighs, and the magic of the Book of Lost Souls was devouring her power. Such was the delicacy of her web, it was prone to unravel at the slightest touch of inimical sorcery. But she could sense nothing now to account for the degeneration.

A mystery for later.

She entered Hex's room. The Augeran lay on his bed, apparently asleep. As Romany approached him, she felt an uncomfortable sensation like the man might open his eyes and look up at her. Impossible, of course. In spirit-form, she would be invisible to the Augeran unless she wanted him to see her. She studied his face. One scarred cheek was smeared crimson. Had it not been for his scars, she might have wondered if the man's skin were truly made from the granite that it looked like. It occurred to her that granite came in more colors than just gray. Black, green, pink . . .

A pink stone-skin? That would be something to see.

It was difficult to imagine this man as a member of a powerful civilization. Or a member of anything, for that matter, except maybe a circus troupe. And it was strange to find him sleeping when he'd been bouncing off the walls in his meeting with Mazana. But then there was little about the man's coming to Gilgamar that didn't puzzle Romany. She was forced to agree with Senar Sol—something she avoided doing as much as possible—that the Augeran's sole purpose was to stir up bad blood between Mazana and Avallon. As if they needed help on that score. Earlier, when the emperor had learned about the meeting, he'd thrown a bottle of wine across his room. Such a waste.

If he was so enraged, though, why hadn't he sought out Mazana to confront her? Why weren't his minions breaking down Hex's door now to question him?

Another mystery. And Romany hated mysteries, unless they were her own.

Jambar's quarters next. The priestess's web was more degraded here than it had been even in Hex's room, but again she could find no reason for the deterioration. The shaman was apparently in the middle of a reading, for on a table at the center of his chamber was his bone-strewn augury board, covered in incomprehensible characters. Jambar circled the board, muttering all the while. He peered at the blood-speckled bones from every angle, trying to unlock the meaning behind their arrangement.

Romany regarded him thoughtfully. Before the meeting with Hex, she'd caught the end of a discussion between Mazana and the shaman, and it had revealed much as to the man's state of mind. The discussion had been about Erin Elal. An edge had entered the Remnerol's look at every mention of Avallon's name, and that edge had left Romany in no doubt as to his feelings toward the emperor. Perhaps, she mused, those feelings explained the patchy nature of the shaman's predictions. Perhaps he'd been pleased to learn of the Augerans' coming, if it meant the Erin Elalese might suffer the same fate as his people had at Avallon's hands. If so, wouldn't he be disinclined to share his forecasts with Mazana, thinking she might pass them on to the emperor?

Whatever riddle Jambar sought the solution to, clearly he didn't like the answer the bones gave him, because he scooped them up and whispered something over them before dropping them onto the board again. More peering, more muttering. Romany wondered if her presence interfered with his reading. She was tempted to make life still more difficult for him by spinning her threads about a bone and tugging it out of position. Something made her hold back, though. She watched Jambar scratch at an armpit, shake his head, stare out of the window for inspiration.

Finally he picked up his bones again. Another cast? Third time lucky, perhaps?

Instead of releasing the bones, he put them into a bag and made for the door. On his way to call on someone, evidently, but who?

More and more interesting.

Romany drifted after him.

His destination turned out to be just three doors distant. Mazana Creed's quarters. The emira was there, reading a book to Uriel, and the sight of the boy reminded Romany to find out who had won the duel between Twist and Strike. Later, though. Something was happening here. Mazana must have sensed it too, because she sent Uriel to his room without Jambar having to ask.

As the shaman started talking, Romany's brows knitted.

Interesting indeed.

Senar's tread was heavy as he climbed the ramp to the Key Tower at the western end of the seawall. He'd left the Alcazar half a bell ago claiming he needed a breath of air, but the reality was he wanted to escape the pressure building upon him from all quarters. The pressure of expectation. The pressure to choose sides. On the *Raven*, Kolloken had said a man couldn't ride two horses at the same time, yet wasn't that what the Guardian was doing? Maybe soon the different courses those mounts took would force him to surrender his hold on one or risk being torn apart. Until then, though, didn't he have to try to keep his seat? *Someone* had to span the divide between the two sides.

Foolishly, he'd come to Gilgamar thinking Mazana would recognize the scale of the Augeran threat and throw in her lot with the emperor. As he was coming to realize, though, he couldn't read her any better now than when they first met. She was shrewd enough to know the worth of the stone-skins' professed friendship, and to know what the fallout would be from her meeting with Hex. So why had she agreed to speak to the man? When Senar had told Avallon of their discussions, the emperor's reaction had been predictably explosive.

What did Mazana hope to gain by goading him? Did she think she could extract concessions as to a future alliance? But concessions on what, exactly?

No, the sad fact was that she thought her best interests lay in abandoning Erin Elal to its fate. And that she did not trust the emperor any more than she did Hex. Senar couldn't blame her. How had Kolloken put it on the *Raven*? *If he has to raze every city in the League to save Erin Elal, he won't hesitate.* Avallon would stop at nothing to bring his neighbors into the conflict, and the maneuverings to that end had already begun. This morning the emperor had met with Gilgamar's Ruling Council, as well as the Sabian survivors of Dragon Day, trying to drum up support. At best Mazana would consider this an intrusion on her patch, at worst a move to undermine her authority.

Then there was the rumor that Cauroy still lived—a rumor Mazana thought Avallon had started.

Senar scowled. There had to be a way to bring the various factions together. To find common ground before the squabbling delivered not just Erin Elal but the whole continent into Augera's hands.

The entrance to the Key Tower was guarded by four Gilgamarian soldiers, sheltering in the shade of its arched gateway. More soldiers slouched in the guardhouse itself, their red jackets unbuttoned against the heat. One man lay snoring against a wall. At a table three soldiers sat playing dice. None of them looked up as Senar walked by. He scratched at the dragon scales on his neck. Overnight the plates had advanced a fingerspan toward his face, but he wouldn't think about them. That way, there was a chance they would just go away, right?

Turning left, he passed through another gateway and stepped back into the hammer of the sun. The battlements of the wall stretched before him, curving to the east. The wind was off the sea to his right, seasoned with salt and hot as the sun's own breath. When he looked down over the parapet, he saw far below a slope covered with blocks of stone. Their purpose was to blunt the break of the sea and to prevent ships—even those riding waves of water-magic—from approaching too close to the wall. The rocks were draped with fireweed, and among them were scraps of wood from vessels that must once have been smashed to ruin on them. Foam hissed and bubbled between the stones.

Senar started along the wall. Ahead was another tower of similar size to the Key Tower—the Buck Tower, it was called—and beyond that he could make out the battlements of the Chain Tower where the mechanism that raised the chains across the Neck was housed. Atop it Senar saw the arm of a catapult pointing out to sea. He halted. To his left the greasy waters of the harbor shifted lazily. Flying at the masts of the ships at quayside, he recognized the flags of Thax and White Wing, Mercerie and Andros. Survivors of the Dragon Hunt, no doubt, now marooned here until their captains found the courage to make a break for home.

A flash of light caught his eye. Docked at the western end of the harbor was the ship he knew belonged to Galantas Galair. Plated in steel, its hull looked like the armored flank of a dragon. Its decks were deserted, as was the quay at which it was berthed, but Senar knew a handful of watchers—both Revenants and Erin Elalese—would be observing the vessel. The harbormaster had reported that its crew was made up of Rubyholters. After docking, those sailors had disappeared belowdecks, and they must still be there now, along with Shroud knew how many stone-skins.

"Striking ship, ain't it?" a voice behind him said in Erin Elalese.

Senar turned to see Kolloken standing a few paces away. "Too striking, perhaps," the Guardian replied.

The Breaker nodded. "Stone-skins were keen their arrival didn't go unnoticed. Clearly they were set on stirring up the manure, and I'd say the emira has played right into their hands, wouldn't you?"

Senar frowned and looked away.

A group of Gilgamarian soldiers walked past him on the battlements. One of them must have been a new recruit, for the red of his jacket stood out starkly against his companions' faded pink. Farther along, two more soldiers threw stones at the limewings diving for fish in the Ribbon Sea.

"Come to inspect the defenses?" Kolloken said.

Senar left enough of a pause to let the man know his presence was unwelcome. "I had some time to kill."

"And this was the farthest you could get from the Alcazar, eh?" The Breaker chuckled, then pointed at the Chain Tower. "You seen inside the fortress—the machinery that raises the chains?"

"No."

"Impressive sight. Each of them chains is as thick as a tree trunk.

They're invested with earth-magic, too. Strong enough to take a battering from a dragon." He stroked his crooked nose. "And it ain't just the dragons they keep out, neither. The highest chain is far enough above the water that even the most powerful water-mage can't lift a ship over it. And even if a ship *did* get past, it'd still have to run the gauntlet of the Neck, with defenders raining down missiles from both sides."

The man had clearly done his homework. "What about an attack from inside the city?" Senar asked.

"You mean could a force take the wall and lower the chains?" Kolloken sucked at his gums. "Don't see how. You've seen how solid the Key Tower is. And if an invader took that, they'd still have to get past the Buck Tower before they even reached the Chain Tower. That's where their problems would really start. The place is locked up tighter than a virgin's corset. Portcullis, barbican, the works. Ain't no way an attacker is getting through to the chains."

"Chains have two ends. And the tower on the other side of the Neck isn't half as impressive."

"Doesn't need to be. All it guards is the stones that them chains are fixed into. And they're invested with earth-magic too, in case you're wondering. No point the chains themselves being unbreakable if the dragons can just rip them from the walls." Kolloken leaned against the merlon. "In fact the only weak point in the defenses is the one that matters most: the men. You know when this wall was last attacked?"

"I have a feeling you're going to tell me."

"Three hundred years ago. Some Corinian Storm Lord turned traitor and was tossed to the dragons on Dragon Day, but he survived and returned with a fleet of devilships." Kolloken spat over the wall. "Three hundred years. How many of the soldiers round here were alive back then, do you reckon? The closest most of them have seen to fighting is putting down a brawl in the ghettos—or starting one, who knows. How long do you think they'd stand if the stone-skins come knocking?"

Senar made a sour face. If the texts from before the Exile were right, no one would be standing before the Augeran military machine.

Kolloken must have guessed his thoughts, for he curled his lip and said, "What, you reckon just because the Guardians got their ass handed to them eight hundred years ago, the Breakers won't put up a fight now?"

"It's not the putting-up-a-fight bit that concerns me. It's the winning. Before the Exile, there were hundreds of Guardians, and we still lost. How many Breakers are there now?"

"Enough."

Enough? There was no way of knowing how many stone-skins were coming, or what they were capable of. Yet apparently Kolloken had already plotted their downfall. "How long have you been learning the Will?" Senar asked. "One year? Two?"

"We'll have more time before the stone-skins arrive. If they've only just started talking to the Rubyholters, they ain't likely to launch a campaign this side of winter. That gives us another six months, maybe nine."

A whole nine months? The Breakers could carve their headstones in that time. "After four years' studying, I was still an initiate. And I was one of the stronger ones. How many of your friends have shown a gift for the Will? How many can wield it at the same time as a blade? And how many of *those* can do more with it than part an enemy's hair?"

Kolloken's eyes were cold. "Perhaps if you'd shared your knowledge sooner, we wouldn't be in this mess, eh? You know, even after the news of the stone-skins broke, none of your Guardian pals would teach what they knew. They'd much rather take the knowledge to their graves, even if it means those graves become *our* graves too."

Because if the Breakers had known the secret behind the Will, they'd have given it up long ago, of course. Because power like that was so much safer in the hands of any deadbeat who could shape a thought. Senar kept his silence, though. He knew better than to bang his head against that wall.

"But you're different, ain't you?" Kolloken went on. "You'll teach me. Hells, we can start now, if you like."

Time to change the subject. "What about the risk of the stone-skins landing along the coast and marching on the city?" Senar said. "The seawall counts for nothing if an enemy can just go around it."

The Breaker was a long time in answering. "East of here there's nothing but rocks as far as Dian. There are bays to the west, but any force approaching that way would have to advance along a corridor of land barely wide enough . . ."

His voice trailed off.

Senar glanced across. Kolloken was looking toward the harbor.

It didn't take the Guardian long to spot what had caught the man's eye. On the quay leading to Galantas's metal-plated ship was a gray-cloaked figure—a Revenant—gesticulating to a companion. As the babble of their voices reached Senar, the second mercenary turned and fled toward the docks. The first figure drew his sword and retreated after his friend.

Senar's belly was sour.

Trouble. It had only been a matter of time, hadn't it?

He trotted back along the wall toward the Key Tower, Kolloken beside him.

CHAPTER 19

MEREL SHIELDED her eyes as she stared north. On the horizon, the topsails of the stone-skin fleet looked like puffs of cloud infused with the dawn. Perhaps Amerel should have been heartened to see those ships after a night spent following nothing more than the glimmer of their lights. But if she could see the Augerans, they would be able to see her too, and since Galantas had ordered his own lanterns doused for the journey, this would be the first the enemy knew about the pursuit.

Soon they would have to give an answer.

The stone-skin commander had pushed his water-mages hard through the night, for not once had the fleet's speed slackened. In order for the vessels to stay together, that speed must have been limited to what the slowest ship could muster. Yet it had been a challenging pace all the same, for while Barnick had had no trouble matching it, the same could not be said of the other Rubyholt mages. With the coming of dawn, Amerel had discovered that, of the other six vessels that had set forth with the *Fury,* only two remained. One was half a league behind, the other a smudge on the southern skyline. She'd heard the *Fury*'s crew muttering that the missing ships had slipped away in the night. Galantas, though, would not believe it. They had merely fallen behind, he insisted, and might yet catch up. For while they could no longer follow the stone-skins by sight, their course was set and could be easily followed to its destination.

Gilgamar. If there had been any doubt before, it was gone now. The city lay just four bells to the north. Last night Amerel had quizzed Noon on the relevance of the place to Erin Elalese interests, but he'd claimed ignorance. She was even minded to believe him. Not difficult to believe ignorance of a Breaker, after all.

The devilship began keening, feeding on the crew's growing anxiety now that the Augeran fleet had been sighted. On the main deck, a handful of men were hunched over the rail, gazing north with furrowed brows. One looked like he was ready to vomit. But fear, Amerel had heard, was a healthy thing when the enemy drew close. It taught you caution. It got the blood pumping round you so you were ready for the off.

Or at least that was the theory.

It hadn't worked that way on the road to Kerin, all those years ago. It had been Amerel's first mission as a Guardian, and she'd been hunting bandits with her then master, Colat. But it had been the bandits who had surprised *them* just as the Guardians were setting up camp. For years Amerel had trained for that moment. Nothing could have prepared her, though, for a dozen screaming savages set on shedding her blood. When the arrows started falling about, she had frozen. She would have died, too, if that missile had found her flesh instead of tangling in her hair.

Looking back now, it was hard to remember how she had felt. Hard to remember anything of the fight that followed, except for the face of the first man she'd killed—the first man she'd ever killed. Or maybe "boy" was a more accurate description. He'd been younger even than she was, with a face wasted from hunger, and all screwed up with the same fear she had felt. She'd tried to disarm him rather than kill him, but somehow she'd run him through anyway. Afterward, by the fire, her hands had shaken so badly she'd spilled the cup of tea Colat passed her. There had been a hint of disapproval in her master's eyes. But then it had all been so simple for him. The bandits attacked, he killed them, end of story. He'd told her the killing would get easier in time, as if "getting easier" were a thing to be prized. And he was right, of course; it *had* gotten easier. Everything did with practice.

He would be proud of her now, Amerel reckoned.

"Two ships coming about!" called a lookout in the rigging.

Tattoo had been standing with the quartermaster by the ship's wheel, but now he shimmied like a chitter monkey up the mainmast to the maintop. He trained a telescope on the northern horizon.

Galantas emerged from the captain's cabin holding a glass of brandy. Seemed a bit early for that. Maybe like Amerel, though, he hadn't been able to sleep last night.

"Two ships, right enough," Tattoo shouted down. "Both shortening sails. And that ain't the only problem we got. We're close to the Rent."

"How close?" Galantas asked.

"Stone-skin ships are hanging over it."

Amerel could see the Rent, now she was looking for it—a darker tinge to the water like the shadow of some monstrous creature lurking in the deep. Not a good place for an engagement, but if she had her way, that would be the stone-skins' problem, not hers. She strode up to Galantas. "Hold your course," she said in a low voice.

He rounded on her. "Back in the Isles, you said there'd be no fighting. You said we'd turn when the stone-skins did."

"When their *fleet* turned, yes, not two ships. How does two ships turning help us if the rest sail on? We need to prove ourselves worthy of the stone-skins' full attention."

"By defeating those two ships?"

Amerel nodded.

"And how are we going to do that? If we were seven ships instead of three—"

"Leave the stone-skins to me."

He snorted. "As easy as that?"

"Yes."

Galantas studied her. "How?"

"You'll see."

"How?"

"Sorcery."

"You're a water-mage?"

Amerel nodded. Anything to shut him up. She couldn't tell him about the glass globes, obviously, in case he'd heard of Erin Elal using them before. "I can destroy both ships, but I need them closer. Turn the *Fury* about if you must, but hold your ground. If I fail, there'll still be time to run."

"Assuming Barnick can outdistance them."

"If he can't, we're dead anyway."

"Captain!" Tattoo shouted. "Enemy are hull down and closing!"

Galantas looked toward the approaching ships, then back at the

two distant Rubyholt vessels and the empty horizon where the other
four should be. He was loath to flee, Amerel knew. He didn't need telling how his opponents would greet the news that he'd run at the first
whiff of trouble. Still, it couldn't hurt to remind him.

"If you turn tail," she said, "what will you have achieved save to
prove your doubters right? Where are the dragons you said would
destroy the stone-skins? Where's the vengeance you promised?"

Galantas scowled and tossed his glass over the rail. His color was
high, and he was breathing hard against the effect of the demon
figurehead's voice. Maybe soon the devilship's bloodlust would over-
ride his instinct to bolt, but not yet. He glanced south again, as if the
missing Rubyholt vessels might have appeared in the last few heartbeats. Then he looked back at Amerel. She could guess what he was
thinking. He'd be wondering how a water-mage—as she claimed to
be—could destroy two enemy ships that were each protected by their
own water-mage. But he *wanted* to believe her. She used her Will to
play on his indecision.

"I'd ask you to trust me," she said, "but I'm not sure I could do it
with a straight face. Just trust that I have no more wish to die here
than you do."

Tattoo descended to the deck. "Captain?" he said.

Galantas ignored him. He closed his eyes. Amerel watched him.
Any more waiting around, and the stone-skins would make his decision for him, but that worked for her. Galantas rubbed a hand
across his face.

When his eyes opened again, there was a new resolve in them.

He nodded to Amerel.

She turned and strode away before he could change his mind.

Noon appeared in the companionway, his eyes heavy with sleep.
The sight of the stone-skin ships roused him, though. Amerel motioned for him to join her as she made her way toward the bow.

"Don't you ever sleep?" he said as he fell into step.

"Just heading below now." She gestured to the Augerans. "You can
deal with this lot, can't you?"

Noon shot her a look. "You could tan leather with that sense of
humor of yours."

The wave of water-magic carrying the *Fury* subsided. Galantas
shouted orders to the crew: to ready weapons, to mop the boards
stained by blayfire oil—again, to run out flags to signal for help from

the other Rubyholt ships. At first his commands were met with sullen silence, but Tattoo backhanded one man, and the others moved grumbling to their tasks. What else could they do? Mutiny? The only way they'd escape the stone-skins was with Barnick's help, and for now the water-mage remained in Galantas's corner.

By the time Amerel reached the starboard cathead, she could make out the two stone-skin ships approaching, side by side on their waves of water-magic. The first was of a size to the *Fury*. The second was bigger still—a fortress with four masts so tall they seemed to scrape the sky. The decks of both ships were heaving with soldiers, and yet more men—archers?—were climbing the rigging to the tops. It didn't look like they intended a polite inquiry as to why the *Fury*'s course coincided with theirs. The larger ship had a catapult on its forecastle, but as yet the stone-skins hadn't loaded it. Perhaps they wanted to take the devilship intact. The *Fury* must certainly have looked an easy prize, undermanned and lolling on the swell.

"What are you thinking?" Noon asked Amerel.

"I'm thinking those ships are a little closer together than is good for them."

The Breaker smiled. "Water?" he said, reaching into his belt-pouch for one of the globes of sorcery.

"Water," she agreed. She'd told Galantas she was a water-mage, after all.

"How do you want to play it? The globe won't smash if we throw it in the sea, but if we wait till the stone-skins get close—"

"We're not waiting," Amerel cut in, holding out a hand.

Noon placed the globe in it.

The rustle of water grew louder as the ships drew near. The ominous beat of drums started up within their bellies, and the *Fury*'s keening went up in pitch as if the devilship was giving answer to the enemy's challenge. Amerel looked across at the figurehead. It resembled the demon hacked into the Rubyholt cliff, but its fierceness was diminished by the apple someone had stuffed in its mouth like it was a pig dressed for the spit. If that person had hoped the apple would blunt its voice, though, they would be disappointed. Any louder, and the thing might shatter the glass globe in Amerel's palm.

And she didn't want that.

She studied the globe. Inside, a blue mist swirled. She'd heard it said that these sorcerous missiles hit as hard as a falling mountain, and she could well believe it, judging by the deep reservoir of power within. So much power, in fact, it was a wonder anyone had managed to cage it in a fragile glass shell. How best to use it, though? If she tossed it down the companionway of a stone-skin ship, the magic unleashed would rip the vessel apart. But why settle for just one ship when there was a chance she could take out both?

Wrapping her Will around the globe, she carried it speeding over the waves toward the onrushing ships. She lost sight of it against the blue, but her Will-sense was as good as her eyes for tracking its passage. The stone-skin vessels had halved the distance to the *Fury*. On their waves of water-magic, they reared high above the devilship. Amerel could now make out the images on their colored sails. The mainsail of the smaller ship showed a denkrakil rising from the waves, while the sails of the larger craft were like the panels of a tapestry depicting the events of some notable's life. It seemed an outrageous extravagance on a working ship. And the Guardian wasn't even the one who'd have to repair the sails if they got torn.

From behind her came the clatter of weapons, Tattoo's bellowed orders, the pounding of feet. Amerel turned to see the *Fury*'s crew lining up along the rails in readiness for battle. Pincushion—the man she'd met in Bezzle—shook his sword at the stone-skins like he thought that might scare them into retreating. Another Islander appeared intent on matching the devilship's shriek. The crew's blood was clearly up, but passion alone wouldn't make up for their lack of numbers. If Amerel's plan failed, they would need the help of their kinsmen on the other two Rubyholt ships to stand even a chance of escaping.

She swung her gaze south. Earlier, the closest Rubyholt vessel had been much nearer to the *Fury* than the two stone-skin craft, yet now with the threat of battle imminent, its progress had slowed. She hadn't thought it was possible to retreat while at the same time moving forward, but the ship's captain was giving it his best shot.

The volume of the devilship's cry rose yet further.

"Anyone got an ax?" Noon said.

The glass globe drew level with the stone-skin ships—a thousand armspans away now, at the edge of the Rent. And just in time, too, for the vessels had started to draw apart, their captains no doubt intending to attack the devilship from both sides. Amerel positioned the globe midway between the ships and an armspan above the waves.

She gripped the rail. "Brace yourself," she said to Noon.

A flick of her Will shattered the globe.

There was a ripping sound, then a roar like an avalanche. The sea between the stone-skin ships erupted, lifting the vessels, tipping and tossing them, pounding their hulls. The larger craft was slapped on its side; the smaller one was hurled clear of the swell and half spun about to come down with a splintering crack of shattered masts. Onboard, the stone-skins were flung about like dolls to fall screaming amid the crashing waves. The blast threw up geysers of spray, and the water seemed to hang in the sky before it came sheeting down on the stricken ships, smothering them in a torrent of gray.

Spray fell on the *Fury*'s boards too, filling Amerel's eyes and open mouth, and tasting of salt and sorcery. She'd thought she had detonated the globe at a safe distance, but perhaps she was mistaken, for through the deluge she saw a wave bearing down on her, as tall as the *Fury*'s bowsprit. Galantas shouted to Barnick, and the breaker began to recede, yet still when it reached the devilship it lifted the vessel so sharply it made Amerel's stomach churn. Another wave arrived just as the ship came down, and it hit the bow like a hammer striking an anvil. The deck pitched. Cries sounded from the crew. A third wave rolled toward them, then another, but all the while Barnick was working to soothe the seas, and the waves started to settle.

Amerel's hands were like claws on the rail. She was so wet she might have been dunked in a barrel. Water spattered down onto the *Fury*'s deck from the sodden sails and rigging. The boards were covered in puddles that stretched first one way then the other as the ship rocked. Beside Amerel, Noon coughed like someone had just given him the kiss of life. The crew were silent, but the demon figurehead continued to keen.

A mist of spray hung over the waves. To the north, where the globe had smashed, the sea heaved and bucked like an unbroken colt. The water was covered by mexin grains and splinters of wood, but the stone-skin ships themselves were gone. The sail with the denkrakil on it was spread across the waves like a shroud. Amid the debris bobbed dozens of motionless bodies. Only a handful of stone-skins had survived the sorcerous blast. Of these, most clung to pieces of wreckage, but some swam north in the direction of their distant fleet, evidently ignorant of the perils of the Rent beneath them. Because as Amerel knew, not even the strongest swimmer could resist the tug of the darkness.

The dead went first, dragged down into the depths. The living went moments after, kicking and shrieking and still clinging to the scraps of wood they held. Only two of the swimmers stayed afloat—the water-mages from the sunken ships, presumably—though even they appeared to be struggling. The dash north must have taxed them beyond the limits of their powers. After a while, they gave despairing cries and vanished from sight.

A rush of bubbles, then nothing.

The blood-dream built like a migraine behind Amerel's eyes.

Galantas wiped water from his face. The force of the sorcerous detonation had left his ears ringing, but he kept his expression even. He could feel his crewmen's gazes on him, and he needed them to believe that he had planned all along to destroy the stone-skin ships. That he was still in control of events. The reality, he knew, was quite the reverse. He'd hoped that when Mokinda left for the Dragon Gate, the Sabian threat would go with him. Now it seemed this Cayda woman was no less a menace. And to think she was supposed to be his prisoner. He'd have to do some rethinking in that regard.

He caught Barnick's gaze, and the mage read the unspoken question in his eyes.

"I've sensed nothing from her before now," he said. "Even when she unleashed that—"

"Could she be another Storm Lord?" Galantas interrupted. "Mazana Creed, perhaps?"

"Mazana Creed is younger. And she's got red hair."

"Then who?"

The mage had no answers.

Scowling, Galantas shot a look at Cayda. Her face was momentarily in profile. Yet again, he got the sense that he'd seen her before, but where?

A call came from the lookout on the main crosstrees. "Enemy are swapping signals, Captain!"

In his youth, Galantas might have scrambled up to join him, but swinging through the rigging had become a good deal harder since he'd lost his arm. He trained his telescope on the blur of colored sails on the horizon. If the stone-skins were halting, it meant he had their full attention. So what next? Somehow he doubted they would continue to throw ships at him two at a time. Would the whole fleet now turn and give chase?

He didn't have long to wait for an answer.

"Stone-skins are moving off!" the lookout shouted. "They're running, Captain!"

Galantas had seen as much already through his glass. *Running?* Weren't they going to check the wreckage for survivors? Would they leave him unharrassed to follow on behind? He understood why they might not be keen to engage the *Fury* a second time, but some nettles just had to be grasped. And up until now, the stone-skins had never shied away from doing what needed to be done.

He frowned. Unless they were in too much of a hurry to waste time playing tag. Why, though? Why should it matter when they arrived in Gilgamar? Had they found out about the dragon blood marking their hulls? Were they racing to reach their destination before the creatures caught up to them? When they got to Gilgamar, they would still have to get past its chains, of course, but if they managed that . . .

Galantas's frown deepened.

That would leave the *Fury* alone outside the city when the dragons came.

Darkness.

Someone had placed a bag over Ebon's head after they'd dragged him into a back room of the embassy. He could feel the cloth against his eyelids when he blinked, feel it press against his lips when he breathed. There weren't even shades of gray to soften the black. But he could still hear. He'd heard his captors close the shutters to stop anyone outside looking in. He'd heard muffled voices in other parts of the embassy, doors opening and slamming. The sounds of the morning should have been getting louder around him, but instead they had died away as if the building was being emptied. Now all was quiet save for the occasional creak from the darkness. And beyond that, at the edge of hearing, Ebon imagined he could make out a restless whisper as if the Vamilian spirits had returned to his mind.

He flexed his fingers. They'd tied him to a chair, wrists bound so tightly his hands tingled from the restricted blood flow. How long had he been like this? He'd heard at least one bell ring, maybe two. Odds were, he was waiting for Ocarn to arrive, for it was surely Ocarn's men who had grabbed him. He swallowed against a thickness in his throat. He'd been so busy thinking on his own plan that he'd never considered the Mercerien might have one too. Someone must have seen Ebon scouting the embassy earlier. Or the woman who he'd talked to had joined up the dots. After, when he'd gone walking with Vale, the Merceriens had arranged an ambush for his return. Had they grabbed the Endorian as well? He wasn't in the room with Ebon, but maybe Ocarn was just keeping them apart so he could question them separately.

If Vale *had* escaped capture, though, perhaps he was outside now, planning his move. Perhaps if he saw the closed shutters he would guess which room Ebon was in.

Perhaps, perhaps.

He felt a flush of helpless rage and started struggling against his bindings. The ropes burned his wrists. He'd failed. Even if he walked out of here alive, Ocarn would already have taken Lamella and Rendale away. But that was the least of Ebon's worries just now. Ocarn had scores he wanted to settle, and what reason did he have to show restraint? No one knew Ebon was in Gilgamar except Vale and Gunnar, and not even they would be able to prove Ocarn was behind his disappearance.

Muffled footsteps came from Ebon's right, swelling louder as a door opened. How many sets? It was difficult to judge. Three people at least, maybe four. Ebon's breath came quickly, hot and moist inside the bag.

Moments later, the bag was snatched away to leave him blinking against the light of a torch. Ocarn was holding that torch. He passed it to someone behind Ebon. All of the others who'd come in with him were behind Ebon, out of sight.

The door shut.

Ocarn grinned at Ebon like they were old friends reunited. His face had thinned since their encounter seven years ago, and he'd dispensed with his apology of a mustache. The blond curls that had once hung down to his shoulders were cut short. He took out a pair of heavy gloves and pulled them onto his hands.

Ebon looked around the room. To his left, the large shuttered windows were bordered by threads of light. A rug that must once have covered the floor had been rolled up against a lacquered desk to leave Ebon's chair standing on stone. He wanted to see how many men were behind him, but when he tried to turn, someone grabbed his head to keep his eyes forward. A pity, that. There was no way Ocarn could know about the powers Ebon had inherited from Galea, but the surprise would last only as long as his first burst of sorcery. If he'd known where Ocarn's men were standing, he could have tried to disable them before turning on their master.

"Prince Ebon Calidar," Ocarn said, "what a pleasure to see you again."

He stepped in close.

Ebon's chair shifted as someone behind him grabbed it to hold it steady. The prince braced himself.

Ocarn's first blow was more of a cuff than a punch. The Mercerien was evidently just warming up, though, for his second strike hammered into Ebon's cheek, snapping his head round so fast he felt a wrench in his neck. He found himself staring down at the floor, forced himself to look at Ocarn again.

In time to meet the third punch. His head exploded with light, and he would have toppled over if he hadn't been held. The whole side of his face throbbed, yet it didn't hurt as much as his scalded pride. Pride, it had always been his curse. He'd need to swallow it a while longer, though, before he retaliated—at least until he'd given Ocarn a chance to brag. He worked his tongue around his mouth, tasted the warm iron of blood.

And looked at Ocarn once more.

"Lord, that feels good," the Mercerien said, flexing the fingers of his punching hand. "For you too?" He stepped back and gestured to the man holding Ebon's chair. "Stand him up."

Ebon's chair was lifted, and he staggered to his feet. Still tied to the chair, he could not stand fully straight and had to look up to meet Ocarn's eyes from a half bow.

"I like that pose," the Mercerien said. "It suits you."

His fist thudded into Ebon's ribs, knocked him back a step, but Ocarn came after him, connecting with a blow to the midsection that folded Ebon in half and snatched the wind from him. He gasped like a grounded fish as Ocarn hit him again and again, right fist, then left, working on his stomach. The Mercerien grunted with the effort, like he was the one being hit, and grunts escaped Ebon's own lips no matter how hard he tried to keep them in. He wanted to tense his muscles against the onslaught, but he was too busy wheezing for a breath that would not come. He thought to jerk forward and butt Ocarn in the face, but instead he took the punishment, curling up as best he could to rob the punches of their weight.

Finally the beating ended, and Ebon sagged back. The man behind him guided the chair down until it touched the floor. Ebon slumped into it, his head lolling forward, his whole body shuddering. He had to swallow to keep his guts from heaving. He channeled his power to his bruised midriff—just a trickle at first to soothe the ache there. Wouldn't want Ocarn seeing how easily his hurt was shrugged off. Wouldn't want him thinking Ebon was ready for another round. The Mercerien grabbed a handful of Ebon's hair and tugged his head up, brought his face close so he could study every line of pain. Rather than meet his gaze, Ebon kept his eyes on the floor. Let Ocarn think he had knocked the fight out of him. Maybe he would move on to the gloating that was sure to come.

Ocarn released him, and Ebon's head fell forward.

"Hurts, does it?" the Mercerien said. "Good. But it's still not enough for the dishonor you visited on my sister. Maybe I'll get my men to bend you over that chair, let them have some fun with you. How does that sound?"

Ebon's voice came out a croak. "Where's Rendale?"

"If I were you, I'd be more worried about yourself. Aren't you curious how I knew you were coming? How I was able to snare you so easily?"

Ebon stared at him.

Ocarn chuckled. "You still have no idea, do you? Then let me tell you a story. Yesterday a man comes to see me at the embassy. Says he has information for sale. Says a woman called Tia sent him. Apparently someone paid her to get them into the Upper City, no questions asked. But Tia's a curious sort, and after she strikes a deal with this person, she has him followed to the harbor. She sees him pay a guard to deliver a false message to me about a fight on my ship, then watches him snatch one of my crew and question him, and, well, it seems even scum from the Lower City can work out what two plus two equals. And since you were stupid enough to believe she couldn't smuggle you across the canal immediately on false papers, she has all the time in the world to send one of her thugs to seek me out."

Ocarn's voice was thick with scorn, and Ebon almost lost his head then. He wanted to lash out with his sorcery and smear the man's smile over the wall behind. But his anger was as much for himself as for the Mercerien. Stupid, Ocarn had called him, and Ebon couldn't deny it. He'd let his desperation cloud his judgment of Tia. He'd thought he was risking only a few thousand sovereigns in trusting her, but now his folly was about to cost him his life. Because there was no doubt in Ebon's mind that Ocarn meant to kill him. When you crossed a certain line, you didn't let your victim walk away after to talk about it.

"She was going to take your money and stand you up," Ocarn went on, "but I convinced her to honor her side of the bargain and deliver you into the Upper City. It cost me a great deal. Five thousand sovereigns she wanted to go through with your agreement, and I must say that seemed a high price at first." Ebon didn't think Ocarn could have stretched his smile any wider, but he managed it now. "But eventually we reached an arrangement."

Ebon was silent, unsure what the Mercerien was hinting at. Then a jolt of prickling cold ran down his spine. "You gave them to Tia," he whispered. It all made sense suddenly. Ocarn had given Lamella and Rendale to Tia so she could ransom them to his father. Earlier, the embassy woman had told Ebon that Rendale was taken away yesterday—taken away to Tia, it now seemed. The irony wasn't lost on him. For the last twenty-four bells, he'd been champing to get into the Upper City, while all the time Lamella and Rendale were likely being held by Tia in the Lower.

"Gave *them* to Tia?" Ocarn said, staring at Ebon through narrowed eyes. "Ah, yes, Rendale's crippled woman." He paused to study Ebon some more, his look calculating. "Except she wasn't Rendale's woman, was she? She was yours."

Ebon's expression gave nothing away. Nothing *more* away, at least.

"I always thought their displays of affection were forced," Ocarn continued. "Or they were to start with." He looked to his guards for a laugh, and they duly obliged. Three laughs, meaning three men, though Ebon couldn't pinpoint precisely where they stood. "Pretty enough girl, your Miela," Ocarn said. "A bit too willing, though, for my taste. She never gave me much of a chase when I came for her.

Claimed it was the leg, but we both know otherwise. She liked to be bent over a chair, just as you will be. Maybe you'll enjoy it as much as she did, eh?"

Ebon was barely listening. The taunts didn't fool him. He was thinking about other things. Strange, he shouldn't have needed an incentive to want to live through this encounter, but the news that Lamella and Rendale were with Tia made it suddenly vital that he get away. Assuming Tia intended to ransom them, how long would it take for her demands to reach Galitia, and for Ebon's father to respond? Months perhaps, with the Sabian Sea off limits. Months held in that cesspit of a Lower City. And when the time came for Tia to release her charges, was she any more likely to play fair with Ebon's father than she had done with Ebon himself?

He looked toward the windows, the shadow of an idea flitting through his mind. There was only one way he was going to escape from this place, and if his plan failed, he would likely suffer all Ocarn had promised and worse. Before he rolled the dice, though, he wanted one more piece of information from his host.

"You know this means war, don't you?" he said. "Between Galitia and Mercerie. When my father finds out you took me—"

"He'll do nothing," Ocarn cut him off. "You forget, I left Mercerie only two weeks ago, which meant I was there when word arrived of the attack on Majack." He stepped closer. "Your people are weak. Weaker now than they've ever been. You think your father will risk a fight while he's threatened by Garat Hallon and the Kinevar? And by the time those threats are resolved, if indeed they ever are, I'll have likely taken my father's throne and struck at Galitia myself."

Ebon held back a smile. Everything Ocarn had said was true, but Ebon had never believed that war was a possibility. That hadn't been the purpose of his question. *When my father finds out,* he'd said, and Ocarn hadn't tried to deny that Isanovir *would* find out. And who alone knew enough of what had happened here in Gilgamar to carry word home to Galitia?

Vale.

Meaning the Endorian had not been captured.

Time for me to do some taunting of my own. "You, on Mercerie's throne?" he said. "Sounds like my father will have you just where he wants you."

Ocarn gave a chill smile. "Well, well. It seems the cock hasn't completely lost his crow. Let's see what we can do about that." He gestured to his man behind Ebon. "Hold him."

"Are you sure you've got that right?" Ebon said. "Are you sure it shouldn't be you doing the holding and your man the punching?"

The Mercerien laughed. "That's funny. I like that. Tell you what, you keep the lines coming. We'll see if they can outlast my punches."

"Or you could try taking a run up this time," Ebon suggested. "Get some extra force behind the blow."

Ocarn did not reply. Instead he flexed his fingers. His cheeks were flushed, and Ebon wanted him hot if that meant he'd hold nothing back when he threw his next punch.

Because when that punch came, a wall of Ebon's sorcery would be waiting to meet it.

Senar descended the ladder into the bake-oven air of the *Eternal*'s hold. The stench of bilge greeted him, and there was a smell of rot too. He stepped down onto the planking above the bilge and turned. An Erin Elalese soldier held a lantern. By its smoky light, Senar saw a wall of barrels and casks to his left. To his right was the mizzen-mast where it descended through the ceiling to join the keel below. Beyond, the vertical beams supporting the orlop deck faded into darkness, black like the trunks of burned trees.

Above the creak of shifting wood, Senar heard the scratch of rats' claws, the metallic thud of the hull bumping into the quay. He stepped forward to make room for Kolloken behind. At the base of the wall of barrels, bodies had been piled into a mound of flesh and gore. *Ruby-holters.* Among them were women and children. All had had their throats cut. Flies buzzed about.

To one side was a smaller heap of four corpses, all wearing gray cloaks—presumably the Revenants who'd been guarding the quay at which the *Eternal* was docked. Their throats, too, had been cut. Crouching next to the bodies was the Revenant subcommander, Twist, his expression as dark as the bruises on his face. A few paces away, standing beside the lantern bearer, was the Erin Elalese water-mage Jelek. His skin glistened with sweat. As his gaze met Senar's, he put a sweet in his mouth. His teeth were brown and rotten.

"Who found the bodies?" the Guardian asked.

The lantern bearer grunted responsibility.

"And?"

The man looked at Jelek as if seeking permission to talk, but the mage just stared back. After a pause the lantern bearer said, "Me and Cutter. We were following that Hex guy down from the Alcazar. He left maybe a bell ago. We watched him skip down the quay and across the gangplank"—he glanced at Twist—"but we couldn't see any Gray Cloaks standing guard. That got us thinking. So we went to check up on our lads in the Bloodfish."

"The Bloodfish?"

"The inn at the end of the wharf. Couple of our boys have been keeping an eye on the ship—you know, watching the Gray Cloaks' backs, and all. Well, we get to their room and find them dead, their throats cut just like these. So we thought maybe we should take a look round the ship, find out what's been going down."

Jelek popped another sweet into his mouth, then pointed to the larger pile of corpses. "These-a souls," he said in his singsong voice, "must be the Rubyholters who sailed the ship from Bezzle. Looks-a like the stone-skins kept hostages belowdecks to guarantee the sailors' cooperation, then killed them all to stop them a-talking."

Made sense. That would also mean, Senar realized, that the Augerans and the Rubyholters were at war, for the notion of Galantas lending his ship to the stone-skins was irreconcilable with the presence of hostages on board. He wondered if Galantas's corpse would be found in the pile. "Easy enough to kill the Rubyholters unwitnessed," he said. "But what about the Revenants? Someone must have seen or heard something."

"Not that they're admitting to," the lantern bearer said.

"You asked at the inn?"

"Aye."

Kolloken said, "If our lads at the Bloodfish had seen someone attack the Gray Cloaks, they would have hollered."

Senar nodded. "Meaning the Augerans must have silenced the Erin Elalese in the inn first. But how? I doubt they get so many stone-skins round here that a few more wouldn't have caught the eye."

"Maybe there weren't no stone-skins to see. Maybe they had friends working for them. Gilgamarian friends."

"Maybe." The Guardian turned back to the pile of gray-cloaked corpses. "But that doesn't explain how four Revenants got butchered without anyone noticing."

Twist looked up from his crouch. "If their throats were cut, they must've been taken by surprise. But they were stationed on the quay. Ain't no way someone could have crept up on them without them seein'." He flashed a look at Jelek like he wondered whether the culprits were Erin Elalese.

It was a possibility, Senar had to concede. For while the Gray Cloaks wouldn't have counted Avallon's men as friends, they wouldn't have counted them as enemies either, to be kept always at spear's length. And if Breakers *had* slain the mercenaries, that would explain why the Erin Elalese soldiers in the Bloodfish hadn't raised the alarm . . . if not why those soldiers had themselves been killed.

No, it had to be the stone-skins.

"Was there any blood on the quay?" Senar asked.

"No," the lantern bearer said.

"Then maybe the Gray Cloaks weren't killed there. Maybe they were lured onto the ship."

Twist frowned as if the suggestion was a slight to his men's professionalism. "All four of them?"

It did seem unlikely, but what part of this mess didn't?

The pitch of the deck made the pile of Rubyholt bodies move. A young woman slid to the boards, causing a cloud of flies to rise into the gloom. Senar tugged at his collar. The heat was making it difficult to think. "No matter how or where the Gray Cloaks were killed, the stone-skins would have needed numbers to do it. So where are they all?" He turned to the lantern bearer. "You searched the ship?"

The man nodded.

"Search it again."

"Search it yourself. They ain't here, I'm telling you."

"A group of stone-skins doesn't just walk down the quay and blend into the scenery."

Kolloken said, "Maybe they lowered a barge over the side and rowed to another part of the harbor."

The lantern bearer spat on the boards. "Already thought of that. The ship's still got its full complement of boats."

"So maybe they brought another with them to throw us off the scent."

Jelek chewed thoughtfully on another sweet. The light from the lantern caught sparkles in his metal piercings. "If they took a barge, they still had to come ashore somewhere."

An idea surfaced in Senar's head. "Unless they went through the Neck and left the harbor."

Could that be it? Had the stone-skins feared Avallon would seize them, and so slipped away while no one was looking? The Guardian wasn't buying it, and judging by the expressions of those around him, neither were his companions. If the Augerans' intent had been solely to flee the city, why dispose of the Rubyholters?

"Daylight," Senar said, his voice betraying his bemusement. "How did they do this in daylight without a soul noticing?" *Unless* . . . "When did they dock this morning?"

"A bell before dawn," Kolloken said. "The harbormaster lowered the chains for them specially."

"Meaning it was dark when they arrived. Could they have slipped away then?"

"They could have done, but then who killed the Gray Cloaks and our boys? They ain't been dead that long. And why did Hex come down to the ship *now*? Odds are, it's because he meant to disappear with his friends—maybe even help them do it."

Twist straightened. "The hows of it will have to wait," he said. "First we got to find out where the bastards went. Because if they're still in Gilgamar, the fact they didn't wait till tonight to pull this stunt means there's somethin' going down—and going down soon." He looked from Senar to Jelek. "The chica and the emperor must be told."

Ocarn threw a punch at Ebon's head, putting his whole body into it, twisting for leverage.

To the sound of cracking bones, his hand struck a wall of Ebon's sorcery and buckled. Such was Ocarn's momentum, his elbow followed through to strike the shield too. He let out a wail of pain, staggered back a pace, and fell to his knees. He seemed to collapse in upon himself, curling up round the blood-smeared hand now clutched to his chest.

Hurts, does it?

Ebon didn't give Ocarn's men a chance to react. Dropping his sorcerous barrier, he gathered his Will and lashed out. Not at Ocarn or at his own bonds—none of his powers could be used to sever them—but at one of the windows to his left.

Glass and shutters exploded outward with a splintering roar. Such was the force of the detonation, the stones around the window were torn loose as well to leave a jagged hole. There was a grating, settling sound, followed by the patter of falling mortar and splinters of wood. Clouds of dust billowed up. Above Ocarn's gurgling whimpers came distant screams, questioning shouts. A good sign, Ebon decided, for even if Vale wasn't already waiting outside, a blast like that was sure to draw him.

Or more of Ocarn's guards, perhaps.

Ebon, expecting the Mercerien guard behind him to strike, threw himself left. His chair jerked free of the man's grasp and teetered on two legs before toppling. The room pitched. Ebon tensed his neck muscles to stop his head hitting the floor. Instead it was his left shoulder that took the impact, sending a spike of pain along his arm.

The room stretched tall above him. Through the hole in the wall he saw hazy shapes in the dust. He waited with held breath for one to resolve itself into Vale, but the shapes weren't moving. It dawned on him then that he didn't know what lay beyond the wall. He'd been dragged into a room at the rear of the embassy. Did the building back onto a road? A courtyard? He cocked his head, straining to hear a crunch of wood or glass that would indicate approaching footsteps. Nothing. He thought to call for help, but the destruction of the window was surely call enough. If Vale hadn't heard that, he wouldn't hear Ebon's shout either.

From behind him came a ringing of steel as swords were drawn from their scabbards. Ebon glanced at Ocarn, still on his knees. The Mercerien looked through the hole in the wall, clearly conscious of the risk posed by Vale. Let him look. His men wouldn't move against Ebon without his say-so, and every heartbeat he spent watching was another heartbeat for Vale to get here.

Then the spell broke. Ocarn shook his head to clear it.

Ebon needed a way to slow him down—to buy Vale more time. "It's not too late to end this," he said to Ocarn. "Release me now and we can—"

Ocarn's growl cut him off. "Xable," he said to one of his men, "get him out of here." He nodded toward Ebon, then clambered upright, cradling his injured hand. "You others, drag that desk over to the wall and block the hole."

Oh no you don't.

Gathering his power again, Ebon struck out at Ocarn. The blow lacked the force of the strike that had shattered the window, but it was enough to send the Mercerien reeling backward. He tripped over the rolled-up rug and fell against the desk. Then the rug slid from under his feet, and he slumped to the floor.

Something thumped into the side of Ebon's chair—a weapon most likely. One of Ocarn's men must have aimed a blow at him, but the chair stole the force of the attack, so that when it hit Ebon in the ribs, it only bumped rather than cut. He lashed out behind with his power. Facing the wrong way as he was, he couldn't see who he was aiming at. With his assailant so close, though, he couldn't miss, and he was rewarded with a hiss of expelled air, a clatter of metal on stone.

Ocarn was back on his feet. With his left hand he drew a dagger—

Vale's battle cry, sped up to double time, seemed to warble as the Endorian leapt through the hole in the wall. His sword, held two-handed, struck sparks off the stone to one side. He slipped as he landed on the carpet of glass and splinters, took a wobbling step to get his balance. An eyeblink was all he needed to read the room. Then he flashed to engage the soldiers behind Ebon, his movements so fast they appeared jerky.

Ebon liked his odds better all of a sudden.

A part of him expected Ocarn to run for the door, but instead the Mercerien surged forward. Light glinted off his knife. If he reached Ebon, he could hold the blade to his throat, make Vale stand down until more guards arrived.

No way Ebon was going to let that happen.

A scream sounded from behind him. One of the soldiers was down.

Ebon made of his sorcery a wall to keep Ocarn at bay, and the Mercerien leaned into it like he was fighting a headwind. Just five paces away now. Four. Three. This wasn't a contest Ebon could win, he realized, and so he lowered his wall abruptly. As Ocarn lurched forward, Ebon lashed out at his lead leg just as his weight came down on it—*crack*. The Mercerien cursed and fell on top of him, sending another jolt of pain through Ebon's trapped left arm.

Ocarn shifted his weight, tried to lever himself off—

Thud.

Ebon felt as much as heard Vale's sword pommel strike the Mercerien's skull. Gurgling blood, Ocarn reeled back on legs as weak as willow reeds before collapsing to the floor. His eyes rolled back in his head.

Dead?

Ebon hoped not.

Vale cut through Ebon's bindings and hauled him upright. The prince's wrists were prickling sore where the ropes had bit, and he rubbed life back into them before stretching out the cramps in his arms and legs. He could hear no movement in the embassy. If more Merceriens were inside they had the sense to keep it to themselves. Ebon caught Vale's eye. It seemed he should thank his friend, but what did you say at a time like this? What words would suffice? Instead he simply nodded, and the Endorian returned the gesture.

"You hurt?" Vale asked.

"No. You?"

Vale shook his head. "We should go."

"One moment."

Ebon scanned the room. Ocarn's three guards were sprawled unconscious, while Ocarn himself lay in a heap at Ebon's feet, his chest stuttering up and down, a lump forming on his brow where Vale had struck him. Ebon rubbed a hand across his throbbing jaw, felt again the sting of Ocarn's punches. Could he complain at his treatment, though, when Ebon himself had planned something similar for the other man? Ebon had told Vale to find a quiet place for them to interrogate Ocarn, had resolved to make him talk one way or another. How far would he have gone if the Mercerien refused to speak? Perhaps he'd been lucky he hadn't had to find out.

What was he supposed to do with him now, though? This wasn't over. When Ocarn came to, he would want revenge. And with Rendale and Lamella in Tia's control, what was to stop him trying to reclaim them? If Ebon had to buy their freedom, he didn't want to find himself in a bidding war. What were his choices? Take Ocarn with him when he left? Something told Ebon questions would be asked if he tried to exit the Upper City with an unconscious man on his shoulder. What did that leave? With Gilgamarian soldiers probably on their way here to investigate the explosion, there wasn't time for anything fancy.

He could kill Ocarn, of course. That would make the problem go away. But only at the cost of another, larger, problem when Ocarn's father found out. For while Galitia could not afford a war with Mercerie, the same could not be said in reverse.

Ebon frowned. Kill Ocarn in cold blood? Was he really considering it?

Beyond the hole in the wall, the dust had settled to reveal a walled courtyard with a gate at the far end. From far off came shouted orders, the jangle of armor. The noises were closing in on the embassy, but Ebon still had time to finish Ocarn if that was what he wanted. He reached down and pried the Mercerien's knife from his fingers. Just one lunge, and it would be over. Such a small thing when you looked at it that way.

Ebon dropped the knife and headed for the door.

At Mazana's call, Senar opened the door to her room. The last quarter-bell had been one of the longest of his life, shared as it was with the executioner in the corridor. Thinking to fill the silence, the Guardian had told the giant about what he'd discovered on the *Eternal,* and about the time he'd spent afterward trying to find someone at the harbor who had seen the Augerans leave the ship. The executioner had taken the news in typically animated fashion. Senar had then made the mistake of suggesting that, with the whereabouts of the stone-skins unknown, the giant would need to be especially vigilant with Mazana's safety. The executioner's only reaction had been a tightening of the lines about his eyes. Considering his usual dispassion, though, Senar reckoned he'd been lucky to escape the encounter unscathed.

He closed the door behind him.

Mazana was collecting wooden soldiers from the floor, and as she crouched she gave Senar a view down the front of her dress. It took him an instant longer than was proper to avert his gaze. Outside in the passage he'd heard her reading to Uriel, but the boy was not present. The closed door to Senar's right doubtless led to his bedchamber.

The emira scooped up the last soldier and placed it on a desk before sitting on the bed. There was something about the way her hair fell across her face that put Senar in mind of Jessca, and he was conscious suddenly of Jessca's ring on his little finger. What moment from his past had sparked the recollection? He couldn't recall. Now when he thought about Jessca, the image that always came to mind was of her lying on a block of stone in the Sacrosanct's crypt. Her face was the color of clay, and the top of her head had been ripped away by some demon's claws. For some reason, the memory was not as raw as it had been when Senar first arrived in Olaire. The realization left him feeling strangely uneasy.

"You heard about the *Eternal*?" he asked Mazana.

She nodded.

"We've tried to find witnesses, but no one saw a thing. Not of the stone-skins leaving, not of the Revenants being slaughtered. The Gilgamarians are making their own inquiries, but in the meantime, the guards on the seawall have been put on alert."

A smile touched Mazana's lips. "The Gilgamarians on alert, eh? I feel safer already."

"You find this amusing?"

"Maybe a little. You know of course that Hex has reappeared? He returned to the Alcazar a bell ago."

Senar stared at her. "Have you talked to him?"

"Sadly, no. By the time word reached me about the *Eternal,* our fidgety friend had disappeared again." She paused. "But then just about everything seems to be going missing these days. And turning up in the most unexpected places, too."

Senar wondered where this was heading. Somewhere with a trap-door and spikes, probably.

"Tell me," Mazana went on, "did you see the bodies of the Erin Elalese soldiers who were killed at the inn? The ones who were supposed to be keeping an eye on the *Eternal*?"

"No."

"Meaning we have only your kinsmen's word that they existed at all."

Now Senar understood. "You think the *Eternal* was Avallon's work. You think he made up the deaths in the Bloodfish to hide his trail." Senar had had the same thought, so he couldn't begrudge it to Mazana. "If the emperor killed the Revenants, though, it stands to reason he seized the stone-skins too. Yet you said Hex came back to the Alcazar. Why would Avallon snatch the man just to let him go again?"

Mazana inclined her head to acknowledge the point. But there was an expectation in her look that told Senar he was missing something.

Someone knocked at the door.

"Enter!" Mazana called.

A young female servant slipped inside carrying a tray on which was a plate of sandfruit slices together with a decanter of red wine and two glasses. Was that second glass for Senar? Or was the emira expecting company? Eyes downcast, the girl made to set the tray down on a table beside the bed. As she passed Mazana, her hands shook, making the glasses rattle.

"Shall I pour, ma'am?"

"Why not? One for you, Guardian?"

Senar hesitated, then nodded.

The servant picked up a glass, only for it to slip in her grasp. She stooped and tried to grab it as it fell. Missed.

It smashed on the ground.

The servant gasped and pulled back her left hand as if she'd been stung. There was a cut to her palm, a shard of glass protruding from it.

Too late Senar saw the danger.

The emira reached out and seized the girl's arm.

The servant flinched, tears in her eyes. Blood ran down her wrist. It reached Mazana's hand, and the emira's skin absorbed it like blotting paper. Senar stepped forward. Mazana was turned away from him, so he couldn't make out her expression. The servant could, though, and her face paled at what she saw. She tried to pull free, but the emira's grip was too strong.

"Mazana," Senar said.

A moment passed as the servant continued to struggle. Mazana turned her head as if to check that Senar was still there. He wondered what would have happened if he hadn't been.

Then the emira released the girl.

The servant staggered back. Where Mazana had gripped her arm, there were white impressions, slow to fade. She hitched up her skirts and fled.

Senar heard the door slam behind him, but he didn't look round. His gaze was still on the emira—or rather on the back of her head, since she remained facing away from him. The girl's blood had left a purple-red blotch on Mazana's arm the size of a sovereign. Senar remembered the last time she'd got blood on her skin, and what had happened afterward in the corridor outside Darbonna's cell.

He braced himself.

The emira kept still. She was trying to gather herself, he suspected. To reestablish control. She tutted as she took in the pieces of glass on the floor. When she finally looked across, her eyes had a glow to them.

"That was your glass she broke, by the way," she said.

No matter, Senar thought. The way he was feeling just now, he'd be happy to drink from the decanter.

Mazana picked a path through the broken glass to the table. She filled the remaining glass with wine, then drained it in one go. After refilling the glass, she returned to sit on the bed. The stain on her arm started to fade. From Uriel's room came a muted cough.

"How far is it from here to the Rubyholt Isles?" Mazana asked suddenly.

The Guardian was slow to answer. The emira would know better than he. "To the Outer Rim? Maybe fifty leagues."

"And to Bezzle?"

"I don't know. Twice that?"

"Let's say one hundred and twenty-five leagues. On the open sea, I could cover that distance in half a day, but if I had to weave a way through the Rubyholt Isles . . . maybe fourteen bells? For a lesser mage the journey could take anything up to a day."

Senar waited for her to get to the point.

She drank from her glass. "I've been thinking more about our friend Hex's appearance this morning. We got here yesterday at around the third bell, yes? And it was another two bells before your esteemed emperor arrived. So, let's imagine the stone-skins had a spy in Gilgamar. Let's imagine that spy left the moment Avallon was unmasked to inform the Augeran expeditionary force—and that he had a Rubyholter on hand to guide him through the Isles. And let's also imagine Subcommander Sunder responded immediately to the news by dispatching Hex to Gilgamar. By my calculations, Hex should have arrived here"—she glanced down, her lips moving silently as she pretended to work it out—"about twelve bells from now."

Senar struggled to gather his thoughts. "You're saying the stone-skins knew the emperor was coming before he arrived?"

Mazana snapped her fingers. "Of course! Why didn't I think of that?"

"That means they must have a spy in Erin Elal," Senar said, his pulse quickening. The spy would have to be one of Avallon's closest advisers too, for the details of his journey to Gilgamar would have been kept secret from all but a select few.

"Or . . ." Mazana prompted.

He looked at her blankly.

"Or Avallon himself found a way to tell the stone-skins he was coming."

"And dig his own grave at the same time? He'd be trapped here, far from home and among uncertain friends."

"But think of what he stands to gain." The emira set down her glass, then rose and crossed to the desk. "If the stone-skins knew he was coming to Gilgamar, they might be tempted to strike. True, Avallon could fall with the city, but equally he could slip away when the assault started. And of course it doesn't matter to him whether the stone-skins take the city or not, because either way the result would be to draw the League into the war."

Senar frowned. There was sense in what Mazana said, but she was seeing only half the picture. "So where is this strike coming from? You're forgetting, the stone-skins who came with Hex can have numbered only a few dozen. I think even the Gilgamarians can be relied upon to repel that threat."

Mazana opened a drawer and removed a scabbarded knife. Fume's knife. "But we can also assume Hex's party isn't the only threat we have to contend with here in Gilgamar."

"Meaning?"

The emira unsheathed the knife and made a show of studying its blade. "Jambar paid me a visit earlier, had you heard? No? He tells me your emperor is planning an attack on the Alcazar."

Senar tore his gaze away from the dagger. "Of course he is. No doubt Jambar saw me fighting on Avallon's side, too."

Mazana moved closer. "Don't be so quick to dismiss the shaman's visions. Some of them have already proved disturbingly accurate. Did you know, for example, that Avallon has brought more soldiers to Gilgamar than were invited? With Jambar's help, Jodren has tracked down a sizeable force to a warehouse in the Lower City."

Senar kept his silence.

Mazana watched him closely. "You hide your surprise well. You are surprised, aren't you?"

"In truth, I am not. As I said, Avallon is far from home and among uncertain friends. You can't blame him for keeping some soldiers close in case you decided to turn on him."

"Or in case *he* decided to turn on *me*."

"Right. The stone-skins aren't enough of a challenge that he wants to make an enemy of the Storm Isles as well. He needs you. He needs your help against the Augerans."

The emira's laugh was dismissive. "Oh, come now, you know better than that. He needs me only as long as I am sympathetic to his cause. And since I have yet to commit to an alliance, perhaps he is tempted to do away with me in the hope my successor proves more accommodating."

"After this successor has seen him betray you?"

Mazana said nothing. She halted a pace in front of Senar, close enough to strike. The Guardian's gaze flickered to the knife in her hand. A single cut would be all it took to seal his doom. Sorcery oozed from the blade like pus from a wound. Senar met the emira's gaze. Would she do it? He didn't think so, but was he prepared to stake his life on it? If he raised a Will-shield against her, would she read that as proof of his guilt?

She studied him. He knew what she was thinking. If he'd suspected all along that the emperor had forces in the city, why hadn't he told her? And what other things might he be keeping from her? Like, say, Avallon's admission in their meeting yesterday that Erin Elal, and not the Sabian League, would be Augera's first target in the coming conflict?

The Guardian swallowed. The fence between the two sides was feeling a lot more uncomfortable to sit on, suddenly.

"If all this is true," he said, "why hasn't Jambar seen the danger before?"

"Apparently he has. Apparently he dismissed it as too remote to bother me with." Mazana examined the knife again. "Perhaps he was too willing to give your emperor the benefit of the doubt. Perhaps I have been guilty of making the same mistake."

"And what has changed that Jambar is now so sure of his predictions?"

"The coming of Avallon to Gilgamar, for one thing. My meeting with Hex, for another. Back in Olaire, there was no foreseeing those two events would come to pass. Now that they have done, a veil has been lifted from the shaman's eyes."

"He sees clearly now, does he? Has he been able to tell you what happened to the stone-skins on the *Eternal,* then? Has he told you where they are now?" Senar paused then went on, "He sees only what he wants to see, Emira. And tells you only what he wants you to know."

Not unlike the Guardian himself, he realized.

Mazana did not respond.

But she didn't sheathe her knife either.

Floating in spiritual form to one side of Mazana and Senar, Romany watched the quarrel play out. Earlier she'd heard Jambar tell the emira about this Erin Elalese plot, but she found it no easier to credit now than she had then. If they'd been plotting something, after all, wouldn't Romany have caught a hint of it along her web?

Unless the plotting had been done *outside* the Alcazar's walls, of course.

She frowned. Events in Gilgamar were moving apace, what with the goings-on at the harbor. She wondered if she'd made a mistake by confining her web to the Alcazar. It was too late to worry about that now, though. Her web within the building continued to corrode, and her priority must be the repair of the existing strands rather than the creation of new ones. Besides, her purpose here in Gilgamar was a simple one: to observe the emira and strike at the appropriate time.

And she had an opportunity to do that now if she wanted to take it.

She had no idea whether Mazana really planned to stab Senar, but if the emira hadn't meant to use Fume's knife, she shouldn't have unsheathed it. Her eyes had that raw red edge that Romany had seen in Darbonna's cell. A memory rose of the old woman's final moments, and the priestess shuddered. Mazana stroked a finger along her dagger's blade. Working herself up to something, perhaps? If so, would Senar try to stop her? Or would he just stand there and look hurt when the knife carved him open?

Romany considered. What to do? The Spider had been reluctant to remove one of her own game pieces from the board, and Romany found herself of a similar mind. Something was brewing in Gilgamar, and it seemed reckless to act before the priestess knew all the facts. The stone-skins were coming, that much at least was clear. But why? And was their target just Erin Elal or all the nations hereabouts? If they'd set their sights on the Sabian League, wouldn't killing Mazana play into their hands? With the other Storm Lords dead, the emira was the only one who could claim to speak for the whole League. If she died, the chance of a coordinated response to an invasion might be lost with her.

Romany shook her head in irritation. She was getting too far ahead of herself. In Olaire, the Spider had left to her the choice of *when* to dispatch Mazana, not *if*—meaning the consequences, whatever they might be, were none of her concern. Perhaps that was just as well too. There were times, like now, when Romany was glad to be able to leave the hard decisions to the goddess. To be shielded from the responsibilities of her actions. And yet there was no denying that her hand would be the one guiding Shroud's blade. No denying either that Romany, by arguing in Olaire for Mazana to be eliminated, might have played a part in the Spider's judgment.

Eliminated. Such a disingenuous word. What she meant was "murdered." Why not just say it?

Romany watched Mazana close to within a step of Senar. The priestess had already squandered a chance to dispose of the woman when she let the Guardian creep up on her at the portal. How long could Romany rely on him keeping quiet about that? How many more opportunities to kill Mazana would she get? And if the priestess needed to harden her heart against the emira, well, all she had to do was remember that strip of skin hanging down from Darbonna's arm.

Remember? Hells, she'd be surprised if she ever forgot it.

An image of Uriel's face appeared in her mind's eye, but she pushed it away. The boy would be better off without his sister in the long run. And Romany could no more base her actions on how Uriel would be affected than she could on her desire to return to her temple in Mercerie.

Taking a breath, she started spinning her threads about Mazana.

And the knife in her hand.

Senar stared at Mazana, struggling to understand what had just happened. One moment the emira had been holding the knife, the next it had twisted in her grasp like it had a will of its own. His eyes widened as a bead of blood formed at the tip of Mazana's finger. He grabbed her hand and pulled her to him, then pressed her finger against his cuff. As if a bit of pressure would defeat the knife's sorcery! He had heard what happened to the palace guard who'd been cut by Darbonna. Would Mazana's wound refuse to close, as the soldier's had? Could she bleed out from so superficial a scratch?

The emira had gone pale. The dagger fell from her hand and clattered to the floor. Senar kicked its hilt and sent it spinning and skittering across the floor. He had to clench his jaw to stop himself shouting in frustration. Hadn't he known the weapon was dangerous? Hadn't Romany urged him to take it from Mazana? Why hadn't he done so? Because it had slipped his mind? Or because he had feared a clash with the emira over it? *And why not?* he thought bitterly. What was the worst that could happen if he put off the confrontation?

In the next room, Uriel started coughing. Mazana tried to take back her hand, but Senar held her firm. He saw his fear mirrored in her eyes. Her breath came quickly. She pulled back again, and this time he relented. On his cuff, where her finger had bled into it, was a mark. Just a small stain, not the large blemish he'd expected. Mazana laid her injured finger across the palm of her other hand. Her gash was thin as a paper cut, and tainted by the same sorcery Senar had detected in the dagger. Blood gathered at its edges. But it did not well up to form a bead. Instead it soaked into the skin around it—just as the servant's blood had done earlier when it came into contact with the emira's hand.

Mazana stared at her finger. Then she brushed a thumb over it. It came back with the faintest smudge of crimson. So the flow hadn't ceased completely, but it wasn't as fast either as when the cut was first made. Mazana turned her finger to see if the blood would gather and drip. It didn't. Senar's thoughts raced. Her finger was absorbing the blood as fast as it seeped from the cut. Did that mean she was taking it back into her body? Did that mean she was . . . safe?

Mazana trembled. Senar sensed something building inside her, sensed her struggling to hold it in. He wasn't sure which of them moved first, but she was suddenly in his arms. Her breathing steadied.

Perhaps Senar should have felt relief at her apparent deliverance. Instead, though, he found himself thinking back to the time he'd held her like this after her run-in with Greave outside the temple of the

Lord of Hidden Faces. Good old Senar, always there to lend a shoulder. Was this all he was to Mazana? A crutch to lean on when she faltered? And what did she offer in return?

A knife in his face, that's what.

If the emira hadn't cut herself, it might have been Senar wearing that scratch, and with decidedly less promising prospects too. Would he have deserved it, though? He'd preached Erin Elal's cause to her at every turn. He'd told the emperor about the Chameleons' mission to Bezzle. That was the problem with trying to be loyal to two masters: you ended up being a traitor to both—

A knock at the door.

Mazana and Senar sprang apart.

Jodren entered, his coral bird perched on his shoulder, trilling. When he saw Senar, his steps faltered.

The emira's voice was tight. "Yes?"

Jodren hesitated, evidently unsure whether his news was fit for the Guardian's ears.

"Out with it!"

He straightened. "I've just received word from Twist," he said. "Seems the missing stone-skins have been spotted in the Lower City. My men are hunting them now."

Romany listened to Mazana order Senar to the Lower City. She wondered if that strange feeling at the back of her spiritual throat was disappointment or relief. She should have inflicted a more grievous wound, she knew. Something that severed a major artery perhaps, or pierced an organ. But that would have called for a more conspicuous manipulation of the knife, and thus risked arousing Senar's suspicions. Then again, why did she think he would have identified Romany as the culprit? And even if he had done, he'd have had some explaining of his own to do to the executioner once he was found alone with Mazana's corpse and a bloody knife.

The priestess sighed. She hadn't been thinking clearly before her attempt on the emira's life. Too many doubts clouding her mind. Now she considered it, instead of trying to cut Mazana, she could have induced the woman to turn the knife on Senar, for with the Guardian out of the way, Romany would have been free to reinvestigate the possibility of luring the emira through the portal.

All just speculation now.

Jodren was talking to Mazana about beefing up the number of Gray Cloak patrols in the Alcazar, and Romany took that as her cue to leave. Back to her quarters to lick her wounds and plan her next move.

When another opportunity to strike came, she would have to be better prepared.

CHAPTER 20

T HERE WAS dust on Senar's tongue as he halted beside Twist. Hanging from hooks in a wall on the opposite side of the street were racks of ribs, black with flies. Beneath, a pair of dogs stood on their hind legs, scratching at the stones in their efforts to reach the meat. In a doorway with a crimson-spattered frame stood a bare-chested man. A line of scar tissue ran up from his left armpit and over his shoulder, so thick it looked like the arm might once have been severed and sewn back on. Farther along, two more Gilgamarians squatted barefoot in the dust, watching Senar.

Twist hawked and spat. On his shoulder was perched Jodren's coral bird. Not for the first time, Senar wondered why Twist hadn't challenged him to a duel when he had challenged everyone else. Because Mazana had told him not to, perhaps? But why?

The mercenary stared at the hooks with their grisly loads.

"Missed breakfast?" Senar asked.

Twist grunted. "Did the chica send you?"

The Guardian nodded. Mazana had insisted he come, more because she wanted him out of the way, he suspected, than because she thought he was needed. And Senar wasn't complaining if it meant he got time to do some thinking. Or should that be *more* thinking? He grimaced. If he took any longer to choose his path, he might end up looking indecisive. "What happened here?" he said, glancing at the blood-framed door.

"Not *here*," Twist said. "At a cantina a few streets away. Nice place. Hey, they even got chairs." He spat again. "Stone-skins stopped by this morning to pay their respects, some time after the seventh bell. Weren't no warnin'. They just walked in with steel bared and started swingin'."

"After the seventh bell? But the *Eternal* only arrived at half past the sixth."

"Busy bastards, ain't they?"

"How many stone-skins were at the cantina?"

"Coulda been four, coulda been forty," Twist said. "By the time we got here, there weren't many folks willin' to sing chapter and verse."

"Anyone you know among the dead?"

"Not as I'd want to admit to, if you gets my meanin'."

"And that's it? No other targets were hit?"

"No."

An old woman shuffled up to buy some meat from the scarred man. When he carved half a dozen ribs from one of the racks, the flies covering it scattered. The woman started screeching like she'd thought they'd been included in the price.

From around a corner along the street, Mili and Tali appeared. They strutted up in their gossamer robes.

"If it ain't the new recruits," Twist said. "Let's hear it."

Tali stretched like a cat. "Plenty of sightings . . ."

". . . of the stone-skins, O Great One."

"But then there have been sightings . . ."

". . . of the executioner, too, along with everyone . . ."

". . . from the Faerie Queen of Imbar to . . ."

". . . the Demon Lord of the Ninth Hell."

Senar considered. "Any chance this talk of Augerans is just a ruse? Any chance someone could have heard about what happened on the *Eternal* and used the stone-skins as a front to settle scores?"

Twist barked a laugh. "You reckon folks round here need a front for that sort of thing? Besides, the timing's wrong. News from the *Eternal* didn't break till after this went down."

The Guardian nodded absently, his thoughts troubled. There was something wrong about this. Assuming the Augerans who'd hit the cantina had come from the *Eternal,* why pick a fight with the locals and advertise their presence? Why come to this nowhere part of the city at all? He looked round again, wondering what he wasn't seeing. Along the street he'd taken to get here, dust hung in the air as if a team of horses had just passed this way. Beyond, the buildings of the Upper City were a distant smudge of white, and if he craned his neck he could make out the battlements of the Key Tower to the southeast. Closer, nothing rose higher from the ground than the single-story mud-brick shanties all about.

"Why here?" he mused aloud, then looked at Twist. "Why would the stone-skins come *here*?"

"Been askin' myself the same question. Ain't nothin' round here but flies and dust."

"What about the Erin Elalese Mazana's had you watching? Are they close by?"

"Close enough. Don't see how the stone-skins coulda known that, though. And even if they did, don't see what they gain by marchin' into that cantina and redecoratin' the walls."

Tali said, "Maybe they *wanted* us . . ."

". . . to know they were here."

Twist nodded his agreement. "Explains the fireworks. City like this, you get a lot of background noise. Stone-skins had to make sure they shouted loud enough to get our attention."

Senar's skin prickled. And why would the Augerans want them looking in this part of the city unless they didn't want them looking somewhere else? *Like a trickster showing the lure with one hand as he lightens your purse with the other.*

"Call off your search," he said to Twist. "Pull your men back to the Upper City."

The mercenary's lips quirked. "Them's the chica's orders, are they?"

"Let's pretend they are. Whatever the stone-skins are planning to do next, it won't happen here. We need eyes on the Alcazar and the seawall. And we can't watch them from here."

Twist nodded, but did not move. He murmured something to Jodren's coral bird, then twitched his shoulder and watched the animal take to the air. It disappeared behind the rooftops. The mercenary's gaze shifted back to the man with the scarred shoulder.

"Was there something else?" Senar asked.

"That depends. Our friend there"—he gestured to the Gilgamarian— "was at the cantina when I showed up earlier. Red to the elbows, like he'd been wieldin' a blade himself. Got me wonderin' where that meat he's been hawkin' comes from."

Senar looked at him. "You thinking about breakfast again?"

"Maybe I am. You join me?"

The Guardian raised an eyebrow, searching the mercenary's expression. The man was probably joking, he decided. Almost certainly.

But he couldn't have sworn to it.

Ebon stared along the waterfront toward the metal-clad ship. On the quay, two carts were being piled with corpses taken from the vessel. A crowd of amputees was clustered around it like someone was handing out new limbs. A cordon of Gilgamarian soldiers tried to keep order. As Ebon watched, one of the warriors slammed the flat of his sword into the face of a man missing both ears. Then he picked him up and tipped him into a cart. That didn't seem to calm the other vultures, but why would it? Now there was just one more body for them to squabble over.

Ebon rubbed a hand across his chin. He'd healed his jaw and stomach since Ocarn's beating, but they still ached. Gods, how he hated this city. It was destined to be his home a while longer, though—at least until he tracked down Tia. He'd tried asking the locals for information on her whereabouts, but he'd been met with hostile looks. She'd seek him out herself eventually; Lamella and Rendale were too valuable an asset for her to squander. First, though, she'd probably want to let Ebon stew awhile so his desperation grew—and with it the bounty she could ask for her prisoners.

Thereby giving Ocarn a chance to make contact with her first.

If Lamella and Rendale died, Ebon would have no one to blame but himself. Since arriving in Gilgamar, he'd taken one half measure after another: the sailor he'd released when he could have silenced him; his decision to let Ocarn live. No doubt some would say that he'd done the right thing, sparing the Mercerien's life. But right for whom? For Ebon's kinsmen in Galitia, certainly. Maybe even for Ebon himself. What about Lamella and Rendale, though? He recalled the moment Majack's walls had been breached by Mayot's undead army. Faced with the choice of rescuing Lamella or going after the Fangalar sorceress, he hadn't hesitated. Why was it that when the hard decisions came, it was always Lamella who lost out? Why did he always sacrifice her in favor of the kinsmen who feared and distrusted him?

Vale had been talking to four men in gray cloaks near the carts. Now he walked over to speak to Ebon.

"What news?" Ebon asked him.

"Those men are mercenaries," Vale said. "Revenants, they call themselves. For some reason they think I should've heard of them. Seems they're working for the emira—that's who we saw arrive yesterday before we questioned the Mercerien sailor."

Ebon stared at him. "Imerle Polivar is here?"

"Imerle is dead. She died on Dragon Day, along with most of the other Storm Lords. Mazana Creed's in charge now."

The prince held Vale's gaze. Ordinarily he couldn't have cared less about Sabian politics, but could he afford *not* to take an interest when the new emira visited Gilgamar just as Mottle warned of an attack?

Vale must have been thinking the same, for he nodded and said, "I thought I should ask a few questions about what happened on that metal ship. Came in before dawn, apparently. The crew's all been slaughtered. Whoever did the killing was on the ship with them, but they've since vanished. Revenants wouldn't say anything about that, so I spoke to a couple of the locals. Seems the Gray Cloaks have been wearing out their boots tramping back and forth, looking for someone who saw the killers leave the ship. Killers with skin that looks like stone."

A whisper of cold passed through Ebon. He'd seen someone with skin like granite near the Mercerien embassy. "And *did* anyone see anything?"

"No."

Of course they didn't. No one ever did, remember.

Before Ebon could say more, four Gray Cloaks pounded past him along the waterfront. A painted lady slow to get out of their way was caught by a shoulder and sent toppling into the harbor. From the western end of the port—the direction the Revenants headed in—came shouts of warning. When Ebon tried to see the cause, though, he found his view blocked by the hull of an Androsian galleon.

The Gilgamarian soldiers protecting the carts abandoned their positions and sprinted toward the Harbor Gate. People started running every way, some toward the gate with the soldiers, some along the quays as if they were late to board a ship just departing. Another

group of Gray Cloaks hustled past Ebon, and he exchanged a look
with Vale before jogging after them. Ahead the waterfront curved
south and west until it met the harbor wall at a tower—the Key Tower,
he'd heard it called. Over the bow of a fishing scow he saw red-cloaked
figures carrying spears and shields pouring onto the wharfs from a
ship in the tower's shadow. He couldn't make out their faces from this
distance, but he didn't need to see them to know their complexions
would be stony.

The approach to the Key Tower was guarded by a ramp and a gatehouse with a raised portcullis. The Gilgamarian soldiers stationed
there had evidently been caught out by the speed of the enemy offensive, because the lead red-cloaked figures were already swarming
beneath the portcullis and into the stronghold beyond. Not a single
sword had been raised against them, though there were archers on
the tower's battlements shooting down at the foe. Ebon saw a man
lean out so far his helmet slipped from his head. A red-cloaked warrior took a bolt through the leg and went down. None of his companions stopped to help him. From within the tower came echoing
screams, a clash of metal on metal. Then a bare-chested Gilgamarian soldier emerged from an archway onto the harbor wall. A spear
thrown from inside took him in the back, and he pitched forward.

Red-cloaked warriors appeared in the archway. They hurdled the
prone figure and dashed along the wall, sunlight glinting off their
spear tips. Ebon looked from them to the Gilgamarian soldiers remaining unmolested on the battlements of the Key Tower they had
left behind.

"They're not attacking up the tower," he said to Vale as he ran
across the drawbridge linking the two halves of the harbor.

"Not enough men, not enough time," the Endorian said. "They'll
want to take as much of the wall as they can while the surprise is
with them."

Ebon nodded. They were going for the chains.

Before they could reach the monstrous Chain Tower, though, they
would first have to negotiate the smaller Buck Tower halfway along
the wall. It was toward this tower that the stone-skin frontrunners
now raced unopposed. The doorway offering access to the fort was
unbarred, but as the enemy drew near, a portcullis began to inch
down over the opening. Why so slow? The first stone-skin fell to a
crossbow bolt shot from the tower's battlements, and the warrior after

him too. But the next attacker reached the gate when it was only half down, and slid into the gloom beyond. A second red-cloaked man followed him under, then a third. As a fourth tried to duck through, though, the portcullis dropped onto him. Its spikes crushed him, screaming, into the ground.

Ebon drew up. Farther along the waterfront the flow of stone-skins coming ashore from their ship had dried up. The last handful now toiled up the ramp, and snapping at their heels were the eight Revenants who had preceded Ebon along the harbor. A look back revealed more Gray Cloaks coming up behind the prince, but their progress had been halted at the drawbridge Ebon had just crossed. That bridge was being raised by a group of Gilgamarian soldiers, no doubt anxious to isolate the Upper City—and therefore themselves—from the fighting. A sharp exchange of views ended with the severed head of a Gilgamarian guard on the ground. Harsh, perhaps, but with the city's fate in the balance, this was no time for careful diplomacy. The dead soldier's colleagues saw the error of their ways and lowered the bridge again. The Gray Cloaks ran over.

Ebon swung his gaze back to the second tower. With the portcullis down, the red-cloaked attackers were bunching up on the wall, and the ones with crossbows among them started up a withering fire to pin down the Gilgamarian soldiers on the battlements. Just three stone-skins had made it inside. And how many Gilgamarians to face them? Surely more than enough, Ebon told himself, but then a burst of fire-magic lit up the windows. Was one of those three stone-skins a sorcerer? Screams sounded inside.

"How many stone-skins do you count?" Ebon asked Vale.

"A hundred, maybe." The Endorian looked at the Chain Tower. "Not enough to take that fortress."

"Are you sure about that? And even if you're right, what about the fleet that's no doubt waiting outside?" Ebon couldn't see anything of that fleet along the Neck, but it had to be there, didn't it? Else why were the stone-skins intent on lowering the chains? "Those ships can provide covering fire for the men on the wall, maybe even cross more fighters over to join the attack."

Vale looked back along the waterfront. More Revenants rushed across the drawbridge spanning the canal, but there were only a dozen of them, and the Gilgamarian soldiers showed no signs of wanting to follow.

"Where the hell are the rest of the Gilgamarians?" Vale said. "This can't be all the men they've got."

"Tucked up in the Upper City, most likely, happy to let someone else do the fighting." The Harbor Gate had been closed, and the battlements above it were thronged with soldiers watching the struggle on the wall. "By the time they pluck up the courage to come out, this could be over. If the stone-skins take the second tower, they'll be able to hold it with a handful of men while the rest attack the Chain Tower. You've seen the Gilgamarians in action. How long do you think the ones in the Chain Tower will survive?"

At the first tower, the portcullis had been lowered to maroon a dozen red-cloaked warriors on the wrong side. A volley of crossbow bolts shot by Revenants landed like a clattering hail on their shields. Meanwhile, at the second tower, the portcullis barring entry to the stone-skins on the wall was rising. The corpse of the impaled man rose with it until two of his kinsmen tugged him free of its spikes. Smoke trickled from the fort's windows.

Ebon swung his gaze back to Vale.

The Endorian grimaced, knowing what was in the prince's mind. "This ain't our fight," he said.

"You think I don't know that?" Ebon snapped. "You think I want to be here?" Just the sound of combat so soon after Estapharriol had chilled the sweat on the prince's skin. "I don't care what happens to Gilgamar, or the League. But if Gilgamar is lost, then so are Lamella and Rendale. And until Tia contacts us, we have no way of tracking them down. If the stone-skins take the city, do you think finding them will get any easier? Do you think Tia is going to worry about keeping them safe if she's busy dodging stone-skins?"

Vale looked across to where the enemy were now entering the second tower. "Shit," he said.

That about covered it. Since arriving in Gilgamar, Ebon had made nothing but bad decisions, and now here he was being given the chance to make another. Join the defense and risk sacrificing his life—and Vale's—needlessly. Or do nothing, and watch the Chain Tower fall. If it did, the rest of Gilgamar would probably follow. With Ebon's record, maybe he should have left the decision to Vale, but when had he ever been content to be ruled by another's judgment?

"There's only two of us," Vale said.

"Gunnar will be on his way here." Ebon had sent the mage to keep an eye on the Canal Gate in case Ocarn tried to get a message to Tia, but he'd have heard the commotion at the harbor.

"Three, then. You think that's enough to make a difference?"

"Against a hundred stone-skins on the wall? Maybe. Against an entire fleet if it makes it past the chains . . ."

He glanced again at the Chain Tower overlooking the entrance to the Neck.

The fort had to hold.

Romany lay back on her bed, rubbing her forehead where her mask had left impressions. She could hear the attack on the harbor, but that wasn't what concerned her just now. Earlier she had respun the corroded sections of her web, only for the new threads to begin degenerating the instant they were woven. And at a faster rate than she'd detected previously, too. Clearly *some* form of power was clashing with hers, yet even knowing that, she had struggled to discern its nature. The key was not to concentrate on it, she found, but to relax her vision. Sometimes things were visible from the corner of your eye that were not evident when you looked at them directly. Such had been the case here, for she had become aware of a cloud of sorcerous particles extending through this entire wing of the Alcazar.

Romany didn't know what unsettled her more about that magical haze: that it had taken her so long to detect it, or that she still couldn't say what it was. It didn't seem to be affecting the Alcazar's inhabitants. Hells, it didn't seem to be affecting *anything* except her web. That raised the question of whether the mist had been fashioned solely to destroy Romany's creation. Possible, she conceded, but unlikely. For in all her years, she had yet to encounter anyone with the wit to detect her network of ethereal strands.

If the nature and purpose of the mist was a mystery, the source could not be in doubt. *Hex.* The stone-skin was back in his quarters, asleep. It occurred to Romany that his constant slumbers might hold a clue as to the nature of his power. It also occurred to her that his true mission here had never been to persuade Mazana to turn on Avallon. It hadn't even been to sow distrust between the sides. No, his audience with the emira had been arranged so he could gain access to the Alcazar. Now he was where he needed to be to instigate his next move.

So what would that move be? Something directed at the emperor, probably, though Hex surely wouldn't pass up the chance to strike at Mazana too. Odds were, his friends from the *Eternal* would be involved somehow. They might even be here already. But no, her web would have warned her if they were inside the Alcazar. Where, then? Somewhere close? Another building in the Upper City?

Again she found herself regretting her decision not to extend her web into the rest of Gilgamar.

What now? Warn Mazana of the threat? After Romany had just tried to kill her? Yes, that would make sense. A better option would be simply to sit back and ride out the impending storm. And maybe look for an opportunity to help the Augerans dispatch Mazana?

A knock at her door roused Romany from her reverie, but she did not answer it. It was Kiapa, she knew, come to summon her to a midday meeting between Avallon and the emira. There'd be lots to discuss now that the attack was under way. Romany, though, had no intention of attending, because if she did so she might find herself in the open when Hex sprung his surprise. Better to remain in her quarters and prepare herself for whatever was coming. After all, just because she wasn't going to go looking for trouble didn't mean *it* would not come looking for *her*.

Another knock, a pause, then Kiapa wandered off.

The first line in Romany's defenses would be a knot of spells in the corridor outside, aimed at dissuading anyone from approaching her door. Before she started on those, though, she had a hunch she wanted to confirm. Freeing her spirit from her body, she floated into the air and sped along her web to Jambar's room.

There were occasions when Romany hated being right. This was one of them. The shaman lay sprawled in death on the floor, clutching his bag of bones. There were no marks on his body, yet his face was frozen in such a rictus of suffering that Romany decided she could rule out natural causes as the manner of his passing.

Hex.

It should have been impossible to murder a shaman as skilled as Jambar. The priestess had a hunch regarding that too, which she would need to check later. Why had Hex targeted the Remnerol, though, of all the people in the Alcazar? Because he might have foreseen what the Augerans were planning, obviously. But if Hex was able to assassinate people with such ease, why hadn't his first victim been the emperor or Mazana? *Because Jambar wasn't surrounded by body-guards. Because to take down Avallon, Hex will need the help of his kinsmen.*

It struck Romany then that there was something absurd about the course of action she'd chosen. The Augerans looked more and more like a genuine threat to the League, and here was Romany about to take their side against Mazana? Why? *Because the emira is a danger to the Spider.* Wasn't she more of a danger to the stone-skins, though? How did Romany balance the need to silence Mazana against the emira's value in a future war with Augera?

Her spiritual face twisted. *Not my concern.* Spider's blessing, hadn't she vowed a bell ago to keep her mind free of distractions?

A part of her wished the goddess were on hand to discuss her reservations. But then the Spider wasn't the sort to change her mind once her course was set, or to welcome a debate on her orders. What was a priestess's role, she would say, if not to carry out the wishes of her patron? What was the point in Romany being a priestess at all if she meant to second-guess the Spider's every command? *What point, indeed.* The destruction of the Sabian League would be of no concern to the goddess. What had she said in Olaire? *Empires rise, empires fall.* What did it matter to her if Romany's temple—or indeed Romany herself—fell too? The Spider's game would just continue on a different board and with different pieces, for it was a game that had started long before Romany was born and would go on long after she died.

And so the priestess must hold her goddess's hand while she was led off the edge of a cliff.

She sighed. With the Spider as a mistress, she should have known it would end this way.

The Key Tower loomed above Ebon. The ramp leading up to it had looked steep from a distance, but up close it looked all but unclimbable. At its base, around thirty Revenants were drawn up. The front rank held shields, while in the second rank Ebon saw two twin sisters wearing thin gauzy susha robes and precious little else. As Ebon approached, the women and a few of their companions turned to stare at him before looking away, uninterested. There was a reassuring calm to their manner, a readiness that said this was just another fight to them, and one they expected to win.

The stone-skins they faced showed no more apprehension. Standing outnumbered at the top of the ramp, they must have known their position was hopeless. There weren't enough of them to make a shield wall across the entire width of the ramp, so instead they had formed a wedge in front of the gate. Three of them held their shields high to protect the group from missiles shot from the Key Tower's battlements. From where Ebon was standing, the stone-skins looked an imposing group, each fighter as large as any man or woman the prince had seen before. Perhaps that was just an illusion, though, created by their elevated position.

A Gilgamarian woman on the ramparts leaned out and pointed her weapon at the stone-skins. Before she could shoot it, though, its bolt fell out of its slot and spun down to clang off a shield. Then shouts started up from the battlements, and the soldier disappeared. A deepening hiss reached Ebon, as of a dozen waves of water-magic drawing closer. The waves carrying the enemy fleet? He was sure of it.

Time was running out.

He looked for the Revenant leader. At the rear of the group stood a man with his arms crossed. He was listening to a companion with an unruly beard and cheeks so red they looked flash-burned. As Ebon came near, he heard their conversation.

". . . been shouting up to the Gilgamarians," Beardy was saying. "Tried to get them to drop a rock on the stone-skins' heads—they got a damned catapult up there, for Shroud's sake—but I may as well have been talking to my old lady for all the sense I got back. They don't know if the stone-skins left anyone in the tower to stop them raising the portcullis, but they sure as hell ain't coming down to check."

"Then let's get this over with," the leader said. "Gonna be like tryin' to pry a limpet off a ship's ass, but if we can double up on the flanks—"

"I can put a dent in their ranks," Ebon cut in.

The leader turned to look at him, and Ebon found himself staring into the blue eyes of a young man with a faceful of bruises. "Who are you?"

"The introductions will have to wait. I can put a dent in the stone-skins' ranks, but you'll have to get your men closer to take advantage."

The mercenary moved his tongue round his mouth, then looked at his bearded companion. "I reckon we can do that."

Beardy squinted at Ebon. "You a sorcerer? 'Cause I ain't smelling anything coming off you."

"I am a sorcerer—of a kind. Now, are we done talking here, or should I pull up a chair and get comfortable?"

The leader chuckled. "We're done. Just make sure you wait for my signal before unloadin' on the stone-skins. Steepness of that ramp, we ain't gonna be skippin' the last way into the breach."

"One more thing," Ebon said. "You'll want to find a place in your front rank for my friend here." He nodded toward Vale.

The two Revenants gave Vale a look.

"He's an Endorian," Ebon explained. "A timeshifter. If you need someone up that ramp fast, there's no one quicker."

The leader grinned like Ebon had offered to double his back pay. "Endorian, you say? Well, first rank it is, then." He slapped Vale on the shoulder. "Name's Twist. Reckon you and me are gonna need a word when this is over, eh?"

Vale stared at him blankly.

"Got ourselves some free help, boys," Twist said as he took his place in the front rank and accepted a shield from one of his men. "Up here with me, Endorian, don't be shy. You want a shield, or is that just gonna slow you down?"

Vale shook his head to the offered shield before moving up to flank Twist. Ebon took a position directly behind his friend. When the time came to unleash his power, the closer he was to the stone-skins, the harder his strike would land. A man to his left kissed a fish-bone charm around his neck, while a woman beside him settled a full-face helmet over her head. Ebon found himself looking for the animal etched into its cheek-piece, but these were no Pantheon Guardsmen, he reminded himself. Home felt suddenly very far away.

The man on Vale's right looked the Endorian up and down. To Twist he said, "You want me to open a book on him now, chief?"

"Up to you," Twist said. "But you might wanna see what punch he packs before you set the odds."

"Whose money are we taking this time?"

Twist's answer was lost beneath a scream from along the harbor wall. The second tower had already fallen, and that scream doubt-less signified that the stone-skin attack on the Chain Tower had begun. Ebon couldn't actually see that attack because the second tower was in his way. He could, however, make out a Gilgamarian officer atop the Chain Tower's battlements, waving his sword as if he were about to lead a charge over the parapet. Easy to be brave, though, when you had a wall and a portcullis to hide behind.

And yet didn't the defenders have every reason to be confident? With the portcullis down, the stone-skins would be forced to assault the battlements. The narrowness of the wall would give them only a limited front along which to attack, and they didn't even have ladders that Ebon had seen. How could they possibly hope to overrun their target?

Something told him they would find a way.

Ebon looked back at Twist to find the man watching him in turn. "Are we ready?" the leader asked.

"We are."

Twist glanced at the mercenaries to either side of Ebon, and it was only now the prince realized that he stood between the scantily dressed twin sisters.

"Recruits," Twist said to them, "you're responsible for our friend here. Try to look after him better than you did your last employer."

The twins scowled at Ebon as if he'd been the one who had spoken.

"I am Tali," the sister to his right said.

"And I am Mili."

"Be sure you don't mistake us . . ."

". . . we shall be testing you later."

Twist raised his voice to carry to his troops. "Okay, listen up. Here's what's gonna happen. Our friend here"—he nodded to Ebon—"is gonna punch a hole in the stone-skins' ranks, then the race is on to see who can fill it first. Keep them engaged on the flanks and make our numbers count. Word is these stone-skins know their business, but let's see for ourselves."

"What if the bastards charge us?" someone said.

"Then we throw them back, of course. And don't go worryin' about them havin' the high ground. Just makes it easier for us to get our weapons under their guard, right?" He started up the ramp, and the troops around him lurched into motion. "Nice and steady," Twist said. "Keep the line straight. Fun don't start till we get in close."

Ebon followed Vale. His heart was thumping. He'd never stood in a shield wall before, and never imagined he would, either—even if it was only in the second rank. Such was the gradient of the ramp, his leg muscles burned after only a handful of steps. From the direction of the Chain Tower came more shouting. It was the Gilgamarian defenders who made the noise. There was an eerie silence about their red-cloaked foes that put Ebon in mind of the Vamilians in the Forest of Sighs who had fought and fallen without a sound. From among the stone-skins at the top of the ramp, there were no orders shouted at the Revenants' approach, no words spoken to give encouragement. But unlike Mayot's undead charges, these stone-skins could die. Ebon had seen the man crushed beneath the portcullis, witnessed two more shot down as they ran along the wall.

There were nine stone-skins in the enemy wedge. The woman at the center seemed to be looking straight at Ebon as if she knew what was coming. He had to fight an urge to draw his sword even though he knew he wouldn't need it.

Twenty paces.

The Revenants inched up the punishing slope, saving their strength for the last dash. Where their line overlapped the stone-skins, the mercenaries edged forward to envelop the enemy formation. Beside Ebon, one of the twins—he'd already forgotten who was who—whistled a merry tune.

Fifteen paces.

The three stone-skins who'd been holding their shields high swung them forward to join the wedge. This would have been a good time for the Gilgamarians to shoot their crossbows, but no one appeared at the parapet. Perhaps they were all staring at the approaching enemy fleet.

Ten paces.

Ebon gathered his power so he was ready to strike the instant Twist gave the order.

Any moment now.

"Go!" the leader shouted.

Ebon lashed out at the woman at the center of the stone-skin formation. His power crumpled her metal shield and lifted her from her feet. She was hurled back into the portcullis with a force that set the gate rattling. Her helmet flew from her head. Then she flopped forward and hit the ground face-first, unconscious. The man to her left was punched from his feet, while the one on her right was sent staggering back to collide with the tower. His shield fell from his grasp. Even the enemy warriors standing outside *them* felt the force of Ebon's strike. They grunted and shifted, their shields clanging at the impact like they'd taken a blow from a mace.

Vale was already halfway to the shattered line, Twist a step behind. The Revenants to either side roared as they surged forward, leaving Ebon alone with the twins. The clash was as good as over before it had even begun.

Or it should have been.

There was something unreal about the way the stone-skins responded to Ebon's attack. There was no moment of disbelief or panic, nor were any orders given. Yet the two stone-skins who had taken the imaginary mace-blows moved smoothly across to fill the space vacated by the men driven back. Meanwhile, *those* two warriors— already recovering—returned to the ranks in new places. *As if they had practiced this scenario a thousand times in training.* Against any foe other than Vale, the stone-skins might have re-formed the wedge in time to meet the Gray Cloaks' charge. The Endorian, though, was too quick for them. He parried a spear thrust, then burst between two shields and into the space beyond.

Even then the red-cloaked warriors reacted with an unnatural unity of purpose. The woman on the extreme right turned to engage Vale while her companions shuffled round to close the gap she had left. For an instant it looked like Vale might be vulnerable, isolated within the stone-skin wedge, but then the Revenants came surging up against their formation, stopping any more of the enemy from turning to attack the timeshifter. Twist was the first to reach the red-cloaked warriors. He swayed around a spear tip before dipping his shoulder and driving his own shield into that of the stone-skin in front of him.

Ebon gathered his power again, ready to strike if Vale needed him. The woman facing the Endorian had dropped her spear and drawn a shortsword. Of the hundreds of opponents Ebon had seen his friend fight, the majority had managed no more than a single block before falling to his blade. The stone-skin, though, parried once, twice, then attempted a shield-bash. Vale side-stepped. That step brought him up against the portcullis. If there had been stone-skins on the other side, they could have attacked him through the bars. But the tower must have been empty, for no spears stabbed out from the gloom. Vale aimed a cut at his opponent's neck, and the woman was slow to raise her shield. She fell in a crimson spray.

Heartbeats later, the clash was over as Vale cut down the remaining stone-skins from behind.

Ebon climbed the slope to join him. Twist, holding a sword with a hooked tip, was frowning at a dead stone-skin as if he might have seen the man before. The mercenary had emerged from the fighting unscathed, but there were plenty among his companions who had taken injuries. Ebon saw Beardy crouch next to a woman with a bloody froth at her lips and a hole in her side. The mercenary's face turned white as lederel milk as the wound closed up to a furious scar. Three Revenants lay unmoving on the ramp. The remaining mercenaries tipped the stone-skin corpses off the ramp and into the harbor, or shouted up to the Gilgamarians on the battlements to come down and raise the portcullis.

Ebon looked along the wall toward the next tower. One down, one to go.

Assuming they could take the second tower before the third one fell, of course.

Senar strode toward the Alcazar. A crowd of soldiers had gathered outside to watch the fighting on the seawall. As yet there was no sign of them going to help their companions, but Senar was sure they'd be sending moral support. Nothing like moral support, after all, to shield you from an enemy's blade.

Inside, a group of men in wigs stood in a circular entrance hall, awaiting their turn in front of whatever council was convened behind a door to Senar's left. The Guardian swung into the corridor leading to the South Wing. A female servant was coming the other way, alternating between a brisk walk and a trot. Senar had to suppress an urge to break into a jog himself, but if the fighting had already spread to the Alcazar, wouldn't he have heard it? Wouldn't the Gilgamarian guards be doing more than simply gawking at the wall?

Like running away, perhaps.

Senar increased his pace. Things came together in his mind. The assault on the wall meant the Augerans were trying to lower the chains, which in turn meant their fleet must be on its way. There were too many stone-skins on the wall to have come from the *Eternal*, suggesting the bulk of the attackers had entered Gilgamar in a second ship—a ship from which Hex had shrewdly drawn attention by arriving in a steel-clad vessel that caught the eye like no other. So was the wall the Augerans' only target here? Senar doubted it. Because if Hex's party had intended to link up with their kinsmen, there would have been no need for the group on the *Eternal* to disappear. Their target must be a different one to the chains.

Avallon. And that would mean striking at the Alcazar.

So where was Hex now? The assault on the wall was surely his signal to attack the emperor, yet the corridors around Senar were still. The only sounds were the squeak of his boots and the distant clamor of combat from the harbor—a clamor that rose as he passed each window, before falling away again. It couldn't last. The stone-skins would be close. Maybe they were even inside the Alcazar. With the South Wing empty but for Mazana's and Avallon's delegations, there were plenty of rooms to hide in. Yet how had the Augerans managed to infiltrate the building without a soul noticing? The same way they'd sneaked off the *Eternal*, probably.

Whatever way that was.

Senar turned into a corridor bright with trapped sunlight. Ahead, two Revenants holding spears—a man and a woman—barred his way. Their expressions were bored. A reassuring presence, to be sure. But there'd been four Gray Cloaks guarding the *Eternal*, and they had died without even putting up a fight. As Senar approached, the mercenaries parted for him. The woman had a ring through her nose; the man a scar that ran over his scalp, parting his hair.

"Trouble?" the woman said as the Guardian strode past.

He nodded. "And we're next."

Senar's mind drifted. How many Revenants were stationed in the South Wing? Two dozen? Three? There was also the executioner, of course, as well as a sizeable number of Breakers. Not to mention Kiapa and the emperor's bodyguard, Strike. Any stone-skin party would have to be strong indeed to overcome such a force. Yet Senar still found himself wishing he'd asked Twist to accompany him back to the Alcazar, rather than sending him and his men to the wall. On the other hand, if the subcommander *had* been here, he would probably have been too busy fighting his own side to pose any threat to the enemy—

The Guardian's musings were interrupted by a crack behind, as if the two Gray Cloaks had slammed the butts of their spears into the ground. Senar swung round, his hand on the hilt of his sword.

And stared.

A portcullis had dropped across the corridor behind the mercenaries—a portcullis he was reasonably sure hadn't been there moments ago. There wasn't even a hole in the ceiling it could have come from.

A close thing, the portcullis falling when it had. Only time would tell if it had been good luck or bad that he'd ended up on this side.

"What the shit?" the female Revenant said.

More cracks sounded from behind Senar, and he turned to see bars descending over the windows. As each one fell, the light in the passage faltered. A deeper darkness gathered beyond the next intersection. It crept toward Senar, bruising the walls, floor, and ceiling. A new world was unfurling, he realized. His first thought was of the portal that Romany had opened yesterday, not far from here. But through that gateway he had spied another land entire, whereas this realm was overlapping the Alcazar rather than replacing it.

Behind him the portcullis rattled as the Gray Cloaks tried to lift it. Senar did not go to their aid. There would be no escape that way, and he wouldn't have even taken it if there had.

The darkness from along the corridor rolled toward him.

As the gloom washed over him, he shivered. About him the walls had darkened to the color of old blood, and there were speckled black patches like mold spores. It was as if the Alcazar had decayed a hundred years in as many heartbeats. Senar lifted his hand, half expecting to see his skin tarnish in the same way. For now, though, it remained hale. He peered along the corridor. The windows were bright squares on the walls, but the sunlight couldn't pierce the shadows in the passage. In the distance, the faintest smudge of red enlivened the gloom. A scraping noise reached the Guardian, like a sword being dragged along the floor.

Then over that suddenly came the clash of weapons, a chorus of competing shouts, one giving way to a scream.

Drawing his sword, Senar set off into the murk.

"Come with me," he said to the two Revenants, but they made no move to follow. He didn't stop to reason with them. If they meant to stay put, he couldn't force them to change their minds.

That darkness along the corridor was a good deal more threatening than he would be, after all.

Ebon looked out through the archway in the Key Tower to see an enemy catapult-stone coming toward him. He ducked back, and it glanced off the side of the turret, setting the stronghold juddering. Splinters of rock pattered down onto the wall. The ship that had loosed that stone was positioned opposite the tower on a wave of water-magic. Ebon could make out the faces of the archers on its decks, see three warriors heave another rock into its catapult's cup. Beyond, the fleet of stone-skin ships stretched out in two lines along the length of the wall. A vessel beyond the Buck Tower had secured lines to the parapet so the foe on board could cross to the wall. No one was making the traverse now, though.

"Move it!" the woman behind Ebon said, and he set off along the wall in a half crouch. As he passed the Gray Cloaks at the arrow slits, he listened to the whip of enemy missiles flying overhead. In front, more mercenaries waited beside the Buck Tower's portcullis. Four had their shields pressed against the bars to stop the stone-skins inside shooting their crossbows out. Another held still a rope hanging down from the battlements. As Ebon reached him, the man thrust the rope into his hands. Up Ebon had to go, the breeze tugging at his clothes, his chest muscles tensed against the arrow he felt sure was coming. To his right, a missile clacked off stone. As he reached a barred window, he caught the stench of burned flesh from inside.

Vale waited at the parapet to haul him over. For a while Ebon lay on his back, staring up at the sky. Then a man to his left shouted, "Shoot!" and Ebon looked across to see a Gilgamarian soldier yank on a cord to release a catapult's arm. The arm snapped forward and released its stone before thudding into a padded beam with a force that set the air thrumming. The rear end of the catapult kicked like a mule and came down rattling. The weapon was manned by half a dozen soldiers. More Gilgamarians stood at the arrow slits on the opposite side of the tower, along with the Revenants who had made the climb before Ebon. To the prince's right, a spiral staircase descended into the tower. Two mercenaries were stationed there to look out for stone-skins attacking from below.

"This way," Vale said.

Ebon rose and followed him across the tower.

He looked down at the stretch of wall next to the Chain Tower.

He'd expected to see the stone-skins attempting to scale the tower's battlements. Instead all he saw was a group of red-cloaked warriors huddled behind their shields. A single rope attached to a grapnel hung down from the Chain Tower's parapet, but even now it was being lifted by a Gilgamarian soldier and cast into the harbor. Arrows flashed down from the turret's arrow slits to clank against stone-skin shields. Beside the enemy warriors, four ropes hooked to the ramparts extended down to a three-masted ship a stone's throw away. But there were still no stone-skins shimmying up the rope to reinforce their kinsmen. What would be the point? Another twenty, fifty, even a hundred warriors wouldn't have been enough to take the Chain Tower.

Ebon frowned. The sight of the enemy clustered helpless on the wall should have inspired relief, yet something about this business smelled wrong. He did a head count. Thirty red-cloaked warriors were on the battlements, with another dozen bobbing lifeless in the harbor. But a hundred had taken part in the attack on the Key Tower, which meant around sixty of the enemy must be sheltering in the tower below him. What were they doing down there, admiring the architecture? Ebon caught the eye of the Gilgamarian soldier at the nearest arrow slit.

"How long have they been like that?" he said, nodding at the stone-skins on the wall.

"Since not long after the attack began," the man replied. "Fools have been giving us target practice. A few strapped their shields to their backs and tried to scale the Chain Tower, but they still made for easy pickings. Highest anyone got was halfway up before they were feathered. It didn't take the others long to realize they were wasting their time."

"Have the ones below us tried to attack up the stairs?"

"No. Feinted to do so a couple of times, but never went through with it."

Ebon looked at Vale. Never went through with it? But there were only a dozen Gilgamarians up here. And surely capturing this tower was a necessary first step to attacking the next, for by doing so, the stone-skins would not only dispose of the archers stationed here, but also gain a position from which to shoot at the Gilgamarians on the Chain Tower. So why hadn't they tried? True, they couldn't have known exactly how many soldiers were posted up here, but to not even test the defenders' strength . . .

Perhaps the stone-skins had gambled on reaching the Chain Tower
before its portcullis was lowered. Or perhaps their intelligence on the
wall's defenses was—

A cheer from one of the Gilgamarian archers interrupted his
thoughts. He glanced over the battlements again. Four stone-skins sat
on the parapet next to the fixed lines, facing out to sea. Their spears
rested on top of the ropes. The nearest to Ebon, a woman, placed her
hands on the spear shaft—one to either side of the cord—then leaned
forward so the weapon took her weight. Legs kicking, she went
sliding down the inclined rope toward the deck of the stone-skin
ship below.

They're pulling out.

Four by four, the red-cloaked warriors zipped along the ropes.
Their kinsmen who'd been sheltering in the tower now emerged onto
the wall, the warriors with shields protecting the ones without.

All of the Gilgamarians cheered now, but Ebon didn't feel like
celebrating. Neither did the Revenants, judging by the fevered conversation going on between Twist and a handful of his colleagues.

"It's a feint," Ebon said to Vale. "This whole attack. They never
really tried to take the Chain Tower because that was never their
target. They just wanted us to think it was."

Vale's expression was characteristically grim. "So what *is* their
target?"

Ebon wished he knew. None of this made sense. The only way the
stone-skin fleet could get into the harbor was past the chains. And
since the mechanism to lower them was on *this* side of the Neck . . .

A grinding sound came from the direction of the Chain Tower,
followed by a splash and a swish of water.

Ebon's blood ran cold.

One of the chains was down.

The Gilgamarians weren't cheering anymore. Had the stone-skins
managed to smuggle a force into the Chain Tower by a different route?
Or were there traitors among the defenders?

No, that couldn't be right, for if the chains had been lowered, they
would have been lowered all together. Whereas Ebon had heard but
a single splash.

Twist headed toward the stairs, and the prince set off after him.
The Chain Tower, that was where he needed to be.

The Chain Tower would hold the answers.

Amerel squinted against the glare of the light reflecting off Gil-gamar's seawall. The stone-skin fleet had deployed in two lines parallel to it, nine ships in each. Even on their waves of water-magic, the vessels weren't able to maneuver their sides flush to the wall, because it was shielded by boulders streaked red with fireweed.

From a distance that fireweed made it look like the stones were daubed with blood, yet there was little enough fighting taking place on the wall. The stone-skins had gained control of the battlements to the *east* of the chains. It was the fate of the Chain Tower on the *west* side that would decide Gilgamar's destiny, though, for it was here that the mechanism to lower the chains was housed. A scattering of Augerans had gathered on the wall below it. Amerel watched four red-cloaked figures cast grapnels up to the battlements. Three missed with their throws, while the fourth managed to climb a mere handspan up his rope before it was cut from above.

The Guardian blew out her cheeks. There was something strangely halfhearted about their efforts. Like they knew they couldn't take the tower and were simply going through the motions. Perhaps their num-bers were too few, but then why weren't more Augerans crossing to the wall? The closest stone-skin ship had secured lines to the para-pet, yet no warriors moved along them to reinforce their kinsmen on the battlements.

Noon leaned on the rail next to Amerel. "Are we just going to sit here and watch?"

"A chair would be lovely, thank you."

Attacking the stone-skin fleet would be suicide, and pointless to boot, since the real fight—if you could call it that—was taking place on the wall. Besides, Amerel had done her part. The rest was down to the dragons if they ever showed up. And if they *did* show up, the last place she wanted to be was close to the stone-skins' ships.

Tattoo climbed to the maintop and peered through his telescope at the city. He called down to Galantas, "It's her, Captain, I swear it. See the glint to the right of the harbor entrance?"

Galantas nodded.

Amerel caught the gaze of the quartermaster at the wheel. "What's going on?"

"Spotted the *Eternal,* is my guess," the man said.

"The *Eternal?*"

"Captain's ship—his old one."

Of course: the metal monster Amerel had seen in Bezzle. When she looked toward Gilgamar, all she could make out above the wall were the masts of the ships at quayside. "That telescope can look through walls, can it?"

"Main trunk is capped with steel," the quartermaster said. "Can spot it a league off. Captain likes to cover it up when we go about our business. But it weren't covered when the stone-skins took her."

So the Augerans had taken the *Eternal* to transport their raiding party here? Not the ship she would have chosen for a surprise attack.

Amerel wiped a hand across her sweat-sheened forehead. On the journey north, the wind of the *Fury*'s passage had cooled her, but there was no breeze now to take the edge off the heat. She looked east. Where in the Matron's name were the dragons? The clash at the Rent had scarcely delayed the Augerans, but still Mokinda should have long since reached the Dragon Gate. Had he had second thoughts about releasing the creatures? Or met resistance from the governors of Dian and Natilly?

Then again, would Amerel even be able to see the dragons before they attacked? What if they stayed below the water until they closed on their targets? What if the first she knew of their coming was when one rose beneath a stone-skin ship?

Or beneath the *Fury*, perhaps.

A nervous glance at the waters off the starboard bow.

Nothing.

A rock thrown by an Augeran catapult ricocheted off the Chain Tower and into the waterway beyond. The concussion sounded across the sea, momentarily drowning out the hiss of the waves carrying the stone-skin ships. On the battlements to the west, the Augerans had started sliding down the lines to the waiting ship. . . .

Amerel frowned. Wait, sliding *down*? Were they withdrawing? Had they already given up on taking the tower?

A scraping, clanking noise reached her, and she watched wide-eyed as the topmost chain slithered free and splashed into the sea. What the hell? The chain hadn't been lowered, it had been . . . cut. And it couldn't have been lowered anyway, since it had fallen on the *eastern* side of the Neck, not the *western* side where the Chain Tower was located.

But cut? How?

Noon whistled between his teeth. "That changes things."

"Not for us, it doesn't."

"If the chains fall, so does Gilgamar."

"We didn't come here to save Gilgamar. We came to watch the dragons destroy the stone-skin fleet."

"And how are they going to do that if the fleet's tucked up in the harbor?"

"Why, by following them in, of course. The Augerans will have cut the chains. Can't just reattach them afterward."

"What if the stone-skins are ashore by the time the dragons get here?"

Amerel shrugged. "So the dragons destroy empty ships, I can live with that. It still leaves the Augerans stranded in Gilgamar, with a Sabian League up in arms around them."

The Breaker looked unconvinced.

It was all academic anyway. Even if Amerel had wanted to help—and could persuade Galantas to do so—how was the *Fury* going to stop the chains being cut? Three more sorcerous globes might account for three more stone-skin ships, but what then? She looked over her shoulder to the south. The encounter at the Rent had enabled the other two Rubyholt vessels to recover ground on the *Fury,* but the subsequent dash to Gilgamar had strung them out again. The closest was half a league away, the next a mere blur on the horizon. By the time they got here, this would be over. Their water-mages were probably powering down now to make sure of it. And even if they *did* arrive in time, how could a mere three Rubyholt ships change the course of the battle?

A lookout shouted, "Two sails bearing down, captain! One to port, one to starboard!"

Amerel started. Stone-skin ships?

She swung her gaze round and saw two vessels approaching the *Fury* on waves of water-magic, a two-master from the east, a three-master from the west. The demon figurehead, crooning softly before now, found its voice again.

"Get us out of here," Galantas said to Barnick.

The mage did not reply. His expression was dark.

"Mage!"

"We're not going anywhere," Barnick said. "Whenever I try to raise a wave, one of the stone-skins cancels me out. Another water-mage. On that ship there." He pointed to the three-master approaching from the west.

Galantas's voice was flat. "A water-mage strong enough to nullify your magic and still conjure up a wave beneath his own ship?"

Barnick scowled.

Galantas looked at Amerel. "What about you?"

Me? Ah, of course, after her exploits at the Rent, he thought she was a water-mage. "My hands are tied."

"What do you mean your hands are tied?" he snapped. "You destroyed two ships at the Rent, but now you've got nothing?"

Yes, that would take some explaining later. "I can deal with one of the ships when it arrives, but the other will likely close with us in the meantime."

Galantas stared at her, then waved his hand in disgust. With the enemy just moments away, it wasn't as if he could argue. "Then target the ship to port," he said, turning away. "Once Barnick's water-mage is dead, maybe we can withdraw before the other ship gets here."

Withdraw. Like this was a tactical maneuver rather than a race for their lives.

Amerel spun about and headed for the bow.

Behind her, Tattoo started screaming orders: "Prepare to repel boarders! Archers to the tops! Axes ready to cut the lines!"

The devilship shrieked its joy.

Amerel weaved a path across the main deck through the sailors scampering to take up positions. She could see the stone-skin ships more clearly now, both smaller than the *Fury*, both crawling with enemy warriors. They were coming in fast, no doubt anxious to close with the devilship before they suffered the same fate as the ships at the Rent. The one to the east—Amerel's target—had a hole in the main topsail where a catapult stone had ripped through it.

Noon caught up to her at the port cathead. His voice was strained from the effort of resisting the devilship's song. "There's another option," he said. "You take one globe; I'll take another. When the second ship gets close I'll throw—"

Amerel raised a hand to cut him off. "And how close would that ship have to get before you could be sure to hit it?" Too close for comfort, probably. "No, we stick to the plan: take the first ship out, hope the other turns and runs. Or that Barnick can keep us far enough away from it for me to take it out after."

"You're the boss," Noon said. He reached into his belt-pouch. "Earth, air, or fire?"

"Surprise me."

The concussion of Cayda's sorcery was so loud it should have left cracks in the sky. The Augeran galleon's oarports blew open, its sides exploded outward, and the quarterdeck, along with the stone-skins on it, was lifted into the air. Overhead, the mizzen yard cracked, and one of the sails was torn free to go billowing into the sky. A red-cloaked Augeran must have been standing above the very point of detonation, for he was launched toward the *Fury* as if he'd been shot from a catapult. He sailed through the air, limbs flopping, before hitting the sea midway between the two ships.

As his body disappeared beneath the waves, Galantas was staggered by a gust of wind from the blast. It tangled in the *Fury*'s sails, and the vessel slewed round. Splinters rained down on deck. Galantas closed his eyes. All about him the air screeched and whistled, but all he could think about was how Cayda had managed to unleash such destruction. *Air-magic.* He'd worked that out all by himself. But wasn't the woman meant to be a water-mage? True, the most powerful sorcerers could manipulate not only their own element but also the element over which it was dominant. Their control over that second element, though, was supposed to be shaky at best. Yet Cayda had demonstrated an equal command over water and air—a command few mages could match over even their primary element.

When Galantas opened his eyes again, the broken remains of the stone-skin galleon were sinking. Within heartbeats, only the bowsprit showed above the surface. Then that too vanished from sight. The wind dropped to a sigh. Corpses bobbed on the drunken waves. A mist of blood hung over them.

Movement from the corner of Galantas's eye, and he looked across.

The other stone-skin ship was still heading toward them. After Cayda's show of force, Galantas had wondered if the Augerans would remember important business elsewhere. Instead they came on more swiftly.

Barnick began to raise a wave beneath the *Fury*.

Galantas put a hand on his arm. "No," he said.

"What?"

Instead of responding, Galantas looked at Amerel. The stone-skin ship was now just fifty lengths away. Was it too close for Cayda to repeat her fireworks without also taking down the *Fury*? And if so, did she have the strength to unleash another blast? Perhaps Cayda was contemplating the same, for she stared at the enemy vessel with an uncertain expression.

Then she met his gaze.

And shook her head.

Galantas's mind worked furiously. A moment ago, he had despaired at his plight, but now he saw an opportunity in it. He'd had enough of running. It was time to make a stand, and that meant accepting the challenge the stone-skins' advance represented. A part of him knew this was madness. Forty Rubyholters against hundreds of stone-skins? More importantly, forty pirates against hundreds of battle-hardened warriors? It didn't matter that the enemy couldn't bring all of those hundreds to bear at once, because force of numbers was sure to tell eventually. This wasn't a fight the Islanders could win.

At that instant, though, Galantas didn't care. It was the devilship's influence, he knew. The demon bound to its frame was poisoning his thoughts, so much so that when an Augeran arrow thudded into the binnacle, Galantas felt the *Fury's* rage as a rush of blood to his face. His crew would feel it too. If they could use that rage against the stone-skins, that would even the odds somewhat. Plus if Galantas took a battle here, might his kinsmen on the other ships be shamed into joining him? He looked south at the *Willow Reed*. At the rate Tub was approaching, he should arrive in time to play some part in the conflict.

But the Needle had only nine warriors with him. Why should he court death now when he'd worked so hard to stay out of trouble at the Rent?

Galantas pushed his doubts aside. Sometimes the odds were stacked so high against you that you *had* to run them. And if he could find a way to win, his name would become legend in the Isles. If he couldn't, well, he wouldn't be around to worry about it.

"No," he said again to Barnick. "We fight."

The mage considered, then shrugged. Of all those aboard the *Fury*,

Barnick had least to fear from a battle, because if the Rubyholters lost, he could simply jump overboard and swim to safety.

The wave beneath the *Fury* receded.

The stone-skin two-master drew closer.

Some of Galantas's crew shouted to him to find out what was happening, but he did not answer. Let them assume Barnick had been prevented from carrying them clear by the stone-skin mage on the approaching ship. In any case, the rising bloodlust inspired by the devilship would soon take his kinsmen past caring.

Galantas retreated to the break of the aft deck.

With the stone-skin ship riding high on its wave of water-magic, all he could see of the enemy was the first line of warriors at the starboard rail. They carried shields that sparkled in the sunlight. More arrows whipped toward the *Fury,* and a choked scream sounded from on high. When Galantas looked up, he saw a crewman with a shaft through his throat tumble from the crosstrees, only for his leg to catch in the rigging. He hung suspended above the main deck. When a drop of his blood fell to the boards, the devilship's response was like a shot of oscura in Galantas's veins.

Someone started singing the Scourge. Within moments the rest of the crew took it up, their eyes fever-bright. Galantas wanted to join in, but a captain had to remain apart. One man dipped his fingers in the dead archer's blood on the deck and smeared it across his cheeks. Others banged the hilts of their weapons against the boards. Some idiot of a Squall decided to show defiance by standing up and twirling his sword over his head. An arrow through his eye shut him up. As he collapsed to the deck, Galantas felt another jolt in his blood.

The quartermaster crouched behind the ship's wheel. "Drefel," Galantas said, "we need a reserve. Pick five men and bring them here."

Drefel nodded and scuttled away.

Qinta took his place at the main deck's rail, and beside him was Noon. The Storm Islander was plainly fighting to keep his emotions in check, for his eyes were closed, and he was taking deep breaths. Cayda, by contrast, stood relaxed beside the mainmast. She seemed in no hurry to take part in the fighting, but her turn would come.

Galantas remembered then the alien sorcery unleashed against the *Lively,* Allott's talk of the ship's rigging coming to life. He glanced at the lines overhead.

Nothing.

"Here they come!" Qinta shouted.

The wave beneath the stone-skin ship receded. The dregs of it slapped into the *Fury*'s hull, throwing up a shower of spray that drenched the men squatting behind the rail. Galantas's bladder felt fit to burst. A dozen grapnels arced out from the Augeran ship. Most were caught by the crouching Rubyholters and tossed back, but a handful bit on the *Fury*'s rail. Someone with an ax rose to chop at a line, only for Qinta to haul him back down.

"Wait till she's made secure!" the Second bellowed.

The ships came together with a thud.

Twenty black-cloaked stone-skins boiled over the gunwale.

The *Fury*'s crew rose to meet them, shrieking as they wielded their swords and boarding pikes. Qinta raised his pike to intercept a female Augeran. A full armspan of the shaft punched through her chest and out of her back, and the Second drove the point into the stomach of another enemy to leave two stone-skins impaled on the same weapon. To his left, a Rubyholter had climbed to the rail and now jumped across to the Augeran ship as if he meant to take it single-handed. He succeeded in carving his sword through an opponent's neck before he was hacked down by a trio of stone-skins.

Galantas sensed Drefel at his shoulder, straining to join the fray.

"Wait," he said.

Sitting up in her bed, Romany watched her quarters transform. There was blood on the walls—spots, splatters, and smears—so old its color had faded from crimson to brown. There was blood on the floor too, sprinkled across tiles newly lined with cracks and edged with grime. There was even blood on the metal bars that had materialized over her window, mixing with darker patches of rust. Outside, the sky was a sharp blue, but inside the light had turned leaden as if the Alcazar were passing into dusk. Romany wrinkled her nose. The air smelled charred. And it wasn't wood burning, either.

She stood up and crossed to the door. Beneath her sandals, the floor felt sticky. From all about came a scuttling and a scratching as if rats moved behind the walls. Then Romany heard the reverberating footsteps of something huge lumbering along the corridor outside. Her spells of deception remained intact in the passage, meaning the owner of those steps probably didn't even notice her door as it approached. Yet still she held her breath. Must be the executioner, to set the floor trembling like that.

Romany wasn't minded to peek outside to check.

The footsteps receded.

Safe for now at least.

She looked about her. For all her shock at what had happened, she still found herself admiring the perverse artistry in Hex's creation. Okay, so the color scheme wasn't one she would have chosen, but there was no denying the man's sense of theater, or the skill with which he'd fashioned his conception. She reached out with her mind toward the wall. Hex's magic was like a skin spread over the stone. Spread thinly, too, but that was hardly surprising if it encompassed the entire Southern Wing. When she tried to pierce it with her sharpened awareness, her sorcery passed through as easily as a needle through mexin. Around the puncture, the blood and grime retreated to reveal a white circle of stone.

Interesting.

Romany's heart started to beat more easily. True, she'd made only a small hole in the Augeran's construction, but there was no reason to think that a large hole would prove more challenging. Escaping this otherworld should be a straightforward matter. If there were bars over the windows, there would probably be gates blocking the exits as well, yet all Romany had to do was find one and punch a hole in it. And while she'd have to pass through the corridors to get there, she'd have what remained of her web to warn her of trouble ahead—plus the skills she'd inherited as an assassin, if it came to a confrontation.

With her way out assured, she turned her mind to other considerations.

The noise of fighting came through her window from the floor below. Sorcerous concussions landed on her web like raindrops on a spider's weave, making the whole thing shudder. But still she was able to detect a concentration of Hex's power below and to her right—a concentration that surely signified the man's conscious will was being exercised. Worth investigating further?

Absolutely.

Returning to her bed, she lay down and let her spirit drift free of her body.

She floated through the door and into the corridor. It was darker here than it had been in her quarters, and beneath the blood and gore on the walls were veins that pulsed with a liquid sound. Romany grimaced. The charms of Hex's otherworld were already wearing thin, but in her spiritual form, those charms were no more dangerous to her than if the stone-skin had conjured up images of moonblossom and honeyheather. *Moonblossom.* She tried to hold that picture in her mind.

She drifted through the floor to the lower level. Explosions came from her left followed by blooms of fire. Fortunately her destination lay to her right, and she hastened in that direction. She could see barely twenty paces in front, which meant she heard before she saw the monstrosity approaching from the other direction: a naked man with a shuffling gait, whose fingers had been replaced with metal claws. Worse still, his head had been twisted round the wrong way and now lolled forward. Or should that be backward?

Romany sped past.

The concentration of Hex's power came from around the next corner, and the priestess knew then what her destination would be. *The room where Mazana met the emperor yesterday.* The room where they had agreed to meet again today. When she glided inside, she found the chamber bore no resemblance to the one she remembered. The desk was covered with so much blood it might have had a body dismembered on it, while the walls looked like leprous skin covered in lesions and blotches and cuts sewn together, the stitches still in place. Those cuts throbbed as if something moved behind them. The air was sprinkled with flies.

A portcullis had fallen across the door barring access to two Gray Cloaks in the corridor. Near the desk stood Mazana Creed alongside Kiapa, Jodren, and the executioner. There was no sign of the emperor or his retinue. Kiapa was stony-faced as he took in his surroundings, Jodren looked like he'd bitten into something rotten, while even the executioner wore a frown, as if he'd taken a wrong turn and was trying to work out where he'd ended up. Mazana's face was pale, yet her gaze was unwavering as she stared at a red-cloaked figure in front of her.

Hex.

Romany floated closer.

The Augeran looked as solid as the other people here, but the priestess sensed she was seeing merely a copy of the man, a sorcerous construct. His cloaked swirled about his legs as he performed an extravagant turn. He was talking to Mazana.

". . . trust you will find your new accommodation to your liking."

When the emira responded, her voice was mild—too mild, it seemed to Romany, considering her predicament. "I assume it's too late for me to take up that offer you made?"

"To deliver the emperor's head, you mean? I think you'll find we never needed your help on that score." Hex's next twirl took him closer to the gated door, and the Gray Cloaks beyond it retreated. "Forgive me if I leave you here, but you'll appreciate my priority must be the Erin Elalese. Never fear, though, I will be back for you sooner than you please. Hee hee!"

"You think you can hold me here?"

"Why not? We're a little far from the sea for you to call on your power."

Mazana smiled. "My power, yes." Then she shifted her gaze to the crimson-smeared desk as if noticing it for the first time. She rested a hand on it. "My, my," she said, looking back at the Augeran, "what do we have here? *Blood?*"

And suddenly Romany understood the reason for the woman's lack of concern. *Spider's blessing, the blood!* And so much of it, too! The priestess swallowed. What had Hex done?

Mazana closed her eyes and opened her arms. All about, blood started coming away from the surfaces across which it was daubed— fat red drops where it was fresh, thin brown flakes where it was dried. It drifted toward her. Where it came into contact with her flesh, it was absorbed. Her skin turned first crimson, then purple-red, then red-black. Her lips parted, and she let out a shuddering breath. The air in the room shuddered with her, the very Alcazar seeming to sigh. Flies alighted on her arms and legs.

Then she opened her eyes to reveal orbs the same hue as her skin.

Jodren and Kiapa, standing to either side, stepped back. The executioner, by contrast, might have not noticed the change for all his reaction. Hex, too, showed no alarm at her transformation. But then the stone-skin wasn't even watching her, Romany realized with a start. Instead he appeared to be looking . . .

Straight at her.

Her heart skipped a beat. No, it wasn't possible!

He winked at her with the eye above that always-bleeding cut. A red tear rolled down his cheek.

Then he looked back at Mazana and gestured.

The sewn cuts on the walls ruptured in sprays of pus and blood. From one, a two-headed . . . thing emerged, dripping slime. From another was disgorged a seething mass of spiders, bloodroaches, and other creatures Romany wasn't hanging around to identify. She'd seen enough already, thank you very much.

She fled back to her body.

CHAPTER 21

SENAR LOPED along the corridor, squinting into the gloom. The temptation to break into a run was strong, but he couldn't see more than a dozen steps ahead, and he wasn't about to pick up his pace if it meant blundering into the laps of the enemy. A staircase materialized from the murk, but he ignored it. The sounds of battle all came from the lower level.

With each step he took, the temperature rose. At times he thought he could hear footsteps tracking his own, yet always when he looked back he saw nothing but darkness. The walls were spattered crimson like someone had gone berserk in a slaughterhouse. There were bloody prints on the ground as well, following the same course he was.

Showing him the way to go.

Round the next corner, a naked figure awaited him. Senar's pulse kicked in his neck. Not a stone-skin, but a man covered in weeping cuts and wrapped in coils of knotted wire. The wire opened up more gashes as he parted his arms to draw the Guardian into a prickly embrace. Senar lashed out with his Will, and the apparition fell against a wall with a screech of metal on stone that set the Guardian's teeth on edge. The man righted himself just in time to meet Senar's sword swing. The blade tore open his throat before snagging in a loop of wire. Senar wrenched his weapon free.

The apparition collapsed. A smell of decay hit Senar like he'd carved a chunk out of a piece of putrid meat. Maggots squirmed in the dead man's cut.

The Guardian screwed up his face and went on.

From ahead came the *thump* of a sorcerous concussion, and the walls of the passage trembled. A rush of air, a patter of mortar. Another figure shambled into view: a woman with a shroud of hair hanging across her face. Along the ground she dragged a mace with a head so large Senar doubted even the executioner could have lifted it. The only thing she'd be harming with that thing was the floor tiles, yet when he drew near, he didn't stay his hand. There was no place for mercy in a battle. The enemy you spared one moment might cut you down the next.

His sword smashed her forehead to splinters. She toppled wordlessly, still clinging to the mace as if her hands were welded to its shaft.

If only all of Senar's opponents today would go down so easily.

Along the wall to the Guardian's right, the doors gave way to windows looking out on a murky courtyard. The sun was a gray smear overhead. Battling figures flitted through the gloom: Breakers, Revenants, and stone-skins, along with a panoply of the grotesque. Senar saw Kolloken amid the throng, his hair and face so slimed with blood and gore he might have sliced open an enemy's belly and shoved his head in. He traded sword strikes with a hunchbacked swordsman whose body twitched so violently it looked like he was seizing.

Beyond, the wall of the yard collapsed into rubble as a blast of sorcery struck it. Over the stones scuttled a woman with two extra arms instead of legs. She sprang at a gray-cloaked spearman, grasped his wrists in two of her hands while her other two reached for his throat. They went down in a tangle, then wrestled in the rubble until a stone-skin swordsman reared up and dispatched them both.

Senar blinked. So the Augerans were fighting the apparitions too? What in the Nine Hells was going on?

He slowed and scanned the yard for the executioner, knowing if the giant was there, then Mazana would be too. But there was no sign of either of them. Through an archway ahead, a swordsman backpedaled from the square into the Guardian's corridor. He wore a sleeveless white jerkin and trousers, and his blade whined as it cut through the shadows.

Strike.

The bodyguard's clothes seemed to glow in the darkness. He faced no fewer than three stone-skin opponents, but by withdrawing through the arch, he had prevented them from coming at him together. As the first—a woman—tried to follow, Strike's blade flickered out. The Augeran reeled back cradling her sword arm, her weapon jarring from her hand.

Then from the gloom along the passage another stone-skin appeared—a man so big he seemed to fill the whole corridor. He had golden spiral tattoos on his cheeks and forearms. Senar shouted a warning to Strike, but the bodyguard had already seen the danger and turned to face this new adversary. His sorcerous blade moved with freakish speed to intercept the Augeran's first stroke, yet still he could manage only a half parry, his opponent's sword bursting through to graze his shoulder. Strike retreated a step, his enemy following.

Senar couldn't use his Will on the stone-skin while Strike was between them. He rushed to the bodyguard's aid.

Too late.

A whirlwind exchange, and suddenly Strike's head was lifted from his shoulders by a backhand swing that seemed to pass through the bodyguard's block. Two jets of blood reared up like snakes from the stump of Strike's neck.

His legs buckled.

Swearing, Senar drew up. Avallon's bodyguard was dead, and he'd lasted no longer than a handful of heartbeats. Senar was under no illusions that he could have defeated the man so swiftly.

His tattooed conqueror was breathing mightily. Keeping his gaze on Senar, he knelt to wipe his blade on Strike's trouser leg, first one side, then the other, leaving crimson stripes on the cloth. Then he straightened. His frown gave him a studious, almost apologetic look, yet there was a note of arrogance too as if he wasn't sure Senar warranted the time it would take to cut him down. The stone-skin glanced into the courtyard. Would he snub the Guardian to join the larger battle? Would Senar let him?

Like hell he would.

He sheathed his sword, then extended his hand and used the Will to call Strike's blade to him. The weapon stuck for a moment in the bodyguard's grip. His sword arm pulled straight, then his body swiveled to face Senar and began sliding across the blood-streaked floor until the blade abruptly came free and flashed through the murk. Its hilt settled into the Guardian's palm. He closed his fingers around it.

The tattooed stone-skin smiled faintly.

A strange reaction, that, to Senar's display of power. In the Augeran's eyes there was a look akin to recognition, but if Senar had met the man before, he was sure he would have remembered. Then understanding came to him. *He doesn't recognize me, he recognizes the Will. He knows me for a Guardian.* There was more to it than that, though. Something in the stone-skin's look suggested Senar should know him too—should know something that had a bearing on their coming clash. Something that went beyond the skill the Augeran had shown in brushing Strike aside.

Senar gave the bodyguard's sword a swing. Its whine was like the buzz of a needlefly. The earth-magic invested in it made it light as a wooden practice blade. He'd owned a sword like this many years ago, a sword he'd taken from a Kalanese pasha that he'd assassinated outside Kal Kartin. Alas, a blade only held its enchantment for a few weeks, and there was never a powerful earth-mage around when you needed one to top up the sorcery.

Earth was dominant over air, meaning the weapon would cut faster through the air than a normal sword, and land with the weight of an anvil besides. Judging by the tattooed stone-skin's size, though— he was almost as big as the executioner—that was likely to afford the Guardian only parity in their duel.

He moved forward and halted in front of the pool of Strike's blood. The Augeran remained still. Who would attack first? Who was most content to wait if it meant keeping the other out of the fight in the yard?

From the opposite side of the square, the thunder of a sorcerous concussion rattled Senar's teeth. He caught a glimpse of the emperor, surrounded by Breakers.

Then the stone-skin kicked Strike's head toward him and charged in after it.

Amerel watched from behind the mainmast as stone-skins swarmed over the devilship's rail. Noon was in the thick of the action, fighting with two swords. The Breaker caught a stone-skin's thrust on one blade, then hacked down with the other, cutting clean through his opponent's shoulder. The Augeran's arm fell to the deck. As he opened his mouth to scream, Noon's shoulder caught him in the midriff and pitched him back into the woman behind. The Erin Elalese slashed his sword across her throat before she could recover. Continuing his swing, he chopped through the ankles of a man on the rail, and the Augeran toppled shrieking back into the close-packed ranks on the enemy deck.

Not bad. For a Breaker.

Up until this point, only black-cloaked stone-skins had been doing the fighting, but now a dozen Red Cloaks came howling into the fray. A woman leapt over the rail and exchanged a series of blows with Tattoo before tripping on the recently severed arm. The Rubyholter's backhand cut split her skull with a clicking sound that Amerel heard even above the tumult. Farther right, another Augeran charged in behind his shield and knocked two Islanders off their feet. For a moment there was a gap in the Rubyholt line, but as the stone-skin pushed through it, one of his fallen enemies grabbed his leg and sank his teeth into it. Maybe he'd missed breakfast. The Augeran bellowed and slammed the rim of his shield down onto his attacker's skull.

A swing of Noon's sword lifted the stone-skin's head from his shoulders, but more of the foe were pressing in behind.

Now, Galantas, Amerel silently urged.

Galantas had been holding back a reserve of men, and—right on cue—he drew his sword to signal the advance. Alas, such was the quantity of blood already on the deck that the charge became a slipping, slithering dash that carried one of the attackers straight onto the blade of an enemy swordsman. Another Islander barreled into a kinsman and knocked him into the Augeran he'd been fighting. All three went down. The two Rubyholters reacted first, grabbing a handful of their opponent's hair before ramming his head into the boards. *Crunch, crunch,* the stone-skin's face dissolved into blood and splinters of bone.

Shouts sounded from the south, and Amerel glanced across to see another Rubyholt ship rushing toward the *Fury* on a wave of water-magic. Improbably, it looked like Galantas's kinsmen meant to come to his aid. The way things were going, though, they would arrive too late. Amerel was needed on the main deck. Of course, she'd have liked nothing better than to wade into that shitstorm. First, however, she had a task to perform that might even the odds a little in the Islanders' favor.

The devilship's wailing made her head throb as she scanned the stone-skin ship. Unlike Barnick, the Augeran mage hadn't obligingly advertised his presence by wearing blue robes, yet picking him out should still be straightforward. . . .

There!

Sheltering beside the binnacle was a red-cloaked man half a head shorter than the two spearmen flanking him. At his hip was a sword with a gilded hilt too ostentatious to be anything but decorative. His eyes twitched this way and that, searching for an arrow with his name on it.

Gathering her power, Amerel reached out and curled her Will around the hilt of a dagger in the baldric of one of the mage's guards. She took a breath.

One movement to draw the knife from its scabbard, another to turn it and plunge it into the throat of the sorcerer.

The mage didn't even see the blow coming. It took him a heartbeat to process what had happened. Then he gave a frothy gurgle and raised his hands to his neck as if he thought he could staunch the flow of blood.

His two minders looked on, slack-jawed.

Amerel withdrew.

"Their mage is down!" Barnick shouted.

Galantas swayed back from a sword slash and felt his opponent's blade cut the air in front of his face. The Augeran blocked Galantas's counter, and their two swords locked long enough for Galantas to get a whiff of the stone-skin's last meal. Then the deck shuddered. That shudder would be Barnick's work, Galantas knew. The mage was stirring up the seas, thinking the Rubyholters were more used to fighting on a pitching deck than their foes. He seemed to be right too, for Galantas's assailant tottered back against the rail, then threw out his arms for balance.

Galantas ran him through. "Kill them!" he yelled. "Kill them all!"

Not that he expected anyone to hear him above the clamor, or be able to carry out his command if they did. His men were now battling just to hold their ground, for if the stone-skins pushed them back from the rail, they would be outflanked and overwhelmed. To his right six Augerans carrying shields had formed a wedge allowing their kinsmen to gain the *Fury*'s deck behind. A red-cloaked swordsman climbed to the rail only to take a Rubyholt arrow in the neck and topple backward. But more would surely follow in his wake.

Recognizing the danger, Qinta hurled himself at the wedge. His sword caught the rim of a shield and made the metal sing. Galantas moved to support him, but before he could reach his friend, a concussion sounded from within the ranks of the Augeran shield bearers. Air-magic. *Cayda*. The warriors staggered. Qinta charged in among them, swinging his sword two-handed. Beside him, the quartermaster, Drefel, aimed a clumsy stroke at another foe, but the stone-skin blocked the attack and retaliated with a cut that lopped off Drefel's left hand. A decisive blow you would have thought, yet Drefel's devilship-inspired madness was such that he didn't even register the wound. He thrust his stump into his opponent's face before dispatching him with a disemboweling cut.

Galantas felt the same madness tugging at him, but he would not yield to it. He had to hold on to his reason—to harness the *Fury*'s rage rather than give in to it. Because Drefel's fate had showed him what happened to those who drank too deep of the devilship's spirit. He threw himself at one of the surviving shield bearers. The man parried his strike, then unleashed a sequence of cuts and thrusts that had Galantas's sword twitching every way. When the feint came, he didn't pick it in time. His blade swung low just as the stone-skin brought his weapon high in a stroke intended to rob Galantas of his remaining arm. He tried to sway back, knew he was too late.

The Augeran's sword bounced off an invisible barrier. Then someone else's blade swung over the stone-skin's weapon and took the man in the throat.

He dropped to the boards.

Galantas glanced across to see who had saved him. Cayda, of course. She was already turning to find the next enemy. For a heartbeat Galantas could only stare after her, too bemused to question what had happened, too relieved to care.

If she kept saving his life like this, he might end up owing her one.

The deck trembled to the pounding of the combatants' feet. To the south, Galantas heard Tub's men singing as the *Willow Reed* sailed closer. Most likely Tub intended to veer off at the last moment, but at least this time he had the decency to *pretend* to attack before retreating. Some of Galantas's own crew were singing themselves. Not the Scourge now, but some new song that set his guts crawling and created an otherworldly harmony to the figurehead's voice. Galantas watched Wex spit its words in a Red Cloak's face even as the stone-skin drove a spear into his chest.

Another Augeran reared up in front of Galantas. The woman was grinning. Then a blow from a Rubyholt mace crumpled her skull, and she lost her smile with the rest of her face. Beyond, the Needle ship rushed closer. For a moment Galantas thought Tub meant to ram the exposed starboard side of the Augeran vessel. Then the wave of water-magic beneath the *Willow Reed* subsided, and the bowsprit swung round so that the two ships came together, flank to flank.

Hells, the man actually meant to attack! With ten fighters!

The *Willow Reed* thudded into the Augeran ship, and Galantas set his feet against the contact. A female stone-skin blundered into him. He pushed her off, then drove his sword through her neck. Black blood bubbled from the woman's mouth, and her lips twitched as if she were trying to speak, but no words came out.

Something caught in her throat, maybe.

Galantas looked for the next foe. More, he wanted more! The *Fury*'s song had taken the heaviness from his limbs so that he could barely feel the weight of his weapon. Through the maelstrom of combatants, he saw Tub's Needles attacking along the opposite flank of the Augeran ship. A brave move, but their numbers were so few the enemy didn't even have to redirect forces from their assault on the *Fury*. The tipping point was close, Galantas knew. For all the ferocity of his crew's defense, the stone-skins' superior numbers were starting to tell. The time to surrender, or at least to offer to, had surely come, but even as the idea came to him, it was swept away on a surge of bloodlust. The figurehead's voice was loud in Galantas's ears, promising him strength if he would only give in to it.

A female Augeran clambered onto the *Fury*'s deck. Galantas's sword thrust had her twisting away. Her feet tangled in a line, but another foe was already hurdling the rail, then another and another. Galantas was driven back toward the steps leading to the quarterdeck. The stone-skins came at him in a huddle, crouched behind their shields. A Squall launched himself at them like a ball at a rack of skittles, taking two of the warriors down.

Then someone behind Galantas shouted something in his ear. Something that quenched his bloodrage as surely as a bucket of water in his face.

It came again.

"Dragon from the east!"

Ebon emerged blinking onto the top of the Chain Tower. To his left the tower gave way to the wall that formed one half of the Neck, while to his right was a section of shattered parapet where a stone-skin rock must have struck it. The Chain Tower had its own catapult—a monstrous construction twice the size of the one on the smaller Buck Tower. The machine stood idle, its operators all crowding the eastern battlements. Ebon joined them and looked down to see the waterway below, fizzing white from the ever-breaking wave of water-magic carrying the nearest stone-skin ship. The chains—spotted with rust, and each so large Ebon couldn't have wrapped his arms around them—emerged from holes in the wall below him and disappeared into holes in the wall opposite. The highest chain had been severed and now hung flush to the wall on this side of the Neck.

On *this* side of the Neck. Meaning it had been cut on the other.

Ebon shifted his gaze to the hole across from him through which the chain had once passed. The stones around the opening looked singed, but there was no flicker of red to suggest a fire had been lit beyond. In any case, what fire could undo steel? On the battlements above, a handful of stone-skins stood about a catapult of equal size to the one behind Ebon. Evidently the enemy had launched a strike on *that* side of the wall as well as this, and with considerable success too. The stone-skins' position across the Neck would be all but unassailable now, assuming they'd captured the other forts along the wall. And of course they didn't need to hold out indefinitely—just long enough to take down the other chains so their ships could enter the harbor.

Ebon had to get across to that tower.

A Gilgamarian soldier hurled across the channel a grapple tied to a rope. It landed with a clatter on the opposite battlements. The soldier hauled on the rope, trying to make the grapple bite on the parapet, but before he could do so, a stone-skin seized the grapple and tossed it over the battlements. The Gilgamarian cursed and reeled it in again for another cast. Might as well not bother, though. Even if he could get a line over the Neck, there wouldn't be many volunteers

willing to pull themselves across it, under fire from the stone-skins
and without a free hand to hold a shield.

"More grapples!" someone shouted. "They can't throw twenty back
at once!"

Where were they going to find twenty grapples, though? How many
were kept in the tower on the off chance the soldiers needed to storm
a battlement instead of defend one? And Ebon suspected that the
stone-skins who'd gone zipping down those lines had been careful to
take theirs with them.

A steady flow of Revenants climbed to the battlements behind him,
and with them came a group of pale-skinned men, hard-faced and
bristling with threat. There was a whiff of bad blood between the
newcomers and the Gray Cloaks, but if they were spoiling for a fight,
they'd get one soon enough when the first stone-skin ship entered the
Neck. "Erin Elalese," Ebon heard one of the Revenants whisper, and
instinctively he looked for Luker Essendar among them—before
realizing the man was hundreds of leagues to the southwest.

With the Erin Elalese was a Mellikian with so many piercings
through his face it made Ebon's skin hurt just to look at him. The
man glided to the wall next to Twist and looked down at the channel below—looked so long that Ebon began to wonder if there was
something there that he'd missed. The rocks the stone-skins had
flung at the Chain Tower showed as wavering shadows beneath the
surface.

"How long since the first chain a-went down?" the Mellikian asked
of no one in particular.

It was a Gilgamarian officer who answered. "Tenth of a bell,
maybe."

"And no sign of a second chain following. That means whatever
the stone-skins are a-doing in that tower, it's taking time."

The Gilgamarian snorted. "Course it bloody is. Those chains are
reinforced with earth-magic. Should be impossible for the stone-skins
to drop them."

"And yet that thing a-hanging down from the wall below us—that
does look a *bit* like a chain, does it not?"

An Erin Elalese woman wearing an eyepatch spoke. "How many
chains have to come down before the stone-skins can get a ship over?"
she asked the Mellikian.

He considered. "Maybe three, maybe two. Depends how many of

their mages combine their wills. And how quickly they react when I
a-counter them."

Counter them? So the Mellikian was a water-mage too?

The woman with the eyepatch looked toward the harbor. "If you
brought a ship over here, we could climb down. Then you could ferry
us across—"

A shake of her companion's head cut her off. "I can't lift a ship as
high as that tower. So you'd still have the problem of a-scaling the
wall. Even if we had enough time to try, we don't have enough men."

"You got a better plan?"

"I do," Ebon said. The idea had come to him while he was looking
at the rocks in the waterway. They'd sparked a memory of a certain
river near Estapharriol, and of a shattered bridge that Galea had restored by raising the stones submersed in the water. "I might be able
to fashion a way across the channel with the rocks the stone-skins
have been throwing at us."

For a heartbeat everyone stared at him.

Then Twist said, "So what are you waitin' for? A Shroud-cursed
drumroll?"

Ebon already regretted opening his mouth. He'd only done this
once before, and that had been under Galea's guidance. "If I can do
this, it won't be so much a bridge as a line of stepping-stones. *Wet*
stones."

"And?"

"And if you slip and fall, I imagine you'll find swimming in your
armor a challenge."

"I ain't gonna slip. Now, are we done talkin' here, or should I pull
up a chair and get comfortable?"

Ebon gave a tight smile.

They made a space for him to work as if they thought the stones
he'd be maneuvering might come raining down around him. Perhaps
they would. Could he really say he knew what he was doing? In
Estapharriol he'd been restoring an old bridge, whereas here he'd
be fashioning something new. Did that make a difference? Should it?
He reached out with his power toward the nearest submerged rock,
and it rose into the air, dripping water. Simple enough, but what
about when he tried to lift another? Would the first one fall as he
shifted his focus to the second? Could he section off his mind enough
times to raise all the rocks he would need to make a crossing?

If this were the first time he'd attempted this—if he'd had to shape conscious thought to do the task—he suspected the answer would have been no. He suspected lifting even three rocks into the air would have been as hard as juggling the same number of balls. Galea, though, had left some imprint on his mind when she'd repaired the bridge in Estapharriol. It was as if she'd gifted him the skills of a master juggler, and now all he had to do was throw the balls in the air and decide in what pattern to make them dance. Up came the stones; five, six, seven, then more. One watery shadow turned out to be not a rock but a crayfish cage tangled with fireweed, another a rusted breastplate. These he let fall again.

He raised the glistening stones so they hovered in front of the battlements, keeping them bunched together so the stone-skins wouldn't know what he planned to do. Maybe they'd think he meant to hurl the rocks at their section of wall. He turned the stones over so the flattest side of each faced upward where a foot would tread. Then he counted them. Fifteen. Not enough to reach across the Neck, so he started adding to their number from the stones protecting the base of the harbor wall. The more rocks he used, the smaller the gaps he'd have to leave in the makeshift bridge.

From across the waterway he heard raised stone-skin voices, saw figures rushing along the battlements. They couldn't know what he planned to do, but they'd know *something* was in the offing. Doubtless they would call to their kinsmen in the tower below, summoning them to the wall.

He had spent as much time on this as he could allow himself.

He pushed the stones out in a line toward the opposite parapet. The spaces between them looked ominously wide until he told himself those spaces were better suited to a running stride.

Twist spoke. "Come on lads, line up. Shields to the front. No pushin', now—you ain't queuin' for your pay." Then, to the Gilgamarians, "Those that are stayin' behind, keep up a coverin' fire on the stone-skins—"

"We know our business," someone interrupted.

"Course you do. And if any craven in a gray cloak gets too precious about crossin' them stones, you have my permission to shoot him, y'hear? Can't have anyone holdin' up those comin' after."

Across the Neck, red-cloaked warriors were gathering at the point that Ebon's stones led to. Whoever was first across would be greeted by a sizable welcoming committee. Vale was in his peripheral vision. Without taking his gaze from the stones, Ebon reached out and put a hand on his friend's arm. "You don't have to go first this time. Let Twist have the honor."

Vale grunted and drew his sword. He already held a shield in his other hand. "If we're doing this, we may as well do it properly. I can take twice the care and still cross as fast as the next man."

As he moved toward the parapet, though, Twist blocked him off. "Not so fast there. Recruits!"

The twins slunk forward.

"Yes . . ."

". . . O Great One?"

"You're up!"

"Yes . . ."

". . . O Great One!"

Ebon frowned. The twins, really? The only ones in the Revenants' ranks who weren't wearing armor? Did Twist mean to use them as arrow fodder? If so, the sisters didn't seem daunted at the prospect, because they grinned as they accepted a shield each from one of their companions.

Ebon's line of stones was ready. The first twin sprang to the parapet, her shield held out before her. She extended a foot and prodded at the closest rock like she was testing the temperature of water. "Will these things . . ."

". . . bear our weight?"

Ebon shrugged. "Step on one, see what happens."

The sister leaned forward to put her weight on her front leg. Ebon tensed, expecting to feel her burden as a pressure in his mind.

Nothing. The stone appeared as solid as if it were anchored in mortar.

"Let's go!" Twist said. "Every moment we waste gives the stoneskins another moment to prepare."

The first twin nodded.

Then she went bounding across the rocks like an alamandra, apparently unhampered by her shield. Her sister followed, ponytail bouncing.

"Go, go, go!"

Vale was next over the parapet, and Ebon watched his friend start along the line of stones. The Endorian crossed in a series of bounds, putting two feet down on each rock before jumping to the next. Yet still he was able to keep pace with the twins. Of all those who would make the crossing, the Endorian was least likely to fall, but he was no less likely to catch a stone-skin arrow. Even as the thought came to Ebon, a missile clanged off Vale's shield. A stone-skin rose above the parapet to fire another shot, only to take two Gilgamarian arrows in the neck. He dropped out of sight.

Twist climbed to the wall behind Vale, while ahead the twins approached the midpoint of the Neck. The stone-skins had assembled to meet them on the opposite battlements. How many did they number? A dozen? Fifteen? The twins' moment of greatest vulnerability would be when they jumped down from the stones and found themselves assailed on three sides.

An idea came to Ebon. Dare he risk it? Yes, the twins had already shown they had the agility to make his plan work.

Focusing on the stones closest to the enemy battlements, he began altering their alignment so the second half of the crossing followed a gentle curve that would deliver the sisters to the left of the stone-skins' position. The first twin had time to see the rocks move and change course. The red-cloaked warriors tried to shift across, but before they could reset their formation, the woman reached the parapet. She launched into a somersault that took her over the head of the nearest stone-skin and onto the tower beyond.

Her sister leapt to the battlements behind her, Vale following.

A dozen Revenants were on the stones now. One man took an arrow in the shoulder that half spun him round and sent him toppling. Another lost his footing on the greasy rocks. As he fell he managed to catch the next stone along, only for the woman behind him to step on his hands. She lost her balance, and both mercenaries dropped shrieking into the water below. Ahead, Twist gained the battlements, but the next man tripped as he cleared the parapet and fell into a swinging enemy sword that took half his head off. The woman behind him had made the crossing with a small loaded crossbow in one hand. She fired it point blank into the face of her companion's killer.

Ebon looked for Vale and saw a flash of his friend, before losing him again behind a merlon. Vale had been fighting with Mili and Tali on either side, not using his sword against his opponents, but merely twitching his shield from side to side as he collected enemy spear thrusts. And how did you get past the shield of a timeshifter intent on defense? Twist and another mercenary, meanwhile, guarded the point where the stepping-stones met the parapet, allowing their fellows to gain the battlements safely.

Sensing the numbers turn against them, the stone-skins backpedaled toward the tower's stairwell.

Ebon risked a glance at the nearest enemy ship. It was difficult to be sure at this distance, but it looked like those on board were staring not toward the tower but east across the Ribbon Sea. A faint trumpeting sound reached the prince, yet he could not see the source. A signal between stone-skin vessels, perhaps? Would the foe turn their catapults on the tower now that their kinsmen were retreating? Would they try to bring more men over, or steer their ship closer to the chains so they could fire on the warriors crossing the stepping-stones?

The first of the Erin Elalese climbed to the parapet alongside Ebon. She made it only to the third rock before slipping and falling. The next man in line went off cursing and high-stepping like he was running on hot coals. After him came the woman with the eyepatch. As she started on her way, a rustling sigh sounded, and the links of the highest chain slithered out of the hole on the far wall like the coils of some monstrous snake. Coming free, it fell and slapped down onto the water before sinking from sight.

Ebon frowned. There went his safety net. How much time had passed between the first and second chains falling? Long enough for the defenders to prevent the third going the same way? He looked for Vale across the Neck, saw him lead a rush around the side of the stone-skin force, trying to flank them. When the battlements fell to the Revenants, Twist and his allies would face a scrap down a stairwell into the tower itself. And something told Ebon he had yet to see the best of what these stone-skins had to offer.

Assuming he got to see it all. If Vale had been with him, he'd have said Ebon had already done his part. That his abilities were best used in keeping the stepping-stones in place so more men could cross over the Neck. When had the prince ever been content to leave his fate in another's hands, though? Or let someone else do work that was rightfully his? He had chosen to help the defense of the city, and when you made a decision, you followed it through. You didn't leave someone else to live with the consequences.

A dozen Erin Elalese were currently on the stones, and a dozen more waited to cross. Yet more foreigners climbed to the battlements from the stairwell to Ebon's right.

He stepped in front of the newcomers.

"I'm next across," he said to the first man. "And I'll be the last."

On returning to her body, the first thing Romany noticed was the perceptions of the senses she had been denied while in spirit-form: the texture of the blanket beneath her fingers; the smell of burned meat that reminded her of the immolation of Mercerie's lepers six years ago. She swung her legs off the bed and stood up. Too quickly, as it turned out, for her spirit had not yet properly resettled in her flesh. A wave of dizziness swept over her. She staggered to the door. Her web told her there was no one outside, but when she tugged on the handle, she was still relieved to find the corridor empty.

It would not remain that way long, Romany suspected. Hex's wink told her not just that he could see her, but also that he knew who, and thus probably where, she was. And while it was unlikely he would come for her straightaway—he'd told Mazana his priority was the Erin Elalese—what happened if the emperor died? The priestess wasn't inclined to wait on the outcome of the fighting downstairs. With her web in its death throes, she felt decidedly vulnerable. If Hex *did* move against her, she wouldn't get any warning. And how was she supposed to defend herself against a wave of creatures like the ones he'd unleashed against Mazana?

She set off along the passage, spinning sorcery about her to create an invisible weave of threads that would absorb the force of any weapon swing aimed at her. She passed an intersection before reaching a staircase leading down. Down was where all the fighting was taking place, so Romany stayed on the upper level.

It was getting hotter. Sweat beaded on the priestess's forehead, and she wiped a hand across it. The feeling of being watched was strong, yet when she glanced back, she saw no one following. Above the muffled sounds of battle, she heard a rhythmic clacking noise like someone tapping a cane on the floor. One moment it appeared to be coming from in front of her, the next from behind. She drew her knife. The next intersection materialized from the darkness. A right turn would lead her to an exit.

She went around the corner.

And stopped. Her stomach tried to claw its way up her throat. Ahead the corridor was barred by a gate. And standing in front of that gate was Hex, smiling.

"Welcome," he said.

Romany smoothly reversed her course and continued along the main passage.

He'd come for her. Spider's blessing, he'd come for her! But why? Was the emperor already dead? And how had the Augeran known she would head this way? *Most likely he hadn't,* she thought. He was a mere sending, after all, not flesh and bone, which meant he would be able to move about this otherworld as swiftly as Romany moved about her web.

This was not good.

She slowed her steps. No point in hurrying now. She hadn't walked away from Hex because she thought she could escape him; she'd walked because she needed time to think. So close to freedom, yet so far! For while she'd had no trouble punching a hole in Hex's sorcery earlier, somehow she doubted it would be so easy if the Augeran was there to contest her will. Did she have any choice but to fight him, though? Having gone to the trouble of intercepting her, he was unlikely to let her wander off.

The clacking noise stopped, and in its place she heard a jaunty humming. From the floor directly below came a retort of metal followed by a scream. This section of corridor was even darker than the others. She could make out the next turning as a square of gray in the wall—

The man came at her out of nowhere. Romany shouted in surprise. It was the freak with the claws for fingers and the head twisted round. Even with her assassin's reactions, she could only half raise her knife to meet a sweep of one taloned hand. . . .

The claws tangled in the threads of her sorcerous wards and stuck there.

Of course, her magical defenses. In her panic she'd forgotten.

Her foe tried to gut her with his other hand, but Romany was ready for him this time. She swayed aside, then countered with a slash to her assailant's throat.

Or where his throat would have been if his head weren't the wrong way round. Instead Romany's blade sliced into the back of his neck. The apparition hissed at her, and the priestess had to fight down an urge to drive her knife over and over into its chest, release the tension that had built up inside her.

As Mazana had done to Darbonna in Olaire, perhaps?

Romany willed herself to calm. When the freak struck out again, the priestess didn't try to block, simply let his attacking hand tangle in her sorcerous defenses. Then she weaved strands about him, pinning him immobile. He struggled uselessly . . . and silently. *Just like the Vamilians.* Was this man flesh and blood as the Vamilians had been, enslaved and summoned to suffer in Hex's cause? Or was he a mere conjuring of the Augeran's tortured mind, no more sensate than the blood on the walls?

Romany stepped past the apparition. Upon reaching the next intersection, she looked to her right.

To find another gate blocking the corridor. Hex was in front of it, spinning about with arms extended as if he were dancing with an invisible partner. Romany glanced from the man to the gate beyond, wondering if the time had come to pit her will against the Augeran's.

Hex must have read her intent, for in front of the gate, another portcullis came down, *crack.*

Romany turned and walked away.

An idea took shape in her mind.

Hex's footsteps followed her. "Not wearing your mask this time?" he said as he caught up.

When the priestess spoke, she was impressed at the steadiness of her voice. "There's no hiding anything from you, is there?"

It occurred to her the stone-skin was close enough for her to drive her knife into his throat, but the man walking beside her was just a sending, and the "real" Hex doubtless wouldn't feel a thing if she stabbed him. She needed to keep him talking, because if he was talking he couldn't also be unleashing his monstrosities on her.

Maybe.

"Haven't you got anything better to do than dog my heels?" she said. "I thought your priority was the Erin Elalese."

"The emperor dies now or he dies in a bell's time, what does it matter? *You* are far more intriguing."

That was the key to staying alive long enough to put her plan into action, Romany suspected: stay interesting. And yet how could she be anything less? "I wonder if your kinsmen fighting downstairs would agree."

Hex ignored the comment. "What does your mask signify?"

"It signifies that I am a priestess of the Lord of Hidden Faces."

"A priestess?"

The man sounded disappointed, and Romany remembered the Spider telling her the Augerans followed no gods. "That is what Mazana Creed knows me as."

A staircase to the lower floor emerged from the gloom ahead, and Romany took the steps down. It should be a simple enough matter to steer a course around the site of the battle she had heard, but she would have to expect to encounter more of Hex's freaks below. Sure enough, she'd barely cleared the staircase when an old woman in rags appeared in front. She held an ax in each hand and started swinging the weapons wildly.

Romany tangled her up in a knot of sorcerous threads and continued on. These puppets, she decided, weren't half so frightening when you could sense Hex's strings moving them.

"I have spent the last quarter-bell considering how best to describe your servants," she said to the Augeran. "The word I settled on was 'inept.'"

"They are not to everyone's taste, it is true. But an artist must be allowed a degree of license in his creation. Hee hee!"

More likely, Romany reckoned, they were inept because anything more would require the stone-skin's constant input. "Just keep them out of my way."

On the floor ahead was a severed foot. Romany could have stepped over it, yet she felt the need to give it a wide berth. The corridors on this level were less gloomy than they had been upstairs, but still dark enough to make it impossible to gauge where she was. Fortunately, enough of Romany's web had survived to guide her course, and she surprised Hex with an abrupt left turn.

The Augeran trotted to catch up once more. He was not so much walking as tapping out a beat with his feet. *Tap, tap, swish, tap, slap. Tap, tap, swish, tap, slap.*

"Our powers have much in common," he said. "The subtlety of our touch, the sweep of our awareness."

"And what makes you think you've seen the entirety of my powers?"

"It is rare for anyone to detect my dreamworld before it is unveiled. Yet I sense that you did just that."

Dreamworld? That explained a few things.

Hex added, "I might not even have noticed your web were it not for the resistance it offered to my expanding realm."

Romany sniffed. "Resistance was not intended. If it had been, it would not have been so easily brushed aside."

"Perhaps. I assume you constructed your web so you could spy on the others here? If so, it is curious that you extended it not just into the emperor's quarters, but the emira's too."

"Isn't it."

In front, the floor of the passage was covered with blood right up to the walls. Not the flaky brown sort either, but the sort that sucked and slipped under Romany's sandals. She suppressed a shudder.

Tap, tap, swish, tap, slap.

"Where are we going?" Hex asked.

"Perhaps I'm going to find your body. Perhaps I'm going to wake you up."

"I think you'll find I am a sound sleeper. Hee hee!"

Romany took a right turn. The chamber where Hex had left Mazana was ahead somewhere, and a blast of bloodred light lit up the corridor to reveal two eviscerated Gray Cloaks thirty paces away. That blast told Romany the emira was still alive and fighting, and the executioner was too, judging by the roar that set the gloom quivering.

"You're going to help your patron?" Hex said. That note of disappointment was back.

"She's not my patron," Romany said, turning into a passage on her left that led her away from Mazana. "I must say it was considerate of you to feed her strength with all that blood."

The Augeran's voice became thoughtful. "The emira a blood-mage. That much at least I did not anticipate."

"And now it's too late."

"Please!" He waved a hand at the red-streaked walls. "If I wanted to, I could dispense with all this in a heartbeat, and thus rob her of her strength."

"Then why don't you?"

"Because for now it amuses me to see her flail about. It amuses me to let her think she might still find a way out. When the time comes to disabuse her of that notion, crushing her will be a simple matter."

"So simple you could do it in your sleep?"

Hex chuckled.

Romany's step had quickened as she neared her destination, and she forced herself to slow. The stone-skin believed that he had her caged, let him think she was aimlessly pacing her prison's confines. There was no way he could have guessed her goal, because if he had done he would have summoned up a firestorm or some other calamitous deluge to bring this to an end.

"Pick a corridor, any corridor," the Augeran said. "If you look long enough, maybe you'll find one I forgot to block."

His tone was still good-humored, but something told Romany he had begun to tire of this game. How long before he returned to his business with the emperor? She needed something to hold his interest, but what? Ordinarily, giving a man a chance to brag would keep him talking until the stars were dust. But in Hex's case she suspected he found flattery as tedious as she did.

Just a little farther. There was the turning ahead.

Tap, tap, swish, tap, slap.

"You made a mistake, you know," Romany said.

"How so?"

She turned into the corridor she'd been looking for. Fifty paces in front was the portal she had opened yesterday.

"By allowing your sorcery to destroy my web."

Hex was silent, thinking about that. Even if he was immune to flattery, he was still a man, and that meant he would be proud enough to want to work out the answer to Romany's riddle. There *was* no answer, of course. By destroying the priestess's web he had rendered her half blind, and at no cost to the Augeran. But every heartbeat it took him to figure that out brought Romany closer to her target.

Forty paces.

Tap, tap, swish, tap, slap. Tap, tap, swish, tap . . . slap.

That hesitation in Hex's step told Romany she was in trouble. Since she was able to perceive the gateway through her web, there was every chance the Augeran could too. And while he wouldn't know what he was sensing, he *would* know that Romany hadn't chosen this corridor without a purpose.

Thirty paces.

Once again she considered driving her knife into Hex's neck in an effort to slow him, but she suspected she'd lose more time delivering the blow than she would gain from it. She had tensed herself in readiness for this moment and now sprang forward.

Twenty paces.

If she'd caught the Augeran sufficiently by surprise . . .

A handful of armspans away, a portcullis slammed down across the corridor.

The tattooed stone-skin leapt at Senar, using Strike's body as a stepping-stone across the puddle of the bodyguard's blood. Senar lashed out with his Will at the corpse as the other man's foot landed on it. The body shifted, and the Augeran's jump turned into a stumble, his left boot twisting as it came down on the blood-slick tiles. Senar surged to the attack, cutting and thrusting while the stone-skin was off balance. An overhand blow from the Guardian—reinforced with his Will—burst through his enemy's block, scoring a nick to the man's forehead. The Augeran was slow to react to Senar's next attack. Senar's backhand cut passed over his foe's attempted parry and swung unimpeded toward his chest.

As easy as that? The Guardian was almost disappointed.

Then his sword passed through the man's body and emerged from the other side. It clipped a spark from the wall of the corridor.

Senar gaped, tottered backward.

The stone-skin's blade came for his throat. No time to block or sway aside, so instead he threw up a Will-shield to halt the stroke.

The weapon hit the invisible barrier and bounced off.

The Augeran came roaring forward, lunging with his sword at Senar's chest. The Guardian turned to let the weapon slide past. He could have tried to grab the blade, maybe aimed a counter at his opponent, but instead he backpedaled, hoping to buy himself time to think. He hadn't just imagined it; his sword had passed through the stone-skin like he was a spirit. Yet the Augeran's blade had been real enough moments later when it crashed into Senar's Will-barrier. He seemed real enough now, too, as he pressed forward again, feinting low before swinging high. The Guardian ducked under the stroke, his mind still turning over. So the warrior had . . . dematerialized as Senar's sword swept toward him, then rematerialized after it exited his body? All in the space of a heartbeat? How was that possible?

The Augeran attacked again. Senar's sorcerous blade came round so fast it was in position before his opponent's weapon reached it, forcing the Guardian to check his stroke.

The stone-skin's sword ghosted through, whistling for Senar's groin before cannoning off another hastily thrown-up Will-barrier.

Great, so the man could make his blade insubstantial as well as his body.

Senar tested his opponent's low guard with a thrust. The Augeran blocked easily. Senar's attack had been tentative, but how could he commit to a stroke when he didn't know whether his foe would be there in body to meet it? His gaze flickered to the stone-skin's face. There had been no tell in the man's eyes when he went spectral, no change in the translucency of his flesh. There had to be some way, though, to read when he employed his power. Some way to anticipate which strokes were real and which illusory.

Through the windows to Senar's right, the battle in the courtyard was a blur. The emperor shouted at the defenders to rally to him, but Senar paid him no mind. His enemy's next attack was a cut at his chest, and the Guardian blocked it with his sword, allowed his foe's weapon to slide along the blade to the hilt. He kicked out at the Augeran's leg, landed a hit on the knee.

The blow might have hurt Senar more than it did his opponent, for all the expression he showed. The stone-skin heaved against their locked swords, hurling the Guardian back.

And came forward once more.

His lunges were his most dangerous attacks, because they gave Senar less time to react if they passed through his parry. The Guardian began employing his Will more and more as a first line of defense. A little extra in his next Will-block forced his opponent's weapon wide, and the Augeran was late to recover it. Most likely his moment of vulnerability was merely bait for another trap, but Senar plunged in anyway, angling a cut at his enemy's throat. His blade beat the stone-skin's attempted block . . . only to meet no resistance as it entered the man's neck.

The Augeran's sword, meanwhile, had changed direction mid-parry. Now it swung for Senar's midriff, ready to fillet the Guardian the instant Senar's blade left his foe's throat.

Which it did not.

Senar had stopped his stroke to leave his sword in his opponent's insubstantial form. He'd been hoping that, when the stone-skin re-materialized, he would find himself choking on a handspan of steel.

The warrior did not re-form, though. Instead he held back his own stroke, his blade hovering short of Senar's ribs.

They remained that way for a while, the Guardian unable to disengage for the threat to his midsection, the stone-skin unable to complete his attack because of the sword in his neck. The Augeran smiled, then cocked his head with a look that suggested they agree to break apart.

To hell with that.

Senar gathered his Will and unleashed it in a blow that sent his spiritual foe reeling backward.

Amerel ran her opponent through and looked for the next. The arrival of the dragons meant her plan to destroy the Augeran fleet had worked, but she would save her celebrations until the *Fury* was free of the stone-skin vessel. Assuming it hadn't caught a dragon's eye already, of course. Even now one of the archers in the tops was yelling something to Galantas. And judging by the panic in his voice, he wasn't shouting down his lunch order.

Amerel needed to cut the lines holding the *Fury* to the stone-skin vessel, but before she could do so, there was the small matter of twenty enraged Augerans in her path. Apparently they hadn't understood the archer's warning, for they showed no signs of ceasing the attack. One leapt at the Guardian, only for the deck to tip beneath him. He was sent tottering back against the gunwale, and Amerel fell against him, her head beneath his chin, her nose in his armpit. He pushed her away, then drew his sword arm back. *Hold!* she commanded with her Will, and he checked his swing for the heartbeat she needed to sway clear. Her own blade traced a line of blood across his throat.

Someone bundled into her from behind. Might have been on her side, but Amerel wasn't taking chances. She reversed her sword and stabbed out, felt the blade sink into flesh. The figure fell away. A Rubyholter teetered past, his face a crimson mask. There was blood in Amerel's eyes too, and blood-dreams rattled around in her head, so sharp she couldn't tell if her hurts were real or imagined. A few paces away, Noon and a stone-skin wrestled over a spear shaft. Amerel was about to strike at the Augeran when the deck pitched again.

Matron's mercy, enough with all the shaking! What was Barnick doing? Mixing up a cocktail?

Then there was a bump and a creak, a scraping noise from the hull, and Amerel realized it might not be the water-mage doing the jolting.

Noon and his opponent broke off their struggle. The stone-skins had finally deduced that something was wrong, because the latest warriors to gain the *Fury*'s deck paused at the rail. Even the demon figurehead had lost some of its bluster. A shadow danced back and forth across Amerel, and she looked up to see a dead archer swinging by one foot from the rigging, an arrow through his neck. A wave slapped the hull. The distant rumble of combat from Gilgamar floated over the sea.

Then the scraping noise returned, moving down the length of the devilship from stern to bow.

The boards trembled.

A dragon's head reared up off the *Fury*'s starboard bow, streaming water. Its silver plates were scratched and tarnished like an old suit of armor, and atop its brow was a crown of scales from which hung strands of fireweed like tangles of hair. Up, up, it went, so high it put a crick in Amerel's neck just tracking it. Its eyes were so large they could have taken in the world, yet they seemed to be looking straight at the Guardian. Its lips peeled back with a sound like a hundred swords being drawn from their scabbards, and it gave a roar that set the foresails shivering.

A Rubyholt archer was on the forecastle. He jumped to the main deck and crashed into a rack of boarding spikes. Around Amerel, the other Islanders stampeded toward the quarterdeck. "Dragon!" someone shouted, like she needed the clarification. One man dived down the companionway. Maybe he thought he would be safe belowdecks, but the truth was, there was nowhere safe while the *Fury* remained here. Their only hope was to flee this place and the dragon with it.

And that meant cutting the devilship free of the stone-skin vessel.

Amerel turned and dashed for the port rail. A pace ahead was a black-cloaked Augeran, running the same way. The Guardian was tempted to cut him down, but just because someone presented their back to her didn't mean she *had* to plant a blade in it. Besides, the stone-skins were now withdrawing to their own ship. Little sense in continuing the fight, after all, when the only prize for the winner would be to get eaten alive by the dragon. Clearly the Augerans were hoping to flee just as Amerel was. Clearly they didn't realize that their water-mage was dead.

"Cut the ropes!"

Amerel hurdled an Islander's corpse, slipped on a patch of gore, and windmilled her arms. There was a shriek from behind, a horrible crunching, but she didn't look round to see who the dragon had taken. It hardly mattered so long as it wasn't her. As she reached the gunwale, the deck tilted and carried her into it. To either side, Augerans clambered over the rail. A boot swished her hair. There was a blood-soaked rope drawn taut next to her, and she swung her sword at it.

It parted.

A breeze chilled the back of her neck as if the dragon was breathing on it. When she glanced round, though, she saw the creature still loitering by the bow. A rumble sounded in its throat. It scanned the people on deck like it was choosing from a menu. Then its gaze fell on the *Fury*'s figurehead. With the combatants' fighting zeal doused, the devilship's voice had dropped to a whimper. Evidently that noise was still enough to grate on the dragon's ears, though, for the creature raised a clawed foot and struck the figurehead. It shattered the wood and sent the painted demon sailing a dozen armspans to splash into the sea.

"Cut the ropes!" someone shouted again.

Three lines remained intact. At one, a man with a harelip held an ax above his head like he was chopping wood, while beside him a woman tried to slice through a second with a boarding pike. Tattoo pushed her aside and severed the cord with a swipe of his sword. Amerel scampered for the third rope, but she was beaten to it by a red-cloaked warrior on the Augeran ship. He slashed through the line with a knife, and suddenly the *Fury* was free.

The two vessels drifted apart.

"Barnick!" Galantas yelled.

A wave of water-magic burgeoned beneath the devilship. Barnick didn't waste time turning the vessel, simply reversed it from the dragon. The beast snapped its teeth at the retreating bow.

Missed.

Beside Amerel, the last stone-skin on the *Fury* scrambled to the rail and tried to leap the gap between the two separating ships. His tired half dive, though, took him only half the distance, and he fell shrieking into the sea. The *Fury* pulled away, rising higher and higher as the wave beneath it grew. There were clear waters now between the ship and the dragon. The beast regarded the vessel with its huge golden eyes. There was no reason for it to follow the *Fury*. It was the stone-skin ship, not the devilship, that was marked with dragon blood. It was the stone-skin ship that bobbed helpless without a water-mage.

But follow the creature did. How unfair was that?

The dragon's body gleamed in the water, half the length of the *Fury*, with spikes along its spine and a tail that snaked behind. It barely seemed to be moving at all, but in the blink of an eye it had quartered the distance to the devilship. Amerel swallowed against a dry throat. Someone shouted at Barnick to go faster—as if the water-mage might have been toying with the creature until now. Still he managed an extra burst of pace that sent Amerel staggering into Tattoo. The wind rushed in her ears.

The dragon drew nearer.

An archer shot an arrow that struck the beast's snout. A second missile took it in the eye, but the dragon appeared not to notice. Just forty lengths away. To Amerel's right, two Rubyholters lifted a stone-skin corpse and tossed it over the side in the hope it would draw the dragon. It didn't. Amerel would have thrown some live meat to the beast if she'd thought that might work better, but there was a glint in the creature's eye that said it was enjoying the chase. If it had wanted easy prey, it would have stayed with the stone-skin ship.

Amerel roused herself. A sorcerous globe down the gullet would show the dragon the error of its ways. True, the beast was much closer than she would have liked, but with the *Fury* pulling away swiftly, perhaps the devilship would escape the brunt of the magic when the glass smashed. Where was Noon, though? Not with the sailors on the main deck. Not on the quarterdeck either. Damn the man. If he'd gotten himself killed, he could at least have had the courtesy to give her the globes first.

"Noon!" she shouted.

No response.

She pushed past Tattoo, making for the prow. A Will-blow wouldn't inflict any lasting damage on the dragon, but it might persuade it to try its luck elsewhere. It wasn't as if she was blessed with other options.

She gathered her power.

That was when she saw Noon at the starboard cathead. His shirt was ragged, the right sleeve torn clean off. He held something in his hand. Something that sparkled as he hurled it toward the pursuing dragon.

Uh-oh.

Amerel made to grab the rail.

An explosion of earth-magic cracked the air, and not for the first time today she found herself lying on the deck, staring up at the sky.

CHAPTER 22

BY THE time Ebon crossed the stepping-stones, the battlements were under the control of Twist and his allies. Half a dozen Erin Elalese had ignored the prince's instruction to remain on the opposite tower and followed him over the stones. But no more were on their way now.

He released the rocks, and they fell into the waterway.

To Ebon's left was a pile of Gilgamarian corpses. Seven motionless red-cloaked warriors were scattered about the tower, and an equal number of Revenants were laid out beside the catapult. Across from Ebon, one of the twins sat with her back to the parapet, her left leg cut to the bone, the skirt of her susha robe soaked with blood. The bearded Revenant healer was tending to her, and Ebon saw her wound close up to a red-beaded scar. Vale stood in the shade of the catapult's arm holding a shield that looked like it had been trampled over by a herd of lederel. His frown conveyed his disapproval at Ebon's presence, but he said nothing as the prince joined him.

To the east, the stone-skins from the next tower must have been advancing this way along the wall, because a handful of Revenant archers had taken up station on that side of the battlements and were sending down a steady fire of arrows. From the south came a trumpeting sound, and over the parapet Ebon saw a silver-scaled dragon erupt from the waves beside a stone-skin ship. Dragons might have been a common sight in these parts for all the attention the mercenaries and the Erin Elalese gave them. Ebon, too, had no time to gawp. Preparations were under way for the attack down the stairs.

Revenants collected ammunition from corpses, or half rolled, half pushed catapult stones to where Twist stood beside the stairwell. The mercenary leader was in whispered conversation with the woman wearing the eyepatch. When it ended, she moved away to join her kinsmen.

Twist raised his hands. "Okay, lads, gather round," he said to his men. "Here's how it's gonna go down. These stones"—he pointed to the catapult stones—"should do nicely to clear away any enemies on the stairs. The lefties among you are gonna be first to follow them down, 'cause the way the staircase turns, you'll be better able to get a swing in if you meet trouble. While we're attacking down the stairs, the Breakers there"—he nodded to the Erin Elalese assembled at the eastern battlements—"are going over the side with the ropes they've brought. Stone-skins below have left the portcullis up to allow for reinforcements along the wall, and we mean to use that to our advantage. While we pin down the enemy at the bottom of the stairs, Breakers will hit them through the arch. Dunno how many swords the stone-skins have got, but judging by the numbers they left guarding these battlements, I'm guessing it's less than we have. Questions?" He didn't give anyone a chance to speak. "Then let's do this. Endorian plus one, you're with me in the second wave."

Ebon stared at the man. "Plus one"—was that him? The mercenary did him too much honor, surely.

A catapult stone was rolled to the top step. A push sent it thumping down the stairwell with a noise like a titan's footsteps.

The left-handed fighters among the Revenants came grumbling forward as if they'd been called to the lash. Their colleagues slapped them on the back and spurred them on with sympathetic offerings. "Save some for us, eh," one man said. "Anything you want me to pass on to your wife and my kids?" The lefties numbered only four, meaning the second wave of attackers—Ebon's wave—might as well have been the first. He could have objected, of course—Twist had no authority over him or Vale. But the truth was, Vale belonged at the front, and Ebon meant to be at his shoulder.

A second catapult stone was sent rumbling down the stairs.

Alongside Ebon, Vale was his usual steadfast presence. The Revenants pressed in close, getting ready to go. A woman with the longest hair he'd ever seen sucked in deep breaths. Twist was chuckling to the man beside him as he reenacted how he'd dispatched a stone-skin in the fight for the battlements. His voice had an edge of excitement to it. Maybe it was an act to put his companions at ease, but if so it wasn't helping Ebon. Normally he didn't feel fear before a fight, yet an iciness was creeping through him as if the goddess Galea had returned to his mind. This once he might have welcomed her back. There were times when he thought that he could sense her in a distant corner of his mind—and that, with the right tug, he could have drawn her to him. But not today.

A third stone followed the second. There had been no shouts from the stairs to suggest the other rocks had met stone-skins on their way down, so Twist raised a hand to halt the man pushing a fourth, before gesturing to the lefties. Ebon swallowed and drew his sword. He needed more time to prepare himself for what waited below, but how was thinking about it going to make it easier? Better just to get on with it. Someone passed him a shield. It felt so heavy on his arm he doubted he'd be able to lift it when the time came.

"Go!" Twist said, and the lefties stormed down the stairwell. Twist tapped each one on the shoulder as if he were counting them off. Then he gestured to the Erin Elalese.

Two Breakers sat in the crenels on the eastern rampart. They dropped ropes over the parapet and disappeared so fast down them, they might have lost their grip on the lines. Shouts came from along the harbor wall—stone-skins calling a warning to their kinsmen in the tower. Too late, Ebon hoped. The next two Erin Elalese climbed to the battlements, but the prince didn't see them descend because one of the Revenants had nudged him forward. He turned back to the stairwell to see Twist vanish after the lefties. Two more mercenaries came next before Vale reached the top step.

Ebon took a breath and followed him down.

The sorcerous explosion sent Galantas staggering back against the port rail, and he grabbed the lower shrouds. One moment the air above the dragon was clear, the next it was filled with roots and dirt. Rocks as big as carts came crashing down around the beast, throwing up spray. Soil and pebbles pattered onto the *Fury*'s decks, and a cloud of dust enveloped Galantas.

Earth-magic? Now Cayda was just showing off.

A fog settled on the sea behind the *Fury*, along with a blanket of leaves. Beneath the surface, the dragon was naught but a shadow. Dead? Unlikely with those impenetrable scales on its back. Doubtless it had merely been stunned by the deluge, which meant Galantas needed to put some distance between himself and the creature before it recovered. The *Fury*'s flight had taken it on a westerly course away from Gilgamar, and Galantas shouted to Barnick to angle the ship closer to the northern shore. The waters would be shallower there, making it harder for the dragon to follow. Hopefully.

Qinta was at his shoulder. "What about the Needles?" he said.

Galantas had forgotten about Tub. The *Willow Reed* had been cut free of the Augeran vessel. The stone-skins were busy dousing the sails with water in order to better harness the meager wind from the west. The *Willow Reed,* by contrast, wallowed on the swell, its decks deserted. Either the crew had been butchered to a man, or any remaining souls were lying low. There was nothing to be gained by rushing to search for survivors, Galantas decided, especially with that dragon skulking in the water between the two ships. He had the lives of his own crew to consider, after all.

He climbed to the quarterdeck and swung his gaze east. Aside from the beast that had attacked the *Fury*, only four dragons were visible—no, make that five, for a monstrous copper head had just come roaring from the deep beside an Augeran galleon. Galantas whistled as the dragon rammed the ship beam-on, caving in the hull and driving the vessel back. Closer, a smaller red-scaled beast surfaced beside a two-decker. It lifted its tail from the sea and shattered the main yard with a clubbing blow. Screams sounded.

The ship's water-mage must have entered the fray at that moment, for the sea about the dragon churned and swirled. The beast was flipped over to expose its belly. A hail of arrows flashed out from the vessel, but the dragon had already sunk beneath the waves.

Galantas smiled. On Dragon Day the Storm Lords might give as good as they got, but the Augerans hadn't come equipped with the sorcerously invested weapons they would need to take down dragons. Their best chance at salvation lay in gaining Gilgamar's harbor, but what of the chains barring their way? Had the stone-skins in the city managed to cut a second one? It was impossible to tell from Galantas's vantage point, because the *Fury*'s passage north and west meant his view of the Neck was obscured by the Chain Tower. But a count of the Augeran ships told him that none had yet entered the harbor. And why would they still be outside unless their way was blocked?

To the west of the Chain Tower, the wall was clear of stone-skins, while across the channel, the battlements of the smaller tower overlooking the Neck were now in Gilgamarian hands. The arrival of the dragons would have buoyed the defenders. They would know they only had to hold out a short while longer before the Augeran fleet was forced to scatter. Would flight save the stone-skins, though? Barnick hadn't been able to outpace the dragon just now, so odds were the Augeran mages, tired by last night's exertions, wouldn't be able to either. Especially since, with their ships' hulls marked by dragon blood, this wasn't a chase the creatures would give up lightly.

"Captain!" Qinta said.

The Second pointed toward the inner line of stone-skin ships. A four-master had risen up on a wave of water-magic and now surged toward the harbor entrance. Its main course showed a woman's face framed in fire, and there was a white square over her cheek where a gash in the sail had been clumsily patched. Galantas licked his lips. The ship was going to try to clear the chains. An act of desperation? Probably, but its captain must have thought he stood at least a chance of success to risk the attempt.

The wave beneath the vessel grew. If one ship made it over, the rest would surely follow, and already a second stone-skin craft was moving into position behind the first. Once in the harbor they would be protected from the dragons by the same chains that had blocked their passage moments before. Galantas looked at the Chain Tower, hoping for some response from the defenders. A volley of arrows raked the decks of the first Augeran ship, but that wasn't going to slow it. What could?

Galantas cursed. The stone-skins were about to wriggle free of the trap.

The four-master drew level with the Chain Tower. It was so high now, the stone-skins in the rigging could have shaken hands with the Gilgamarians on the battlements.

Then the wave beneath it started to subside. An armspan lower, three, five. Galantas lost sight of the ship as it entered the Neck.

Heartbeats later, he heard a tortured squeal of metal, screams, a crack of wood.

Not encouraging sounds if you were a stone-skin. The vessel must have hit the chains.

The defenders on the Chain Tower cheered.

"Well, well," Barnick said.

"What just happened?" Galantas asked.

"Someone threw their Will against the wave under that ship. Someone strong." He nodded toward the Chain Tower. "Looks like the Gilgamarians have got themselves a water-mage up there."

Senar's Will-blow had driven the stone-skin to one knee. A string of bloody drool hung from his mouth, and he wiped a sleeve across it. Along with the cut over his eye, that made it two strikes to nil in Senar's favor, but what mattered was who landed the last blow. There was a newfound respect in the stone-skin's eyes, and he nodded as if to acknowledge the Guardian's merit. All very civilized. It was easy to forget they had been trying to kill each other moments before, and would likely be moments from now too.

This pause allowed Senar to consider his options. The Augeran's ability to phase in and out of existence made him an opponent unlike any that the Guardian had faced. Was there a way he could turn the man's gift against him? Earlier, Senar's sword in the stone-skin's neck had prevented him from rematerializing. Would any . . . impediment have the same effect? Even dust? A few Will-blows to the ceiling might loosen a cloud of plaster. A handful of soil would also work, though Senar doubted his foe would stand idly by while he entered the courtyard to do some gardening.

His thoughts turned to the dragon scales on his right arm and shoulder. If he waited until his opponent aimed a hit at that part of his body, he could sacrifice a block in exchange for an attack. And yet if the Augeran's strike was with an insubstantial blade, the scales would not stop it any more than Senar's sword would.

In the yard, the emperor continued to urge on his troops. Along the corridor behind the stone-skin, meanwhile, a figure emerged from the darkness—a man with ragged hair, clutching an ax with a wooden shaft. His lips had been cut away to reveal the teeth and gums beneath, giving him a permanent feral smile. The tattooed Augeran half turned as the man approached, then frowned and stepped aside to let him pass. The axman ignored him, his gaze fixed on Senar.

Meaning they *were* on the same side?

If so, the stone-skin must have seen his ally more as hindrance than as help, for as the apparition drew level, the Augeran drove an elbow into his temple. It landed with a wet crack like the sound of an egg breaking. The axman collapsed.

The stone-skin bent down and pried the ax from his fingers before straightening.

With a shout he attacked, swinging ax and sword together. Senar blocked the ax with his Will, the sword with his own blade, but the Augeran's weapon slid through it. The Guardian swayed backward, the sword's tip passing a hairbreadth from his chin. The ax came at him again, and this time when he parried, his sword crashed against the weapon. The head of the ax hooked the blade, pinning it for a heartbeat and forcing Senar to block the next sword thrust with his Will. The stone-skin followed up with a kick to the midsection. Senar didn't have time to gather his power again. Instead he tried to fold with the blow, took a thump to the gut that scrambled his insides and set the air hissing between his teeth.

The Augeran surged forward again, golden tattoos flashing in the gloom. His next stroke passed through Senar's parrying sword, then his next and his next too, until the Guardian found himself using only his Will to block his enemy's strikes. At times the swish of the stone-skin's weapons had him convinced he could tell the physical attacks from the spiritual ones. But just because a stroke started out "real" didn't mean it would end that way. And of course if he used his sword to try to block it, that just made it more likely his foe would turn his own weapon insubstantial. . . .

An idea formed in Senar's mind. A long shot perhaps, but that was better than no shot at all.

His use of his power was starting to take a toll. Each impact of his foe's weapons on his Will-shield was accompanied by a needle-prick of pain in his skull. He flinched with each blow, making no effort to conceal his discomfort. Let his opponent see he was suffering. Let him think victory was close. The Augeran's attacks developed into a rhythm like the beat of a galley's drummer. Given time he would have battered through Senar's defenses, but the Guardian wasn't going to allow him the chance.

An overhand stroke from the stone-skin's sword gave him an opening. He sidestepped the attack. His opponent's ax was already sweeping round.

Now Senar needed a touch of luck.

He swung hard with his sword—at the ax rather than its wielder, hoping the weapon was real and not insubstantial. Its whisper through the air suggested it was, but until it actually met his sword—

Senar's blade cut cleanly through the ax's shaft, and the metal head thunked to the floor to leave the stone-skin holding nothing but an armspan of wood.

Growling, he tossed it away.

Senar kicked the ax-head past his foe, then sprang to the attack. The Augeran raised his sword to block Senar's cut, but the Guardian used a nudge of the Will to slow the weapon. For an instant, he thought he had his man.

His sword passed harmlessly through the stone-skin's flesh and out the other side.

The Augeran smiled, stepped back out of range.

Senar held his ground, waiting.

And suddenly his opponent wasn't smiling anymore. For unbeknownst to him, Senar had used the moment afforded by his foe's retreat to fix his Will on the fallen ax-head, and slide it across the floor beneath his adversary's right foot. The stone-skin hadn't felt it because his foot was insubstantial as it came down. When he re-materialized now, though, it was with a chunk of metal imbedded in his heel.

Senar watched the man's expression twist from incomprehension to shock.

Then the pain hit him, and his eyes bulged. He clamped his teeth shut, but still a blubbering wheeze escaped his lips. He sank to one knee, his left hand reaching down to touch the ax-head sticking out from the back of his heel like a sandclaw's talon. A sheen of sweat appeared on his forehead.

Then his features smoothed, the agony passing.

He's made himself insubstantial, Senar realized.

The Guardian wondered if his victory would be short-lived. Could the Augeran pluck the ax-head from his spiritual flesh? Or had the metal fused to skin and bone in a way that could not be undone? The answer, he decided, lay in the stone-skin's look: a look that was bale-ful but also heavy with foreboding. A look that said the Augeran knew the game was up. For while the man's spiritual form seemed to offer relief from the pain, it was only by returning to the flesh that he would be able to kill the Guardian.

And Senar suspected a lump of agony in his foot might restrict his fighting style.

Just then, the walls of the corridor shimmered.

Romany had been expecting Hex's portcullis to come down, and she struck out at it with her awareness. She had only had a heartbeat to gather her power, and rather than fashioning an opening big enough for her to run through, she could create just a hole an armspan in dia-meter. While her conscious mind hesitated, her assassin's instincts took over. She dived through the opening before rolling on one shoul-der and coming to her feet again. Her blood-caked sandals skated on the floor as she pushed off, and she stuttered into a run again.

Fifteen paces from the portal.

Something struck and tangled in the weave of sorcerous threads at her back. Something Hex had thrown at her? She did not look round. To either side the walls swelled and darkened to resemble the leprous skin Romany had seen in Mazana's room earlier. Large wrig-gling forms like oversized maggots pushed through lesions in the flesh. They flopped to the floor before rupturing to release buzzing shapes as big as Romany's fist. Hornets. One flapped about her face, and she lashed out with her knife, missed. Her breath snorted in her nose. Just hold it together a few moments more.

Ten paces.

Ahead the corridor was empty of obstructions, yet Romany doubted it would remain that way for long. She veered toward a door on her left, hoping that Hex might mistake it for her destination. As she reached for the handle, a knot of barbed wire sprung up about it. *Good,* she thought as she swerved away. The time he'd wasted con-juring up that wire was time he could otherwise have spent creating another portcullis.

Five paces.

She opened the portal with a thought. There was a snapping sound like a ship's sail in a gale, and the gateway burst open to fill the corridor in front. Smoky orange light shone through it, bright enough to make Romany's eyes water.

That must have been why she didn't see Hex's second portcullis until she was upon it. There was no time to strike out with her power, and she skidded into the gate, half turning to take the brunt of the contact on her shoulder. Still her head struck the bars. She reeled backward, lights flashing before her eyes, hands grasping out to seize the metal and stop herself falling. Even disoriented as she was, she could sense the portal just beyond the portcullis. Waves of wind-tugged dust melted into shadow at its edge. If she had reached a hand through the bars, she might have touched the gateway, for all the good that would have done her.

Fortunate, then, that she had deliberately opened the portal to only a fraction of its full size. Now she let it creep a few armspans forward until the brightness engulfed her.

She lurched through Hex's portcullis as if it were made of mist and into the world beyond.

She halted, doubled over with her hands on her knees. She'd run only twenty paces, yet from the way the air sawed in her throat, she might have sprinted the length of the Alcazar. Blood trickled down her temple from the blow to her head, but she ignored it. *I made it!* No way Hex could reach her here. The fact she'd been able to walk through his portcullis told her his sorcery couldn't pass through the portal. And even if he did find a way to make his dreamworld manifest here, he wouldn't be able to grow it faster than Romany could run away.

The air of the new world was hot against her skin. It felt heavier somehow, as if the sky were pressing down on her. She shielded her eyes against the grit on the wind. There was no more to see of the place now than there had been the last time she'd opened the portal—just rocks and dirt and that dazzling distant glow of the sunset. But at least none of Hex's abominations were here. Relief tingled through her.

Safe.

Was that even true, though? Hex might not be a threat anymore, but how long could she hope to survive in this alien world with nothing but a dagger and the clothes on her back? What guarantee did she have that this world's inhabitants would be friendlier than the stone-skins? More important, how far was she from the nearest water, the nearest food? She shook her head. Odds were she'd have to return to her world in a day or two, and that meant passing back through this portal to the Alcazar. If the Augerans' attack on Gilgamar succeeded she might find Hex waiting for her when she arrived.

This wasn't over yet. The first part of her plan had been accomplished, but the hardest part was still to come.

She straightened. Above the whistle of the wind, she couldn't hear Hex's footsteps behind, but she knew he was there all the same. He'd be hurting from her escape. He'd be curious about the portal, and why his sorcery couldn't pass through it when Romany could. She would have to play on that inquisitiveness as she had done on the walk through the Alcazar. At worst, she might detain him long enough to give Mazana and Avallon a chance against his kinsmen. At best . . .

At best? Well, that was why she still hadn't fully opened the portal yet, wasn't it?

A final breath, then she turned to face him and adopted a suitably disdainful look. That, at least, came easily enough. Hex stood a prudent distance from the portal, his image misted by the dust on the air. The walls of the corridor were similarly indistinct, overlain by a boundless rocky plain streaked with orange light. Romany's robe flapped in the wind, but the Augeran's cloak was still. Behind him was a swarm of the oversized hornets. His expression was indecipherable in the murk.

Romany said, "I seem to have found one of those exits you forgot to block."

The Augeran's gaze scanned the realm beyond the gateway before coming to rest on the priestess. When he spoke his voice was a mere whisper above the wind. "You think you are safe because you have passed through a portal? I have worked my power through gateways before."

"You want to try? Go ahead."

One of the hornets buzzed toward Romany. She raised a hand as if to deny it entry. With or without her intervention it wouldn't have been able to journey through the portal, but if Hex thought that some conscious effort on Romany's part had denied it passage, he might also think that her resistance could be overcome. The hornet moved close enough to the priestess for her to see the gleam of its eyes, and for an instant she wondered if she had made a mistake.

Then the creature melted from sight as it flew along the Alcazar's corridor and past the opening to the portal.

"My turn," Romany said. She spun her threads about one of the hornets, tangling its wings. It fell twitching at Hex's feet. "Or how about this?" Extending her senses toward the wall on the Augeran's right, she pierced a hole through the sorcerous skin. A circle of white stone appeared amid the diseased flesh. "See? That wasn't so hard. Perhaps you should have another go."

Hex edged forward. *Yes, come closer.* He looked pensive, but not angry. A shame. Anger would have been easy to play on. He raised a foot and brought it down with a squelch on the hornet Romany had snared.

"Curious," he said. "This portal is one you opened, yet did not create or define. Meaning your destination beyond is one of convenience, not design."

He'd taken the first step toward realizing the precariousness of Romany's position, but she wasn't about to let him go the rest of the way. "How perceptive," she said. "In return, it seems only fair I share with you some of the things *I've* learned about *your* world." She pointed to the white circle on the wall. "Spreading your dreamworld over an entire wing of the Alcazar has left it vulnerable to attack, particularly since it doesn't restore itself once it is breached. Imagine what other wounds I might inflict from this side of the portal where I am free to experiment beyond the reach of your power. Of course, there is little damage I can do while you remain here to contest my will, but if you are *here,* you can't also be where the fighting is. And if your kinsmen should lose to Mazana's and Avallon's forces, how long do you think it will be before your sleeping body is tracked down?"

Hex shuffled forward again, and this time Romany responded by stepping back as if she feared him. If he thought her afraid, he might think he still posed a threat to her, and that he might thus be able to reach her beyond the gateway. A smile split his patchwork face. "No portal has ever resisted me before."

"So you've already said. If you keep saying it, maybe that alone will be enough to crack my defenses." Romany pretended to hesitate. "In any case, even if you *were* somehow to breach them, what's to stop me from closing the portal?"

"And still affect my dreamworld from beyond?"

"And wait until you go elsewhere before reopening it," she corrected him.

"How would you know I'd moved on, pray tell? How could you know I wasn't waiting to bid you a last farewell?" His feet tap-tapped as he capered to within an armspan of the portal. He reached out a hand as if to test the boundary between the two worlds, then thought better of it and lowered his hand again. Clearly his confidence was back, yet he had the sense to remain beyond the borders of Romany's realm.

And there he might have stayed if the priestess had previously opened the portal to its fullest extent. She hadn't, of course. But she did so now, and the gateway snapped open.

To bring Hex within the glare of that dying sun.

At the same moment, Romany lunged toward the Augeran, not with physical fingers, but with spiritual ones. Her target was not his body, but the soul inhabiting it. So great was his surprise that he didn't try to evade her. She seized his wrist.

And collapsed the portal, isolating his spirit on this side of the gateway.

Ebon blinked against the gloom in the stairwell. The edges of the steps were rounded with wear and made more treacherous by splinters of rock left by the falling catapult stones. Vale had already disappeared from sight below, and Ebon pounded after him, his bones rattling, the edge of his shield scratching against the wall. Echoing shouts. A stab of light from an arrow slit, a glimpse of sea beyond. Then a flash of orange smeared the walls, and he felt a blast of heat. Yells and screams came from below, followed by a pop and crackle of sorcery. *Fire-magic.* But from someone on Ebon's side or the enemy's?

The orange glow faded, and Ebon squinted for the next stair down. The clash of weapons started up. He was gripping the handle of his shield so tight he suspected someone would have to pry his fingers free when this was done.

The wall on his left gave way to an arched doorway, movement beyond.

Ebon plunged through.

Fractured images of a huge chamber, all blurring into one: a shield spinning on the floor; Twist leaping to engage two stone-skins; flames flickering in the enemies' eyes. Protruding from the wall to Ebon's left were blocks of stone into which the chains had been set. Beneath them stood a robed man with hands wreathed in black sorcery, two guards beside him. Ahead, more stone-skins were drawn up in an inverted U. The warrior at the bottom of the formation had golden spiral tattoos on his arms and cheeks. Three Revenants lay motionless on the ground, another burned and shrieked.

A sword whistled down from Ebon's right, and he brought his shield round to take the blow. The impact set his arm trembling. He surged forward behind the shield, making room for the Revenant at his back. Beyond the stone-skin who had attacked him, Breakers poured through the archway from the seawall. Red-cloaked warriors turned to face them, and their ranks rippled as if they'd been struck by an invisible force. Air-magic? The force of that sorcery must have struck Ebon's attacker too, for she bundled into him, sent him stumbling back. His feet tangled, and together with his assailant, he crashed to the floor.

The female stone-skin landed on top of him. There wasn't space for her to wield her sword, so she dropped it and grabbed Ebon round the throat instead. They clawed and strained and wrestled. A bead of her sweat fell onto his cheek. He tried to lever her off, but her weight bore down on him. He focused his power for a strike at her face. The blow was weak, though, and she rolled her head with it, then came down on him with redoubled fury. Her nails dug into his neck as if she meant to rip out his windpipe.

Click.

The top of her skull disappeared to a sword stroke as a gray-cloaked shape—Ebon's savior—hurdled the prince. The stone-skin's blood washed into Ebon's nose and mouth. He turned his head, gagging and spitting, then wiped a sleeve across his eyes to clear them. The stone-skin was even heavier dead than she had been alive, and it took all his strength to push her away. He clambered to his feet, recovered his shield. There had been no chance to thank the Revenant who had saved him. Ebon couldn't pick him out now amid the chaos and the gloom.

The room wobbled. For an instant, he thought it was just his legs quivering. Then a grinding sound reached him, a scream of metal, and he realized something had hit the chains outside. A stone-skin ship? A dragon? It didn't matter so long as it hadn't got past.

Where was Vale? To Ebon's right, one half of the enemy U formation had disintegrated under the attack from the Breakers. The stone-
skins there now fought in pairs against an ever-increasing number
of foes. As yet none of the bodies on the ground wore red cloaks, but
it was just a matter of time before the Erin Elalese overran their ad-
versaries. When that happened, the other stone-skins would be
forced to surrender, wouldn't they? But how could they do that if it
meant condemning their fleet to the mercy of the dragons?

Ebon's gaze was drawn to the stone-skin with the golden tattoos.
Wielding two shortswords, the man was whip-quick. His right blade
appeared to pass through an opponent's parrying weapon as he dispatched the Revenant he fought. Ebon could see Vale now, bearing
down like a whirlwind on the tattooed man. The stone-skin stood
calm before the Endorian's furious motion, his swords flickering out
with a speed that seemed—impossibly—to match the timeshifter's.

Then Vale was falling.

Ebon's throat constricted. No, it couldn't be. The Endorian must
have just slipped. But the strings of blood whipping from the stone-
skin's blade told a different tale, and the timeshifter crumpled to the
floor.

"No!"

Ebon surged toward Vale. He took an elbow in his ribs, shook it
off with a grunt. All he could think of was that he'd sacrificed Vale
for Lamella and Rendale. Not deliberately, perhaps, but he'd known
the risks of joining the city's defense. He'd known Vale would bear a
greater part of that risk than Ebon himself. And why had Ebon just
stood there stupidly while his friend fought the tattooed man? It didn't
matter that the exchange had been over in heartbeats. If Ebon had
struck out at the stone-skin with his power, he might have created
an opening for the Endorian.

A red-cloaked warrior reared up. Ebon lashed out at him with his
sword, hammered down at his opponent's blade before another
sword—an ally's—plunged into the stone-skin's throat.

Ebon was past before the body hit the ground.

The next enemy was on to him. Ebon tried to barge the man aside,
but he might as well have been trying to push over a wall. He was
thrown a step backward, deflected a sword stroke with his shield,
then lunged forward with his own blade only to find his assailant
had been whisked off by the tide of battle. A woman was now in her

kinsman's place. She unleashed a barrage of cuts that had Ebon huddling behind his shield and retreating all the while. He stepped on a fallen shield, felt it dimple beneath him. He stepped back again and kicked it toward the stone-skin as she pressed forward. There was a scrape of metal as it slipped beneath her foot. She staggered toward him, scorn showing in her eyes even as he slammed the rim of his shield into them. Her legs buckled.

Ebon had lost his bearings in the clash, but he spotted the tattooed man again, trading blows with the woman wearing the eyepatch. There was no doubt about it this time, his backhand cut passed *through* his opponent's sword before opening her throat, and the Breaker fell in a welter of blood. From somewhere came a voice— Twist's?—shouting for people to leave the tattooed man to him or else, but two Erin Elalese—a man and a woman—had already engaged the warrior. The woman seemed to breach his defenses, only for her blade to pass through his head. The stone-skin's counter carved open her stomach, and her guts tumbled out. Her friend thrust his shield forward, his sword stabbing under it, but the tattooed man was already gone, long gone, and the Breaker was suddenly down on his knees coughing blood. Ebon hadn't seen the attack that killed him. But then how did you defeat a warrior who was smoke one moment and steel the next?

With sorcery, of course.

Ebon cared nothing for revenge against the stone-skin. All he wanted was to reach Vale while there was still a chance he could heal his friend. The stone-skin wasn't just going to watch, though, as Ebon dragged the Endorian to safety, and so the prince advanced upon the man, his grief and rage building. The tattooed warrior noted his advance and turned to face him. In his gaze was a touch of sorrow as if he recognized Ebon's loss and regretted it. Ebon gathered his strength. In Mayot's dome he had drawn on every last scrap of himself to keep Mayot's sorcery at bay, and he now drew upon the same and more, drew it in until he felt an icy tingle in his extremities.

Then he released his power all at once, focusing it on the stone-skin.

There was a rush of wind, a rip and a roar as if he'd conjured up the Furies themselves in this place. The combatants around Ebon staggered and swayed. It was the tattooed man, though, who caught the worst of the attack, as it landed with the sound of a fist behind driven into a palm. He was hurled back. The wall of the tower behind him was a dozen paces away, but he covered the distance in an eye-blink to strike the stone. . . .

Except he did not strike it; he passed through it like a phantom. Perhaps he'd made himself insubstantial, or perhaps he'd been that way before Ebon's power hit. What was on the other side of that wall? The Neck? The harbor? Would he recover and return to the fight?

What would be the point? The battle was over, Ebon realized. Only a handful of stone-skins in the tower remained upright. As echoes of Ebon's sorcery continued to whistle about, a red-cloaked warrior was forced to the ground by two Revenants. A female mercenary stood with one foot on the body of the mage who'd been working on the chains, as if he were some big game she'd brought down. Had she got to him before he could bring down the third chain? Was the battle for Gilgamar over, or just starting?

Ebon let go his power, and the wind died away like a door had been closed on a storm.

Where was Vale? Ahead the twins were hugging each other. Ebon weaved around them, then stepped over a fire-charred corpse. Breathy whimpers came from a Breaker with a sword in his leg. Someone else was coughing like they'd had their first taste of juripa spirits. From the direction of the portcullis, a voice began shouting, taut with excitement. The survivors gave a muted cheer—more a tired exhalation.

Victory?

Ebon hardly noticed, for he'd seen Vale lying on the ground to his left. Tears streamed down the prince's cheeks, because beside his friend knelt the bearded mercenary healer, smiling reassuringly up at Ebon as their gazes met.

From the quarterdeck of the retreating *Fury*, Galantas stared over the waves. The Augeran ships had maneuvered into line for their turn to enter the harbor, but their way would now be blocked by the vessel that had hit the chains. Its stern was visible at the entrance to the Neck. A three-decker had been following hard on its heels. It tried to draw up to avoid a collision, but the two ships came together with a thud, a crack, and a chorus of screams. All music to Galantas's ears. Behind, a third vessel approached. Plenty of time for this one to heave to, but as it did so, a gold-scaled dragon rose beneath it, tipping the ship and pitching dozens of stone-skins into the water. A second dragon, another gold, surfaced amid the figures and scooped a shrieking Red Cloak into its jaws.

The *Fury*'s crew cheered.

A fourth Augeran ship closed on the pair of golden dragons, and the archers onboard let loose a storm of arrows that pinged off the beasts' armor like hail off a copper roof. Galantas shook his head. Brave, but stupid. *How often the two go together.* A scorpion mounted on the vessel's forecastle shot a bolt that disappeared into the larger dragon's mouth, but the creature merely growled before spurting a jet of water from its nostrils that hammered into the soldiers manning the weapon. Farther east, another dragon—steel-colored this time—had surfaced. The stone-skin ship closest to it turned tail and fled south. Heartbeats later, a horn blast sounded across the water, and another enemy vessel took flight, then another, and another.

Galantas's crew cheered in earnest now. He cast his eye over them. Fourteen survivors if you included Galantas and the two Storm Islanders. Fourteen out of the forty who had met the stone-skin attack: seven Spears, two Needles, two Squalls, as well as that Raptor krel, Toben Stark. Squint grabbed a Squall and led him on a jig about the deck that ended in raucous laughter when the two men slipped on a pool of blood. A flask of spirits was produced and passed round. Some of the Spears whooped and chanted Galantas's name. Hells, even the Raptor was shouting.

Galantas had endured enough boos in his time that a cheer would never lose its appeal. On this occasion, though, the adulation rang hollow. *As hollow as this victory.* For while his men might be content merely to have survived the day, Galantas had set his sights higher. And once the initial flush of success had faded, how would his crew view today's events? Most important, how would the Needles, the Squalls, and the Raptor view them? For it was their account—as opposed to that of Galantas's Spears—that would carry most weight. Galantas knew what Kalag would say: that the victory here was Cayda's, not Galantas's. That it was Cayda who had destroyed the three stone-skin ships that the *Fury* had tangled with. That it was Cayda who had driven off the dragon when it attacked. And who could argue with him? By contrast, what had Galantas done today, save ferry the woman about like some captain for hire? Even the audacity of his decision to fight the stone-skins would be overshadowed by what came after.

His words to Qinta at Clinker's Bay came back to him: *We need some way to turn this into a victory, not just over the Augerans but over the Storm Islanders as well.*

His gaze moved to Cayda and her companion, now standing at the rail to his right. He recalled the invisible barrier she had conjured up to save him from that stone-skin's sword stroke. And a light went off in his head. Air-magic, he'd thought at the time, but there was another possibility . . .

Pieces of the puzzle started falling into place.

He looked across at Qinta. If he was going to act, he would have to do so quickly.

"Qinta," he said, then indicated Cayda and Noon with a flick of his eyes. "Our friends over there . . . Perhaps you could invite them to join me."

The Second nodded in understanding.

Senar squinted. The gloom about the corridor had fallen away, and all was searing light. The blood and grime were gone, along with the body of the axman behind the tattooed Augeran. Senar looked at the stone-skin's heel, fearing the ax-head embedded there might vanish too.

It did not.

He listened to the moans of the wounded in the courtyard, the distant clamor from the seawall. Evidently the battle for the harbor was still going on, but the fact that the tumult sounded no closer indicated the defenders were holding their own. In the yard, the grass had been trampled into a red-brown soup of mud and blood. Bodies lay all about. There was no sign of the emperor or Kolloken, but Senar saw Lindin Tar's corpse draped over the ruin of a bench, a hole in her chest the size of a sandfruit. At the center of the square, four red-cloaked Augerans stood in a huddle, surrounded by a ring of Gray Cloaks and Erin Elalese soldiers. One of those soldiers called for the stone-skins to surrender their weapons, but they did not obey. They looked at the warrior Senar had crippled, seeking instructions.

The tattooed man did not acknowledge them.

From along the corridor, two figures appeared. There was no mistaking the executioner's form, and in front of him strode . . .

Mazana.

Senar's expression soured. The emira's face, arms, and legs looked scalded, and her eyes held a tinge of bitter red like cooling embers. Darbonna's knife was pushed through her belt.

When the executioner saw the tattooed stone-skin, he reached for his sword.

"Stay back!" Senar said. "You too, Mazana."

The emira halted. She looked from Senar to the Augeran. "If the two of you are busy, I can come back another time." She sounded giddy. Power-drunk.

When the stone-skin spoke, his voice was so low it seemed to come all the way up from his feet. "No for need. I is just leaving."

"I *am* just leaving," Mazana corrected him.

The man probably didn't hear her, because he was already stepping back through the west-facing wall of the corridor. Ahead and to Senar's left was a door in the same wall. The executioner threw it open and looked into the room beyond. Plainly the Augeran had moved on, though, for the giant slammed the door shut again moments later.

"What's happening at the harbor?" Senar asked Mazana. "Do I need to get down there?"

"I think not. Remarkably, it seems the dragons have been able to scatter the stone-skin fleet without your help."

Dragons? "And the wall itself? Does the Chain Tower still hold?"

"As far as I could make out from a glance through a window."

"Where's Kiapa? Jodren?"

Mazana made a careless gesture. "When I left him, Kiapa was looking a bit gnawed, but he'll recover. The same for Jodren—except for the recovering bit, of course."

"And Uriel?"

For a heartbeat the emira stared at him as if she didn't recognize the name.

Then the color drained from her face, and she set off at a run along the corridor.

Hex stood before Romany as pale and insubstantial as a specter. From his expression his mind was still trying to catch up to the sequence of events that had brought him here. He shook his arm free of her grasp.

A mistake.

He must have realized it too, for he snatched out for her again.

The priestess slapped his questing aside. If he reestablished the link between them, she wouldn't be able to return through the portal without taking him with her. And she had no more wish to let him hitch a ride back than she did to be stranded here with him. He came for her again, his face screwed up in rage as he tore at the weave of her sorcerous defenses. Romany backpedaled. She didn't need to fight him, just keep him at arm's length long enough to escape.

Another flick of her mind reopened the portal. As she retreated through it, the heat of the dying sun faded. Hex came after her, ripping through her wards as easily as if they were cobwebs. Just a few more paces. The whistle of the breeze and the touch of the wind-swept dust fell away to be replaced by the still air of the Alcazar. Hex tried to follow, his spiritual fingers clawing at her. But she had moved beyond his reach now, and he might as well have been trying to catch a cloud in his hands. She waved a farewell. His roar of fury filled her ears.

Then silence as she closed the portal again.

Home sweet home.

Romany leaned back against the wall. Hard to believe it was over. There was no way that Hex could open the portal without her help, yet still she found herself counting off the heartbeats, waiting for the inevitable *tap tap* of his steps, or the whisper of a "hee hee!" in her ear. *Foolishness*, she berated herself. *I've won; just accept it.*

With Hex gone, his dreamworld had vanished from the Alcazar—the portcullis, the hornets, the darkness. Romany decided she much preferred this Alcazar to the other one. A pity she couldn't have spent more time gloating over the Augeran, but with an enemy as dangerous as Hex, you didn't take chances. And to think the fate she'd inflicted on him was the one she'd originally intended for Mazana! There was an irony there if she was minded to look for it. For now, though, all she wanted to do was put the memory of this episode behind her.

There was dust in her hair and on her clothes. She brushed herself down. A bath was in order, she suspected. A solitary clash of distant swords told her there was still fighting going on in the Alcazar, but she had already done her part and more.

It was time to find somewhere quiet to watch the rest of the drama unfold.

Mazana was a dozen paces in front of Senar, head down, sandals slapping on the floor tiles. Her dress had a tear on the shoulder he hadn't noticed before, and the cloth flapped as she ran. The Guardian dashed after her. He was still holding Strike's sword, and the blade whined as he pumped his arms. He passed the spot where he'd cut down the woman with the mace. There was a puddle of blood so large he had to jump to clear it. His heel caught the edge, and he slipped and skipped a step before finding his feet again.

Behind him came the thump of the executioner's footsteps. The giant bounded past Senar, closed the distance to Mazana in a handful of paces, and fell into step behind. She reached a staircase to the upper floor and took the steps three at a time, shedding a sandal halfway up where the steps switched back on themselves.

Senar reached the top a moment after her. The corridor was deserted. Mazana's footsteps echoed along it as she sprinted toward her quarters. Doors flew past to either side of Senar. There were no bodies blocking the way, no blood to suggest the fighting had spread here. And that had to be a good sign, right?

Then he saw the door to Mazana's room lay open.

There was an acid taste at the back of his mouth.

The emira plunged through the doorway, the executioner pausing on the threshold. Senar pushed past the man to get inside.

He halted.

A dead woman in a gray cloak sat slumped against a wall, her hands cupped over a wound to her stomach. A bodyguard? To one side stood Mazana. Senar could hear her breathing. She looked through the door to her brother's room, and the Guardian followed her gaze.

Matron, no.

Uriel lay curled in a pool of blood, his red hair soaked a darker shade of crimson. Behind, the wall was spattered with drops that were trickling down like rain on a window. *Still trickling.* Meaning the boy had died only a short time ago, maybe even just heartbeats before the nightmare world faded—and with it, most likely, the apparition that had slain him, for surely no Augeran would have wasted time on the boy while the battle raged in the courtyard.

Senar struggled to breathe. It felt like he'd been punched in the gut. He shifted his gaze to Mazana. She was facing away from him, her hands hanging slack at her sides. For a while she stood motionless.

Then she sank to her knees.

Amerel heard a footfall behind, then felt a blow cannon off the Will-shield she had thrown up earlier. She sighed. So predictable. But then to anticipate Galantas's next move, all she had to do was consider what she'd have done in his place. She turned. Tattoo stood a step away, a cudgel in one hand, his gaze flickering from Amerel to Galantas. Galantas himself watched from beside the binnacle, Barnick alongside.

She wagged a finger. "Treachery, Galantas? I'm shocked."

Galantas looked unabashed. "I rather suspect you beat me to it. I saw the way you fought the stone-skins—the way your opponents' weapons bounced off you, just as Qinta's did now."

"Bounced off *you* too, as I recall." She was starting to regret helping him, but at least this time her mistake had been *saving* someone's life.

Galantas studied her. "You're a Guardian, aren't you?"

"Let me guess—you're a fan."

"When you came to my cabin yesterday, I was sure I'd seen you before. I managed to persuade myself I was mistaken, but then it came to me. That Erin Elalese trade delegation nine years ago. Your hair and eyes were different then, but it was definitely you."

"If you say so."

"And if you lied to me about where you're from, I have to wonder what other parts of your story aren't true. Such as what you were doing in Bezzle the day the stone-skin commander died."

"You think I was responsible for that? Even though I wasn't there?" Amerel waved a hand. "But you're right, what should that matter? Why let a small thing such as facts get in the way of a good theory?"

Galantas held her gaze, then shrugged. "Tell me now or tell me later, it's all the same to me. But you *will* tell me. Just as you will tell me the real story behind how you got the dragon blood, and what part Mazana Creed played in all this."

Amerel did not respond. No point in trying to argue her innocence any further. There were too many details working against her.

Blood ran into Galantas's eyes from a cut below his hairline. When he wiped it away, he left a red smear across his forehead. "You can't win here," he said. He glanced at Noon. "Even if your friend is a Guardian, too—and I'm guessing he's not—there are only two of you against twelve."

"You're forgetting this," the Breaker said, raising the remaining sorcerous globe between thumb and forefinger. "Maybe you saw me throw one of these at the dragon before the explosion."

Galantas stared at him.

Amerel said, "Come on, Galantas, work it out. We used water-magic at the Rent, air-magic against the stone-skin ship, earth-magic against the dragon. Guardians aren't elemental mages. And even if my *friend* here were"—the word "friend" tasted unpleasant on her tongue—"three different elements from the same mage? That's impossible unless you're a Fangalar." She gestured with her head to the globe. "Except it isn't, with these."

"If you throw that thing at me, you'll die as well," Galantas said.

"Whereas if we surrender to you, we're sure to live forever."

His expression did not waver. "You're bluffing."

"Am I? If I'm dead anyway, might as well take you with me. And if I choose to fight, I might not even need the globe. There are just three of you on this deck. How long do you think you'll survive once the swords are drawn? How many of your crew will come running when you call? It's been a whole quarter-bell since they survived a scrap with the stone-skins. I'm sure they're just counting the breaths till they can spit in Shroud's eye again."

Galantas made to speak, but Amerel talked over him. "There's another way to resolve this," she said. "You lend us a boat to get to shore, we wave our good-byes and part as friends. You even give us your water-mage to man the boat—just in case a sudden squall blows in before we get to land. Then afterward you forget this conversation ever happened, and you sail back to the Isles in glory." The time had come for her to employ her Will. "You'll be the man who destroyed the stone-skin fleet. The man who survived Liar's Crossing. A hero, some will say. Who better to lead the Isles when the stone-skins next come calling? Who better to take the throne that has been so tragically vacated by his father? Seems a shame to risk all that on whether I'm bluffing. But if you're *sure* I won't use the globe . . ."

Galantas's face was blank, but she knew she was winning him over. He wanted to live more than he wanted vengeance against her. Vengeance only mattered if you'd lost something you cared about. And what had Galantas lost except his father and a few hundred of his kinsmen? The real problem, Amerel knew, was the *Fury*'s crew. More particularly, what they might have seen of the confrontation taking place here. Galantas looked down at them on the main deck. A handful still stared east toward Gilgamar, but the majority had moved on to relieving their kinsmen's corpses of valuables.

"I don't think you need worry about them," Amerel said. "They were too busy celebrating to see your man here"—she nodded to Tattoo—"trying to take me down. And they're too far away now to hear what we're saying. Which means you won't lose face if you let me go. As for my part in today's events . . . Let's just say it would serve both our purposes if I were to be written out of the tale."

Galantas continued to look at his crew. Two men were dragging out a spare sail to cover the dead. If anyone felt their captain's gaze on them, they didn't turn to meet it. Maybe they really hadn't seen Tattoo attack Amerel. Or maybe they knew they were only useful to Galantas if they returned home with a happy story. A story that didn't mention him being outwitted by the woman he'd tried to incapacitate moments earlier.

Amerel rubbed a hand over her eyes. After another night without sleep, the only thing that had sustained her through the fight with the stone-skins was adrenaline. Now her limbs felt like mud. A cut to her left arm stung as if someone had rubbed salt in it. She leaned back against the rail, tried to look like she didn't much care what Galantas chose to do, provided he did it quickly. He fiddled with his shark-tooth necklace. Amerel treated him to a last touch of her Will.

"Take your time," she said, keeping her voice light. "If you can't decide what to do, I'm sure another dragon will be along soon to offer an opinion."

Galantas watched Barnick steer the boat up onto the pebble beach. The wave of water-magic deposited the craft just short of the ridge of shells and seaweed that marked the height of the winter tide. Then it melted away. The two Erin Elalese clambered over the gunwales before staggering up the beach as if the ground pitched no less than the boat had done.

"You had no choice," Qinta said from beside Galantas.

Was that true? Galantas replayed in his mind his conversation with Cayda. Was there anything he could have done differently? He'd hoped to catch her by surprise with that attack, but the woman had expected his betrayal. Should he have called her bluff over the globe? With his crew's blood still up, he reckoned they'd have been happy to attack her and add another coat of red to the *Fury*'s deck. But they wouldn't have reached her before Noon threw that glass globe. The Erin Elalese could have jumped overboard as the thing shattered. Maybe they would have survived the resulting explosion, and maybe they wouldn't. But Galantas himself would have died, that much was clear.

No, he couldn't have played things differently. Yet that knowledge didn't ease the sting of his humiliation—a sting that was made all the sharper by the fact the confrontation had been played out in sight of the *Fury*'s crew. Galantas looked again at his men on the main deck, all busy with their tasks. Had anyone witnessed what happened? Perhaps it was his imagination, but the Raptor, Toben Stark, seemed a little too anxious to keep his gaze from meeting Galantas's. Could Galantas afford to take a risk on the man's ignorance? It wasn't just Galantas's own future at stake, after all. Everyone in the Isles stood to lose out if they were robbed of the unity that would come from his leadership. The needs of the many outweighed the needs of the one, and all that. Unless that one was Galantas himself, of course.

"What now?" Qinta said.

Good question. Galantas opened his telescope and looked east. The stone-skin fleet was in full flight, the dragons in pursuit. Three ships remained beneath Gilgamar's wall, including the two vessels that had collided at the entrance to the Neck. Both were studded with arrows. Those missiles must have accounted for the ships' water-mages, because the vessels weren't trying to flee. A third craft lay on its side to the west of the Chain Tower, a hole in its hull. What remained of its crew climbed onto the stones at the base of the seawall, or swam for the safety of the Neck while a bronze dragon glided among them through the debris-covered waves.

Galantas reached a decision. "We go west. Find a bay where we can lie low and wait for nightfall."

"And after?"

"After, I thought you and I might pay a visit to Gilgamar with Barnick."

Qinta regarded him skeptically. Then understanding dawned. "The *Eternal*."

Galantas nodded. It was possible Gilgamar's Ruling Council might give him the ship as a reward for his role in defeating the stone-skins, but Galantas wasn't going to ask for something that was his by rights. More important, after what had happened with Cayda, he needed more than ever to score a victory over the Storm Islanders. Stealing the *Eternal* from under the Gilgamarians' noses surely counted as that.

Reaching the ship would be the easy part, he knew, for the Gilgamarians would have more important things to worry about than guarding a vessel in their harbor. The hard bit would be escaping the city. It might be some time before the chains were lowered to allow ships to pass through the Neck. Galantas, though, would have surprise on his side. No one would expect someone to try to break out of the harbor, especially when the dragons, and what remained of the stone-skin fleet, were at large in the Ribbon Sea.

He swung his telescope south.

And stiffened. A ship with black sails was visible on the horizon. The *Karmight*? Alongside it was a three-masted vessel that looked like the *Scion*. A Falcon ship. Maybe they'd hung back in the hope of arriving late to the piece, or maybe their mages had genuinely been unable to match the *Fury*'s pace. Either way, they would now find themselves in the path of some stone-skin ships and their pursuing dragons. A thought came to Galantas. Might his kinsmen's slowness work to his advantage? If the two ships' captains survived their brush with the enemy—and even now they changed course to take themselves out of the Augerans' way—they would know nothing about Cayda destroying the three stone-skin ships, or driving off the dragon. All they would know was that the Augeran fleet had been put to flight. That Galantas's plan had worked. In other words, all the good bits, with none of the inconvenient qualifications.

Assuming, of course, they heard nothing to the contrary from the *Fury*'s crew.

Galantas closed his telescope and looked again at Toben Stark. There wasn't a crewman on board who had escaped the fight with the stone-skins without a scrape or three, and the Raptor had a gash to his chest that had stained his shirt crimson. "Nasty cut our friend has got there," Galantas said to Qinta.

"Gonna sting," the Second agreed.

"Still, a few stitches, and he'll probably be good as new." He paused. "Though it never ceases to amaze me how the most innocent of wounds can go bad. Be a shame if that happened to the krel's cut."

"Damned shame," Qinta said.

He actually sounded like he meant it, too. Oddly Galantas found a part of him sharing the Second's regret. But being a leader brought responsibilities, and one of those was to take hard decisions when they had to be taken. Harder on Toben than on Galantas, perhaps, but there it was. "Before you call on the Raptor," he said, "maybe you could listen to the rest of the crew's chatter, see what they're saying about Cayda." If anyone *had* seen her clash with Galantas, the *Fury*'s stores of Elescorian brandy were sure to loosen their tongues.

Qinta made to say one thing, then seemed to change his mind. "There'll be eyebrows raised if we get home without a single survivor from the other clans on board."

"Then let's hope it doesn't come to that."

Qinta's gaze strayed to the sky as if seeking confirmation of the wisdom of Galantas's command. Galantas wondered what the birds would have to say about the sense in questioning his orders. Nothing, it seemed, for the sky was empty.

Barnick was on his way back to the *Fury* now, his long hair streaming behind him as the barge swept over the waves. Cayda and Noon remained on the beach.

Qinta followed Galantas's gaze to the Erin Elalese. "This spells trouble, don't it? The emperor and the emira working together."

Galantas nodded. It also made it all the more important that he become the next warlord, for what chance would the Isles stand against the twin threats of the stone-skins and an Erin Elalese–Sabian alliance if the divisive figure of Kalag was at the helm?

"The Storm Isles' part in this, I get," Qinta went on. "They've got a score to settle with the stone-skins after Dragon Day. But what about Erin Elal? What's their interest here?"

"Perhaps they feared they were the Augerans' true target, and not the Storm Islanders."

"But why? Stone-skins attacked the League on Dragon Day, not Erin Elal."

Galantas had no answers, but he meant to find out. Maybe there was something between the Augerans and the Erin Elalese he could use when he next crossed paths with them. Bad blood, perhaps. Maybe even old blood. *The sharpest kind.*

"And what about this Cayda woman?" Qinta added. "Why'd she pretend to be from the Storm Isles if she was really a Guardian?"

"To hide the fact Erin Elal and the League were working together."

"You still think she was the one who took down the stone-skin commander?"

It made a certain sense, yet it left a host of questions unanswered, not least of which was how she had managed to kill Eremo without being near him. And how she had known the stone-skins would be returning to the fortress at precisely the hour they did. An inside source, perhaps?

Galantas shrugged the questions aside. His priority for now was retaking the *Eternal,* and then launching his bid to become warlord. Later there would be time to consider the implications of the partnership between Erin Elal and the Storm Isles, as well as Galantas's response to it. Who knew, perhaps there was still a deal to be done with the Augerans. Perhaps when they learned who had been responsible for Eremo's death, they would be willing to resurrect the pact they made with Dresk. The events of the past twenty-four bells would surely have taught them the folly of picking a fight with the Rubyholters. True, Galantas would still have to sell any possible deal to his own people. But if any of the clans had cause for grievance against the Augerans, wasn't it Galantas's own Spears? If Galantas could find it in himself to forgive their transgressions, doubtless the other tribes could do so as well.

And he suspected that, given time, he *could* forgive the stone-skins for the killing of his father and Galantas's subsequent rise to the leadership of the Spears.

The sacrifices I make for my kinsmen.

Amerel watched through spirit-eyes as Barnick hooked the boat onto the *Fury*'s chains and climbed to the main deck before crossing to join Galantas and Tattoo. If she'd been minded to, she could have listened to their conversation, but it didn't matter now. She floated for a time, staring at the Islanders but not seeing them, as if they were but a memory of something that had gone before. A memory that would plague her like all the others when this day was done.

Amerel felt a grudging respect for the Rubyholters. It was a miracle any of them had survived the clash with the stone-skins. They had proved themselves surprisingly capable in repelling their stronger and more numerous foe, and while the devilship had played a role in firing their blood, that did not detract from the skill they had shown. Earlier she'd suggested to Galantas that his crew wouldn't have helped him if he attacked her. She knew better, though. Pirates they remained, but with what they had come through today, they had taken the first steps toward becoming . . . something more. Maybe they deserved better than what fate intended for them. But this was war, and war cared no more for right and wrong than Amerel did.

She looked east. At the entrance to the Neck, a dragon clambered onto a stone-skin ship as if it were trying to escape something in the water. The vessel began to tip, the masts swinging down until they hit the water with a slap of canvas. Screams sounded, cries for help, the joyous trumpeting of the dragon. The other Augeran ships had scattered, no two of them heading in the same direction. One was on a course that would bring it close to the *Fury*. Galantas must have seen it too, for he gave the order to set sail.

The *Fury* rose on a wave of water-magic and set off west.

No more delays. Amerel had put this off long enough already.

She focused her Will on the remaining sorcerous globe, now hovering over the devilship's quarterdeck.

And shattered it.

She opened her corporeal eyes in time to see a blinding white flash. It was followed by a crack like a mountain breaking on an anvil. A ring of fire bloomed outward. The *Fury*'s sails burned in sheets of flame before collapsing into ash. The decks, too, were alight, and the boards that had been soaked in blayfire oil burned fiercest of all, sending plumes of purple-gray smoke into the sky. Even on the beach Amerel could feel the hunger of the flames. A furnace-wind swept up the shore with a roar like some creature from the Abyss. It stung her eyes and knocked her back a step.

The urge to look away was strong, but she forced herself to witness the destruction. Cries sounded from the *Fury*'s decks. The lucky ones among the crew would have died instantly, but a handful of unfortunate souls cavorted about like living firebrands before hurling themselves into the sea. No relief to be found there, though. The waves round the devilship hissed and steamed like a pot on the boil. The swimmers sank beneath the surface and did not reappear.

"You had no choice." Noon said from beside Amerel. Like he thought she might need reassuring.

She didn't. Galantas dead was the only way to be sure her involvement in the assassination of Eremo remained secret—to be *sure* Augera remained the Isles' enemy and not Erin Elal. It had to be done; no sense fussing over it. She remembered the time eleven years ago in Helin, at the dawn of the Confederacy, when she'd received her first orders to kill in cold blood. Her target then had been a Helinian councilor. A good man. A man of principle who had argued against joining the Confederacy because he had feared—reasonably—that his city would become Avallon's plaything. A young and inexperienced Amerel had failed to sway him in three days of talks, even with her Will. Yet still when the order to kill him came, she had sat up through the night, reading and rereading the Guardian Council's dispatch like the words might have changed since she last looked. And for what? The task hadn't needed doing any less the next morning.

Erin Elal had been safer for the councilor's death, she'd told herself afterward. It was either him or who knew how many of her kinsmen. There comes a time, though, when the excuses run out. When the weight of your actions defies justification. After the Helinian councilor had come that guild master in Mezan. Then the Kalanese pasha and his household. Each one a small step, perhaps, but if you took enough of those steps, you were apt to look back one day and wonder how you'd come so far in the wrong direction. Sometimes your steps took you to a place beyond any hope of returning. Sometimes you lost your way entirely.

The *Fury*'s mizzen yard crashed to the deck, shattering the starboard rail and throwing up sparks. A blood-dream bubbled up in Amerel's head, but she forced it down. She felt Noon's gaze on her and looked across.

"You look terrible," he said.

"Thanks. That means a lot, coming from you."

A wave broke against her sandaled feet. She bent down to scoop up some water, then splashed it on her face. When she rose again, Noon was still watching her.

"Ever think we'd make it this far?" he asked.

"Sure. Right from the moment we stepped off Barnick's boat just now."

"Gotta hand it to you, you get the job done. Not how I'd have done it, maybe, but that hardly matters." He extended a hand. "It's been"— he paused—"an interesting experience working with you, Amerel."

She blinked. Had he just used her name? She looked at his hand, then at him. "Let's not get carried away."

Noon gave a half smile and lowered his hand. "Where next? Gilgamar?"

"Gilgamar," Amerel confirmed. It would be a long walk to the city, but at least they wouldn't be meeting any dragons on the road. Maybe when she got there, she would find out why the stone-skins had come this way, but she couldn't pretend she cared. She just wanted to get back to Erin Elal, and Lyssa. Admittedly there wouldn't be many captains willing to risk the Ribbon Sea while the dragons were about, but Amerel reckoned she might be able to persuade one. . . .

Lyssa. It was a strange feeling having someone to return home to after a mission. Strange, but not altogether unpleasant.

She turned to climb the beach.

"You know," Noon said as he followed, "I've been thinking about those globes of sorcery. Any idea where they come from? Or how many more the emperor's got?"

"No."

"With enough of them things, you could destroy a stone-skin fleet. Destroy *every* stone-skin fleet. If you surprised them in their home harbor, maybe. Or if you knew where they were going to land."

As if things would be that easy. "You'd still need a Guardian to set them off at a distance. And what are the chances of the emperor entrusting a Guardian with that many globes?"

"Or of finding a Breaker and a Guardian willing to spend enough time in each other's company to get the job done?"

Amerel considered for a moment, then nodded. "We're doomed."

Senar knocked at Kolloken's door and entered at the man's call.

The floor of the Breaker's room was crisscrossed with bloody foot-prints. Kolloken sat on a chair with his left leg stretched out on a low table. His trouser leg had been torn away to reveal a gash to his thigh. He cleaned the swollen skin around the cut with a wet cloth, his pinched lips the only indication of his pain.

The doors to the balcony were thrown open against the heat, and Senar looked outside. The Alcazar was afire with talk of dragons, but beyond the chains there was no sign of the beasts, just a stone-skin ship slumped at the entrance to the Neck, its sails hanging limp. In the harbor itself was a scattering of corpses. The bodies had drawn snakes from the canal, slithering atop the water like an oil slick. Boats moved among the dead as scavengers picked over the corpses.

"Still got Strike's sword, I see," Kolloken said. "Emperor's gonna want that back."

Senar glanced down at the blade in his scabbard. "Then he can come and get it himself."

The Breaker finished cleaning his wound. He'd washed his face of the gore Senar had seen on him in the courtyard, but there were still smears of blood under his eyes and nose. His gaze on the Guardian was appraising. "I'll pass that on."

"Who was that stone-skin I fought?" Senar asked. "*What* was he?"

"A Syn, most likely. They're mentioned a few times in the old texts. Augerans used them as assassins mainly, and who can blame them? Walk through a wall, stab your blade through your enemy's parry—there ain't many who can defend against that, eh?"

"Then we're fortunate he didn't think to target the emperor before the fighting started."

"Who says he didn't?"

Senar studied him. "You drove him off? How?"

"Emperor got lucky, is all. When the shit came down, he was on his way to meet the emira, had plenty of men around him to keep the Syn from closing."

Men with the Will, presumably. And well-versed in it too, to have survived the encounter. But it stood to reason *some* of the Breakers in Avallon's party would have a talent for the power. Senar closed the balcony doors. "I hear that the meeting with Mazana won't be happening now. I hear you're leaving as soon as the Gilgamarians drop the chains, even if that risks a confrontation with a dragon."

Kolloken's gaze flickered to the doors, then back to the Guardian. "What can I say? Avallon's a sensitive soul. Doesn't want to intrude on the emira's grief."

"Either that or he's already got what he came for."

The Breaker said nothing.

Senar curled his lip in disgust. "Mazana was right, wasn't she? The emperor planned this all along. He let the stone-skins know he was coming so he could lure them into attacking Gilgamar." It explained a lot of things—like Avallon's downbeat reaction to hearing Mazana had sent the Chameleons to Bezzle. The news should have come as a boost to the emperor . . . unless he had already told the Augerans he would be in Gilgamar, and thus drawn their fleet away from where the Chameleons were going.

"Don't know what you're talking about," Kolloken said. Then, "But if that *was* Avallon's plan, I'd say it worked out pretty well, wouldn't you? Imagine the picture a couple of weeks back when he finds out the stone-skins are planning to meet Dresk. The eastern seaboard's exposed. The hammer could fall at any time, and the emperor with no one to hold his hand when it does." Kolloken swung his leg down from the chair. "I'd say them storm clouds are looking a good deal less threatening now, eh? Avallon sends Amerel to pay her respects to Dresk, then he drops in for a visit with his friends in the north"—he spread his hands to take in the Alcazar—"and suddenly the stone-skin fleet has gone to Shroud, with both the Rubyholters and the League helping to send it on its way. Not a bad week's work, all in all."

"Is that why you killed Uriel?"

Senar had hoped to see shock or indignation in Kolloken's look, but the Breaker's expression showed nothing.

"When that otherworld fell away," Senar added, "I didn't see you in the courtyard. Where did you go?"

Kolloken kept his silence.

"The blood on the wall in Uriel's room was fresh. And no one else on the upper floor was killed—I checked."

A hint of a smile touched the Breaker's lips. "Sure looks like someone targeted the lad. Don't mean it was me, though."

Senar felt the heat build in him. "You killed a boy."

"Why don't you say it a bit louder, Guardian? I don't think they heard you outside."

"You killed a boy!"

"He was already dead!" Kolloken spat. "They all are, even that red-haired bitch of yours—especially her." He tossed aside the cloth he'd been using to clean his leg, then pushed himself to his feet with a grimace. Blood trickled down his injured thigh. "I heard what happened when she met Avallon yesterday. Emperor laid everything out before her, all nice and tidy. But the emira was too busy playing clever to listen. Then she goes and meets that stone-skin Hex, rubs our noses in it like this is some Shroud-cursed *game*." The Breaker's voice was rising all the while. "Emperor gave her a chance, and she shoved it right up his ass. If anyone's to blame for what happened to Uriel, it's her."

Senar clenched his hands into fists. "Why did you have to kill him? You'd already won when the stone-skins attacked the city. The League was never going to risk Gilgamar falling into enemy hands."

"Ain't enough," Kolloken said. "Not nearly enough. The emira could just have put her strength into Gilgamar, thinking she was safe so long as the city held. Can't see her sitting back now when the stone-skins come, eh?"

"Mazana's no fool. She may not have noticed you missing in the courtyard, but she's been suspicious of Avallon from the start. If it hasn't already occurred to her that he's behind Uriel's death, it will do soon."

"Then it's lucky we got you here to convince her otherwise, ain't it? What, that pricks your conscience? You mean you ain't done worse in your time?" Kolloken shuffled closer. "What do you reckon'll happen if the emira gets it in her head that Avallon killed her brother? You don't think she'll come at us with all she's got? Who wins if she does that?"

Senar scowled, but there was no denying the force of the Breaker's logic. If Mazana turned on Avallon, the empire would fall. The Sabian League too, after. And for what? Would knowing the truth about Uriel's death ease the emira's grief? Would Senar himself feel better to see the injustice answered?

The injustice. He shook his head. What had Kolloken said? *You mean you ain't done worse in your time?* Senar had, of course. More often than he would like to admit. You didn't serve as a Guardian for twenty years without getting some dirt under your fingernails. Senar had got good at burying the memories deep, but he still caught a whiff of them sometimes. And all done in the name of the same empire that Avallon was trying to protect now. *But I never hurt a child,* he told himself. Wasn't that more by accident than design, though? If he'd been in Kolloken's place, what would he have done? If the order to kill Uriel had come from the Guardian Council, would he have hesitated?

The Breaker wiped his bloody hands down the front of his shirt. "I warned you on the crossing from Olaire. I warned you the emperor wouldn't pull his punches. You should've listened. You should've picked your side like I told you to, but instead you had to go mooning round after a pair of tits."

"Screw you."

Kolloken stabbed a finger at his chest. "You think the emperor's not playing fair? You think the people back home are gonna thank him if he keeps his hits above the belt? He did what he had to. To protect Erin Elal. To win this Shroud-cursed war. So what's it going to be? You gonna tell the emira the truth and watch Erin Elal burn? 'Cause I reckon that'd be hard to stomach, even for a turncoat like you."

"Turncoat," Senar said, his voice empty. "Avallon destroyed the Guardians. He sent me to die through the Merigan portal. So you tell me, who betrayed whom?"

Kolloken's only response was a smile.

He knows he has me, Senar thought. For all the Breaker's talk of turncoats, he knew Senar was caught on the horns, else he wouldn't have told him the things he had. What could the Guardian do with the knowledge? Confront Avallon? Like the emperor would care. Lash out at Kolloken? That would be naught but an empty gesture, petty in its impotence. The man would take the blow and laugh in his face. *And he'd be right to.* Petty or not, Senar felt an urge to plant his fist in the Breaker's smile, and he had to turn away to stop himself. He made himself walk slowly to the door, his head held high. As if by doing so he could disguise the completeness of his defeat.

Outside, he leaned against the wall. The passage seemed to be spinning. Why in the Matron's name had he come here? What had he hoped to achieve? He would have been better off living with the suspicion of Kolloken's crime than the certainty. Now he'd opened a door he could not shut.

His thoughts seethed. Somewhere downstairs, Avallon would be toasting the success of his schemes. But if he believed he could predict how Mazana would react to Uriel's death, he was wrong. He knew nothing about Fume or the Founder's Citadel. He knew nothing about Dardonna's knife and the power it gave. What reason did Mazana have not to use that power now? And there was no guarantee it would be the stone-skins who bore the brunt of her fury. For when the storm of her grief blew over, her suspicions would turn to the emperor, as Senar had said. Did he have it in him to allay her distrust? To look her in the eye and swear Avallon was blameless?

He wasn't that good at lying. He wasn't even sure he wanted to try.

The Guardian rubbed a hand across his face. He felt tugged in all directions. How could he go back to Mazana and offer her comfort? How could he pretend his conversation with Kolloken had never happened? Maybe he was better off not returning at all, but wouldn't that be just another form of betrayal? Who else did Mazana have to turn to if not Senar? Romany? The executioner? And if he left this place, where would he go? Back to Erin Elal? Back to the emperor?

He listened to the voices on the floor below. A female servant crossed an intersection to his left, not looking at Senar as she passed. He closed his eyes. Mazana or Avallon, Avallon or Mazana. The choice seemed no clearer now than it had ever been. The future offered two paths, but what did you do when you wanted to walk both, you wanted to walk neither?

The answer seemed obvious suddenly. You made your own path, of course. A new path entirely.

He opened his eyes again. In the room behind, Kolloken was whistling.

You mean you ain't done worse in your time?

Senar pictured Uriel sitting next to Mazana in Olaire, learning to use water-magic. The Guardian hadn't known the boy well. In truth, he'd never tried to get to know him, but that didn't mean he couldn't feel the sting of his death. Maybe in Kolloken's place he would have done the same; he didn't know. What he *did* know, though, was that he wouldn't have been whistling about it afterward. He wouldn't have blamed Mazana for what happened like he was the one who'd been wronged.

A coldness settled on him, and he pushed himself away from the wall.

Then he turned and went back into Kolloken's room, closing the door behind.

Cradling her glass of wine, Romany sat back on the bench in the courtyard of the Spider's Gilgamarian temple. The malirange trees about her gave off a heady scent that made her think of her own shrine in Mercerie. Beyond the temple's walls, the city was hushed. The same stillness had pervaded the corridors of the Alcazar earlier, making it easy for Romany to slip away. Doubtless no one had noticed she was missing. Would anyone notice, she wondered, if she never came back?

In the windows to her right were a host of female faces, their attention fixed not on Romany but on two nearby figures: the Spider and the high priestess of this temple, Lexal. A casual observer would not know who was the goddess and who the disciple, for the Spider's garb was typically unassuming, whereas Lexal's robe was spun from a radiant weave of damask, and she wore a gold circlet with a centerpiece of a redback spider made of duskstones. From the glances the woman cast Romany's way, it was plain she resented having another high priestess in her shrine. To be fair, though, she *had* provided Romany with a glass of Corinian honeywine. Not one of the finer vintages, alas, but perhaps it was just the priestess's mood souring the drink.

Uriel was dead. She hadn't spared the boy a thought when Hex unleashed his dreamworld on the Alcazar. If she'd taken Uriel with her when she made her break for safety, he might have escaped with her through the portal. Then again, how would she have got him through the portcullises that Hex conjured up to block the corridor? *I wouldn't. I would have been forced to leave him behind.* Hex would have used the boy to try to lure Romany back into his clutches. And what would she have done when faced with the choice of saving Uriel or saving herself?

The Spider finished speaking to Lexal. She approached Romany and sat on the bench beside her. "Why, High Prrriestess," she said, "you look positively piqued. Was it something I said?"

"Not everything is about you, my Lady."

"Among some of your fellow priestesses, such a statement would be considered blasphemy."

"And where are those priestesses now?" The gods knew, Romany would have given anything to trade places with one of them just then. "If you'd wanted another lackey to stroke your ego, you wouldn't have brought me back from the dead."

The goddess struggled to hold back a smile. And failed. "Am I to assume this ill temper is because of Uriel's demise?"

"What else?"

The Spider sighed. "Why is it that people get so insufferably emotional over the fate of a child? I will never understand it. There is a simple cure to such sentimentality, and it requires just a subtle change in perspective. Instead of brooding over today's doe-eyed boy, consider instead the small-minded tyrant he would doubtless have become."

Romany shot her a look. Could the goddess really be so cold? Strange how after so many years in her service, the priestess didn't know her well enough to judge. How could Romany follow a goddess she did not understand? Why did she do it? *There is a simple cure to such sentimentality.* Romany wanted to believe the Spider was better than that, but what other reason could there be for the goddess's words? Was she teasing Romany? Over the death of a child? Such a wellspring of comedic possibility.

The Spider said, "Do you think Uriel is the only child who died today? Dozens will have passed away in Gilgamar alone. Will you mourn them too? You knew them only slightly less well than you knew Uriel." She held Romany's gaze a moment longer, then gave a despairing shake of her head. "Have you ever heard of a goddess called the Healer from back in the Third Age? No? She must have woken one morning touched by the moon, for she decided to devote her days to soothing the ills of mankind. Thirty years she spent trying to set the world to rights. All around the globe she traveled. And do you know what she found when she got back to where she started?"

"Nothing had changed."

"Nothing had changed," the Spider agreed. "Well, that's not quite true. In some cases she had actually made things worse. In one notable instance two formerly peaceful nations had all but wiped each other out over the ambiguities in a treaty she had imposed on them."

"So what is your answer to"—Romany struggled for the right words—"all this? To the iniquity and the suffering?"

"What makes you think there *is* an answer? Or that *I* would know it if there was? I'm only a goddess, after all."

Yes, in retrospect the Spider was probably the last person Romany should be asking. To the goddess there was no such thing as right and wrong, just interesting and uninteresting; no good and evil, just useful and useless. And even if the Spider *had* given Romany an answer, why should the priestess have accepted it as true? What made the goddess's judgment any more valid than Romany's own? What were immortals, but beings who wielded more power than the unfortunate souls they made their playthings? Did that power give them a moral imperative? *No more than it does any tinpot dictator.* "So what happened to this goddess, this Healer?"

"No one knows. Unsurprrrisingly, her experiences left her disillusioned. One day she just disappeared. And she has never shown her face since."

"Misery loves solitude," Romany said, looking at the goddess pointedly.

The Spider seemed not to notice. She stretched out her legs. "I believe congratulations are in order for the way you outwitted that dreamweaver. Hex, wasn't it? For a while there, I thought he had you."

"You were watching? You saw his dreamworld, then?"

"Yes, I wonder what sort of childhood *he* had."

"Is he actually dead? Has Shroud taken his soul?"

"Somehow I suspect the Lord of the Dead might pass on that one."

Romany sat up straighter. "You mean he could steal someone else's body and come back?" His old body had already been burned, the ashes scattered.

"Like you've done, you mean? It is possible."

The priestess couldn't tell if the Spider was telling the truth or just goading her. "Let me try you with something easier, then. Did Hex interfere with Jambar's readings before he killed him?"

"It seems likely."

"And planted the idea of the emperor's treachery?"

The Spider shook her head. "There is no way Hex could have known the configuration of bones needed to cast suspicion on Avallon. Most likely he disrupted *all* of Jambar's readings and left the shaman blind."

"So Jambar just made up the bit about the emperor attacking Mazana?"

The goddess shrugged. "Perhaps he really did see that happen in one of the futures. Or perhaps he foresaw Avallon's treachery, but was wrong about the form it would take."

"Did the emperor intend all along to kill Uriel?"

"If the stone-skins attacked, yes. Oh, he couldn't have known for sure that Mazana would bring the boy to Gilgamar. But he must have thought it likely, just as he'd have thought it likely he wouldn't be able to turn the emira to his cause. Uriel was his plan B in case he failed to persuade her. And all things considered, you'd have to say he played his hand rrrather well. He assassinated the Augeran commander and put an end to an alliance between the stone-skins and the Rubyholters. He lured the new subcommander into a hasty strike at Gilgamar, thus drawing the League—probably—into the war on Erin Elal's side."

"But if not for me, Avallon would have died in that strike—he and everyone else in the Alcazar."

The Spider's mouth quirked. "Yes, there is an irony in that, don't you think? I send you to eliminate Mazana, and instead you save her from the stone-skins. Odd, isn't it? In the Forest of Sighs, you had no trouble dispatching seventeen of Shroud's disciples—"

"Eighteen."

"Yet here you seem unable to dispose of even one simple target."

The priestess sniffed. "As I recall, you left the timing of Mazana's death to me."

"So I've interrupted you in your work, have I? Are you heading back now to finish the job?"

It was a thought. At this moment, death might be a blessing to the emira.

Romany swirled the wine in her glass, but did not drink it. A dragon's trumpeting came from the south. With the city so still, it sounded like the beast was just on the other side of the cloister wall. One of the watching priestesses started at the sound and bumped her head on a window frame.

"How much of the stone-skin fleet survived the dragons?" Romany asked. "How many ships will make it to port?"

"A handful, no more. Their water-mages pushed themselves hard to get here when they did. Not many will have enough power left to outpace the dragons."

"Will the stone-skins feel their loss? Have we hurt them enough to make a difference?"

"Harrrdly. After our discussions in Olaire, I made a start at extending my web across the Southern Wastes to Augera. From what I can make out, the stone-skins have been preparing this invasion for decades. This fleet is but a small part of their power, easily replaced. Next time they come, they'll come hard and in greater numbers."

"They'll come here? To Gilgamar?"

"Not for a while. Erin Elal will be their first target."

"Can they be beaten?"

"No."

Romany's mouth was dry. As simple as that? The Spider hadn't paused to consider her answer, hadn't qualified it in any way. And while the goddess wouldn't claim to be an expert on military matters, she had doubtless seen enough conflicts—had *started* enough of them—to be able to judge their course with a degree of authority. "Even if the Sabian League allies with Erin Elal?"

"Even then."

"Then shouldn't we be doing something to help?"

"By 'we,' I assume you mean 'me.'" Then, "Perhaps you think I should intervene to thwart every conqueror that turns on a weaker neighbor. Why stop there, though, why not put an end to all war? The Healer would apprrrove, don't you think?"

Romany scowled, but she could hardly disagree with the Spider's sentiments. Had it been any other empire in the stone-skins' sights, Romany would have been the first to wash her hands of it. "In Olaire you told me the Augerans had outlawed the worship of any god. If they win here, you might find it hard to play your games with pieces of just one color on the board."

"And if I neglect my other concerns in order to fight the stone-skins, you think my enemies in the Pantheon will go easy on me? Maybe even join me to repel the hated aggressors?"

This was getting Romany nowhere. Trying to make the Spider look past her own interests was the definition of futility. "So you'll do nothing, then?"

"I didn't say that." The goddess's fingers drummed against the bench. She looked about the courtyard, apparently considering her next words. "I am minded," she said at last, "to lift my judgment on Mazana Creed, at least for now. Even if Fume's influence continues to grow, I suspect the emira will be too busy trying to avenge Uriel to worry about me." The goddess watched Romany closely, awaiting her reaction. When it did not come, she said, "What, no objections? In Olaire you were adamant she must die."

"Circumstances change."

"But the woman's a monster! A monster, I tell you! Or at least I think that's what you said."

"But a monster on our side." It felt a betrayal to speak the words, but a betrayal of what, of whom? Who was Romany to judge Mazana? And how might someone judge the priestess's own actions of the past few days? "The stone-skins are coming. If you won't challenge them, someone has to."

"How admirably pragmatic of you." The Spider's voice had a note of approval in it that might have lifted Romany another time. "And since you seem so keen to oppose the Augeran threat, I assume you'll have no complaints about returning to the emira now. Where better to meet that threat than at Mazana's side?"

Romany nodded. She'd expected the goddess to send her back. What she hadn't expected was to find herself not entirely distraught at the prospect. "Is that to be the sum of your aid against the stone-skins? Giving me to Mazana?"

"Isn't that enough? High Priestess, you do yourself down. And those are words I never thought I'd say." Her fingers fluttered. "As it happens, I've been considering how best to raise Mazana's spirits after her brother's death. I was thinking a change of scenery might help. A trip to somewhere farrr from Gilgamar, where she can put all this death and conflict behind her." The Spider gave a dark smile. "Somewhere like the Forest of Sighs, for example."

Romany stared at her. *The Forest of Sighs?*

The goddess gestured, and a hazy image appeared before the priestess. It showed Mazana on a dais, crouching. There were blocks of stone around her, an upturned rusty throne to one side. *Mayot's throne*, Romany realized. The emira used a hand to brush away the grit on the floor. She must have located whatever it was she was looking for, because at that moment her hand stilled. The lines about her dead eyes softened a fraction. With Uriel gone, that was probably the closest she would get to an expression of satisfaction.

Romany squinted. What had Mazana found? A fragment of the Book of Lost Souls? Some token from one of the powers who had fought in the dome? No, there was nothing on the ground. Just a blotch that looked like dried blood. Mayot's blood, perhaps? Would Mazana be able to steal some of his power from it? That didn't seem worth a journey of two hundred and fifty leagues, even if that journey would have taken her only heartbeats along the Spider's web. . . .

Her breath caught. For suddenly she knew whose blood it was—remembered him cutting his own palm to seal a deal over the fate of the Book of Lost Souls.

Shroud.

Romany swallowed. The blood of a god. And Mazana a blood-mage who had taken in part of Fume's spirit.

The emira extended a finger toward the stain. This time when the blood was absorbed into her skin, it turned the flesh not crimson, but black.

Abruptly the image faded. Lexal approached, and she halted before a still-shaken Romany. "There's a man outside the temple," she said. "A Guardian called Senar Sol. He wants to speak to you." She looked from Romany to the Spider. "To both of you."

Ebon leaned back in his chair, his gaze shifting over the common room. A line of men sat at the bar, laughing and banging their glasses down in unison. Ebon wished he could have some of what they were drinking if it would stop his hands trembling. He didn't trust the barman to serve him what he asked for, though, so instead he put his hands in his lap. It didn't hurt to look edgy, he decided, just as long as he held his nerve when the time came.

He had asked to meet Tia on neutral ground in the Lower City, but he'd already recognized her tongueless minion at a nearby table, engaged in a drinking contest with two scantily dressed women. Doubtless there were more of her crowd scattered among the tavern's other patrons. Certainly Ebon was drawing a lot of looks for a man sitting alone minding his own business. Everyone in the room seemed to be carrying a weapon, all except a raggedy-haired girl who shuffled among the tables with palms outstretched.

Behind Ebon, Vale coughed to signal Tia's arrival. She halted at the door to inspect the room before making her way toward Ebon's table. Her hair was piled atop her head, and she wore a shimmering black gown, as if she'd stopped off on her way to a ball in the Upper City. Fifty sets of eyes followed her progress across the polished clay floor.

She sat down across from Ebon. "Ah," she said, looking between him and Vale, "if it isn't the two heroes from the wall. Word of your exploits has reached us even here. I can't tell you what an honor it is to see you again."

Ebon did not respond. He'd resolved to say as little as possible until he saw Lamella and Rendale. Less chance of mistakes that way.

Tia glanced at the empty floor under the table. "You seem to have traveled light."

"Ten thousand sovereigns would have been a bit heavy to carry through the Lower City." Ebon took from his pocket a flat leather case a handspan long and put it on the table. "Instead I brought stones. Dawnstones, to be precise."

"Notoriously difficult to value, those stones."

"Which is why I took them to a jeweler in the Upper City this afternoon." He nodded to the leather case. "In there you'll find an envelope sealed with wax containing both the stones and a certificate of value. For ten thousand three hundred and fifty sovereigns, if I remember rightly."

Tia looked from Ebon to Vale, then back again. "Sounds eminently reasonable. Assuming I can rely on the integrity of this jeweler, of course."

"Yes," Ebon said, "so hard to find people you can trust these days."

The woman laughed. "Who is he?"

"Tattagill. He seemed confident you would have heard of him."

"Tattagill, yes." She paused. "I must say I'm impressed you managed to raise ten thousand sovereigns so quickly. Makes me think I didn't charge enough to get you into the Upper City."

"Oh, I don't know. Three thousand sovereigns to be betrayed sounds about right." Tia watched him, still waiting for an explanation, and he added, "I had some change left over from the assets

I liquidated to raise the three thousand. I also received a reward from your Ruling Council for the part I played in defending the city. Apparently they think Gilgamar owes me a debt—something you might like to consider when you get a chance."

The woman snorted and reached for the case.

Ebon put a hand on it. "After I see Rendale and his . . . partner." It stung to say those words. Could he blame them, though, if some feeling had developed between them? Doubtless they both thought him dead. Who knew what they'd been through these past three weeks? Who else but each other could they have turned to for comfort?

Tia sat back in her chair, searching his eyes. Then she scanned the common room as if she'd misplaced someone. Was she about to change the terms of their agreement? Demand more money? It was just a matter of time, surely.

A man sidled over and put a glass of spirits on the table in front of her. She took a sip. "You know," she said to Ebon at last, "there's something about this that bothers me. After our first meeting, I thought you were a fool to trust me with three thousand sovereigns. Then I found out from that Mercerien prince—Ocarn?—that you were a prince yourself, and I realized three thousand sovereigns meant nothing to you. To come here now, though, after I betrayed you the first time . . ." She tapped a finger on the rim of her glass. "Remind me why I shouldn't grab you and ransom you *and* your brother to your father. Because I'm having trouble remembering myself."

"I wouldn't advise trying," Ebon said.

"Really? Oh, Ocarn warned me about your timeshifter friend here, but I have to say he's looking a little peaky right now. Still suffering from the after-effects of that wound he took on the wall, no doubt—yes, I heard about that too. Is he fast enough to match six of my men? Ten?"

"Maybe, maybe not. But he's certainly fast enough to get to *you* before anyone stops him."

"And how about the man holding a knife to your brother's throat at this moment?"

This was not going as Ebon had hoped—as he'd expected perhaps, but not as he'd hoped. "So you've got a knife to Rendale's throat, and I've got a knife to yours. You could roll the dice if you like, see what numbers come up. Or you could take the ten thousand sovereigns on offer, and congratulate yourself on a good day's work. Seems a simple enough choice to me, but maybe the view's different from your side of the table."

Some of the people at nearby tables were moving away. Either they'd overheard the conversation or they could sense the tension bubbling up like a pot coming to the simmer. The tongueless man interrupted his drinking game with the two women to lift an ax from below his chair and place it on the table. Across the common room, Tia's other minions could be picked out from the way they started edging closer, or put their hands on the hilts of their weapons. Maybe ten of them in all.

Good of them to identify themselves like that.

The beggar girl chose that moment to approach Ebon's table. She held her hands out to him, and he placed a coin in them. The girl turned to Tia, and the woman ruffled her hair . . . then took Ebon's coin from her hands and pocketed it. The girl smiled and moved away.

"Should I deduct that from the ten thousand?" Ebon asked.

Tia's mouth did not so much as twitch, but a little of the tightness had eased from her expression. "How do you deduct a sovereign from a dawnstone? Scratch it with your nail?"

She had a point. Ebon put his elbows on the table, clasped his hands together. "Where is my brother?"

The woman held his gaze before gesturing to a black-haired man by the door. He disappeared outside. "He's close," Tia said in answer to Ebon's question. "You'll forgive me if I felt the need to keep him somewhere safe until I had a chance to look around and make sure you hadn't done something stupid. Like dress up a few Gilgamarian soldiers in civilian clothes and plant them in the room. Someone tried that once, if you can believe it. Thought I wouldn't notice. But soldiers have a particular smell that sticks out in a place like this. Of course, you'd never do anything so stupid as to invite soldiers to a private gathering."

"What would be the point? I've seen how your Gilgamarian soldiers fight."

Tia smiled—not so much at his words, he suspected, as at Ebon himself. His voice had a tremor to it, hope and anticipation and dread all squeezing the breath from him as if he were wrapped in a boa's coils. It didn't seem possible the next people to enter the room might be Lamella and Rendale. But would Tia let them walk out with him afterward? His knife at her throat lasted only as long as she sat at this table. Who was to say she wouldn't swap the captives for the jewels, get up and move out of Vale's range, then order her men to take the Galitians captive?

The door opened, and Black Hair reappeared.

Behind him came a haggard-looking Rendale. He caught sight of Ebon across the room and stopped, blinking stupidly. But just because Ocarn and Tia knew Ebon was alive didn't mean they had shared that information with Rendale, or told him why he was being brought here. Lamella came next, shuffling on her twisted leg. When she saw Ebon the color drained from her face. She put her hands over her mouth. Her strawberry-blond hair looked a shade darker than Ebon remembered it, her eyes more deep-set, and there were lines to her face he didn't recognize. His skin was flushed. He felt a prickle all over. But even then, he realized he was watching her to see if there was guilt in her look to go with the shock and relief.

He tutted his disgust.

Lamella's shoulders shook silently, and Tia cocked her head. "My, my," she said to Ebon. "Look what you've done to the poor woman. And I thought it was just me that had that effect on people."

Ebon hadn't known how he would react to seeing Lamella again, or she to him, but he had never imagined this. He forced himself to break her gaze. If Tia was to guess there was something between them . . . Behind Lamella and Rendale, Peg Foot entered the tavern, grinning as if he were the one Ebon had come to free. He grabbed Rendale's arm and muscled him forward. Lamella followed with Black Hair. More people drifted away from Ebon and Tia's table, while the men at the bar watched them with expressions gone sober.

"That's close enough," Tia said to Peg Foot when he had closed to within ten paces. Her gaze was still on Ebon. "At least until I've seen these jewels you've brought."

"Of course," Ebon said.

He had to buy himself time now, so he scratched an imaginary itch on his leg, then pretended to fumble at the clasp of the leather case before finally pulling it open. They were all watching him, even the beggar girl. Just how he wanted it. With exaggerated care, he unfolded the case once, twice, three times to reveal . . . nothing. The case was empty.

He looked at Tia.

She looked back at him.

Silence.

"Well, this is embarrassing," Ebon said.

"What?"

"I seem to have left the stones behind."

Tia stared at him as if he were speaking a foreign language. Then she bared her teeth and gestured. Around the common room, her minions drew their weapons. Peg Foot produced a knife from somewhere and held it to Rendale's throat. What little conversation remained in the room now died away. An overturned glass hit a table, and Ebon heard the *drip, drip* of spilled liquid falling to the floor.

Tia said, "I don't know what game you're playing, but it won't work."

"You misunderstand—"

"Let me guess, your reward from the Ruling Council included the hire of some soldiers, and they're on their way here now?"

"Please, you've got it all wrong."

Tia's eyes burned. "You don't think I guessed you might try something like this? You don't think I've got men watching every damned road leading here?" Her voice shook with fury. "By the time your friends arrive—"

"Please," Ebon cut in, raising his hands, "I'm telling you the truth. I don't have any friends on their way." Then he leaned forward and added, for Tia's ears only, "That's because they're already here."

Before he'd finished speaking, a woman behind Peg Foot had grabbed the man's hand holding the knife at Rendale's throat and twisted it behind his back. A sweep of Peg Foot's leg, and he was on the floor, face pressed to the clay. Black Hair, meanwhile, took an elbow from another man that snapped his head back. He dropped like a stone. The tongueless man reached for his ax, but one of the women he'd been drinking with—the twins—had already snatched it up. The other sister rose and delivered a kick to his forehead that sent him toppling backward in his chair. Around the room, Tia's other minions were being similarly disarmed and subdued by the Revenants.

Ebon had not moved. He was watching Tia. The woman sat upright in her chair. Points of color had formed on her cheeks. The muscles of her neck stood out as she swallowed.

"Well, this is a turn up," Ebon said. "It seems your nose is sensitive enough to sniff out soldiers, but not mercenaries. Hardly surprising, since I've found these particular mercenaries to be an altogether superior breed. Allow me to introduce Twist, commander of the Revenants." Twist sauntered in close and drained Tia's glass of spirits. "If you look hard enough, you might just be able to see him under all the bruises."

Twist pulled Tia to her feet and patted her down for weapons, found a knife in her boot, and slung it away. "We ready to move?" he said to Ebon. "Seems a shame to turn in early, but I reckon we've outstayed our welcome."

"The men she said were watching the roads . . . ?"

"Dealt with."

"Then let's go." Ebon pushed back his chair and rose.

"What do we do with her?" Twist asked, pointing at Tia.

"Bring her with us. At least as far as the Canal Gate. She can be our hostage against her men's good behavior—in case any of them think to try and follow us when we leave."

The commander nodded, then looked at Vale. "You feelin' better, Endorian? Hope you ain't forgotten that duel you owe me."

Vale grunted. "How could I, with you reminding me every quarterbell? Though I *am* struggling to remember ever agreeing to it in the first place . . ."

Ebon stopped listening. He was looking at Lamella and Rendale. Rendale rubbed his neck where Peg Foot's knife had touched it, his expression pained. Lamella wiped her eyes. Whatever strength had sustained her since she'd fled Majack must have been leaching away, for she swayed on her feet, had to reach out to a table to stop herself falling. They were both watching him, and he looked at them in turn. Not the joyful reunion he'd imagined, but sometimes when you'd wanted a thing for so long, the reality couldn't live up to the expectation. He thought of all the ways he'd let Lamella down in his search, all the half measures he'd taken.

But his doubts melted away as she came shambling toward him. A faltering smile broke out across her face as she closed the distance between them and buried herself in his embrace.

EPILOGUE

EBON CONCENTRATED on the distant presence. He felt a moment's disorientation as his spirit covered the leagues separating him from Luker Essendar, then blinked and found himself looking out through the other man's eyes.

To find a fist swinging toward him.

He tensed.

Luker was already raising an arm to block. He retaliated with a right cross that thundered into his attacker's chin and sent him reeling. More figures swarmed about him like bees round a honeypot. There was a fireplace to his right, crude tables and benches. A common room, then.

Ebon spoke in Luker's mind. "I've caught you at a bad time."

If the Guardian was surprised to find the prince in his head, he gave no indication. "Just give me a moment." He'd gotten a woman by the neck and was holding her at bay. She couldn't reach him with her punches, but that didn't stop her from flailing about, her teeth bared, hissing in fury.

"I don't think she likes you," Ebon said.

"Oh, you noticed."

Luker grabbed her between the legs with his free hand, then lifted her up and hurled her across the room. She landed on a table, and it collapsed with a crack sending glasses and tankards flying.

"Do you mind?" said a woman's voice from out of picture—Jenna's? "Some of us are trying to have a drink here."

Luker scowled. "Do you think you could save the wisecracks for later, maybe give me a hand?"

The next man was on to him—a bald man with bloodshot eyes and drooping jowls. The Guardian swayed back from a punch, kicked his attacker in the groin. Baldy doubled over. A thrown tankard—Jenna's?—thunked into his head, spraying ale. His eyes clouded.

Luker shoved him into the path of a woman coming up behind. "This about Parolla's mother?" he asked Ebon. "Shroud tell you where she's been reborn?"

Ebon nodded. "One of his disciples just paid me a visit."

Luker must have heard something in his voice, for his expression darkened. He picked up a chair and broke it over a man's head. "I'm not going to like this, am I?"

"No," Ebon said. "No, you're not."

ACKNOWLEDGMENTS

Many thanks as usual to my editors, Marco Palmieri and Natalie Laverick, and to my publicists, Ksenia Winnicki and Lydia Gittins, for their efforts in promoting this book and the series as a whole.

I should also say thank you to the readers who have gotten in touch to share their thoughts on my books, or recommended them to others. I am grateful as well to the bloggers and reviewers who have hosted me for interviews or guest posts, and thus helped to provide a signal boost for the series. Particular thanks are due to Wendell Adams and Bob Milne who were beta readers of this book, and who came up with some very useful comments to help me fine-tune the manuscript.

Finally, thank you to my wife, Suzanne, for her support, advice, and encouragement. I really couldn't do this without her. And thanks to my son, James, for being his wonderfully entertaining self. This book is for him. I'm looking forward to the day when he will be able to read it.